The

COLLECTED
STORIES

of

EVAN S.
CONNELL

COUNTERPOINT
WASHINGTON, D.C.

The author gratefully acknowledges those who published or
broadcast many of these stories in slightly different form: *Accent*,
The American Mercury, *Antaeus*, *Boston University Journal*,
Carolina Quarterly, *Denver Quarterly*, *Escapade*, *Esquire*, *Flair*,
Foreign Service, *Gent*, *Glimmer Train*, *Greensleeves*, *Lillabulero*,
National Public Radio, *New Mexico Quarterly*, *New World
Writing*, *The New Yorker*, *Paris Review*, *Première*, *Saturday Evening
Post*, *Southern Review*, *Story*, *The Threepenny Review*, *Today's
Woman*, *Tomorrow*, *The Transatlantic Review*, and *Western Review*.

Lyrics from "Big Rock Candy Mountain" in "Filbert's Wife"
on page 429 are quoted by permission of Robbins Music
Corporation, New York.

Library of Congress Cataloging-in-Publication Data
Connell, Evan S., 1924–
     [Short stories. Selections]
     The collected stories of Evan S. Connell.
     1. Manners and customs—Fiction.   I. Title.
  PS3553.05A6   1995
  813'.54—dc20   95-33080
ISBN 1-887178-06-6 (alk. paper)

FIRST PRINTING
Book design by David Bullen
Composition by Typeworks
Printed in the United States of America on acid-free paper that
meets the American National Standards Institute Z39-48 Standard.

COUNTERPOINT
P.O. Box 65793
Washington, D.C. 20035-5793

Distributed by Publishers Group West

For Gus and Elizabeth Blaisdell

The Collected Stories of

Evan S. Connell

CONTENTS

Contents

Contents

Great problems are in the street.
NIETZCHE

The

COLLECTED
STORIES

of

EVAN S.
CONNELL

ARCTURUS

Verweile doch, du bist so schön.
Linger awhile, thou art so fair.
— GOETHE

THE CHILDREN, Otto and Donna, have been allowed to stay up late this evening in order to see the company. Now with faces bewitched they sit on the carpet in front of the fireplace, their pajama-clad legs straight out in front of them and the tails of their bathrobes trailing behind so that they look somewhat like the sorcerer's apprentice.

Outside the wind is blowing and every once in a while the window panes turn white; then the wind veers and the snow must go along with it. Automobile horns sound quite distant even when close by. Aside from the hissing, sputtering logs which are growing black in the fire, and the alluring noises of the kitchen, the most noticeable sound is a melancholy humming from the front door. Otto and Donna are convinced a ghost makes this dreadful wailing and no amount of explanation can disprove it. Their father has lifted them up one after the other so that they can see it is only a piece of tin weather stripping that vibrates when the wind comes from a certain direction, and they have felt a draft when this happens, but their eyes are dubious; wind and metal are all very well but the noise is made by a ghost. It is a terrible sound, as no one can deny, and upon hearing it Otto shivers so deliciously that his little sister must also shiver.

"What does company look like?" he inquires without lifting his gaze from the burning logs. And is told that company will be a gentleman named Mr. Kirk. Otto considers this for a long time, wiggling his feet and rubbing his nose which has begun to itch from the heat.

"Is he coming to our house?"

Otto's father does not answer. Lost in meditation he sits in his appointed chair beside the bookcase.

Presently Otto sniffles and wishes to know why the man is coming here.

"To visit with your mother."

A cloud of snowflakes leaps to the window as if to see what is going on inside but is frightened away by the weather stripping. How warm the living room is! Donna yawns, and since whatever one does the other must also do, her brother manages an even larger yawn. The difference is in what follows: Donna, being a woman, does not mind succumbing, and, filled with security, she begins to lean against Otto, but he is convinced that sleep is his enemy and so he remains bolt upright with a stupidly militant expression that tends to weaken only after his eyes have shut. Though his enemy is a colossal one he accepts without concern the additional burden of his infant sister.

"Why?" he asks, and looks startled by his own voice. It is doubtful he can now remember what he wishes to know, but why is always a good solid question and sure to get some kind of response.

"Because your mother wrote him a letter and begged him to come see her."

Again follows a silence. The clock on the mantel ticks away while the good logs crackle and the coals hiss whenever the sap drips down upon them. Otto is remotely troubled. For several weeks he has sensed that something is wrong in the house but he cannot find out what. His mother does not seem to know, nor does the cook, who usually knows everything. Otto has about concluded the nurse is to blame; therefore he does whatever she tells him not to do. Sometimes he finds it necessary to look at his father, or to sit on his lap; there, although they may not speak to one another, he feels more confident. He is jealous of this position and should Donna attempt to share it he is prone to fend her off until orders come from above.

In regard to this evening, Otto has already gotten what he wanted. He does not really care about Mr. Kirk because the value of a visitor lies simply in the uses to which Otto can put him, whether it be staying up late or eating an extra sweet. All at once Donna topples luxuriously into his lap. His hand comes to rest on her tiny birdlike shoulder, but through convenience only. At the moment he is careless of the virgin beauty; her grace does not intrigue him, nor does he realize how this tableau has touched the heart of his father across the room. Somberly Otto frowns into the fire; almost adult he is in the strength of such concentration, though one could not tell whether he is mulling over the past or the future. Perhaps if the truth were known he is only seeing how long he can roast his feet, which are practically touching a log.

"Is he coming *tonight?*" Otto knows full well this is a foolish question, but there lurks the fear that if he does not show a profound and tenacious interest in the whole business he will be sent to bed.

With ominous significance his father demands, "Why do you think you two are up this late?"

Otto stares harder than ever into the fire. It is important now that he think up something to change the subject in a hurry. He yawns again, and discovers that he is lying down. He sits up. He inquires plaintively if he may have the drumstick on Christmas.

His father does not reply, or even hear, but gazes at the carpet with a faraway expression somewhere between misery and resignation and does not even know he has been spoken to by the cook until she firmly calls him by name.

"Mr. Muhlbach!"

He starts up, somewhat embarrassed. Cook wishes to know at what time the guest will be arriving. Muhlbach subsides a little, takes a sip from a tumbler of brandy, and is vague. "Ah . . . we don't know exactly. Soon, I hope. Is there anything you want?"

But there is nothing; she has finished all preparation for the dinner and now is simply anxious for fear that one delicacy or another may lose its flavor from so much waiting. She looks at the children on the carpet before the fireplace. Otto catches this look; he reads in cook's stern face the thought that if she were their mother she would have them in bed; instantly he looks away from her and sits quite still in hopes that both his father and the cook will forget he is even there. Seconds pass. Nothing is said. Cook returns to the kitchen with an air of disgust.

Now the suburban living room is tranquil once again, much more so than it was two hours ago. At that time there were tears and reprimands and bitter injustice, or so the participants think. Otto especially felt himself abused; he was the object of an overwhelming lecture. He did not comprehend very much of it but there could be no mistake about who was in disgrace; therefore he rolled over onto his stomach and began to sob. Surely this would restore him to the family circle. No one, he thought, could refuse to comfort such a small boy. It was a fine performance and failed only because he peeked up to see its effect; at this he was suddenly plucked from the floor by one foot. He hung upside down for a while, gravely insulted, but found it impossible to weep effectively when the tears streamed up his forehead, so after a fit of coughing and bellowing he was lowered to the carpet. On his head, to be sure, but down at any rate, and for some time after he occupied himself with the hiccups. He still believes that his punishment was not only too stringent but too prompt; one appreciates a few moments in which to enjoy the fruit of one's evil-doing. Furthermore all he did was take a stuffed giraffe from his sister. It is true the giraffe belonged to him; the trouble came about because he had not thought of playing with the giraffe until he discovered she had it, and when he had wrung it away from her he put it on the table out of her reach. So, following the administration of justice, he was ordered to kiss his little sister on the lips, a penance he performs with monstrous apathy, after which the living room was turned into a manger for perhaps the twentieth time and the father magically transformed himself into a savage dog, growling and snarling, keeping everything for himself. Donna and Otto are spellbound, so terrifying is their father in the role of a dog. In fact he is so menacing and guards the cushions and pillows with such ferocity that the point of the fable is invariably lost. On occasion they have even requested him to be a dog so that they might admire his fangs and listen enraptured to the dreadful growls. But perhaps they are learning, who can tell?

Now the lesson is ended and, as usual, forgotten. The giraffe is clamped upside down beneath Donna's arm; it is fortunate in having such a flexible neck. She no longer cares that a visitor is on the way; she does not listen for the doorbell, nor does she anticipate the excitement that is bound to follow. By firelight her hair seems a golden cobweb, an altogether proper crown. Blissfully asleep she lies, despite the fact that her pillow is one of Otto's inhospitable knees. Barely parted and moist are the elfin lips, while her breath, as sweet as that of a pony, sometimes catches between them, perhaps betokening a marvelous dream. She cannot be true, Botticelli must have painted her. Her expression is utterly pious; no doubt she has forgotten her miniature crimes. One hopes she has not dwelt too hard upon those miniature punishments which followed.

Now comes a stamping of feet just outside, an instant of silence, and next the doorbell, dissonant and startling even when one expects it. Company is here! Otto is first to the door but there, overcome by shyness, allows his father to open it.

Here is more company than expected. Kirk has brought along someone he introduces as Miss Dee Borowski, an exotic little creature not a very great deal larger than Otto although she is perhaps eighteen. One knows instinctively that she is a dancer. She is lean and cadaverous as a greyhound, and her hair has been dyed so black that the highlights look blue. She draws it back with utmost severity, twists it into a knot, and what is left over follows her with a flagrant bounce.

They have entered the Muhlbach home, Sandy Kirk tall as a flagpole and a trifle too dignified as though he will be called upon to defend his camel's hair overcoat and pearl-gray homburg. He has brought gifts: perfume for the woman he is to visit, its decanter a crystalline spiral. For the master of the house something more substantial, a bottle of high hard Portuguese wine. With a flourish and a mock bow he presents them both to Muhlbach. He apologizes for his lateness by a rather elaborate description of the traffic in the Hudson tube, and as if a further apology may bring a smile of pardon to Muhlbach's face he adds in an almost supplicating way that Borowski was late getting out of rehearsal. Immediately the dancer confesses that her part will be small; she is third paramour in a ballet production of *Don Juan*. Well, she is feral enough and will probably mean bad dreams for the young men in the audience, but there is something ambivalent about her as though she has not quite decided what to make of her life. Her eyebrows, for example, do not grow from the bony ridge that protects the eye; someone has plucked the outer hairs and substituted theater brows that resemble wings. She pauses beside the lamp and a shadow becomes visible high on her forehead—it has been shaved. Now she has decided to take off her new mink jacket; underneath is a lavender sweater that clearly intends to molt on the furniture, and a pair of frosty-looking tailored slacks. Quite rococo she looks, and knows it too. But to complete this ensemble she is carrying a book of philosophy.

Replies Muhlbach, conscious that his own voice must be a monotone, "My wife is upstairs. She will be down in a few moments. This is our son and there asleep by the fire is Donna."

Kirk has been waiting for this introduction because he has presents for the children too. To Otto goes a queer little stick-and-ball affair, a game of some sort. Otto receives the device without enthusiasm but minds his manners enough to say thank you. For Donna there is the most fragile, translucent doll ever seen. It is not meant for her to play with, of course, being made of Dresden china, not for years yet. Kirk places it on the mantel.

Miss Borowski has stooped a little so that she and young Otto look at one another as equals. Otto wishes to appear self-sufficient but despite himself he likes what he sees; then, too, she is considerably more fragrant than his mother, who always has an odor of medicine. He decides to accept the overture. They are friends in an instant and together, hand in hand, they go over to inspect Donna, who has found the carpet no less agreeable than her brother's leg. Otto does not object to anyone's admiring his baby sister; there are times when he discovers himself seized by the desire to tickle her ribs or her feet. He does not know this is love. So much the better, for if he knew he might stop. Nor is he unaware that she is the beauty of the house, though he takes comfort in the memory of her astonishing helplessness. He fails to understand why, despite his instructions, she cannot learn to put on her shoes or even go to the toilet when necessary.

Sandy Kirk meanwhile has been appraising the home and he has learned something: the supper table has been set. Only then does he recall the invitation was for supper. Unfortunately he and the dancer stopped to eat before coming over. Muhlbach hands him a cocktail, which he accepts with a serene smile; he waits to see if there will be a toast, but there is none. He notes that Borowski is giving the little boy a taste of her drink and he sees Muhlbach frown at this.

Into the room, supported by a nurse, comes Joyce Muhlbach, and the attention of everyone turns to her. She is unsmiling, clearly suffering deep pain. She is dressed but there is about her the look and the fetid odor of someone who has been in bedclothes all day. Her eyes are febrile, much too luminous. Straight across the room she moves, clutching the nurse's elbow, until she reaches the invited guest. Kirk, who is about to tap a foreign cigarette on the back of his wrist, seems paralyzed by the sight of her. Her husband turns around to the fire and begins to push at a log with his foot. And the dancer, who is holding Otto by the hand, stands flatfooted with the prearranged expression of one who has been told what to expect; even so her greedy stare indicates that she is fascinated by the sick woman's appearance.

Joyce now stands alone, and while looking up at Kirk she addresses her son. "Isn't it about time for little boys to be in bed?"

Otto assumes that nasal whine which he feels the best possible for all forms of protest, but he knows the end has come. Still a token argument is necessary. He knows they expect one. He reminds his mother that he has been given permission to stay up tonight; the fact that it was she who gave the permission seems not especially cogent. With strangers present his pride forbids the wheedling and disgraceful clowning which is sometimes successful, so he is reduced to an obstinate monologue. He watches his father pick up Donna, who is quite unconscious; she could be dragged upstairs and would not know the difference.

All of a sudden Otto gets up from the corner where he has been stubbornly crouching since bed was mentioned, and the churlish whine disappears. He owns a rifle. It is on the top shelf of the hall closet where he cannot reach it; nevertheless it belongs to him, and if Miss Borowski has a fancy for rifles his father might bring it out. Otto has reasoned no further than this, indeed has done nothing but look crafty, when his father remarks that there will be no showing of the gun tonight. Otto instantly beseeches his mother, whom he considers the more sympathetic, and while his back is turned he feels himself caught around the waist by that inexorable arm he knows so well. His head goes down, his feet go up, and thus robbed of dignity he vanishes for the night.

There follows one of those queer instants when everything becomes awkward. Otto has taken away more than himself. Is it affectation that causes Dee Borowski to sit cross-legged on the floor? Time is running out on them all.

Joyce begins: "Well, Sandy, I see you got here."

The moments which follow are stark and cheerless despite the comfortable fire. A flippant answer could make things worse. One listens moodily to the poltergeist in the door. But Muhlbach re-enters to save them, re-enters briskly with a cocktail shaker and says, while filling the dancer's glass, "A month ago my father died." And he proceeds to tell about the death of young Otto's grandfather. Nothing about Muhlbach suggests the poet—certainly not his business suit, not his dictaphonic sentences, least of all his treasury of clichés. His story unwinds like ticker tape, yet the visitors cannot listen hard enough. Even Borowski has forgotten the drama of herself, and if one should quietly ask her name she might reply without thinking that it is Deborah Burns.

And the urbane Sandy Kirk, who has found his way around half the world, by this recital of degeneration and dissolution he drifts gradually into the past, into profound memories of his own. Unlike the ingénue, death is not unfamiliar to him, death is not something one mimes on cue; Kirk once or twice has seen it look him sharply in the eye and finds he does not care for that look. As the story progresses he begins to empathize with Muhlbach; he is gratified that this man does know some emotion, and he wonders less why Joyce married him. When he read her letter, read the sardonic description of her husband, he was astonished to perceive that beneath the surface she was utterly in love with the man, a man who until now has seemed to Kirk like a shadow on the water. He did not much want to come for this visit because he is afraid of Joyce. Their relationship never brought them any kind of fulfillment, never carried them to an ocean, as it were, but left them stranded in the backwash of lost opportunity. No matter how many years have since intervened she has had the freedom of his heart as now it seems he has had hers. Kirk has not been able to resolve his feelings about Joyce; he was never able to place a little statue of her in his gallery as he does with other women. No, the letter put him ill at ease; he did not want to see her ever again but there was in her appeal such urgency that he could not refuse. However, he has come prepared. He has thought everything out. He has brought along this terribly serious little ballerina for protection. He has only to say the magic word, that is, he need only mention ballet or the theater and Dee Borowski will take over, destroying all intimacy without ever knowing what she has done. It is a shrewd device, one Sandy Kirk has used in other clumsy situations; all the same he knows that Joyce will not be deceived.

Now Muhlbach, seated like the good merchant that he is, shaking up his trousers so as not to result in a bulge at the knee, continues in his oddly haunting style, telling how young Otto was invited to the sickroom but was not informed he would never see his grandfather again. And they talked a little while, did the boy and the old gentleman who was dying; they talked solemnly about what Otto had been doing that afternoon. In company with two other neighborhood gangsters he had been digging up worms. At the end of this conversation Otto received a present all wrapped up in Christmas tissue, though Christmas had hardly come into sight. It turned out to be a primer of archaeology, and while Otto held this book in his hands there beside the bed his grandfather sleepily explained that it was a book about the stars. After a momentary hesitation Otto thanked him. Muhlbach, standing on the other side of the deathbed, was carefully watching his son, and many times since that afternoon he has mulled over a curious fact, the fact that Otto could recognize the word "archaeology" and knew its meaning. Indeed the book had been chosen for him because he had sounded interested in the subject; furthermore Otto has always had fewer qualms than a Turk about displaying his accomplishments. What restrained him from correcting his grandfather? It was a marvelous opportunity to show off. The father does not know for sure, but he does know that the boy is preparing to leave the world of childhood.

And so Muhlbach, without understanding exactly why either of them did what they did, hurried out to buy his son a rifle. In a sporting-goods store he handled the light guns one after another, slipped the bolt and examined the chamber, raised the sights, caressed the stock, and in fact could hardly contain his rapture, for he has always been in love with guns. To one side stood the clerk with arms folded and a mysterious nodding smile. "This is a twenty-two, isn't it?" Muhlbach asked, though naturally it was not a question but a statement. However he bought no ammunition because even pride must genuflect to reason.

From the bedroom comes the querulous voice of Otto, who has been abandoned, and he wishes to know what they are talking about.

"Go to sleep!" orders his father.

In the bedroom there is silence.

Every few minutes the cook has peered out of the kitchen, not to see what is going on but to announce her impatience. She has allowed the door to swing back and forth; she has rattled silverware and clinked glasses. She cannot figure out why people linger so long over a drink. She herself would drink it down and be done with the matter.

Kirk is now obliged to confess that both he and the dancer have eaten. Pretense would be impossible. He turns helplessly to Joyce with his apology and she feels a familiar annoyance: it is all so characteristic of him, the tardiness, the additional guest, the blithe lack of consideration. How well she remembers this selfish, provoking man who means so much to her. She knows him with greater assurance than she can ever know her deliberate and, in fact, rather mystic husband. She remembers the many nights and the mornings with a tenderness she has never felt toward Muhlbach. Thus Sandy Kirk finds her appraising him and he glances uneasily toward her husband: Muhlbach is absorbed by the snow clinging to the window panes.

It is decided that the guests shall sit at the table and drink coffee while dinner is served the host and hostess; there is no other solution. And they will all have dessert together. The cook thinks this very queer and each time she is summoned to the dining room she manages a good bourgeois look at the ballerina.

Around the mahogany oval they sit for quite a long time, Muhlbach the only one with an appetite. Once Joyce Muhlbach lifts her feverish gaze to the ceiling because the children's bedroom is just overhead and she has heard something too faint for anyone else, but it was not a significant noise and soon she resumes listening to Sandy Kirk, who is describing life in Geneva. He says there is a tremendous fountain like a geyser in the lake, and from the terrace of the casino it is one of the most compelling sights in the world. Presently he tells about Lausanne farther up the lake, its old-world streets rising steeply above the water, and from there he takes everyone in seven-league boots to Berne, and on to Interlaken where the Jungfrau is impossible to believe even if you are standing in its shadow.

Muhlbach clears his throat. "You are probably not aware of the fact, but my parents were born in Zurich. I can recall them speaking of the good times they used to have there." And he goes on to tell about one or two of these good times. They sound very dull as he gives them, owing in part to his habit of pausing midway to cut, chew, and swallow some roast beef. It occurs to him that Kirk may speak German so he asks the simplest question, *"Sprechen Sie Deutsch?"* Conversation in German affords him a kind of nourishment, much the same as his customary evening walk around the block, but aside from his mother, who now lives in an upstate sanatorium, there is no one to speak it with him. Joyce has never cared much for the language and it appears that Otto will grow up with a limited vocabulary.

Kirk replies, *"Nein. Spanisch und Französisch und Italienisch."* To Kirk the abrupt question was disconcerting because he had fancied himself the only one capable of anything beyond English. He has come to this home with the expectation of meeting a deadly familiar type of man, a competent merchant who habitually locked his brain at five o'clock, and Kirk is trying to remain convinced that this is the case. Muhlbach admits to not having traveled anywhere dangerously far from the commuter's line, south of Washington, say, or west of Niagara, and it is one of Sandy Kirk's prime theses that a stay-at-home entertains a meager form of life. The world, as anyone knows, was made to be lived in, and to remain in one place means that you are going to miss what is happening somewhere else. All the same Kirk sports a few doubts about his philosophy and so he occasionally finds it reassuring to convince other people that he is right. He has a talent for evocation and will often act out his stories, tiptoeing across the room and peering this way and that as though he were negotiating the Casbah with a bulging wallet. Or he will mimic an Italian policeman beating his breast and slapping his forehead over the criminal audacity of a pedestrian. Very droll does Sandy Kirk become after a suitable drink; then one must forgive his manifold weaknesses, one must recognize the farcical side of life. Thus he is popular wherever he goes; it is a rare hostess who can manage to stay exasperated with him all evening.

He seems to present the same personality no matter what the situation: always he has just done something wrong and is contrite. He telephones at a quarter of eight to explain that he will be a little late to some eight o'clock engagement. "Well, where are you now?" they ask, because his voice sounds rather distant, and it turns out he is calling from another city. But he is there by midnight and has brought an orchid to expiate the sin. Naturally the hostess is furious and wishes him to understand he cannot escape so easily but her cutting stare is quite in vain because he can no more be wounded than he can be reformed. One accepts him as he is, or not at all.

Now he has taken them though the Prado, pausing an instant in the gloom-filled upper chambers where Goya's dread etchings mock the very earth, gone on to Fez and Constantine and swiftly brought them back to Venice, where a proper British girl is being followed by a persistent Italian. She will have nothing to do with this Italian, will not speak to him, nor so much as admit he lives, despite the most audible and most extraordinary invitations. Now a man must maintain his self-respect, observes Kirk with a dignified wink, so all at once the frustrated Italian seizes her and flings her into the Grand Canal, and wrapping his coat like a Renaissance cloak around his shoulders he strides regally off into the night. Such are the stories he tells in any of a hundred accents, and no one can be certain where truth and fiction amalgamate, least of all the narrator. He speaks incessantly of where he has been, what he has done, and the marvels he has seen. Oh, he is a character—so exclaims everyone who knows him. It is amazing that such a façade can exist in front of a dead serious career, but he is a minor official of the State Department and puzzles everyone by mumbling in a lugubrious way that his job is expendable and when the next election comes around they may look for him selling apples on the corner. Still, he travels here and there and draws his pay, rather good pay, no matter who is elected. It is suspected that he is quite brilliant, but if so he never gives any evidence of it: one second he is a perfect handbook of slang, the next he becomes impossibly punctilious. It is difficult to decide whether he is burlesquing himself or his listeners.

The Muhlbachs are content to listen, regardless, because there is little enough drama at home and this visitor floats about like a trade wind of sorts, bearing a suggestion of incense and the echo of Arab cymbals. His wallet came from Florence—"a little shop not far from the Uffizi," he will answer—and his shoes were made in Stockholm. They can hardly equal his fables by telling how sick young Otto was the previous summer even though he spent several weeks in a hospital bed and required transfusions. It was a blood disease and they were fortunate that one of Muhlbach's business partners had contracted the same thing as a child and could supply the antitoxin.

Nor can they explain the curious pathos everyone felt over a situation the doctor created. It happened on the worst day of the illness, when they had at last come to believe he could not get well. While the doctor was examining him Otto became conscious, and to divert him the doctor asked how he would like to attend the circus that evening. Otto thought that would be fine and managed enough strength to nod. So they agreed that the doctor should call for him at six o'clock sharp that they might have time to reach the grounds ahead of the crowd and secure the best possible seats. Otto then relapsed into a coma from which he was not supposed to recover, but one eye opened around five o'clock in the afternoon and he spoke with absolute lucidity, asking what time it was. There could be no doubt that the speaker must be either Otto or his reincarnation because he has always been fearfully concerned over the time. By five-thirty he was certain he should be getting dressed and by six o'clock he had begun to sob with frustration because the nurse prevented him from sitting up. When they sought to pacify him by means of a teaspoonful of ice cream he rejected it with pitiful violence. His father's promise of a trike when he got well was received with an irritated hiccup. In vain did they explain that the doctor had been teasing; Otto knew better. Any moment the door would open and they would all be dumbfounded. The clock ticked along, Otto watching desperately. The hand moved down and started up, and finally started down again. Then he knew for the first time those pangs that come after one has been lied to.

But perhaps it was not unjustified; they had thought he would leave them and he did not, and scars on a heart are seldom seen.

MEANWHILE the cook has been acting superior. Around the table she walks and pours fresh coffee with her nose in the air as though its fragrance were offensive. She stumbles against Miss Borowski's chair, does this sure-footed cook. What can the matter be? And she is so careless in pouring that coffee slops over the cup into the saucer. It is true the cook apologizes, but her resentment is implicit and there follows a baffled silence at the table.

Joyce Muhlbach perceives the cause. The cook is jealous of the ballerina. But who can imagine the cook in tights? It would take two partners to lift her. Here is an amiable creature shaped like a seal, beloved of her employers and playing Olympian roles to a respectful audience of Otto and Donna, yet unhappy. She has found a soubrette at her master's table and is bursting with spite. She too would be carried across a stage and wear mascara. Rather great tragedies may be enacted in the secrecy of the heart; at this moment something very like a tear is shining in the cook's artless eye.

Joyce again is listening to a sound upstairs. She is attuned to nothing with such delicacy as to the events of the nursery. Donna will cough only once, muffled by the pillow, yet her mother hears, and considers the import. Is it the cough of incipient disease, or nothing but the uncertain functioning of babyhood? Accordingly she acts. To her husband everything sounds approximately the same, but that is the way with husbands, who notice everything a little late. Good man that he is, he cannot even learn how to tell a joke, but must always preface it with a hearty laugh and the advice that his listeners had better get set to split their sides. Of course it is all one can do to smile politely when Muhlbach, after ten minutes of chuckling and back-tracking and clearing his throat, gets around to the point. Kirk would tell it with a fumbled phrase and be midway through another tale before his audience caught up with the first one.

She surveys them both as though from a great distance and knows that she loves them both, her husband because he needs her love, and Kirk because he does not. She half-hears the dancer asking if Sandy has changed since she knew him.

Again comes a stamping on the walk outside, but heavier than were the feet of Kirk. This is the sound of big men thumping snow from their boots. Everyone hears and looks through the archway toward the front door—that is, everyone except Joyce, who has instantly looked at her husband. Kirk from the corner of his eye has taken in this fact and for the first time becomes aware of the strength of this marriage: no matter what happens she will look first of all at her husband and react according to him. There is something old and legendary about this instinct of hers, something which has to do with trust. Kirk feels a clutch of envy at his heart; when he and she were together she did not necessarily look to him whenever anything happened; he had always thought her totally self-sufficient. Now Muhlbach turns back to the table, frowning, and considers his wife, but when she cannot supply the answer he crumples his napkin, places it alongside his plate, and goes to the door. They hear him open the peephole, call someone by name, and immediately swing open the door.

Cold and huge they come in, two men. Duck hunters they are. One is John Grimes and the other is always referred to as "Uncle." Muhlbach, appearing over-joyed, insists that they come into the dining room, so after a few moments they do, though "Uncle" is reluctant. Both men are dressed in corduroy and heavy canvas. Grimes also wears a brilliant crimson mackinaw to which a few flakes of snow are clinging, and while he stands there boldly grinning the snow melts and begins to drip from the edges of his mackinaw onto the dining-room carpet. His pockets bulge with shotgun shells. His gigantic hands are swollen and split from the weather.

Behind him, away from the circle of light, stands Uncle, who is long and solemn and bent like a tree in the wind. His canvas jacket is open, revealing a murderous sheath knife at the belt; its hilt looks bloody. Dangling by a frayed strap over one of his bony shoulders is a wicker fishing creel, exhausted through years of use, from which a few yellowed weeds poke out. He has a bad cold and attends to it by snuffling every few seconds, or by wiping his nose on the cuff of his jacket. Obviously he is more accustomed to kitchens than to dining rooms, nor would he seem out of place in overalls testifying at a revival. He grins and grins, quite foolishly, exposing teeth like crooked tombstones, and when he speaks there is always the feeling that he is about to say something bawdy. But he is considered a great hunter; it is a rare animal or bird that can escape from Uncle. At present he is gaping at Miss

Borowski. Uncle recognizes her as an unfamiliar piece of goods but is not altogether certain what. Borowski returns the stare with contempt.

Both hunters smell acrid and salty. About them wells a devastating aboriginal perfume of wood smoke, fish, the blood of ducks, tobacco, wet canvas, beer, and the perspiration of three inchoate weeks. Sandy Kirk got up slowly when they came in. No longer the center of attention, he stands with his napkin loosely in one hand and watches what goes on, making no attempt to join the bantering conversation. Astutely he measures John Grimes. With one glance he has read Uncle's book but this Grimes is anomalous: he might be a politician or a lawyer or some kind of professional strongman. Above all this duck hunter is masculine. The cumbersome mackinaw rides as lightly on him as does the angora sweater on Borowski. His very presence has subtly dictated the terms of the assembly: he rejects the status of guest and demands that he be distinguished primarily as a man; therefore Joyce and the dancer find themselves reduced to being women. By way of emphasis there looms behind him that sullen scarecrow known as Uncle with a few whiskers curling under his chin, in his awkwardness equally male.

The duck hunter feels himself scrutinized and swiftly turns his head to confront Sandy Kirk. For an instant they gaze at each other without pretense; then they are civilized and exchange nods, whereupon the hunter smiles confidently. Kirk frowns a little. Whirling around, Grimes makes a playful snatch at Uncle's chin as if to grab him by the whiskers. "Try to kill me, will you?" says he, and turns up the collar of the mackinaw to display a tiny black hole caused by a shot. At this Uncle begins to paw the floor and to protest but at that moment is petrified by an oncoming sneeze which doubles him up as though Grimes had punched him in the stomach. He emerges with a red beak and watery eyes and begins hunting through his filthy jacket for a handkerchief, which turns out to be the size of a bandanna.

John Grimes snorts and grins hugely, saying, "Missed the duck too!" This further mortifies Uncle. The two of them look as though they can hardly restrain their spirits after three weeks in the forest and may suddenly begin wrestling on the carpet.

The cook has pushed open the kitchen door and is having a necessary look. Everyone is aware of her; she is not subtle about anything. She seems particularly struck by the fact that both men are wearing knitted woolen caps—John Grimes' is black as chimney soot and Uncle's is a discolored turtle green. It is curious what a cap will do. A cap is like a beret in that when you see someone wearing it you can hardly keep from staring. Cook has seen these men dozens of times but looks from one to the other in stupefaction. She is not unjustified because the headgear causes

Uncle to appear even taller and skinnier and more despondent than he is; if ever he straightens up, the pompom of his cap must certainly scrape the ceiling. At last, conscious that she herself is beginning to attract attention, though she knows not why, cook allows the kitchen door to close.

But another rubberneck is discovered. Near the top of the stairs a pinched white face looks through the railing, and of course it is Otto come out to see what this is all about. He resembles a lemur clutching the bars of some unusual cage, or a tarsier perhaps, with his impossibly large ears and eyes wide open for nocturnal prowling. Like the cook, Otto finds himself on display; he becomes defensive and starts to back out of sight, but is asked what he thinks he is doing up there.

"I want a drink," says Otto piteously, and quite automatically. He has been on the stairs for ten minutes listening without comprehension to a description of the camp in the forest. He comes partway downstairs, holding on to the banister, and as the chandelier light falls upon him it may be seen that if there is anything on earth he does not need it is a drink: his belly is so distended with water that the front of his pajamas has popped open. Unconscious of his ribald figure he asks, "Who are all those men?" He cares who they are, more or less, but the main thing is to turn the conversation upon someone else. While his mother is buttoning up his front he is trenchantly introduced to the hunters.

"Are they company?"

They are. The lack of repartee following his question implies he is unpopular, but Otto scintillates.

"What are they *doing?*"

It should be clear to anyone that the hunters are standing at the mahogany sideboard where the good cook has poured them each a cup of coffee. They are too wet to sit down anywhere. Otto studies them from top to bottom and says he thinks Donna needs to go to the toilet. Will someone come upstairs and see? The nurse is upstairs. If either of them needs anything the nurse will take care of the matter. Otto feels the balance of power swinging away from him; unfortunately he cannot think of anything to say, anything at all. He stands on the bottom step with his belly out like a cantaloupe and those dark eyes — the gift of his mother — wondering. There is nothing special on his mind when he complains that he wants to see the ducks; in fact he hardly knows what he said and is startled that it has gotten a reaction.

Grimes and Uncle have bagged a few over their legal limit, to be sure, but that is not the reason they have brought some to the Muhlbachs. At any rate two fat mallards are lying on the front porch and Otto is allowed to watch through the closest window while Uncle goes outside to get them. Otto mashes his hot moist face against the chilled glass and is quiet. They do not look like ducks to him, but that is what his father said; therefore they must be ducks.

Uncle stoops to catch each mallard by a foot. Already the birds are freezing to the step and when he pulls them up they resist; Otto sees that a few feathers remain on the concrete. The front door opens for a second while Uncle comes in, each bird hanging by one foot so that its other yellow web seems to be waving good-by. The heads swing underneath. The male looks almost a yard long—it cannot be that big, of course, but Grimes and Uncle, who is still snuffling, agree it is the biggest mallard they have ever seen. Around its green neck is a lovely white band; Otto reaches out hesitantly to discover if it is real. The neck feathers are cool and soft. The female is a mottled brown and buff, a small one, not much more than half the length of the male. They are dead, this Otto knows, but he is not certain what death is, only that one must watch out for it.

John Grimes takes each bird around the middle and everyone is a little surprised when the heads rise, just as though they had finished feeding, but the reason is simple: the necks have frozen. Grimes holds both mallards up high; he cracks the cold orange beaks together and smiles down at Otto.

"Quack! Quack!" blurts Uncle.

Otto knows who made the noise and pointedly ignores Uncle, but he cannot get enough of staring at the refulgent bodies. He has never seen anything so green, or of such tender brown. The breasts are full and perfect; to find out what has killed them one must feel around in those feathers, parting them here and there with the fingertips, until the puncture is suddenly disclosed.

Otto is subdued, and when the episode of the ducks is ended, when they have been taken roughly into the kitchen and nothing more can be said of them, he must struggle to regain his plaintive tone. Now there is not a chance it will be successful but he says he thinks Donna would like a drink. It is not successful. However, there are two big guns that Otto always keeps in reserve; one is that he believes he is getting a stomachache and the other is that he is afraid the stars are falling. He is no fool, this Otto, and realizes that if he tries them both on the same evening he will be found out. He studies his bare feet like a politician and estimates which question would be more effective, considering the fact that there are some ducks in the house and that his mother has been in bed all day. He begins to look wonderfully ill at ease.

"Are the stars falling down?"

Always that is good for an answer, a long melodious one, always. But tonight it is met by a grim stare from his father. He looks hopefully at his mother; she is not so ominous but equally firm. There is about the atmosphere something that tells Otto he might soon be turned across his father's knee. He elects to retreat and backs toward the stairway, wondering if he could reasonably ask for the dog-in-the-manger again. His father places both hands flat on the table, which means he is going to stand up. Otto abandons all hope, and, wearing a persecuted face, goes up the stairs as rapidly as possible, which is to say in the manner of a chimpanzee.

Almost immediately there is a crash in the upstairs hall followed by the unmistakable sound of Otto falling. Once again he has forgotten about the hall table. Originally there was a vase on this table but after he destroyed it while hurrying to the bathroom they reasoned that sooner or later he would take the same route; hence there is nothing but a lace doily on the table. In fact, Muhlbach finds it a senseless place to put a table, but his wife wants it there though she cannot explain why. Otto is bellowing. To listen to him one would be convinced that in all history no individual has ever experienced such pain. He varies pitch, rhyme, and tempo as he recalls the tragedy; it is a regular Oriental concert. The footsteps of the nurse are heard, and the matter of her scientific soothing, but he will have none of this professional.

Joyce gets up from the table, but in passing behind Muhlbach's chair an expression of nausea overspreads her face and she almost sinks to the floor but recovers without a sound. Kirk starts to cry out, and upon seeing her straighten up he emits a weird groan. Dee Borowski and Muhlbach gaze at him very curiously.

Otto can still be heard, although the sincerity of his dirge may now be questioned. At any rate he has been carried to bed, where the nurse swabs his bumped forehead with mercurochrome and covers it with a fantastic bandage that he seems to enjoy touching. Still he is so exhausted by the hour, the splendor of the ducks, the strange men, and the accident in the mysterious hallway that it is necessary to continue whimpering. This self-indulgence halts the instant he becomes aware that his father has entered the room. Otto prepares himself like any rascal for he knows not what judgment, and cannot conceal his apprehension when his father draws up a chair and sits wearily beside the bed. They talk for a while. Otto does not know what they are talking about. Sometimes they discuss his mother, sometimes himself, or Donna. He industriously maintains his end of the conversation though he feels himself growing sleepy, and in time he is neither displeased nor alarmed to feel the hand of his father stroking his head. Somewhat groggily he inquires if the stars are falling. In addition to being a useful question Otto is moderately afraid of just such a catastrophe. He did not come upon this idea second-hand, but thought of it himself. The first time it occurred to him he began to weep and though a number of months have gone by so that he trusts the sky a little more he is still not altogether confident. One cannot be sure when a star is falling. Clearly there is nothing to hold them in place. Why should one not suddenly drop on his bed?

Countless nights, in winter and spring, autumn and summer, have Otto and his father gone out of doors, or sometimes driven toward the country far enough that the city lights were less obtrusive, and here, with the boy on his father's lap, they have considered what was above. At first there was a certain difficulty in communication. For example, Muhlbach discussed the planets and stars while Otto listened with profound concentration. Muhlbach was impressed until Otto, after a period of deep thought, inquired if Donna was a star, a question that might be answered in various ways, of course, depending. But with practice they began to understand each other so that after several months Otto grew familiar with the elementary legends and was apt to request his favorites, such as Andromeda, or The Twins. Or he might ask to hear that wonderfully euphonious index to the Great Bear, which goes: Alkaid, Mizar, Alioth, Megrez, Phecda, Merak, and Dubhe.

"What does the bear eat?" he asks, and this is certainly a question packed with logic. His father's faith is renewed; the lessons continue. Not far behind the bear— do you see?—comes Arcturus, its warden, who follows the animal about. This happens to be the father's personal favorite among the stars because it was the first one he himself ever learned to recognize, and was taught him by his own father, the very same who gave young Otto the archaeology book. Muhlbach hopes that Otto will learn Arcturus before any other. This is the reason he points to it first of all. He directs the flashlight beam toward this yellow giant, so many times larger than the sun, and though Muhlbach has searched the heavens with a flashlight numberless times he is yet amazed that this light appears to reach all the way.

We can never go there, Otto. It is too far. Muhlbach includes a few statistics and is again deluded by his son's intelligent expression because it develops that what Otto wishes to know is whether or not Arcturus is farther away than downtown. Still, hope springs eternal, and after smoking half a cigar Muhlbach has recovered from the blow enough to try again. Once upon a time—yes, this is the right approach—once upon a time Arcturus came flying straight toward the earth! What do you think of that? Otto is shaken by the premise; in his father's lap he sits erect and anxious, no doubt pondering what will happen when they meet, or met, since it is all in the past. Half-a-million years, for that matter, and Muhlbach, now savoring parenthood to the utmost, adds with a sportive air that the sole observers were troglodytes. Otto lets this pass. Now Muhlbach hesitates because he has pumped up his story; the full truth is that Arcturus was also drifting a bit to the side as it approached and even now is passing us so there is not to be a collision after all. Fortunately Otto considers the telling of greater value than the tale. He is not much gripped by explanation or hypothesis; he would as soon just look. One would think he was gazing into a mountain lake. According to his father they can see perhaps three or four thousand stars in the sky; Otto again looks up and is stunned, though for a better reason. He is a pure voluptuary, a first-rate knight of the carpet. Sidereal time, relative motion, and years of light are all very well—astronomy, in short, can come or go, so Otto feels—but stars are magnificent. Briefly he is held by the constancy of Arcturus, then he loses it. There are a great many things in the sky. How shall he hold fast to one? When he is older he will distinguish more clearly but now a light is a light, each about as effective as its neighbor. Now he has been seduced by Mars. It seems bigger and more suggestive. What could he not accomplish if only he held it in his hand! As there is no moon, and Sirius is down, nothing can be more glamorous. How red it is! How wondrous bright! In vain does Muhlbach point out Pollux and Castor, Procyon, Regulus.

In his bedroom the little boy sleeps with one arm raised and a fist clenched as if in triumph, on his helpless face a stubborn look, his forehead all but invisible under the preposterous mercurochrome-soaked bandage. Muhlbach sits beside his son, watching and thinking. The bedroom is silent but for the breathing of the two children. The nurse has gone downstairs. After a while Muhlbach rises and walks soberly across the room to stand above his daughter; her pink jade lips are parted and it is clear her dream is a serious one. Muhlbach wonders if she will sleep until spring. He longs to pick her up, somehow to unfold himself and conceal her deep within, and he bends down until their faces are an inch apart.

He hears the front door close, the faint after-knock of the brass lion's head on the outside of the door. He moves on tiptoe to the window and looks down at his two friends, the duck hunters, who elect to tramp across the snowy lawn even though the walk has been shoveled. He looks at his watch to discover he has been up here almost a half-hour. He very much wanted to go hunting this year, possibly more than ever before; each time this thought comes to him he feels unutterably disgusted with himself.

Uncle and Grimes leave dark symmetrical prints on the snow and as always Uncle is one step behind. There is no reason for this; it is just the way they are. It comes to Muhlbach that John Grimes is leading his afreet by a chain round the neck. He watches them get into Grimes' car, sees the headlights flash and thus notices that the snow has stopped falling, and moodily he looks after the burning red tail lights until the street is again deserted. That snowy rectangle over which they walked oddly resembles the eight of spades; and now the half-moon comes floating above the rooftops as if to join in this curious game. Much higher—well along in the night—kneels the father image, Orion. While Muhlbach stands at the window the moon's light descends calmly upon his troubled face and reaches beyond him into the nursery past Donna's crib to the wall poignantly desecrated by paste and crayon scribbles. There a swan is in flight. Otto has seen fit to improve this wallpaper swan. What could be gained by telling him its elegance is perhaps impaired by the measles he has added? Muhlbach thinks over the shards remaining from his own childhood, but is conscious mostly of how much has perished.

Some time longer he stands there steeping himself in this restorative moonlight, and looks around with approval at the knotty pine toy shelf he has knocked together and varnished, and again remarks the silence of this night which is counterpointed by the breath of his children. An unimpressive man he is, who shows a little paunch and the beginning of a stoop, though otherwise no older than forty warrants. People do not ever turn around to look at him on the street. At cocktail parties no feminine gaze lingers on him. When it comes to business there are men who find it worthwhile to seek out Muhlbach for an opinion; otherwise he is left alone.

Quietly but without disappointment he leaves the nursery, shuts the door, and descends the staircase hopeful that his wife has recognized the futility of this evening. It strikes him as incredible that she can maintain interest in a man she has outgrown.

When he enters the living room the nurse slips back upstairs. Sandy Kirk and Joyce are making no attempt to communicate; they sit side by side on the sofa but behave like strangers seated together at a movie. Borowski appears hypnotized by the embers; she has taken off her shoes and placed them neatly like an offering on the marble hearth. Muhlbach finds her naïveté wearisome and he thinks that if she does anything else ingenuous he will lose his manners and become rude. She does not even blink when he strides past; she does nothing but dully watch the subsiding flames, her mouth idiotically open. From his chair beside the bookcase he glowers at her, and it suddenly occurs to him that he is sick of the cook, too, and sick of the relentless nurse. He is sick to death of life itself, and of solicitous neighbors, and he has forgotten whatever is not despair. Too much is happening to him, whereas all he wants is to be left alone that he may regain some measure of his inner strength. Even one hour, uninterrupted, might be enough. He thinks he cannot pretend much longer. His thoughts turn upon Goethe, from whom he is remotely descended, and he visualizes that man interminably searching himself for power while playing to his sycophants a stiff-legged excellence.

All at once his wife trembles; she bites her lip over some private thought, and looking at him she remarks, just loud enough to be heard, that John Grimes and Uncle left a few minutes ago.

Muhlbach, struggling against disorder, allows himself a few seconds before replying, "I know, I know."

Sandy Kirk rouses himself, picks up a magazine and fans his cheek as if only now he realizes how suffocating the room has become. Muhlbach, watching Kirk, is filled with hatred; it seems to him that never before has he encountered a man he despises as much.

"They missed you," his wife continues, "but I told them you'd go hunting again next year."

In this speech there is a note of self-pity that causes Muhlbach to shut his eyes and throw up his hands, though he does not say a word.

"I told them I was being selfish but I want you with me every minute of the time. Next year they'll have you the same as before." Having started she cannot stop; she turns swiftly upon Sandy Kirk and presses one of his limp hands to her breast. Her eyes fill with tears but except for this she appears peeved, resentful, and she talks compulsively. Words pour from her nerveless mouth without meaning and Kirk is obviously terrified. He stares at her out of the corner of his eye like a trapped animal; he is powerless to recover his hand. Muhlbach scowls at Dee Borowski who has turned around to watch, and he knows that she is aware of him, but she cannot get enough of the nauseating scene; she must look and look. Muhlbach springs out of his chair and rushes into the kitchen.

Sandy Kirk turns his head this way and that to avoid looking at Joyce. All the precautions he took, they were no good. She has not respected any convention; she had lunged through every defense and taken him. Even under the circumstances it was not decent of her to do that. She has always shocked him one way or another, even the first time they met. He had been a college student then and one afternoon was standing on a snowy bluff overlooking a river that had frozen close to shore. He had brought along a sled and was wondering if he dared coast down because the slope was studded with pinnacles of rock; furthermore, if he could not stop in time there was a very good possibility of crashing through the ice and drowning. Then he noticed this girl trudging up with a sled. When he warned her it was unsafe she replied, "Mind your own business," and without hesitation flung herself upon the sled, hurtled down among the rocks, and reappeared far out on the ice, wriggling to a stop not five yards from the water. That was the way she did everything. Now she is twenty-nine years old—an aged, wasted old woman who can scarcely walk without assistance. Her arms have shriveled to the bone and the veins are black.

Kirk is furious that Borowski has not reacted the way she was supposed to. When at last he had gathered the will to speak, to interrupt the horrible monologue, and pointedly mentioned *Don Juan*, the dancer only looked at him in stupefaction. So he has not distracted Joyce, she has still got him, hanging on; but then he recovers his voice, that familiar ally, and all by itself his voice starts to tell about something funny that once happened in Switzerland. Kirk waves his free arm and rolls his eyes comically toward the ceiling until at last, thank God, Muhlbach comes out of the kitchen. It is over. Joyce loosens her grip and he begins to pull his fingers away one at a time.

With an ingratiating tone Sandy Kirk addresses Muhlbach, who gives back a clinical stare and stretches out his hands to the fire. Seeing this calm gesture of self-assurance, seeing as it were, a true *Hofmeister*, Kirk suffers a familiar malaise, for among diplomats and intellectuals, or artists of any description, he feels established, but faced with a solid pedestrian he loses confidence in his own wit and commences to doubt the impression he is making. It has always been so, though for the life of him Sandy Kirk fails to understand why. And this Muhlbach is indestructible, a veritable storm cellar of a man. No catastrophe will ever uproot him or confuse him, this man of the flatlands with a compass on his forehead. Kirk is envious, and also contemptuous. He is a little afraid of Muhlbach. He has finally managed to draw the captive arm away from Joyce, yet she clings mutely with her eyes. He feels sorry for her and wishes he could feel more, but there it is: she seems to him unreal and distorted, not the girl he once knew. This sick woman is distasteful. In the future he may feel some compassion but this evening she has driven him backward till he has begun to grow violent. If she does not soon release him altogether he will throw a fit. He cannot stand being forced this way, being accustomed to having what he wants only when he wants it. During intolerable situations Sandy Kirk always envisions himself in some favorite locale thousands of miles away. It is a form of ballast. And now he decides to imagine himself in Biarritz seated regally on the hillside on his favorite bench. From there he would contemplate the Atlantic sun shining on red tile rooftops, and after an expensive supper he might wander into the casino to luxuriate in the sound of clicking, rattling chips and the suave tones of croupiers.

Otto has wakened; he can be heard talking to the nurse about something, no doubt vital. A jack-in-the-box will go down for the night more easily than will Otto. Recently he has taken to singing in the middle of the night; he disturbs everyone in the house with his pagan lament. "What are you singing about?" he will be asked, but he always refuses to answer.

Just then the telephone rings. Who could be calling at such an hour? Sandy Kirk, like a doctor, must always leave word of his whereabouts, and so does the dancer, though with more hope than expectation. As usual the actual message is less exciting than the suspense. Joyce, whose call it was, returns to the living room almost immediately. She seems more vexed than she has been all evening and after resting for a minute she mimics the inquisitive neighbor.

" 'I saw your lights were still on and simply thought I must find out if there was anything I could do.' She got a couple of ducks, too. Your friends are dreadfully generous."

Muhlbach makes no attempt to reply. He shakes his head as if he can endure nothing more.

Joyce Muhlbach's voice begins to rise unsteadily. "I told her not to telephone! I told that woman to let us alone!"

Borowski has emerged from her private reverie long enough to gobble this up and Muhlbach, who was watching her, is again filled with loathing. Little by little everyone in the room becomes aware that a group of carol singers is approaching, and finally, in passing the Muhlbach home, their song is clear. The voices are young; most likely a group of students.

After they have gone Joyce slowly resumes twisting her wedding ring; it is loose on her finger and slides off easily, hesitating only at the knuckles. She takes it off and puts it on and all at once remarks that she has received an ad from a mortuary. In this there is something so ghoulish that it is almost impossible not to laugh. Her husband of course knows about the advertisement but the guests have a tense moment. Joyce glances from one to the other in a malicious way, twisting her ring and sliding it off, waiting to see if either of them dare smile.

Borowski becomes flustered. "Sandy has told me everything about you." This gets no response at all. Borowski turns red, and says that Joyce meant a great deal to Sandy years ago. Neither was that the proper speech so Borowski glares at Sandy Kirk because it is his fault she has gotten into this situation.

Joyce is suddenly aware that Donna has wakened, and though not a sound comes from the upstairs nursery this same knowledge reaches Muhlbach a second later. Both of them wait. He glances across the room to her and she catches the look solidly as if she had been expecting it. Kirk guesses they have heard one of the children and he recalls that earlier instant when they reacted as a unit, causing him to sense how deeply they were married. He is a little injured that they mean this much to each other; he feels that Joyce has betrayed him. He knew her long before Muhlbach ever did. It is as if something valuable slipped away, disappeared while he was preoccupied. Now he thinks that he intended to come back to Joyce. They would have gone well together, and he knows that whatever Muhlbach may have brought her he did not bring something she has always needed—excitement. This intelligent, sober, prosaic man escorted her into a barren little room, a cool study where she has withered. Kirk feels himself growing embittered over the way life has treated him. This woman was rightfully his own, even if she refused to admit it. There were instances, it is true, when she became tyrannical, but later she would always repent; and if he should abuse her he had only to hang his head until her eye grew milder. To his mind comes the observation of one of those lugubrious Russians: that from the fearful medley of thoughts and impressions accumulated in man's brain from association with women, the memory, like a filter, retains no ideas, no clever sayings, no philosophy, nothing in fact but that extraordinary resignation to fate, that wonderful mercifulness, forgiveness of everything.

The longer Kirk sits in the room with Muhlbach's wife the more does he perceive how terribly he is still in love with her. He has been afraid this would happen. She is one of those legendary creatures whom the French have so astutely named *femme fatale*. One does not recover. Kirk permits himself a furtive look at the husband. Yes, he has been stricken too.

What kind of a woman is she? One talks to her a little while of this or that, nothing remarkable is said, nothing in the least memorable, and one goes away. Then, all uninvited, comes a feeling of dreadful urgency and one must hurry back. Again nothing is said. She is not witty, nor is she beautiful; she is in fact frequently dour and sullen without cause. Periods of gloomy silence occur, yet no sense of emptiness, no uneasiness. She seems to wait for what is about to happen. It is all very confusing. Sandy Kirk broods, puzzles, gazes hopelessly into space for vast amounts of time thinking of nothing, unable to formulate questions worth asking himself, much less answer, feeling nothing at all but a kind of dull, unhealthy desire.

He steals another look at Muhlbach and discovers in that stolid face a similar misery, which makes Kirk feel better. He remembers with embarrassment certain phone calls during which he was unable to speak. "Hello," he will mumble, already despondent at the thought that she is listening. "Is that you?" And when she replies, sounding stubborn, or irked that he has telephoned at such an inconvenient hour, then every single thought explodes like a soap bubble. He waits anxiously to hear what she will say next, which is nothing: he is the one who has called, it is up to him to manufacture a little conversation. But he is destroyed by aphasia, he finds nothing humorous about life, not a thing worth repeating. What has he been doing? Well, quite a lot but now, thinking about it, what is worth the effort of describing? He summons all his strength: "What have *you* been doing?" He has just managed to mutter this. She replies in an exhausted voice that she has not done anything worth mentioning. This is impossible! He mumbles something about the fact that he has been thinking of her and called to find out what she was doing—what a stupid thing to say, he realizes, and discovers to his amazement that he is clutching the telephone as if he were trying to strangle it. The wire has been silent for five minutes. He prays no operator has decided to investigate this odd business or he will be locked up for insanity, and in a voice more dead than alive he demands, "Are we going out tonight?" He is positive she will say no, and that is exactly what she does say. Instantly he is filled with alarm and wants to know why not; she replies callously that she doesn't want to see him ever again, but offers no explanation. He subsides. He leans against the wall with his eyes closed. He has not eaten all day but is not hungry. Minutes pass. Neither of them speaks. It is raining, of course; water splashes dismally on the window ledge and life is implacably gray. One cannot imagine sunshine, laughter, happiness. He staggers and understands that he was falling asleep. He whispers good-by and waits. She immediately answers good-by. Neither hangs up. Love is not supposed to be like this. He announces his good-by again with renewed vigor just as though he were rushing out to the golf course, but the mummery sickens him. There is no significant click at the other end of the line. What is she waiting for? Will she never release him? Can she possibly expect him to hang up first? Life is a wretched joke. He cannot abide the sound of his own name. Still she refuses to hang up the receiver, and it goes on and on, a long, dreary, stupid, inconclusive affair. These calls have on occasion lasted a full hour or more though neither of them said a good minute's worth. How desperate was the need to communicate, how impotent the message. So when he sees her he wants to know why she does not talk to him over the telephone, and she looks at him without a smile.

Kirk decides he is losing his mind. Has Muhlbach, that barn of a man, disgraced himself in a similar manner? Because normal men do not ignore their pride. Yet look at those tormented eyes! It is clear that he, too, has fallen apart in front of her. There could be no other explanation.

Kirk will never forget one night he went shambling through the streets without enough energy to lift his head until all at once, as though he had been handed a telegram, he started rapidly across the city, rushed through Times Square with his eye fastened on Forty-fourth Street, and just around the corner there she was!

What fantastic perception could account for this? And she seemed to be waiting—expecting him! Yet she was anchored securely to the arm of some nondescript man in a bow tie. As they passed each other he nodded curtly and stalked into the crowd. What a lover does he make! What happened to the celestial phrase? He is the sort of man who would address the wrong balcony. Even his agony is fraudulent because he is hoping everybody on the street notices his tragic face. He thinks he could not be more obvious with the stigmata; still, nobody paused when he strode somberly toward the river. Well, he has been through no grimmer night than that one. It might have made sense if she had been a famous beauty, but even in those days no one ever picked Joyce out of a group. She never was quick on her feet, or had a musical voice, nor did her skin ever take the light as the artists say. And how did they know—both of them—that they were destined to meet just around that corner?

At this instant the cook appears, not in her black uniform but in a rather shocking dress. She has finished every dish and emptied the garbage and now she would like permission to go home. Muhlbach calls a taxi for her. Cook bids good night to everyone, to everyone except the ballerina, and then she returns to the pantry where she will sit like a monument on her favorite stool to brood until the taxicab arrives. All have noticed her going upstairs a few minutes ago with a sweet for the children. She wakes them up to feed them something that will ruin their teeth; nothing can break her of this habit. Neither explanation nor threat of dismissal deter this cook, not even the formidable nurse. Cook is of the opinion the children are her own and it is clear that her heart would fall open like an overripe melon if Muhlbach ever made good his threat. The nurse and the cook look upon one another as hereditary enemies and neither questions that this should be so. Nurse dislikes going into the kitchen and while there is apt to sit with arms crossed and a severe expression. Cook feeds her without a word, stinting just a little, and afterward scrubs the dishes quite fiercely. She has never seen this nurse before; who can tell how reliable the creature is? Cook believes this nurse is neglecting the babies and thus it is she sneaks upstairs at least once a night. That is why, when Muhlbach calls for something, there may be silence in the kitchen.

All at once comes the sound of a shot. Conversation stops in the living room. There are no cars on the street, so it could not have been a backfire, and besides it sounded as though it were in the house. Muhlbach is about to investigate when at the head of the stairway appears the nurse, dreadfully embarrassed, to explain that she has been listening to a gangster story on the radio. She hopes they were not alarmed. She just now looked into the nursery; the children were not awakened.

No, they are accustomed to sounds like that. Machine guns and bombs are natural toys nowadays.

Well, so much for the shot; cook has not committed suicide after all.

Presently the taxi may be heard crunching up the street. One expects it to climb the little drive, but it does not, even though Muhlbach has sprinkled rock salt from the street to the garage. Cook expertly flickers the porch lights but this taxi driver is leery of hillsides and does no more than blink his headlights by way of announcing that if she wishes a ride she must take the risk. That is the way of cab drivers nowadays; one must bow to their high-handed manner or simply do without. And should you fail to tip them they may slam the door on your fingers. Cook often tells about the friend of a very good friend of hers who lost a thumb just that way and almost bled to death. Oh, it is a gruesome tale indeed and always concludes with the cook nodding darkly, hands folded severely over her white apron. She believes in a day of reckoning with as much faith as she attacks her Sunday hymns in the kitchen. These hymns have made her a neighborhood celebrity; whenever she is mentioned someone invariably adds, "—the one who sings in the kitchen." The cab driver, ignorant of the future, states his position by lighting a cigarette, and at this the cook capitulates. She lets herself out the screen door—so useless in winter—and is heard walking cautiously down the icy steps. One can see her getting into the back seat of the cab. The door is closed and she is taken away, unhappy woman.

The children—"my babies," she calls them—are undisturbed that she has left. They are never sure whether they dream of her nightly visit or whether they really do wake up and eat something. No matter, they will see her the following morning. Just before noon she will arrive, lumbering and scolding without even waiting to learn what they have done wrong. If they have been really bad she will frighten them by saying she is going to California. Their eyes open wide. It is the word alone that Donna has come to fear; the sound of it is enough to make her weep. Otto knows it is a place far off in the direction of downtown where people go when they are angry, and he knows that no one ever returns from California, so he too begins to sob. Oh, there is no punishment worse than when cook starts packing her suitcase.

But they are sleeping now. Otto is a little boy, there can be no question of that, but Donna, what is she? She is so small! Can anything so tiny be what she will one day be? Will there come a time when she would abandon her father and her brother for the sake of someone they have never seen? Someone perhaps as impossible as Otto, or even more so? Surely no one more obstinate and militantly ignorant than Otto can lay claim to being human. Only wait and see! He will come for Donna with biceps flexed and a hat crushed on the back of his head. Most likely he will be chewing gum. He will converse like a cretin, yet how accomplished will he think himself. Will Donna think as much? Will she peer into her mirror and suffer anguish over the shape of her chin or the cut of her gown? She could not be more perfect yet she will despise herself because of him. Perhaps he will even be tattooed! He is so clever and so handsome, she thinks, how can it be that her father pokes fun at him? Well, her father has grown old and does not know about the latest things. In fact Donna is mortified that he chooses to wear the kind of collar and necktie he does; it might have been very well in Mother's day, but that was twenty years ago. "How just positively incomparable!" she cries at the sight of her girl friend's new dancing slippers. By next month, though, every thing has become "beautific." Her father mulls over the expense he has gone to in sending her to a decent university. All in vain. She might as well have been educated by comedians. Yet how lovely she is! Muhlbach feels tears surging to his eyes, but of course nothing shows. Why not? Why is he unable to weep for beauty that is positively incomparable? And he thinks of her mother, and when Donna twirls about the living room for him with flushed cheeks Muhlbach cannot trust himself to speak.

Who can say whether this will all come to pass? Is that the way it is to be, or will panic annihilate them all? Perhaps such horror will occur—bombs and irresistible rays not yet invented, a holocaust even the comic-books have not conceived—that Donna will never be stricken by this ludicrous young god. In view of the damage he is sure to inflict perhaps it would be just as kind if she died in the wreckage of war. Well, they will all find out.

Now, this starry night, she lies serenely sleeping, a Botticellian morsel, the cook's beloved, an altogether improbable object, cherished above life itself.

Otto, being masculine, cannot afford to be so complacent as his sister, not even in dreams. His fists fly back and forth, he cracks his skull against the wall and does not feel a thing, he thrashes, mutters, climbs mountain peaks, vanquishes his enemies in a second, and above all else he frowns. Not for him the panacea of Donna's rag doll. A gun may be all right for a time, a puppy is even better, a picture book is good too, and attempting to climb the willow tree is a worthy project, but there seems to be no final answer. He must investigate one thing and then another, and in each he finds something lacking. Here he is scratching at the screen door again though he wanted to go outside not five minutes ago. His nature is as restless as the nose of a rabbit. No one can be certain what he is seeking.

He is wakened by something happening downstairs. The voices have changed. There is the sound of coat hangers rattling and of people moving around. Company is going. Otto looks groggily at the ceiling and tries to stay awake although he does not know just why. He would like to get up and look out the window but the room is cold; then too the nurse would probably come in and he does not especially like her. He has thought up some grisly tortures that he intends to try on the nurse, such as flooding the bathroom and when she runs in to turn off the water he will lock the door so that his father will think she did it. Otto has a great bag of schemes for the nurse. He is certain to drive her away. Meanwhile he must concentrate on the noises and so understand what they are doing downstairs. Donna is breathing passionately at the moment and Otto is annoyed by this interference; he props himself up on both elbows.

The front door opens and people can be heard talking outside. This is really too much; Otto is wide awake and out of bed, creeping to the window. There he crouches, his brilliant eyes just above the sill. The winter air makes his eyes water so he grinds his fists into them, the best remedy ever. And he shivers without pause. He has come unbuttoned again.

Muhlbach is following the guests down the icy walk to Kirk's car. Its windshield is a mound of snow and while the guests are getting into the car Muhlbach reaches out and brushes off the windshield. This is no instinctive action: for the past hour he has been thinking about this gesture. When he opened the door for Grimes and Uncle he noticed the snow still falling and saw that it was about to cover the other car. Not long after that he hit upon the proper method to end the evening, a simple act not only cordial but final. It should express his attitude. Now he has done it but too fast; Kirk was not even looking.

The engine starts up. The diplomat has fitted on his elegant gray gloves, settling each finger, and now pulls the overcoat across his knees while waiting for the engine to warm. Beside him the dancer is already beginning to look snug; she has drawn her rather large strong feet up onto the seat and tucked her hands deep inside the mink sleeves of her jacket. She is only waiting for the instant the wheels begin to turn, then she will lean her head against his shoulder and like the wheels she will roll toward a conclusion. She is always touched by this moment when the acting is done, the curtain comes swaying down, and life takes over. Each time, however, she is a little frightened, a little doubtful that she can survive.

Muhlbach, standing soberly beside the hood, brushes more snow from the edge of the windshield and receives a faint shock when Kirk acknowledges this by glancing out at him; for an instant the man looked older, much different, the hair on his temples appeared silver. Muhlbach is well aware that Kirk is eight or ten years junior, yet he cannot escape the eerie feeling that he saw a man distinctly older than himself.

Throughout the evening these two have avoided each other, and so it is destined to end. Circumstances have set the limit of their association. They must be neutral forever. Sandy Kirk has divined the truth of this while Muhlbach was thinking it through. They nod. The car starts forward but immediately slips sideways into a rut where the wheels spin ineffectively. Kirk, tightening his grip, presses the gas pedal to the floor and Muhlbach realizes the man is a poor driver. The tires are screaming on the ice. Muhlbach waves both hands, shakes his head, goes around to look, and sees that he must get out his own car to give Kirk a push. In a few minutes it is done; they are safely away from the curb.

The visitors have gone. Muhlbach eases his car once more into the garage and closes the door, but despite the extreme cold he cannot bring himself to go inside the house right away. While he stands forlornly gazing down at his shadow on the moonlit snow he hears the voice of his son crying timorously into the windy night.

Muhlbach lifts up his head. "Go to sleep, Otto."

And the apprehensive Otto, peeping down from the nursery window, hears this faint reply. It is the voice of his father saying everything will be all right.

1954

NAN MADOL

U NCLE GATES and Aunt Ruth lived in Springfield and every so often they came visiting, but I do not remember having much of a conversation with Uncle Gates until I was about nine or ten years old. One evening he stared across the dining room table at me and asked what I intended to do with my life. I told him I wanted to become an archaeologist. If that is true, he said, you must pay attention in school. I didn't like Uncle Gates as well as my father's younger brother Rodney who could pull a silver dollar out of my nose and throw animal shadows on the wall by manipulating his fingers in the lamplight. Once when Uncle Rodney was visiting us he winked at me and turned a back flip. Uncle Gates, who resembled a parrot, did not care about magic tricks or back flips. He taught history and literature at Springfield College and I remember thinking that I would hate to be in his classes.

Almost every summer he took a trip, usually with Aunt Ruth, sometimes by himself. He had traveled around Canada and Mexico and the Caribbean and Europe and once I asked my father how Uncle Gates could afford so many vacations. He made a killing in the market, my father said. I had no idea what the market was, or how one could earn money by killing something in it, but the explanation sounded reasonable.

Now Uncle Gates was on his way home to Springfield after touring the South Seas and my father had written to let me know that he would be stopping overnight in San Francisco. I was expected to entertain him.

He was seated in the hotel lobby gazing straight ahead when I saw him for the first time in twenty years. He had retired from teaching and he appeared much older. Wattles hung from his jaw. The backs of his hands were spotted. For a moment he did not recognize me. Then he exclaimed, William! You gave me quite a start. You are beginning to look like Rodney.

It had occurred to me that we could drive across the Golden Gate Bridge and take the road up Mt. Tamalpais for a panoramic view of San Francisco Bay. Uncle Gates thought that sounded like an interesting excursion. First, though, he wanted to get a coat.

I am unaccustomed to your foggy climate, he said. Come along, I'll show you my room. This is a splendid hotel. I knew right away that I would like it.

He had trouble getting to his feet, which annoyed him. He frowned and steadied himself on the back of the chair.

Your parents may have told you about my accident, he said as we walked through the lobby. It happened a year ago last Christmas. I slipped on a patch of ice and went down like a ton of bricks. I was knocked unconscious. My balance hasn't been too good since then. I thought I would get over it, but I haven't. Now let's see, where's the elevator? Ah! No, isn't that the fire exit? I seem to be a little turned around.

An African couple entered the elevator ahead of us. The man wore a conservative English suit but the woman was dressed in an elaborate flowing gown. Uncle Gates studied them while the door closed and we started up. I could not tell from his face what he was thinking. He cleared his throat.

The elevator stopped at the fifth floor. He looked puzzled. Then he remembered the Africans. He shuffled to one side and politely asked if this was where they wished to get off.

As we walked along the corridor to his room he seemed to mistrust the carpet, lifting each foot higher than necessary. Inside the room, after fumbling for the light switch, he went to the window and pulled the drapes apart. There lay the huge sparkling bay, the bridge to Oakland, Treasure Island, the Berkeley hills.

You have a distinctive city, he said. What a shame these young people in California fail to appreciate it.

How do you know they don't? I asked.

Just look at them, he said. Now don't chide me, William. I am aware that times change. However, we should not ignore fundamentals. Would you like a glass of water before we start? Or perhaps you would care to make use of the bathroom?

No, I said, I'm fine.

I envy you those kidneys, he said. Pardon me. He walked into the bathroom, shut the door and turned on the shower before using the toilet. All right, young fellow, he announced when he came out, let's tackle that mountain.

While we stood waiting for the elevator I remarked that it was a handsome couple we had met on the way up.

He nodded. Yes. I wondered where they might be from. I know very little about the regional costumes of Africa, despite visiting several of those countries a few years ago. All kinds of people seem to stay at this hotel. It's practically a United Nations. I can't imagine a crowd like this in Springfield. He pressed the button again and shook his head.

The Africans were talking to a clerk at the desk when we came out of the elevator, but Uncle Gates after one glance paid no attention. I suspected he had filed them in his mind under the appropriate label and that was that. He walked unsteadily but with determination toward the revolving door which was moving slowly, like the paddlewheel of a steamboat. These damn things, he said, you never can tell what they're up to.

Outside the hotel I told him I would get the car and bring it around, but he insisted he didn't mind walking. I remembered a dozen motorcycles parked on Geary in front of a liquor store and I hoped that by now the bikers would be gone, but they were loitering on the sidewalk—black leather jackets with steel chains and painted insignia, boots, beards, mirrored sunglasses. Uncle Gates glared at them.

What the devil is the matter with those bums? he demanded. Why aren't they at work?

Come on, I said and took him by the arm to prevent him from stopping. A couple of the bikers had noticed us.

He had trouble getting into the car. I am sorry to inconvenience you, he said while backing toward the seat. I am not as limber as I was at your age. After sitting down he lifted one leg with both hands and pulled it inside, then the other. My God, he muttered, there used to be a time when I could walk all day.

As we drove toward the Golden Gate he sat with his arms folded, oblivious to everything. At the corner of Van Ness and Lombard we slowed down for some police cars and a crowd of people, but he looked straight ahead.

Who on earth buys those knickknacks in the gift shop? he asked suddenly. I should think a place like that would go broke. Doodads! Nothing but doodads!

Well, it's none of my business. What's the name of this place we're going to? Mount something-or-other.

Tamalpais, I said. Tamal Indians used to live around there. Tamal country. Tamal pais.

I understand Spanish, he said.

This surprised me a little, although I did not know why. He had traveled in a number of Latin countries so I should have realized that he would understand Spanish. He may have guessed what I was thinking because he remarked that languages weren't difficult. We talked about this for a while. He had learned to read and speak several European languages, but did not consider himself a linguist. Also, he had begun to study Mandarin. I asked if Mandarin would be of much use in Springfield and he replied that it had not the slightest value.

However, he went on, the process of learning can be remunerative. What a shame that most people wish merely to be diverted. There is greater satisfaction in a single page of Tacitus than you are apt to find in twenty-four hours of ephemeral entertainment.

He sounded very much like a professor. I was afraid he might start questioning me about Tacitus so I asked if he wanted the window rolled up. Fog obscured the bridge towers and it was getting cool.

I am quite comfortable, he said. Do as you please.

His answer reminded me of the Midwest where polite indifference signified good manners. I thought about his courtesy to the Africans and about his courteous response when I had suggested we go for a drive. I wondered if he really did want to go driving or if he would rather have strolled around Fisherman's Wharf or listened to the bongo drummers in Aquatic Park. Maybe he would have liked to explore Mason Street and ogle the hookers. I wished for Uncle Rodney who probably would have said the hell with a scenic drive, let's see what's happening in the Tenderloin. I imagined Uncle Rodney walking into a strip joint and astonishing everybody with a back flip.

Ahead of us stood the lopsided cone of Mt. Tamalpais, regarded by some as California's attempt to copy Fujiyama. Uncle Gates, communing with himself, did not see it until I pointed. He emitted a volcanic rumbling which I took for approval, and retreated to his meditations. I tried to think of him as a young man before the clay hardened. I had seen him any number of times when I was a child, but he had been my uncle, an adult, whose face and form I knew without knowing anything else. What was he like when he married Aunt Ruth? Well, I thought, why not ask?

Tell me something that happened many years ago, I said. Anything you remember.

He turned his head and considered me with a grave expression. What have you got up your sleeve? he asked. Why should you inquire about my youth?

Because I don't know you, I said. I was always your nephew.

A foolish escapade. Is that what you have in mind?

No, I said. Anything. Something you've never forgotten.

This may have amused him because I heard a noise similar to a little cough. Then he said, You must give me a moment to think. You've knocked me off balance. I don't believe I've been asked such a question before. All right, sir, now that you've jogged me, I do recall a curious incident—my encounter with the Hungarian princess. It occurred in New York when I was twenty-five or so. Yes, twenty-five ought to be about right. I was studying for my doctorate and for some reason found myself at a party in an enormous apartment overlooking Central Park.

He paused. What was I doing there? he wondered aloud. Who invited me? Lord, it's been so long. Well, it hardly matters. Now about the "princess." I doubt if she was a princess, William, I suspect she belonged to some lesser order of nobility, but that is how I choose to think of her. At all events, the woman had more money than you could shake a stick at. The size of that apartment! Great God! Room after room after room. She lived alone. There wasn't another soul in the place—except for servants. And you will not believe this, but the woman took a fancy to me. She persuaded me to stay after the other guests departed. She was attempting to seduce me! What do you make of that, eh? I don't mind telling you, William, I was shocked.

But you must have known, I said. Why else would she want you to stay?

Uncle Gates hesitated. Finally he said that at the time the idea was inconceivable. He could recall feeling puzzled by her interest because she was several years older, and he felt intimidated by so much wealth.

Now what was her name? he continued absently. Hanlika. Magyana. Something of the sort. In any case, there I was sipping cognac in the middle of the night while doing my best to make conversation. We were seated on opposite sides of the room. She was lounging on a sofa covered with the skin of a polar bear and I suppose she expected me to join her. I didn't know what to do. There happened to be a large gilt mirror on the wall behind me and I became aware that she was watching herself while we chatted. That struck me as odd. It made me a bit uneasy.

And did you join her?

Ha! cried Uncle Gates and clapped his hands. I knew you would ask. I was a lusty young buck so it is natural to assume that given the circumstances I would take advantage of such an opportunity. However, I must say that woman revolted me. She might have been ill—I don't quite know. She was listless and pallid. She may have suffered from anemia. Or I suppose she could have been tubercular. Whatever the reason, I stayed put. Another thing. She crossed her legs frequently while watching herself in the mirror. It was most unpleasant. I wanted to leave, but I was afraid of seeming rude. And now I recall something else. She rambled on about the Hohenzollerns and Hapsburgs as though they were family friends and whenever she mentioned one of those names she would throw back her head and laugh like a jackass. To this day I recall seeing the inside of that woman's mouth. I could see black fillings in her teeth and strands of saliva. Most unpleasant.

Was she an impostor?

I think not. She brought out an old photo album with pictures of her father and mother and grandparents and I don't know who else. There were carriages and family retainers and horses and what appeared to be the wall of a castle. The grandfather was a burly fellow wearing a fancy military uniform with a chest full of medals. He had a great curling mustache and she told me he never missed a social event at the court of Franz Josef. The woman's father, I believe, had become some sort of industrial magnate. Impostor? No, I think not. In any event, William, there's my story of the princess. Nothing much happened. It didn't amount to a hill of beans.

Have you wondered what might have happened? What if you had decided to join her on the sofa?

No. No, I have never considered that. I was out of my element. As the saying goes, I felt like a fish out of water. Thank goodness I had sense enough to realize it. I would only have made a fool of myself.

Where do you suppose she is now?

Oh, he said after a pause, I rather expect she's gone.

The Sausalito art festival had just opened and I thought he might enjoy it, so I asked if he would like to stop on the way back from Mt. Tamalpais.

Uncle Gates stared through the windshield without expression. He was slightly deaf so he might not have heard.

A few minutes later I remarked that on top of the ridge we would be able to see the bay on one side and the Pacific on the other, but there was no response.

Those motorcycle bums! he said abruptly. What do they do all day?

They scare the wits out of everybody, I said, that's what they do all day. They ride up and down the coast like a swarm of hornets. I wish Picasso had drawn them.

That fellow was a Communist, said Uncle Gates. That man was a Communist.

I had hoped Picasso would give us something else to talk about. I tried to think of another subject. We could discuss relatives, but I didn't want to. I remembered how my parents would talk for an hour about cousin somebody from Leawood who married the daughter of somebody whose brother-in-law had bought the Spruance house on Wornall Road across from the Presbyterian church, or the youngest son of the couple from Grandview whose Chevrolet caught fire on Ward Parkway the summer before last who was engaged to the niece of Lucille Nordgren whose first husband had been promoted to vice-president of something. I remembered lying on the porch swing with a glass of lemonade and asking myself why adults did this.

William, Uncle Gates said. Those little fishing boats we saw while driving across the bridge and now these tile-roofed homes clinging to the hillside—I am reminded of southern France. However, I've seen no vineyards. Nor, might I add, a single weathercock.

Stay another night, I said. We can drive up to the Sonoma vineyards tomorrow afternoon.

He answered politely that he wished his visit were not so brief. Then, folding his arms, he remarked that he had been to Europe several times and always looked forward to France. Germany, though, was different. As soon as one crossed the Rhine one knew it was Germany. I expected him to go on, but he seemed lost in thought as we climbed out of the eucalyptus groves toward the ridge. Hawks were soaring above the steep flower-covered slope and the Pacific looked like a puddle of aluminum.

How was your South Seas trip? I asked.

Nan Madol, he said. Now that was an experience! Not altogether pleasant, mind you. The humidity of those tropic islands—Lord, I could have been mistaken for a wet sponge. Those islands are worse than Springfield in August. I spent a week on Ponape and let me tell you that jungle is a steamer. I do recall one amusing moment. Some fellow arrived a day or so after I did and when he first showed up on the lanai he was a regular fashion plate. He must have watched too many movies. From the way he was gussied up he must have been expecting to meet Hedy Lamarr or Dorothy Lamour or one of those other movie sirens. I don't mind telling you, it was all I could do to keep from laughing. Privately I called that fellow Sir Gerald Poobah.

And what about Nan Madol?

Ha! Getting there was quite an event. I had met a British couple who wanted to visit the place, so the three of us got together and arranged for a guide with a motorboat. Well, the lagoon wasn't rough but the way that motorboat hit the waves was like sliding on your gazimpus down a washboard. I was afraid I had injured myself.

Nan Madol. Nan Madol, I thought. It could be something spoken in a dream.

I don't recall what the name signifies, Uncle Gates said. I inquired, but whatever I was told has slipped my mind. It is remarkable how age creeps up on a fellow, almost before you can say Jack Robinson. He sat erect and motionless, frowning at the road.

From Ponape you crossed a lagoon?

He blinked as though waking up. Yes. I apologize. I was woolgathering. Yes, we reached the place after quite a rough motorboat ride, as I believe I mentioned.

Then he told me about Nan Madol. Just when it was constructed and by whom is unknown, except that the builders could not have been Micronesian because skeletal remains are those of a long-limbed race physiologically different from present-day islanders. Nor is it known how many centuries ago the fortress was abandoned. What has been learned is that the immense basalt pillars forming the walls were quarried from the volcanic summit of Ponape, but how they were carried down the mountain and through the jungle to the islet remains a mystery.

My British friends suggested levitation, Uncle Gates said, which may be as plausible as anything else. My God, those basalt logs must have weighed a ton apiece and they were piled on top of one another to a height of twenty or thirty feet. And a sinister place it is, William! I shouldn't care to spend a night there. Indeed, I was told that early in this century some Dutch or Danish anthropologist did just that, despite being warned not to. He went to sleep in a stone cist which may have been used to hold prisoners. Well, shortly before dawn the natives on Ponape heard a roaring noise as though an army of men were blowing conch shells and when they paddled out to get the anthropologist they found him dead. Now I don't know how much of that yarn to believe. What's your opinion?

I'm a believer, I said. But why was the fortress built? Who were they afraid of?

Exactly! Whom did they fear? What did they fear? According to legend, three hundred and thirty warriors kept watch over the sea beyond the reef, so it is clear that they anticipated an attack. Now who might their enemy have been? It's mysterious. Quite mysterious. He chuckled and nodded. Oh, another thing. The walls of Nan Madol are alive with lizards. Our guide said they taste like chicken, but I suspect he was joshing. The crabs, though, should be palatable. We saw hundreds on the tidal flat scuttling here and there. At all events, I'm glad I had sense enough to wear a hat, otherwise that sun would have finished me.

He quit talking suddenly. He looked exhausted. We had come to a view point on the ridge and I was gazing across the Pacific when I heard him say something else.

The walls of Nan Madol are black, William. Black as the very devil. Then he continued in a different tone: I consider myself fortunate. I have seen more than most people. Tourmaline, amethyst, emerald.

I wondered what that last remark implied, but he did not explain. Mt. Tamalpais was rising directly ahead of us. He clucked with approval.

Your Aunt Ruth would appreciate this. I wish she could be here. Your parents may have notified you that she has been experiencing difficulty with her gastrointestinal system. The doctors don't agree on just what is wrong. Her spirits are good and I do my best to pretend, but I must admit it is discouraging.

Where will you go next summer? I asked.

That depends. I should like to stroll among the ruins of Persepolis.

There was very little traffic on the mountain road and not many cars in the parking lot. I pointed out the trail and told him that if we walked several hundred yards we could see more of the bay.

I expect I can manage, he said. Now you might give me a hand getting out of the car.

I helped him to his feet but he seemed reluctant to start walking. He frowned at the pavement.

All right, he said at last, more to himself than to me.

When we came to a bench on the trail he decided that was far enough, so we sat down. He grunted with satisfaction and laced his fingers across his belly.

A fellow could sit here till the cows come home, he remarked. Yes, sir, it's a sight. He removed his glasses and polished them with his handkerchief. There was a little indentation on the bridge of his nose where the glasses had worn away the bone. Without the glasses he looked much less formidable. Carefully he hooked them on, cleared his throat, and said: The Germans have a legend about Frederick Barbarossa.

Barbarossa meant Red Beard and I knew it had been the nickname of a German emperor. I thought Barbarossa had led one of the crusades, but I couldn't remember anything else.

In a pedantic voice Uncle Gates asked: Do the ravens yet fly over the mountains?

I understood that he was quoting and I tried to identify it. Nothing reasonable came to mind. I felt pretty sure he wasn't quoting the Bhagavad-Gita, but I had no idea what it might be.

Once upon a time, Uncle Gates continued, a lowly shepherd stumbled upon the entrance to a cave in the Kyffhäuserberg—which is a mountain in Thuringia, William, as you may know. At any event, the shepherd followed this passage deep into the heart of the Kyffhäuserberg where he found the Holy Roman Emperor and six of his knights asleep at a stone table. The sound of the shepherd's footstep awakened Frederick from his slumber. Lifting his head, he asked: "Do the ravens yet fly over the mountains?" And the shepherd responded: "Sire, they do." Then Frederick said: "We must sleep another hundred years."

That's quite a story, I said.

I have not finished, said Uncle Gates. The conclusion might be noted. When the emperor's beard has grown three times around the table Frederick and his knights will emerge from the Kyffhäuserberg to exalt Germany above every nation of Europe.

I waited for him to go on, but that seemed to be all. I said I didn't care for the end.

Nor do I, he said. When Frederick awakens let us hope there will be no Germany. We have met with more than enough knighthood, I believe. Yes. More than enough.

We sat on the bench and watched the afternoon. I suspected he might be thinking about Aunt Ruth.

Finally I said, I hope you don't mind but I invited a friend to join us for dinner.

I do not mind in the least, he said, provided you had the wisdom to invite an attractive young lady.

I told him she was a dancer and her name was Rachel, but I wasn't sure if he heard. He appeared to be watching a ship moving toward the Golden Gate. One of his hands began to tremble; he covered it with the other.

I doubt if your great-aunt Megan is more than a shadow, he said. She passed away when you were quite small. A most intolerant creature much addicted to Old Testament morality—an eye for an eye and so forth. Yet she was honest enough according to her lights and the absolute soul of kindness. I find that the memory of her returns more often as time goes by. Perhaps it is because she symbolized the dichotomy of our estate. We humans seem to contradict ourselves, yet we do not contradict the truth—as Demades so perspicaciously observed some centuries past. Maybe that is it. Well! he exclaimed, slapping his knee. Enough nonsense! If you would assist me to my feet, young man, we might wend our way toward the city. I am a trifle chilled.

It had been windy where we were sitting and I asked if he felt all right. He assured me that he was fine.

"Do the ravens yet fly over the mountains?" I asked myself as we started back along the trail. It was a musical question. Uncle Gates, I said, do the ravens yet fly over the mountains?

Sire, they do, he replied. Ah, William, half a century has elapsed since I came upon those resonant lines.

Music of a different sort began to reach us en route to Sausalito but Uncle Gates did not offer his opinion until we came within sight of the amplifiers.

I fail to understand, he said, enunciating each word, how a sensible person could tolerate such noise. I should think it would kill every cat in the neighborhood.

I had planned to look for a parking spot but now it did not seem like such a good idea. Apart from the boiler factory music, I guessed that his taste for painting and sculpture did not extend much beyond the Old Masters.

Perhaps we should return to San Francisco, he said. At what time are we to meet your friend?

I told him she would meet us in the hotel cocktail lounge at six o'clock. He made a rumbling noise and consulted his watch. I asked what sort of food he would like. Chinese? Mexican? Fisherman's Wharf?

It makes no difference, he said. My appetite is robust, although I do not care much for gizzard and liver. The young lady may have some preference. You told me her name.

Rachel.

Ah! I was thinking "Hazel." As Caxton observed in the suffix to his first book: "Age crepeth on me dayly and feebleth all the bodye." So you must indulge me, William. This has been a pleasant afternoon. My one regret is that I will not be here long enough for an excursion to those vineyards you mentioned.

He turned to look at the fog spreading across the bay toward Oakland and I expected him to say it looked like a blanket, which was the usual tourist remark, but he said: Well, that Middle East business worries me. Those sheiks have us in their pocket. I don't know what's going to come of it. I doubt if anybody does— certainly not those nincompoops in Washington. We've got to have a decent supply of oil.

He appeared to be falling asleep as we drove across the bridge, but as we passed through the toll gate he lifted his head. Did I tell you about George Neidlinger? You didn't know Mr. Neidlinger, of course. He represented some oil exploration outfit, though I don't recall the name. We had lunch together once a month at the Oxbow Grill for years and years. He died last August. He was a gentleman through and through.

I had not told Rachel much about Uncle Gates, only that he was a retired professor on his way home after a trip to the South Pacific. I thought it might be an awkward evening because she was reticent with strangers while he was a thicket of stubborn convictions and meditative silences. What were we going to discuss? Picasso had been eliminated. Oil sheiks? Frederick Barbarossa? I found myself wishing for Uncle Rodney with his bag of tricks.

You must have known Agnes Barstow, he said as we approached Union Square. Agnes and Howard were friends of your parents. They divorced quite some time back. Well, she took Howard for every cent. The judge awarded that woman everything—left him a pauper. It isn't fair. Howard worked hard all his life, yet the court sided with her. Agnes is a bitch! I apologize William, for such a pejorative, but it happens to be appropriate. Howard Barstow ended up without a dime!

He was enraged by something that had occurred years ago. When he looked at me his lips were set. I felt shocked by the angry brilliance of his gaze. His right eye burned more brightly than the left and I remembered having read that this also was true of Czar Nicholas—that his eyes burned unevenly and made him terrible to confront.

All at once he cackled and poked an elbow into my ribs. I suggest you drop me at the entrance before parking the car, young fellow. I would like to spruce up a tad before supper.

When we stopped in front of the hotel he said, I propose that we kick up our heels this evening. You and your lady friend shall be my guests at the restaurant or nightspot of your choice.

I argued that since he was the visitor he should be my guest, but he would not hear of such a thing.

A doorman helped him out. Uncle Gates stooped a little, peered over his glasses and slapped the hood of the car. I am feeling a bit friskier, he said. Toodle-oo!

By the time I got back to the hotel it was after six o'clock and I felt guilty about having invited Rachel. I hoped Uncle Gates would not start telling her about his dying friends and my elderly relatives. It occurred to me that he might have decided to lie down in his room for a while, which would give me a chance to talk to her.

In the cocktail lounge five men sat at the bar like department store mannequins, not moving, not speaking, all five heads turned the same direction, which meant that Rachel must have arrived. Indeed she had. She was wearing an apricot jumpsuit. Furthermore, she was talking with Uncle Gates. Her features always reminded me of Nefertiti—sleek, balanced, imperious. And being a dancer she walked boldly, with her back arched. Strangers asked if she was in show business; if they were sufficiently ill-mannered they would ask if she was famous. She had danced supporting roles with several ballet companies and frequently appeared in local productions, but the wheel of fortune only hesitated before moving on. She did not quite illuminate the stage. So, when her bank account dipped toward the horizon she would go to work processing orders at a securities firm.

Where have you been keeping him? she demanded and I had never seen her more radiant, which puzzled me. One time at a party I saw an old psychoanalyst almost as ugly as Uncle Gates surrounded by attractive women. It was curious.

We have been discussing the intricate polyphony of creation, said my uncle.

Well, I said, don't let me interrupt.

You didn't tell me you were driving to Mt. Tam, said Rachel. You should have invited me.

For goodness sake, William, sit down, said Uncle Gates. Don't just stand there. He contemplated me for a few moments with the frank indifference of an owl and then winked at Rachel. Now be that as it may, he said to her, continuing whatever they had been talking about, the in-dwelling spirit—the animus—will not be denied. Which puts me in mind of a remark by Nietzsche to the effect that an evening of music would be followed next morning by a cascade of insight and inspiration. Nietzsche wrote: "It is as if I had bathed in a natural element." And this, my dear, reflects your comment on the ballet.

Rachel did not lift her eyes from him. Or if she did glance at me it was as though she felt obligated. Uncle Gates would not let up. He started telling her about a performance of Stravinsky's *Firebird* with Maria Tallchief that he had seen in Paris forty years ago. I thought about trying to climb into their conversation, which might have been no more difficult than swimming to Oakland. Clearly they did not want to be interrupted so I ordered a drink and listened. It occurred to me that his memory had improved quite a lot. When he was talking to me he apologized for getting old and fumbled around for details as though he had lost something in the attic, but now he seemed to have no such trouble. Rachel sat erect with clasped hands and it appeared to me that she was not breathing.

Wagner. Wagner and Liszt, he said. Ah! "A storm of enthusiasm raged between us and we filled eight days with so powerful a content that I am now stunned by it." Thus, Rachel, the intermingling of creative faculties may prove explosive. Nor is the Wagner-Liszt eruption unique. After a meeting with Schiller, Goethe wrote: "You have renewed my youth and have made me a poet again, which I had all but ceased to be." Yet you speak of feeling shattered by that encounter with the prima ballerina.

My God, Rachel said, what are you telling me? You ask me to doubt my own senses!

Let us transpose this to the realm of literature, Uncle Gates said as though lecturing a student. Consider Stendhal reading two pages of the *Code Civil* each day before resuming work on *La Chartreuse de Parme.* Or the effect of von Humboldt on Darwin's chef-d'oeuvre.

I began to think about going for a walk. Neither of them would have noticed. I also thought it might be a good idea if I listened to Rachel more attentively. Her classic profile and the elegance of her carriage had persuaded me that not much else mattered. However, the vigilance with which she followed the mind of my decrepit old uncle was disconcerting. I looked at his bent shoulders and sagging face, the forehead like an onion, the brittle jaw, the feathery hair and liver spots, the ears that had lengthened while the rest of him shriveled. I thought of how he had felt his way down the hotel corridor, tottering on his heels.

Rachel asked him about Europe. She wanted to spend some time there, maybe a long time. She might get an apartment in London or Paris and become a celebrated dancer. If dreams came true this might happen. However, that is not the fundamental nature of dreams and she was smart enough to know it. Her ambition and talent did not lack intelligent direction, so it was odd that her career advanced in a circle. From stage to stage, then a tour of duty at the securities firm. I suspected she might be a little too intelligent for the dream.

France is powdered with the dust of centuries, my uncle told her. At noon the caravans of clouds whipped by a sea wind, the pink tile roofs, the rust-colored little roses. And the wisteria spreading—ah! Rachel, you must see those vineyards blue with spray and poplars bordering the roads. One night at a festival not far from Aix when the streets were decorated with paper lanterns I danced with the prettiest girl in France. This is your moment, Rachel. Do not lose it.

I looked at the expression on her face and found myself wishing Uncle Gates would go home. He reminded me of the wicked old magician in fairy tales. His glasses had slipped down his nose and his bright eye burned furiously.

Let me ask you a riddle, he said. If many things seem beautiful to us, what is more beautiful than any of these?

Tell me, she said.

More beautiful than any of these, Rachel, is what we have learned. Yet what can be more beautiful than what we have learned?

Tell me, she said again.

That which we do not comprehend.

Rachel looked at him very seriously. I had no idea what their conversation meant, but I had a feeling she would never be quite the same.

I will tell you where to find the crowns of three Visigoth kings, he said.

Where? she asked.

In the Musée de Cluny. They are made of hammered gold, Rachel, and the embellishment does not look precious to us—agate, rose quartz, rock crystal, irregular pearls of weak luster, and a few unpolished emeralds. They were recovered from the Guarrazar fountain near Toledo.

Is this another riddle? she asked. What do the crowns represent?

I cannot begin to imagine, Uncle Gates replied while stroking the tip of his nose. As Montaigne informs us, ideas are wont to follow one another, yet they do so at times from a distance and gaze upon each other but with a sidelong glance.

It seemed to me that he was getting insufferably professorial and there might be no end to it. I pointed out that regardless of how they felt, I was hungry.

You have developed into a sensible young fellow, said Uncle Gates, contrary to what I anticipated. Where shall we dine?

I had a moment of inspiration. Sire, I announced and thumped the table with both fists. I am a great eater of beef!

He eyed me sharply. Unless I am mistaken you are drawing upon *Twelfth Night*.

I didn't know. I thought he might ask for the next line or tell me I was getting a C-minus in the course.

If you scholars would excuse me, Rachel said, and Uncle Gates at once began struggling to his feet. He remained standing until she had left the table.

After seating himself he continued briskly: William, if I were your age I would grab that girl quick as a wink. There is some unique felicity to marriage, as your Aunt Ruth and I have concluded from many years of attachment. Socrates, to be sure, when asked if it were wisdom or not to take a wife, responded that whichever a man does he will repent of it. Still, you are not Socrates. Take my advice and marry that woman, you young squirt.

Rachel had scraped enough barnacles off his hide to fill a basket and I would not have been surprised if he suggested we all go dancing till dawn. But then Uncle Gates sagged and looked vacantly into space. I thought he had forgotten me. One of his hands quivered. Something seemed to be flowing through his mind or spirit like an underground river. I wondered again if he might be concerned about Aunt Ruth, whose illness sounded threatening, or about the emptiness ahead. They did not have children.

The African couple entered the lounge. Their almost iridescent skin and distinctive bearing caused people to look, but my uncle did not notice. The years Rachel dispelled had returned swiftly and he began talking less to me than to himself: Ned

Scowcroft was the fellow who called the ambulance after my accident. He's all right. His daughter works for the government, although I have forgotten just what she does. He and several other men carried me to a park bench. I failed to get their names or I would have thanked them. Ned Scowcroft is a gentleman, but I can't say as much for his brother. Charles Scowcroft isn't worth a hoot! Uncle Gates slapped the table for emphasis. Then, lifting his head, he peered across the room. William, he said after a long pause, my eyes are not what they used to be. Does this place serve niggers?

Rachel was approaching, so he began to get up.

Please, she said and touched his shoulder.

He would have none of this. With an effort he got to his feet and there he stood, loyal to a moribund convention—one hand trembling—as he stood throughout his life in the presence of a lady.

1992

LION

T HE BAWLING ANIMAL was part of a dream, but then Katia opened her eyes and heard it again. She lay in bed listening. Again she heard it. There were no cattle this high on the mountain. She threw the blankets aside and rushed to the window. At the edge of the clearing a pregnant cow was lurching up the slope, its eyes wild with terror. It stumbled against a log, fell to its knees, and got up clumsily. Strands of frothy saliva swung from the cow's muzzle. Katia watched it urinating and dropping pies while it attempted to run. The cow seemed to be trying to go downhill but for some reason it could not. The animal bawled and turned frantically toward the left and then toward the right, all the while staggering higher. She could not understand what was wrong with the cow, which plainly had lost its mind—rearing and flinging its head around as if that might solve the problem. Then she saw the lion. It was not a very big lion, not fully grown, but it was no bobcat. This was four times the size of a bobcat, with the heavy grace of a lion and the features of a lion, but the way it followed the cow was unnatural. It did not behave the way a lion should. Twenty yards behind the cow, which now and then jumped awkwardly, crept this adolescent lion, which did not appear to be excited or even very much interested, as though the two of them were circus animals trained to act out a scene. We do this every night, the lion seemed to say, what a bore. So he would lift one paw and set it down, then another, crawling forward without enthusiasm. Showing his broad lion face and stubby ears, his tail brushing the rocky ground like a rope, playing his part almost with embarrassment, he looked from side to side as though expecting the trainer's whip. His face gleamed with life and it was clear that he thought while he looked about. Oh yes, he said, we've done this many times. And a paw reached forward tentatively because the hard ground was littered with pine cones and he was a domestic lion unaccustomed to the wilderness. The morning is cold, he explained. The wind flows down from the peaks and I am hungry, but I will have breakfast pretty soon. Oh yes. All of this he seemed to be saying while he guided the hysterical cow up the mountain. Then out of the snowy pines flashed an irritated bluejay, but the lion paid no attention; troubled by something on the wind, disturbed, inquisitive, the lion swung his face toward the cabin and Katia knew beyond doubt that he was aware of her behind the glass. His focused glare was turgid with meaning—elemental, undisclosed, sealed within his nature. She wondered if the lion's expression might be different if her husband stood beside her at the window. And if at this instant the lion should speak, what would he say? Perhaps he would explain why he was guiding the cow up the slope. Well, don't you see? I was hungry and have found what I went looking for. I am within my rights. That is what the lion might point out. Then, having observed Katia, he slid forward like a snake because he did not want to step on a sharp rock or a pine cone. Oh, he was within his rights, yes, this almost affectionate lion who ignored the frantic creature just ahead. Katia saw that he had no intention of leaping on the cow, which seemed horrible—as though the lion had acquired a human brain. Each time the cow turned one way or the other so that she might go down the mountain, well, this patient young lion would lope the same direction far enough to prevent her from doing as she wished. And if she stopped for a moment because she was out of breath, well, he would pause, stroking the air with his tail. He was not in a hurry. Nevertheless, they ought to keep moving. Let us proceed, he suggested. Before long the journey will end. Oh yes, pretty soon. Five minutes. Ten minutes. Have you rested enough? Then suppose we climb a little higher. Come now. Katia realized that although she was in no danger she was shuddering with fright as well as from the cold. She thought about getting a sweater or jacket, but she could not leave the window. Now they were dancing—the immensely gravid cow lunging this way or that, her elegant partner following, the terrible dance whirling always a little higher. Oh, higher, if you please! Yes, that's right, that's where we shall go, whether you agree or not.

And you will not see your friends or your home again because I am planning to eat you. You understand, don't you? Of course you do. You are not very smart, but you realize that you are going to be eaten. I can tell from the way you act that you know what I have in mind. Now let's be on our way. A little higher, not much. I could if I wished eat you right this moment, but I detect the presence of enemies so we must continue up the mountain until I decide we have reached a proper spot for breakfast. And you are the breakfast. Oh yes! Ho ho! Now let's be off. So they danced across the clearing. They had emerged from a grove of aspen behind the stream and Katia guessed that the cow had been driven from Gus and Betty Pruitt's ranch. Or maybe the cow unwisely decided to take a walk. Whatever happened, they must have been climbing quite a while because the Pruitt ranch was far below. From a granite outcrop beyond the shed it was possible to look down and make out black dots in the valley, which were cattle. She might have seen this particular cow, although she hoped not. It shouldn't matter, but for some reason it did. Now they had stopped because the cow was blowing. The lion acted less considerate. Katia thought she heard him growl. Maybe the lion did growl because the cow bucked stupidly—a queer, futile bucking motion—and threw her muzzle at the sky before she resumed the climb. Katia wondered if the lion remembered the cabin, if it remembered seeing her inside. Perhaps it would bound across the clearing snarling and screeching to crash through the glass. It could do that. It might. She felt the solid thumps of her heart, she knew she was vulnerable and mortal. She watched the lion pick up one hind leg and daintily extend it a few inches while the half-developed body eased forward. The cow sensed this. She knows, Katia thought. What else does she know? Almost nothing. She can't be intelligent. And it seemed to Katia that the dance of death was not merely horrid but unjust—terrifying because the lion was going to eat both the cow and the unborn calf. She thought about running to the storage room for her husband's rifle and running outside to confront and kill the lion. She imagined doing this. Yet she disliked and mistrusted the rifle, which was a hateful object. Not once had she fired it. She had never touched it. Her husband would be able to kill the lion, she felt certain of this, but he was in Glenwood Springs for the twentieth reunion of his high school class and he would not come home until tomorrow. He would run outside and shoot the lion, but he was not here. I might be able to hit it, Katia thought. Suppose I shot the awful thing, then what? She looked through the glass with a troubled expression as though she were in a box at a theater and could do nothing except watch. She resented the fact that she was not a man. It occurred to her that she might open the window and shout at the lion and wave her arms. Or she could get a frying pan from the kitchen and beat on it with a spoon. Maybe the lion would run away. No, it would not. Whatever she did would be useless; she could not prevent the lion from doing what it had resolved to do. This seemed intolerable. She realized that she had covered her mouth with both hands to keep from screaming, and just then she noticed a quick movement outside. There on a tree stump sat a chipmunk. He sat upright, clasping a seed between his paws. He, too, was watching. He sat on the stump like a little person, fascinated by what was happening beyond the woodpile on the opposite side of the clearing. He sat erect, dumbfounded, one glossy eye appalled and shocked. Katia suddenly felt stronger because the chipmunk agreed with her. And leaning against the stump was an ax. The ax could be used as a weapon. But if she did not dare shoot the rifle, what good was the ax? With a furious squeak she hurried to the closet for a jacket, seized the camera, threw open the door and ran outside because at least she could take a picture. If there was a picture of the lion following the cow she could explain everything to her husband and he would believe her. He might become enraged. Maybe he would track the lion and catch up with it and kill it, so at least there would be some justice. He would skin the lion and they would use the skin as a rug in front of the fireplace. That would not make things right, but it would help. She had run almost as far as the woodpile when she smelled fried potatoes. She had been watching the ground for rocks because she had forgotten her moccasins and her last glimpse of the lion was his profile; now she was looking directly into the blunt triangular face. He crouched motionless as stone, yellowish and detached, like a carved marble lion in a museum. She tried to remember who had told her that you are much too close to a mountain lion if you smell fried potatoes when there aren't any. Sid might have told her. He had grown up on a ranch and knew about animals. He might have told her, but she did not think so. Somebody else had mentioned the peculiar smell. Maybe it was a joke because she had known absolutely nothing about wild animals when she moved to Colorado and married Sid. Or maybe she imagined the smell, but it was very strong. Now the lion was contemplating her with an acute dangerous gaze, with perfectly human lucidity. His mind had been aroused, he was thinking. If he decided to attack, she would not have time to get back to the cabin. He would move so fast that she might not even see him, she would be struck down almost where she stood. When Sid got back from Glenwood Springs he would find her body, or what was left of it, and the knowledge that her flesh might be eaten was an inconceivable idea. She watched the lion raise his head like a cat wishing to be stroked while he appraised her with luminous eyes and she fled to the cabin. After bolting the door she rushed to the window to take a picture but discovered that she did not have the camera. It lay on the ground near the woodpile. Both animals were higher on the slope. The chipmunk, too, had moved; he clung upside down to the side of the stump as though outraged or amazed. His tail arched over his back, one eye glowing like a gemstone. He was too alarmed to do anything. And at the base of the stump Katia noticed a miniature yellow flower with heart-shaped leaves. She was astonished because the flower had not been there yesterday. The tiny announcement struck her as a reproach, although she did not know why. She felt that in some mysterious way she had failed, as if by abandoning the cow she diminished herself. But this did not make sense. She glanced at the monstrous elk antlers Sid had picked up and wired to the top of the shed. The antlers were disembodied, oracular, beyond comprehension. She realized that she despised and feared this mountain where so much exceeded her ability to understand, where the boundaries established for civilization did not exist. She placed both hands on her belly. She, too, was pregnant. Winter had swept in arrogantly, fiercely; but now the valley stirred, triumphant with life. The tremendous promise of another season was imminent. The confident flower, the chipmunk clutching his precious seed, the grumpy bluejay—beyond doubt they were anticipating spring; but the desperate cow with a calf whose eyes had not yet opened—for these two the promise would end horribly among aspen shadows or beneath an enormous spruce or on some granite ledge and the murder would find an equal place in the cycle. I hate it, Katia thought. She felt sickened. What was about to happen could not be right. She watched grimly as the cow lurched and plunged, bawling, slobbering. Its expression seemed to have passed beyond fright; the cow appeared to be insane. And what of the lion? Did he appreciate his own intelligence? They were traveling toward a place he knew, which belonged to him, which he considered his inheritance, where the dreadful play would end. Was he conscious of himself? For a while he had been puzzled by what the wind reported so he had stopped, doubtful, estimating the danger. But what came forth? Not much. Oh, not very much. The lion's conceit infuriated her. Because he was powerful, because he terrified everything on the mountain—except perhaps the bears—because of this the lion went about his business lazily. If I could kill you! she said aloud. Deliberately the lion had frightened the cow away from the ranch, he had directed her to climb the mountain, and a little above the clearing would be an exciting place for breakfast. Oh yes! So he plodded back and forth, this way or that, a shepherd minding his charge, exerting himself only enough to let her know she could not go home again. Once he lashed his tail to prove he was still on the job, a fact he wished to emphasize. And like a good shepherd he kept his distance because if she collapsed with fear and could not get up, well, he would have to drag her to the table. That would be hard work. Even for a grown lion that would be difficult. So he whipped his tail and grinned. Almost shyly he crept closer, not too close, and she reared again and tripped over a stone and let fall another pie; and when she tossed her head to look for some escape he was vastly amused. He lifted his grinning muzzle. He stared at her with friendly eyes. You won't forget me, will you? I'm right here and you must do as I say. All right, keep moving. Climb a little higher. When the time comes—if you have been a good obedient cow—it will end quickly. I'm not quite grown, you see, I'm not strong enough to drag your carcass up the mountain and that is why I decided to let you do the work. Ho ho! We must climb a little more, we two. Of course you're terribly upset, but never mind, we're almost there. Before you realize it I will be on your back. Yes indeed! Stop complaining. And don't think you are clever enough or swift enough to escape. No no! But the cow lifted its muzzle, lowing for help, and Katia who stood at the window with both hands protecting her belly thought she could guess what dull recognition stirred its brain: the cow feared not only for its life but also, dimly, for another life. Then it stopped, exhausted, drooling. The lion snarled. Katia was positive she heard this. However, the cow did not move. The lion waited. At last they resumed their obscene journey, the cow staggering between two evergreens while the lion followed attentively, and then all at once they were gone. Katia looked for the chipmunk; he, too, had vanished. But after a moment he popped up on the stump and continued nibbling his seed, or another, while he kept watch, knowing quite well that the world is mutable and deadly and it is wise to avoid mistakes. Oh yes, he knew quite a lot about lions and humans and owls and nuts. He had observed the performance but he did not care any longer, he had important things to do. Katia looked at the evergreens which stood unperturbed, quiet, absorbed by their own reality. She felt an urgent desire to leave the mountain—this prehistoric ridge where nothing mattered except food. She hated the granite boulders and the violent rain, the medieval forest, the grotesque shapes emerging at dusk, the unexpected barbaric music, the hideous shrieks of creatures annihilated by passion or by the claws of predators during the merciless night. She hated this unfeeling, amoral existence. She wanted to return to the city where at suppertime she might arrange silver heirlooms on a linen tablecloth, where it was possible to discuss poetry or attend fashion shows and concerts of classical music, where the values of the mountain could be denied. Overhead two red-tailed hawks slanted with the current. Perhaps they could see the cow and the lion. If so, what did the spectacle mean to them? Or were they, like the chipmunk, indifferent? She could not understand why she felt as she did, why she felt some responsibility toward the pattern of life; surely this must be the utmost conceit, yet she could not feel otherwise. She wished her husband would come home, and while she thought about him she heard a distant bellow and a scream.

1994

AT THE CROSSROADS

A RED-BEARDED TRAMP with quick blue eyes and an old woman who calls herself Letty are standing at the intersection of two highways in the desert. The old woman feels death not far away so she is returning to West Virginia where she was born, but the tramp sees a different future—he is headed for California where he believes his luck will change.

It is almost noon. Old Letty, with head bowed, does not move, but the tramp is growing restless and begins to kick at the gravel. Now and again he shakes his head in despair. All at once Letty turns to him with a beseeching expression; she has just found out she cannot make it back to the town in the Cumberland Mountains where she was born. She has waited too long. Death is following her and will not wait. It does not seem possible. She is both weakened and thrilled by the idea, yet there can be no mistake—her time has come. Presently she is obsessed by a singular desire: she must explain to someone what life actually is. Now that she has been overtaken it is dreadfully important that someone remember her, remember and never forget that she too was once here on earth. A lazy vagabond is not the audience she would have selected but such is the will of God and to this man, therefore, whoever he may be, she intends to confide the meaning of her life.

Without preamble she walks over to him and begins in a quavering voice, "There was a time in Ely, Nevada, when the Lord appeared in the bright sunlight and said I was doing about as well as could be expected."

The tramp gazes at her incuriously; he wonders if she can be mad. He does not know where this old woman is going or where she came from or why, and cares not the slightest. His own plans are much too absorbing. It is very strange how any man should have all the bad luck he has had, very strange indeed, but if only he can reach the coast things will be different. He thinks about the many stingy people there are in the world; while he broods on how they conspire against him his lips puff out through his beard. Shading his eyes, he squints along the broad federal highway that comes sweeping out of the waterless eastern hills, but all he can see is cactus standing on the slope with arms uplifted like railroad signals. He looks north along the graveled state highway to an abandoned borax flat and beyond that to a low blunt range of old brown mountains upon which no snow ever falls and where nothing lives. There is not a sign of movement on either road, and when he squints to the south he cannot see much because the horizon is swimming in waves of heat. He feels a tug at his belt and looks down at the old woman with some irritation, noticing once again that she has an envelope fastened to her dress with a safety pin. Women are apt to do things like that; his mother used to leave messages pinned to a lace curtain in the parlor. So he is not particularly surprised or amused; however, he is a cautious man and after studying her anxious face he thinks he will keep her in sight. It might not be wise to turn his back on her any more.

Letty has forgotten what she meant to say to him and so draws herself up with a severe expression; but when at last it comes back to her she cannot repress a smile. All memories cause her to smile no matter what they might be. Her chin begins to tremble and then without warning her eyelids close. Now she is prepared to tell her companion all about it, but upon looking up she is distressed to find he has crossed the highway and she realizes that she has just had a little nap. She picks up her satchel and begins walking after him. It seems that the intersection is completely under water but she knows this is only an illusion caused by the desert heat, and so with her satchel firmly in one hand and her bamboo stick in the other she marches against the waves which obligingly recede very much as they did for the oppressed Jews.

The tramp, squatting in the gravel, is considerably interested in something he has just discovered. At first he thought it was the metal casing of a machine gun bullet but it turned out to be a lipstick cylinder. He pulls at the cap which comes off with a plop, he twists the base to see how much is left and then smears his thumb with it, and with a sly expression he lifts his pink thumb to his nose: the odor takes him by surprise even though he expected it. Assaulted by memories, he jumps to his feet and throws the lipstick as high and as far as he can. It comes down in a mirage out among the cactus—a dry lake bed has filled with rippling water and a black-tailed jackrabbit is leaping through it. He watches the rabbit jump out of the water and go leaping away over the brush. Now the lake is dry again, exposing its cracked, sodium-crusted bed. Everything is illusion. The tramp sits on his knapsack, bitterly discouraged, and holds his hands above his head to combat the sun.

Letty thinks he is listening to the story of her life. She goes on talking to him and he does not move. She tells the tramp about her brothers, Noah, Jonathan, Ephraim, Willard, and Thomas, and at the mention of their names her shameless eyes begin to weep. She fumbles for the letter at her breast. It is securely pinned and her old fingers do not very much care what she orders them to do—they go dancing away to the side—but after a while she gets the pin undone. Now the frayed, yellowed envelope is in her hand. She turns it about until she has located the flap, and a moment later she has the message itself, folded and unfolded so many times that it is in two pieces. She holds it out to the tramp, but he only looks at her in astonishment. Lifting one half of the brown spidery script close to her eyes, she commences to read aloud as though she were giving him a lecture:

> Jonathan's going was a blessed release for there was, of course, no hope that he could ever get better. We held the funeral right at two P.M. this afternoon and then Melinda, Jackie Lu, and I drove to Blue Springs to bury him. As you know, Aunt Letty, your own father, grandfather, and great-grandfather are buried there, and young David was most curious about all those graves. He's come to resemble a picture in the album of Grandfather Shelby except for the beard, and has the meanness of menfolk. We think that he will be a big one like his great-uncles. It was but last night whilst we were gathered on the porch the child stood by my knee and gravely asked when you are coming home, so I kissed him and pushed back his hair and said to him it will be soon. . . .

She cannot read any more; the sunlight is shattering. The letter wanders about in front of her eyes. She decides to tuck it away but the envelope has disappeared. Now she locates the envelope lying in the gravel near her feet. She is afraid to bend down and she does not know what to do. Alkali dust has gotten all over her shoes. The highways weave and shimmer. For a moment she is a little girl and her twin brother Ephraim has just waked her by saying, "Letty, Mamma is dead, and I think he is too." So she got out of her bed and went with Ephraim, and what he had said was true—they lay there in each other's arms, neither of them smiling, and nobody ever could understand what had caused them to die at the same time. Noah and Ephraim had pulled down the shades in the bedroom but the windows were open and as the wind blew in gustily the shades billowed and flapped as if waving good-bye to the dead. She could hear Noah out of doors crying and working the pump, but Ephraim stood dumbly beside the deathbed with his mouth open and his hands thrust into his pockets. She heard the dogs howling in the cellar and presently noticed how the hair on Ephraim's neck was standing straight out. She lifted the shade from the back window and found the sun had just started through the notch in the mountains. Overnight the snow had been melting; the barn roof was almost clear. The young sow lay motionless in her pen and her head was half-buried in a mound of snow and straw. Some chickens were picking their way across a patch of red mud beside the cistern where Noah in his overalls was still pumping water, though the bucket had long since filled and now each time he leaned on the pump handle the bucket overflowed.

Next she dreams of visiting Willard who is in the state penitentiary for life. He has grown into the biggest man of the family, taller than Noah, yet as strong as Thomas. She has brought him a sack of black walnuts which he likes and which he will crack in the palm of his hand, but all the time she is visiting he complains of the warden's yellow hound which bays at night just outside the wall. Willard believes the hound is challenging him to escape.

Now she is with a strange young man who limps, whose name she has forgotten. They have been walking somewhere for some important reason and he is tremendously excited by the election of President Hayes; they stop to rest on a fallen log but he is unable to sit still; he goes limping around the clearing while he tells her of the election and what it is going to mean, and often he looks over his shoulder at her with radiant eyes to see if she comprehends. The air is piquant with the odor of turpentine from slashed pines nearby and while she is reaching for a sprig of wild mint beside the log he cries, "Oh, Letty! Aren't you listening?" But for the election she cares nothing; she wants to get married. A look of shock appears on his face when she suggests he marry her. They gaze at each other in dismay.

The tramp does not hear a single word of it. This old woman has been talking for an hour but it would take some kind of a professor to understand her. He has listened enough to know that she preaches for a living, not in a church but along the wayside, and in the satchel she carries along with her other belongings a tambourine for taking up the collection. Well, he thinks, there is nothing more satisfactory than the gospel—he has shouted himself drunk and jumped in the water at more than one meeting. Preachers lead a good life. There are times when he thinks about stealing a Bible and going into the business.

Briefly he listens to her reedy little voice, quavering and righteous and alone in the desert. She is talking about one of the grandsons she has never seen. He cannot imagine why she talks so much, but women are like that and he has long since realized that the less they say the more sense they make. He decides to eat an apple which is in his knapsack.

Letty feels some time has slipped away. The letter, dated nineteen years ago, is back in its envelope and again is pinned to her dress although she cannot remember doing it. She looks around for her companion and finds him across the road eating something—she watches steadily but cannot make out what it is. Soon she forgets this terrible afternoon and stands content at the crossroads, swaying a little, her eyes closed. Minutes drift by without a sound. On the desert nothing moves. Old Letty dreams, and occasionally speaks out in a sharp, critical tone, but if the tramp hears whatever she says he makes no attempt to answer. He dreams very seldom but when he does there is certainly no doubt about the meaning: principally he dreams of finding money while running through a forest. Joyously he flings himself high up among the cool dark boughs and then with moist leaves brushing his cheeks he comes floating down very casually, though somewhat reluctantly, clutching in both hands an impossibly thick clump of dollars. For some reason a few of these notes always float out of his grasp and with a sudden movement flatten themselves against the bark of passing tree trunks. A few more of the bills wad themselves up and are sucked into the forks of branches where they disappear like leaves spinning into a whirlpool. He realizes it is idle to do nothing but stare at this money while it gets away, and proof lies in the fact that his hands are empty every time he touches the ground, still he cannot stop himself in the air or turn around, or even reach for it, because once again he finds himself graciously descending, wrenching loose from the boughs these turgid clumps which break off like heads of lettuce in rich black loam. Whenever the tramp thinks about this particular dream his beard begins to quiver and he is apt to choke or cough, and often he looks narrowly over his shoulder to see if anyone has read his thoughts.

Letty is awake again, looking sternly at her companion because she imagines he has just insulted her. Her fear is confirmed when she notes that his beard is moving gently, as though he were laughing deep in his throat. She knows what he thinks of her—that nobody has ever loved her. Why should anyone laugh at that? Besides, it is not true. Almost immediately she has the facts to make him change his opinion. She intends to tell him about just a few of the bold young gentlemen and she will conclude her triumph by letting him know that she spurned every suitor and of her own free will chose God, yet even as she begins to speak the truth comes flying home, and trembling a little, she must stop. She staggers into the middle of the highway to gaze at him. Cautiously the tramp returns her look as if he reads her desperation at last and wonders what can be wrong.

Letty nods and smiles at him. She beckons to him.

The tramp becomes embarrassed. He kicks at the gravel and looks away, scanning the empty highways, and when after some moments he looks around at her again she has bowed her head. He plucks thoughtfully at his beard.

It is late afternoon now. The heat is stupefying, and for a long time the tramp has been squatting on his heels sifting hot pebbles and sand through his fingers while he thinks how much better life will be in California. Impatiently he waits; surely someone besides himself is going that way. It occurs to him that the old woman has stopped talking—he squints over his shoulder. She is on her feet but asleep, and while he is watching her she wakes up, stares at him blindly, and closes her eyes again.

Death is very close now. Very near to her, only a few minutes away. She is thinking of a morning eighty years ago. Someone had propped her up against a rail fence and there she was waiting for something, or someone, and presently two little boys came clambering over the fence. She knew they were her brothers Noah and Willard. They were climbing out of the field where they had made cornstalk fiddles. They walked up to her and Noah said, "Here, Letty, we have brought you one too," and placing a fiddle and bow in her hands he showed her what to do. She saw they were smiling down at her, so she began to laugh and they joined in, and she was sure the frogs and crickets and birds joined in while they performed upon their father's land.

1956

I CAME
FROM YONDER
MOUNTAIN

BEYOND THE UPCOUNTRY of the Carolinas, farther back in the hills where the clay looks blue and the wild carrot and yellow lily cover the scars of crumbled sawmills, where thunder has the high rattling sound of pebbles in a wood bucket, there the ridges are hung with scented air in the heart of the afternoon and there if you wander into a hollow sometimes you'll catch a far-off smell of sweet bay or see the pendant bells of a honeycup swinging in the wind. There the red spruce and the paintbrush grow, bordering trails that spiral down the mountains, and if the long clouds resembling cliffs of slate appear in the west then there will fall drops of rain big around as acorns.

It was on such a day that a girl wound down the trail to a town called Keating, which was a town shaped like an oak leaf with a railroad track for a stem. The girl's name was Laurel Wyatt and she carried under one arm, wrapped in a crazy-patch quilt, her baby which did not very often move. She did not look at the baby, but once in a while she spoke to it, as though it were a grown person.

"'Tis a piece," she said in that fashion, looking mildly ahead.

A wind shook the sides of her black sweater and twisted those strings of her hair not bound by the ribbon behind her neck. Cinnamon squirrels sailed along the tree limbs considering her through quick eyes, while in the woods flickers called and bloodheads knocked suddenly and then were answered by thunder sounding far in the west. The sun overhead filtered through the southern pines like streamers of yellow gauze; insects with wings thin as spotted tissue flickered in the light.

A raindrop thumped the crazy-patch quilt. Another pounded into the trail, thereby causing a dust umbrella to open beside the girl's foot.

"Powerful day," she said to the baby.

Across log bridges where excited water popped and slipped on rocks, past raccoons who stopped their dark and slender hands to watch her, softly on a pad of brown pine needles Laurel moved down toward the town of Keating. The streams as she passed over them were white and green, and moss tails which were stuck to the rocks swayed in the current. Once one broke free and wiggled quickly downstream as though it were alive. Once as she crossed a log bridge there fell from its underside a chain of fat bugs which floated gravely away. Water spiders skated in pools behind rocks; bits of pine branch also revolved and sometimes a stiff cone.

She came to a stream where on the far side a baby hog bear sliced the water again and again and each time looked in wonder at its empty paw. Laurel stood by a hollow stump and at last the bear sat up and, seeing her, trundled away into the woods like a small barrel.

Thunder rattled as she moved over a bald. Rocks in her path were speckled with mica which threw back the light of the sun, and by them copper thorns overhanging the trail grabbed at her ankles but each one slid over her stiff skin. In the woods again, she set her baby on the ground in order to fasten the little buttons of her sweater. Then on she went, and down.

When she came to the clearing of a cabin she stopped by the cistern there and with a porcelain dipper took water from the bucket. Brown smoke rose a few feet above the cabin and then spread out like a toadstool. A man in brown coveralls sat in the cabin doorway and raised one hand to her but she did not see him. She put the dipper back in the bucket and walked past the clearing and on down the trail.

A flarehawk coasted over with tail spread and beak hooked bitterly: in the branches and on the ground nothing moved. Wandering clouds crackled, shot quick forks at one another which sometimes bent down to test the strength of the red spruce trees, and once as Laurel Wyatt crossed a charred tract there floated silently from one cloud a ball of green fire.

"This heart of Judas," she said. And scarce looked at it though the fire followed her to the trees.

Beyond another bald a shower caught her, and her black sweater sagged with water. On she walked, across ridges where the false loblolly grew and down through the following hollows by a preacher's message painted on a flat stone, on until at last she came to the doorstoops of Keating whereon lay bent rakes and barrel hoops and dozing hounds with mange. Through the town she went to the railroad platform and there she laid the baby beside her on a bench, crossed her legs, and sat looking straight ahead.

On the platform stood a man with a pink face and eyebrows like scrolls of birchbark; behind him sat a woman who wore a dress with three-cornered buttons. The man ducked his head and squinted at Laurel.

"Oh, stop clowning," the woman said.

He strode the platform with his lips pressed together.

"Must you eternally pace?" she asked.

"There it is. It can't get up the hill."

"Must you say something funny every minute?"

Then nobody spoke for a long time until down the line the train gave a hoot and chuggled up the tracks with feathers of steam spurting out from the engine wheels. The number on its hood was 7. The wheels squeaked as the train prepared to stop. When this had been done all that moved was the iron bell atop the cab which swung back and forth emptying itself drunkenly over the platform. Then a coach door clanked and the conductor stepped down, a tiny man with hook-and-lace shoes and a nose like an orange rind.

Quickly the man picked up two suitcases and the woman pushed a parcel, a gourd, and a canvas jacket under his arm.

"Sweetheart, you're tired?" he asked. She climbed the steps and he followed, staring at the back of her head. "You're tired?" he asked, disappearing into the coach.

The conductor smelled of stout tobacco. He walked up and down the gray boards dragging one foot and rubbing his arms while the iron bell on the cab clanged and rolled north, clanged and rolled south.

"What you going to wear for a wedding coat?" caroled the conductor in a sharp voice. He walked to the end of the platform where he spit onto the tracks and stood looking behind the train at the western mountains. Sparks and ashes drifted above him. He turned around and walked back along the railroad platform. "Old chin whiskers of a billy goat," he sang. He stood at the other end of the platform for several minutes, came back, and climbed aboard the train.

Laurel Wyatt sat with one hand resting on her crossed thighs. The bottom of the pale dress was above her knees.

The conductor banged half of the door, and Laurel's eyes focused. She walked to the closed train door where she said, "I am locally."

Came the voice of the conductor: "Too late."

"I have come to train travel," she said.

The conductor slowly opened the door. Laurel Wyatt went into a coach and sat down, putting the baby beside her. She sat as on the bench with one hand resting on her thigh and the other on the seat.

The couplings rattled, clanked, the coach knocked backward then forward and began to move.

The toes of the baby curled but it made no sound. About its wrist was tied a string with seven knots.

"For I'm a-going—I'm a-going away—" In came the conductor, the black leather of his hook-and-lace shoes squirking. "Whereabouts you folks headed?"

"Out of these queer hills," said the man. "That girl's cracked. I can't understand her. She gives me the creeps."

"Everything gives you the creeps."

"You're tired, sweetheart? You're not feeling good again?"

"They're like that. Yes, sir. They are. I seen them time and again. Time and again do it. They think the train waits specially for them. But it don't. No, sir!" The conductor went along the aisle patting the top of each seat. "For to stay—a little while—"

He stopped beside Laurel. "Them folks inform me you been sitting there nearabouts an hour waiting on this train. You deef? What's the matter with you? We set by that station there eight minutes, you didn't get on. I expect largely you be a deef one. Hey? This train come up the hills, set by eight minutes, you don't fleck a muscle. Only got a number of minutes in Keating. They's a storm fixing to swamp us. People think trains set by all day long waiting for them specially, they don't, don't do nothing specially. Not for nobody. I expect you know that. Hey? Don't you? Don't that appeal to you? Eight minutes is all. You be deef. Ain't you? What's the matter with you?"

"I presume largely I forgot it," Laurel said, but she did not look at the conductor.

"You do! You do! Ahahah!" The conductor pinched the end of his nose in rage. "Give me your money. Whereabouts you headed? Tipton? You mountain people always go to Tipton. That's where you be headed. Tipton'll cost you exactly a dollar and ten cents."

Laurel cautiously folded her hands.

"Whereabouts you headed? Tipton?"

But she did not answer.

"You be headed for Tipton."

"I came from yonder mountain."

The conductor bent his knees and sank down a little to peer out the window. "Deef or no deef, give me the money for Tipton."

"I have that money," Laurel said, reaching into the pocket of her sweater. "And here. 'Tis the money for a train travel to Tipton town." She added, "I have quite a considerable of this money." And then she sucked in her lips and looked at the floor of the coach.

The conductor put the money in his coat pocket and moved along dragging one foot. "But I'm a-coming back—if I go ten thousand mile—if I go ten thousand mile."

LAUREL RESTED her hands in her lap and watched the telephone poles go by. She did not move, but sat mile after mile in that same fashion while the train clicked along with the rhythm of a galloping horse, and all that showed she was not a stone girl was a softness to her cheeks when the train screeched around a curve and the late afternoon sun touched the pale hairs of her face.

As the train sank and moved south the clay cutbacks became stippled with gravel and changed in color; they were almost white, then pink, and when the train clacketed over a bare patch the clay had broken through the topsoil in a scarlet web. The train rolled between wooden sheds on which were nailed crusty tin medicine signs, and crossed a street where bells were ringing and a man swung a lantern. Then the train was dark, for clay banks rose beside the windows, and when these banks dropped to let in the sun there was no town.

Laurel Wyatt stood up. The train swayed and she fell into the seat. She stood again and held on to the baggage rack above the seats. With her hands high above her head she looked around the coach.

"Tipton town?" she asked in a voice very low.

Her body swayed with the motion of the train and as she hung almost by her hands the pale printed dress pulled above her knees. Her legs were short and solid. Below her knees the skin was tan and stiff, but higher it was white and soft.

"Oh, my Lord!" she said.

As the train went around a curve her hip bumped the window and then she swung out into the coach. She looked over the seat toward the corridor at the rear where the conductor had disappeared. She was standing tiptoe, her fingers hooking through the wire mesh of the rack. She clung there as the tracks curved twice more.

Then, "Smoke Hill 'twas," she said, unhooked her fingers from the mesh and dropped into the seat.

It was as she sat down that rain came tapping softly on her window, and the sky braided with clouds. The fields which had lain flat by the wheels humped into ridges and were now the sides of a trough wherein the ashes of the train collected, and the coaches tipped downward with squealing wheels while orange sparks flicked by. Through the trough with windows rattling, couplings banging, went the train. Then only flat fields it rushed, and there was Tipton.

The iron bell rang and turned east and rang and turned west.

"What'll the wedding supper be?" the conductor sang. Laurel's sweater caught on the door handle and he pulled it free for her to step down, singing, "Dogwood soup and catnip tea."

Beyond the platform in the distance rose the eagle's beak of the mountain. Turning until it overhung her left shoulder, Laurel Wyatt entered the city of Tipton, cheeks sucked in, dropping each foot as though into a deep hole. A hedge grew before her; she pushed through it while people watched, then on through flowers bound to stakes. Her feet dragged over a slab of writing. On she went, looking to neither side, by a wrought-iron bench, under the broken stone sword of a horseman riding north.

Beyond painted lines she entered a street and she paused, looked over her shoulder again for the eagle's beak. Then on till a building was in her path. She stopped, struck once at the door, and stood waiting.

There came through the shutters above a woman's voice. "What do you want? His office is closed."

Laurel Wyatt stood by the door.

"Come back tomorrow."

As the day darkened the voice called out again, "I told you to go. I said tomorrow."

Much later: "Good Lord, you still there? Oh, I'll tell him."

Later still, by the landing window a light was carried; a lamp turned on. In the doorway the doctor buttoned his vest. "Well, girl?"

He took off his glasses, twirled them slowly by the white ear pieces, looked at the baby. "You know that child is dead. You know that."

To the door came a nurse with a soft doughy face. She stood beside the doctor, looking at the baby. "I should think it is dead."

"Blister plasters," muttered the doctor. "If it wasn't dead before, you'd have murdered it with those plasters. You know that, don't you?"

"I doubt if she does," said the nurse.

"Somebody ought to go back in those hills and teach you people. Everybody knows I'm too busy, but somebody ought to."

"I told her. I said, 'Come back tomorrow.'"

Though Laurel spoke the words could scarcely be heard.

"'Tis dead."

They watched her for a moment.

"Why didn't your husband come along with you, girl?"

"He's probably drunk," said the nurse.

"Where are you from?"

"She doesn't even know."

"You've come a long way down out of those hills, girl. A long way. You got enough money to get back? You do, don't you?"

"She hasn't got any money. She hasn't got anything."

"You take that child back. You give it a fine burial."

"She doesn't even hear you."

"Nobody ever hears what I say. Nobody ever does. All right, girl. Give it to me. I'll see it's done."

"She'd probably drop it in a ditch."

Laurel stood looking beyond their shoulders and the lamp in the hallway darkened the sockets of her cheeks, caught a glisten in her eyes. A raindrop came down her temple and the cheekbone, rested on her jaw. Slowly, slanting into the doorway where Laurel Wyatt stood, the heavy rain began to fall. Water streamed down her arms and curved through her empty palms, dripped from her fingertips. The pale dress, wet, wrapped slowly around her legs.

THROUGH THE RAIN she moved, past the sloshing window ledges of shuttered buildings, through boundaries of sticks and paint, beyond the stoppered mouths of settling cannon, beyond awnings and wires whereon the bulbs of Tipton flickered, upon the black and silent cinders until they had sunk in clay, and on, with the rhythm of a slow pulse beat, into the edge of a forest where at last among trunks of spruce the sound of her passage was lost in the rain.

1949

THE FISHERMAN
FROM CHIHUAHUA

S ANTA CRUZ is at the top of Monterey Bay, which is about a hundred miles below San Francisco, and in the winter there are not many people in Santa Cruz. The boardwalk concessions are shuttered except for one counter-and-booth restaurant, the Ferris-wheel seats are hooded with olive green canvas and the powerhouse padlocked, and the rococo doors of the carousel are boarded over and if one peers through a knothole into its gloom the horses which buck and plunge through summer prosperity seem like animals touched by a magic wand that they may never move again. Dust dims the gilt of their saddles and sifts through cracks into their bold nostrils. About the only sounds to be heard around the waterfront in Santa Cruz during winter are the voices of Italian fishermen hidden by mist as they work against the long pier, and the slap of waves against the pilings of the cement dance pavilion when tide runs high, or the squeak of a gull, or once in a long time bootsteps on the slippery boards as some person comes quite alone and usually slowly to the edge of the gray and fogbound ocean.

The restaurant is Pendleton's and white brush strokes on the glass announce *tacos, frijoles,* and *enchiladas* as house specialties, these being mostly greens and beans and fried meat made arrogant with pepper. Smaller letters in pseudo-Gothic script say *Se Habla Español* but this is not true; it was the man who owned the place before Pendleton who could speak Spanish. From him, though, Pendleton did learn how to make the food and this is the reason a short fat Mexican who worked as a mechanic at Ace Dillon's Texaco station continued eating his suppers there. He came in every night just after eight o'clock and sat at the counter, ate an astounding amount of this food, which he first splattered with tabasco sauce as casually as though it were ketchup, and then washed it farther down with beer. After that he would feel a little drunk and would spend two or three dollars playing the pinball machine and the great nickelodeon and dancing by himself, but inoffensively, contentedly, just snapping his fingers and shuffling across the warped boards often until Pendleton began pulling in the shutters. Then, having had a suitable evening, he would half-dance his way home, or at least back in the direction of town. He was a squat little man who waddled like a duck full of eggs and he had a face like a blunt arrowhead or a Toltec idol, and he was about the color of hot sand. His fingers were much too thick for their length, seemingly without joints, only creases where it was necessary for them to bend. He smelled principally of cold grease and of urine as though his pants needed some air, but Pendleton who did not smell very good himself did not mind and besides there were not many customers during these winter months.

So every evening shortly after dark he entered for his food and some amusement, and as he appeared to contain all God's world within his own self Pendleton was not disinterested when another Mexican came in directly behind him like a long shadow. This new man was tall, very tall, six feet or more, and much darker, almost black in the manner of a sweat-stained saddle. He was handsome, silent, and perhaps forty years of age. Also he was something of a dandy; his trousers, which were long and quite tight, revealed the fact that he was bowlegged, as befits certain types of men, and made one think of him easily riding a large fast horse, not necessarily toward a woman but in the direction of something more remote and mysterious—bearing a significant message or something like that. Exceedingly short black boots of finest leather took in the cuffs of his narrow trousers. For a shirt he wore long-sleeved white silk unbuttoned to below the level of his nipples which themselves were vaguely visible. The hair of his chest was so luxuriant that an enameled crucifix there did not even rest on the skin.

These two men sat at the counter side by side. The tall one lifted off his sombrero as if afraid of mussing his hair and he placed it on the third stool. His hair was deeply oiled, and comb tracks went all the way from his temples to the back of his thin black neck, and he reeked of green perfume. He had a mustache that consisted of nothing but two black strings hanging across the corners of his unforgiving mouth, ending in soft points about an inch below his chin. He seemed to think himself alone in the restaurant because, after slowing licking his lips and interlacing his fingers, he just sat looking somberly ahead. The small man ordered for them both.

After they had eaten supper the little one played the pinball machine while this strange man took from his shirt pocket a cigarillo only a little bigger than his mustache and smoked it with care; that is, he would take it from his mouth between his thumb and one finger as if he were afraid of crushing it, and after releasing the smoke he would replace it with the same care in the exact center of his mouth. It never dangled or rolled; he respected it. Nor was it a cheap piece of tobacco; the smoke ascended heavily, moist and sweet.

Suddenly the fat Mexican kicked the pinball game and with a surly expression walked over to drop a coin into the nickelodeon. The tall man had remained all this time at the counter with his long savage eyes half-shut, smoking and smoking the fragrant cigarillo. Now he did not turn around—in fact all he did was remove the stump from his lips—but clearly he was disturbed. When the music ended he sat motionless for several minutes. Then he lifted his head and his throat began to swell like that of a mating pigeon.

Pendleton, sponging an ash tray, staggered as if a knife had plunged through his ribs.

The Mexican's eyes were squeezed shut. His lips had peeled away from his teeth like those of a jaguar tearing meat, and the veins of his neck looked ready to pop. In the shrill screams bursting from his throat was a memory of Moors, the ching of Arab cymbals, of rags and of running feet through all the market places of the East.

His song had no beginning; it had no end. All at once he was simply sitting on the stool looking miserably ahead.

After a while the small fat Mexican said to Pendleton, "Be seeing you, man," and waddled out the door. A few seconds later the tall one's stool creaked. He put on the high steepled sombrero as though it were a crown and followed his friend through the door.

The next night there happened to be a pair of tourists eating in the back booth when the Mexicans entered. They were dressed as before except that the big one's shirt was lime green, and Pendleton noticed his wrist watch—fastened not to his wrist but on the green shirtsleeve where it bulged like an oily bubble. They took the same stools and ate fried beans, tacos, and enchiladas for half an hour, after which the short one who looked like his Toltec ancestors gently belched, smiled in a benign way, and moved over to his machine. Failing to win anything he cursed it and kicked it before selecting some records.

This time Pendleton was alert; as the music ended he got ready for the first shriek. The tourists, caught unaware, thought their time had come. When they recovered from the shock they looked over the top of the booth and then the woman stood up in order to see better. After the black Mexican's song was finished they all could hear the incoming tide, washing softly around the pillars of the pavilion.

Presently the two men paid their bill and went out, the short one leading, into the dirty yellow fog and the diving, squeaking gulls.

"Why, that's terrible," the woman laughed. "It wasn't musical." Anyone who looked at her would know she was still shuddering from the force of the ominous man.

Her husband too was frightened and laughed. "Somebody should play a little drum behind that fellow." Unaware of what a peculiar statement he had made he formed a circle of his thumb and forefinger to show how big the drum should be.

She was watching the door, trying to frown compassionately. "I wonder what's the matter with that poor man. Some woman must have hurt him dreadfully."

Pendleton began to wipe beer bracelets and splats of tabasco sauce from the lacquered plywood counter where the men had been eating.

"We're from Iowa City," the woman said with a smile.

Pendleton had never been to Iowa City or anywhere near it even on a train, so he asked if they would like more coffee.

"Those two fellows," her husband said, "do they come here every night?"

Pendleton was seized with contempt for this domestic little man, though he did not know why. He walked stiffly away from their booth and stood with both hairy hands on his hips while he listened to the sea thrashing and rolling in the night.

"Who?" he demanded. "Them two?"

The couple, overpowered by his manner, looked at each other uneasily.

On the third night when the Mexicans sat down at the counter Pendleton said to the one who spoke English, "Tell your buddy no more yowling."

"Tell him yourself," the Toltec replied. "Eight tacos, four beers, and a lot of beans, man."

"What do you think this is, buster, some damn concert hall?"

For a moment the little Mexican became eloquent with his eyebrows; then both he and Pendleton turned their attention to the silent one who was staring somberly at the case of pies.

Pendleton leaned on his hands so that his shoulders bulged. "Now looky, Pablo, give him the word and do it quick. Tell him to cut out that noise."

This enraged the small man whose voice rose to a snarl. "Pablo yourself. Don't give me that stuff."

Pendleton was not angry but set about cleaving greens for their tacos as though he was furious. While the blade chunked into the wood beside his thumb he thought about the situation. He did not have anything particular in mind when all at once he slammed down the cleaver and with his teeth clenched he began bending his eyes toward the two.

"*No debe cantar*," said the little one hurriedly, waggling a negative finger at his companion. "*No más.*"

"All right, by God," Pendleton muttered as though he understood. He wished to say something in Spanish but he knew only *mañana, adiós,* and *señorita,* and none of these seemed to fit. He resumed work, but doubtfully, not certain if the silent one had heard either of them. Without turning around he explained his attitude: "People come here to eat supper."

Abel W. Sharpe, who had once been county sheriff and who now lived in a retirement home, came through the door alone but arguing harshly. He took a stool beside the tall Mexican, looked up at him twice, and then ordered hot milk and a waffle. While he was pouring syrup into the milk the nickelodeon music stopped and the black Mexican did it again.

At the first note the old man jumped off his stool and crouched several feet away, a spoon in one hand and his cup of sweet milk in the other. "Can't hear nothing," he said angrily to Pendleton. "The bastard deefened me."

The Toltec, who was playing pinball, paid not the least attention because he had lighted four pretty girls which meant he probably would win several games. His friend, now motionless, sat on the stool and gazed ahead as though he could see clear into some grief-stricken time.

Not until the eighth or ninth night did Pendleton realize that the restaurant was drawing more customers; there would be half-a-dozen or so extra for dinner, maybe more.

Then there came a night when the Toltec waddled in as usual but no one followed. That night the restaurant was uneasy. Things spilled, and while cleaning up a table Pendleton discovered a menu burned through and through with cigarette holes. By ten-thirty the place was deserted.

Pendleton said, "Hey, Pablo."

The Toltec gave him a furious look.

"All right," Pendleton apologized, "what's your name?"

"What's yours?" he replied. He was insulted.

"Where's your buddy?"

"He's no friend of mine."

Pendleton walked down the counter behind a damp rag, wrung it over the sink, and then very casually did something he never even thought of doing: he opened a bottle of beer and indicated to the Mexican that it was free.

Toltec, though still aggrieved, quickly accepted this gift, saying, "I just met the guy. He asked me where to get some decent food."

Pendleton wiped a table and for a while appeared to be idly picking his teeth. When he judged enough time had gone by he said, "Got tired of my grub, I guess."

"No, tonight he's drunk. Man, he's out of his skull."

Pendleton waited a couple of minutes before saying, "He looks like a bullfighter I saw once in Tijuana called Victoriano Posada."

This proved to be a shrewd inquiry because after drinking some more of the free beer the fat Mexican remarked, "He calls himself Damaso."

Pendleton, wondering if some other information would follow, pretended to stretch and to yawn and smacked his chops mightily. He thought that tomorrow, when the tall man arrived, he would call him by name.

"Know what? He goes and stands by himself on the sea wall a lot of times. Maybe he's getting ready to knock himself off."

"Tell him not to do it in from of my place," Pendleton answered.

Through the screen door could be seen a roll of silvery yellow fog with the moon just above it, but the sea was hidden.

"These Santa Cruz winters," Pendleton said. Opening the icebox he chose a beer for himself and leaned against the counter, far enough away that his guest might not feel the friendship was being forced. Peeling off the wet label he rolled it into a soggy gray ball which he dropped into a bucket. "Singers make plenty money, I guess."

The Mexican looked at him slyly. "What are you talking about?"

Pendleton, after scratching his head, yawned again. "Huh? Oh. I was just thinking about what's-his-name. That fellow you come in here with."

"I know it," the Mexican said, laughing.

For a while Pendleton studied his beer and listened to the combers, each of which sounded as if it would smash the door. "Feels like something standing up in the ocean tonight," he said. "I could use a little summer."

"You want the town full of tourists? Those sausages? You're crazy. You're off the rocks."

Pendleton judged that the Mexican was about to insult the summer people still more, so he manipulated the conversation once again. "Somebody told me your friend got himself a singing job at that night spot near Capitola."

"Look," said the Toltec, patient, but irritated, "I just met the guy a couple of weeks ago."

"He never said where he's from, I guess."

"Chihuahua, he says. That's one rough town. And full of sand. That Chihuahua—it's noplace."

Breakers continued sounding just beyond the door and the fog now stood against the screen like a person.

"What does he do?"

The Mexican lifted both fat little shoulders.

"Just traveling through?"

The Mexican lifted both hands.

"Where is he going?"

"All I know is he's got a pretty good voice."

"He howls like a god-damn crazy wolf," Pendleton said, "howling for the moon."

"Yah, he's pretty good. Long time ago I saw a murder down south in the mountains and a woman screamed just like that."

Pendleton opened the icebox for two more beers. The Mexican accepted one as though in payment for service. For some seconds they had been able to hear footsteps approaching, audible after every tunnel of water caved in. The footsteps went past the door but no one could be seen.

"Know what? There was an old man washed up on the beach the other day."

"That so?" said Pendleton. "Everything gets to the beach sooner or later."

The Mexican nodded. Somewhere far out on the bay a little boat sounded again and again. "What a night," he said.

Pendleton murmured and scratched.

"Know something, mister? That Damaso, he ain't no Mexicano."

"I didn't think so," Pendleton lied.

"No, because he's got old blood. You know what I mean? I think he's a gypsy from Spain, or wherever those guys come from. He's dark in the wrong way. He just don't *feel* Mexicano to me. There's something about him, and besides he speaks a little Castellano."

Both of them considered this.

"What's he howling about?" Pendleton asked. "Some girl?"

"No, nothing like that."

"Then why the hell does he do it?"

But here the little Mexican lost interest; he revolved on the stool, from which only his toes could reach to the floor, hopped off, and hurried across to the nickel-odeon. Having pushed a nickel through the slit he studied the wonderful colors and followed the bubbles which fluttered up the tubes to vanish; next, he dialed "Tuxedo Junction" and began shuffling around the floor, snapping his fingers and undulating so that in certain positions he looked about five months pregnant.

"Who knows?" he asked of no one in particular while he danced.

The next night he again came in alone. When Pendleton mentioned this he replied that the dark one was still drunk.

And the next night when asked if the drunk was going into its third day he replied that Damaso was no longer drunk, just sick from being so, that he was at present lying on the wet cement having vomited on his boots, that probably by sunrise he would be all right. This turned out to be correct because both of them came in for supper the following night. Toltec, smiling and tugging at his crotch, was rumpled as usual and smelled human while his tall companion was oiled and groomed and wearing the white silk again. A good many people were loitering about the restaurant—every booth was full—because this thing had come to be expected, and though all of them were eating or drinking or spending money in some way to justify themselves, and although not everybody looked up at the entrance of the two Mexicans, there could be no doubt about the situation. Only these two men seemed not to notice anything; they ate voraciously and drank quite a few beers after which the Toltec began playing pinball and Damaso remained on the stool with his long arms crossed on the counter.

Later the nickelodeon lighted up. When at last its music died away there was not a sound in the restaurant. People watched the head of the dark man bow down until it was hidden in his arms. The crucifix disentangled itself and dropped out the top of his gaucho shirt where it began to swing to and fro, glittering as it twisted on the end of its golden chain. He remained like that for quite some time, finally raised his head to look at the ticket, counted out enough money, and with the sombrero loosely in one hand he stumbled through the door.

The other Mexican paid no attention; he called for more beer, which he drank all at once in an attempt to interest a young girl with silver slippers and breasts like pears who was eating supper with her parents, but, failing to win anything at this or again at the machine, he suddenly grew bored with the evening and walking out.

The next night he entered alone. When asked if his companion had started another drunk he said Damaso was gone.

Pendleton asked late in the evening, "How do you know?"

"I feel it," he said.

Then for awhile Pendleton stood listening to the advancing tide which had begun to pat the pillars like someone gently slapping a dead drum. After taking off his apron he rolled it up, as he always did, and put it beneath the counter. He untied the sweaty handkerchief from around his neck and folded it over the apron, but there his routine altered; before pulling in the shutters he stopped at the screen door and looked out and listened, but of course did not see or hear any more than he expected.

Sharply the Toltec said, "I like to dance." And he began to do so. "Next summer I'm really going to cut it up. Nothing's going to catch me." He read Pendleton's face while dancing by himself to the odd and clumsy little step he was inventing, and counseled, "Jesus Christ, he's gone. Forget about it, man."

1952

THE CONDOR
AND THE GUESTS

I N P E R U a female condor was staked inside a wooden cage. Every so often a male bird would get into this trap and would then be sold to a zoo or a museum. One of these captured condors, however, was sold to an American, L.R. Botkin of Parallel, Kansas.

It cost Mr. Botkin a great deal of money to get his bird into the United States, but he had traveled quite a bit and was proud of his ability to get anything accomplished that he set his mind to. At his home in Parallel he had a chain fastened about the bird's neck. The other end of the chain was padlocked to a magnolia tree which he had had transplanted to his back yard from the French Quarter of New Orleans on an earlier trip.

All the rest of that first day the condor sat in the magnolia tree and looked across the fields of wheat, but just before sundown it lifted its wings and spread them to the fullest extent as if testing the wind; then with a slow sweep of utter majesty it rose into the air. It took a second leisurely sweep with its wings, and a third. However, on the third stroke it came to the end of the chain. Then it made a sort of gasping noise and fell to the earth while the magnolia swayed from the shock. After its fall the gigantic bird did not move until long after dark when it got to its feet and climbed into the tree. Next morning as the sun rose it was on the same branch, looking south like a gargoyle taken from the ramparts of some cathedral.

Day after day it sat in the magnolia tree without moving, but every sundown it tried to take off. A pan of meat left nearby was visited only by a swarm of flies.

Almost a week following the bird's arrival Mr. Botkin was eating lunch at the Jupiter Club when he met his friend, Harry Apple, and said to him, "You seen my bird yet?"

Harry Apple was a shrunken, bald-headed man who never had much to say. He answered Mr. Botkin's question by slowly shaking his head. Mr. Botkin then exclaimed that Harry hadn't lived, and clapping him on the shoulder said he was giving a dinner party on Wednesday—a sort of anniversary of the condor's first week in Kansas—and asked if Harry could make it.

After the invitation had been extended Harry Apple sat silently for almost a minute and stared into space. He had married a tall, smoke-haired ex-show-girl of paralyzing beauty and he understood that she was the reason for the invitations he received.

At last he nodded, saying in his melancholy voice, "Sure. I'll bring Mildred, too."

Mr. Botkin clapped him on the shoulder and proposed a toast, "To the condor!"

Harry sipped his drink and murmured, "Sure."

Mr. Botkin also got the Newtons and the Huddlestuns for dinner. He was not too pleased about the Huddlestuns: Suzie Huddlestun's voice always set him on edge and "Tiny" was a bore. He had asked the Bagleys, but Chuck Bagley was going to an insurance convention in Kansas City. He had also asked the Gerlachs, the Ridges, and the Zimmermans, but none of them could make it, so he settled for Suzie and Tiny. They were delighted with the invitation.

On the evening of the party "Fig" Newton and his wife had not arrived by seven o'clock, so Mr. Botkin said to the others—Mildred and Harry Apple, and Suzie and Tiny Huddlestun, "Well, by golly, this calls for a drink!"

With cocktails in their hands the guests wandered down to the magnolia tree and stood in a half-circle, shaking the ice in their glasses and looking critically upward. The men stood a bit closer to the tree than the ladies did in order to show that they were not afraid of the condor. The ladies did not think the somber bird would do anything at all and they would rather have sat on the porch and talked.

Tiny Huddlestun was an enormous top-heavy man who had been a wrestler when he was young. His larynx had been injured by a vicious Turk during a match in Joplin, so that now his voice was a sort of quavering falsetto. He bobbled the ice in his glass with an index finger as big as a sausage and said in his falsetto, "That a turkey you got there, Botkin?"

His wife laughed and squeezed his arm. Even in platform shoes she did not come up to his chin, and the difference in their sizes caused people to speculate. She never listened to what he said but every time she heard his voice she laughed and squeezed him.

Mildred Apple said a little sulkily, "L.R., I want it to do something exciting." The cocktail was making her feel dangerous.

Mr. Botkin snapped his fingers. "By golly!" He swallowed the rest of his drink, took Harry's empty glass, and went back to the house. In a few minutes he returned with fresh drinks and a green and yellow parrot riding on his shoulder. Solemnly he announced, "This here's Caldwell."

"Caldwell?" shrieked Suzie Huddlestun, and began to laugh so hard that she clutched Tiny's coat for support.

Mr. Botkin was laughing, too, although he did not want to because he disliked Suzie. His belt went under his belly like a girth under a horse and as he laughed the belt creaked. It was several minutes before he could pat the perspiration from his strawberry face and gasp, "By golly!" He turned to the Apples who had stood by politely smiling, and explained, "Old Nowlin Caldwell at the Pioneer Trust."

"Caldwell," the parrot muttered, walking around on Mr. Botkin's shoulder.

Tiny Huddlestun had been hugging his wife. He released her and cleared his throat. "You going to eat that bird at Thanksgiving, Botkin?"

Mr. Botkin ignored him and said, leaning his head over next to the parrot, "Looky there, Caldwell, that condor don't even move. He's scared to death of you. You get on up there and tear him to pieces."

THE PARROT JUMPED to the ground and ran to the magnolia tree. The tree had not done well in the Kansas climate and was a stunted little thing with ragged bark and weak limbs which were turning their tips toward the ground. The parrot hooked its way up the trunk with no trouble, but at the lowest fork paused to watch the condor.

Mr. Botkin waved a hand as big as a spade.

The parrot went on up, more slowly however, stopping every few seconds to consider. Finally it crept out on the same limb and in a burst of confidence clamped its bright little claws into the wood beside the condor's talons. Then it imitated the black giant's posture and blinked down at the guests, which caused all of them except Harry Apple to break into laughter. The chain clinked. This alarmed the parrot; it whipped its head around and found itself looking into one of the condor's flat eyes.

"Eat 'im up!" Tiny shouted.

But the parrot fell out of the tree and ran toward the house, flailing its brilliant wings in the grass and screaming.

While his guests were still chuckling Mr. Botkin pointed far to the south where thunderheads were building up and said, "That's what the Andes look like."

The guests were all studying the familiar clouds when Fig Newton's sedan squeaked into the driveway. Mr. Botkin waved to Fig and his wife and went into the kitchen to get more drinks. To the colored girl Mrs. Botkin had hired for the evening he said, "Ever see a bird like that?"

The colored girl looked out the window immediately and answered with enthusiasm, "No, sir, Mr. Botkin!" But this did not seem to satisfy him so she added, "No sir, I sure never have!"

"You bet your sweet bottom you haven't." He was chipping some ice. "Because that's a condor."

"What's he eat?" she asked, but since he did not answer she felt it had been a silly question and turned her head away in shame.

Mr. Botkin shook up the drinks, bumped open the screen door with his stomach, and carried the tray into the yard. After he had greeted Fig and Laura Newton he said, "That little darky in the kitchen is scared to death of this bird. She wouldn't come near it for the world."

Fig answered, "Generally speaking, colored people are like that." He had a nervous habit of twitching his nose each time he finished speaking, which was the reason that hundreds of high-school students spoke of him as "Rabbit" Newton.

"Make him fly, L.R.," Laura said. "I want to admire his strength!" She was dressed in imitation gypsy clothes with a purple bandanna tied around her hips and a beauty mole painted on her temple. She did a little gypsy step across the yard, shaking her head so the gold earrings bounced against her cheeks. She lifted her glass high in the air. "Oh, make him fly!"

"Yes, do," added Mildred Apple. She had finished her drink quickly when she saw Laura's costume and now she stood on one leg so that her hips curved violently.

Mrs. Botkin, an egg-shaped little woman with wispy white hair that lay on her forehead like valentine lace, looked at her husband and started to say something. Then she puckered her lips and stopped.

Fig had been waiting for a pause. Now he drew attention to himself and said in measured tones, "Ordinarily the Negro avoids things he does not understand."

There was a polite silence until his nose twitched.

Then Mr. Botkin, whose cheeks had been growing redder with each drink, said, "You know what its name is?"

"What?" cried Suzie.

"Sambo," put in Fig, imitating a drawl. A laugh trembled at his lips, but nobody else laughed so he tasted his drink.

"Sherlock Holmes?" guessed Laura. Only Suzie tittered at this and Laura glanced at her sourly.

Mr. Botkin finally said, "Well, I'm going to tell you—it's Samson."

He waited until the guests' laughter had died away and then he told them that the name of the female in Peru was Delilah. He joined the laughter this time, his belt creaking and the perspiration standing out all over his face. When the guests had quieted down to head-wagging chuckles he said, "Well, by golly, I'll stir this Samson up!" He picked some sticks off the grass and began tossing them into the magnolia. At last one hit the condor's chest, but the huge bird seemed to be asleep.

"The damn thing won't eat, either!" he exclaimed in a gust of irritation.

"Won't *eat?*" shrilled Suzie Huddlestun, standing in the circle of Tiny's arms. "Gee, what's it live on if it don't eat?"

Mr. Botkin ignored her.

Fig cleared his throat. Pointing upward he said, "If you will look at that branch you'll see it is bent almost like a strung bow."

Mrs. Botkin suddenly turned to her husband and laid a hand on his sleeve. "Dear—"

Everybody looked at her in mild surprise, as always happened when she decided to say anything. She pressed a wisp of hair back into place and breathed, "Why don't you let the bird go?"

There was an uncomfortable pause, which Laura Newton broke by dancing around the back yard again. The candy-stripe skirt sailed around her bony goose legs. "How many want the condor to fly?" she asked, and thrusting her glass high in the air she cried, "Vote!"

Tiny Huddlestun had been squeezing his wife, but now he held his glass as high as possible without spilling the liquor and looked around with pleasure, knowing that nobody was tall enough to match the height of his ballot. Suzie's glass, clutched in her childlike hand, came just above his ear.

Mildred Apple sulkily lifted hers and so did Fig. Mr. Botkin had been watching with a curious sort of interest. His glass had gone up as soon as Laura proposed the vote. He looked at his wife and she quickly lifted hers.

"Harry?" Laura cried.

Harry Apple continued drinking.

Mrs. Botkin murmured, "I think dinner's ready." She fluttered her hands about in weak desperation but nobody looked at her.

Laura asked in a different tone, "Harry?" She was still holding the glass above her head.

Harry stood flat-footed and glared at the ground. A little drunkenly he swirled the ice in his glass.

After a few seconds of silence Mrs. Botkin coughed and started toward the porch; the guests filed after her. Mildred Apple was wearing white jersey. She got directly ahead of Laura and walked as if she were about to start a hula. Suzie and Tiny swung hands. Mr. Botkin, scowling, brought up the rear.

DURING SALAD Laura Newton talked mostly to the people on either side of Harry. Burgundy wine from France was served with the steaks and while they were beginning on that the sun went down. Then one by one the guests stopped cutting their meat and looked through the porch screen.

Fig Newton twisted the Phi Beta Kappa key on his chain as he watched the condor lift first one foot and then the other from its branch. Tiny Huddlestun leaned his ham-bone elbows on the table and raised himself partly out of his chair in order to see over Mrs. Botkin's fluffy white head. Of the guests, only Harry Apple did not look; he stared at his wine glass, turning it slowly with his fingers on the stem. Mr. Botkin's eyes had narrowed in anticipation; he waited for the flight like an occidental Buddha.

The condor's wings spread, brushing the leaves of other branches, and at the size of the bird Laura dropped her fork. Nobody picked it up, so it lay on the flag-stones, its tines sending out a persistent hum.

The black condor lifted its feet again. This caused the chain which dangled from its neck to sway back and forth.

The dinner table was quiet. Only some June bugs fizzed angrily as they tried to get through the screens.

Mildred Apple said abruptly, "I'm cold." Nobody looked at her, so she went on in a sharp tone, "Why doesn't somebody switch off that fan? I tell you I'm cold. I won't sit here all night in a draft. I won't!"

Mr. Botkin did not turn his head, but growled, "Shut up."

Mildred was shocked, but she recovered quickly. "Don't you *dare* tell me to shut up! I won't stand for it! Do you hear?" Mr. Botkin paid no attention to her, so she turned petulantly to Harry; he was looking at his glass.

"Switch it off yourself," murmured Laura.

Mildred's eyes began to glitter. "I will not!"

"I'm sure nobody else is going to," Laura said in a dry voice.

Fig was getting ready to say something when Suzie Huddlestun gasped, "Oh!"

The condor took off so slowly that it did not seem real; it appeared only to be stretching, yet it was in the air. When its immense wings had spread and descended a second time its talons rose above the top branches, curling into metal-hard globes. For an instant the condor hung in the purple sky like an insignia of some great war plane, then its head was jerked down. It made its one sound, dropped to the warm ground, and lay without moving.

Laura Newton observed sourly, "What a simple bird." She looked across her tack-hammer nose at Harry.

Tiny grinned. "Now's the time to cook that turkey for Thanksgiving, Botkin." He looked all around the table but nobody chuckled and his eyes came back to Suzie. She laughed.

Fig took a sip of water and then cleared his throat. "Fowl," he said, after frowning in thought, "are not overly intelligent."

Twilight was ending. The guests could not see the condor distinctly, but only what looked like a gunny sack under the dying magnolia. Much later, while they were arguing bitterly over their bridge scores, they heard the condor's chain clinking and soon a branch creaked.

1948

THE BEAU MONDE
OF MRS. BRIDGE

Parking

THE BLACK LINCOLN that Mr. Bridge gave her on her forty-seventh birthday was a size too long and she drove it as cautiously as she might have driven a locomotive. People were always blowing their horns at her or turning their heads to stare when they went by. The Lincoln had been set to idle too slowly, and in consequence the engine sometimes died when she pulled up at an intersection, but as her husband never used the Lincoln and she herself assumed it was just one of those things about automobiles, the idling speed was never adjusted. Often she would delay a line of cars while she pressed the starter button either too long or not long enough. Knowing she was not expert she was always quite apologetic when something unfortunate happened, and did her best to keep out of everyone's way. She changed into second gear at the beginning of any hill and let herself down the far side much more slowly than necessary.

Usually she parked in a downtown garage where Mr. Bridge rented a stall for her. She had only to honk at the enormous doors, which would then trundle open, and coast on inside where an attendant would greet her by name, help her out, and then park the formidable machine. But in the country-club district she parked on the street, and if there were diagonal stripes she did very well, but if parking was parallel she had trouble judging her distance from the curb and would have to get out and walk around to look, then get back in and try again. The Lincoln's seat was so soft and Mrs. Bridge so short that she had to sit very erect in order to see what was happening ahead of her. She drove with arms thrust forward and gloved hands tightly on the large wheel, her feet just able to depress the pedals all the way. She never had serious accidents but was often seen here and there being talked to by patrolmen. These patrolmen never did anything, partly because they saw immediately that it would not do to arrest her and partly because they could tell she was trying to do everything the way it should be done.

When parking on the street it embarrassed her to have people watch, yet there always seemed to be someone at the bus stop or lounging in a doorway with nothing to do but stare while she struggled with the wheel and started jerkily backward. Sometimes, however, there would be a nice man who, seeing her difficulty, would come around and tip his hat and ask if he might help.

"Would you, please?" she would ask in relief, and after he opened the door she would get out and stand on the curb while he put the car in place. It was a problem to know whether he expected a tip or not. She knew that people who stood around on the streets were in need of money, still she did not want to offend anyone. Sometimes she would hesitantly ask, sometimes not, and whether the man would accept a twenty-five-cent piece or not she would smile brightly up at him, saying, "Thank you so much," and having locked the Lincoln's doors she would be off to the shops.

Minister's Book

IF MRS. BRIDGE bought a book it was almost always one of three things: a best seller she had heard of or seen advertised in all the stores, a self-improvement book, or a book by a Kansas City author no matter what it was about. These latter were infrequent, but now and again someone would explode on the midst of Kansas City with a Civil War history or something about old Westport Landing. Then, too, there were slender volumes of verse and essays usually printed by local publishing houses, and it was one of these that lay about the living room longer than any other book with the exception of an extremely old two-volume set of *The Brothers Karamazov* in gold-painted leather which nobody in the house had ever read and which had been purchased from an antique dealer by Mr. Bridge's brother. This set rested gravely on the mantelpiece between a pair of bronze Indian-chief heads—the only gift from cousin Lulubelle Watts that Mrs. Bridge had ever been able to use—and was dusted once a week by Hazel with a peacock-feather duster.

The volume that ran second to *The Brothers Karamazov* was a collection of thoughts by the local minister, Dr. Foster, a short and congenial and even jovial man with a big, handsome head capped with soft golden-white hair which he allowed to grow long and which he brushed toward the top of his head to give himself another inch or so. He had written these essays over a period of several years with the idea of putting them into book form, and from time to time would allude to them, laughingly, as his memoirs. Then people would exclaim that he surely mustn't keep them to himself until he died, at which Dr. Foster, touching the speaker's arm, would laugh heartily and say, "We'll think it over, we'll think it over," and clear this throat.

At last, when he had been preaching in Kansas City for seventeen years and his name was recognized, and he was often mentioned in *The Tattler* and sometimes in the city paper, a small publishing firm took these essays which he had quietly submitted to them several times before. The book came out in a black cover with a dignified gray and purple dust jacket that showed him smiling pensively out of his study window at dusk, hands clasped behind his back and one foot slightly forward.

The first essay began, "I am now seated at my desk, the desk that has been a source of comfort and inspiration to me these many years. I see that night is falling, the shadows creeping gently across my small but (to my eyes) lovely garden, and at such times as this I often reflect on the state of Mankind."

Mrs. Bridge read Dr. Foster's book, which he had autographed for her, and was amazed to find that he was such a reflective man, and so sensitive to the sunrise which she discovered he often got up to watch. She underlined several passages in the book that seemed to have particular meaning for her, and when it was done she was able to discuss it with her friends, who were all reading it, and she recommended it strongly to Grace Barron, who at last consented to read a few pages.

With ugly, negative books about war and Communists and perversion and everything else constantly flooding the counters this book came to her like an olive branch. It assured her that life was worth living after all, that she had not and was not doing anything wrong, and that people needed her. So, in the shadow of Dostoevski, the pleasant meditations of Dr. Foster lay in various positions about the living room.

Maid from Madras

THE BRIDGES gave an evening party not because they wanted to have cocktails with a mob of people, but because it was about time for them to be giving a party. Altogether more than eighty people stood and wandered about the home which stood on a hillside and was in the style of a Loire Valley chateau. Grace and Virgil Barron were there, Madge and Russ Arlen, the Heywood Duncans, Welhelm and Susan Van Metre looking out of place, Lois and Stuart Montgomery, the Beckerle sisters in ancient beaded gowns and looking as though they had not an instant forgotten the day when Mrs. Bridge had entertained them in anklets, Noel Johnson huge and by himself because she was in bed suffering from exhaustion, Mabel Ong trying to start serious discussions, Dr. and Mrs. Batchelor whose Austrian refugee guests were now domestics in Los Angeles, and even Dr. Foster, smiling tolerantly, who appeared for a whisky sour and a cigarette while gently chiding several of the men about Sunday golf. There was also an auto salesman named Beachy Marsh who had arrived early in a double-breasted pin-stripe business suit instead of a tuxedo, and being embarrassed about his mistake did everything he could think of to be amusing. He was not a close friend but it had been necessary to invite him along with several others.

Mrs. Bridge rustled about the brilliantly lighted home checking steadily to see that everything was as it should be. She glanced into the bathrooms every few minutes and found that the guest towels, which resembled pastel handkerchiefs, were still immaculately overlapping one another on the rack—at evening's end only three had been disturbed—and she entered the kitchen once to recommend that the extra servant girl, hired to assist Hazel, pin shut the gap in the breast of her starched uniform.

Through the silver candelabra and miniature turkey sandwiches Mrs. Bridge went graciously smiling and chatting a moment with everyone, quietly opening windows to let out the smoke, removing wet glasses from mahogany table tops, slipping away now and then to empty the onyx ashtrays she had bought and distributed throughout the house.

Beachy Marsh got drunk. He slapped people on the shoulder, told jokes, laughed loudly, and also went around emptying the ashtrays of their cherry-colored stubs, all the while attempting to control the tips of his shirt collar which had become damp from perspiration and were rolling up into the air like horns. Following Mrs. Bridge halfway up the carpeted stairs he said hopefully, "There was a young maid from Madras, who had a magnificent ass; not rounded and pink, as you probably think—it was gray, had long ears, and ate grass."

"Oh, my word!" replied Mrs. Bridge, looking over her shoulder with a polite smile but continuing up the stairs, while the auto salesman plucked miserably at his collar.

Laundress in the Rear

EVERY WEDNESDAY the laundress came, and as the bus line was several blocks distant from the Bridge home someone would almost always meet her bus in the morning. For years the laundress had been an affable old Negress named Beulah Mae who was full of nutshell wisdom and who wore a red bandanna and a dress that resembled a dyed hospital gown. Mrs. Bridge was very fond of Beulah Mae, speaking of her as "a nice old soul" and frequently giving her a little extra money or an evening dress that had begun to look dated, or perhaps some raffle tickets that she was always obliged to buy from Girl Scouts and various charities. But there came a day when Beulah Mae had had enough of laundering, extra gifts or no, and without saying a word to any of her clients she boarded a bus for California to live out her life on the seashore. For several weeks Mrs. Bridge was without a laundress and was obliged to take the work to an establishment, but at last she got someone else, an extremely large and doleful Swedish woman who said during the interview in the kitchen that her name was Ingrid and that for eighteen years she had been a masseuse and liked it much better.

When Mrs. Bridge arrived at the bus line the first morning Ingrid saluted her mournfully and got laboriously into the front seat. This was not the custom, but such a thing was difficult to explain because Mrs. Bridge did not like to hurt anyone's feelings by making them feel inferior, so she said nothing about it and hoped that by next week some other laundress in the neighborhood would have told Ingrid.

But the next week she again got in front, and again Mrs. Bridge pretended everything was all right. However on the third morning while they were riding up Ward Parkway toward the house Mrs. Bridge said, "I was so attached to Beulah Mae. She used to have the biggest old time riding in the back seat."

Ingrid turned a massive yellow head to look stonily at Mrs. Bridge. As they were easing into the driveway she spoke, "So you want I should sit in the back?"

"Oh, gracious! I didn't mean that," Mrs. Bridge answered, smiling up at Ingrid. "You're perfectly welcome to sit right here if you like."

Ingrid said no more about the matter and next week with the same majestic melancholy rode in the rear.

Frayed Cuffs

ORDINARILY Mrs. Bridge examined the laundry but when she had shopping to do, or a meeting, the job fell to Hazel who never paid much attention to such things as missing buttons or loose elastic. Thus it was that Mrs. Bridge discovered her son wearing a shirt with cuffs that were noticeably frayed.

"For Heaven's sake!" she exclaimed, taking hold of his sleeve. "Has a dog been chewing on it?"

He looked down at the threads as though he had never before seen them.

"Surely you don't intend to *wear* that shirt?"

"It looks perfectly okay to me," said Douglas.

"Just look at those cuffs! Anyone would think we're on our way to the poor-house."

"So is it a disgrace to be poor?"

"*No!*" she cried. "But we're *not* poor!"

Equality

MRS. BRIDGE approved of equality. On certain occasions when she saw in the newspapers or heard over the radio that labor unions had won another victory she would think, Good for them! And, as the segregational policies of the various states became more and more subject to criticism by civic groups as well as by the federal government, she would feel that it was about time, and she would try to understand how discrimination could persist. However strongly she felt about this she was careful about what she said because she was aware that everything she had was hers through the efforts of one person: her husband. Mr. Bridge was of the opinion that people were not equal. In his decisive manner of speaking, annoyed that she should even puzzle over such a thing, he said, "You take all the people on earth and divide up everything, and in six months everybody would have just about what they have now. What Abraham Lincoln meant was equal rights, not equal capacity."

This always seemed exactly what she was trying to point out to him, that many people did not have equal rights, but after a few minutes of discussion she would be overwhelmed by a sense of inadequacy and would begin to get confused, at which he would stare at her for a moment as though she were something in a glass box and then resume whatever he had been doing.

She invariably introduced herself to members of minority groups at gatherings where she found herself associating with them.

"I'm India Bridge," she would say in a friendly manner, and would wish it were possible to invite the people into her home. And when, among neighborhood friends she had known for a long time and who offered no unusual ideas, the increased means of certain classes were discussed, she would say, "Isn't it nice that they can have television and automobiles and everything."

In a northern town a Negro couple opened a grocery store in a white neighborhood; that night the windows were smashed and the store set afire. Newspapers published photographs of the ruined property, of two smirking policemen, and of the Negro couple who had lost their entire savings. Mrs. Bridge read this story while having breakfast by herself several hours after her husband had left for work. She studied the miserable faces of the young Negro and his wife. Across the newspaper the morning sun slanted warm and cheerful, in the kitchen Hazel sang hymns while peeling apples for a pie, all the earth as seen from her window seemed content, yet such things still came to pass. In her breakfast nook, a slice of buttered toast in hand, Mrs. Bridge felt a terrible desire. She would press these unfortunate people to her breast and tell them that she, too, knew what it meant to be hurt but that everything would turn out all right.

Gloves

SHE HAD ALWAYS done a reasonable amount of charity work along with her friends, particularly at a little store on Ninth Street where second-hand clothing that had been collected in drives was distributed. In this store were two rooms; in the front one a row of card tables were placed together, behind which stood the charity workers who were to assist people seeking something to wear, and in the back room were several more card tables and collapsible wooden chairs where Mrs. Bridge and her fellow workers ate their lunch or relaxed when not on duty in front.

She often went down with Madge Arlen. One week they would drive to their work in the Arlens' Chrysler, the next week in Mrs. Bridge's Lincoln, and when this was the case Mrs. Bridge always drew up before the garage where her parking stall was rented. She honked, or beckoned if someone happened to be in sight, and shortly an attendant whose name was George would come out buttoning up his jacket and he would ride in the rear seat to the clothing store. There he would jump out and open the door for Mrs. Bridge, and after that he would drive the Lincoln back to the garage because she did not like it left on the street in such a neighborhood.

"Can you come by for us around six, or six-fifteen-ish, George?" she would ask.

He always answered that he would be glad to, touched the visor of his cap, and drove away.

"He seems so nice," said Mrs. Arlen as the two of them walked into their store.

"Oh, he is!" Mrs. Bridge agreed. "He's one of the nicest garage men I've ever had."

"How long have you been parking there?"

"Quite some time. We used to park at that awful place on Walnut."

"The one with the popcorn machine? Lord, isn't that the limit?"

"No, not that place. The one with the Italians. You know how my husband is about Italians. Well, that just seemed to be headquarters for them. They came in there to eat their sandwiches and listen to some opera broadcast from New York. It was just impossible. So finally Walter said, 'I'm going to change garages.' So we did."

They walked past the row of card tables piled high with soiled and sour unwashed clothing and continued into the back room where they found some early arrivals having coffee and éclairs. Mrs. Bridge and Mrs. Arlen hung up their coats and also had coffee, and then prepared for work. The reform school had sent down some boys to assist and they were put to work untying the latest sacks of used clothing and dumping them out.

By two o'clock everything was ready for the day's distribution. The doors were unlocked and the first of the poor entered and approached the counter behind which stood Mrs. Bridge and two others with encouraging smiles, all three of them wearing gloves.

Robbery at Heywood Duncans'

THE BRIDGES were almost robbed while attending a cocktail party at the Heywood Duncans'. Shortly after ten o'clock, just as she was taking an anchovy cracker from the buffet table, four men appeared in the doorway with revolvers and wearing plastic noses attached to horn-rimmed glasses for disguise. One of them said, "All right, everybody. This is a stick-up!" Another of the men—Mrs. Bridge afterward described him to the police as not having worn a necktie—got up on the piano bench and from there stepped up on top of the piano itself where he pointed his gun at different people. At first everybody thought it was a joke, but it wasn't because the robbers made them all line up facing the wall with their hands above their heads. One of them ran upstairs and came down with his arms full of fur coats and purses while two others started around the room pulling billfolds out of the men's pockets and drawing rings from the ladies' fingers. Before they had gotten to either Mr. or Mrs. Bridge, who were lined up between Dr. Foster and the Arlens, something frightened them and the one standing on the piano called out in an ugly voice, "Who's got the keys to that blue Cadillac out front?"

At this Mrs. Ralph Porter screamed, "Don't you tell him, Ralph!"

But the bandits took Mr. Porter's keys anyway and after telling them all not to move for thirty minutes they ran out the porch door.

It was written up on the front page of the newspaper, with pictures on page eight, including a close-up of the scratched piano. Mrs. Bridge, reading the story in the breakfast room next morning after her husband had gone to work, was surprised to learn that Stuart Montgomery had been carrying just $2.14 and that Mrs. Noel Johnson's ring had been zircon.

Follow Me Home

HOW THE SCARE actually started no one knew, although several women, one of whom was a fairly close friend of Madge Arlen, claimed they knew the name of someone who had been assaulted not far from Ward Parkway. Some thought it had happened near the Plaza, others thought farther south, but they were generally agreed that it had happened late at night. The story was that a certain lady of a well-known family had been driving home alone and when she had slowed down for an intersection a man had leaped up from behind some shrubbery and had wrenched open the door. Whether the attack had been consummated or not the story did not say; the important part was that there had been a man and he had leaped up and wrenched open the door. There was nothing in the paper about it, nor in *The Tattler*, which did not print anything unpleasant, and the date of the assault could not be determined for some reason, only that it had been on a dark night not too long ago.

When this story had gotten about none of the matrons wished to drive anywhere alone after sundown. As it so happened they were often obliged to go to a cocktail party or a dinner by themselves because their husbands were working late at the office, but they went full of anxiety, with the car doors locked. It also became customary for the husband-host to get his automobile out of the garage at the end of an evening and then to follow the unescorted matrons back to their homes. Thus there could be seen processions of cars driving cautiously and rather like funerals across the boulevards of the country-club residential district.

So Mrs. Bridge came home on those evenings when her husband did not get back from the office in time, or when he was too tired and preferred to lie in bed reading vacation advertisements. At her driveway the procession would halt, engines idling, while she drove into the garage and came back out along the driveway so as to be constantly visible, and entered by the front door. Having unlocked it she would step inside, switch on the hall lights, and call to her husband, "I'm home!" Then, after he had made a noise of some kind in reply, she would flicker the lights a few times to show the friends waiting outside that she was safe, after which they would all drive off into the night.

Never Speak to Strange Men

ON A DOWNTOWN STREET just outside a department store a man said something to her. She ignored him. But at that moment the crowd closed them in together.

"How do you do?" he said, smiling and touching his hat.

She saw that he was a man of about fifty with silvery hair and rather satanic ears. His face became red and he laughed awkwardly. "I'm Gladys Schmidt's husband."

"Oh, for Heaven's sake!" Mrs. Bridge exclaimed. "I didn't recognize you."

Conrad

WHILE IDLY DUSTING the bookcase one morning she paused to read the titles and saw an old red-gold volume of Conrad that had stood untouched for years. She could not think how it happened to be there. Taking it down she looked at the flyleaf and found "*Ex Libris* Thomas Bridge."

She remembered then that they had inherited some books and charts upon the death of her husband's brother, an odd man who had married a night-club entertainer and later died of a heart attack in Mexico.

Having nothing to do that morning she began to turn the brittle, yellowed pages and slowly became fascinated. After standing beside the bookcase for about ten minutes she wandered, still reading, into the living room where she sat down and did not look up from the book until Hazel came in to announce lunch. In the midst of one of the stories she came upon a passage that had once been underlined, apparently by Tom Bridge, which remarked that some people go skimming over the years of existence to sink gently into a placid grave, ignorant of life to the last, without ever having been made to see all it may contain. She brooded over this fragment even while reading further, and finally turned back to it again, and was staring at the carpet with a bemused expression when Hazel entered.

Mrs. Bridge put the book on the mantel, for she intended to read more of this perceptive man, but during the afternoon Hazel automatically put Conrad back on the shelf and Mrs. Bridge did not think of him again.

Voting

SHE HAD NEVER gone into politics the way some women did who were able to speak with masculine inflections about such affairs as farm surplus and foreign subsidies. She always listened attentively when these things came up at luncheons or circle meetings; she felt her lack of knowledge and wanted to know more, and did intend to buckle down to some serious studying. But so many things kept popping up that it was difficult to get started, and then too she did not know exactly how one began to learn. At times she would start to question her husband but he refused to say much to her, and so she would not press the matter because after all there was not much she herself could accomplish.

This was how she defended herself to Mabel Ong after having incautiously let slip the information that her husband told her what to vote for.

Mabel Ong was flat as an adolescent but much more sinewy. Her figure was like a bud that had never managed to open. She wore tweed coats and cropped hair and frequently stood with hands thrust deep into her side pockets as if she were a man. She spoke short positive sentences, sometimes throwing back her head to laugh with a sound that reminded people of a dry reed splintering. She had many bitter observations in regard to capitalism, relating stories she had heard from unquestionable sources about women dying in childbirth because they could not afford the high cost of proper hospitalization or even the cost of insurance plans.

"If I ever have a child—" she was fond of beginning, and would then tear into medical fees.

She demanded of Mrs. Bridge, "Don't you have a mind of your own? Great Scott, woman, you're an adult. Speak out! We've been emancipated." Ominously she began rocking back and forth from her heels to her toes, hands clasped behind her back while she frowned at the carpet of the Auxiliary clubhouse.

"You're right," Mrs. Bridge apologized, discreetly avoiding the smoke Mabel Ong blew into the space between them. "It's just so hard to know *what* to think. There's so much scandal and fraud, and I suppose the papers only print what they want us to know." She hesitated, then, "How do you make up *your* mind?"

Mabel Ong removed the cigarette holder from her small cool lips. She considered the ceiling and then the carpet, as though debating on how to answer such a naïve question, and finally suggested that Mrs. Bridge might begin to grasp the fundamentals by a deliberate reading of certain books, which she jotted down on the margin of a tally card. Mrs. Bridge had not heard of any of these books except one and this was because its author was being investigated, but she decided to read it anyway.

There was a waiting list for it at the public library but she got it at a rental library and settled down to go through it with the deliberation that Mabel Ong had advised. The author's name was Zokoloff, which certainly sounded threatening, and to be sure the first chapter was about bribery in the circuit courts. When Mrs. Bridge had gotten far enough along to feel capable of speaking about it she left it quite boldly on the hall table; however Mr. Bridge did not even notice it until the third evening. He thinned his nostrils, read the first paragraph, grunted once, and dropped it back onto the hall table. This was disappointing. In fact, now that there was no danger involved, she had trouble finishing the book. She thought it would be better in a magazine digest, but at last she did get through and returned it to the rental library, saying to the owner, "I can't honestly say I agree with it all but he's certainly well informed."

Certain arguments of Zokoloff remained with her and she found that the longer she thought about them the more penetrating and logical they became; surely it *was* time, as he insisted, for a change in government. She decided to vote liberal at the next election, and as time for it approached she became filled with such enthusiasm and anxiety that she wanted very much to discuss government with her husband. She began to feel confident that she could persuade him to change his vote also. It was all so clear to her, there was really no mystery to politics. However when she challenged him to discussion he did not seem especially interested, in fact he did not answer. He was watching a television acrobat stand on his thumb in a bottle and only glanced across at her for an instant with an annoyed expression. She let it go until the following evening when television was over, and this time he looked at her curiously, quite intently, as if probing her mind, and then all at once he snorted.

She really intended to force a discussion on election eve. She was going to quote from the book of Zokoloff. But he came home so late, so tired, that she had not the heart to upset him. She concluded it would be best to let him vote as he always had, and she would do as she herself wished; still, upon getting to the polls, which were conveniently located in the country-club shopping district, she became doubtful and a little uneasy. And when the moment finally came she pulled the lever recording her wish for the world to remain as it was.

1954

MADEMOISELLE
FROM KANSAS CITY

Grand Entrance

"FIRST TRIP to New York?"

Ruth turned to look at him—the stranger and opportunist—without surprise. He was furtive; he was cheap. "I've always lived here," she said. "Now hop on your scooter and roll. Make it fast."

He hurried along the street. She picked up her suitcase and climbed the brownstone steps. Already she felt at home in New York. Kansas City?—it was as though she had lived there once upon a time. The Midwest belonged to another life, it had not meant very much. One day she would go back to visit. Yes, and what bitter pleasures there would be! Someday, yes, she would go back, just long enough to be seen, to be talked about. She pressed the bell and waited.

"The room looks fine. I'll take it," she said, and paid for the first week.

And then for half an hour she sat on the edge of the bed and gazed down into the street thinking only that here in New York, at last, she belonged. The room was not fine, it was not half so fine as it sounded in the newspaper, or by telephone; it would not do for long, but it would do until she could find a job and learn the city.

As for the Wenzells—"I've written them to expect you," her mother had said at the station, "but of course they won't know where to find you." No, the Wenzells didn't know where to find her, thank Heavens. "Be sure to look them up!" her mother had called—anxious, waving. "They're awfully nice! Have a good trip! Don't forget to write!" Yes, Mother, yes, yes. Ruth kicked off her shoes and fell backward across the bed. The ceiling, she noticed, was stained. A scrap of paper hung down. But it would do; yes, anything at all would do for a little while. The heat, now, in mid-June; the sleazy, filthy men like spiders on the street; garbage and papers in the gutter—even this was preferable to life in Kansas City. Now, she thought, shutting her eyes, it would be four o'clock in the afternoon and her brother would be swimming at the country club, diving from the high board to impress whoever cared enough to watch. And sister Carolyn?—playing golf, beyond doubt. And her father?—still at the office, perspiring, or perhaps at court again. Nobody thought about him between breakfast and supper. Yet that was not so; her mother must think of him. And what would Mother be doing now?—lying on the sofa with a damp cloth over her eyes, the shades of the house pulled down, the house cool and dank, insufferable as a closed museum!

In New York it was growing dark. Ruth lay on a strange bed. What was past was soon to be obscured. She had not lived until now. And was it not strange, she wondered, that the first words she should speak in this new home had been a lie?

The Victim

EARLY one Sunday morning, before dawn, Ruth was wakened by someone tapping at the door. Then there was silence. Whoever it was, she thought, had gone away. But the tapping resumed and she heard her name whispered, and knew that Lenny was outside. She lay motionless, with clenched teeth, and waited for him to leave; but he tapped louder, and called her by name. "I've got to see you!" he said. "Ruth, I'm going to shoot myself!" She turned over in bed, the springs creaked. "I know you're in there," he said, and rapped sharply on the panel. "Let me in, please! Ruth! Ruth!" His voice was becoming hysterical. "I need you! Christ! Christ! It's Lenny, Ruth, it's me!" She did not answer; and the man who lay next to her, whom she had met a few hours before, was wakened by the noise. Ruth could not think of his name; when she tried to remember it but could not she felt a rush of hatred against him, against all men for their lack of discretion, their indelicacy, because they could not control their passions—they seemed to her despicable and contemptible for eternally running after women. Then she thought of his name, Howard, but remembered nothing else about him. His body was rigid with fright; in the darkness she smiled, knowing that he was wondering now, as he had not bothered to wonder earlier, who she was, if the man knocking at the door was her husband. Ruth lifted one hand to his face to comfort him because he had started to tremble. From the corridor came the sound of Lenny weeping, then a furious hammering at the door; she turned her head to look at the man beside her but could not make out his features. He was shaking with fear and she decided that whoever he was she would never see him again. She reached across him to the night table for a cigarette, then sat up in bed with her chin resting on her knees, smoking and waiting. She imagined herself in another bed, in another woman's place, and wondered how she would feel if that woman returned in the middle of the night. It was difficult to imagine. It would not happen, but if it did happen what would she feel? Not fear, certainly. No, I would be angry, she thought. I'd be infuriated.

After a while there was silence in the hall. She sensed that Lenny had gone away.

Monday morning, at coffee, she saw the story on the second page, and a photograph of Lenny. He had gone into Washington Square and sat on a bench until almost noon, then suddenly stood up, pulled the gun from his pocket and killed himself. There was no explanation, except that offered by his landlord—he had seemed despondent for several weeks.

Ruth looked with distaste at his picture, the familiar supplicating smile, the enormous soulful Jewish eyes that once had seemed to her so beautiful. Now the face looked merely weak, vaguely hopeful. There weren't enough bones in him, she thought. Why should he have gotten so upset about me? We didn't mean anything to each other, I told him that.

Later, when she happened to think about him, less and less frequently, as days and weeks went by, she would think that she ought to feel some sense of regret. She might have spoken to him through the door, she might have done that much at least, for she had known that he did mean to kill himself if she rejected him. At that hour there had been only one person on earth who could have saved him— that had been herself, but she had preferred to sit in bed smoking a cigarette and waiting for him to go away. She asked herself if she would have opened the door to him if she had been alone, and it seemed to her that probably she would have allowed him in and would have talked to him, tried to console him without becoming involved. But this was an idle thought; she had not been alone, she had been with someone, therefore she could not let him in. Lenny had been a victim of circumstances, that was all.

Messalina

THIS ONE was no different. She listened, feigned a smile, accepted the drink he poured, which was, as she had known it would be, as it always was, too strong— not a drink so much as a poison, an attempt to relax her, to drug her, so that he might do more as he wished, might half-live the absurd masculine fantasies. She swallowed the drink and looked about the room; like the man himself, the room was no different. She looked for the closet and got up and walked across the room to open it, as she always did, feeling his eyes greedily upon her. I despise you, she thought. If only you realized how I despise you! Before she touched the handle of the closet door she knew that nobody was hiding inside; so, at the last instant, she turned toward the window as if that had been where she intended to go, and stood, holding the curtain aside, staring down into the mid-city night. She knew he was watching her from his chair and that he was quietly starting to remove his clothes. A shoe bumped on the carpet but she did not turn from the window. This is the scene, she thought. This is the hour, the place, the tragedy. This is where the unhappy girl opens the window and the music rises to a crescendo as she plunges to her death. How does it always end? The final scene? Focus on the salesman, briefly, see his shocked expression. But only briefly because he's not important. Do we close with a crowd gathering on the street? Fade out. Ruth unlatched the window and pushed it open. Would he be alarmed? She turned; he promptly smiled. She did not think he had been worried, he had been staring, staring at the flesh he had bought for a little while, but then, seeing her smile, he must pretend that she was human.

"Gettin' late!" he grinned.

"Well now, do tell," she said, and saw the effort he made to conceal his displea- sure—his southwestern accent, her mimicry. "Where are you from?" she asked. Then he said he was from Kansas City. For a moment of horror she glared into him, into the gelid green eyes, but saw no malice, nothing.

"I guessed you were from Texas," she said.

"Folks do," he remarked, and for a moment she almost understood everything about him. He meant no harm. There would be a family back home, he was away from his wife—perhaps he loved her, or perhaps she had bored him for twenty years—what did it matter? Ruth looked at him more softly.

"Truth is," he said, and he was ready to talk, and she saw that he might talk for an hour, "truth is, now, I come from Louisiana. Saint Charles, Louisiana. Know where it's at?" Ruth shook her head. "Sleepiest place ever was, full of moss and bugs. I lef' some time back, though. Lived lots of places. Thinkin' I might move to Noo Yawk!" He laughed; it was a joke; and yet he wished to know if she would encourage him to move here. Now, *that* would be something to talk about back home. Pretty little whore wanted me to move there. His voice echoed from the sleepy towns of the past; she remembered Harrisonville and Joplin, darkened lobbies of old hotels, yellowing magazines untouched in the stained oak racks.

"Tell me about Kansas City," she said.

"Been livin' there these past two years," he answered, chuckling. "Man's got to go where the company sends him. Don't give a man no choice in the matter." He poured himself another drink and wagged his head. "Nice enough. Lord, I suppose. Lakes and trees. Hot in summah, though. Hell, on the other hand I don't mind that so much. It's them cold wintahs that freeze up a man like a drum."

"Two years you've been there," Ruth said. "You must have friends. You must know a great many people by now."

"I meet easy," he said, nodding. "That's how come I'm in this good position. That whole territory belongs to me. I know how to put people at ease. That's always been m'strong sellin' point. People meet me and think to themself right off, why, I think I met that man somewhere before. You'd be surprised," he added and suddenly, seriously, looked up at her where she stood leaning against the wall.

"I feel the same—as though we'd met before," she told him. Immediately she regretted saying this, even before he answered. She had meant this as an insult too subtle for him to perceive. He had not perceived it, but it reminded him of his purpose. He would not forget again. He winked at her and patted the bed.

"If we ain't met befo', I'm sure that's my errah. Come along now, little lady, you sweet thing."

"I'll take the money first," she said, and snapped her fingers for emphasis. Always she had asked for it before she undressed, but never like this, never directly. She glanced at herself reflected in the half-opened window and for a moment thought she was seeing someone else.

"It's a powerful lot of money, what they told me it would be," he said, and waited. He was hopeful. She knew she should not have talked to him; it was a mistake to ask about Kansas City.

Don't argue, she thought, gazing down into the street. For God's sake, don't be one of those!

"Well, sho," he said at last and cautiously took his wallet from an inside pocket of his coat. She walked across the room and stood silently in front of him while he counted the bills into her hand, wetting his thumb before releasing each one, wrinkling each one to be sure that another had not clung to it; and she wondered if when he had finished she would crumple them and throw them at his face. Then he was through counting; she folded the money, tucked it into her purse, and without hesitation reached back, unzipping her dress and pulling it over her head before he could try to help. She did not want his hands to touch her clothing.

When, soon, she lay beside him, both naked, and he set to fondling her, kissing her body and whispering suggestions, she pretended that he was arousing her. She listened to the noise of the midnight street and imagined herself walking to the theater. Some night it would happen, and crowds would follow. The unimportant people of the world would point to her. She turned her face aside from his kiss, caught her breath when he lunged. Underneath the heaving obese body, insulted by the odor of cheap talcum, disgusted by his clumsiness, she heard with indifference his groans of ecstasy. Now she did not need to pretend; his face was pressed into the pillow while he labored. She opened one eye and gazed at the ceiling, waiting for him to be satisfied. She wondered if she really did despise him, and decided that she did not. She felt nothing in relation to him, nothing at all. Now for a little while she was free; there was no need to talk to him, and she began to think of her mother, of a different time, and values that were lost.

Heavily, flabbily, like a sea lion he moved across her, clutched at her shoulders, at her breasts, choking and trembling, crying softly in his agony that he loved her, and begged her to love him. Then Ruth sighed, brought back regretfully through the years from her dream of childhood, which was the dream she always dreamt, of a summer evening, her brother yodeling from the darkening heart of an elm in the green yard, her sister meticulously skipping rope, seventeen, eighteen, nineteen, twenty! and the enormous moths batting patiently against the screen door while her parents waited on the porch swing for a cool breeze—evening that would never end. Beneath the spasms of the corpulent, aging body which she could neither hate nor love she wondered what had driven him to this. What futile need possessed him? Why was he here? Is this, she wondered as he grunted and tried once more to kiss her lips—is this the image of my father? Never before had she needed so deeply to understand, yet this man had not the wisdom to explain. Had anyone? If the nature of man was always to be a mystification, what had she to hope for? And it seemed to her that it would be unnatural, in the face of their mystery, to do other than acquiesce.

1960

LEON & BÉBERT

I T WAS just past noon and Leon, dressed in white duck trousers and a striped red shirt, was quickly finishing breakfast. He had been up until two o'clock playing cards at the Po-Po Club, then had gone around the lake to visit friends, so had not gotten to bed until dawn. Now Bébert was coming by for him at any minute. Already the lake was dotted with boats, sailboats for the most part; only here and there the white froth lengthened behind a motor. Leon, spreading marmalade over a piece of toast, squinted attentively at the motorboats. Just then he heard Bébert's station wagon climbing the hill; the noise was unmistakable. He stuffed the toast into his mouth, took a drink of coffee and hurried to the door, pausing just long enough to put on his nautical cap.

The door, however, would not open. Apparently it was locked. Leon did not remember locking it. He turned the knob again and frowned. He had been mildly drunk when he came home and there was a possibility that he had done something clever, had played a trick on himself for no comprehensible reason. Or, of course, there was the possibility that a practical joker had stopped by and done something to the door. He took the knob with both hands and tried to turn it, but it would not move. Just then Bébert honked. Leon rattled the door and banged the knob with his fist.

Bébert honked again. "Come on!" he shouted. "Are you asleep?"

"I'm coming, save your breath," Leon muttered. He could not understand why the door would not open.

"Let's go, Leon!" Bébert called.

Leon switched the lock back and forth and tried the door again.

"What's going on in there?" Bébert called.

"Stop shouting, I can hear you," Leon said. Then raising his own voice, he called: "The door's stuck!"

"What's that?" Bébert sounded astonished. A moment later he came walking down the gravel path toward the house.

Leon looked at his hands which were beginning to feel swollen from twisting the knob. He took hold of it delicately with two fingers and tried it, but it would not open.

Just then Bébert rang the bell.

"For God's sake!" Leon said. "I'm right here, what are you doing?"

"Do you know what time it is?" Bébert called. "Almost twenty past twelve!"

"That isn't my fault," said Leon angrily. "You told me you'd be here by twelve at the latest. Now this damn door is stuck."

"Where are you?"

"Here. Standing right next to you, obviously. Is anything wrong outside?"

"What do you mean? I don't understand."

"I mean," said Leon, "does it appear to you that somebody has wired my door shut, or anything like that?"

"No, it looks just fine."

"Then would it be too much to ask if you'd take hold of it and see if you can get it open? I'd appreciate it very much. I seem to be locked in."

"That's so," said Bébert a moment later. "It won't open. I guess you'll have to open it from inside."

"Which way did you turn the knob?"

Bébert was silent. "I tried it again," he said finally. "Both ways. It won't budge."

"Do it once more. I want to watch and see if it moves on this side."

"All right. Here goes!"

"Well, it's jammed," said Leon thoughtfully.

"You'd better hurry up and get it open," said Bébert. "Otherwise we'll miss our ride. They said they were going to start at twelve-thirty whether we were there or not."

Leon seized the doorknob and struggled to turn it, but it would not move.

"You'd better go without me!" he said furiously. "I can't get out, that's all there is to it! This damn thing is broken and I'm trapped."

"Is this the only door?" Bébert asked. "I remember there's a door opening onto your sun deck."

"Yes, and what else do you remember about it?"

"That's right," said Bébert. "It's quite high off the ground because of the hillside. I forgot about that."

"Approximately twenty feet, to be exact. Personally I wouldn't care to break a leg by leaping off the sun deck like a musketeer or somebody. Perhaps you would, but I wouldn't. Not even for a speedboat ride."

"What are you going to do?"

"There's nothing I can do, my hands are already practically blistered. You try it. Take hold of the knob and rattle it. I'll kick the door from inside. Maybe it's slightly sprung."

"I should say so!" Bébert laughed. "That's the major understatement of the week! No, it simply won't budge," he added. "You're right, it certainly is 'slightly sprung.' "

Leon gave the door a savage kick.

"I can just see you!" said Bébert, laughing. "There you are hopping up and down on one foot, clutching your toes in an agony of pain."

"Oh, don't be stupid," said Leon. "Do you think I'm subnormal? I kicked it with my heel."

"And a lot of good it did! I can see the door's still closed. Who's talking about being stupid?—that's what I say."

"Well, I suppose you could stand around out there all day and amuse yourself at my expense, but in the meantime that isn't going to get this door open."

"True. However, I'm not a locksmith. I don't know what you expect me to do about it."

"There's an idea," said Leon quickly. "Why don't you run down the hill and get a locksmith?"

"It's Sunday."

"Doesn't that old man in the bicycle shop stay open on Sundays?"

"That old man with the wooden leg?"

"No, no," Leon said impatiently. "He hasn't got anything to do with the bicycle shop."

"I've seen him there several times."

"Well, maybe he's a friend of the locksmith. The locksmith is the old man with the Scandinavian accent."

"Oh, yes, I know who you mean. I had no idea he was the locksmith."

"Well, he is!" said Leon, glaring at the door. "Now why don't you jump in your car and go down and see if you can find him."

"I doubt if he's there on Sunday."

"Maybe he is, maybe he isn't! Having you got a brighter idea?"

"Don't shout at me, Leon. We're not twenty-four inches apart."

"I'm sorry. I'm getting claustrophobia. I want to get out of this place."

"I'd certainly like to see you out. Don't think I wouldn't."

"Splendid," said Leon. "We're agreed. Now, tell me what time it is."

"Close to twelve-thirty!" Bébert exclaimed.

"We'd better work fast. Listen. You can make it down the hill to the dock in three or four minutes. They won't have gone by then. Tell them we'll be there but we'll be a few minutes late. They'll wait for us, I'm sure. Then go over and get the locksmith."

"Telephone. That would be simplest. Call up Rick and—ah, no, that wouldn't work because he'd already have left his place. He must be at the dock."

"It also wouldn't work because I don't happen to have a telephone."

"I just now remembered that," said Bébert. "Why don't you have one? Every-body else does."

"It's a long story. I had an argument with the company, but I didn't want one anyhow. I never did like telephones. But let's not get into that. Now will you please jump in that station wagon and hurry down the hill? Maybe Rick knows some-thing about locks. Bring him back with you. The main thing is, to let them know we're going to be late."

"Can't you get out a window?"

"Well, I painted the house a few months ago and all the windows are stuck. Now listen, Bébert, would you please—"

"My watch is wrong! I'd forgotten, but it stopped the other day and I simply took a guess when I set it. I think actually it must be about twelve-fifteen."

"Wait," said Leon. He ran into the bedroom and looked at the alarm clock. "You're right," he said, returning to the door. "It's not quite twelve-fifteen. That gives us a little leeway."

"Good! I've been thinking. Do you have a piece of wire? A hairpin, for instance. You must have thousands of them in there," said Bébert, laughing.

Leon clutched his head and rolled his eyes. "I could find one. What do you want with a hairpin?"

"I used to be pretty good at picking locks. Nothing spectacular, of course, but once when I was about nine or ten my brother couldn't open the lock on his bicycle so I picked it. Everybody insisted I'd been practicing. My father said I'd end up in the penitentiary."

"That's very amusing," said Leon.

Bébert was silent.

"What's the matter?" Leon asked.

"Not a thing," Bébert replied. "Not a thing. I can't say that I particularly care for your sarcasm, but otherwise there's not a single thing the matter."

"I'm sorry. I shouldn't have spoken like I did, but I'm getting nervous. I never could stand being trapped anywhere."

"I know how you feel. I accept your apology. I get the exact same feeling in elevators. They give me the willies. But it's odd that you should feel trapped in your own house."

"Here, I found a hairpin! What'll I do with it?"

"Slip it under the door."

"It won't go."

"How strange. There's a crack on this side. It ought to slide right under. Try again."

"It won't go, I tell you! I'm sorry if I sound edgy, Bébert. This hairpin's too big. It's one of Sheila's, I think. Anyhow, I can't get it through."

"I used to date a girl in Philadelphia who had the most monstrous hairpins I ever saw in my life. One evening we were at a very nice restaurant eating mackerel *au fenouil* when one of her hairpins fell out and dropped on the plate with the loudest clink you could imagine. A couple at the next table actually turned around. She was so embarrassed she wanted to sink through the floor."

"We're going to miss that boat," said Leon, "I can feel it."

"It's my fault, I'm awfully talky today, I don't know why. Now you try to pick that lock and meantime I'll scout around out here and see if I can find something."

"I'm no good at this," Leon said. "I'm too nervous. He gave the door another kick. "Bébert, listen, this is a complete waste of time. Bébert? Bébert! Are you still there? We've got to do something. I'm going stark raving mad. Where are you?"

"I'm out in back!" Bébert called.

Leon ran through the house to the sun deck and looked down. There was Bébert wearing sneakers, Bermuda shorts and a suède jacket, with a pair of binoculars hung around his neck.

"Any luck?" cried Bébert.

"I don't know how to open things," Leon said. "I'm worse than a woman. I'm helpless. God, how useless I feel!"

"Maybe you should take a trip. Ordinarily that helps."

"I should take a trip," said Leon, leaning on the rail. "I can't even get out of my own house, but I should take a trip."

"Well, you *are* in a bad state, I can see that."

"I'm ready to jump."

"This ground's not as soft as it looks."

"I don't care," said Leon.

"I must say I've never seen you so changeable. A few minutes ago when I suggested jumping off the deck you said you didn't want to break a leg. By the way, did you know that Winston Churchill once jumped off a train trestle? It's the truth. I read about it somewhere. When he was a boy he was playing with some other boys and they chased him up on some high trestle and were about to capture him, so he simply waved his arms and leaped off. As a matter of fact, I think he did break his leg or something. He's an amazing man."

"If I stay in this town much longer," said Leon, "I'm going to go berserk. I'll be as mad as a hatter."

Bébert, shading his eyes, looked up with an expression of concern. "What did you say? I couldn't hear. Are you all right?"

"Of course I'm all right!" Leon shouted. "It's a beautiful day! I'm in perfect health! The government just sent me a tax refund, what more could anybody ask? Certainly I'm all right. I just would like to get out of this god-damned house and go for a speedboat ride, that's all I want, but I can't. I don't know why I can't, it doesn't seem like it's asking a very great deal. Does it seem to you like that's asking a lot? Please do speak frankly."

"I can't understand a word you're saying. You puzzle me."

"Ah well," said Leon. "Ah well, the hell with it. I'll go inside and try to unscrew the hinges."

"That's not the way to do it."

"What do you mean that's not the way to do it?" Leon exclaimed. "Just who the hell gives you the right to tell me that's not the way to do it? What do you know about it? If you'd come by when you said you would, why, we'd be at the dock by now."

"How so? I admit I was late, I admit that, but what does that have to do with your front door being stuck? Is that my fault?"

"At least that would have given us time enough to open the door."

"I've got an idea. Let's figure out some way to get me inside, then I'll open it."

"What makes you think you can open it?"

"I don't know, but I think I can. It's just this feeling I have. There must be something wrong with the inside. You got in last night without any trouble, didn't you?"

Leon nodded.

"Then that means that the trouble isn't on the outside, it's on the inside. That makes sense, doesn't it?"

"I guess it does," said Leon. "I don't know. I'm so frustrated I can't think."

"Of course it does. Now, how can I get up there? Do you have a ladder?"

"There's a ladder next door but the people are away and they have a big dog in the yard."

"Where do they keep the ladder?"

"Well, wait a minute." Leon cautiously climbed up on the rail of the sun deck and peered through the trees. Then he got down and said, "Usually it's in the yard beside the fence. I thought I might be able to see it, but I couldn't."

"If that's where they ordinarily keep it, it must be there. They wouldn't be taking it with them."

"I don't think you'd better go over there," said Leon. "That dog is vicious."

"What kind of a dog is it?"

"It's an Airedale. A couple of months ago it bit the gas-meter reader."

"I used to have an Airedale," said Bébert. "They're friendly dogs. I'll have a try at it."

"I wouldn't if I were you," said Leon.

Bébert walked across to the fence and stood on tiptoe.

"Is he there?" Leon asked.

"I don't see a soul," replied Bébert.

"What about the ladder?"

"Yes, it's here. Do you have a box of any sort?"

"A box? What for?"

"I have to get over the fence in order to borrow the ladder, don't I? I can't simply leap it. I'm not the athletic type."

"There's a wooden packing crate underneath the deck, I think. Unless somebody's stolen it."

"That should do. Let me look." Bébert disappeared beneath the deck. Presently he backed into view, dragging the crate. "This ought to be just right," he said, and dragged it over to the fence. After testing it with both hands he climbed on top and had another look into the neighbor's yard. Leon watched silently. Bébert whistled and then called, "Here, poochy! Here, poochy!"

"Is he there?"

Bébert shook his head.

"Well, I'd be careful anyway. He could be hiding somewhere waiting for you to get over the fence."

"It certainly is warm down here," Bébert said as he began to climb the fence. "It's much warmer than it was in front."

"There's never much of a breeze where you are," said Leon. "All that shrubbery. Don't snag your fly."

Bébert suddenly stopped with an expression of terror and then fell backward into Leon's yard. There was a scuffling and clawing and the fence rocked. The neighbor's shrubbery rustled.

"I told you," said Leon. "That's how he got the gas-meter reader. Are you all right?"

"Yes," said Bébert, sitting up. "I believe I'm all right. I'm just a little shocked."

"He's a funny dog. He doesn't bark. He just lies in wait like a serpent and then *pow!*"

"I don't think he's an Airedale. He's too big."

"Well, he is. They've got a bunch of silver cups in the house with his name inscribed on them."

"My dog was the friendliest thing," said Bébert.

Leon belched. "I guess they're like people. You get decent ones and then you get these onery sons-of-bitches. It makes you wonder."

"Look! Isn't that a hummingbird?" asked Bébert.

"Yes," Leon said. "Quite a few birds live around here in these trees. I don't recognize too many of them, but it gives the place a sort of cheerful atmosphere."

"I'd say you have an absolute little Garden of Eden!—that's what I'd say."

"Well, it's pleasant," Leon admitted. "I like it here. Sometimes there are so many birds and bugs and squirrels and cats and God knows what else that you'd think it was Noah's ark, but generally it's restful. Except right at this moment I've got a bellyful of it. I want to get out."

"I understand," said Bébert. "You know, I believe I've torn my trousers."

"I thought I heard something rip," said Leon.

Bébert was examining himself. "Maybe not," he said finally. "I've simply got to shed a few pounds, though. All of my clothes are tight."

"Isn't that a new jacket?"

"Yes, do you like it? I bought it day before yesterday. Gump's was having a sale. In fact I bought it with today in mind. I'd been wanting something new and I said to myself that this speedboat ride was a perfect excuse."

"We'll never make it," Leon said, squinting at the lake. "You'd better go without me. Go ahead. Don't pay any attention to me. I've been on a speedboat before."

"But you've been saying for the past three weeks how you'd love to wangle a ride on the *Sea Bishop*."

"The *Sea Bishop* isn't the reason. The real reason is that I want to meet that movie starlet Phluger runs around with."

Bébert was amazed. "Seriously? I had no idea. I thought you admired his boat."

"It's a nice enough boat," said Leon.

"Well, this is quite a surprise. Although now that I think of it, I might have known. It's so typical of you."

"Bébert," Leon said, "did you ever get a good look at that broad?"

"Only from a distance. She swished into the post office one afternoon dressed up like a zebra while I was on my way to the laundromat. That's as close as I've ever come to her, and it was altogether close enough, thank you."

"If I ever get within six feet of that broad," Leon said, "I'll explode. I'll go off like a two-dollar skyrocket."

"Will she be on the boat?"

"I guess, I don't know why not. She's Phluger's house guest, isn't she? Where he goes, she goes."

"And *that's* the reason you've been so bearish! I should have guessed."

"I'd been counting on this afternoon. Oh, God, when I think of it! I could weep, Bébert. This is cruel."

"We can make it, if we hurry."

"There's not a chance. I'm locked in. You'd better go."

"I won't! We're going to get you out of there and furthermore we're going to make it on time. I can feel it in my bones."

"That's nice of you, Bébert," Leon remarked, smiling down at him. "You're a very sweet guy."

"Now don't be silly," Bébert answered, waving his hands. "You'd do the same for me, if not more."

"A little while ago when you came by and that door wouldn't open I almost went out of my mind. I thought it was a plot. I thought Phluger had discovered what I was really after. I could have committed murder, I was that infuriated."

"It's not my business, of course, but in a way I don't think you're being very honorable."

Leon took off his cap and scratched his head.

"I heard you pretending such an interest in the *Sea Bishop*," Bébert continued. "You said one flattering thing right after another. It was embarrassing."

"I was embarrassed too," Leon admitted. "But Rick was talking about going out today and said Phluger had told him to bring along some friends and all of a sudden I couldn't stop myself. I just had to get an invitation."

"Well, we're frittering time away. Let's see. How am I going to get up there? Don't you have a rope? I could climb up."

Leon shook his head. "What about that box? If you put it directly beneath here and stood on it I might be able to reach down and get your hand."

"Then what? You'd need a windlass to haul me up. Besides, you couldn't reach me."

"Let's try it."

Bébert went to the fence and came back dragging the crate. "Our hungry friend's still there," he remarked. "I could see him watching me through the bushes. I haven't been so startled in years."

"You've got new sneakers," Leon observed.

"Yes," said Bébert, and climbed up on the box. "Now, see if you can reach me."

Leon stretched out on the sun deck and put one arm over the edge.

"You see? We're not even close."

"Jump."

"Don't be ridiculous. I doubt if I could reach you and if I did I'd break your arm or pull you off the deck. You're strong, I admit, but I wouldn't say you were a professional trapeze artist."

"Try it. If it doesn't work you can let go."

"Oh, all right, but just this once," said Bébert. "I certainly hope nobody's watching us. We must look like perfect fools."

He took off his binoculars and set them on the packing crate. Then he crouched and gazed up with a determined expression. Leon, holding to the rail with one hand, reached down as far as possible, clenched his teeth and nodded, Bébert leaped and clutched at him, but failed.

"You can jump higher than that," said Leon.

"I don't trust this box," said Bébert. "This whole idea is absurd, in fact. I mean, honestly, Leon, suppose you were a stranger watching."

"Try it again. Really jump. Put your heart into it."

"I've never felt so imbecilic in my entire life. I just know this isn't going to work." He crouched again and looked up. "Ready? Here I come!"

"Wait a minute!" Leon cried.

"What's the matter?"

"One of your shoestrings is untied."

Bébert knelt and tied it while Leon watched.

"All right, that takes care of that," said Bébert. "Get a good grip on that rail now because I'm heavier than I look."

Leon took several deep breaths. Bébert rubbed his hands together.

"Set?"

Leon nodded. Bébert cleared his throat and sprang but he did not get much closer.

"I suppose you're right," Leon said. "What'll we do now?"

"Why don't you knot a sheet and let it down?"

"I doubt if that would work either."

"Of course it would work. It's done all the time."

"No, I think that's one of those fables like boiling water when a woman's about to have a baby."

"What do you mean a fable? I don't understand."

"Just that it isn't necessary."

"Boiling water?"

"Yes. It's not essential."

"Is that a fact! I always supposed they needed it for some reason."

"No. For years I thought the same, but then recently I read that this was merely a dramatic convention in the movies."

"That's interesting," said Bébert. "I never knew that."

"Yes, and I suspect that this business about escaping from resort hotel fires by means of a knotted sheet is pretty similar. It doesn't sound plausible. What I mean is, it *does* sound plausible. Too plausible, if you follow me. It sounds much too easy, like boiling water. The sheet would rip, I think. But I don't know. On the other hand, it might be feasible. I guess we could try it, there's nothing to lose. I've got to get out of here someway. All right, why not?" Leon jumped to his feet and went into the house and came out with a sheet.

"Three or four knots," Bébert suggested. "They ought to strengthen it and give it a ropelike quality."

Leon sat down on the sun deck and gathered the sheet in his lap.

"I can't see what you're doing," Bébert said, "but it occurs to me that the smartest way to do it would be to roll the sheet into a sort of roll before tying the knots."

Leon, who had not thought of this, quietly got up and spread the sheet across the deck and then began rolling it.

"It certainly is warm down here," Bébert said. "By the way, did you know there's a wasp nest under the deck?"

"I can't hear you."

"I say, there's a nest of wasps directly underneath you."

"Yes, I know," said Leon. "It's abandoned."

"No, it isn't either."

"I can't hear you, Bébert. You're mumbling."

"I said there are about a thousand wasps crawling all over that nest. I'd do something about it, if I were you."

Leon got to his feet and came over to the railing and looked down. "Are they excited? Did you bother them?"

Bébert laughed. "You must think I'm an idiot. Nobody in his right mind would disturb a nest of wasps."

"Then why did you suggest I do something about it? Do you want me to get stung?"

Bébert gazed up at him in astonishment.

"You resent the fact that I'm not able to get out, don't you?" Leon persisted.

"I haven't the foggiest—"

"Please don't interrupt! The truth is, you know we're not going to get to the dock on time and you blame me for it."

"That's not true."

"Yes, it is. I can see your side of the matter, Bébert. If I were in your position, I'd be extremely resentful."

"You would?"

"Even though I might recognize that the door getting stuck wouldn't be your fault, still I couldn't help blaming you. Consequently you see that I understand your attitude."

"But I don't have any such feelings, I swear!"

"Never mind," said Leon and went back to the sheet. "Let's just not discuss it. I appreciate the fact that you've stayed this long. That was decent of you. I'll get out somehow, tomorrow maybe. You go on down to the boat. They're waiting for you."

"I've got a good mind to stir up those wasps right this moment."

"Yes, you do that. You can run away from them, but pretty quickly they'd come swarming up on the deck and into the house."

"If you keep speaking to me like that I certainly will! In the meantime, why don't you stop feeling sorry for yourself and finish tying those knots."

"Here, it's done," Leon said, coming to the rail with the sheet. He threw one end of it over and looked down. "That's too short. It won't work."

"I'll be able to reach it if I stand on the packing box. You just tie your end around the post. Make sure it won't slip."

"If you want to stir up those wasps," Leon remarked while he was tying the sheet, "kindly direct them to the Airedale."

"Oh, he's just lonesome," said Bébert. "He's a good dog."

"I didn't see you trying to pet him. Well, grab hold of your end and try it. Don't start climbing yet, because I'm not sure whether this knot's going to hold. Just pull on it."

"I've never done anything like this," said Bébert. "I'm glad I'm wearing sneakers."

"How does it feel? Does it feel strong?"

"It feels pretty good," Bébert said uncertainly. "How does it look up there? Is it slipping?"

Leon was silent. At last he said, "Maybe it's just drawing itself up tighter. Knots will do that sometimes. Pull on it harder. Swing on it. Be sure to keep your footing."

Bébert cautiously lifted himself from the box and dangled for a few seconds, then lowered one foot and gave a gentle push. The railing began to creak.

"I don't like the sound of that!" he called. "What about it, Leon? Is it safe?"

"I think so."

Bébert was slowly revolving on the sheet. "I'd rather you were positive!" he called.

"There isn't anything particular to worry about," Leon said. "Come on up."

"All right. You'll tell me if it starts to slip. I haven't done any climbing in years," Bébert added as he started up the sheet. "I must say it's rather stimulating."

"You're doing fine," Leon said. "Keep at it. I've got a finger on the knot so I can feel if it gives way."

Bébert stopped to rest. "I'd almost forgotten how to climb. We climbed ropes in school during the gymnasium period but that was a long time ago. There was a certain way you used your feet. Listen, can't you stop the sheet from turning around? I'm afraid I'm getting dizzy."

Leon peered over the edge of the deck. "Well, you really are turning, aren't you? I didn't know it was going to do that. Are the wasps bothering you?"

Bébert laughed. "No, no. They've got better things to do. This *is* fun, although I feel terribly foolish. How's the knot?"

"It's in pretty good shape," Leon said. "However, if I were you I wouldn't wait too long. I mean, I don't want to get you excited, but it wouldn't be a good idea to hang there all day."

Bébert glanced down at the box and then up at the sun deck. After some hesitation he continued climbing.

"This is a mistake," he said. "I'm just sure I'll regret this entire affair."

"Hurry up," said Leon. "Please hurry up."

"I don't think I'm going to make it," said Bébert. "I think I'm going to fall."

"Well, whatever you do, don't land on that box. If you have to fall, fall on the ground."

Bébert stopped again.

"You're almost here," Leon said. "Two or three more and you've got it. Don't give up now. I've got my foot on the knot."

"Yes, but I'm slipping," said Bébert desperately.

"There's nothing to worry about, only get a leg or an arm on the deck as soon as you can. In fact, the sooner the better."

"All right, here I come. Keep your fingers crossed."

"Upsy-daisy," Leon said. "Climb! That's the boy. Again! You've got it now, Bébert. Once more!"

"I'm absolutely exhausted," Bébert said, hooking his chin over the edge of the deck. "I believe I'll just park right here."

"It would have been easier if you'd taken off your jacket."

"Yes, I should have. It's awkward and it's so warm. I'll take it off as soon as I get up."

"Will it help if I give you a pull?"

"No, I don't want you to upset my balance. That's what happens to mountaineers. They go along all right but then some outside force throws them off balance and they're killed."

"I hadn't thought about it," said Leon vaguely. "You look more like a burglar than a mountaineer. What are you going to do with the binoculars?"

"Oh, I just thought I'd bring them along. Can you see anything from where you are?"

"Phluger's boat, you mean? No, the trees are in the way. Listen, Bébert, I do wish you'd stop dangling there like something on a Christmas tree and make an effort. You really should get up here on the deck. It's dangerous clinging to a sheet."

"I'll try," said Bébert. "Incidentally, I didn't need to climb up this sheet, you could have climbed down."

"You're right! You're absolutely right. I never thought of that. Isn't that strange?"

"Neither did I until just now."

"H'm'm. Well, anyway, as long as you're here you might as well come on up."

Bébert, after several deep breaths, climbed a little higher and grasped the railing; Leon reached down, took him by the belt and lifted him up onto the deck.

"Well, that was something!" Bébert exclaimed as he got to his feet and began brushing himself off. "However, all's well that ends well. Now let's have a look at that door. What did you do with the hairpin?"

"It's stuck in the lock."

"All right, sir, let's have a look," Bébert said, rubbing his hands. He took off his jacket and marched into the house.

"Do you want a beer while you're working?"

"No, I've got a wicker basket full of beer in the station wagon. I thought it would be nice to drink on the lake."

"I'll take a few bottles out of the icebox so we'll have plenty," Leon said. "By the way, if you need anything like pliers or a hammer you'll find them in the kitchen drawer."

"I'll need a screwdriver to work on the catch."

"It's there too. In fact there are so many gadgets in that drawer I'm afraid to open it. I get a feeling they're alive. It's like some kind of mechanical zoo. Well, anyway, I'll be on the deck untying the sheet."

A few minutes later Bébert called: "Did I ever tell you that I once met an actress?"

"Not that I remember."

"She was very famous. It was about eight or ten years ago. I was interviewing her for our school paper. I can't think of her name at the moment, but the boys were mad about her, of course, and when I returned from my interview they asked if she had seduced me. They couldn't believe nothing had happened."

Leon, who had been sitting cross-legged on the sun deck with the sheet in his lap, looked around with an expression of interest.

"What *did* happen?"

"As I say, not a thing. It was terribly disappointing. She offered me a cup of tea, then I asked which movie she had most enjoyed working in and she said she enjoyed them all, she loved working in the movies and hoped to become a better actress. That's all there was to it. I only stayed about five minutes. She had an appointment of some sort. At least that's what she said. I believe she simply wanted to get rid of me. But of course nobody took my word for it. They thought I was trying to conceal the fact that we'd had an orgy."

"In five minutes?"

"I can't hear. What did you say?"

"I say, it seems like that would be a rapid orgy."

Bébert didn't reply.

"What about that lock? Are you making progress?"

"I think so. Yes, I think I am."

"Speaking of orgies, suppose we drown Rick and Phluger and have that movie starlet to ourselves. How would that sit with you? Could you handle that Hollywood stuff, Bébert?"

"Oh, from what I've heard she'd be too much of a problem for me. She's so gaudy, I'd be frightened out of my wits. Leon, do you know, I'm beginning to understand this lock? I do believe I'm actually going to get it."

"Keep after it. You've got me almost convinced. By the way did you ever hear of Chace Pine?"

"Of whom?"

"Chace Pine. He was a famous eighteenth-century roué who invented a machine that would flog forty girls at a time."

Bébert was silent for quite a while. At last he said, "I disapprove of those things."

"Well, *chacun à son goût.*"

"I suppose," Bébert said, "although my taste runs to a different direction. Why forty, do you imagine? Why not fifty?"

"I don't guess anybody knows," Leon said. "At least in this book I was reading they didn't offer any explanation."

"Chace Pine. What a peculiar name. He sounds Welsh, or mid-European possibly. What made you bring up that subject?"

"Oh," said Leon, who was folding the sheet, "I was just thinking about orgies. Those were the good old days, Bébert. They had every imaginable kind of activity. Now everybody merely copies everybody else. I frankly doubt if you could locate a genuine orgy anywhere within a hundred miles. Housewives darting back and forth, husbands creeping around when they're supposed to be at the office, secretaries and that sort of thing, naturally, trysts in the supermarket, but it's pretty pallid, it seems to me. And the parties you go to, why, maybe they smoke a little bit of marijuana and think they're doing something fantastic, and even then some pitiful little experience like that, why, you're apt to get arrested."

"Leon, you're not going to believe this," said Bébert, "but the door is open."

Leon sprang to his feet and rushed into the house, and it was true, Bébert had succeeded.

"Let's go!" he shouted and ran outside. "What time have you got?"

Bébert glanced at his watch. "Nearly a quarter to one but I don't think they've left, I haven't heard the *Sea Bishop*'s motor."

"I forgot the beer," Leon said, running back into the house. He hurried into the kitchen, filled a paper bag with bottles and ran outside.

"You shouldn't have slammed the door," said Bébert.

"What difference does it make? Let's go!"

"Well, but you may not be able to get back in."

"I thought you fixed the lock."

"No, no, you misunderstood. I just got the door open, that's all. I didn't say I'd fixed it. You shot by so fast I didn't have a chance to explain. I won't guarantee that you'll be able to get back in."

"I'll worry about that when the time comes," said Leon. "I'm so glad to be out of that house I don't care if I never get back in. What are you standing there for? Come on, come on!"

"I'm thinking," said Bébert.

"We haven't got time for that!" shouted Leon, who was already halfway up the path to the station wagon.

"Yes, but, I think," Bébert called weakly, "that I've left my keys in your house. They're in my jacket."

Leon ran a few more steps up the path and then gradually sank to his knees with the bag of bottles nestled in his arms.

"I'm awfully sorry," said Bébert. "You don't know how ashamed I am."

Leon, still on his knees, put down the bottles and stretched out full length on the path. An instant later he lifted his head and shouted:

"The door! Bébert, try it! Maybe it works!"

Bébert rushed to the door and seized the knob; Leon watched him for a few moments and then rolled over.

"I just wish the earth would open right up and devour me," said Bébert. "You have no idea how this makes me feel, words just couldn't begin to convey it. I'm so embarrassed."

"You haven't got an extra key to the car, by any chance?" Leon asked without looking at him. "No. No, of course you haven't. I can tell."

Bébert didn't answer.

"I suppose it could have been worse," Leon said. "You could have fallen off the sheet and broken your back, for instance."

"That might have been best," answered Bébert, who was sitting on the step with his head in his hands. "I don't know if I can ever forget this day. Truthfully, if Chace Pine were here right now I'd give him permission to flog me."

Leon, who had been plucking dandelions from the hillside, said, "I feel degraded somehow. I don't know exactly why. I keep thinking about last night, how I spent half an hour flattering Rick in order to get this invitation. Now I see that it was wasted. All on account of a little casting couch actress, damn her soul."

"Well, there she goes!"

"What do you mean, there she goes?"

"The *Sea Bishop*. Hear the motor?"

Leon lifted himself to one elbow. "Is that it? Are you sure?"

Bébert nodded. "That's Phluger's boat. Probably we'll be able to see it when it gets out further on the lake. But I don't think we could have made it even if I hadn't left the keys inside."

"Yes, we could have," Leon said grimly. "We could have been on the *Sea Bishop* this very minute and I could have been sitting right next to that—oh, Jesus, Jesus!" he exclaimed and slapped the ground. "Why must I torture myself! It's over, the chance of a lifetime. Gone! Gone, Bébert. All on account of a miserable key. It's so senseless."

"A key, perhaps, or a door," Bébert remarked. "Then too I was a few minutes late, so you might even say that was the cause."

"I ought to move out of this town," Leon said thoughtfully. "I've been here much too long. Do you know how long I've been here?"

"How long?"

"Six years."

"Well," said Bébert, "that's what I thought. I've been here almost as long. But I must admit I like it."

"Where are you from, by the way?" Leon asked, looking at him curiously. "It occurs to me we've known each other all this time but the fact is, we're strangers."

"Yes, that's odd. So many people seem to congregate in this town and they see each other practically all the time and then they disappear one way or another and you realize you never did know the first thing about them. It's a bit frightening."

"Remember that juicy broad with the Dutch-boy haircut that used to come into the Po-Po Club every night? Every time she came in I was afraid to move for fear I'd fracture myself. Do you remember that one?"

"I think I do," said Bébert. "But there are so many girls. It's utterly impossible to keep track of them all."

"It was a year ago last spring she was around. Some oaf that looked like a pro wrestler always had hold of her by the arm so I never got a chance to meet her. Then all of a sudden she disappeared. Her name was Ingrid, that's all I could find out."

"Yes, well, that happens," said Bébert. "I was attracted to a girl who used to eat supper every Wednesday at the Fiddler. I thought she was one of the most appealing things I'd ever seen."

"So?"

"Nothing came of it. I was afraid it would be conspicuous if I spoke to her. I should have, I suppose. I'm such a coward. I think she liked me. But then, too, there was something else. I happened to see her downtown one afternoon at the grocery store with her hair done up in pink plastic curlers and whatever feeling I had for her simply evaporated, once and for all. She looked like an absolute tramp. It made me rather angry, to tell the truth. Don't you think it's common for a girl to chase around in public like that? I do. It's not only insulting but vulgar, that's my opinion. Andrea tells me it's a 'class' thing. At any rate, it's too late now. She's gone, whoever she was."

"Balls, balls, balls," Leon said, sighing heavily. "I don't know which way to turn. I really ought to get out of this idiotic town. I need to go somewhere and actually accomplish something, that's my trouble. It's ridiculous and degrading to lie around here all the time. If I had the guts God gave a celluloid duck I'd pack up and leave. I'm in a horrible rut. Sail around on the lake, go to the Fiddler or Lamott's for dinner, then end up at the Po-Po Club practically every single night. It's monotonous and humiliating and stupid. I mean, it *is*. Do you know what I mean?"

"I agree wholeheartedly," said Bébert, nodding. "In fact, it's a vicious circle."

"I've decided to get out. I'm not going to waste my life here, you can bet on that!"

"When are you going?"

"Next winter."

"We'll miss you. The club won't be the same without you."

"I'm not leaving right this moment."

"I understand. But I do want you to know that I'm terribly sorry about what happened just now. Our afternoon's ruined and I can't help thinking it was my fault."

"All right, it's your fault. I'm in no mood to argue about it."

"What do you think we ought to do now?"

Leon slowly got to his feet. "Go to the Po-Po Club, I suppose. It's cool there, anyway. We might sit on the patio and have a beer. I can't think of anything else."

"Do you have plans for supper tonight?"

"No. I wasn't sure what time we'd get back from the speedboat ride so I didn't make any plans. Have you got an idea?"

"Oh, nothing exciting. But this is Sunday and I rather like to eat at the Fiddler on Sundays."

"All right, that suits me. We can spend the afternoon at the club and then walk over to the Fiddler. Somebody said they've got a new waitress."

"Yes, that's so."

"What does she look like?"

"She's quite pretty, but too flamboyant for my taste."

"Is that a fact!" said Leon, looking at Bébert with interest. "What's her name?"

"I don't know. She waited on me twice last week, but I neglected to ask her name."

"H'm'm," said Leon. "I haven't been to the Fiddler in quite a while. That sounds good. That's a good idea."

"All right, let's get started. How are we going to get in?"

"Get in? Get in where?"

"Into your house. I've got to get my keys."

"Oh my God," said Leon. "Not again."

"Well," said Bébert crisply, "I'm not looking forward to it any more than you are. Maybe you have a better suggestion. Shall we walk?"

"Why don't we coast down the hill? We could coast almost into town."

"Yes," said Bébert. "Then my car would stop somewhere along the edge of the lake and the keys would still be up here in your house. That would be sensible now, wouldn't it?"

"I don't know what to do," Leon said. "I'm so frustrated and exhausted I can't think. Nothing makes sense any more."

Bébert was studying the house. Finally he said, "I hate the very thought of this, but I suppose I could climb up that sheet again."

"No, you can't, because I folded it and put it in the bedroom."

"In that case, how are we going to get it?"

"I think it's impossible," said Leon.

"It's not impossible," said Bébert. "There must be a way."

"There's one very easy way. Just hop over that fence again and make friends with the dog so you can borrow the ladder."

"If only we had a piece of meat to give him."

"There's meat in the icebox," said Leon, "but if you can get to the icebox you don't need the ladder, if you follow me. You're putting the cart before the horse. Anyway, if you want my opinion, throwing that Airedale five pounds of meat would only whet his appetite. You've got a better chance of making friends with a hammerhead shark."

"Let's walk around to the back, there's obviously no way to get in the front."

"If there's one thing on earth I don't want, Bébert, it's to get back into that house right now."

"I know, but it's imperative. We simply don't have any alternative. I realize how anxious you were to get out, Leon, but we've just got to get back in."

"I know, I know," said Leon gloomily. "All right, let's have a look. Maybe I could stand on the packing crate and give you a boost, or something."

1964

^A COTTAGE
NEAR TWIN FALLS

Dear William Koerner:
I have long been an ardent admirer of your novels and it has occurred to me
that I may render a small service in return for the many pleasurable read-
ing hours your books have afforded me. It so happens that I have a summer
cottage near Twin Falls, which, owing to the exigencies of business, I shall be
unable to occupy this summer as is my usual custom. If you would care to
"get away from it all" for several weeks I would feel honored . . .

Koerner scanned the rest of the letter, rolled a sheet of stationery into his typewriter, and quickly tapped out:

Dear Mr. Oates:
Thank you for your letter and your kind invitation to spend several weeks at
your cottage near Twin Falls. I'm sorry that at present I'm unable to accept
your offer. I do appreciate the invitation.

> *Cordially,*
> *William Koerner*

Having signed it, Koerner put the note in an envelope just as the telephone rang.
"Hello, Koerner! MacChesney. Am I disturbing you?"

"Hello, Mac," Koerner said. "I was answering the mail."

"Fan letters?"

"One."

"How's the Great American Novel coming along?"

"You, too?"

"Did I say something wrong?"

"Everybody asks the same question."

After a pause MacChesney said, "Koerner, old man, what should I have asked? I was just curious."

"Sorry I flinched," Koerner said. "Jumpy nerves. Have you been out of town? I haven't heard from you in a while."

"Right here. Nose to the grindstone. *Comme toujours,* as the French say. In fact I'm at the office right now. Listen, there's a cocktail party tonight and I was wondering if you'd like to come along. Chances are it would bore you stiff but I thought I'd ask. If you want to stay home and work, don't hesitate to say so."

"A cocktail party sounds wonderful," Koerner said. "I'd love to go."

"You would?"

"I haven't been to a party in six months."

"Really?"

"I'd love to get out."

"Really? I'll be damned!"

"Who's giving it?"

"Bibi and Dennis Pratt."

"I don't know them. Would they mind if you brought me?"

"Bibi asked me to ask you. She's a great fan."

"Oh," said Koerner.

"Well! Well!" MacChesney said. "This is a surprise. I was positive you'd turn it down. I'll drop by for you at eight o'clock."

"I'll be waiting," Koerner said.

MacChesney arrived a little after nine. On the way to the party he said, "Seriously, old man, how's the new opus coming along? Just curious."

"*Ça va,* as the French say."

"Picked out a title, or does the publisher do that?"

"We're discussing it. I want to call it *Old Man Goriot* but the publisher thinks it would sell better if we called it *War and Peace.*"

"*War and Peace,*" MacChesney said. "That's been used before. I don't think the other title is very good."

They had been at the party only a few minutes when somebody said, "I understand the title of your new book is *The Old Man and the Sea.*"

"No," Koerner said. "I wish it was."

"Hal Shaw," another voice said. "Honored to meet you, Mr. Koerner. Something I've been wanting to ask: what do you think of Ian Fleming?"

"I haven't read any of his books."

"You a writer and don't read Fleming?"

"Once upon a time I read a Mickey Spillane," Koerner said. "It was fascinating. I didn't realize an hour had slipped away."

"What's your opinion of Agatha Christie?" asked an old lady who was clutching what appeared to be a glass of undiluted bourbon.

"I haven't read any of her books," Koerner said. "Do you enjoy them?"

"No," the old lady said. "They bore the bloomers off me. I just wondered what you thought. Do you like Belva Plain?"

"Do you write every day?" somebody else was asking.

"Where do you find your inspiration? Does it come naturally?"

"Let's get together for lunch one day next week," said a man who, after shaking hands, would not let go. "I got an idea for a novel but I don't have the knack of putting things down on paper. It's a great story, been in the back of my mind for years. Needs to be ironed out but you could make up a plot and knock it together in no time flat. We'll split fifty-fifty."

"My niece wants to become a writer," said another voice, "but apparently you don't stand a chance unless you know the key person. She's written a novel but for some reason it was rejected. I've read the first chapter and it certainly is more interesting than a lot of things being published. If I have her send it to you will you read it and give her some professional criticism?"

A young man who had been leaning against the mantel with a dignified expression suddenly was at Koerner's elbow, saying in an undertone, "Got time to read my stuff?"

"William Koerner?" a new voice inquired. "Let me shake you by the hand, sir. Enjoyed your book from beginning to end. My sincere congratulations."

"Thank you," Koerner said. "I've written several. Which one did you like?"

"*Deadly Gambit.*"

"Oh. That's not mine."

"I thought your name was Koerner."

"Yes, that's right."

"You're not the author of *Deadly Gambit?*"

"No. I . . . "

"You didn't write *Deadly Gambit*? Somebody told me you did. You claim you didn't. What's going on around here?"

A woman in a Norwegian ski sweater asked if William Koerner was a pen name or if it was real.

"I don't know," Koerner said.

"Is your book in bookstores? Or might you have an extra copy?"

"I'm absolutely dying to ask you one question," said a gaunt woman with a Dauphin haircut. "How do you invent your ideas? Do you make them up or do they come to you naturally?"

"You a writer?" asked an old man with shaggy eyebrows.

Koerner nodded and took a drink.

"Published?"

Koerner nodded.

"Written any best-sellers?"

"No."

"Let me give you a bit of advice, young fellow. Write about real people."

"You wrote a book?" asked a woman who resembled a chipmunk. "Is it fiction? Or is it a novel?"

MacChesney came back with two friends, one of whom looked frightened, while the other, after hanging an arm around Koerner's shoulders, breathed into his face and said, "Tell me the truth, how much do you guys make? Not being nosey, understand, just curious. How much you guys make? In round numbers how much?"

"What do you think of Iris Murdoch?" asked a plump woman who giggled.

"I haven't read any of her books," Koerner said.

"She's simply wonderfully good. Do you care for Ayn Rand?"

"We haven't met," Koerner said and took another drink.

"That's odd! What time of the morning do you get up?"

"Excuse me for interrupting," said a woman with a face as round as an onion, "I'm Dodie Truehorse. We have mutual friends—the Boppetts."

"Boppett?" said Koerner.

"Surely you remember them. You met at a gathering in Los Angeles four years ago. They've talked about you often. I'm not going to detain you, but of course they'll skin me alive if I can't tell them what your new book is all about."

"I didn't catch your last name," Koerner said. "It sounded like Truehorse."

"That's correct. People assume I'm an Indian, but I'm not, although I was born in Montana."

"Montana," Koerner said. "That's one of my favorite states. Do you know what happens when a workman falls into a vat of molten copper?"

"Good Heavens! What?"

"The company ladles out a certain amount and lets it cool into a brick and then conducts a funeral service and buries it. However, the price of copper keeps going up so the bricks get smaller and smaller. I don't know how big they are now, probably about the size of a sugar cube."

"That's revolting!" said Dodie Truehorse.

"He sounds like a pinko," said another woman. "He should be investigated."

"I admire you," said a man with bleary eyes. "Never read anything you wrote, but I admire the hell out of you."

"Composition must be excruciating," said an elfin creature. "You must feel utterly exhausted."

"Not in the least," Koerner said. "I . . . "

"Billyboy! How you doing?"

The man looked familiar, but Koerner could not think of his name.

"Skip Gershman. We went to high school together. Used to play tennis at the old Armour Fields court. I knew you 'when,' Bill, so don't big-shot me. Great to see you. How does it feel to be famous?"

MacChesney returned with another friend who shook hands uncertainly and said, "I haven't read anything you've written, but I promise to go to the library first thing in the morning."

"Hey, Billyboy," Gershman continued, "why don't you keep in touch with old friends?"

"The last I heard of you," Koerner said, "and this was about fifteen years ago, I ran into somebody who mentioned that you were selling fire insurance."

"Bingo! On the button! Same office as little Joe Pacelli. How's that for coincidence? Remember Pacelli? Had a sister named Gloria with hairy legs. Now listen, Billy. I want to tell you a true story about what happened last summer to my brother-in-law. It's a riot. You'll die laughing. Put this in print and I guarantee you'll make a bundle. I'm going to let you have it for nothing—not asking a cent. I'd jot it down myself, but I'm busy."

Koerner stared into his drink until the story was over.

"Not asking a cent," Gershman repeated. "Give me a credit line, that's all I want. Great seeing you again. Keep up the good work."

"I understand you're an author," somebody said. "What do you do for a living?"

Koerner pushed his way through the crowd into an alcove beside the bar.

"What do you think of Maxine Hong Kingston?" a little voice inquired.

Koerner looked around and discovered that he had been followed by the Iris Murdoch lady.

"I think Maxine Hong Kingston is mysterious," he said. "What do you think of Han Suyin?"

"I prefer Amy Tan."

"What about Hamilton Basso?"

"Koerner," said a man with a crushing grip, "Nowosielski's the name. Friend of a neighbor of yours, Pete Foukas. What I want to talk to you about is my kid. He got this crackpot idea he wants to be some kind of artist, all the time painting pictures. I tell him it's a waste but he don't listen. Maybe you could beat some sense into him. I want you to come over to my place and put on the feed bag. Meet the missus. Get the kid straightened out. Right now I got to make a pit stop but I'll get back to you."

"Have you written for the stage? If not, you must," said a bald young man with horn-rimmed glasses and a cigarette holder. "You honestly must."

"This may sound terribly rude," somebody else began, "but I wasn't altogether satisfied with the conclusion of your last book. It seems to me it should have ended on a different note."

MacChesney came back with a girl in a turtleneck sweater and a rope of African beads who said, "Are you writing at the moment?"

Nowosielski reappeared. "Listen to this joke about two Irishmen. It'll kill you. Put it in a book."

"Who do you admire above everyone else in the world?" asked a lady with a southern accent. "Eudora Welty or William Faulkner?"

"Jack Dempsey," Koerner said.

"Don't remember me, do you?" asked a grinning fat man. "Bet a dime you don't."

After looking at him Koerner said, "No, I'm sorry. I can't remember. Where did we meet?"

"Mister," the fat man snarled, "you just go to Hades in a handcart."

"How marvelous to be talented," the southern lady said. "Do you write all day or do you wait for inspiration to strike?"

"And your name, sir?" asked a scholarly man wearing a Dartmouth blazer.

"William Koerner."

"Frankly, that means nothing," the man remarked with a pleasant smile. "Have you done anything I should know about?"

"No," Koerner said. "But tell me, what is your opinion of Ivy Compton-Burnett? Is she as significant as Clorinda LeCoq?"

On the way home from the party MacChesney said, "Well, sport, did you enjoy yourself?"

"I'd almost forgotten about cocktail parties," Koerner said.

"You might not know this," MacChesney said, "but you're potted."

"I didn't make it up," Koerner said. "It just came naturally."

MacChesney coasted to a stop in front of the apartment. "Ardyce and Poom are throwing a bash tomorrow. They asked me to invite you."

"Ardyce and Poom?"

"He's a top gun at Dixon, Wechsler, Katz, Pomerantz and Figgie."

"Uris, Christie, Rushdie and Puzo," Koerner said. "Spillane, Plain and Tan."

MacChesney sighed.

"Tell me the truth," Koerner said as he began climbing out of the car, "have you read Danielle Steel's latest? Had brunch with Leo Tolstoy? Played badminton with Barbara Taylor Bradford?"

"You're absolutely soaked," MacChesney said. "There's no point in talking to you. But seriously, do you want to go? Ardyce is a great fan. And Poom's not bad, once you get to know him. How about it?"

"Tell Ardyce and Poom that I appreciate the invitation," Koerner said, "but I'll be out of town. I'm eloping with Dodie Truehorse."

1966/1994

THE GIANT

H IS NAME was Alden Hauserman. He was almost seven feet tall. He weighed three hundred and forty pounds. His jaw, his hands and his feet, even in proportion to the rest of his body, seemed too large. He was altogether bald, the yellowish scalp ribbed and furrowed. The great ridge bone above his eyes threw back the cast of his face thousands of years; yet the brain of a civilized, passionate man stared out of the deep sockets. He was a gentle, affable giant, and exceptionally verbose. There was, in fact, nothing he enjoyed more than talking, although few people could endure listening to him—he alarmed everybody he approached. To people of the usual size he was not a man but a primitive idol resurrected; and when, as was his habit, he waved his hands as though conducting music while he talked, the listeners were subdued, half terrified.

He would talk about anything, but most of all he enjoyed talking about the future of humanity. Bending down until his head nearly touched the listener, Alden would ask, as though he were a supplicant, "Truthfully, don't you realize?"

The listener, staring up at his head, vaguely horrified at finding a smile on the lips, was apt to gasp, "Realize what?"

"Stop a moment and think," Alden would continue, spreading his lips in what he thought must be a friendly grin, "just stop right where you are and think. Now, I'm going to tell you something. As a matter of fact I'm going to make a prediction. Listen to this. Someday, although you and I won't live to see it, people exactly like ourselves are going to be masters of the universe! Ah, but you answer, what *is* the universe? Define your terms, Mr. Hauserman. That's what you answer, am I right? But who can define the universe? Certainly I can't, and I'll venture to guess that you can't. Am I right? You can't tell me where we are, or what we are, any more than I can tell you. What does this mean? It's obvious. You and I are simply too small to comprehend. In a sense we're no larger than pygmies. Have you ever seen one of those dreadful shrunken heads? Well, I have! And I don't mind admitting to you that I couldn't sleep for a month afterward."

Then he might lean down closer, gently grasping a lapel, or perhaps an arm of his spellbound victim, for he was serious and he was anxious to communicate.

"Now, listen to me. One of these days our descendants won't be living on the earth, did you ever think of that? It's a mathematical certainty that because of the rate at which we reproduce ourselves we'll be obliged to populate the other planets. We don't have enough food, we don't have enough space. You know for yourself that what I'm saying is true. Do you drive to work? How do you find a place to park? You can't. Already we've run out of room for ourselves.

"Do you suppose anyone at all will remain on earth? I don't know. It's interesting to speculate. Perhaps we'll elect to destroy this little home of ours simply because we'll have no further use for it. Or we might take it with us as we wander through the universe. Certain nights of the year—I don't know why it is, unless it has something to do with the atmosphere—certain nights the moon isn't a disk, it's actually a sphere. Do you know what I'm talking about? It makes me feel that I could stretch out one arm and take the moon between my fingers as though it were a glass marble.

"I have a telescope mounted on the roof of my apartment building. I often spend half the night up there examining the moon and the stars. Did you know, by the way, that some astronomers claim the universe is expanding at a tremendous rate, while others claim it's not? How can anyone perceive the truth? Even these learned scientists argue among themselves! So there you are. What do you think about that? And speaking of expansion, our old everyday sun has a few tricks up her sleeve. Take those incandescent sheets of gas—why, they'll suddenly stretch out forty or fifty thousand miles into space! Knots and streamers of fiery gas come pouring out of certain prominences toward some invisible center of attraction in the chromosphere. Apparently they're drawn by some vast electrical or magnetic force we know nothing about.

"But if it's size that interests you, pure and simple, you just can't ignore that dark giant revolving around Epsilon Aurigae. Why, it's so big we can't even draw a picture of it to the proper scale. If we drew a circle representing that star, we'd need a microscope to find the dot representing the sun. It's near Capella, just three degrees away. Come over to my place some night and I'll show you. Listen, if man is capable of exploring the universe, what is he incapable of? You think I'm joking, don't you? I can tell that you think I'm toying with you, but I'm not. I'm dead serious. Look at it this way. You and I don't know exactly what's going on. We're the masses, so to speak. Yet right this moment in Washington, in London, in Moscow, and here in New York there are brilliant men plotting our future. These midget satellites are nothing! Scientists have scarcely begun to comprehend our potential. I wish I could make you understand! Try to imagine what life will be like in the future. We'll accomplish things that now would seem like miracles. But I can see that you think I'm exaggerating. You're laughing at me. You are, aren't you?"

No one ever accused him of exaggerating, and nobody had ever been known to laugh at him. Few people even tried to comment on anything he said, but looked for an excuse to get away, nodding and agreeing.

If, as occasionally happened, someone appeared with the courage or the tranquillity of spirit, or whatever it was that was necessary to sustain the impact of his size, then Alden would become jovial and boisterous, but even more determined to express himself, so that when the gathering broke up he would insist on making a date for luncheon or for supper in order to continue the discussion. In spite of this no one could dislike him. Whenever his name was mentioned people spoke enthusiastically of him, saying how interesting he was to listen to, and how remarkable it was that he seemed completely unaware of being different.

Often when a party was ending there would come a strange and unfortunate time: Alden invariably stayed to the last and hunted the center of the dwindling crowd as though he wished to preserve it; yet each time he located it and insinuated himself into its center it dissolved like a cluster of organisms seen under a microscope that are touched by a needle—the components swam away, recreating their unity somewhere else, leaving him once again outside, gazing upon them in silence.

1959

THE TRELLIS

INSPECTOR POLAJENKO stood in the middle of the street with his gloved hands cupped around his mouth as if he were shouting through the rain; actually he was only shielding his cigar. While he smoked he gazed at a purple stucco cottage which indicated by an absence of lace curtains that a man lived there alone, and according to a sign on the front gate the man was a silversmith named Tony Miula.

Though it was only a few minutes after dawn there were lights in almost every neighboring house and faces could be seen at upstairs windows. A cluster of motorcycles and a police sedan were parked before the yellow brick Colonial house next door to Tony Miula's cottage.

Inspector Polajenko splashed across the street, unhooked Miula's gate, and walked toward the front door with a bemused expression, like a philosopher who has stumbled on a great truth. The door opened before his fist had touched it and Polajenko, who was not a little man, looked up at Tony Miula.

Calmly the inspector said, "I've heard about you," wiped his shoes on the mat, and stepped inside the cottage.

"What have you heard?" asked Miula in a nasal tenor. He had been cutting pictures out of a magazine and still carried the scissors.

Polajenko walked to a window where he could see the sleeping porch of the neighboring house. After a few seconds he walked to another window from which he could again see the sleeping porch and a part of the back yard where, in a corner, stood an arch of white latticework interlaced with rose bushes. Elegant red and yellow blossoms burst everywhere through this trellis, some of them touching the legs and back of a wicker chair in which an obese, bald-headed man was sitting.

"Just your name," he said, and a friendly little smile came onto his face.

Tony looked relieved.

"How much do you pay for this bungalow?" Polajenko asked, moving to another window where he continued to stare at the bald-headed man, who was wearing a raincoat over some gaudy pajamas and who seemed very much at peace because his legs were crossed and one hand rested casually in his lap. On one knee hung a checkered golfing cap. His head was tilted back as though he sat in a dentist's chair, while the September rain streamed steadily down his face.

"The rent is five hundred dollars a year," replied Tony, following the inspector with glittering eyes, "but I think that's too much so I just pay four hundred and ninety-nine, and every year the landlord gets furious."

"I keep forgetting the name of your neighbor," said Polajenko.

"I don't believe you," Tony said, snapping the scissors, but as the inspector did not comment he finally muttered, "Allan Ehe."

"Ah, yes," Polajenko said, looking from the trellis to the screened-in porch, "now I remember."

"Do you know what I did during the war?" Tony asked.

"I'm a little afraid to guess," Polajenko answered and continued twisting the left side of his mustache.

"Every day, all day, for more than three years I cleaned out the officers' latrines. Do you know why? Because I refused to fire a weapon even for practice."

"Well, Tony, it is a fine idea to object; however you must pay for the luxury."

"I cannot possibly fire a gun."

"Did I say you killed Allan Ehe?" Polajenko assumed a pained expression.

Tony Miula crossed his legs and sat down regal and serene as a yogi. Around him the carpet was littered with magazine pages and metal staples he had pried from the bindings in order to dismantle each publication completely.

"How do you make your living, my friend?" inquired the inspector, standing at a window with his back to Tony Miula.

"I'm a bachelor, as you know, with little living to make."

"How do you know I know?"

Tony ignored him.

"Let us suppose you had a wife, my friend, how would you pay for her?"

"I would work with my hands."

"Would you make those sandals you wear?"

"Yes, I would," said Tony after some thought. "Furthermore I might tool leather belts and engrave silver buckles. Possibly you noticed the sign in front?"

"Ah," the inspector said, snapping his fingers, "I remember now that I did." From his vest he took a new cigar and began carefully sliding it from the cellophane. "Have you known this neighbor very long?"

"Years and years. We were introduced when he was thirteen and I was nine. He immediately hit me in the eye."

"Have you been fighting ever since?"

"Yes, indeed. I always got the best of him."

Polajenko had crumpled the cellophane in his fist and now dropped it to the carpet.

"Pick that up," Tony ordered. "It's not the same as a clipping."

Polajenko hastily did as he was told, and while putting the cellophane in the pocket of his raincoat he asked, "Do you drink a great deal?"

"Whenever I cannot handle the weight of the world."

Polajenko was sympathetic. "How often is that?"

"Never."

"You don't seem very strong to me."

"You'd be surprised," said Tony, not looking up from his magazines.

"Where do you sleep?"

"I sleep on the lawn in summer."

"Will you tell me why?"

"To watch the cardinals which live in a bush nearby."

"Well, my metronomic man, where do you sleep in the winter time?"

"On a cot by the kitchen stove."

"You are a strange piece of goods," the inspector said. "I must get to know you better."

"You will," said Tony, prying out a staple with the tip of his scissors.

Polajenko began to wander around the room with his head bowed and hands behind his back. Tony glanced with annoyance at the drops of water his raincoat was shedding but said nothing. The only sounds in the bungalow were the snip of the scissors and a damp squeaking of the inspector's shoes as he circled the man on the floor.

"I've seen thousands of hands," Polajenko resumed. "Like a face, a hand has a few lines in the play. In you I discern a little of Baudelaire, and believe me, my friend, there is nothing farther from the soul of a decent American than Baudelaire."

"Inspector," said Tony after a pause, "would you like to know why the man is dead?"

"Why else would I be here?"

Tony dropped his scissors, crossed his arms on his chest and looked up at the inspector. "That's not worthy of you, sir. Neither of us is a fool."

Polajenko looked apologetic but said nothing.

"I cannot tell you all the reasons he is dead, but I can tell you more than anyone else, more than his wife, or more than his mother, of whom I am very fond and for whom I always create something nice at Christmas time. I can tell you what insults he never forgot and why, about Jeanne Williams and Jean Williams, or the treasure hunt by which I delayed his suicide. I am able to analyze his friends; I knew them infinitely better than he ever did or could. Friendships begin by accident but end on purpose. It is true that a foolish hostess may cry, 'Martin Gorst, this is George Boom. You two will be inseparable!' But if Gorst and Boom look at one another favorably it will come to pass in spite of their introduction and no one will know why. Though it may be true that providence can separate two men for life still they are friends and will remain so until the chemistry of their relationship has changed, which is not an accident. Sometimes the two who were bound in this way understand why they are no longer so, but sometimes they do not, knowing only that they will inconvenience themselves to avoid any sight or sound of the other. Then again, one may perceive and one not perceive—which is the way it generally was with myself and this unstable individual who is now being removed feet first from the back yard."

Inspector Polajenko, who had been looking out the window, instantly turned around but Tony was still seated on the floor.

"Tell me, my friend, just how do you know he is being carried away?"

"I hear them talking in the back yard," replied Tony. "There are three men. Two of them are subordinates."

Polajenko closed his eyes and cocked his head, but he could hear only the splash of water from the eaves and the tick of the watch deep in his vest.

"They've forgotten his cap," Tony added.

Immediately Polajenko looked out the window. The lieutenant was just stooping beside the trellis where Ehe's golfing cap lay upside down in the wet grass. Two motorcycle policemen walked across the back yard with the body on a stretcher.

"I must get to know you better," said Polajenko tightly.

"I told you you would," said Tony.

With a thoughtful expression Polajenko suggested, "I have a friend who would like to meet you."

"He has a good practice, I'm sure."

Polajenko looked dourly at the silversmith.

"When Allan was very young he did a cruel thing," Tony said, and disgust ran lightly across his face.

"Who has not? The trick is to feign ignorance of it."

"These two girls named Williams were not related but they lived on the same street and one was very popular. Allan lacked the courage to approach her so one night he opened the telephone book, found a Williams on the proper street, and made his call. He was stupefied by the immediacy with which she accepted an invitation. So away he went on the appointed evening, was welcomed by the parents, and sat himself down. Up he jumped as he had been taught to do when he heard her coming down the stairs. When she came around the curve of the staircase he had no idea who she was because she was cheerless and plain, and one of her legs was in a brace. There followed what is known as the painful silence, or the awkward pause, while he gazed at her hopefully as if she and her treacherous parents might suddenly vanish and his problem be solved, for it had come to him at last that he had got the wrong girl. Without a word he walked to the door. But here he could not figure out the latch and then the crippled girl, half-dead with pity, limped to his side and showed him how."

Polajenko was standing across the room examining the contents of Allan Ehe's billfold. He did not seem to be listening.

"Three decades later he mentioned that evening. He could not forget what he had done because he knew in his heart that he was still capable of a similar act. Standing by my work bench he asked if I remembered, and when I said I did, he bitterly shook his bald head."

Polajenko folded a piece of paper into an airplane and sent it gliding across the carpet where it landed beside the magazines. Tony unfolded it and read:

> I long ago lost a hound, a bay horse, and a turtledove, and am still on their trail. Many are the travelers I have spoken to concerning them, describing their tracks and what calls they answered to. I have met one

or two who had heard the hound and the tramp of the horse, and even seen the dove disappear behind a cloud, and they seemed as anxious to recover them as if they had lost them themselves.

"Thoreau," said Tony, who always read things that did not interest anyone else. "From his wallet. Shall we study it under a microscope?"

"The typewriter is in his den and you can see the end of its carriage from where you are standing. If you don't believe me, turn around and look."

"If I didn't believe you, my friend, I would look," replied Polajenko. "I suppose you realize that certain people in this neighborhood are of the opinion you have two heads."

Tony answered with indifference. "I have a great deal to think about."

"Why is it you wear such formal clothes?"

"Why not?"

"But do you know anyone else who wears a frock coat and a top hat in the house?"

As if the inspector's question had disturbed him Tony took off the hat, looked it over, and finally put it back on his head. Polajenko continued to smoke in silence.

Once, scarcely loud enough to be heard, he asked, "Don't you symbolize something?"

And Miula answered, "Nothing whatsoever."

By this time Allan Ehe was on his journey to the morgue. His wife had been removed to the hospital in a catatonic state, and their four children were being fed by another neighbor.

"Altogether he was as fond of his wife as a man is apt to be of the one who substitutes for his genuine love, even though she was the most undistinguished woman who had ever aroused him. She was a devout Protestant named Winifred, a broad and tame creature with a hoarse voice and a detachable blonde coronet that framed her serene violet eyes. He had married her less than a month after being jilted by a thin, chilly little person who taught ballroom dancing."

Tony got up from the carpet like a giraffe, his eyes enormous with concern, and hurried into the kitchen. Presently he returned with two fragrant cups of coffee on a bamboo tray. Then, sitting down in his favorite position, he began a vague, wandering account of the year Ehe had spent in Greenwich Village, a year during which he fancied himself a poet.

"You see, my inspector, the idea came to him right after his elder brother died of leukemia, leaving behind a ten-thousand-dollar insurance policy. Allan flew de luxe to New York where he took a four-dollar-a-week room because he was of the opinion one must suffer in order to write poetry. While walking through the Village one rainy night, thinking how coarse people were, he happened to meet a Ukrainian girl named Natalie who also possessed a soul, so they began living together. They moved into a garret from which one could see a few yards of the Hudson providing there was not too much laundry on the lines, and there he wrote poetry while she decorated the walls with spirals and cubes and odalisques, meanwhile telling him about the slavery endured by women of the old Ukrainian families. In turn he told her how much he disliked Illinois, except for squirrel hunting and the wiener roasts on certain October evenings when the poplars and oaks stood about in the smoky dusk in attitudes of grave meditation. He never told her he had ten thousand dollars.

"They bought the worst available phonograph in a junk shop and took it to her father who was a butcher in the Bronx. The butcher was very good at mechanical things, whereas Allan was an artist, and soon had the machine repaired so they returned to their garret and began playing 'Where the Bee Sucks There Suck I,' meanwhile making a joke of everything that happened, no matter what.

"Her murals were rather muddy but as all their friends were similar to themselves no one criticized this fact. In the center of the attic hung a mobile which everyone admired and which turned idly around this way and that as though keeping an eye on so much happiness. They drank red wine and white wine at the proper times, looking critically at the glasses, ate smoked cheese and crackers and a great deal of spaghetti which Natalie cooked and invariably said was not successful. Throughout the evening they would play with each other, calling one another darling, and wandering about the garret holding hands. Often she would curl up in his lap and twist a lock of his hair around her fingers while their guests watched with casual sophistication. He learned to tell jokes about how naïve she had been when they began living together. Idly, sipping the wine, he dissected her as though she were on a table for everyone to enjoy, while she murmured in mock embarrassment, 'Do stop, Randy,' which was the name she had decided to call him.

"At about this stage they bought a dozen heavy white porcelain mugs to replace the glasses. In this way everyone could use two hands to drink the wine, meanwhile smiling with relief at having escaped the world of the Philistines.

"Late at night they usually went for a walk beside the river with their closest friends, a couple named Jones. This couple was unable to get married because his previous wife refused to divorce him, so she had gotten her last name changed from Langendorf to Jones. They lived in a basement near Washington Square and if no trucks were parked in the way they could see half of the arch. She wrote free verse while he spent the day designing heroic statuary."

"Tony! Tony, let me rest," begged Polajenko.

"Of course, Inspector. I'll tell it in the third person. Tony visited Allan and Natalie. One evening, together with a girl friend of Natalie's who was fond of saying she would like to be a man, they went for a serious walk. Through the smoke and grit and roaring automobiles they sauntered, thinking what a fine thing it was to exist at the center of the universe, and presently the girl, whose name was Alec, became playful. She scooped up some water from a fountain and threw it on Tony, clutched him by the hand, and cried to the night, 'Why don't we run?' Tony refused to run. Therefore she dashed back and forth pulling up tufts of grass, pausing now and then to gaze thoughtfully at the stars. When they sat on the concrete revetment of the river she sat a little apart and with chin cupped in her hands she looked mournfully across to Jersey, as though she perceived more than neon lights and the omnipresent rumbling.

"With the candor of intimate friends Natalie inquired how much money silversmiths could make; Tony replied so brusquely that she was offended. Allan smiled dryly; he had not warned her about Tony. Alec soon inquired when he would be moving to New York and when he said he would not she looked at him in stupefaction. On their way home to the Village she walked beside him with extreme dignity, as though they were going down the aisle, but suddenly exclaimed, 'How do you expect me to write a book?' Natalie instantly cried, 'Oh, but you must! You have so much to say.' And Alec closed her eyes in pain, saying quietly, 'But I have not even closed a single episode. I must close an episode before I write my book.' Natalie shivered. 'I should feel intellectually naked afterwards.' There came an opening in the boulevard traffic; all four clutched hands and dashed to safety. The girls could not run very fast because they were wearing tight knickers.

"Some weeks after this evening Tony Miula, back among his metals and clippings, began to receive a series of incoherent letters from Allan. The letters told of going to a university psychiatrist, of envy and despair and most of all confusion. Natalie told him repeatedly that he was the greatest living poet in the English language, and to him at night she would whisper, 'You need me now. I'm the stronger.'

"Allan enclosed some lines he had written:

> *In the day I have blamed you,*
> *In the night have I shamed you,*
> *Chill abbess I love.*

"And that was mostly what his life in the Village consisted of. His poems were all very short and related to her. She was large and bony with luminous brown eyes like those of a nocturnal animal. He wrote of the gas that seeped into their garret from a broken pipe somewhere in the wall, and later, when they shared the basement with the Jones couple, of how clogged his head felt every morning.

"He wrote more and more often, until each mail brought two or three letters; then all at once when he was near to madness the clouds lifted for an instant that he might see himself on the cliff. The next day he left New York. Back home he spent week after week shuffling through the streets, and each afternoon he lay face down in the grass of the public square while the sun turned his neck as black as an old walnut. If anyone spoke to him he would begin to weep. Then one evening shortly before sundown he stood up, felt his jaw, and lurched across the square to a barber shop. The following week he had a job and was playing cards with his neighbors."

"Excuse me," said Inspector Polajenko, "but nobody behaves like that. Whose story is this? I seem to see not him but you as the poetaster."

Tony answered with a benign smile. "The point is that artistic garrets are full of people playing 'Where the Bee Sucks There Suck I.' Here is the land where this man was born and where he died. God give me to say what he suffered."

"I hate to seem stupid," said the inspector with a sigh, "but why is it you detour around honesty? You are verbal and clever enough, but your vision is perverse and astigmatic. All rays must converge at the retina, else we are lost." He stopped pacing the floor and stood a while gazing down on Tony, who met his look with equal strength.

"Actually, I respect you, Mr. Polajenko."

"Don't apologize when you say it. Do you know you look just like my brother?"

"But I *am* your brother."

"When you talk like that," Inspector Polajenko said grimly, "I can't understand a single word you say. You were telling me he went to a priest for advice. Go on."

There followed a long silence. Rain dripped steadily from the eaves.

At last Tony replied, "I never said that, but he did. He was told the Savior loved him."

"And what do you think of that?"

"It's all well enough provided a few mortals do too." He dipped his tongue into the cool coffee and closed his eyes. "Inspector, do you know, the first time you looked at me I knew a lot about you."

"To be understood is about the most fascinating thing I know," answered Polajenko. "But quite frankly, my friend, your assurance is irritating, particularly in one who understands the world not from practice but speculation. You sit astride it all with such disdain, a cavalier upon a nag. Come now, once in a while there must be empty bottles in your trash barrel."

Tony vigorously shook his head.

Polajenko examined the end of his cigar which he had chewed as flat as a paint brush.

"Just two things interested Allen as much as astronomy. One was a woman addicted to pornography, the other was building something. Still and all, each soul is a flower in the Master's bouquet."

"Please be lucid. Are you able to tell me what our subject did after he failed as a poet?"

"He operated an elevator. I often went downtown in order to ride in that elevator. Up and down we'd go. He had a beautiful speaking voice. One knew he believed he should have been a radio announcer. When calling the floors he modulated his tone and stood so erect. I would stand directly behind him and murmur, 'Your diction is superb. If I were a producer I would make you famous.' Such things do happen, you know; if they did not you would probably have more suicides than you have now. Good fortune, good fortune. It's like the truncated pencil sellers who deny their estate by hanging about their necks a placard which says, 'Keep Smiling.' Or the blind minstrels who quaver that happy days are here again.

"He did drink. Oh, how he drank! After a few he would become solemn and forthwith dispense his soul like a box of chocolates. Off he would go on business trips now and again, but always registered under an alias at a hotel with wooden walls. In his room he immediately took out his pen knife and began boring peepholes. He carried with him a role of adhesive tape to insure his own privacy when he so desired. Do you find him evil?"

Polajenko shrugged, his eyes returning casually to the scissors with which Tony was prying out staples.

"I, myself—" Tony continued, but here he belched, pressed a hand to his chest, and exclaimed, "Excuse *me!* Now I myself began as a thin child with wind-tossed hair and brilliant gypsy eyes, and did not fill my pockets with junk or go skating on the mill pond, so of course had I done the things Allan did the world would have brayed 'I told you so.' One of our instincts is to produce a play, which is the reason he did not shoot himself in the bedroom, say, but yonder among the roses."

Polajenko's eyes fastened greedily on the gangling silversmith, while about his red lips there formed the trace of a cynical smile.

"He gave the impression that he was living his life in order to have done with it.

He became interested in foods and wines to pass the years away. Oh, he thought a good bit, but he never had any worthwhile thoughts. Mostly he brooded over women, and I grant you it sometimes does appear that the world and all consists of anatomy and not one stroke more. But with Plymouth obstinance we ignore the nature of man, then look what you have! Why is everyone so astounded when a child is ravished?" Tony sat up straight and began tapping his lips with his fingertips as if trying to remember something.

"Oh, yes! He used to stand in corners with his arms folded, if that tells you anything. And I would see him walking in the garden holding lofty dialogues with himself. He felt that time was passing and he seemed vaguely baffled and resentful of the fact, for he knew he had not done much. He was commencing to grow old in the most commonplace way. He attracted no notice. One thought of him as aging, nothing more. He did not grow majestic, or even confident. He just went down that road feeling bad, do you understand? And he wasn't going to be treated—oh, never mind, never mind." Tony looked gloomily at the carpet. "Last year about this time I was awake before dawn. I remember how the shadows lightened. On their sleeping porch I saw his wife rolling about as if something troubled her dreams. Her breasts poured heavily like flowing batter around and around while he sat on the edge of the bed glaring down at them as if his destiny were his death as well."

"Common enough," muttered Polajenko with a melancholy smile.

"That morning the bull was bellowing against his forehead. By some divining instinct he knew that life was happening to him. It was this knowledge he denied for so long in New York. There he grew a beard like an old-time Bolshevik; even so I remembered most clearly not the symbol of virility but his uneasy eyes, timid and frightened, of robin's-egg blue, or like those of a drowned man under water. I understood then about the ferocious beard, why he had grown it."

"I wish," said Polajenko wearily, "that you would put a hoop around each story so that I might gather them up."

"And you would like them labeled, too."

"That would make my job easier," Polajenko admitted. "Pardon me for saying this, but you're not quite real."

"That depends."

"You don't understand. What I say is that I never met anyone who acted like you. You don't talk like anybody I know. Furthermore you don't live the way people do."

"You just haven't watched closely," said Tony, getting to his feet. "By the way, did you count the cigarette stubs under the trellis? He smoked all night. What did you find in his bathrobe?"

"Chewing gum, a comb, and an empty match box. I find myself wondering if he would still be alive if he had found some more matches."

"So you conclude I am not a murderer after all!"

"Ah," said Polajenko with regret. "That is the trouble with you. A person says a word and it echoes from you as a paragraph."

"Stop showing off to yourself."

Polajenko winked slyly, as though the two of them shared an agreeable secret.

"Is there anything else you want?" asked Tony with a rather stiff countenance.

"As a matter of fact, yes," said the inspector, "but I doubt if you will give it to me."

They stood a few seconds almost back to back. Tony Miula's eyes glittered ominously. "All right!" he burst out. "What is it? What is it?"

"Your scalp."

"Of course! You caught me that time. Why am I so stupid?" He slapped himself on the forehead.

The inspector turned around to gaze at him in mild surprise, and then looked down at the sallow, bony hands as if they confirmed something he had always suspected. Idly he said, "They tell me you are a great hunter."

"That's a lie!"

Polajenko peeled the cellophane from a smaller cigar and after licking one end he replied, "It is a lie and I am sorry. I'll never lie to you again. All the same, why don't you hunt? There is squirrel and quail in the woods just over the ridge. I often go there. Men are like that. They must kill a little or go insane from humiliation and despair. Why don't I meet you there sometime?"

"Then you accuse me!" He slapped himself again and announced to the ceiling, "Ah, God, that I should chop tiger hair for the gruel of an ass!"

Inspector Polajenko sighed wearily. "What a fellow you are! I don't see why we can't be friends."

"Shall I tell you? Because I'm smarter than the people you deal with—all the lonely bats and thugs. I may even be a watt brighter than you."

At this Polajenko stepped swiftly up to Tony Miula and pulled the horsy face down until it was touching his own. "Queer fish, I am going along with you," he whispered, threatening, then he stepped backward and blew a puff of smoke.

"You hurt my feelings," said Tony, rubbing his throat where Polajenko's powerful hand had caught him. "I won't tell you any more."

"Oh, really!" the inspector said in a good humor again. "Do you want me to give you the third degree?"

Tony looked petulant. "Your center of gravity is outside yourself. I thought you were more of a man, but you're just like Allan. Give you a push and down you go."

Polajenko groaned. "You exhaust me."

But Tony was already into a fresh narrative and as usual did not feel it necessary to connect one thought to the next, believing that anyone worth speaking to would contribute his own power. The incident took place at a country-club dance on New Year's Eve when Allan Ehe was twenty-two. He escorted to the celebration a girl no one there had ever seen, who at first was rumored to be a famous Continental beauty. However, the minute she opened her mouth it was obvious she came from some midwestern town enclosed by wheat sheaves, and in fact she turned out to be the niece of his sister-in-law up for a visit. But if her varnish had an apparent crack, Allan's had not. He danced around the floor once in a while with fearful dignity, disdaining all rhythm but the waltz, which meant they spent most of their time at their table, she a little baffled but trying to match his somber expression. Following each waltz he would lead her to the Louis Quatorze mirror, encircled by gold leaves and bucolic angels. There without a smile he would adjust his white necktie or pick lint from his lapel. Everyone watched him. He ignored his friends or bowed severely like a timid ambassador. He told no jokes; he relaxed not an instant. Never again in his life would he command such a gathering of people. He made only one mistake; he accepted an invitation to join a party. There the cardboard trumpets and paper hats did their appointed work, and when Tony all at once exploded a sack of confetti on his head he was destroyed, for his dignity was conscious.

"I caught up to him by the mirror," Tony continued. "He wasn't looking at himself this time, believe me. He was heading toward the safety of the men's room where he intended to lock himself in a cubicle. Frankly I had intended to finish him off but I saw he was dying and where is the sport of a *coup de grâce*? I enjoy the slaughter of Titans, but I do not shoot squirrels."

"Did you feel at ease with him?"

"I called him by his first name."

"I am not going to put up with you much longer."

Tony shrugged, as if to inquire what better the inspector had to do. "Analogies, like epigrams, are stronger in poetry than verity, all the same Allan Ehe was somewhat analogous to a spider that remains visible so long as it is not endangered, but retreats when assaulted. After his crucifixion at the country club he was not seen for almost a week." Tony plucked irritably at the carpet with his scissors and eventually admitted, "I had hoped right up to the last that he would learn something from me. He died for lack of strength. I saw the beastly gun drop from his hand into the wet grass. I saw the robins spring from the trees all around and fly off in alarm—"

"Pardon me, but how tall are you."

"Six feet and seven inches. In the morning."

"Goodness!" exclaimed the inspector grimly. "That means we would be the same height if I should cut off your head. How tall are you at night?"

"Just a little shorter. During the day our cartilage is compressed."

"All the same," the inspector answered without much inflection, "most people don't find it necessary to mention such a fact. As for the robins you think you saw, they have no nests in that back yard. But go on, though Diogenes has passed you by."

"We were playing bridge on the train when a strange young woman hurried past. She was not much to look at but as she was alone he immediately began to follow her. Now he was handsome enough at twenty-six, though already showing a slight baldness and the ambitious belly of which he was so vain, for it signified success, and he loved to boast of his conquests, being of the opinion that I envied him. We followed her to a Pullman near the end of the train and there she sat down opposite two nuns who were amusing themselves with a game of string—"

Tony held up his hands to demonstrate how they had been weaving the string.

"—which is a good game to play for a few seconds, but the nuns played it by the hour. Frankly I was ashamed so I returned to the vestibule but he was undismayed; he sat down beside the quarry. He was a master of fatuity, even the crows would listen when he spoke. However he had some difficulty here and soon came back to the vestibule for a cigarette. I goaded him very well, I think; he swelled up like a toad but could not think of anything to say. So long as he succeeded at anything he could be taunted endlessly, responding with an imbecilic grin, but when he failed he lost his humor. I knew this but I continued because I always played the footman to this fat Don Juan and got a little tired of it. When he started to reach out the window in order to knock the ashes from his cigarette I was seized with hatred and struck the cigarette out of his hand—like that! The wind would have blown the ash into my face, at least I think it might have. I could have stepped backward as quickly as I slapped, but I did not and that was the point. Allan perceived in my action a rather cogent truth, which is that the illuminating act is the instinctive one, and in a fraction of a second may refute the manner of a lifetime. In this particular case it did not refute anything but simply stated in italics that I, of all persons, had never respected him. He was always tender as a scallion. The days of life we shared were sweet and rich for me. He never knew I sucked the very liquid of his soul. He did not learn a thing from me. Well, his death was not the first time I ate the bitter herb of heartbreak and neglect. Under a skylight in Greenwich Village I have been betrayed. When you have written the name of your love in the sand and presently watched the tide return, what more can you see?

"He spoke of suicide on dreary nights. Those who speak of it may do it, textbooks be damned. Once he came tapping on my door and handed me his will. He was a fraud that night, still I engaged him in a treasure hunt. I hid bits of tissue paper here and there and gave him the first instruction to open the dictionary at a certain page. There he found the second bit of tissue directing him to a picture on the wall, and behind this there was another telling him to peep under the sofa. From there he went to the icebox and from there to the medicine cabinet. Eventually, in the wastebasket, he found his will which I had torn in half. That is the way to do it, I said to him, let the policemen chase you a while."

"You know," said Polajenko with a bemused expression, "I'm sorry we gave the Salvation Army our iron maiden."

"But he loved her," Tony complained.

"Our rapport is breaking down, my friend. Whom are we talking about?"

"She fed him and kept him warm, woman's first concern for man."

Polajenko took off his glasses and pinched the bridge of his nose. "Are you talking about Natalie?"

"No, certainly not. I'm telling you about Winifred."

"I can't remember all these people."

But Tony was speaking at the same time. "Every Tuesday morning she goes into the back yard with a creaking wicker basket full of wet clothing and hangs it up to dry. I always hope for a windy morning; then the sheets pop like flags and the water runs down her forearms and drips from her plump elbows while she clips the washing to her line. I watch through the hedge more dead than alive, for she stands so—astride the basket—arms raised in triumph! Ah, that I might be a sculptor! The rope would go, to be sure, and the basket and the frock. But that all requires a noble mind. It suits me better to work with leather and chips of second-rate Mexican jade. But before I die I will hold one day in my hand a chisel, and I shall see beyond it an obelisk of marble from the quarries of Carrara, and no god known shall stop me. One day I will walk in Paradise. Now like a murdered actor do you look, in life's adroit facsimile of death! But I've no pennies to waste upon your eyes. . . . "

"I *have* been looking at you, it is true," replied Polajenko, "and now I know for the first time what it is has puzzled me. I have seen the shadows pass over your face, but did not know what they meant. It is not love itself you want or need, like other

The Trellis

men, but only its image. If the curse of manhood had not dried up all my tears I think I could weep for you."

Struck by the inspector's tone Tony Miula hesitantly raised his eyes and found that Polajenko was looking at him with love, and a feeling long unfamiliar came into his heart as silently as the tide.

"Excuse me," said Polajenko, "but if you were awake and watching when the gun dropped from his hand then you must have seen him examine the weapon and raise it to his temple. Now if that is so, why did you allow it to happen? Or are you not your brother's keeper?"

"He had been lifting that gun for decades and it was my opinion that only he could lower it. I knew that something awful was happening to him, that some dread hour had come."

"I'm sorry, but that doesn't satisfy me."

"Well," Tony argued, "with the copious wisdom of hindsight I think next time I might do something about it. I might scream. However he was obstinate, as little men are apt to be, and having decided to shoot something he might as well have let go at me. Why don't you get out and leave me alone? I'm tired and have nothing more to say. Leave!"

Polajenko leaned backward in astonishment. But upon recovering from his surprise he recalled that he was not a guest to be ordered about; he grew angry and said he would leave when he pleased.

"But you are persecuting me," Tony whimpered.

"You! You sound an eerie chord, my friend, minor and foreign to the ear."

Before the last consonant had died away Tony's barbaric scissors whirled and flashed across the room, struck Polajenko flat on the breast and dropped almost reluctantly to the carpet. After a long silence during which the men looked away from each other Polajenko whispered, "You have thrown scissors before. . . . You could have hit me with both blades."

Tony nodded sullenly.

"That's enough," Polajenko muttered, buttoning up his raincoat.

"Yes or no?" said Tony. "Tell me if I am accused."

"Why should I tell you? You won't go anywhere." Polajenko began to grin. "Why, any time I want you I'll have you. I'll ring the bell and you'll hurry to let me in."

"I know things you will never learn from anyone else."

"But you garnish everything! Give you a pat of dough just large enough for a biscuit and you try to make a wedding cake." Polajenko considered the scissors which had stuck in the carpet. "Tony, you react like a woman. A man would have been careful not to alarm me."

Tony made a wry face. "It is easier to master desire than grief."

Polajenko grinned maliciously. "And some enjoy their guilt. Come now, you marionette, aren't you a little pleased he's dead?" Taking off his glasses again he began to squeeze his eyes. "It is easy to feel poetic about the tragedy of others. To know poetry when we ourselves have been victimized requires a peculiar mind."

"The sentiment is lovely, but I doubt the facts. The limbs of my neighbor are stiffening by the instant. Why don't you leave me?"

Polajenko sighed, as he had done from time to time, and made no attempt to answer, and his exhausted expression did not change, as though he were through with all struggling forever.

"The poles were established in the first act. For him the experience of others could not provide a solution. This garden so formal to the eye, who sees beneath the soil where roots go spiraling down in search of greater life, enfolding rocks, relics, or bones with indiscrimination, plunging through burrows in their hunger? His life was a feckless search for manhood.

"Do you know what caused him to fall in love? First of all it was her nose, which is long and bony. He would often feel of it in a kind of fascination and so she thought him quite strange indeed. Then one day he happened to toss her a pomegranate; she clutched, as women do, but managed to hang onto it. This surprised him. He had been prepared to laugh; instead he grew sober, looked at her in a melancholy way but said nothing. Later he alluded to the incident and she realized that somehow the fact that she had been able to catch a pomegranate had made him love her more than anything else she had ever done."

"Excuse me, but he seems to have told you a suspicious lot."

Tony looked at him in surprise. "But I collect stamps!"

The inspector considered this for a little while and finally said, "Ah, yes. So did he. Over stamps and wine rare confidence passes. Lord, I feel so unnecessary."

"But he never outgrew the insecurity of youth. It's a pleasure to be a little older and not so fearful of ridicule. But Allan went hunting like Ponce de León and his quest was the more stupid because he saw only the beds of various motels. That was when he sold automobiles. For two years he stood around rocking on his heels and gazing numbly at the floor or the ceiling, sometimes touching his bald spot or coughing gently into his fist. I would walk by the showroom and grimace; he would stare at me as through a mist of chloroform. He was just barely a success because, like all merchants worthy of the name, he was stupefied by anything that did not come with a set of directions. He did not know, nor did he care, that its name is Betelgeuse, or that it could annihilate the sun. But he spoke with authority; thus even when he was dead wrong few persons dared contradict him, for he sounded so right.

"He made excellent bait. There is nothing I would rather have for breakfast than the disposition of a bigot. One morning I strolled into the drugstore where he worked for a while. The instant he saw me he looked suspicious and uneasy. Strange—he never trusted me. I handed him a broken fountain pen. He said they were out of stock on that pen and wouldn't be getting repair parts. 'It's a hundred-year pen,' I said. 'Every part is guaranteed unconditionally for a hundred years.' He said, 'This particular model has been discontinued.' And I said, 'Then what good is the guarantee?' He was furious, but finally said he would give me another pen. I said I didn't want another, I wanted this one fixed, and I waved the guarantee at him. You should have seen him. I told him he should see a psychiatrist about that temper. The pen only cost nineteen cents and I broke it deliberately, of course. Allan suspected me right from the first. That night he slipped into my garage and released the air from the tires of my bicycle. Isn't that childish? He was a jealous and greedy man, and every time I stung him he ran off waving his arms and screaming."

Polajenko interrupted. "Now listen to me. Here is a man felled like a tree. Something has cut him down. You have shown me his branches, but where is the trunk? I want something to grab hold of."

"You must be very nervous to constantly tug your mustache like that."

"Oh, that's nothing," muttered the inspector. "The only thing that annoys me is I always pull the same side and take out so much hair I look lopsided. Now where were we? You're such a Pagliacci that you and your dead neighbor are inextricably tangled in my mind. In all you say about him I seem to find you."

"If the nails the carpenter hammers form an interesting pattern, is the carpenter responsible? When we are young we value nothing we cannot eat or put into our pocket, and when we are old if we value nothing more, there comes a sorry end. So he fell in the summer house, above his blind eyes an intricate lattice with its roses. I hear the tramp of many feet. Look out the window there! See how the trellis shakes? Mark this well. We are coming to break ourselves a souvenir—a thorn or a blossom to remember him by. Yet time was, time is, time will be, so the Magi say. Allan lost three things. Are we not as anxious to recover them as if we had lost them ourselves?"

Polajenko had gone to the window while Tony remained cross-legged on the floor. In the next yard many people were standing about, gazing now at the police, now at the trellis where the wicker chair lay on its side, and as these people walked around they left their footprints in the wet and bending grass. One stooped, sudden as a hawk, having found a cigarette butt unguarded, and put it in his pocket.

Polajenko stood by the window a long time with his hands gripping the lapels of his raincoat, and finally he said, "Now you have told me an *avant-garde* story, you gadfly. I am not sure that I like it. I may think it over or I may presently cut off your head. How would you like that?" But he was burlesquing himself.

Tony smiled happily. "It is a waste of time to think, I assure you, my inspector, for whether we concern ourselves with a thousand hounds or a turtledove, the heart remains generalissimo."

Inspector Polajenko turned from the window with a shrug and passed out into the rain, and was never seen by the silversmith again.

1957

THE MOUNTAINS
OF GUATEMALA

S O IT IS Christmas night. Warmer than the paper has predicted, overcast, there is a stasis to winter. Muhlbach, having locked the door, stands a moment on the horsehair welcome mat and considers his neighborhood. Celebrations persist, but they are subdued now; packages were opened this morning and already certain gifts have come to seem a trifle stale, not totally wanted. Drinking continues, music is heard across fences dark beneath the clouds, Christmas trees illuminate windows that face the street, and yet this holiday is dying. Tomorrow the offices reopen.

If it's a little sad, says Muhlbach aloud, loud enough that the next-door cat pauses to look toward him, then finishes the sentence to himself: if it's a little sad, well, at least the children have been satisfied. Sugar plums and peppermint canes — these they anticipate. Candles and tissue stars and reindeer dancing down the blue north wind — all of this they discover, for it is Christmas to them. Nor could you tell them different, assuming there was a purpose. They'll find another side to Christmas soon enough. Or is it for ourselves that we remark this day? Once each year we attempt to recall the first solemn joy of biting a candy stick as hard as a chicken bone. At all events, this festival has come to us again. Now it closes.

Muhlbach, settling the gloves against his fingers, walks deliberately, with a thoughtful expression, between the soggy drifts of snow. There is no one else in sight.

At the second corner he pauses, extends an arm beneath the street light to look at his watch. Six-fifteen. Six-fifteen precisely! There is nothing to indicate the annoyance he feels. Within five minutes the bus will appear, another ten minutes and he will be at Eighty-third Street. Therefore he will reach his destination just when he is expected, as though he had calculated his arrival to the moment. But, of course, they expect him promptly; they know him. They realize that he is never late, never early.

Six-fifteen and a spattering of seconds. It would be nice, thinks Muhlbach, if just once the bus might not be on time; I'd have something to say, an excuse to make. As it is, I've no excuses, no apologies, no debts. I suppose I should ask for nothing more. I'm well off, in good health. I am not threatened in any way, unless it is by the knowledge of how quickly time passes. Very little happens to me. Seldom does anyone inquire how I am, they assume I must be fine. No one asks how business is going, not more than once do they ask. Who cares to know the details of yesterday's transaction? Would you be particularly interested in the clauses of a policy worked out this past week between Metropolitan Mutual and Algonquin Savings and Loan? Ah, I see, someone just now has called you to the telephone. Well, some other time, he concludes, addressing the street light.

Across the way a door opens, but no one steps outside; he hears music and laughter before it closes. Now the silence is profound.

The bus is not in sight. He wonders if the noise of its engine will carry to him before it turns the corner. Or has the bus a flat tire? Is it stuck in a snowdrift? In any case, he thinks, the bus will be late, thank God, and so shall I.

Six-seventeen, almost.

Who'll be there? A small gathering, Dolly has insisted, nothing presumptuous. But that could mean—let's see, last year she assured me of this with some similar phrase, but there were sixty guests. Still, a crowd means anonymity; I can leave early, if I choose. Who'd miss me? However, she did say this would be for supper, meaning there won't be more than ten or twelve. Eula will be there, no doubt, she's a close friend of Theodore. Then, too, she's after me, no mistake, though I should think that by now she'd have given up. Is it specifically me that Eula wants, or am I just a suitable candidate? Perhaps I should ask. Either way, I've had enough marriage for a while. That's not the truth: ours was richly arranged, a medieval tapestry, ornate patterns of each coming and going, bugles from afar. The prince arrives, the queen departs. Stags, hounds and cats, and Greasy Joan to keel the pot. That life was more plentiful than this, I've not had half enough. Be honest. But how would it be with Eula? Certainly it's marriage that she wants, passionately desires; and if I am to be the necessary adjunct without which she cannot achieve this blessed state—if I am that but nothing more—could I not benefit even so?

Ah, here it comes. No, not the bus. A truck! A truck is driving along this isolated, snowbound street. How strange! At this hour, in this place, altogether strange. He watches the truck turn a corner and disappear, looks down at the tread imprinted on the recent snow and finds that he is affected by the strength those tires have registered. Few machines are more convincing than a truck. He feels envious of the driver, who knows not merely the direction he is traveling, but why.

As to the supper, who'll be there? Eula Cunningham by reason of the mysterious, or not so mysterious, conspiracy of womankind; yes, Eula will be present, very much present, solid as sausage firmly wrapped in satin, as ripe as last Sunday's gardenia. The Forsyths, probably. If so, all right; if not— A dark fleet shape, a bird, perhaps, twists violently overhead and is gone. Muhlbach wonders if it may have been some midwinter hallucination. No sensible creature, he reflects, would leave its nest.

He looks once again at his watch, looks to the end of the lifeless, snowy street. The night is immense, the earth turns evenly on its course. Voices float down the river wind.

Motionless beneath the streetlight he hears, but does not wish to, as though they stood next to him, a woman talking with a man. Such a feeling of segregation rises in him that he grinds his heel on the ice. Reaching out a gloved hand, he slaps the metal post as militantly as though he wore a gauntlet. How useless, how foolish; he is startled by his own act and wonders that any man such as himself, long used to self-control, can be simply turned to abstract gestures. Anyone observing him—what must they think? Here is a man handsomely muffled in an expensive overcoat, scarfed and hatted sans reproach, patiently standing at the bus stop, who, for no evident reason, reaches forth and smacks the streetlight. There's no doubt that such a man is mad, no doubt at all.

Very well, he thinks, I am mad. I am damned and I am mad. What next? One supper party follows another. Why do I accept?

He thinks of the previous night, remembering the squandered hours. Worse than merely squandered, how altogether disagreeable that evening was! Insults enough for twenty. It might have been a plot, except that plots imply some basic logic. No, it is just the nature of that couple; they might be archetypes of the coming era. Katherine's interminable narrative of the doctor's visit—the rectal thermometer—a gross anecdote at any time, why did she choose to tell it during the meal? Yes, all of us are mad. It's that, or else I'm out of joint, he thinks. Do I belong to another age? I might have lived more at peace in the tranquil humors of some Edwardian salon where men got to their feet half-religiously each time a lady entered. I think that may be so, and my quotidian difficulties are simply mine. It is I who am at fault. It's the fashion nowadays to speak of anything at all, under any circumstance. Now it's not poor taste to speak of physical examinations while your listeners are at supper. Thermometers, bedpans, sexual encounters, ad infinitum.

Six twenty-one, and Muhlbach smiles. The bus *is* late. He stamps his feet to learn if they are freezing; it is colder than he thought when he first stepped out the door. But no, stamping causes them to sting a little, that's all. His thoughts return to last night's supper, to the abominable tablecloth—it had not been pressed after it was washed, and that was many meals ago. Is this the newest sophistication? Stains, ashes, dirty napkins, broken furniture, what's the sense of it? Is it that Katherine doesn't care? Or that she chooses in this manner to debase herself and, by implication, her husband?

Muhlbach glances up. There's the bus.

Once aboard, he settles himself by a window, stretches his legs beside the heating vent, and looks about. There are no other passengers. Well, this is luxury indeed, a private bus. The driver did not speak while he was paying the fare, not even the expected Merry Christmas, but there is no sense of animosity. We will ride along in silence, very good. It's a splendid way to travel.

Muhlbach looks out the window. Trees, colored light bulbs, houses. The bus is quiet and it is warm. He begins to wish that he might go riding all night long; he is overcome with respect for the grace and majesty of this bus that voyages through the snowy waste beneath two omnipotent wires. Who could have devised such an excellent machine!

Stuyvesant Avenue, the intersection. A red signal dangles above the arctic. Not a car in sight, but still we must wait. How marvelously red, how powerfully red, is the light. No doubt it is true that habit dulls the edge of perception; there are things we seldom notice. How many times have I waited for this light? Yet only now, for the first time, as though I always had been blind, have I seen its color. Magically, it is green! Nor have I ever seen a lighted glass one tenth so green.

The bus rolls forward and it seems to pull itself carefully around the corner to Seventy-ninth Street. Muhlbach leans back, feeling the resistance of the scarred leather seat, and shuts his eyes.

He thinks of Katherine's silver gown and wonders how she contrived to get inside it. There's a chance that Dominic wrapped it around her like a flag about a skeleton and unraveled her when the last guest had gone. Her outer elegance was grotesque, if not worse, beside the filthy table. Dominic and Katherine, formidably sophisticated, referring to this holiday as the People's Midwinter Festival, exchanging presents one day early so that on Christmas Eve their guests cannot help but feel somewhat bourgeois. Yet, what is the point of this? And his thoughts return insistently to the stained, rumpled tablecloth. Having eaten upon it only last night, still he has trouble believing that it was not a foul dream.

But take the apple. More indescribable than soiled linen. Resting loosely on the table, associated with nothing, an apple that somehow had been dirtied, as though gravy had been spilled on it, or it had fallen to the floor and rolled through the poodle's mess.

Muhlbach, frowning as the breath from his nostrils faintly steams the window, tries to discover some logic in the previous night, but cannot. There was chaos, no sense of preparation. One would say that Dominic and Katherine had not been expecting guests. And further, that their rooms revealed as much as her metallic sheath. It must be, he thinks, that I am no longer at ease in this world, at home only with the dead. Like Goethe, perched far back in the limbs of the family tree, I find that I take on a certain Teutonic, stiff-legged excellence.

Yes, that may be. But is it unreasonable to feel insulted by such a reception? How difficult to remain civil in the face of low affronts. What is man's sensibility, if not to be employed, if not to generate response? I half believe I might prefer a deft, deliberate insolence; at least some malediction worth reply. But this! Oh, this was common. These must be the peasants of our age that live within glass walls, surrounded by symbols of their pigs and chickens. I wonder if the least and sourest medieval serf could show such disrespect.

And he next considers an oddly baked pie, fallen to a stagnant puddle, watery and rancid, a squalid plate of pumpkin that was presented as a dessert.

Think of the children, two boys, growing toward cruelty with the approval of their father. Was it not shameful that Dominic should be amused by their latest prank? They went fishing on the beach, but for gulls instead of fish. The trick is this: one baits a hook and casts it on the sand. Presently a gull comes waddling up, looks stupidly all around, scoops the bait and starts to fly away. Then one sets the hook, the gull flies desperately higher and the game begins.

So, these future pillars of the community have outwitted a gull. Naturally the bird was killed. Not that it will be missed; one must assume that ten thousand gulls each day meet a death at least as painful. Perhaps it is the dense levity of Dominic that makes the incident as embarrassing as it is disgusting. In regard to the boys, they might even be more intelligent than mandrills. Who can say? They are, according to both parents, "real kickers"—whatever that may signify. Why do Katherine and Dominic depend on such expressions?—slovenly argot more appropriate to their juvenile siblings. The speech of Dominic is interchangeable with that of Katherine. One cannot tell the man from the woman by the words they use. And both affix themselves in a rather maggoty way to the current phrase; they would not stoop to the glib patois of six months past, and indeed it does change that quickly, as though language were a style of jazz. The word "hep" has transmogrified to "hip," and whoever says "hip" must be regarded as "hep," although anyone who speaks the word "hep" is regarded with contempt. That is, such individuals could not be "hip." As though it mattered. But so be it, and to Katherine and to Dominic all this seems to matter very much, very much indeed. Gasser, gassy, gas. Well, and what else? Recalling these fatuous malaprops is tedious, remembering them spoken is insufferable. When their currency is peeled away, lo!—here is yawning vacancy.

What else? He thinks of the aged white poodle beneath the dining room table, shaking its rhinestone collar and coughing up food.

The half-eaten licorice deposited in his lap by Katherine's youngest child, the get of previous marriage; and each indignity suffered by a guest is called amusing.

But most of all he finds that he resents the filthy tablecloth; of the many strange and incomprehensible vilifications, this was the worst. For the cloth is the symbol of hospitality.

It would be charitable, he thinks, to remind myself that Dominic and Katherine are not malicious, only imperceptive, just that and nothing more. But I cannot be certain. Years ago there were occasions when my parents were invited out and I invited to accompany them; it seems to me that from the first I knew that we were being honored. That is why I never objected when my mother instructed me to get washed and dressed. Nor did it matter, at least to me, if my suit was bare; it was clean, and my mother had it pressed. In the same way, I think, our hosts were careful to honor us. When we said good night we were not bewildered. All in all, it may have been no great measure, but it did possess a dignity that I have yet to find among these people. Last night, full of talk and smoke, they did not walk with me to the door. I accepted this as though I were a derelict, but I would have liked them to stand together just inside the door and, holding a candle overhead, say the night is dark and storm clouds gather, yet God will watch over you and fare you well.

Perhaps they do mean well; in these times it is hard to say. The miracle is that we are not more unbalanced. There was, in the first place, and do not forget this, an invitation. What if their motives were muddled, what grant have I to conclude they are not pure enough? Is the marriage decomposing like their filthy home?

Six twenty-eight. And at this moment he feels the bus skidding. The ponderous machine arches toward the curb. Silently, with a shock as though the earth had trembled, it stops. The driver's cap sails graciously off his head and a cascade of snow shaken from a maple tree thunders against the roof. The driver leans down from the seat to pick up his cap—that's the important thing, the cap. Then, turning around, he inquires if his passenger is all right.

Muhlbach nods, too startled to speak.

She's kind of slippery tonight, the driver says apologetically.

Yes, says Muhlbach, recovering. Yes, it is, isn't it!

Away they go, shooting a yellow light as though the driver wishes to demonstrate that the accident has not spoiled his nerve.

Well, there's a topic. Though if tonight's supper is as frenetic as Dolly's previous affairs it won't be necessary to speak a word. It may be more of a carnival than a supper.

All at once Muhlbach gives up. Sickened by the artifice of Katherine and Dominic, a trifle shocked by the accident, the discipline of a lifetime slithers away—grotesque ideas crowd eagerly into his brain: as though from some remote belvedere he gazes pensively across the water to an island swarming with leaping, gesticulating monstrosities. Figures out of lost centuries are reveling, and why not! They are as real as the usual world. Reflectively stroking his chin, Muhlbach observes the scene, knowing quite well that the island is his brain, the monsters his desperate thoughts released, soon to be summoned underground again, there to struggle against their chains and mutter in the night. Now they are free. He watches them; he is neither surprised nor alarmed by their liberty—they are isolated and cannot swim. He sees one glare madly at the rippling surface, feels his vitals contract. Has one learned? But the dwarf flings up its hands, shrieks and goes bounding back into the dance: Muhlbach realizes that he has just then drawn a heavy breath. He sinks against the seat, eyes half-shut. Roasted sheep, a camel, veiled women, tambourines, jugglers, huge Negroes capering and hooting with laughter, acrobats furiously somersaulting across the fire—but now, as if it were dawn, they fade, retreat, the gibbering and howling grows less distinct, the flames have shrunk, the sky in the east is violet. Light sparkles through a window.

The bus has stopped again.

Muhlbach, looking toward the front, discovers another passenger, bundled to the ears in a raccoon coat. From the bottom of this coat protrudes a pair of red rubber boots. Mildly curious, he watches. Yes, it is indeed a girl, mascaraed eyes and pale pink lipstick. She does not appear to notice him, but seats herself across the aisle. He continues to look at her. He cannot imagine why she is alone; a quality about her indicates some need for male companionship. She would be impressed by college boys, would dream of being on the stage. Is she en route to a lover? Could she be a chorus girl just now starting off to work? She is possibly nineteen, though it is hard to guess because so little of her is visible, and most of that is painted. Or perhaps she is a student at home for the holidays. He studies her profile, which is both delicate and resentful; the grottoes of sex may already have tainted her spirit. She turns to look directly at him, hatred gleaming in her crystal eye. She stands, without a word, quickly walks down the aisle to be near the driver.

Muhlbach resumes looking out the window, but sees nothing; he knows that if he had so much as said hello to her he would have been in danger. The humiliation is poisonous; it clings like a roach crawling up his sleeve. What have I done? he asks himself. What forces have met to build such a nation as this? Is it my fault that the pleasure of the trip has been destroyed? Of what am I guilty? He stares at his hands, mildly folded in his lap, regarding himself as the most respectable of men. I have violated nothing, he thinks. All my life I have represented civilization, now I am threatened. I have been touched and warned. She has ordered me to hold my eyes averted; if I do not, I risk a serious penalty. One word to the keeper of the bus: this man has been molesting me. Then what? Is my reputation so precarious? Must it balance on the equanimity of each strange woman?

Angrily, suffocated by this condition, he glares along the aisle, but sees nothing more than he did at first—the enormous coat. That and the shining hair. Her head is turned aside in order to conceal the contour even of her cheek. Yet the silence is a charged, living oath; her thought is bent against him. I have only to make one gesture, he reminds himself; this callow child has power enough to finish me.

Presently he begins to wonder: how differently does she see him? He gazes at his reflection in the window—at the translucent face which comes and goes, dependent on passing lights. Say this is a stranger's face, what is there? No beard, no badge of individuality, no suggestion of a bacchanal. Here sits a man some forty years of age who might be a research chemist, or a physician, appropriately dressed for a winter night, spectacles fixed firmly on a bony, ascetic nose, the nose of a librarian or of a Jesuit. There's nothing to see, nothing. One might guess that such an ordinary man puts in his days at Metro Mutual.

So that is all she could have found. Or did I speak to her? Have I been so preoccupied that, not knowing what I did, I spoke? Without meaning to, I might have spoken. But I know I'd have heard my voice, certainly I would have heard myself. In fact, I've done that before. So I didn't speak, she loathes me because I have looked at her too steadily. How subtle are the senses. This suggests I should be cautious. But halfway to the grave can any man afford such diffidence?

Muhlbach reaches inside his coat, feeling the way clumsily because of his gloves, and finds the travel brochure that he has been carrying about for several weeks. He unfolds it and looks at the map of North America, no bigger than a postcard. The map is colored like a rainbow. Honduras is the color of a tangerine, Mexico is lemon yellow. Guatemala stands out magnificently, as pink as coral. Guatemala appears by far the handsomest and most attractive of these central nations; all routes converge on Guatemala. Muhlbach studies the local map. Antigua. Lake Atitlán. Tajumulco. Puerto Barrios. There's no doubt that Guatemala is the place to go. And so easy to reach. Only three hours by air from New Orleans, four hours from Houston or Los Angeles.

Contemplating this waxy advertisement, he wonders why he picked it up. Because it was available? Because while walking through the lobby of the Bergmann after a particularly stultifying business lunch he saw it, brighter than a fresh flag at the ends of the earth?

Well, the climate in Guatemala is marvelous. Ask anyone who has been there. The highlands with an altitude of five thousand feet enjoy a year-round temperature in the seventies. The traveler will be comfortable in a lightweight coat or sweater in the evening. The exchange of money is simple since the units of Guatemala correspond to those of the United States, the quetzal on a parity with the dollar. Language is no problem. Although Spanish is the language of Guatemala, English is widely spoken and every employee of the Bergmann El Mirador is bilingual. Tourist cards may be obtained through all airlines serving the area. This and a smallpox vaccination are the only documents you need. Should you be traveling on business, a passport and visa will be required.

Muhlbach studies a photograph of a typical room at El Mirador in Guatemala City. It is decorated in red and saffron with draperies from ceiling to floor, furniture quite modern, flowers in a vase, telephone, and a balcony giving out to the famous mountains.

Here is a world of comfort and quiet where tasteful décor blends with contemporary convenience and luxury, with sprightly Central American color and native materials. The dining room offers superb cuisine—from exciting flaming specialties to delicious native dishes—all expertly prepared by master chefs from carefully selected foods. In the evening, romantic Latin music and entertainment set the mood for a wonderful night of relaxing, listening, and dining. A wonderful experience in hotel living awaits you in this picturesque country of timeless heritage. Luxuriously furnished guest rooms, de luxe and quiet, away from the bustle of the city. The colorful cosmopolitan bar serves your favorite beverages prepared with the finest liquors. You'll want to prolong your stay in this welcome retreat from daily cares.

He examines other pictures. The private banquet hall, bleak and rectilinear, as though previous to remodeling it had been used for storage. Its murals have a calculated look. The cocktail lounge, with swollen red leather seats and a silver framed painting of a matador on one knee narrowly eluding a prodigious black bull. The bartender wears a jacket with huge lapels; morosely he gazes toward the camera. Beside the swimming pool a waitress in native costume delivers drinks to a handsome young Nordic couple, striped umbrellas in the background. Finally there is a panorama of the central dining room, but there are not quite enough diners; it has the desolate air of all dining rooms in all resort hotels off season.

The bus slows down, skidding a little, and Muhlbach, very sensitive now to this motion, glances toward the driver as the surest indication of whether they are headed for another accident. But the driver does not look tense, just watchful.

Muhlbach puts his face to the window and discovers that he has ridden three blocks too far. He pulls the cord, gets off—it is much colder now—and crosses the street. It will be a frosty walk back to Eighty-third but probably quicker than waiting for another bus. Only then he remembers the malevolent girl. It is a relief to be away from her; chances are they'll never meet again. It would, in fact, be awful if they should.

Six-forty, he notes the time, and begins his walk.

I could arrange to go, he thinks. I could exchange the dollar for the quetzal. I could take a room at El Mirador.

He waits for several cars to pass, then crosses deliberately against the light. A few flakes of snow twirl in front of him, as pristine as any that fell on Walden Pond. A siren in the distance; but the waves are long, diminishing. By the time he has come to Eighty-fourth he is aware of the silence and listens to his shoes grind the salt that somebody has tossed along the sidewalk.

Brownstone apartments look alike; he pauses to search for the number, slowly wanders down the street, squints against the gathering snow. It has been a year since he was in this neighborhood, yet it is close enough that he might have walked over here one idle evening.

There's the number. There are lights and moving silhouettes on the second floor. Cautiously he goes up the steps, settling each foot; new snow has an innocent look but underneath there might be a skin of ice.

At the entrance he hesitates, knowing that he has been followed by a woman. It is a coincidence, of course; whoever she is, she is merely going the same direction, so he has not looked back. But now he turns around and is astonished to see the raccoon coat. Even from this distance he can tell that she is watching him. She stops walking and pretends to hunt for something in her purse. Muhlbach is suffused with rage. Why is she following him?

With his thumb he presses the button and, stamping his feet, waits for the outer door to open. When it does he quickly steps inside and pushes it shut.

The hall, sumptuously carpeted, smells of radiator heat and of damp woolens as though someone had entered just a moment before.

He removes his gloves, slapping them together although they are dry, folds them and slips them into his pocket, takes off his coat and then his hat and scarf, crosses the hall and rings for the elevator. Evidently someone upstairs is holding the elevator because it does not arrive.

He frowns at himself in the rococo mirror, annoyed by the wait; whoever it is upstairs probably is chatting with a friend.

Just then the front door springs open and Muhlbach sees her in the mirror: at the same instant she sees him. Her face shows no surprise, only bitterness set upon her features. It is plain that she knows—having realized it sooner than he—that they both are invited to this party. Yet even now this knowledge has not softened her; if anything, she looks more furious and suspicious than before.

Muhlbach turns away from the mirror, rings again for the elevator. She stands just inside the door, waiting. They are as far apart as they can be within the confines of the narrow entrance.

It must be my age, he decides. That is the reason she hates me. If I were ten years younger, she might have smiled.

Down comes the elevator and halts with a mechanical thump. The cage slides open all of itself. Marvelous indeed is the prescience of machinery. Muhlbach stands aside. She steps in without a word, as though he did not exist, enveloped by a cloud of hostility. He steps in and a moment later the magical cage encloses them. We are, he thinks, a lion and a tigress being transported to the circus.

The elevator halts again, the cage rumbles back and they are released.

Along the corridor side by side, with nothing to say to each other, and so they reach the apartment very much as though they were man and wife. Muhlbach solemnly touches the rectangular gold button and once again they wait, transfixed by still another closed door. What if it does not open? What then?

Moments go by. What is the magic phrase? This must be the place. God help me, he thinks, if I'm mistaken. He is careful not to look at her. If she intended to come here, why did she ride past the stop? My own reason was simple enough—I forgot. But it's unlikely she did the same. She rode beyond Eight-third Street for a purpose and I can think of nothing except that she did not want to get off first, afraid that I might follow her. How much farther would she have traveled in order to lose sight of me? Yet here we are; this must be a curiosity she could have done without. As for me, I'd say the same.

This door is opened by a maid. The hostess is not far behind, Dolly, à la mode with pearls and diamonds. Stretching forth both wrinkled, maculated hands, she cries out harshly, like an elderly blue heron rising through the cypress glades: Lambeth, dear! Do come in! I see you two have met.

There seems no point in contradicting her. Then, too, she's right, says Muhlbach to himself. It's true we've met. So let us enter as a couple, and never were two more estranged. I suspect we'll search out different corners.

First there are a dozen introductions, whoever is unfortunate enough to be close by.

Sandy Kirk. Ah, but you know each other, of course. I'm utterly absent tonight. And Dee Borowski.

Yes, we've met before.

Already she's going, beginning to sidle away.

Lambeth, sweet, help yourself to the food. We're doing it buffet this year. And do try to scare up my Theodore. He was here not a minute ago.

I will. I'll find my way.

Do you know Eula?

Certainly. We're old friends.

Marvelous! And this is Jack Baxter.

How do you do. Have we met somewhere?

Yes, yes. Quite so.

The British auto salesman. Of course. Jack Baxter. Strange, I remember nothing about him but the face and the accent. It was in September or October that we met, a situation very much like this. The professional Englishman right down to the mustache and tooth. I wonder if I might ask how many Austins he's sold since then.

Jack Baxter, smiling, wanders away just as Eula returns with a drink and something to eat.

Tell me, Eula, the personage across the room who is wearing the scarlet vest, who is he? With the silky Van Dyke a bit discolored by nicotine and the gold chain slung across his paunch, with a voice that rumbles like a Napoleonic cannon so that we hear him under the chattering of two dozen voices, who wears a seal ring like a brass knuckle, and lightly depends on a carved ivory cane, tell me now, Eula, what's that fellow up to?

I thought you knew, she murmurs. I though everyone knew.

I do not, says Muhlbach brusquely, peeved by this assumption. I never have laid eyes on such a man.

Few of us have, Eula confides, leaning closer. But still, I thought you'd know. He's the raison de etra, so to speak.

Come, come, Eula. Is this Beelzebub? You've lost me. What's the fellow's name?

That, she whispers, is A. Telemann Veach. Which implies that one should be knowledgeable enough to recognize a lion.

Well, well! Muhlbach answers. So Dolly has bagged a new celebrity. Does she keep a chart upstairs on which these conquests are listed? Still, it's not a wicked hobby, no worse than collecting postage stamps.

Yes, Eula is saying like an echo, that is he.

And just who is A. Telemann Veach? He does not look like the radio repairman. What's his game? Is he a high diver? Does he escort maiden schoolteachers through Africa? I cannot quite imagine Mr. Veach doing much of anything nine-to-five. Be good enough to tell me, for I dislike being kept in ignorance.

Eula is reluctant to come straight out with information.

Perhaps he is wealthy?—the grandson of the man who invented something, say the hairpin or the paper clip. And that is why he is entitled to wear a scarlet vest.

He's *quite* the literary figure.

Indeed? replies Muhlbach, glancing again toward the great panjandrum who, unfortunately, just then happens to be looking at him. Embarrassed, Muhlbach turns half away and promptly is irritated with himself for doing so—the movement seemed to indicate a certain deference. What sort of figure? he asks. By that I mean, is Mr. Veach a critic for some august journal? Is he a professor of Literature?

Eula gazes up at him with dismay. Why, I thought you knew, she repeats. I thought surely you'd have him placed by now. Mr. Veach is the author of numerous books, many of which have been translated into foreign languages. Everybody knows who he is.

This is a point of dispute, thinks Muhlbach, but says nothing. Then he cannot resist a small temptation. Tell me, that initial, what does it stand for? What is Mr. Veach concealing?

Eula falters, uncertain. I believe it stands for Abercrombie.

Impossible! Out of the past swarm those fearful names, names to haunt a boy during his climb to eminence, names no one forgets. And all at once Muhlbach discovers that he feels no further animosity toward Abercrombie Veach. There's a man in anguish. Shades of Fauntleroy. Curses on every parent.

I'd like to meet him, I think.

He's quite rude.

Do you know him?

We were introduced just before you arrived. By the way, who is Lambeth?

I haven't the slightest idea.

Stop being silly. I want to know everything about her.

Muhlbach doesn't answer; the thought of discussing Lambeth bores him. Why do you say Veach is rude?

All celebrities are rude. There is something gauche about attracting attention to one's person at the expense of others. How long have you known her?

For many years, since you insist.

Not too many, she's just a child. Ordinarily I believe whatever you say because you have no sense of humor, but now I suspect you of lying.

And Eula continues. Muhlbach does not listen attentively, it is all too familiar. He is aware that in common with the other guests he has conformed to the regulations of the evening, that even the rhythm of his speech has altered, that he has not been quite his true self since he walked through the door. Now, and for a while— already it is nearing eight o'clock—he has committed himself to easy responses, to the exercise of useful platitudes.

Gazing about, munching on the food that Eula has brought, affably nodding whenever she pauses for breath, he observes that there is a schism in the party. It is divided by two magnetic poles. A flash of scarlet proves that Abercrombie attracts one crowd, one cluster of neutrons. But who or what is the force behind this other? Some new delicacy? The anchovy dip? No, it's a person—a diminutive male, a Latin fitted to a pin-stripe suit, with eyes twice brighter than a squirrel's, and a nose like Pinocchio. He smiles, this one, he is obviously agreeable, smiling ever more brilliantly. Could he be a Captain of Industry from the banana latitudes? Now who, Muhlbach demands of Eula, is that? She knows, of course.

Señor Rafael López y Fuentes.

This is altogether too much. Really, this is just a bit unreasonable. In one corner there is Abercrombie Veach, with Señor López y Fuentes opposite. Who—are you paying attention, Eula?—who is *he?*

The ambassador from Honduras.

Not so, according to a nearby voice, interrupting with authority. Señor López y Fuentes is the former Honduran vice-consul, now acting as special representative of the president.

In any case, he is running second to the burly novelist. Muhlbach observes them both, wondering if they are conscious of how they have torn the party. It is hard to tell. Neither glances toward the other. Pride? Apprehension? Does the runner risk a glance over his shoulder? Or to each of them is this a matter of indifference? Each in his own fashion is a celebrity, accustomed to being half surrounded like a rare leopard in a zoo, the one by virtue of his odd accomplishment, the other because he represents a Power. He is, this latter specimen, judges Muhlbach, equal in magnitude to the president of Yale, let's say, or the chairman of the board of a moderately large steamship company. And God's lonely man, the renowned author of numerous novels translated into foreign languages, what is his equivalent? An Olympic middleweight boxing champion? A paroled gangster? A metropolitan disc jockey? The first Sherpa to scale Everest? Well, who knows?

Eula, what is your frank opinion of Abercrombie's books? Ah, I see. Very little time for reading, to be sure. Well, then, what are the titles of them? Ah, yes, of course, I'll do so. Yes, no doubt the librarian could give me a complete list.

From across the room Lambeth has been watching. During the instant that they look into each other's eyes he learns that she is no longer hostile; it must be that she had made inquiries, has been told he is not Bluebeard. So she has been thinking over the situation, appraising him. Muhlbach cannot restrain a moment of fantasy. What might happen if they meet again. But they will not. Such a relationship would be blocked by more than age; indeed, that never was the cause. It's altogether possible that one fine day Lambeth will go to live with a man older than himself, each to indulge their heart's desire. Silks, gowns, and a box at the theater for her; the limpid sexuality of youth for him. No, it is not a problem of age, he reflects. When I was twenty I met her, but she found me dull, dull and a little strange, my spine too rigid when we went dancing, my conversation clamped. I would talk of astronomy or of Hegel. It's not much wonder that I lost.

Around him the people gather and disperse; he speaks to those who speak to him. Eula seldom leaves his side.

She is almost my interpreter, he continues to himself. I'm like a traveler in this place, who understands a different language. If I recite a poem of Asia, the new moon lying on her side, what does Asia know of me?

Then all at once, as if summoned by a thought, A. Telemann Veach bulks overhead, far more portly than any human has a right to be, stinking of cigars and gin, one blistering blue eye trained on Muhlbach, the other eye wandering.

You're in the market, announces Veach, and it carries weight. I want to talk to you.

Does he mean the stock market? Says Muhlbach: I'd guess you have me confused with someone else.

What's your trade?

Metropolitan Mutual. I'm considered an expert on corporate fire insurance. Here, let me give you my card. Feeling absurd, moved by a force he does not understand, he offers the card.

Veach without a glance tucks Muhlbach's card into a vest pocket; obviously it will soon find a home in the ash tray. Eula was right; the man is rude. He discovers that she has disappeared. What did Veach say to her? Or did he make an obscene gesture in response to some prosaic question? It's not unlikely.

The minute you came in I figured you for a broker.

You're not too wrong. I was, at one time.

Veach stops scowling. Good! What do you know about a stock called Taggo?

I'm not familiar with it.

That's what I figured. Some son of a bitch has been touting me. Veach grinds the tip of his cane into the Persian rug. You make a few bucks and they start crawling out of the woodwork. Jesus Christ, if it ain't one thing it's sure as hell another. You wouldn't believe what I put up with. Last week it was an abandoned silver mine in Arizona. The metal's there, this nance tells me, only there's water in the shaft. They need five grand to pump out the water. Five grand to pump out the water! Bull.

What information have you on this Taggo stock?

They make a labeling gadget they sell in the dime store. Sell millions of them. They don't pay any dividend. I got three wives to support, what am I gonna do with a stock that won't pay me a dividend? It'll go up, this tout swears on a Bible. You never heard of it, eh? I'm not surprised. What did you say your name was?

Muhlbach.

Is that a fact! There used to be a Muhlbach's grocery store in my neighborhood when I was a kid. You know, I don't belong in this crowd. I've gone around the world twice but I still don't belong. Veach glowers at a woman who is about to approach; she takes a step backward, staring at him uneasily. Veach tugs his beard.

Aw, he says, I'm from a little town. Every once in a while I think maybe I ought to try it again, but hell, I wouldn't make out any better there, maybe worse. It's been so long. He shrugs, displaying his great fat back to another admirer. God damned sycophants, he mutters. You wouldn't believe what I put up with. The only decent thing that happened to me all year was the Horizon Book Club. He inspects Muhlbach to see if this brings a reaction. You don't know my stuff, do you? Christ, I can tell. You're a morning-paper man, financial section, editorial, no comics. That's about the size of you. Sure, sure. You read murder mysteries?

Occasionally, as a soporific.

That's what I figured. I know all about you. You haven't read an honest book in the last five years.

Muhlbach answers that he does little reading, contemporary works especially.

What's the matter with contemporaries?

How does one explain? Say that today's authors seem tortured, frenetic, and shallow? Empty of *fond*? Say that they do not know how to write of the world and its magic, but merely of themselves? Say that they are, in a word, tiresome.

This interests Veach. I'll be a son of a bitch, says he.

Muhlbach, stimulated, decides to continue. When he reads, it is apt to be the essays of Hazlitt, or perhaps a novel as richly variegated and weathered as an autumn leaf. In these books he discovers dignity and grace, qualities now scorned; eloquence, chastity of mind, intellect, a conviction never doubted that on tomorrow the sun will rise, and courtesy. These things exist, old authors knew them. Now they have been abandoned. Now it is stylish to shock the reader, but therein lies a fallacy; for in these times all sensitive men have been benumbed, and no further shocks are conceivable. In any case, says Muhlbach, he seldom reads, but listens to music, when there is time enough. Possibly music and reading serve a similar need. Haydn, Handel, Grillparzer, Lully, there are so many, each as remunerative as his neighbor.

That's all right. Hell, says Abercrombie Veach, music's fine. You don't have to read.

Does he know of Telemann? Probably. He's not a fool. If he doesn't care for music he must have acquaintances who do, who would have given him for some birthday the Passions, the suites for woodwinds, strings and horns, the sonatas of his namesake.

Hell, maybe you're better off, I mean it. There's too much garbage in print. I know, I'm responsible for enough of it. Take these dumb broads—he gestures at the nearest woman—they buy any sort of crap. But I work on something I can be proud of, you know what, Muhlbach? They don't touch it! I've had three novels and a travel book on the national lists, over a million copies so far on one of them, and not one worth the time it takes to scan the jacket blurb. I made so much money you wouldn't believe it. Gross, not net. After the government's finished you might as well be a drugstore clerk. I've hired a dozen lawyers but the Feds still crucify me. It's unbelievable. Also, try chopping up your royalties among three wives and count what's left. It wouldn't feed a terrier for a week. Anyhow, Jesus Christ, I guess I do better than most. I don't know, I just don't know. Veach heaves himself around uncertainly. He upends his cane and seems to be examining the tip. You by chance got a cigar?

Muhlbach shakes his head.

I could send one of these old nannies down the street to fetch one, but I'm sick of the whole reeking schmuck. Listen, it's a god-damn funny business, Muhlbach, when a man can work his heart out and be ignored. Take these harlequins that are supposed to be critics. Critics! Eastbay minnow fishermen. They wouldn't know an original work of art if it grabbed them by a nipple. You know how they refer to me? The aging challenger. I spent four years on a novel, revised it, rewrote the son of a bitch till my eyeballs felt like bubble gum. Did the critics realize what was in that book? Confused! That's what they decided. Can you imagine? Mr. Veach's latest attempt is, to put it kindly, confused. How the hell do they know? Three-fourths of them would get confused by McGuffey.

This is what he wants, thinks Muhlbach. The approval of critics, that is what he needs. Money and publicity—aren't they enough? He has both, more than other men dare to anticipate. Why should he be suffering?

Mister, you're what the Frogs call a poseur, says Veach almost gently; and Muhlbach looks at him in absolute astonishment.

Sure, sure. The muscles of your face give you away, tell all about you. And how you stand, too erect. Well, stalk around like a god-damned bloodless statue if you want, that won't save you. Nothing saves you. Women, friends, money, nothing's strong enough. Listen, nobody gives a damn about you any more than they give a damn about me or about the Pope. Nobody cares. Once you're dead, you're through. Believe it. But I don't know, hell, I got a view of Central Park and I stand there by the hour diddling my whiskers, so maybe it's all the same. Veach stabs the rug with his ivory cane, thrusting here and there, half-mortal blows. Then, as though still on the subject of royalties, he announces he'll go through the buffet again. With no other salutation than a meditative belch he limps toward the array of silver platters and bowls.

Eula promptly reappears. She has not been visible, but it is clear that she was nearby and has been waiting for the author to go away. She does not mention him, Lambeth is on her mind. She has been gone for perhaps fifteen minutes and has come back with a complete dossier.

Lambeth wears a size ten dress and has been seen shopping at Gimbel's. She attended City College, studied dramatics, did not do well, left after three semesters. Lambeth is twenty years old, her last name is Brent. She once lived for several months in Greenwich Village. She was engaged this past summer to a naval aviator who was killed at Pensacola; they already had made the first payment on a tract house near the Anacostia naval station where he was soon to be assigned. Lambeth is a heavy drinker. Indeed, she is now in the kitchen, en route to being drunk, talking to the servants, who are embarrassed. But getting back to essentials, Lambeth even at this tender age has a shady reputation. There are rumors that she gave something of a performance at an affair for naval aviators in the Hotel Commodore.

Muhlbach listens with amazement; this is like a recording.

Lambeth's mother is living in Brooklyn Heights, her father died two years ago of a heart attack. He was considerably older than Lambeth's mother. He was in the garment business. He lost a small fortune during the crash of twenty-nine. Lambeth has a sister, eighteen, whose name is Judith, and a brother whose name Eula does not know, who is either fourteen or fifteen and is attending some military school in Wisconsin.

Eula pauses for a gracious sip of bourbon, and continues. Lambeth's eye shadow is by Helena Rubenstein, mascara by Topique. Coiffure by Mister Francis. She goes dancing at the Peppermint Lounge. She is fickle, she is badly spoiled. She wants above all else to become a high-fashion model.

And what is it, Eula, above all else, that you want?

The question is not asked, nor would a response be necessary, for it is obvious. Marriage. Eula is ripe, and ripeness implies a slow descent toward maturation. Under the circumstances, namely that one isn't married, it's hardly a good thing. Statistics are not encouraging. Less than 8 per cent at Eula's present age will marry within the year. This isn't good. Constant endeavor is required to join that fortunate minority. Next year the percentage will be worse. So, press the case, call on past experience. Fill the gentleman's wassail bowl and bring him meat.

These offerings Muhlbach accepts in a neutral spirit. Remarriage someday is not impossible, but now his desire is weak. Nor is the fair Eula a likely prospect, though of course such things are left unsaid, to be divined. That Eula fails to divine them is her principal liability. Perhaps, though, she does recognize his attitude and believes she'll alter it. So much the worse for her. It can't be done.

Nine-thirty. The maid approaches, bearing a tray of odds and ends, the sort of tidbits a cannibal might recognize.

Thank you, no, says Muhlbach. But it seems the tray, at this moment, is not the reason for her approach.

Señor López y Fuentes would like a word with you, sir.

Muhlbach glances across the room. Señor López y Fuentes is not where he was a few moments ago. He is nowhere in sight.

I'm sure you're mistaken.

No, sir. Will you follow me?

The question is hardly a question; Muhlbach looks attentively into her chocolate eye. No expression answers him. Subdued by years of domestic service, her thoughts are utterly concealed. For all the good it would do he might as well address himself to a Kikuyu mask.

This way, sir.

She has taken two steps, positive that he must follow. He does, deeply puzzled. She does not look back. He could follow her through the crowd without his eyes, by the musky scent.

Señor López y Fuentes is standing alone in the corridor and appears nervous. Quickly he smiles, extends his hand.

What does he want? Muhlbach wonders while they exchange names and pleasantries. Does he think I'm a stockbroker? No, he wants me to undertake some diplomatic mission. Why not? God alone knows what intrigues are met at parties such as this. Here he stands, anxious to speak privately. Now, what do I know about Honduras? Nothing. I should be able to remember a little something. I think it was a nest of spies during the war, so near the Canal. There were spies all over Port-au-Prince. That's not far away. What can he want?

Señor López y Fuentes coughs delicately into his fist. What I have to say, he begins, should be regarded as confidential. I hope you will not misunderstand.

Muhlbach nods and waits.

It is not often that I find myself at a loss for words. I am, as possibly you are aware, a member of some slight significance of the diplomatic corps.

Yes.

It seems we have the reputation, deservedly or not, of being not merely discreet but articulate.

True.

I regret that I am a disgrace to our—what is it to be called—profession? Very well. For, as you observe, I am overcome with difficulty in expressing myself.

Muhlbach, gazing down at the fragile, punctilious Latin, feels himself to have grown too tall. He feels large and obvious, as though at this moment he were speaking to some precocious child. I should hate to think that diplomats were never at a loss for words, says he.

Señor López y Fuentes greets this with another smile, but does not reply.

How strange! thinks Muhlbach. He really is uneasy. Whatever it is that he wants, why can't he give me a hint? Then, because they cannot stand there silently, he asks:

Tell me, señor, are you familiar with Guatemala?

Guatemala! the diplomat barks with such rapidity that it becomes scarcely more than a syllable. Yes. Very familiar. Of course. And he smiles again. Guatemala is our neighbor, naturally. Why do you inquire?

Muhlbach finds himself absorbed by the russet gaze, and can think of no answer. What a ridiculous question; he does not know why he asked it. Only an utter fool could reply that he has asked because he happens to have in his pocket a travel folder. Well then, what?

Guatemala is much more extensive than my own country, yet we of Honduras consider size to be of little virtue. For you here in the enormous United States each of our Central American republics must seem tiny. But you should visit and see for yourself the many splendid examples of architecture and other things of which we are so proud. I have enjoyed the splendid beaches of California and also of Florida, for example, when it comes to recreation, but may I assure you, Mr. Muhlbach, they are not more enjoyable than those we possess.

The speech concludes as abruptly as it began. Señor López y Fuentes looks up and down the corridor.

I have wished to speak to you, he murmurs, because I can tell from looking at you that you are a man of the world. Please, don't say a word. Don't protest. Excuse me if I boast, but I have had a great deal of experience in appraising the nature of men. I know without finding inquiries necessary what you are. Please believe, I have asked no one about you. I judge for myself. You are sophisticated. You are unusually intelligent. Above all, you are a man who respects confidences. You have, furthermore—permit me to say this—the most discriminating taste. This is evident not merely in your fashion of dress but becomes unmistakable in your choice of companions. That is to say, I noticed you the first instant you entered the room, preceded by your charming companion.

So subtly is the final reference included that for a moment it does not reveal itself. Muhlbach almost overlooks it. But then, mute with astonishment, he understands. Intrigue, yes. Of the simplest and oldest sort. One might even say that López y Fuentes does, in effect, want him for a diplomatic mission. What he wants is, of course, Lambeth.

You are to be complimented in the highest terms, Mr. Muhlbach. I have no wish to sound extravagant, but rarely if ever have I been privileged to admire a more attractive young girl. You must accept my sincere congratulations as well as my utmost envy.

Thank you, says Muhlbach. How is it that I never guessed? he thinks. How could I have failed to guess? Now I realize, each time I looked at him he was facing the direction where she was.

If I may say so, it is a young girl of this particular type who can ruin a man before he knows what has become of him. It often happens. I do not pretend this is a catastrophe. There is always a certain degree of honor attached to the man who is bold enough to destroy himself for love. In my country such young girls are very much in demand. One may conclude that the Honduran is not unlike the man of sophisticated European circles. Certainly both have the good sense to appreciate Nature's divine creation. I have no fear of saying, because I know you will not take offense, a young girl of this type is enough to drive a man insane, as the expression goes. I wish to congratulate you again.

He seizes Muhlbach by the hand.

Thank you. The dream has popped. Here is reality.

Let me be honest. I tire of pretending to these dowagers that what is of concern to me is the state of our world. Believe this or not, Mr. Muhlbach, I have reached the point where international affairs are to me insuperably boring. I do not care! I wonder if even in the past I have cared. There are times when I do not know. I am like the young man who inherits his father's medical profession, whether or not he has wished to become a doctor. I am, myself, from a family of nobility. My paternal grandfather was a relative of Carlos the Great, and often found himself invited to the palace. Naturally, even as he, I have taken advantage of what opportunities have afforded themselves. It is foolish to do otherwise. Life is difficult, at best. Tell me, this young girl, is she a movie starlet?

I think not.

You think not. To say that you are discreet, Mr. Muhlbach, does not do justice to your many circumlocutions. Surely it is not too much to expect a more revealing answer.

We're not well acquainted.

You and I, Mr. Muhlbach?

No, the girl and I.

It is regrettable that you will not give me information.

I have none to give.

It would please this young girl greatly to know how you are protecting her reputation. In fact, everything. She, too, has perceived that you are a man of integrity, to say the least. One in whom confidence is never misplaced. Otherwise, she would not have taken you for her lover.

Think whatever you like.

I am sorry if I offend you. I would not have approached you on a matter of such intricacy if I had not observed from the beginning how, as we say, love takes wing.

How is that? I don't understand.

Forgive me, but I have observed how seldom you wonder what she is doing, and equally that she pays you slight attention. I therefore have said to myself that nothing ventured, nothing gained, López. It does seem to me that a favor of such insignificance as a young girl's telephone number would not be a serious difficulty.

I think you yourself had better ask her for that number.

You refuse to give it to me?

Let's say that I do not know her number.

Incredible. I have no choice, Mr. Muhlbach, except to salute such gallantry. You understand, of course, how it would be impossible for me to approach a young girl directly. In my position I must not summon her. Nor, unfortunately, am I able to obtain the information that I wish to have while there are others present. You appreciate the ramification?

I do, but I'm afraid I can't help you.

A moment of silence. López shrugs. There are days when nothing goes right.

That she was in the movies, I was positive. She reminds me of aspiring actresses I have known. Now you tell me that she is not.

So I was told.

López y Fuentes regards him carefully.

All at once I find that I believe you, Mr. Muhlbach. I believe that you are not acquainted with this beautiful young girl. I cannot explain to myself why I believe this is the case. He hesitates, and then: Is it possible that she might have accepted roles in moving pictures that are not viewed by the public? Would you know about this?

No, I would not, Muhlbach replies sharply.

Señor López y Fuentes offers a beaming smile. Let us drop this subject, since it embarrasses you. Mr. Muhlbach, your people are distinguished for many things, but among them is not the passion of my people. It's just as well. We are different, yes, and yet we are brothers after all. We do as we must. As for myself, I am so bored by the life that I am forced to lead I would give anything to escape. You have no idea, sir. You cannot begin to guess how I am stiffled.

Stifled?

That's it, thank you. Stifled. Do you speak Spanish?

Very little. Only a few words.

Muy poco. What a pity. We have a most beautiful language.

I'm sure it is.

French, however, is the language one employs to address a young lady. On certain occasions there is no substitute for French. I'm sorry you will not give me the least information.

Her name is Lambeth. Lambeth Brent. She has a brother who is attending military school in the state of Wisconsin and who is reputed to be either fourteen or fifteen years of age. She recently purchased a size ten dress at Gimbel's department store, and the name of her hairdresser is Francis. Possibly these items interest you. Her mother lives in Brooklyn Heights, but I do not know that telephone number either.

Such ill temper, Mr. Muhlbach, does not become you. It is not appropriate. However, I recognize that it is the result not of your passion, but of my own. Accept my apologies. It is plain that you are a sensitive man, that you have resented interrogation. We will drop the subject. Be good enough to let me explain myself, in order to clear the air.

López y Fuentes steps nearer.

What I have wished throughout my life is to become a movie producer. I would give anything for this experience. Anything in the world! However, fortune seems to be against the fulfillment of my desire. By coincidence, do you have friends or close acquaintances in Hollywood?

Not one.

A pity. One hears very much of Hollywood. Confidentially, I am thinking of resigning from my present position in order to go to Hollywood. What do you think? Should it be possible there to form acquaintances who would pave the way?

Muhlbach perceives that López y Fuentes no longer is talking to him, but to himself; answers will not matter. So here again is the dream.

I am not unique, remarks López crisply. What your personal desire might be, sir, I could not presume to say. I am not your patron. But there is something. In this respect we are alike. Life, in my opinion, is just beyond the finger tips.

Muhlbach discovers that the diplomat is holding out his hand. Is it a salutation, or does he wish to say goodbye? Swiftly, sleek and full of smiling purpose, like a nocturnal carnivore López y Fuentes has gone. Is he once again in search of Lambeth? Or has he retreated to the security of the ordered rank, scarred but unrepentant? Five years hence will he be met in Hollywood behind smoked glasses, or in Geneva wearing striped pants?

It's time to leave. It is not late, not long after ten o'clock, but late enough when each hour can be predicted.

Searching out the hostess, Muhlbach says good night. Good night to Eula, too. She is a trifle peevish to see him escape once more, but there'll come another time. Good night to Lambeth, wherever she is; good night in absentia, and may we not meet again. Good night to the famous author, who left the party half an hour before.

Those are good nights enough. And so, having dressed himself for the journey home, he rides down within the gilded cage, springs open the door and stands for a moment on the top step. Overhead the clouds have parted somewhat, hinting at the constellations.

Pulling shut the door behind him, he once more faces the night. I must go, he thinks a little wildly. The year is almost over.

1961

THE UNDERSIGNED, LEON & BÉBERT

L EON, DRESSED in a striped red shirt, white tennis shorts and blue sneakers, sat on the balcony railing and peered through binoculars at two sailboats in the middle of the lake. A puff of smoke appeared beside one of the boats. The other boat veered away.

Bébert reclined on the lavender chaise longue reading a newspaper and occasionally sipping a Ramos Fizz. He was wearing checkered trousers, sandals, sunglasses, and an Italian sport shirt that resembled a fishnet. His lips moved as he read.

"There are times when I honestly believe the sky is falling," he said. "Just listen: 'Militant students today demanded the immediate resignation of Chancellor Dibble.' The *immediate* resignation, if you please. Isn't that the limit? A person would think the students owned the university. Of course I haven't the slightest idea whether their grievances are legitimate or not, but assuming they do have a right to be heard, it seems to me that going to such extremes won't clear the air. I'm the last person on earth to condemn radicals, I've always been such a radical myself. But on the other hand we've got to maintain at least a semblance of respect for authority."

Leon did not answer. Bébert lowered the newspaper and saw that he was still watching the boats.

"Those imbeciles," Leon muttered.

Another puff of smoke appeared. Bébert sat up for a better view.

"It's Clark and I think the other one's McCrindle," Leon said. "Since when has he had a cannon?"

"They were shooting at each other last Tuesday," said Bébert. "I thought at first they were serious, but I believe they're just shooting strips of old rag. I'm sure we'd see geysers of water if they were using cannonballs. However, it certainly is a strange way to amuse yourself. At least that's my opinion." He watched the boats for a few minutes, but then settled back on the chaise longue and continued reading the paper.

"Here's something else. Listen. 'A prehistoric Indian campsite has been discovered near Staunton; however, the real-estate developer who owns the property has refused to allow archaeologists to excavate. He's clearing the land for a series of tract homes and doesn't want bone-collectors, as he calls them, getting in the way of the bulldozers. He ordered them off his property, even though archaeologists say the village is one of the most complete they have ever seen. Massive stoneware, delicate shell beads, human burials, and numerous other artifacts dating back at least five thousand years were unearthed. Now the diggings have been covered with piles of brick and lumber.' I think that's sickening! Why in the world couldn't they have held up construction long enough for the archaeologists to do whatever it is they wanted to do?"

"The reason is the almighty buck."

"Yes, I suppose. I just wish there was some way I could tell that real-estate developer what I think of him. Doesn't it upset you?"

Leon carefully stood the binoculars on the rail. He picked up a can of beer and took a long drink. Then, after wiping his lips, he said, "It's none of my business."

"You're so detached. Nothing excites you."

"That bird in the white leather boots excites me. I think I'll spend the evening at the Po-Po Club. She might come in again."

"Why didn't you speak to her the other night when she smiled at you? I think you missed your golden opportunity."

Leon gazed down the hillside with a thoughtful expression. At last he said, "I assumed she was smiling at somebody at the table in back of us. By the time I realized nobody was in back of us it was too late. Maybe she'll be there tonight, though."

"Perhaps. Perhaps not. Women are notoriously unpredictable. If she attracted me I assure you I wouldn't be so lackadaisical. I'd find out where she lives and phone her."

"I don't know her name."

"Giacomo should be able to tell you. He knows all the habitués."

Leon nodded and took another swallow of beer.

"You may or may not be aware of this," Bébert said critically, "but you're putting on weight."

"I do that when I drink too much," Leon said. "That could be why I've felt sluggish recently."

Bébert turned a page of the newspaper and continued reading.

Leon blinked sleepily. He picked up the binoculars and studied the hillside. He could see into the patio of the Po-Po Club. At the round center table sat a group of tourists. Midge stood beside them with a tray in one hand, apparently taking their orders. Barbara and her cousin from New Brunswick were seated on a bench in the shade. Kozlenko and Saqui were playing chess in the corner. Giacomo's cat was curled up on a flagstone.

Beyond the club, in the triangular park at the center of town, a fat woman wearing a muumuu was leading a child toward the drinking fountain. A pack of dogs, presumably male, were trotting closely behind another dog which turned around every few seconds to snarl at them. Several shaggy teen-agers dressed like birds of paradise lounged on the grass in front of an old man with a long yellow beard who was playing a flute.

Bébert made a clucking sound. "Just listen. 'Conditions at the state hospital for the mentally retarded were described yesterday as being disgraceful. More than six hundred patients are being cared for in a facility equipped for a maximum of three hundred and forty. Many patients are forced to sleep on the bare floor. There are not enough showers and not enough recreational equipment. Additional funds, urgently needed, according to Dr. James E. Lawton, Director, were summarily cut from the budget last January. Governor Burns' press secretary, reached for comment, stated that a blue-ribbon panel, appointed last year to study the situation, had not yet submitted its recommendation.' Isn't that disgusting? Really, it's so true what they say about a committee being a horse put together by a camel, or whatever. It's the other way around, I suppose, but the point is the same. You know what I mean. And why must every committee be referred to as 'blue ribbon'? They don't deserve a ribbon of any color. They never accomplish anything. If ever they do submit a recommendation you can be sure it will be ignored."

Leon shrugged.

"Well, it disturbs *me*," Bébert remarked crisply.

Leon raised the binoculars to examine a jet high above the lake. The plane was headed for Canada. He watched until it disappeared beyond a bank of clouds.

"I could push you right off the edge," Bébert said, "without a qualm. There are times when you are absolutely infuriating."

Leon shrugged and turned around so that he could see into the neighbor's backyard. He focused the glasses on the doghouse.

"You're such a voyeur."

"Whenever possible I get my hands on it," said Leon.

"You spend most of your time loitering at the Po-Po Club. That's hardly 'getting your hands on' anything, it seems to me."

"You waste as much time at the club as I do. Maybe more. You spent all of last weekend there from the minute Giacomo opened the joint Saturday morning. I at least played tennis Sunday afternoon."

"What are you looking at now?"

"That Airedale. He's gnawing on a big bone. He's watching me while he eats it. He thinks I'm going to try to take it away. He's one mean son of a bitch."

Bébert laughed. "I couldn't begin to count the number of times I've heard you use that expression. For once, thank Heavens, it's apropos." He went back to reading the paper.

Leon watched the dog for a while. Then he considered the houses higher on the hill, the trees at the summit, the sky, and another airplane. Finally he resumed his observation of the town.

"Students aren't the only ones," Bébert said thoughtfully. "There are the blacks, as they choose to be called, and there are the whites. Then we have legions of people protesting our Asian policy while others object to the money spent on the moon. And of course others are terribly critical of the welfare program, and birth control, and the destruction of natural resources, and highway planning, and goodness knows what else. It's gotten so I dread reading the paper. If it isn't one thing, it's another."

"What puzzles me," Leon said, "is why the blacks are all of a sudden huffy about being called anything except blacks. They're insulted to be referred to as Negroes. Before that they didn't like to be called Colored. Before that it was a grave insult to say Darky. Before that they didn't want to be called blacks, so we're almost right where we started. It wouldn't surprise me if next year we're supposed to say Darky again. However, that's their problem, not mine."

"It's part of the emerging pattern of national heritage," Bébert said. "But I've always considered a person a person, regardless of race, creed, or religion. For instance, I myself don't mind being referred to as Caucasian, or white, although I suppose I would resent being called a Honky, or whatever the current term of opprobrium is."

"Everybody's jumpy."

"Not you, certainly."

"I may give the appearance of being relaxed but the fact is, I'm a bundle of nerves."

Bébert sniffed. A few moments later he said, "Billy Graham yesterday told a crowd in Madison Square Garden that Jesus may return at any given moment. I'll quote verbatim: 'I've gotten into the habit of asking myself when I go to bed if He is going to arrive during the night. When I wake up in the morning I wonder if He is coming that day.' Well! There's food for thought: I'm scarcely a fundamentalist, but with things going from bad to worse by absolute leaps and bounds he might not be altogether wrong. We just could be on the eve of the Second Coming. I wouldn't be overly surprised."

Leon made a hissing noise and Bébert glanced up with a look of alarm.

"There she is," Leon muttered.

"You scared the wits out of me. Who?"

"That bird in the white leather boots."

Bébert smiled. "Is she performing a striptease in the park?"

Leon hooked one foot around the post to keep himself from falling off the balcony and leaned forward with the binoculars pressed to his eyes.

"She's going into the laundromat."

"While you simply sit here."

"Bébert, did you ever take a close look at that meat? I mean, did you ever get a good look at that stuff?"

"I consider her fat."

Leon did not answer. He hunched on the rail like an eagle and peered at the entrance to the laundromat.

Bébert sipped the Ramos Fizz. He gazed around for a while with a languid expression, a cigarette held lightly in his teeth. Then he turned a page of the paper.

"Well!" he exclaimed. "Now this truly is appalling. Drew Pearson reports that during the Joseph McCarthy era the Madison *Capital Times* in Wisconsin circulated a copy of the Declaration of Independence among a Fourth of July crowd and requested signatures. Of one hundred and twelve people approached, only one agreed to sign his name. Those who refused to sign called the document 'Communistic' and remarked that 'the F.B.I. ought to check up on this sort of thing.' There's a lesson to be learned."

"What is?"

"Why, that we can't stand pat and assume our democratic form of government will automatically perpetuate itself. There are times when we have to stand up and be counted."

"I don't mind being counted," Leon said. "Just don't ask me to stand up. Anyhow, whether we're counted or not doesn't make any difference. The status is going to remain as quo as it ever was."

"That's defeatism, wouldn't you say?"

"I don't deny it."

"What would become of civilization if everyone felt the same?"

"What civilization are you talking about?"

"Be as cynical as you like. I happen to believe things can be changed for the better, if we make ourselves heard."

"Save the Republic. All together now, let's hear it for Mom and apple pie."

Bébert was silent for a long time. Finally he asked, "Don't you ever feel the urge to *do* anything?"

Leon removed one hand from the binoculars and deliberately lifted his middle finger.

Bébert shook his head. "I'm serious. So many people make the same suggestion, but of course that's merely a form of self-indulgence. It accomplishes next to nothing."

"It expresses my attitude."

"No doubt. But it's destructive. Don't you agree that criticism should be constructive?"

"If anybody would listen to me," Leon said with heavy emphasis, "I would construct so much criticism of this stupid country they would need a forklift to handle it."

"Then why not make your views known? Really, all you do is drink yourself into a stupor at the Po-Po Club and quarrel with Andrea, or sit on the rail peeking at people."

"What we have got here by virtue of this instrument," Leon said, "is a kind of little microcosm."

"Are you still spying on the laundromat?"

"I am. People keep going in and coming out, except that bird. I can't understand what she's doing in there. She must be talking to somebody. Why else would she spend all that time in there?" He lowered the binoculars long enough to rub his eyes, and said irritably, "She didn't take a bag of clothes in, so that means she only went in to get her stuff. Why doesn't she come out? She's been fifteen minutes in there. Women are so slow it's incredible. Really incredible."

"You ought to get married."

"I ought to. I guess I should. You're absolutely right, Bébert. What about you? Don't you ever think about marriage?"

"Girls don't affect me as they do you. I suppose it's a deficiency on my part. I doubt if I'll marry, certainly not in the foreseeable future. I value privacy so much."

"Very possibly I will get married. After Christmas might be a good time. After the parties."

"Andrea?"

"Andrea. Sally. Midge. Barbara. Lisette. Julie. Claudine. That bird in the white leather boots, whatever her name is. I don't care. It's pretty much the same."

"You'll go on and on just as you are. Watching. Peeping. Waiting for the right girl. But you'll never find her because you're afraid to become involved."

"A cop just went into the laundromat," Leon said. "What the hell is happening in there?"

Bébert got up from the chaise longue with a look of annoyance and said, "I believe I'll fix myself another Ramos."

"Bring me a beer," said Leon.

Bébert walked into the house while Leon continued to observe the laundromat. A few minutes later Bébert returned and placed a cold can of beer on the rail. Then he settled himself on the chaise longue, and after sampling his drink he clasped his hands behind his head and contemplated the clouds drifting above the lake.

"Isn't this a gorgeous afternoon? It's enough to make you stop and think. Here we are living virtually in the lap of luxury within arm's reach of anything our hearts desire, while at the same time we're sitting on a powder keg, so to speak. Of course it's next to impossible to get a clear picture of the world situation, but there seems to be little doubt that things are rapidly deteriorating. I've always been struck by the fact that the man in the street finds it easier to close his eyes to the issues confronting him than to take whatever steps are necessary. I suppose it's true that the average man is principally concerned with his own creature comforts. Oh, I can sympathize. It requires a great deal of intestinal fortitude to walk right up and seize the bull by the horns. However, as the old saying goes: Since it is not granted us to live long, let us transmit to posterity some memorial that we have at least lived."

"I didn't follow that," said Leon.

"Nothing could be simpler. For example, look at the schism within the Church. Viewed from any perspective this is beyond doubt one of the most pressing problems of our century. The Pope doesn't know which way to turn and of course it isn't only the Catholics. Protestant theologians are finding themselves in equally hot water. The entire religious community appears to be on the brink of revolution. It's hard to imagine what tomorrow will bring."

"Maybe so. I don't pay much attention to religious controversies. I haven't been to church since I was twelve."

"Well, then," said Bébert, "what about the Medicare program?"

"I haven't looked into it," said Leon.

"I'm going to lay the matter right on your doorstep. Taxes. You can't ignore taxes. Tell me honestly, aren't you angered by those dodges and loopholes enjoyed by the giant corporations? To say nothing of the millionaires who get off scot-free. Don't you think these tax loopholes should be plugged? Some of the wealthiest people in the country never pay one red cent in taxes. How do you feel about that?"

"I never thought about it."

"But you understand as well as I do that the less they pay, the more you and I have to foot the bill. Or think about the people forced to live in abject poverty. So don't you feel this problem bears a relationship to you as an individual?"

"Remotely."

"Does nothing upset you? Are you content to go through life just as you are? It seems to me you're being terribly selfish."

Leon let the binoculars hang from the strap around his neck.

"Bébert," he said, "like I explained earlier: how I personally feel about what's going on in the Vatican, or in a state hospital for the mentally retarded, or even in this screwed-up town is irrelevant. Can I alter the course of events? No. That's why I've never voted. My vote doesn't matter. I'm canceled because there's only one of me while there are two billion of them. We're pawns in a game we can't control. All of us. You. Me. Kozlenko. Saqui. Midge. Barbara. Her cousin from New Brunswick. We're helpless. We've been had—past and present. In the future we're going to get had again. Neither you nor I is in any position to spearhead a drive for Utopia. That's how it is. That's life."

"There we differ," said Bébert. "Now I'll tell you a little something that may surprise you. I, for one, don't intend to remain a passive spectator. It seems to me that if we, as individuals, lack the initiative to come to grips with the problems confronting us we won't be able to avert a national tragedy on a scale that would have been incomprehensible to an earlier generation. There's no sense beating about the bush. We've got to put our own house in order before we attempt to tell the people of other nations how to live. Furthermore, I don't believe I'm alone in my conviction. People from all walks of life are starting to speak up, and what they are saying goes far beyond what might be expected. In certain respects, I feel, the people may be several light years ahead of their elected representatives. You may or may not agree. I'm not trying to force my opinion down your throat, but I feel very strongly that something must be done—the sooner the better. I realize it would be the height of conceit to pretend that I have the final answer, and certainly a spokesman for the government would be quick to point out that I don't know what's going on behind the scenes. I admit there may be another side to the coin. Just the same, myriads of people think our government is not living up to its responsibility. They're saying the time is long past when the government can go on doing business in the same old way, heedless of the demands of its citizens. They're saying the time has come to start paving the way to a better life, and I heartily agree."

"I'll buy that," said Leon.

After a pause Bébert said, "I had some point to make, but for the moment it's slipped my mind. Oh! I remember. This may very well shock you, Leon, but I'm planning to issue a manifesto. A statement of my position on the problems confronting us. I fully intend to have it printed and distributed publicly. I realize such a step may affect my entire future, but that's a gamble I'm prepared to take. I can't go on as I have in the past. I feel an urgent need to become actively involved. I'm not sure if you can appreciate this. I invariably vote, even when I have no preference. I frequently sign petitions, if they seem to be in support of a good cause, and I've written more than one letter to the editor of the *Herald,* though in all honesty I must admit that after reading them over I tear them up. However, you are looking at a new Bébert. From now on I intend to be a different person. I've been wondering what I could do, short of outright revolution, and the day before yesterday, while I was at the Fiddler for lunch, I was waiting on the salad when this idea arrived and I've been unable to get it out of my head. I really do feel it's appropriate and could have considerable impact."

"You are one of the true believers," Leon said.

"Is that all you have to say?"

"No. You are a cornerstone of our great nation. A pillar of society, that's what you are. A hewer and a builder. Let me be the first to congratulate you. We're proud of you, every man jack among us."

"How can you be so blasé?"

Leon sighed. "I've explained, you cannot fundamentally alter the course of events. I'm concerned, don't get me wrong. However, what can you or I do? Let me put it this way. You've somehow got the cart before the horse. I hate to use such a hackneyed expression to express what I mean, but the truth of the matter is that you envision yourself as the horse, whereas in actuality you're the cart. In other words, you and I have no control over the situation. Why can't you grasp a simple fact?"

"Oh, but I so profoundly disagree," Bébert exclaimed. "Oh, if I believed as you do I couldn't go on living. We aren't mere victims of life. We possess a free will. We're human beings, Leon, not protozoa."

"Life's a swindle," Leon said without bitterness. "You get no choice. Call it Destiny. You're no better off than a protozoa, maybe worse. At least they're unconscious, which now and then can be a blessing. Look at us. We're aware of what's happening around us, yet we're swept along like leaves in the current. A prime example is the War Department. I heard on a newscast the United States sells or gives away more weapons than anybody else in the world. Fifty billion dollars' worth, if I remember correctly, just in the past few years. Figures like that are like the number of miles to a star. You can't make any sense of it. But what it boils down to is that everywhere from here to Macao people are blowing each other's brains out with guns they got from us. You remember the Pakistanis and the Indians blasting away with Sherman tanks? The banana republics, Africa, everyplace. Those bloody primitives in Washington—I don't know whether to laugh or cry or puke. So what can I do? Face facts, Bébert. We've got no more chance of influencing those military bastards than that flock of sheep in Utah."

"You're as wrong as can be," said Bébert firmly. "What's more, I just might be able to prove my point. If I draw up a manifesto, will you sign?"

Leon thought about this. At last he said, "You understand you're asking for trouble."

"How so?"

"The F.B.I. photographs things of that nature, which means they have your signature on file. Word could get back to the bank. You could lose your job."

"Nonsense."

"It is not. You be careful what you say and do in the U.S. of A. You run around waving your opinions and all at once you're out of work. You bug Washington and you end up in a sling."

"Of, by, and for the people. That's exactly what Abraham Lincoln said. I'm surprised at you, Leon. You sound as cautious as those people who were alarmed by the Declaration of Independence during the McCarthy era. I assumed you were more courageous."

"Even the cops have changed," Leon said meditatively. "It used to be you said good morning to a cop. No more. Them mothers is mean. They'll stop you for questioning. These days you have to justify yourself. More than once I've thought it would be smart to get out of this country till it cools off."

"You said a while ago you weren't afraid to be counted. I'll ask again. If I draw up a declaration, would you be willing to sign your name?"

"No."

"But it's a recognizable and legitimate form of protest. Those artists who loiter around the sidewalk cafés in Europe are forever issuing proclamations. In fact, that's where I got my inspiration."

"What possible effect could it have on the masses?"

"One never knows, of course. But it might very well stimulate a number of people to think for themselves. After all, that's the function of a democratic society."

"Balls," Leon said. He slapped at a fly buzzing around his head.

"There truly is something that disturbs you. I can tell."

"What?"

"In a word, the Pentagon."

After a while Leon said, "You touched a sore spot. Those bastards."

Bébert smiled. "Are you prepared to sign?"

"I don't know."

"Think it over."

Leon scowled. Bébert watched attentively.

"May I ask your opinion of our admirals and generals?"

"Those murdering amoral bastards. I'd like to give each one of them a taste of napalm."

Bébert removed his sunglasses. "I hardly expected you to be complimentary, but I must admit your attitude is extreme. I doubt if you should condemn them like so many peas in a pod. I'm sure some of them are quite decent and humane. I'm not a rabid patriot, by any stretch of the imagination, but they do have a thankless job. It's a terrible responsibility."

"My dear child," Leon said. "You are naïve. This nation is solidly in the grip of certain men who have not got the brains or the moral perspective God granted a dinosaur. Any R.O.T.C. cadet, for instance, knows you do not invade Russia or get yourself engaged in a land war in Asia, but it would not surprise me if tomorrow the Pentagon landed an expeditionary force in Vladivostok. That is the kind of men who are running this nation, Bébert. They have got our leader by the short hair and the people know it. That is what is tearing us to pieces. Make no mistake about it. Furthermore, the Pentagon has cranked out so many lies it couldn't tell the truth if Jesus Christ materialized on the Washington monument with a flaming sword. As far as I am concerned, I would breathe easier if the Pentagon and everybody inside was washed away by the Potomac."

"I can't altogether agree. I feel that the Defense Department does the best it can under extremely trying conditions. I wouldn't care to be in their shoes."

"War Department. Tell it like it is."

"Since you feel this strongly, why haven't you the courage of your convictions?"

Leon was silent. He scratched the tip of his nose and he gazed across the lake. The fly settled on his knee, but he did not seem to notice. At last he said, "This manifesto, are you including the Pentagon?"

Bébert said quickly, "You write that paragraph yourself."

Leon reached for his can of beer and drank until it was empty. Then he said, "You got me. I'm in."

"Marvelous!"

Leon suddenly leaned forward, peering at the laundromat.

"Here she comes," he muttered. "Somebody's with her. My God, it's Shiffman," he said furiously, and clutched at the rail to keep from falling off. "What's she doing with Shiffman? What's Shiffman doing in the laundromat? What's been going on in that place? Neither of them's got any clothes."

"What!" cried Bébert. "Oh, for an instant I thought you meant neither of them had any clothes."

"Here comes the cop."

Bébert hopped out of the chaise longue and hurried to the rail where he squinted down the hillside. "That far away everything becomes an absolute blur. What's happening?"

"The cop's talking to that bird in the white leather boots. Now he's turned around and he's talking to Shiffman."

"This is exciting," said Bébert. "I love intrigue."

"They're walking away together."

"Who?"

"Shiffman and the bird."

"What's the police officer doing?"

"Well," Leon said after a pause, "he appears to be just standing on the curb scratching his ass."

Bébert returned to the chaise longue. He arranged himself comfortably and picked up his drink.

"Let's talk about our declaration. It's time we began to get organized. I'd like to know your thoughts on the subject. My own feeling is that we ought to be concise. I've always been impatient with wordy petitions. I think, too, we should be respectful. But at the same time we should strive to be eloquent and firm. Uncompromising, yet dignified. That, it seems to me, should be our attitude."

"You might as well include something about the draft," Leon said. "It needs to be overhauled."

"I should say. And I also mean to include an indictment of that real estate developer who interfered with the archaeologists. Whenever I think about that I become furious."

"You could put in all kinds of things," Leon said. "This country is so fouled up." Shiffman and the girl had disappeared into the flower shop and not much was happening in the park or along Bridgeway, so he focused the glasses on the Po-Po Club. Kozlenko and Saqui were still playing chess, but the tourists were gone. Barbara and her cousin were now talking to a man with a tangled beard and hair down to his shoulders who was dressed in an Indian costume. He wore beaded moccasins from the supermarket and a necklace of shells.

"There's that narcotics agent," Leon said.

"Oh? Is he back? I was wondering what became of him. A number of people have inquired. I rather like him."

"He's not a bad sort. I think the assignment embarrasses him. He drifts around pretending to be high on grass and asking where he can score, but he knows everybody knows what he is. It's kind of pathetic. Maybe you should include a paragraph about the narcotics bureau. I sometimes get a feeling the head narco is Mickey Mouse."

"Giacomo despises undercover agents. I'm sure he'd jump at the chance to write a statement. And it occurs to me that that electrician with the bushy red eyebrows might do a paragraph about the prison system, which I'm told is rotten to the very core. Sexual perversion, bribery, brutality, and Heaven knows what else. The electrician is a former convict. At least, so I hear."

"I've heard that. He looks to me like a rapist. Anyway, instead of just distributing this around town, why not send copies to Washington? Send it to senators and congressmen. Let people in the capital know how we stand on these issues."

Bébert nodded. "I agree one hundred percent. I believe I know the names of our senators, but to be perfectly frank with you I haven't the faintest idea who our congressman is."

"Hell, nobody knows who congressmen are," Leon said. "What you do is look it up in the library. The thing I'm worried about is how do we get this printed? Printing's expensive. Maybe mimeographing would be better. Haven't you got a mimeograph at the bank?"

"We have one of those gigantic copiers, but Miss Permaneer is simply insane on the subject. She regards the machine as her own. It's actually quite Freudian. Everybody at the bank feels this is because she has no children. In any case, I'd be afraid to touch it. And of course if she so much as suspected I wanted to copy a political manifesto—well! I don't like to imagine the consequences. No, we've got to find another solution."

"Andrea used to work for that printer in the industrial building. He could run off a few hundred without any trouble. Maybe Andrea could get us a reduced rate."

"Perhaps. Though it seems to me she once said the printer is extremely conservative. I doubt if he would have anything to do with a liberal statement, even if money were involved."

"Well, those are minor matters," Leon said. "They can be taken care of when the time comes. You know, Bébert, this really is starting to excite me. In my whole life I've never concerned myself with civic affairs or politics. It feels odd."

"You're less skeptical than you were."

"That's true. I've been considering what you said and I think in some ways you may be right, and maybe I was wrong. I guess I should apologize for ridiculing you. As you pointed out, it's easy to be cynical. And you were right, it doesn't accomplish anything. I do tend to lie around and jeer at anybody who tries to sincerely accomplish something constructive. So I owe you an apology, Bébert. I apologize. I'm sorry. I was wrong. I see that now. Maybe printing a manifesto isn't going to do any good, barring the unforeseen, but at least you're right about making an effort. It's the spirit that counts."

"No apology is required. But thank you, Leon."

"You've caused me to realize I'm a slob. I feel as though I've been wasting my life. Here you are concerned enough about various problems to actually decide to put yourself on record, while in the meantime what have I been doing? Playing dominoes at the Po-Po Club, lying around, occasionally getting in a set of tennis.

That's fruitless and unproductive. So I'm glad you woke me up. I honestly do appreciate your stimulating me."

"You're welcome," said Bébert. "But I haven't done much."

"More than you'll ever know," said Leon. "You couldn't begin to guess the effect this conversation has had on me. This is a real awakening."

"If so, that makes me very happy."

"I've wondered before, of course, about various matters, but now they suddenly acquire another dimension. Take these germ-warfare laboratories. Well, now I feel that I'd like to teach those men. I wonder if they realize what they're doing. How can they do what they do? How can they rationalize it so every evening at five o'clock they take off their white coat and their rubber gloves and go home to the suburbs? How are these men different from Hitler's technicians?"

"Individually they're probably no different than you or I. I'm sure they're decent, ordinary people."

"I'll have to give that some thought," Leon said.

"I think it's time to give a little thought to our statement. How should we begin?"

Leon frowned. He picked up the beer can and rolled it between his palms, and at last he said, "I'm trying to recall some of the famous documents of history. The only one that comes to mind is the Gettysburg Address."

"Yes, I'm having the same difficulty," Bébert said. "I can't seem to get the Lord's Prayer out of my head."

"We better trot over to the library and read a few of those very celebrated documents. How soon does the library close?"

Bébert looked at his watch. "In a few minutes. We'll just have to wait till tomorrow."

"I think ordinarily those documents tend to begin with 'We, the undersigned . . . ' and go on from there. Also the people who draw them up frequently sign their names in a circle."

"A circle?"

"So the king or tyrant couldn't tell who signed first. The Magna Carta was like that."

"What would it matter who signed first?"

"Maybe he would be punished more severely, or be the first one executed."

"I doubt if we stand much chance of being executed." Bébert laughed.

"There's another thing to include in the declaration. Capital punishment."

"Are you for or against?"

"Against. Unequivocally."

"That's a relief, because I am too. All right, we'll include a strong condemnation of capital punishment. Which should create quite a stir around town. Giacomo considers it a deterrent, as do certain other parties I could name. There may well be a public outcry when we make our position known."

"Incidentally, why doesn't Giacomo put some leather pillows out on the patio? Those benches are hard. I like to lie down there on warm afternoons, but after about half an hour my spine hurts. I should think he could kick out a few bucks for some nice leather pillows."

"To say nothing of splinters. Have you suggested it?"

"That stingy mother? He clears a fortune on that saloon, but would he spend, say, thirty dollars for some pillows? He'd cut his wrists first."

"It's worth a try. You never can tell. But getting back to our manifesto, I believe the very worst that could possibly happen would be, as you say, to lose my job at the bank. And if it creates as much of an uproar as I suspect, we just might be fingerprinted. So we are running a risk."

"I enjoy taking a few chances," Leon said. "Another thing we've got to look up in the library is where to send these copies to the senators and congressmen. It might not be delivered if it was addressed simply to Senator Schmuck, Washington."

"Senators should be addressed as The Honorable John S. Doe, Senate Office Building, Washington, D.C. Representatives are addressed as The Honorable James K. Roe, House Office Building."

"Honorable," said Leon. "There's hypocrisy for you. With a capital H."

Just then the telephone rang. He swung his legs over the rail, hopped down and walked into the house. Soon he came out and gestured to Bébert. "Somebody named Hadley Cushing."

"For goodness sakes!" Bébert said as he got up from the chaise longue. "Hadley is with Dockstader, Weeks, Smith and O'Leary. He's the one who tipped me off to that General Electric acquisition last month. I understand he made quite a killing on it. And of course in my own small way I didn't do too badly. I wonder what he wants."

He went into the house carrying his drink and was gone for quite a while.

"Guess what?" he said when he reappeared on the balcony.

"The Pentagon is going to acquire General Electric."

"No. Hadley's invited us to go for a sail tomorrow. Isn't that marvelous!"

"I thought we had some business in the library tomorrow."

"Yes, I realize. I told Had about our project and he told me he did something similar a few months ago. He dictated an eight-page letter suggesting various means to alleviate racial tensions and bring about better understanding between the generations, provide adequate housing, help the handicapped, improve living conditions, and I forget what else. His secretary mailed copies to both senators as well as to the congressman from this district, whose name, by the way, is Peter Gonzales—isn't that strange? I so rarely see a Mexican person. At any rate, he told me quite frankly that the world situation had brought him to the point of absolute nervous collapse, which is why he dictated his letter. He says right now he's extremely depressed by Mid-East tensions, and also by the supersonic booms. He says a priceless Wedgwood compote fell off the mantel. Apparently a jet was responsible."

"If I'd cleaned up in the market I wouldn't be having any nervous collapse," Leon said. "I'd be on the Riviera living it up with that crazy bird."

"Hadley is very sensitive. He sometimes writes poetry on the weekend."

"There's a waste," Leon said, and belched. "Jesus, this beer. What response did he get to his letter?"

"He never heard from the senior senator, but the junior senator and the congressman both replied. He suspects the congressman might actually have read it, judging from the response."

"What'd the junior Senator say?"

"It was a form letter thanking him for his interest and assuring him that the matter would be investigated at the first opportunity. Hadley was quite disappointed."

"That more or less confirms my previous view," Leon said. "Nobody's going to listen. Nobody cares."

"It isn't encouraging, I admit. Just the same, irregardless of whether or not his letter affected the course of events, he did put himself on record. I think that matters."

"Regardless. Not 'irregardless.' There's no such word."

"I've used 'irregardless' for years. I love it."

"Well, there's no such word," Leon said impatiently. "Now are we going to go sailing, or not?"

"Which would you rather?"

"We could go to the library the day after tomorrow."

"That's a holiday. Would the library be open? Of course if it's closed we could postpone our research another twenty-four hours. However, I'll leave the matter up to you."

"What sort of a boat has he got?"

"It's that lovely ketch tied up at pier six."

Leon focused his binoculars on the pier.

"I thought that ketch belonged to Marcie's brother-in-law."

"It does," said Bébert. "But I understand Hadley and Marcie have begun going together. I suppose that explains the situation."

"Well," Leon said, "you're putting me on the spot. I've admired that boat since I don't know when. I've always hoped for a chance to get aboard her. To be perfectly honest, Bébert, I'd rather go sailing, but I'd feel a sense of guilt if I did. Which would you rather do?"

"Since you're being frank, I will be. I love to sail. If we do, though, I'd feel every bit as guilty. What do you think?"

Leon studied the ketch. Finally he lowered the binoculars and shrugged.

"We might as well go sailing. It isn't as though we need to do everything tomorrow. Those problems we were discussing have been around a long time."

"That's an understatement if ever I heard one," Bébert said. "All right, if that's how you feel, suppose I tell Hadley we'd be delighted. After all, Rome wasn't built in a day."

1968

OCTOPUS,
THE SAUSALITO QUARTERLY
OF NEW WRITING,
ART & IDEAS

FOR AT LEAST twenty-five years the retired ferryboat *Sierra* had been sinking into a Sausalito mudflat. It listed to the left, the decaying prow rode several degrees above the stern, various cats lived somewhere within the hull, and at high tide the ancient side-wheeler moved a bit as though struggling to rise from the muck and live again those glorious days when it ploughed majestically across the bay to Oakland. A fat Greek artist named Philiátes leased the front end of the *Sierra*. Philiátes was seventy or eighty years old with a pair of green olives for eyes and a pockmarked nose that nearly met his chin and he loved to give parties.

During one of these parties, according to what I was told, Willie Stumpf decided to explore the rotting bowels of the ship. The interior was gloomy and Willie was drunk, but after stumbling around for a while he emerged at the stern, which offered a spectacular view of San Francisco Bay. From the stern he climbed a ladder to the quarterdeck, where he was rewarded with an even more dramatic view. He inspected the captain's cabin. Despite mildew, gull droppings, spiderwebs, and the remnants of a dead cat, he thought it would make a suitable office for the literary magazine he intended to start. His intended editor-in-chief, Cal Bowen, happened to be at the party, so Willie described what he had found. Bowen, clutching a bottle of vodka, followed Willie on a tour of the wreck and declared everything to be perfect, after which they seated themselves on the collapsing fantail to discuss the future. The magazine would be called *Octopus*. It would be published four times a year. Willie suggested that when circulation reached 100,000 they could publish six times a year. Bowen thought that sounded reasonable. Later, as circulation increased, Willie said, they could go monthly. All right, said Bowen. *Octopus,* said Willie as he reached for the vodka, what a great name! Absolutely a great name!

The captain's cabin was hosed down and fumigated. New plumbing was installed, worm-eaten wood and shattered windows replaced, everything repainted. Willie bought ads in the trade journals announcing that a vibrant innovative West Coast literary quarterly, *Octopus,* welcomed submissions from new or established writers and graphic artists.

Manuscripts began to arrive not long after the editorial office opened. Manuscripts continued to arrive. Every day the postman dropped off another heap. Willie was subsidizing *Octopus*—paying the rent, utilities, and so forth—but he was less than rich. When the first issue was ready to go to press he would have to buy paper, etc. In other words, as Bowen explained the situation to me, there would be no money to pay an associate editor if someone wished to become an associate editor. In other words, I said after thinking about this remark, you are asking if I would like to work on the magazine without being paid. We might have a drink and discuss that, said Bowen. Let's go to O'Leary's.

There's one problem, he said after we had spent a while at O'Leary's and I had agreed to become the associate editor. The problem is Willie. Willie considers himself an editor. He thinks of himself as the new Max Perkins, the new Cowley, the new Mencken.

He's the publisher, I said. He's the businessman. He's supposed to take care of business. You are the editor-in-chief and I am the associate editor. We decide what's going to be published. Why don't you tell Willie to keep his hands off the manuscripts?

I did, said Bowen. I told him to stay away from my desk and stop picking through the manuscripts. I reminded him I was the editor-in-chief.

What did he say?

He said he was the publisher and I was a word man.

A word man?

That is correct, said Bowen. How long have you known Willie?

Maybe a year, I said.

Long enough, Bowen said and took another drink. The main thing, however, is that he can't tell *Moby Dick* from the latest potboiler. In other words, he is about as discriminating as a high school freshman. He thinks the magazine should have lots of cartoons.

I resign, I said.

You can't resign, Bowen said. You promised. Besides, he does have some good ideas. Not very many, but once in a while.

For example, I said.

He thinks that after we get the magazine off the ground we should expand into book publishing. He says there's a market for worthwhile books. He thinks we should publish books of high literary quality.

That's not a good idea, I said.

Well, said Bowen, it's Willie's money. Have I told you about the swindler?

The swindler, he explained, had mysteriously appeared on the ferryboat with a briefcase that was never opened, an engaging smile, and a proposition. He, the swindler, although that was not how he referred to himself, would, in exchange for five thousand dollars, obtain stock certificates worth one million dollars from a bank in Los Angeles. These stock certificates he would lend to Willie, who could use them however he wished—as collateral, for instance, to borrow money to finance the development of this exciting literary venture. He, the swindler, was enthusiastic. There was every reason to believe, he told Willie, that the *Sierra* could become the pulse and heart and soul of a highly profitable publishing empire. All it required was capital. With the money that could be borrowed on stock certificates worth one million dollars the sky was the limit—although that was not the expression he used.

Willie's scared to death, Bowen said. He wants to get his hands on those stock certificates but he's afraid the guy is a crook.

What's your opinion? I asked.

Well, said Bowen, this crook gave two references—a company in New York and another in Florida. Cheryl called them both. The New York number is disconnected. The company in Florida never heard of him. Also, this crook doesn't know where he lives.

I asked who Cheryl was and he explained that she was a graduate student at Berkeley. She came in three times a week to empty wastebaskets, take packages to the post office, type rejection letters and so forth. She wanted to get into publishing and thought *Octopus* would be a wonderful place to learn what it was all about. She would be listed on the masthead as an editorial assistant.

Let's get back to the swindler, I said. Why doesn't he know where he lives?

That's an interesting question, Bowen said. He told us he bought a house but he can't remember what street it's on because he just moved in.

If you want my opinion, I said, it sounds as though he could be a swindler.

That's possible, Bowen said. He's coming back tomorrow and they're going to sign the agreement. Willie agreed to advance him one thousand so he can drive to L.A. and pick up those stock certificates.

We had been drinking at O'Leary's for quite a while and it seemed to me that certain fundamentals of a logical conversation were being neglected. The swindler doesn't know where he lives, I said, but Willie intends to give him one thousand dollars. Or do I misunderstand?

You are beginning to get the idea, said Bowen.

Let's talk about something else, I said.

Working on the ferryboat is not like working in an ordinary office, Bowen said. It's picturesque. For instance, you know when the tide comes in because pencils roll off the desk. Also, if the tide is high you see lots of cats on the quarterdeck, especially if the moon is full. The other night I was reading manuscripts when I got this peculiar sensation so I went outside to look around and there were all these cats and a suspicious object floating in the moonlight near the stern. I almost called the cops, but Willie doesn't want cops or fire inspectors or health inspectors on board. For one thing, the wiring is bad. He did some of the electrical wiring himself to save money and that ship might be a hundred years old.

I considered this. You are telling me the *Sierra* might go up in flames? Is that what you are telling me?

Bowen looked thoughtful. Well, he said at last, even if it did you wouldn't be in much danger. The bay isn't deep so you could jump off the stern. If the tide happened to be out you'd land in the mud.

Suppose we talk about the manuscripts, I said.

There's one thing I ought to mention before I forget, Bowen said. We've been having a little problem with this crazed photographer. Maybe you know him. Lucky Pizarro. He cruises around San Francisco on a motorcycle and takes pictures of accidents. He carries a gun and last year he shot out half a dozen streetlights on Lombard. He got ninety days or something. It was in the *Chronicle*.

I remember, I said. I didn't realize he was out of jail. What's the little problem?

He brought over a portfolio of his pictures and wants us to publish them.

Accidents?

Accidents, Bowen said. All of them. There were about a hundred. He said if we didn't publish his pictures we might wish we had.

I think he got the wrong magazine, I said. Did you explain to him that *Octopus* is a high-quality literary magazine?

Willie talked to him. Willie said Lucky said we'd better publish those pictures.

What are you going to do? I asked.

We can't publish them, Bowen said. I couldn't finish looking at them. I almost threw up.

He might torch the *Sierra,* I said.

That's conceivable, Bowen said. I hadn't thought of it, but you could be right.

Are there any other problems? I asked. I get the feeling you haven't told me everything.

Nothing important, he said. I told you the union was threatening to picket us.

No, you didn't tell me, I said. Why is the union threatening to picket us?

Willie hired a non-union printer who charges about half as much as union printers.

You could get Lucky Pizarro to take a picture of the *Sierra* after the union goons have trashed it, I said.

That's very funny, Bowen said. You were asking about manuscripts. The truth is, I wasn't expecting much because we don't pay anything, but three or four really good things have come in, which is encouraging. And Willie says after we start making money we can pay the contributors.

When we start making money does the associate editor get a salary?

I wouldn't care to speculate, Bowen said.

I asked what he had in mind for the first issue. He summarized a few stories that sounded worthwhile and said he had accepted five etchings by a Stinson Beach artist. There were other possibilities: an excerpt from a novel about Chicano gangs in Bakersfield, some nature poems by a Salt Lake City schoolgirl, a scholarly essay on the evolution of German opera. *Octopus* would not be doctrinaire, nothing would be predetermined, nor would its embrace be limited. All that mattered was quality. I doubted if that kind of a magazine could sell 100,000 copies or anything like it, but you have to respect idealists; and besides, as Bowen had pointed out, it was Willie's money.

One thing does make me uncomfortable, he said. Willie thinks we should publish the memoirs of Philiátes.

I knew Philiátes only slightly. There were endless rumors about him and no doubt he had led a remarkable life, but listening to him talk was like listening to somebody who had been marooned on an island for fifty years. If he wrote everything down, I said, maybe it would make sense. On the other hand maybe not.

As a matter of fact, Bowen said, Willie thinks if *Octopus* published the memoirs in Greek it would attract a lot of attention.

He's absolutely right, I said.

He's right, Bowen agreed, but ten pages of Greek would be suicidal. Maybe I can talk him out of it. Actually, not all of Willie's ideas are bad. He thinks we ought to publish recipes—recipes by well-known painters and sculptors and novelists and poets. As far as I know, that hasn't been done. We might have a page of recipes in each issue.

I thought about this. It was unexpected. However, as Bowen insisted all along, nothing would be predetermined. We would print whatever we chose to print. Willie's next idea was equally odd, but again, it was unusual enough to be worth considering; he had told Bowen that we might devote one entire issue to the artwork and writing of criminals.

He met some guy from Oklahoma who's out on parole. This guy did a stretch for holding up a hot-dog stand in Tulsa. He wears shiny wing-tip shoes and a pinstripe suit and slicks his hair straight back. He reminds me of somebody—Pretty Boy Floyd or Dillinger.

Listen, I said. With a bona fide swindler financing us and Lucky Pizarro and Pretty Boy Floyd and one issue devoted to criminals, that ferryboat is going to be visited by more than a Sausalito cop or a wiring inspector. What does this pinstripe stickup artist want?

Strangely enough, Bowen said, he doesn't seem to want anything. Willie wants him to represent us on campus.

I'm not going to believe any of this, I said, but go ahead.

Bowen explained that Willie thought *Octopus* could become the favorite magazine of college students everywhere. It would be sold in campus bookstores and coffee shops and on newsstands. He envisioned students from Harvard to East Quackenbush State discussing the latest issue, eagerly buying subscriptions, urging their classmates to buy it, mailing it home to their parents. And this ex-stickup artist from Tulsa would travel from campus to campus in his pinstripe suit and wing-tip shoes to promote it. I tried to imagine our representative heading out of Sausalito in a station wagon loaded with copies of the first issue featuring a scholarly essay on the evolution of German opera, etchings by a local artist, ten pages of Greek, and some recipes.

What's his name? I asked.

Fingers.

Fingers. That's all?

That's what he told us to call him. Just call me Fingers, he said.

Does he remember his address?

I can't answer that, Bowen said. All I know is, Willie told me he's from Oklahoma.

I wondered about the connection between Fingers and a criminal-man issue, but by this time it didn't seem important. I had very mixed feelings. On the one hand, Bowen was serious about publishing a respectable literary magazine and I thought that with two hundred and fifty million people in the United States there might be two or three thousand who wanted more than drivel. On the other hand there was Willie. I was impressed by Willie's confidence and energy and by the fact that he would subsidize such a precarious venture, but then I would think about him calling his editor-in-chief a word man. He had been joking, but I felt uneasy. I asked Bowen if we had received any subscriptions.

Eight, he said, counting my dotty aunt.

Eight, I thought. Eight subscribers. Still, the first issue hadn't come out and the advertising campaign was just getting started. It was impossible to predict what might happen. Quite a bit would depend on the first issue.

Bowen plucked an ice cube out of his drink and began sucking it. I suspected from his expression that he had something to tell me but wasn't sure how to phrase it. Finally he scratched the tip of his nose and asked if I knew Babydoe Slusher. Only by reputation, I said. And then he told me she had given Willie a list of people who might subscribe or who might help subsidize the magazine. This made no sense. I wondered why she would do that. For one thing, everybody on the list would deny knowing her.

Maybe she has an ulterior motive, Bowen said. Anyway, Willie's decided to put her on the masthead as a contributing editor.

Babydoe? I said. Babydoe Slusher will be on the masthead?

Willie thinks it's a smart move. He says she's on what might be called intimate terms with practically all the men in California—movie stars, bankers, lawyers, civil rights leaders, congressmen, scoutmasters—just about everybody.

Congressmen, I said. Listen, I don't know if I want this job. I'm having very serious second thoughts. What about the guy from Oklahoma? Will he be on the masthead?

Presumably, Bowen said. I presume Fingers will appear on the masthead. Also, Willie is drafting letters to some big names in contemporary literature—critics, major novelists, poets, artists. He says having them associated with *Octopus* will give us prestige.

I thought about a critic for the *Times* looking down the masthead and finding himself squeezed between Babydoe Slusher and Fingers somebody.

Willie can be persuasive, Bowen said. I was skeptical about a Sausalito literary magazine, but he talked me into it. I wouldn't be surprised if he talks some of those big names into joining us. By the way, did I tell you that Spook will be a contributing editor?

Spook?

He comes in here once in a while—sad little guy with sleepy eyes and a Fu Manchu mustache. You may have seen him.

I've seen him, I said. What will Spook contribute?

That's an interesting question, Bowen said.

What does he do? I asked. Is he a journalist?

Bowen gazed dustily toward the ceiling. I believe Spook is a small-time drug pusher. That's what I've heard. He's very polite. You hardly know he's in the room. Did I tell you about Doc Arbuckle?

I'm not sure I want to hear about Doc Arbuckle, I said. Who is Doc Arbuckle?

He's from New York. Willie says he's a hotshot advertising salesman. He used to work for one of those Madison Avenue agencies. He's going to be our advertising representative.

Why did he leave Madison Avenue?

Actually, I have the impression there may have been a scandal, Bowen said. I met him a couple of days ago. He's all teeth and hair.

Doc Arbuckle, I said. That sounds like an alias.

According to Willie, Doc is a firecracker. According to Willie, Doc will put us on the map.

It occurred to me that *Octopus* was going to be on the map with or without Doc Arbuckle. Maybe what we should do, I said, is run a photo of Babydoe Slusher in the buff on the cover.

It's curious you should mention that, Bowen said. You won't believe what Willie has in mind.

I'd rather not know, I said. Let's get back to this Madison Avenue hotshot. Has he sold any ads?

Bowen didn't answer. He was looking at the door and there was a strange expression on his face.

What's wrong? I asked.

Bad news, he said. Lucky Pizarro. I'm afraid he's seen us. He's coming this way.

Listen, I said. I'm not sure I have time for this job. To be honest with you, I have serious reservations about a number of matters concerning the magazine and besides I've got a lot of things to do.

Now don't be hasty, Bowen said. Think it over.

1994

BOWEN

H E CAME out of a skeletal midwestern town beside the Mississippi and
his favorite novel was *Huckleberry Finn*. Instead of floating down the
river on a raft he joined the merchant marine, but until the day he
stripped himself naked on a cliff overlooking the Pacific and just after dawn
stepped forward to eternity he imagined himself as Huck—only more sophisticated and intelligent, maddened by genius. I never knew the source of his roman-
ticism, which had about it the appealing innocence of another era. Stern-wheel
paddleboats roiled the Mississippi not long before he was born and perhaps he
could hear them churning around the bend.

I first saw him in Paris, seated on an old-fashioned trunk in the hotel suite of a
famous southern author, grande dame of American literature. He had begun writing a novel about his voyage to New Guinea aboard the freighter *Pelican* and he
had come to pay homage, perhaps to divine the secret of her eminence. I remember that he sat motionless on the ancient steamer trunk and his eyes were crystal
gray.

Three years later I saw him in California. *Voyage of the Pelican* had been published with unusual success. Reviews were excellent. He had been interviewed on

radio and television. A movie producer was going to option the book. Several paperback houses were interested in reprint rights. He told me it was selling better than anybody expected. He had married a porcelain English goddess named Felicia, they were buying a little house in a eucalyptus grove near the Golden Gate, and he believed his days as a merchant seaman were over.

About that time he met another dislocated midwesterner, Willie Stumpf, in O'Leary's bar and grill. Stumpf had inherited a few thousand dollars, he admired Bowen's novel and thought the two of them should publish a literary magazine. He would be the publisher. Bowen could be editor-in-chief. They discussed it until O'Leary's closed. Bowen said the magazine should be called *Octopus* because nothing escapes the grasp of this remarkable creature, and they ought to publish it quarterly. Willie Stumpf said that was a great idea, he would rent an office. They shook hands. Both of them were very drunk.

Marriage turned out to be more expensive than Bowen anticipated; he learned that women require all sorts of things. Then, as if by magic, Felicia became pregnant. He was astonished and dismayed. It seemed to him that life was happening too quickly. Next, the Hollywood producer rode off into the sunset without a word of explanation, as movie producers tend to do. Bowen had started another novel and after contemplating the situation he decided to ask his New York publisher for an advance. The publisher agreed, although with some reluctance, and the advance was rather stingy, considering those good reviews. Then Willie Stumpf discovered that because *Octopus* would cost quite a lot to print, there might not be enough left over to pay the editor-in-chief's salary. Bowen cursed the universe with particular emphasis on Hollywood producers, New York publishers, and Willie Stumpf, after which he got drunk as he often did when fortune showed her ugly face, and concluded that his days as a merchant seaman were not over.

Aboard the oil tanker *Gulfport* somewhere west of Jalisco he missed a step on a gangplank and fell to the deck with such force that he split a kneecap. When I saw him next he was limping, but cheerful. Insurance had taken care of the medical bills, he and Felicia now had a charming daughter, Willie Stumpf had promised $300 a month as soon as *Octopus* showed a profit, and a national travel magazine had commissioned him to write about the San Francisco waterfront. As if this were not enough, *Voyage of the Pelican* would be translated into Swedish. It was strange and wonderful how one's luck could change.

He wrote a colorful description of the waterfront for which he was handsomely paid, so he got drunk and bought a dog. Every now and then somebody who had read the novel or the waterfront essay would compliment him. Once in a while a stranger asked for his autograph. His name appeared in newspapers. A columnist said he was the best writer in California. The public library asked him to give a reading. Felicia was happy. Day by day their tiny daughter Aurora grew more beautiful. Except for the fact that he was having trouble with the second book, life could hardly be better.

The first novel had almost written itself so he did not understand why *Harvest* should be difficult, but the longer he worked on it the more dissatisfied he became. Ideas evaporated. Words would not fall into place. No sooner did he write a line than he scratched it out. The narrative had no logic. Emotions that he tried to evoke seemed false. He began to wonder if he might be arguing against himself, if consciously he might be opposing his unconscious. He remembered a comment by Jung to the effect that a faulty interpretation encourages feelings of stagnation, opposition, and doubt. This, he said, was exactly how he felt, and he thought a change of scene might give him a new perspective on the novel. Unexplored streets, unfamiliar faces — if he could get away for a couple of weeks he might interpret the problem correctly.

He went to Mexico. In Oaxaca he rented an airy whitewashed room with a big overhead fan, a view of the plaza, and a window screen to keep out mosquitoes. He decided to stay for a month because it seemed like a perfect place to work on *Harvest* and life south of the border was cheap.

Oaxaca, he discovered, was full of pleasant surprises. Scarcely had he gotten settled when he met a Sacramento kindergarten teacher on vacation with the result that he did not get very much sleep and found it hard to concentrate on the manuscript. Then, during the second week, Oaxaca turned unpleasant. Eighty dollars vanished from his duffel bag. He suspected the chambermaid because she had a key to the room and she avoided looking at him. After a few more days, exasperated and restless, unable to work on the book, he came home. Although he had lost eighty dollars he did receive something in exchange — a stomach disorder that would afflict him the rest of his life.

The first issue of *Octopus* appeared with the title of an essay on Baudelaire printed upside down. Nobody could understand how this happened. The printer claimed it was not his fault. The proofreader said everything had been rightside up when she went over it. The poetry editor, Troy Dasher, said he had nothing to do with printing the magazine, he merely accepted or rejected poems, so he was innocent. Wendy, the part-time associate editor who scanned unpromising manuscripts, wrote letters of rejection, and made coffee, said she had nothing to do with it. Willie Stumpf accused Bowen, who, as editor-in-chief, must have neglected his duties.

This annoyed Bowen, who said he had done everything expected of an editor-in-chief. Besides, it was the publisher himself who had delivered final proofs to the printer. Why hadn't the publisher bothered to look at what he was delivering?

All of them adjourned to O'Leary's bar where the argument continued. After enough drinks Willie and Bowen vowed to settle the matter outside, so everybody marched across the street to a parking lot. O'Leary's bartender telephoned the police station, which was not far away. A policeman walked over to investigate. The publisher and the editor-in-chief, between insults, had begun shoving each other, so Troy Dasher attempted to separate them just as the policeman arrived and mistook Dasher for the cause of the trouble. In spite of being a poet, Dasher was heavily muscled. When some unknown party grabbed his arm he flung the assailant against a parked car. The entire staff of *Octopus,* as well as the printer, was then escorted to the police station where the publisher, editor-in-chief, and poetry editor were charged with fomenting a public disturbance.

Not long after this incident a small paperback house bought *Voyage of the Pelican,* which was good news, although Bowen had been expecting a sale to one of the international giants. The first printing would be 10,000 copies instead of perhaps ten times that many, but the size of the printing was unimportant. If the paperback drew a large audience they could go back to press.

Meanwhile he continued to work on *Harvest* and he predicted that it would do even better than the first book. It was going to be a very long novel about midwestern America with dozens of significant characters. Because of the length and complexity there were technical problems, but he felt confident that he would soon have everything under control. In order to receive the advance he had signed a contract, but he wanted his agent to negotiate with the publisher for better terms. This novel, he said, might very well be a classic.

Bad luck came visiting once again. Outside of O'Leary's one night he was stopped by a derelict who asked for money. He responded by calling the bum a bum, and for declaring an obvious truth got his nose smashed. Nature had endowed him with a beak in place of a nose and the assault crumpled it. However, on his craggy midwestern face it did not seem inappropriate. He never had been vain, not in the usual sense, and except for the humiliation he felt at having his nose bloodied in a street fight the grotesque encounter meant very little. He was vain only of his talent.

The technical problems, whatever they might have been, were at last resolved and he mailed his second book to New York. The manuscript probably weighed as much as a metropolitan telephone book because he said it was almost nine hundred pages long. He looked forward to an excited call from his agent, but she did not finish reading it for nearly a month. Then she sent a note explaining that the office had been swamped and she would let him know as soon as there was any news from the publisher.

After a long silence he heard from New York. It had been accepted.

By coincidence, the publication date of *Harvest* was his twenty-ninth birthday. A celebration seemed like a good idea, and O'Leary's bar the logical place. Bowen invited everybody and told the Canterbury Bookshop to provide a stack of copies, which he would autograph.

He began drinking before the party started. In the past he had been able to drink throughout an evening with amiable sobriety, but he had done it too often. His body could absorb no more. His eyelids drooped and his mouth hung open. In a display of arrogance or contempt he propped his feet on a table, patted his crotch, and mumbled that he had written a superb book, a masterpiece. Among the guests was another writer he had always liked; but now, focusing on him, Bowen deliberately belched.

Harvest failed to attract much notice. When the first book came out he was identified as a promising young writer, but not this time. Reviewers were disappointed. One or two offered tepid praise and expressed hope for his next work. When I saw him a few months later I asked if there had been any movie interest. He said an important director was reading it.

He was angered and puzzled by the reaction to his second novel. He had visited a number of bookstores to discuss it with the clerks and he urged them to promote it. He suggested window displays, and he autographed every copy in stock so that none could be returned to the publisher. He telephoned book critics to complain that they had not understood what it was about. He said they were fools who could not appreciate anything more complex than a children's story with a moral set in italics. Originality befuddled them. He explained all of this while slumped in a corner of O'Leary's patio drinking beer. Finally the waitress asked him to hold his voice down and keep his boots out of the flowers.

When another issue of *Octopus* rolled off the press everything was rightside up, but Willie Stumpf felt dissatisfied. He thought more copies could be sold if the magazine had cartoons and Bowen told him he should be marketing codfish instead of literature. As a result, the next issue was indefinitely postponed.

Still, the planets must have been aligned in Bowen's favor. A philanthropic organization dedicated to helping artists, writers, and musicians awarded him a three-month fellowship at a bucolic retreat in southern California. He had not applied for it; indeed he had never heard of the organization that awarded these fellowships, but he saw no reason to decline a gift. The fellowship did not provide for wives or children, so Felicia and Aurora would stay at home.

When I next saw Bowen he was asleep in a Santa Monica hospital. He had told me to call the foundation if I happened to be in the neighborhood, so I did and was informed that he had been taken ill. At the hospital they directed me to his room. The door was open. When I saw him lying on his back with his face the color of parchment and his hands folded on his chest and that broken beak of a nose jutting from the blanket like the prow of a sunken ship I thought he had died. I hurried down the corridor and talked to a nurse. She said he was asleep. I said he might be dead, or almost dead, and perhaps she ought to have a look, but she insisted he was taking a nap. I went back to the room. He had not moved and he resembled a corpse, but I could hear a gentle snoring.

A few days later he was out of the hospital. I found him in a rustic cabin where he was busily typing up a short story. Life in the cabin had stimulated him to write stories, he said. As for the illness, an ulcer had developed during his tenure as editor-in-chief of *Octopus* but it didn't amount to much. It gave his stomach something to think about other than the mysterious Mexican ailment.

He wrote five or six stories while he lived in the cabin. His agent had sold one to a men's magazine for a respectable amount by the time Thanksgiving came around, but the others were gathering rejection slips. An excerpt from his celebrated first novel had appeared in a textbook on the art of writing, which was complimentary, but payment was meager, and royalties had declined to the point that Bowen referred to them with amazement. His ulcer muttered, his entrails bubbled with the Oaxaca flux, and the bank had warned him about overdrafts. He no longer sounded cheerful.

He told me that he had a recurrent dream of silver dollars littering the beach while he floated indolently from one shining heap to the next. He said it was a marvelous dream. Awake, he dreamed that some New York literary panjandrum would discover his neglected second novel, catapulting it to the peak of the best-seller list where it stayed month after month. He imagined Hollywood executives wondering if he could be persuaded to write a movie script. Telegrams from Lotusland offered rich contracts, each proposal more extravagant than the last. His career had opened like a morning glory. Why should it fade? He compared himself not unfavorably to Conrad and Melville.

Felicia handed him a cigar on Christmas Day. Bowen was not thrilled. I heard that on the day after Christmas he sold a pint of blood.

And I heard about his affair with the olive-eyed Eurasian girl, Wendy, part-time associate editor of *Octopus*. She had come to the golden state of California looking for adventure. She was in her twenties, although she seemed no more than fifteen, and she must have become pregnant not long after Felicia.

Felicia learned about Wendy. I do not know what she said to Bowen, but he moved out of the eucalyptus grove and into Willie Stumpf's apartment where he was less than welcome. After a series of drunken arguments during which Bowen called his host an illiterate huckster, a mediocrity, a bumpkin, a cultural adolescent, a cartoon-lover, an undergraduate intellectual with a tin ear, and whatever else came to mind, he was evicted. He then lived for a while in the vacant garage of another friend where he started to write an existentialist novel about his experiences aboard the tanker *Gulfport*. His duffel bag and a few other possessions lay on a shelf alongside some camping equipment, a used battery, assorted wrenches, sections of pipe, garden hose, and a sack of fertilizer. His desk was a packing crate. The author himself could be observed seated in a canvas chair on the oil-soaked concrete, fashionably dressed in dungarees, moccasins, and a San Francisco Giants baseball cap. On warm days he typed without a shirt, exhibiting a flaccid paunch for whoever cared to look.

Occasionally he interrupted work on the novel to write a travel essay, which he could do without much effort by recalling the odors and sounds and activities of distant ports and by describing in humorous, picturesque language the human flotsam he had met. And he wrote sketches of small town life, affecting the style of Sherwood Anderson. A few of these sketches sold to midwestern journals, but they reeked of plagiarism. What animated Bowen to write at a level beyond understanding was the mythic quality of life at sea.

Felicia at last relented, so he moved back into their untidy little house among the trees. When they were first married she had attempted to cook and she had managed to keep the house reasonably clean, but now the center of what had drawn them together was sliding askew. She had put on fifteen or twenty pounds that sagged like tallow from her delicate bones and her English porcelain face was beginning to wrinkle. Somebody described her as a premature grandmother. Day and night she served spaghetti, Bowen said, and she was feeding Aurora peanut butter sandwiches. He could remember what he had loved about her once upon a time, but it no longer affected him. He, himself, was noticeably less attractive. He had lost a front tooth and in order to save money he did not have it replaced; or perhaps he took pride in his raffish appearance—the reincarnation of Huck.

Now and then some newspaper asked him to review a book, usually a novel about the sea. When *Voyage of the Pelican* was first published he had been called upon frequently, and because he knew the subject his criticism was perceptive. But little by little his reviews grew venomous, as though he resented competition. Then he began to mention his own work while commenting on the work of someone else, so that calls for his service had become less frequent.

However, the gods of Olympus look indulgently on poets and dancers and sculptors and scribblers. Bowen must have been a favorite because he was offered the position of writer-in-residence for a year at a distinguished New England college. Living quarters would be furnished, he would be required to teach a workshop once a week, the rest of the time would be his own. Felicia, Aurora, and the baby could go with him. It sounded like an easy job, the salary would more than pay his bills, and campus life was relatively civilized. He remembered his days at the state university—tweedy professors and sycamore trees and football games and bonfires and pretty girls everywhere—so it did not take him very long to decide. Most of all he liked the promise of so much free time. He hoped to complete his *Gulfport* novel before the academic year ended.

Bowen's reign as writer-in-residence did not go well. It did not begin auspiciously, nor did the situation improve. At a cocktail party intended to welcome him and the new artist-in-residence he got drunk, he neglected to zip his fly after a visit to the men's room, he attempted to kiss a glamorous young teacher of Romance Languages, and he called the artist-in-residence a comic book illustrator who couldn't paint a catsup bottle. At another ceremonial affair he again drank too much and called the wife of the Dean of Admissions a babbling frump. And it was said that he became involved with one of the girls in his literary workshop. The college no doubt was relieved when he went back to California.

A few months later Felicia stabbed him. According to what she told friends, he used vulgar language and threatened to strangle her so she picked up a bread knife to protect herself but he paid no attention, which is how it happened. Bowen's account was different. They had argued, so in order to get away from her he went for a walk in the eucalyptus grove. When he got back to the house she came at him with a steak knife in each hand. Whatever happened, Felicia called the police, who dispatched an ambulance to the scene of the crime and Bowen was rushed to the hospital because he did not have very much blood left.

When I saw him he looked better than he did in Santa Monica. He was flat on his back again but he sounded optimistic. He did not blame Felicia. Neither did he blame himself. I asked how he was getting along with *Gulfport*. He stared at the ceiling with a thoughtful expression and licked his lips as though anticipating a drink. Oh, he said, there were a couple of problems, nothing important. And the ulcer? Oh, nothing to worry about. On the doorstep of middle age with a bad kneecap, watery entrails, fading eyesight, a missing tooth, an explosive stomach, quite possibly a damaged liver, and now a couple of stab wounds, he seemed to think himself invulnerable.

Bowen's publisher rejected *Gulfport*. He was shocked. He had been expecting a large advance. Thousands in the bank would solve nearly all of his problems. There would be no more arguments with Felicia about paying the bills. He would buy a roll of tarpaper and fix the leak in the roof. He would visit the dentist. He would pay off the mortgage. He would get a new muffler for the car, which thundered and smoked like an old diesel and swayed through the eucalyptus as though the tank had been filled with whisky. He might even get a new car. Thousands in the bank would restore his confidence, which had been unspeakably abused. *Gulfport* was a major book, he insisted, maybe the best novel written in America during the past fifty years. The rejection made no sense. And he disparaged a recent novel that had been critically praised, saying the author had a tin ear and the critics should be reviewing science fiction.

The long he thought about being rejected, the angrier he became, and having worked himself into a rage he decided to commit suicide. His death should be a lesson not only to the idiots at the publishing house but to all the newspaper hacks who had dismissed his second book. After he was gone they would realize their mistake. He pointed out that *Remembrance of Things Past* had been rejected by an editor with a tin ear.

So, one night when the moon was full, he wandered away from the house with a bottle of whisky, a bottle of sleeping pills, and a copy of the scorned manuscript tucked under his arm. When he came to an appropriate site overlooking San Francisco Bay he seated himself and uncorked the whisky. Some time later he opened the bottle of sleeping pills, washed them down, and stretched out with *Gulfport* clasped to his breast. He would not be found until the next day, which was unfortunate because his death would seem more tragic if searchers discovered his body beneath a full moon, but it couldn't be helped. Next day a peaceful corpse would be found among the towering eucalyptus. News that Bowen had killed himself would stun the literary world. It would be the subject of intense discussion from Greenwich Village to Beverly Hills, and posthumously his novel would be published to enormous acclaim.

He awoke on a bright sunny morning with birds twittering through the eucalyptus grove and found himself covered with vomit. The pills had made him sick.
The pages of his manuscript were scattered. He crawled around collecting them
and then he decided to read the opening of *Gulfport* to see if it was as brilliant as he
thought. The first page proved that he had not been mistaken. He read the next
page, and the next, and he did not stop until he had finished the opening chapter.
It was good. Here and there a few lines might be improved but they were easy
enough to fix, so he went back to the house, took a shower, and started to work.

The bungled suicide left him disgusted and humiliated. I don't even know how
to kill myself, he said. I can't do anything right.

He resembled the youth with crystal-gray eyes who sat on a steamer trunk in a
Paris hotel, but it was no more than a resemblance. His eyes appeared rheumy, as
though something inside had been melting. He wore glasses for reading. The fine
tawny hair was a disorganized cobweb. Occasionally his lips twitched.

The god of misfits looked upon Bowen with pity, or maybe it was the god of
malice. *Voyage of the Pelican,* by now half-forgotten in the United States, was sold
to a Dutch publisher. But a short time afterward Bowen's agent called to explain
that there had been a misunderstanding. The terms were not as generous as first believed. In fact, the advance against royalties would be little more than a gesture.

He vanished. He had done this before when he was discouraged or enraged, so
Felicia paid no attention. Somebody told her that he was loitering around the waterfront wheedling drinks and money from strangers, but she merely shrugged.

When I saw him again he wanted to talk about the town where he had grown
up. He ran the fingers of one hand through his uncombed hair and said the town
lay on a marshy point thick with osier. He described the Methodist church and a
feed store and chicken coops behind the houses and a Bible with gilt edges. He
could remember antimacassars on the sofa in the parlor where shades were always
drawn against the afternoon sun, willow branches touching the river, red-winged
blackbirds, an old steamboat landing at the foot of Main Street. He talked about
people gathering to watch a channel dredge that groaned and thumped and
spouted sandy mud. In August the creeks ran dry, he said, and his grandmother
would sit on the porch swing with a rag dipped in camphor tied around her head.
He remembered whippoorwills and wild geese and the south wind and a clock
ticking in the public library. His mother belonged to the Epworth League, she had
a pink conch shell that gave out the roar of barbarous foreign seas. His father
worked as a Rock Island brakeman. And while I listened I had no idea what he
meant. He was talking to someone else—some biographer commissioned to pre-

serve each fragment of his mosaic. I understood that he was trying to explain something, but only he knew what it was.

Then he said he might ship out again. He thought he would write another realistic novel like *Voyage of the Pelican*. His stomach lapped over his belt.

Nobody was surprised when Felicia divorced him. Bowen himself was not surprised; he cheerfully admitted that he had not been a faithful husband, that he drank too much, that he had not earned enough. What seemed to trouble him most was the failure of literary critics to understand the significance of his work, and public indifference to everything he had written since that first novel. He mentioned Hart Crane plunging into the Gulf of Mexico.

That was the last time I talked with Bowen. Considering the number of beer bottles he left on the cliff he must have spent quite a while up there. Just when he made his decision is a mystery because he was alone. Sometime after dawn he took off his clothes and folded them. In each moccasin he placed an empty bottle and before the final step he put on his glasses. When I heard about the glasses, which lay on the sand near his body, I wondered why he had worn them; but of course he wanted to see where he was going.

1992

HOOKER

KOERNER STOOD beside a eucalyptus tree with both hands stuffed into his jeans, listening to the distant foghorns and watching. Fog seeped over the ridge above Sausalito. Before long the Golden Gate Bridge would be engulfed, then San Francisco. Everything would be submerged. In a little while, he thought, we can walk on the bed of the ocean like Captain Nemo and Monsieur Aronnax. Tomorrow the city would reappear, perhaps by noon, or it might not. In late summer one never knew. A cool breeze was pushing ahead of the fog like a pilot fish ahead of a shark. Koerner buttoned his jacket.

Well, now the problem was where to eat. I should learn to cook, he said to himself. Going out every night is bad for the stomach. And he began to think about his usual restaurants, but rejected them all, one after another. Gilhooley's—they must have a blacksmith in the kitchen, you need a hammer to crack the bread and the meat is tough as a sponge. Angelo's—that waiter glides around like a reptile and the minestrone tastes like furniture polish. Wimbledon—they slice a bar of laundry soap and call it cheese. I'd rather eat at the city jail. Then he remembered The Flying Dutchman. He had not been there in months.

The Dutchman's lounge was empty except for a girl drinking wine in front of the stained glass window. She had made herself the center of an art nouveau com-position and almost certainly she knew it. Koerner hesitated. She wore a Stanford sweatshirt and a knitted cap pulled down until it concealed half of her face, but there was no mistaking the unusually long nose and the crazed turquoise eyes.

She glanced up, apparently surprised, although the expression was not quite true. After gazing at him for a moment she said, "*Je ne parle pas Anglais.*"

Koerner laughed and walked over to the table.

"Vaya!" she muttered, scowling. "*No hablo Ingles.*"

The deep nasal voice was familiar. And those insane eyes—there could be no mistake.

"Aye vant," she said, enunciating each word, "tew bee alone."

He looked at her deliberately. "I met you in Taos several years ago."

"I used to be a circus contortionist," she said. "Maybe that's where you saw me."

"At the Taos Inn. We drank at least a gallon of Carta Blanca. We ate guacamole and enchiladas and then we drove out to the Rio Grande bridge and I played 'Sewanee River' on the harmonica because I couldn't think of a number about the Rio Grande. It was freezing. You howled at the moon. Your name is Maria Czermak."

"During a performance the elephant went into musth and grabbed the fat lady," she said in her almost masculine voice. "It was terrifying."

"I've lost my appetite," Koerner said. "Circus or no circus, we knew each other in Taos. You haven't forgotten. You remember that night as well as I do."

She lit a cigarette and murmured through the smoke. "My name is Gloria Wonderlips." Then she tamped out the cigarette. "Listen, I'm Marla Jarecki. I can't talk to you. I have an appointment. Don't ask me to explain."

"How about tomorrow?"

"That's impossible."

"I'll call you."

"Don't even try."

"How will I find you?"

"Give me your number."

He printed it on a cocktail napkin. "I'll be here tomorrow—just in case."

"I know you," she said and brushed his cheek with one finger. Then she was gone.

He could not get over a feeling of disbelief. He had never expected to see her again. He remembered that while they were splashing hot sauce on everything and laughing and feeding each other spoons of guacamole and talking about places they had been—in the midst of all the frivolity it had seemed that something important was happening. He remembered thinking that his life was about to change because of this half-civilized creature with turquoise eyes.

She had been to Mexico. She had visited Campeche where he lived for six months. She knew about the hawks sailing along the sea wall with their white legs pressed together and how the Gulf lay flat as a slice of blueberry pie. The Mexicans built that wall to keep out pirates and Englishmen, he had said, and she laughed. They talked about the smell of gasoline after a fishing boat chugged by, and the terrible restaurant on the beach with fans nailed to the pink plastered wall and a mosaic tile floor and the TV set perched on top of a broken refrigerator. She remembered palm trees struggling against the afternoon breeze, and truck fumes and yellow-and-blue stucco houses and idiotic crowing roosters and flowers and tin shacks and jars of Nescafé and painted wheelbarrows and a troop of Catholic schoolgirls with gold-capped teeth. She had seen the Maya ruins at Palenque, so they talked about that—lime-streaked glyphs, the unexpected drip of water from stalactites in gloomy passageways, mosquitoes, warm rain showers, orange and black lichen scaling the mottled white temples. He felt astonished that they had gone to the same places and had experienced them in the same way; and it had seemed to him that night in Taos while they drank Mexican beer and talked about Campeche and mysterious temples in the jungle that their separate travels must have brought them together for a purpose.

So he remained for a long time in front of the stained glass window with his elbows on the table and his chin cupped in his hands.

Finally he got up and wandered out to the deck. An immense threatening shape obscured San Francisco. Lugubrious foghorns groaned through the darkness. The Oakland bridge was being swallowed. Without doubt the end of the world was near. However, the fog did not seem to be drifting north and dinner was being served outside. He chose a table overlooking the yacht harbor.

"Stay away from that bitch," said a voice.

Somebody in a straw hat was smiling disagreeably. The stranger wore a necklace of Italian glass beads and a polo shirt with an alligator on the pocket. He stood like a woman, swaying just a little, with one hand propped on his fleshy hip. He reeked of deodorant.

"She is not a nice person," the stranger continued, pushing the words out of his mouth. "Do you mind if I sit down? My ankle is killing me. Of course it's none of my business," he went on after seating himself, "but you obviously were entranced by that slut. And I refuse to apologize."

"Who are you?" Koerner demanded.

"Clem Figgie. Oh, you're such a grouch! I've noticed you around town. Was she pretending to be Alexandra Nowosielska?" His features oozed contempt. "Czermak? Maria Czermak? Or did she pose as Marla Jarecki? Isn't she the darling?"

"Jarecki," Koerner said, annoyed with himself for answering.

"She married Jarecki when she was a child, so I'm told. Listen, dear fellow, that sweet thing stole my mother's wedding ring and six hundred dollars. Oh, the money doesn't matter. Well, it does. I'm not that rich." He sighed. "You don't believe one word."

He owns a boat, Koerner thought, I can smell the bay underneath that putrid chemical. He's never had a job, it's inherited—bonds, coupons, stocks, maybe a patch of the hillside. I don't like anything about him. That Fourth of July hat, the sulky voice, the beads, the alligator. He's a mound of grease and pastry.

"Well, she did," Figgie continued, twisting his necklace. "I assure you she did."

I'm losing my appetite again, Koerner thought. That deodorant is suffocating. "What makes you so sure?" he asked. "Just how do you know?"

"Who else? Quite foolishly I invited her to brunch at my place on Saint Swithin's Day and that same evening I discovered the theft. I've no idea why I should unburden myself to you, I can tell you dislike me. Oh, never mind. I was presented to Miss Alexandra, diamonds and all, at a Pacific Heights supper. She can pass, you know. Or did you? Nob Hill. Tenderloin. North Beach. Whatever she chooses to be. Tonight she is the Stanford graduate. And I'm not Clem Figgie, no indeed, I'm the Crown Prince of Nepal." He fanned himself with the menu. His plump boneless face glistened. "Suppose we go for a sail some afternoon. Imagine what a spanking time we might have. Would you like that? Now what do you say?"

"I get seasick in a bathtub."

"Oh! Oh! How amusing!" Figgie cried. "Well, sweet thing, I must be off. My friends are waiting. Bye!" he exclaimed, flourishing one hand. "If I can just manage with this ankle . . . " He eased himself from the deck chair, gasped, and hobbled inside.

I should have let him talk, Koerner said to himself. That was stupid. I could have learned a few things. Alexandra. Marla. Maria. The elephant assaulted the fat lady. What next?

On the following night when he pushed through the frosted glass door of the Dutchman's lounge he told himself she would not be there, but he could not prevent himself from looking. At her table sat an inscrutable Japanese tourist slung with cameras. This is absurd, he thought. I haven't seen her for at least three years, I see her for three minutes, she gives me an alias, pats me like a dog, waltzes off to some appointment and I lie awake half the night wondering when I'll see her again. Well, I'll have a drink before dinner and concentrate on other things. Baseball. Politics. Travel. Yes, that's an idea, I could plan another trip. Think about the Canary Islands or Tierra del Fuego.

The bartender arrived, wiping his hands on a towel. "Are you by any chance William Koerner?"

"I guess so," Koerner said.

"Marla called. She's going out of town for a while."

"Anything else?"

"She'll be in touch."

"Thank you. I'd like a double martini."

No sooner had the bartender turned away than a voice asked: "Is Marla a friend of yours?"

The voice belonged to an earnest young man with pimples and a cowlick. He wore a blue nylon windbreaker that might have come from a drugstore and clipped to the breast pocket stood a platoon of ballpoint pens.

"My name's Orin," he said timidly, extending his hand. "I didn't catch yours."

"Bill," Koerner said without enthusiasm and accepted the hand, which was moist and felt like a tongue.

Orin grinned, exhibiting ragged teeth. "Hello, Bill. It's a pleasure to make your acquaintance. Do you come here a lot?"

"Not very often."

"I come here all the time. It's expensive, but it's a wonderful place to make friends. I was pretty sure I hadn't seen you because I've got a good memory for faces. I hope I'm not intruding but I wanted to introduce myself because Marla used to be my girl."

Koerner looked at him again. Brown glass eyes, expressionless wooden features. Orin resembled Pinocchio.

"Can you guess where I work?" he asked. "Can you?"

There was a medicinal smell about him, but that proved nothing. After a drink Koerner said, "I give up."

"The animal shelter!"

"Well," Koerner said.

"Yep," said Orin. "This sounds funny, but I like animals better than people. Do you have a pet?"

"At the moment, no, but I may get a Chihuahua."

Orin grew tense. "You should buy two."

"Why should I buy two?"

"Because they don't eat much!" Orin cried and slapped Koerner on the back. Then he became serious. "Bill, I'm studying for my vet's license. In fact, I already thought up a name for my clinic. I'm going to call it Orin's Pet Hospital."

"That's a good name," Koerner said. "Tell me about you and Marla."

Orin frowned. "I don't know why she doesn't call anymore. I can't figure it out. Maybe she thinks I don't amount to much but she's going to change her mind when she sees my clinic." Carefully he wiped his nose on the back of his hand. "I'll tell you something else that puzzles me. We always went to the movies in Novato or someplace like that because she didn't want to go into the city. She knows a lot of those bohemians in North Beach and I thought it would be fun to meet them, but she didn't want to. She knows Christopher Lloyd. He's a poet. They went to Stanford together. His picture was in the *Examiner* a couple of months ago because he took a swing at a cop. Did you ever read his poems?"

"A few."

"I don't have time to read. Working at the shelter—wow! You can't believe how busy it gets. Last week it seemed like everybody lost a cat or found a cat. Things always come in bunches."

"How did you meet her?"

Orin's carved head swiveled toward the dartboard, an arm came up and one finger pointed. No, he's not alive, Koerner thought, somebody pulled a string.

"Right there," Orin said happily. "She was watching me so I challenged her to a game."

"And you won?"

"Easy. I'm pretty good. I can beat everybody around here except Dave Aretino. You think you can beat me?"

"I'm out of practice."

"I'll give you a handicap and bet you a dollar."

"Not tonight. So you invited her to the movies?"

"Yep. She sells leather goods and she had an appointment, but she promised to call me. I was afraid she'd forgotten because she didn't call for a long time. She's really strange. Sometimes she dresses up like a gypsy with gold earrings and a bandanna." He stopped to squeeze a pimple. "She told me not to give her any presents, but I wanted to anyway."

My God, she devoured him, Koerner thought. He doesn't know what happened. He dreams about the two of them caring for sick puppies at Orin's Pet Hospital. She scrambled Figgie, too, but six hundred dollars is less than he spends on Halloween. I wonder if she did rob Captain Alligator.

Orin pulled out his wallet. "Bill, I'm going to show you something personal because I trust you, but you can't tell anybody."

The wallet was manufactured plastic that unfolded with a harsh ripping noise. Orin thrust two fingers into a pocket and triumphantly brought out a Polaroid snapshot, which he slapped on the bar face down.

"Go ahead. Turn it over."

Marla was lying comfortably naked on a couch, smiling for the camera. Koerner stared at it. What she had done was to arrange herself exactly like Goya's Duchess of Alba.

Orin chuckled. "Boy, was I surprised when she gave that to me! You could have knocked me down with a feather. She got some friend of hers to take it—some girl-friend." He slipped the picture back into his wallet. "She made me promise never to let anybody see it because her parents might find out. She lives in the city on Pacific Heights and her father is president of a bank. You know, Bill, this is going to sound funny, but after I get my clinic I'm going to ask her to marry me."

It was like something from an old fairy tale. The youth invited the lady to eat his heart, so she obliged. And how does our lady amuse herself this evening? Koerner wondered. Does she wear a short tight skirt as she prowls the Tenderloin? Does she play Alexandra with diamonds on Russian Hill?

Then it seemed to him that he had guessed where she was—in North Beach sipping cappuccino at a sidewalk café, or discussing poetry with Christopher Lloyd in the Literary Lights Bookshop. No doubt she had met Chris Lloyd. His cultural status would attract her. He was, after all, a celebrated North Beach poet.

He remembered seeing Lloyd at Raphael's Café surrounded by unpublished disciples—an arrogant little magistrate with tousled hair and the nose of an Aztec prince, full of himself to the lip, as though the universe spiraled about his pen. There, it was said, at that secluded table in the nook, half-hidden by potted ferns, he held court if the mood settled upon him. Oh yes, quite by accident she would have met Christopher Lloyd. And how did he respond?

She would be out of town—that was the message. Pinocchio waited for her to call, but why should I wait? Koerner asked himself. Tomorrow I might sidle around North Beach and see what develops.

When he drove across the Golden Gate Bridge on the following night he could see fog beginning to obscure the city, and by the time he got to North Beach everything was damp. Coffee at Raphael's seemed like a good idea. Lloyd might show up.

Wallace the giant bartender wore a prodigiously loose Russian peasant blouse and Koerner once again felt amazed that a man could be so wide and thick. When he was not mixing drinks or keeping the peace Wallace liked to draw imaginary creatures to which he gave imaginary names and homes. He drew brendels and absquiths and mergolyns and presips and cocoranths and a great many others. He drew them with exquisite delicacy on the best Japanese paper and everybody who had seen him do these things with a pen lightly between his fingertips was reduced to silence. Koerner remembered several years ago when there had been trouble outside—a junkie waving a meat hook, threatening customers at the sidewalk tables. He could remember Wallace rolling toward the junkie with the massive conviction of a truck rolling downhill. The junkie swung the hook and connected, which may have been the worst mistake of his life. Wallace chose not to kill him, but when a siren came screaming out of the Broadway tunnel a few minutes later the junkie still slept his dreadful sleep on the pavement.

"You haven't been around," Wallace said pleasantly.

"Not for a while," Koerner agreed. "How's Raphael?"

"Oh, you know," said Wallace, and swept imperceptible motes of dust from the lustrous wood. "What can I get you?"

"Nothing right now. Have you seen Chris Lloyd?"

"Half an hour ago he went by."

"Which direction?"

"Columbus."

"Thanks. Tell Raphael hello for me."

Wallace nodded.

Lloyd probably was heading for the Bagel Shop or maybe the Triumvirate. He would be someplace in that neighborhood.

At the corner of Broadway and Columbus stood Reece—a mahogany totem pole. He wore tattered sneakers and a greasy unbuttoned overcoat displaying four hundred soup stains and he smelled worse than a cage at the zoo. He had grown a wretched billy-goat beard, perhaps to compensate for several missing teeth. His mouth twitched. He won't notice me, Koerner thought. He fried his brain so long ago that nothing matters.

"Hey, man," Reece said in his very deep voice, "got a cigarette?"

"Gave it up," Koerner said. "What are you doing on this side of the street? You used to be on the other side."

"Corners," Reece muttered, studying the traffic light. His tickets to Paradise had been counterfeit and now he stood on corners watching the signals change. Green. Yellow. Red. Green. Yellow. Red.

"You know Chris Lloyd, don't you?"

"Uppity Jack."

"Come on, Reece. Do you know him?"

"I know him."

"Seen him tonight?"

After a while Reece lowered his gaze to the fireplug. That seemed to be the end of it. Either he did not want to talk about Lloyd or he had forgotten the question.

"Marla Jarecki. Do you know her?"

"Ted Bristol."

"Come on, how about it?" Koerner said, lifting his voice above the traffic. "Marla Jarecki."

"Ted Bristol."

"He knows her. Is that what you're saying?"

"Ted Bristol Bones."

"How would I find him? Where does he hang out?"

Reece vanished, speeding toward some nebulous galaxy accessible to no one else. At last he returned: "Lights."

This could mean the traffic signal, but probably it meant the bookshop. "What does he look like?"

"George Washington."

"All right, George Washington. Now what does Ted Bristol Bones look like?"

"I told you," Reece said, as though speaking to a child.

"Anything else? Could you describe him some other way?"

"Cops," Reece answered lazily, "bug him."

"Cops bug everybody. Come on, now."

"Watch cap. Pea jacket."

"Good. Will he talk about her?"

Reece considered the fireplug. "Cops bug him."

"I'm not a cop."

"I understand that," Reece said.

Well, I could go either direction, Koerner thought. I could walk up Grant and hunt for the bard of North Beach, or walk down Columbus to the bookshop.

The signals changed and it occurred to him that he had seen Ted Bristol some-where—playing chess in the park, maybe. He did resemble George Washington. Pea jacket. Watch cap. And somebody had said that Bristol was an ex-Communist who worked on the waterfront and knew Harry Bridges. Yes, well, he might be worth a trip. The signals changed again.

"Hey, man," Reece said, "got a cigarette?"

Koerner wagged his head.

Reece began to giggle; he covered his rotting mouth with a pair of leathery hands and he stamped his feet with joy.

Meanwhile the traffic stopped and started like a mechanical caterpillar. Green. Yellow. Stop. Red. Green. Start. Well, Koerner thought, I don't want to stand here until midnight. I see why Reece likes it, but I'd better track down Mr. Bones.

Beneath the peppermint-stripe awning of Literary Lights a bin of used books leaned against the wall. Ten cents apiece. He paused to look at the titles. *Great Golf Courses. Beginning Jiu Jitsu. Prehistoric Astronomy in Cambodia. Sailing for the Novice. Fix It Yourself. How to Bowl 300! Zulu Odyssey.*

He opened the Zulu book. There, dressed for action in pith helmet and rumpled white suit, the corpulent author sat enthroned like a provincial governor—a swagger stick across his knees—facing the camera with dignified reserve after what must have been an adventurous trip through Zululand. His eyes bulged, his formidable mustache drooped.

Koerner looked at the copyright page. The book was privately printed in Philadelphia in 1912. The spine was cracked, the faded linen binding spotted by rain.

On the title page beneath his name, Charles Duckett Grubb, the author had written with a graceful hand:

Millie—Dear Love

Charles

After reading a few sentences Koerner dropped *Zulu Odyssey* in the bin and continued to the entrance. No doubt this African journey had been the most exciting experience of Mr. Grubb's life, but the wearisome prose and the mind responsible for it explained why the narrative was privately published.

Inside, as always, Huong sat like Buddha on a high stool beside the cash register.

"Huong," he said by way of greeting.

The shining slit eyes did not move, nor did Huong speak, nor did anything about that oracular brown face appear to change.

Koerner went down the narrow staircase to the basement and looked around. There—beneath a wildly painted social protest mural—sat George Washington in watch cap and rimless spectacles, his pea jacket folded on a chair. He sat behind a three-legged marble-topped table with a tiny cup of espresso and he was reading Plato. He glanced over the top of his glasses with a suspicious expression.

"Are you Ted Bristol?" Koerner asked.

"Bones, that's me."

"I wonder if I could talk to you."

"Show me your badge."

"I'm no cop."

"IRS?"

"Neither one."

"What's on your mind?"

"Marla."

Bones did not close the book. He did not look friendly. Then he said: "Who wants to know?"

Koerner introduced himself and explained that he had met her in Taos. Bones considered this information. He rubbed his jaw. He had not shaved for a couple of days.

"You're a cop."

"Maybe I look like one."

Bones shut the book, leaving a blunt finger inside to mark the page. He had not made up his mind.

"Why should I talk to you?"

"Can I sit down?"

"You might be straight," Bones said. "You might be anything. She's got trouble enough. I don't want something bad happening to her." He waved at a chair. "You god damn better be straight." Although he did not sound hostile, neither did he sound well disposed.

Koerner pointed to the espresso. "How about another?"

"No. First off, her name is Mikki Novak. I don't like people calling her Marla. Maria. None of that crap. Her name is Mikki."

"Why does she call herself Marla?"

Bones sucked his teeth. He peeled off his glasses and held them up to the light. Apparently they were clean enough. He hooked them back in place. At last he said, "I never knew one to be satisfied."

This could refer to women, but there were other possibilities. I don't want something bad happening to her, he had said, and the George Washington lips barely moved. If anything bad happens to her now, Koerner thought, a couple of waterfront goons will come looking for me. I don't know what she means to this character and I don't know why I'm trying to play detective. Maybe I should go home and wait for her to call.

"Mikki wasn't always wild," Bones said, reaching for the espresso. "Could have been her ma. She was nuts. Smart old broad, but crazy as a sow on ice."

And what about you? Koerner wondered. How do you fit into this?

Bones got to his feet with difficulty and limped around the corner to the toilet. When he came back he said, "Who told you where to find me?"

"Reece."

"That hophead."

"He can surface if he wants to."

"How do you know Reece?"

"I used to hang around North Beach. He was always in the Bagel Shop."

Bones looked attentively at nothing. Then he said, "Reece was a good sculptor. Why did he blow his head apart? What a waste."

"I never knew he was a sculptor."

"Years ago. All right, sport, listen. Bad things came down I won't talk about, but I'll tell you this much. Mikki was a nice kid. I hear things about her I know aren't true. Max and Hilda taught her right. Then she had to go and get married before she grew up. Stupid."

"Jarecki?"

"They lived together. She was sixteen. I told Max to kill Jarecki." His expression changed. Evidently he had decided to say nothing else.

"Was she ever in North Africa?"

"What's North Africa got to do with it?"

"Well," Koerner said, "I'm a little embarrassed about this. We got sort of drunk in Taos and started speaking French. She has an unusual accent."

"You may be straight," Bones said with a smile like a razor blade. "Until now I didn't think so. She learned French in Martinique. I don't know about North Africa." He took a sip of espresso and all at once he appeared older. "I don't see her much these days. Once in a while she comes around if she wants to talk. Usually it's some bastard making trouble."

"Can you tell me anything about her father?"

"Doing time. It was a bad rap. He worked with me at Eckholm's shipyard for thirty-six years. I know Max." Bones opened *The Republic*. His grizzled face tightened.

This seems to be it, Koerner thought, he doesn't want to say anything else. She tells Orin her father is a bank president and they live on Pacific Heights. Attended Stanford with Chris Lloyd. She told Figgie her name was Alexandra something. In Taos she was Maria Czermak. I wonder if she lies to Uncle Bones.

He remembered meeting her at the Taos Inn on a frigid January night. He had been almost asleep beside the fireplace when she walked through the lobby dressed like a stylish Navajo in purple velveteen with a hammered silver concho belt and soft tawny deerskin boots. He remembered staring at her because of the insinuating walk and those oddly tilted, expressionless eyes. She was aware of him, he knew, and she had walked past him with the long full Navajo dress swirling around her boots. And when he followed that swirling Navajo dress into the bar he was surprised to find her alone.

They had talked about Campeche and Palenque, and Tulum above the emerald water, and Isla Mujeres, and the wonderful Mexican menus that tried to make things easy for American tourists by offering beal cutle and sirloing steack and hors d'aeuvre and red snaper. Had she been to Copán? Yes. Ceiba trees under a white-hot sky, tin-roofed shacks beating back the sun. And while she was there a boy with a flute walked out of the tropical green fields like some antique Mayan god and seated himself on the sloping wall of the prehistoric ball court.

Then he had mentioned Petra.

Where is that? she said.

Petra, the rose-red city half as old as time. It lies below Amman, below the Dead Sea, in south Jordan.

Have you been there? she asked.

Yes, he said. It's a city carved out of a cliff two thousand years ago by Nabataean Arabs. In Jerusalem I met three Australians who were back-packing around the world. We hired a taxi to Petra.

I want to go there, she had said. Take me there.

Koerner blinked and stood up. "All those questions—I don't blame you for being suspicious. Thanks for talking with me."

Bones peered over his glasses. "You're no cop."

"No? Why not?"

"I saw Huong in the can. I asked about you."

He's almost friendly, Koerner thought. I might as well try one more question. "What can you tell me about Chris Lloyd?"

Bones removed his spectacles. He examined them for dust. He considered. At last he said: "Lloyd couldn't write his way out of a paper bag. Stevens. Pound. Jeffers. Those are poets. I still think you're a cop."

"Huong tells me you're a narc."

Bones, after one long indecipherable look, returned to Plato.

A fanfare of trumpets welcomed Koerner to the street and a patrol car with flashing lights contributed to the argument at Broadway and Columbus. Reece had not moved from the fireplug, but his hands were in the pockets of his coat and he had turned up the collar. He appeared to be on another space trip, so Koerner walked by without speaking.

Christopher Lloyd was not at the Triumvirate nor at the Bagel Shop nor Beethoven's Goose nor anywhere in the neighborhood. Well, then, possibly at Raphael's.

And there the poet reigned, uncombed, lordly, all but enshrined. There the bard of North Beach presided over his discussion table in a fern-shrouded nook, properly attired in a turtleneck sweater. Koerner hesitated. No. No, it would be impossible to join that clique. Some other time, perhaps, when Mr. Lloyd was offstage. Then it occurred to him that Wallace might know her.

Wallace, not quite as big as a buffalo, was drying wine glasses.

"Cappuccino," Koerner said. While waiting for it he folded his arms and studied the bottles behind the bar. Cointreau with a red ribbon. The frosty green Courvoisier. Dark brown Tía Maria. Black Jack Daniel's almost hidden by Wallace's tip jar. Galliano. Chivas Regal. The opulent Chambord liqueur surmounted by a gold crown.

"I've been wondering," he said when the cappuccino arrived, "does Marla Jarecki come in here?"

Wallace replied with a massive shrug and began rinsing a carafe. It was obvious that he did not want to talk about her.

I think I've blundered into a spiderweb, Koerner said to himself. This is becoming a very strange night. I should go home before something awful happens. Or maybe I'm imagining. He looked across the bar at the great Scottish slab of a face and the tightly curled ringlets. Wallace had a large head, but it seemed uncommonly small above his shoulders. From the side he resembled a giant turtle.

"How's the menagerie?"

"Oh," Wallace answered in his pleasant voice, "various creatures come to mind."

Just then the door opened and a squad of tourists entered, unmistakable vacationers from the midwest, dressed for August in Wichita on a chilly night in San Francisco. They were damp. Koerner glanced outside to see if the mist had turned to rain and found Christopher Lloyd glaring through the ferns. His orange hair flew in all directions and his reddish eyes burned. He looked like a crazed parrot.

Koerner swung around to the bar. There could be no doubt that Lloyd recognized him. But how? They had never met.

Somebody was approaching. The rapid click of heels sounded like a woman, but the poet wore elevated shoes.

"I saw you in Taos," Lloyd snapped. "Marla pointed you out." He had the fierce eyebrows of an old man. At the tip of his nose a crusty wart stood out like the stub of a broken horn.

My God, Koerner thought, I had a feeling she was there with somebody, but not this dervish. "How about a cappuccino?" he asked. And to his surprise Lloyd hopped up on the next stool.

Wallace floated toward them with the peculiar buoyancy of enormous men.

"Remy," Lloyd commanded, folding his arms. After the cognac had been delivered he tasted it and approved. Then he said, "She is a nymph. Furthermore, she is unstable. Did you know that? Until recently she was hospitalized at the Marquis Emerson clinic. They should not have released her. She is capable of destroying herself. I tell you for your own good because she is capable of destroying not only herself but anyone who fails to recognize her condition." He lifted the cognac smoothly with his palms as though elevating the Holy Grail. "You assume that you met a charming fauve, but she is distraught and dangerous. I might add that I saw you talking to that shipyard intellectual. Whatever Bristol told you should be disregarded." He paused, scowling. Then all at once he waved impatiently. "Suppose we get this over with. When Marla was a child she was used by her father. Not once, mind you, not twice, but indiscriminately. Her father is a degenerate who has been sentenced to a long prison term. There is no way of predicting what may happen if he gets out. Do you understand? Now I have one more thing to say, but first, let me thank you for the cognac. Three days ago Marla and I were married." He sprang off the stool, made some incomprehensible gesture with both hands, and stalked out the door.

The discussion table was empty. Their guru having flown, the disciples scattered. Or perhaps they were congregating at another café. Well, Koerner thought, I can't guess what this is all about but I know that maniac is lying. They aren't married.

Then he began to think about Taos. Most of what happened was easy to remember because one scene led to the next; but later, when they were alone on the snowy plateau with Taos a distant sprinkle of lights, fragments were missing. He remembered that while she stared into the canyon he had looked carefully all around because of something malignant in the night. He remembered that he took out the harmonica and began to play, and invented a clumsy little dance on the bridge—as though this might appease the gathering presence—although he could see nothing unexpected except the oval moon riding over Taos mountain. And during the night while they slept together it had seemed to him that a mystery was resolved; but when he awoke in the icy Taos dawn she had vanished. She might have been a violent dream except for a hairpin on the floor.

"Hello," said a voice that was almost masculine.

He looked in the mirror. "*Je ne parle pas Anglais*," he said to her reflection.

After a moment she smiled. "Did you get the message?"

He turned around, startled by how close she was. Tonight, as Figgie would say, she had decided to become the Montmartre Apache—black leather cap, black leather pants and jacket with chains and metal buttons, little black boots.

"If it isn't raining we might take a walk," he said. "I have so much to tell you."

After a questioning glance at Wallace she agreed.

"Where do you want to go?" she asked when they were outside.

"Where? Oh, anywhere. It doesn't matter in the least. Why don't we go to the circus? I'm worried about the fat lady. No, I have a better idea. Let's go to the bookshop. Did you know you lost a hairpin in Taos? I kept it for at least a year, maybe two years. What do you suppose that means?"

"Taos was a long time ago."

He laughed. "Yes. I've tried to forget. No, that's a lie." I'm not making sense, he thought. "Did you know Lloyd was at Raphael's just now?"

She smiled again. "I waited until he left. You're the one I wanted to be with."

"Let's go to Campeche. We could have lunch in that terrible restaurant—that old radio blaring and those tiny paper napkins. Arroz con mariscos and cheese pie and Nescafé. My God, it was awful! Those yellow plastic glasses and bent forks and a bottle of toothpicks—I never thought I'd want to have lunch there again, but now I do. I remember that card table with a splintered leg and the mangy little brown and white mutt that was always scratching and will you come with me to Campeche?"

"Before you start packing, one or two things will have to be straightened out."

"Yes," he said. "And we can spend a while in Villahermosa. It's lovely. There's a fancy painted bandstand in the park and flowers and flowers and flowers and have you been to Villahermosa?"

"Stop dreaming."

"Will you come with me to the hermosa villa?"

"I might."

"I want to hear you say yes."

"Maybe. It depends."

"Maybe. All right, maybe," Koerner said. "Will you come with me to visit the stone deities of Tula? They stand on a pyramid like Egyptian pharaohs supervising the town and there was a guard wearing baggy blue trousers sitting in the shade reading a newspaper and a pig tied to a tree and while I was eating a taco the church bells began to ring and there were orange peels and roosters and Mexico everywhere. Will you—ah! We're here. Charles Duckett Grubb. I want you to meet him. This is his book. This is what he bequeathed to posterity. This is the chronicle of Charles Duckett Grubb."

She was faintly amused. "Is he important?"

"Nobody could be less important. I'm not sure how to explain. Listen." After pretending to clear his throat he began: "Since early childhood in a leafy suburb of Allentown it had been my fondest wish . . . "

"You idiot," she said, with an arm around his waist. "You won't get through the first chapter."

"I don't plan to," Koerner said. "Read the inscription."

"Millie—Dear Love," she read aloud. For a moment she was silent. Then she looked up with a friendly expression. "You sentimental fool. Who believes in love anymore?"

"Close your eyes and pick out something. Anything. I'll buy it for you."

"Now I remember," she said. "The guy with the harmonica." Obediently she closed her eyes and reached for the books. "All right, sailor, what next?"

"Try again."

"Did I pick something awful?"

"*Lost Horizon,*" he said, expecting her to laugh.

"How about it, sailor? Will you help me?"

Koerner felt his breath catch. He took her hand and guided it toward another book while she stood close beside him with her head tilted. A streetlight shone on her sleeping face under the black leather cap. The wide cheekbones, long nose, and protruding upper lip were deeply sensual, a Slavic sculptor's dream of Aphrodite. When he let go of her hand she picked up the book he had selected.

"What's my little gift?" she whispered, slowly lifting her blind face. "What will you buy Marla?" Then unexpectedly she opened her eyes. "Oh, how sweet! *A Scarlet Treasury of Confessions.*" She began to read: "The Countess gleamed white and naked in my arms—well, now really!"

"Who is the Countess entertaining?"

"Nietzsche. Would you like more? It was in the greenhouse that the Countess first lured me to my fall, behind the back of her husband. Oh, my goodness! We ought to read this in private."

"Mikki," Koerner said, "you have no idea how often I've thought about you."

"And I've thought about you. But first, cowboy, let's get things straight."

"I don't understand," he said.

"Who told you my name was Mikki?"

"Bones."

"I thought so. He tells people he used to know my father."

"What are you talking about?" Koerner demanded. "Mikki, will you stop lying?"

"My name is Gloria Wonderlips," she continued in a musical voice. "That old man used to be in the merchant marine but he was horribly injured during a collision. I can't imagine why he tells people he knew my father. You can't believe a word he says. My father died years ago. He was a wealthy land developer in Pasadena. I grew up in Pasadena. I'm rich. Have you heard of Encantada Estates? The homes are incredibly expensive. That was one of my father's projects. Did I tell you his name?

"No," Koerner said. "What was his name?"

"Alexis Masaryk. His grandfather was related to the Tsar of Russia. They were cousins."

"Your great-grandfather was the Tsar's cousin?"

"Yes. My great-grandfather was a Romanov."

She went on talking and he understood that she was mad—or half-mad—and to enter that turbulent world would be another form of madness. She had moved closer. He felt her thighs press against him and he could smell the black leather.

"Let's take the ferry," she said with her arms around his neck. "I know we can agree on a price before we get to Sausalito. I have an appointment, but I'd rather be with you."

Suddenly the gentle weight of her arms became intolerable. Koerner held his breath.

"If that's how you feel," she said, "I've changed my mind." She released him and wandered away.

1991

THE SUCCUBUS

A VERY DISTINGUISHED old gentleman with a white mustache sat
down beside me and crossed himself for a safe voyage over the Atlantic.
"Permit—" he began with a smile, but at that moment the engines
started up, one after another, and the fuselage of the airliner trembled from the
vibrations.

"Permit me to introduce myself," he resumed when the roaring diminished. "I
am—" But just then the airliner swung around and went trundling heavily down
the taxi strip. With an anxious expression the old gentleman fastened his safety belt
and then sat looking straight ahead, his withered bony fingers playing nervously
over the surface of a handsome Florentine leather portfolio on his lap. When we
headed into the wind he closed his eyes tightly and appeared to be holding his
breath. Not until we were several hundred feet in the air did he relax.

"A miracle!" he exclaimed, opening his eyes. "And now, if the airplane is kind
enough—I am Signor Salvatore Brancato. This flying, is it not indeed a miracle?
We are above the birds! Yet, to be frank, my heart is not at peace. It has been my
privilege to cross the Atlantic Ocean many times, for I do business in America, and
the pilots are good enough to explain to me why it is possible—why the machine

does not remain on the ground. I understand what they are saying. Yes, everything. Even so, I think to myself each time when the engines begin: The machine will not move. But it does! And my heart sinks."

"If flying makes you uneasy, why don't you go by ship?"

"I refuse!" he said emphatically, lifting one finger.

"Does it take too long?"

"At my age a man finds he has all the time in the world. Earlier, he did not think there was enough. No, that is not the reason. I allow you to guess." And he added, smoothing his mustache while he eyed the stewardess: "One guess."

"Could it have anything to do with a woman?"

Signor Brancato immediately turned to me with surprise. "I thought you were American!"

"I am," I said.

"But—"

"Do you think Americans don't care about anything except money?"

He shrugged. "With you the enjoyment of women is never an occupation."

"Are you suggesting that a man should devote his life entirely to women?"

Signor Brancato paused to consider this, and finally admitted, "If possible."

"But Signor Brancato, when eighty years, let's say, have gone by and a man has nothing except memories of—"

"Stop!" he exclaimed, holding up both hands. "Permit me to tell you. Nothing is of greater value. Nothing! It is, in fact, because of a woman I do not cross the ocean by ship. I will tell you what happened. If I were a young man I could not tell. Because of a young man's pride, you understand. But, as is the way of life, my own is concluding. And with my life concludes my pride. I believe it will do no harm to anyone to speak of what once happened to me. I swear my story is true, although you may smile. If you have ever been in such a situation, you will appreciate my feelings. If you have not, no amount of explanation will be of the slightest value. By the way, are you married?"

"No, Signor."

"It does not matter one way or another, my young friend. We are all men in this business together. Very well. Here, then, is the story. *Attenzione.*

"First, there is the ocean, do you understand? The sun is shining. Our ship is leaving the beautiful Mediterranean. Gibraltar becomes nothing. We are in the open sea. Next, among the hundreds of passengers, there is a girl. Of course, there are many girls aboard the ship, but only one could I see. Listen, I will describe her to you. No! No, later I will describe. It will take your breath away. For now, remember only that we looked at one another and could not speak. Later I will give the details. First, therefore, we have the sea, which I came to look upon as my true friend."

Signor Brancato, placing a hand on his heart, gazed down at the Atlantic far below the wing of the plane.

"How different from here! Aboard the ship one is lulled this way and that, as in a cradle, awakening the earliest memories. So it was on that magnificent day when Gibraltar faded into Spain and over the bow of our ship the spray came flying. I, who was very young, walked the deck in great enthusiasm, licking the taste of salt from my lips and making myself dizzy with deep breaths. Very soon I came upon this girl who looked at me steadily. Unfortunately she was escorted everywhere by an old man with a stout cane. This, I discovered, was her father. What was I to do? The old man, I could tell, was less friendly than a shark. He seemed to know, after one glance at me, that I was hunting his daughter."

Signor Brancato stroked his luxuriant white mustache and nodded at the memory.

"The old man was right. All the same, I began to make plans. I was, when the young girl stared at me, filled with the ardor of which the poets write. However, I might say, poets do not get to the point. Nightingales. The moonlight. It may be that such things occur to women, but they do not to men. No. A young man loves more in the condition of a beast to whose nostrils have come the seasonal odor. That is to say, he has no doubt about what is tormenting him. The flesh of a glorious young woman. Excuse me, it is true. The problem, naturally, as is always the problem, is how to achieve the flesh. In my case there was this old father with the big cane. A terrible weapon. For years—I do not know how many years—I have dreamed of that stick of wood.

"So! What was to be done? The ocean, my good friend, came to the rescue. I will tell you how. At first it was, as the saying goes, like glass. It was that smooth. But on the second day there was a bulge now and then, and the father of the girl did not feel so well. I could tell. I was watching him carefully. He sat down in a deck chair, and presently forgot about his daughter, who wandered out of sight. Then, naturally, I was upon her like a hawk. I spoke to her. I found her responsive. Her name was Gabriella. But we had not been talking five minutes when her father came looking for her. Gabriella was terrified. She pleaded with me to leave her before we should be seen together. I wanted to stay. I swore I would never leave her. I was lying, of course. I could not get away fast enough. Yet not before we had arranged to meet again.

"I then passed a restless night. In the darkness I paced back and forth like a tiger, thinking of what lay in store for me. That is to say, not being killed by the old man's cane, you understand, but it was the thought of Gabriella that aroused me. I knew—how I knew this I could not say—but I knew that before the ship would dock in New York I would have my way with her. There was no deceit in this girl. Right away I could tell. I thought of nothing else.

"On the next morning I was overjoyed to feel, before opening my eyes, the ship rolling back and forth. This would mean Gabriella's father would get sick. Then, of course, thinking only of himself, he would not care what was happening to his daughter—who was, I swear, the flower of all Italy. Joyously I considered how miserable the old man would be.

"What, then, was my astonishment and rage to find that he did not get sick at all! From a distance I watched. Gabriella and her father strolled about the deck, laughing and chatting. Only once in a while, when his back was turned, would she direct toward me the most deliberate and appealing gaze. I clasped my hands. I swore. I blew kisses to my Gabriella. Otherwise I did not know what to do. I did not want to get the cane broken across my head. I began to fear he would guard her all the way across the ocean, and then, in New York, God knows, she would disappear and we would never see each other again. In my anguish I prayed for a giant wave to wash her father overboard. And, in fact, the ocean was stirring as though it had been asleep for a hundred years.

"Our ship began to rock. To bury the prow, for seconds at a time, deep into the water. Waves came thundering against the sides and swept like rain across the deck. Everybody went inside, and during the afternoon Gabriella's father sometimes drew from his coat a handkerchief and wiped his forehead. Another day, perhaps, and he would retreat to the stateroom, after which Gabriella and I would be free. I took to watching my friend the ocean as, in later years, I watched the stock market.

"By evening, unfortunately, he felt better. He walked about the deck and shook his fist at the ocean. Gabriella, as always, followed obediently one step behind him. Yet he seemed to suspect her of some perfidy—I do not know why. Occasionally he would glare all around. Then he would glare at her. I knew I must be careful, yet it would not do to have Gabriella think me timid. Something must be accomplished.

"The next morning, to my dismay, the sea was calm and oily, and I reflected to myself: The old man will be alert and vigorous. This is a day to be cautious. We were, you understand, getting well into the middle of the ocean, and except for one brief meeting with Gabriella I had achieved nothing. If a few more such days went by, days in which I could not advance my position, I knew—for women do not like to remain too long in abeyance—I knew that the desire of my Gabriella would vanish like the mist. She would turn her attention elsewhere, having decided that I lacked the resource and the courage to gain what I wanted. She would think I was afraid of her father, whose shaggy head filled me with hatred and alarm.

"Ah, but that very afternoon, my young friend, can you guess what happened? I will tell you. For luncheon we were served a peculiar meat, and because of the strange appearance of the ocean, her father went staggering into his stateroom. However, to my astonishment, Gabriella, instead of rushing into my arms, also went to the stateroom to take care of him. I could not believe this treachery! I was furious with her. Had she forgotten me? Had she only been playing with my affections? I could have beaten her. It was shameful to be treated in this way. Now, I thought, now if she comes to me, I will refuse her! I was, of course, lying to myself, because I would devour her with kisses. Yes, and I would carry her off to my little cabin and lock the door. I would, then, make love to my Gabriella until everyone went tramping down the gangplank into New York.

"However, I did not see her again for two whole days. We were then more than halfway across. You can imagine my desperation. I resolved on violence, but while I was still resolving, striding up and down with clenched fists, there was a miracle. Yes! A note handed to me by the steward. It was from Gabriella. She had not forgotten. Tomorrow evening she would be in the library between seven and eight o'-clock, but if I should see her father there I was not to speak, or to make the least sign.

"I thought the hour would never come. Never. I thought, too, of her father being there and everything ruined. Well, the hour did come. I entered the library. There was nobody. Yet not a moment passed before she appeared, smiling, but cold. I hurried over to clasp her hands. We sat down together. I pressed her chilled fingers to my lips. She kept watching the door with an uneasy expression. I implored her to come to my cabin, and she kept shaking her head. But, do you know, after a while she ceased to object, and in a few more minutes I managed to obtain from her a promise to come to me there on the following evening. At this promise I could no longer control myself. There in the middle of the library, with books all around us—I remember quite well—I embraced her. Just in time we broke apart, for she heard the tapping of her father's cane in the corridor. I snatched a large book; she opened a newspaper. In came her father, coughing, muttering, filled with suspicion. I gave him a look of innocent surprise. And Gabriella? She looked up from the newspaper with a smile of the utmost affection. I was astounded by her duplicity, and thought to myself: Is this all a dream?

"I could not be sure. Still, I remembered the taste of her lips, and throughout the day I found myself trembling with anticipation. This evening, I was convinced, she would be mine. Everywhere I looked I seemed to see her, though in truth I did not see her all day long. I began, then, to fear that her father had learned of what was to occur, and had locked her up. But, naturally, I dared not inquire. More and more I became anxious. There was, however, nothing to do but wait until evening and see if she would come scratching on my door.

"Once more the hour arrived. I sat alone, perspiring, in my dark little cabin beside the propeller. My hands shook with the agony of desire. I swallowed continually. I could hear, very close by, the waves sloshing heavily against the porthole. We were running an ugly sea again.

"Just before eight o'clock I heard stealthy footsteps approaching. I rose to my feet, breathless. The footsteps paused. I could tell they belonged to a woman. She was outside the door. She must be trying to read the number of the cabin, I thought, or perhaps she has forgotten the number and is doubtful. She was not very bright. But just then, do you know what happened? I will tell you. There came a little scratching noise. Yes! However, it was not at my door. She was scratching on the cabin of someone else! What next? That door opened! This was incredible. Furthermore, I heard whispering, and then do you know what occurred? The door closed. She had gone into that cabin.

"I could not believe this. Was she in the darkness with someone she had mistaken for me? Oh, no! I must do something, quickly. But what? Then it occurred to me, that woman was not Gabriella at all. It was a terrible coincidence. I would wait and see. But you have no idea of the horror of waiting hour after hour in those circumstances. Perhaps it *was* Gabriella in there. If so, had she learned by this time that her lover was not I? On the other hand, did she care?

"Ah, how often during those hours did I beg for death to end my despair! I was very young and no one came to my door. Sometime during that fearful night I heard the door of that cabin open for a moment and then close. I immediately peeped like a thief through the ventilator, and I saw a fat little woman of perhaps fifty go tiptoeing down the corridor.

"Gabriella, as it turned out, was seasick. She was, as you Americans say, dead to the world. For three entire days she did not emerge from the stateroom. And I? I abandoned hope. My misfortune was eternal. I was not lucky in love. Some men are fortunate, others are not, and that is all there is to be said on the matter.

"When, at last, our ship was practically across the ocean, Gabriella emerged; and it could not be said who looked the more exhausted, this treasure I had never possessed, or I myself. Which of us had undergone the greater ordeal? Her father, I regret to say, was in marvelous health. Up and down the deck he went, taking the air and stopping every few steps to see if anyone was after Gabriella. She followed him everywhere, as pale as a young ghost, obedient and solemn; however, her eyes were bright. She was recovering. She seemed, in fact, to be looking for me. At length our eyes met. And I saw her little red mouth saying, *'Domani.'* Tomorrow she meant to come to me! It would be the last night of the voyage. Then we would be in New York.

"You would think I would be filled with happiness. No. I was too exhausted. A man can stand only so much. All the same, when I read her lips I nodded eagerly. That's the way a young man is.

"And so it was, my young friend, that on this final evening I waited in my cabin exactly as before. Incredible? Not when we are that age. But not exactly as before, because by this time I had endured so much disappointment that the most violent catastrophe would only amuse me. So I thought. I had no idea what was in store. If I had known, believe me, I would have opened the porthole and flung myself at once into the ocean.

"Well, late in the evening I heard someone tiptoeing down the corridor. My heart leaped. An instant later I clenched my fists. If it should happen to be the fat woman visiting her lover again, I intended, I promise you, to strangle them both. Just as before the little footsteps paused in front of my door. I was, you comprehend, practically insane by this time. I could hear someone breathing just outside. No, I thought to myself, this can not be Gabriella. This sounds like a cow. This is the fat woman. No, it can not possibly be my little Gabriella.

"But it was. I heard a scratching at my door. I groaned aloud. I do not even remember opening the door. I only remember how suddenly she was in my arms. My nose buried itself in her hair, which was damp and cold from the ocean wind. She must have come by some intricate route so that her father could not know where she was. I felt her soft heart beating just beneath my own. I tell you, I thought we should both expire at that moment. Such happiness is too much to endure. I made no attempt to speak. Gabriella, however, being a woman, knew what she was doing. She ordered me to close the door. It was, in fact, swinging back and forth, bumping into us every time the ship rolled. For an instant I was obliged to release her. I locked the door. After which I clasped her in my arms so tightly that she grunted. We were in ecstasy, I assure you.

"How long we stood there groaning with passion, I do not recall. She was chilled from the spray, and trembling—but her little brow was hot with desire. Her hands, almost like the hands of a baby, except for fingernails like needles, were clawing my back. My young friend, believe me, it was a moment which comes often enough to men in their dreams, but few indeed are those who experience even once in their entire life a woman ardent as a succubus. Well, the ship, at this moment, was pitching back and forth so we could hardly stand. The water hissed and splattered against the porthole, a moment later rushing over it entirely, while I, looking down, could see nothing except the whites of Gabriella's eyes gleaming in the darkness of my cabin. I was, to be frank, almost alarmed. For the first time I understood why her father kept such a close guard.

"And now, my young friend, as we are men together, and life is brief, permit me to describe her to you. But for an instant only, as such things are better left to the imagination. You must first visualize the cabin — my tiny home. With arms extended I could touch the opposite walls. That was the size. And it was in darkness practically total, except as the ship rolled to one side and the porthole was no longer submerged. Then, my friend, a pink phosphorescent light faintly illuminated my Gabriella, giving her the terrifying appearance of a demoness. My heart pounded, not only with desire but with horror — I do not know why. Was she real? Perhaps she and her father were drowned long ago, and had but now arisen to mingle with the living for a little while. We were running in a storm, and once — I shall never forget — as we stood there clasping each other with the strength of ten lovers, lightning fled like an arrow over the raging sea, and at that moment Gabriella, I swear, was afire.

"She was sobbing, whispering urgently to me. I felt on my breast her tears dropping one at a time. Gabriella had opened my shirt. She was, in a word, real.

"I do not intend to be too explicit about what happened next. That is not worthy of a man. If, now, I were convinced that she was a demoness, I would not hesitate to describe each particular, but a man can never be sure, and therefore I refrain. Let me say only, incoherent with desire, I begin to draw over her head various articles of lace and silk, spectral garments. And Gabriella? She holds up her arms as if to Heaven — or in defiance of it — the tiny fists clenched with the agony of waiting. She has on more clothing than I expect. It seems to me I remove eight or ten layers. The cabin is soon piled high with her clothing. To this day, I tell you, I do not quite understand where it came from.

"Well, at last it is done. How fiercely she embraces me! I am by this time more dead than alive. The musky odor of her is overpowering. I shudder. I am unable to breathe. Have you ever beheld the contortion of a moth which finds itself suddenly entangled in the web of the spider? That is how I feel. I do not know what is to become of me. Never again in my life have I experienced such a feeling. I vow I will remain forever with this creature, no matter in what world she exists. I will abandon my soul for this love. She may do what she likes with me. In return, naturally, I will have the same privilege. I, therefore, pick her up in my arms. She is, I tell you, as solid as an apple. I become wild with joy and necessity. I cry aloud and gently lay her down. The sea comes rushing at the porthole, stopping only inches from us. The supreme moment is at hand. Gabriella lies quite still, her eyes shining with anticipation.

"It is not until years afterward that a singular thought occurs to me, risen from what depths I cannot say. Let us be frank. Does a woman admit love with her eyes open? No. Particularly such a woman as Gabriella? Never!

"But to continue. The moment for which I have longed is now at hand. My feelings are impossible to describe. Let me say only that I am filled with enthusiasm for the task ahead of me. The voyage has been long and desolate. Is it not just that I am to have my reward?

"Now do you know what happens? You can not possibly guess, so I will tell you. Even now, after half a century, I find myself believing it is only a fearful dream. Who can say? Here is what occurred: I become aware—not exactly of the ocean—but of what the ocean is doing. I pause for one instant to listen. Do not ask me why. I have no idea why. I hear a bottle of drinking water in a rack by the basin. I have left the stopper off, and I now hear the swish and slop of this little bit of water in its bottle. I turn my head to gaze at the porthole, and as the ship descends I am, naturally, obliged to lean in that direction. I see the black ocean slide up the glass of the porthole like a shroud. I lean backward. Then, although I do not want to, I lean forward again. Above the door is a little fan, whirring steadily. I have always thought to myself: What a pleasant little noise. But now I think I can not listen to this noise another second. However, I discover that I am too weak to reach up and turn it off. From the ventilator comes an odor of sour red wine and Camembert cheese. I discover I am hanging against the wall, staring into the porcelain basin. My mouth drops open. My eyes are dull. I stagger forward. I stagger backward, cracking my head soundly against the light bracket, but this means nothing to me. I am feeling no pain on the outside. A taste like metal has come into my mouth, as though I have been drinking citrus juice from a tin can. I swallow. I touch my forehead, finding it unpleasant to touch myself. I am freezing to death, yet I am perspiring at the same time. Ah, that villainous sea! I lean over the basin.

"Gabriella? I do not know when she left my cabin. Perhaps at that moment. Perhaps in an hour. When I awoke I was no longer ill, but it was dawn and New York, like a vast cathedral, was visible outside."

Signor Brancato, having finished his story, brushed his mustache with a finger-tip, first to one side and then the other. Finally he said, "It has been a long time, but still it seems to me, my young friend, as if it occurred last night." He gazed down on the Atlantic, several miles below the wing of the plane, and remarked, "See how the water gleams, as if in satisfaction. I could not bear to cross by ship again. A man is created to endure so much, but no more."

"I suspect Gabriella was real," I said.

"I believe you are right," Signor Brancato replied seriously.

"Did you ever see her again?"

"Fortunately, I did not," he answered. "For that, at least, I am grateful."

"But you were the victim of circumstances. Surely she understood that you had become seasick."

"Perhaps. Who can tell? One never knows."

"Suppose, by some chance, you meet her again?"

"Now?" he exclaimed. "What could I do?"

"What would you do?"

"Ah! My young friend, what could I do? No, it is over. Time will pass you by. The elements are merciless."

"But at least, if you should see her again, you would find that she has forgiven you."

"I think not," replied Signor Brancato, smiling, but sad. "You see, there are situations altogether understandable which are, just the same, unforgivable."

1956

ON THE VIA MARGUTTA

NGUS WAS not only a poet, which meant he had no money; he was a poet's poet, which meant he would never have any money. He had not had any money when he was a child in Glasgow, none in London, none in Paris, and now he did not have any money in Rome. This condition did not surprise him; it certainly did not surprise any of his friends, who, if they ever thought about the matter, would probably have been distressed by the idea of Angus with a pocketful, the reason being that his character was largely founded on his poverty, and he was, therefore, reliable. On the other hand, if Angus got hold of some money nobody would know what to expect. However, his friends did not worry about this, while Angus, as astute as he was shabby, surely perceived and gloried in his destiny.

Rome he liked. He liked many things about it, but most of all he liked the fact that it did not get as cold as Glasgow, London, or Paris. Angus was always cold, even in summer, and often spoke of moving further south, but he never did because he was of the opinion that the Tiber marked the southern boundary of civilization, and there was never a more civilized man than he.

He was ugly enough. Poets come in all shapes and sizes and degrees of beauty, of course, but the most successful ones are either repulsive or quite beautiful; those who look like ordinary people may write poems as good as the best, but no legend is apt to rise from the ashes of their life. Angus could not be considered hideous, not even properly revolting, but he was fairly ugly; he had a bush of coarse, dry, red hair, a nose like an owl, and a prominent Adam's apple which, for some reason of its own, was always in motion. All the same, the more one grew accustomed to Angus the more satisfying his features became, in particular his crystalline gray eyes—merciless as the eyes of a highwayman.

If he was insignificant physically—and indeed it was hard to realize that Angus had a physique because no one ever saw anything except the fierce red hair, the eyes, the beak, the Adam's apple, and a long black overcoat much too big for him—if, therefore, nature had been unjust, or whimsical, in fashioning him on the outside, Angus had been compensated with the gift of a mind as perfect as a wheel, or as a snowflake, one of those star-shaped, pristine flakes, six-rayed, like a flat wheel with six spokes, each spoke a carefully constructed little pine tree in shape, arranged around a central spangle: one of those flawless flakes that come wheeling down like the wrecks of chariots from a battle waged in the sky.

And knowing that such a mind was his, Angus had no qualms about putting it to work; he liked nothing better than an argument. Along the via Margutta there were a number of people who had accepted his intellectual challenges and who still bore the scars of the encounter. Not many of them cared to try a second time. They found it was not much fun to be made fools of in front of their friends. Among the least equipped to do battle with Angus was an American, a Texas American, a tall, soft, knock-kneed man named Stu Embry who made quite a lot of money writing novels. He had emerged from the war with material for one substantial book; having written it, sold it to Hollywood, and established a reputation, he had continued to write books of steadily decreasing eminence, which, all the same, people bought and read. Wherever and whenever Angus and Stu Embry encountered each other they would stop and begin to argue about something, and inevitably in the course of the argument Angus would let Stu Embry know that the books he wrote were fatuous. This never failed to enrage Embry who would promptly lose what little control he had, and would hop up and down with his fists clenched, shouting: "I write them! You only talk about them!"

In front of everyone Angus made it quite plain that Embry was a commercial hack and a militant fool, and yet there was in the character of Angus something which prevented him from saying any such thing when Embry himself was not present. The same was true of Embry. It seemed they did not want anyone else butting into their war.

They fought mostly about literature, but the argument would sometimes veer off to one side—onto politics, for Angus was a Communist, or onto religion, or anything else that occurred to Stu Embry as a means of getting back on his feet after an intellectual pratfall. Unfortunately for him the implacable Scot had read voraciously, knew more about everything, and, to say the least, was relentless. When it became embarrassing to everyone listening, and at last became obvious even to Embry that he was once again losing, he would laugh with false heartiness, as though it were of no consequence, and would call Angus some obscene name, turning away as he did so. Then there would appear in the hard gray eyes of Angus a twinkle of amusement, and his lips might twitch as though he were about to show a fang.

One evening, after having assiduously skewered Stu Embry on his own ineptitude, Angus found himself still unsatisfied and cast about for some additional means of humiliating him. Presently his unblinking gaze came to rest on his enemy's mistress, whose name was Giulietta.

When the two of them, Embry and Giulietta, got up to leave, Angus volunteered to walk with them to their apartment. Giulietta studied him for a moment, Embry said nothing, and so they set off along the via Margutta, Angus walking with his hands behind his back and his head bent in meditation.

Upon arriving at the apartment Angus followed them up the stairs and inside, whereupon Stu Embry stalked into the bedroom, shut the door, and did not reappear. Angus, surprised and rather delighted at this bit of good fortune, immediately set about the seduction of Giulietta, calling to mind Shakespeare's counsel that he who cannot win a woman with his tongue is no man at all. Giulietta, a wise and good woman, asked if he was hungry. Angus admitted that he was. He was always hungry, as everyone knew. Sometimes he went without a meal for three days.

Giulietta got up from the couch and walked into the kitchen, and as Angus refused to let go of her waist he was, perforce, dragged into the kitchen too. Once there he consented, rather sulkily, to keep out of the way while she scrambled eggs and fried bacon the way Embry had taught her to do. When the meal was ready Angus was equally ready, for the odors had set his belly to growling; he was so hungry that his eyes had begun to water. Giulietta had cooked six eggs. Angus ate them all, and he ate all the bacon. Giulietta, who had learned very early in life almost everything there is to be known about men, had stopped at a bakery on the way home and there she had bought nearly a pound of thick Italian pastry.

Now Angus was stuffed so full of eggs and bacon and milk and toast that whenever he moved he gurgled, but he could not resist Italian pastry. One piece after another went into his mouth while his eyes glowed in triumph. Not only was he about to win Giulietta, but he was eating sweets as well. After the pastry was gone she prepared him a cup of warm, sugared cocoa, and she watched while he grew more and more stupefied. Before long he began to nod.

Giulietta then walked into the bedroom where she wakened Stu Embry. Together they carried Angus to the couch. Giulietta pulled off his badly worn shoes, loosened his necktie and his belt, and covered him with a blanket. He was already asleep.

In the morning, as soon as he awoke, Angus wrote a poem.

1957

END
OF SUMMER

ACROSS BARCELONA the clocks strike nine. Pigeons wheel and settle, clapping their dusty wings while echoes roll toward the mountain. Marcello, finishing his chocolate, slides a frugal tip beneath the saucer, stands up, straightening his necktie, and wanders through the early sunshine on the plaza. Children are rolling hoops and sailing boats in the fountain. A fine Spanish day, a typical day, he thinks, for everyone but me; and it looks as though things are going to get worse. What's going to become of me?

On the opposite side of the plaza he sits down and folds his arms, unable to decide what to do. The mistresses of the previous summer, two of them, have announced, separately, not knowing of each other, their imminent arrival in Barcelona. Polly is tired of skiing in Austria and writes that she is coming to live with him. Huguette is tired of the Parisian winter and writes that she is coming to live with him. Polly writes that she will arrive on Tuesday. Huguette does not know exactly on which day she will arrive, but very soon, early in the week.

They'll get here on the same day, says Marcello aloud. They'll be on the same train, it's inevitable. Sharing the same seat. It's what the philosophers call Fate. Either a man has no woman, or they're all over him like pigeons.

There is no possibility of getting in touch with either of them. Huguette plans to visit her grandmother in Bordeaux, from there straight to Barcelona. By the time you get this letter, she writes, I'll be on my way. What a wonderful time we're going to have, Marcello! You must show me Barcelona from top to bottom! I'm so anxious to see you!

Polly must also be on the way; the return address on her letter gives the American Express office in Barcelona. How I've missed you, she writes. No one can dance like you. No one else I've met has been half as much fun as you, Marcello. I'm sorry I got angry with you last summer and I'm going to make it up to you, wait and see. All my love.

So there it is. I'm as helpless as a squab, thinks Marcello. I can't do a thing. One or the other of them will kill me, I can feel it. Maybe they'll get together and finish me off. I should have gone to Sardinia. He stands up, scattering the pigeons which in a moment settle stupidly right back where they were, and begins walking down the avenue toward the harbor.

Well, at least they aren't apt to be on the same train—if one looks at the situation realistically instead of romantically. There's no such thing as Fate. Call it Fortune, instead. And we make or lose a fortune, according to our nature. It's that simple, and something to be thankful for. Huguette is coming from the north, from Paris via Bordeaux; she'll get here by way of Bayonne. Polly will be coming through Marseilles, along the Mediterranean coast. They won't meet, at least not until they're here, which means I have a chance. The one that gets here first can move in with me, there's half the problem solved. Now what about the other half? No, it's hopeless. I'm like the man that falls off the building and people hear him say, as he comes shooting past every floor, so far so good.

But suddenly there is the sign: VIAJES COLON.

Marcello steps into the office and says without hesitation: I want a ticket on the boat to Majorca. I want to leave immediately. The sooner the better.

Running away really is quite simple. Once it occurs to you, every other solution seems unnecessarily difficult and unpleasant. You merely go to the clerk and say you want a ticket somewhere, he makes it out, you pay for it, then somebody comes looking for you but you aren't there any longer.

All right, so far so good, thinks Marcello as he emerges from the office reading his ticket. What an insignificant scrap of cardboard and yet how valuable. He reads every word that's printed on it and tucks it away carefully in his wallet. There's just time enough to pack the suitcase, get a bite to eat, catch a taxi to the pier, and tomorrow morning we dock in Palma. From there one can get a bus across the island to Cala Ratjada. Who'd think of going to Cala Ratjada? It's a little town, according to the map, and nobody will be there. I'll be the only foreigner. There must be a hotel of some sort, or a boarding house. There'll be fishermen, a sea wall, sunshine, fresh air, freedom. I won't even leave a forwarding address. If anybody else writes to me, that's too bad. I'm not obligated to anybody. I might even take a different name. Why is it that you no sooner meet a woman than you feel obligated? It's this quality about women that makes you dislike them.

Everything goes according to schedule, even the boat departs on time. Marcello leans on the rail at the stern. Forming a circle with his thumb and finger, he peers through it while Barcelona gets smaller and smaller. Now let them come on the same train, let them meet, let them discover they are chasing the same unfortunate, it makes no difference to me. The fact is, one shouldn't worry so much. One ought to take decisive actions, that's all.

Marcello walks to the bow of the steamer and stands a while gazing ahead.

The sun goes down, the moon rises through the water, and the night is cold, very much colder than you'd expect. Furthermore, there's no cabin space available; a deck chair is the only thing. Marcello rents a chair and pushes it into a corner out of the wind. Even so, it's too cold to sleep; he turns up his collar and spends the night shivering. He thinks of the monkeys in the forest that almost freeze every night, and every night promise each other that as soon as the sun comes up they'll start building a nest; but of course as soon as they get warm they don't worry about the cold. Then the night comes again and they promise themselves that tomorrow they'll do something. That's the way it goes, and it's the same with love. All night long he asks himself: How did I get myself into this situation?

In the morning it's warm and there just ahead is the cathedral of Palma. Barcelona seems part of another life.

Marcello stops long enough for coffee and buns and goes for a short walk along the paseo. Already the morning is hot, a few clouds drift overhead and the Mediterranean appears much darker than it does from the mainland. There is a feeling of isolation, of being surrounded and protected by the sea. Marcello congratulates himself. He sets off briskly toward the bus station.

Luck is running with him; no sooner has he bought a ticket than it's time to go. He hands up his suitcase to a flunky on top of the bus, gets inside and discovers the last vacant seat. It's like an escape movie. The bus stinks of the countryside and everybody seems to be eating fried chicken and cheese. Marcello smokes and stares out the window. The highway is full of bumps and holes, with long unpaved detours, and he discovers every now and then that he has fallen asleep. The island looks practically deserted. The bus stops in one town after another, but there's nobody on the street, the houses are shuttered as though the villagers were away. Around a bend in the highway, up, down, by scrubby trees, past the motionless windmills, through the bleak Spanish noon and all of a sudden there's Cala Ratjada, the end of the road.

One person is there to meet the bus, a boy about twelve years old. His name is Hector and his parents, Marcello is positive, operate a boarding house.

Perhaps, Hector begins, bowing, the moment he discovers Marcello among the peasants, I may be of service?

Perhaps, says Marcello, dusting his sleeves. But perhaps not.

You're Italian! Hector exclaims.

Did you think I was a German? asks Marcello.

I know a German when I see one, says the boy. I ought to know one, certainly, because there are twenty-five of them here right now.

Marcello looks at him in dismay.

Art students, Hector continues. But don't worry, they won't interfere with your pleasure. They're always off somewhere, they go everywhere together. One hardly knows they're on the island, except at supper time, of course, when they bother everybody by singing.

Marcello discovers the boy has picked up his suitcase and that they are walking along the street. Where are we going? he asks, but does not really care. Obviously they are going to get him a room somewhere.

My uncle owns the Casa Madrona, explains Hector. It's the best hotel this side of Madrid. I hope to become an architect, he adds, but I think I'll practice in Granada because they say the women of Granada are the most beautiful. I've never been to the mainland yet and I don't want to spend my life here in this hole. You can't blame me for that, can you?

My friend, this is Paradise, says Marcello.

Paradise, eh? You live here as long as I have and you'll think different. What's it like in Italy? I might go there someday. They say the women are magnificent, much handsomer than Spanish women.

I hate to tell you, says Marcello patting him on the shoulder, but here or there you don't find much difference.

Things could be worse.

Tell me, at your age why are you so concerned with women?

What's the sense of waiting till you're old?

Like me?

Hector shrugs. Thoughtfully he wipes his nose on his sleeve.

Let me give you some advice, Don Juan Hector. You'll be better off if you wait till you're ninety.

Hector looks up at him and sniggers, but does not say anything. Silently they march through the middle of the village. There's an odor of pines, and between the houses Marcello catches a glimpse of the Mediterranean.

Tell me, how much does your uncle charge for a room at the best hotel this side of Madrid?

Practically nothing. You'll be amazed.

There must be other hotels in town?

Not one you'd care to stay at. Hector is walking faster. Marcello sees that he has shifted the suitcase to his other hand so there would be a struggle for possession of it.

The Casa Madrona is as pink and white as a seashell, as clean as if it had never had an occupant. Perhaps there are none. Uncle is reading a newspaper and for a moment cannot conceal his surprise that Hector has found something on the bus.

How much are the rooms?

Very reasonable.

Is there one with a nice view?

One from which you can practically see Africa.

For the next five days Marcello stuffs himself on lobster and squid, watches the fishermen spreading their nets to dry on the embarcadero, and goes for long walks through the pine trees. On one of these walks he discovers a little beach of pure white sand without so much as a footprint on it. He comes to regard this beach as his own. It forms a perfect crescent and is concealed by a heavy growth of trees and shrubs. To the north the trees grow almost to the edge of the water, and to the south the beach ends at the base of a cliff. There is no trail to the top but by picking his way through the underbrush and using tree limbs for support he is able to reach the promontory, and here he spends hours examining the horizon. It is like a shelf in Paradise. Each time he descends to the beach and returns to the Casa Madrona by way of the pine forest he feels mysteriously purified and serene, so that even the Germans with their haversacks and leather pants and pickled Northern faces do not disturb him.

Hector, sensing a cousin in Marcello's dark features, often approaches him on the subject of women. Marcello readily offers advice. You've got to be prepared for them, he says, you've got to seize the initiative, my friend, otherwise you're a dead pigeon. Believe me, they'll trample all over you.

Then one morning he looks out his window at the bus arriving from Palma and is horrified to see Polly and Huguette. He knows immediately that this is no accident, they've been after him and have found him. Worse, it seems they've become friends. Hector, of course, leads them straight to the Casa Madrona.

Well! Well! exclaims Marcello, smiling brilliantly. Just look who's here!

They smile and that's all.

How about a swim? he asks, and goes on to describe the marvelous beach he has discovered.

Wonderful, they say, after looking at each other. They've been riding on the bus all night, they'd like nothing better than to relax on the beach. They'll get their suits and meet him on the patio.

Tia, who's seldom out of the kitchen, packs lunch for three in a big wicker basket and they set off toward the beach. The girls walk together, talking and laughing. Marcello brings up the rear, carrying the basket.

Well, it's not bad, he thinks. So far so good. I was expecting trouble. I don't understand these girls. Anybody would think they're up to something, but maybe not. Still, I ought to ask a few questions to find out just how matters stand. They're clever, both of them. They've agreed on a few things, I can tell that. How did they meet? How did they learn where I was? On the other hand, maybe it would be smarter not to ask. Take things as they are. What causes all the trouble is that people never accept life as it comes, they've got to ask questions. All right, I won't open my mouth.

The path winds through the forest and Marcello studies the girls as they saunter along. Huguette's bathing suit has a fringe that sways very attractively, counterpointing her lanky stride. She's thin, with flat hips and unusually long legs that have a strange, lifeless quality to them, almost as though they were carved out of soap. Marcello listens to her big sandals crunching the twigs and dried needles. He looks at the calluses on her heels and at the stringy hollow in the back of each knee. She is all sinew except for the plump bulge of female flesh around the borders of her suit. She has the legs of a distance runner. There's a soft dark fuzz on the back of her thighs. He watches her taking one step after another—the tender mound of flesh hurrying out of sight under the swaying fringe and a moment later returning obstinately.

He compares her to Polly, who is half a head shorter, who walks much more briskly, no doubt because she has such short legs. Polly has the tough little buttocks of a schoolgirl. Marcello, staring at them, wants to rush forward and seize them, one in each hand, because they are so demanding. He decides they are alive, two sturdy individuals living side by side who have nothing to do with Polly, except that they are obliged to follow her. She wears a tight, two-piece rubber suit that attempts to flatten her stubborn curving muscles. It's as though her compact little body and the rubber suit are struggling with each other—first one appears to be winning and then the other. Her shoulders are brown as an Indian, her arms unexpectedly delicate and graceful. She is barefoot. Marcello wonders how she is able to walk over the rough ground without flinching. Sometimes she steps on a rock but hardly notices. Possibly her feet are tough because she has gone barefoot as a child in California. She has grown up with six huge brothers, Marcello remembers, for she once showed him a snapshot of them. They taught her to shoot and to fish and to ride horseback. She must have learned very early to be afraid of nothing. She's not in the least afraid of men. He remembers how she frankly approached him in a beer garden. Her attitude is very simple, very direct. In some respects she's much like a man.

Huguette, on the other hand, could not possibly be anything except a woman. In Paris she was the complete Parisienne; it is only here on the beach, away from the French, that she assumes this angular peasant quality. Marcello looks at the fringe swinging rhythmically below the erect, flat cradle of her hips. She carries a straw cylinder in which there are oils and lotions, her bathing cap, sunglasses, paperback books, a towel, a packet of tissue, and God knows what else. Polly carries nothing but a towel looped around her neck, not even a cap to keep her hair dry. Huguette could not imagine what it is like to be a male. Polly, with her short, tightly-braided blonde pigtail, would have been equally satisfied to be a man, it makes no difference. It's life that matters and you take pleasure in the other sex, it's very simple. But Huguette, now, everything depends first of all on being a woman; only after that are you a person. With Polly there are just people, and some happen to be male, others female. With Huguette, ah, first there are men, then there are women, and incidentally they are human.

Huguette stops walking. She stands clumsily on one foot, reaches back, pokes a bony finger into her sandal. Marcello is hypnotized by the angles, she's more awkward than a Degas woman climbing out of a tub. She frowns. Polly, too, has stopped, a few steps ahead, and has turned half-around, looking over her shoulder; she is watching Huguette. A beam of sunlight breaks through the trees and illuminates the path beyond the motionless girls. Marcello is fascinated. They are poised as though the artist has just completed them. Frowning, oblivious to all else, Huguette reaches into her sandal; Polly, expressionless, watches and waits.

Out pops a pebble.

They resume walking along the path.

Marcello realizes that he has been holding his breath. They're good girls, he thinks, I'm glad to have them here. And he begins to feel protective. I'm like the good shepherd. I'm the shepherd taking care of his lambs. They trot obediently ahead. They're not concerned. They trust me. They'd be lost without me. He looks at them affectionately. Huguette is smoking a cigarette.

Which of my sheep do I prefer? he asks himself. Which is more valuable, more precious to me? Well, I can't say. The fact is, I love them both. Then he begins to think about the ways in which they choose to give and receive the comforts of their flesh. Polly wants first of all to get rid of her clothing, every scrap of it; she's never satisfied when she's dressed. They must live like savages in California. She's a plump little savage, tough as an acorn. She rides horses, goes swimming naked in rivers, climbs snowy mountains and skis down them. It's all the same with her, every-thing's a part of life and it's there to be enjoyed. Yes, he thinks, she finds so much in life that is wonderful. Of course, it's easier when you're rich. Next year she'll prob-ably be in Egypt riding a camel out to see the pyramids.

What about Huguette? Would she go riding on a camel? No. Yes, he corrects himself. But with Huguette it will be a very different sort of experience; she'll feel the camel between her legs and will probably tell her girl friends what it's like hav-ing a camel down there. She's the child of Huysmans or Baudelaire. There are shad-ows in her soul. She lives in the modern world and thinks thoughts that are never imagined by savages. The fact is, Huguette might enjoy visiting the pyramids on a litter carried by four Nubians wearing plumes. Still, she doesn't have the body to play that part—her feet would stick out beyond the litter. Anybody would think that just owning those feet would keep her from dreaming, but probably it doesn't. She thinks she's Cleopatra. Maybe she is, with those rope sandals. Anything's pos-sible.

Polly, without stopping, hardly breaking stride, scoops up a stone and throws it at a stump. She throws very well, not quite as fluidly as a man, but for a woman she throws hard and straight. The stone flies past the stump and bounces from another tree.

Marcello picks up a stone and hands it to Huguette. She stops, takes careful aim, and flings it at the stump but the stone flies high in the air another direction. Huguette shrugs. Throwing stones is not for women. She continues along the path a little more rapidly, jiggling the fringe of her suit.

Could you hit a man like that? Marcello asks Polly.

She looks at him strangely and runs to catch up with Huguette.

Yes, he thinks, she would hit me, while Huguette would scratch. It could be the difference between America and France. Who knows? He picks up a stone and throws it at the stump, but misses. He looks ahead to see if they have noticed, but they are nearly out of sight among the trees. My little sheep, he murmurs, and hurries after them.

Presently they come to the crest of the path and there below, just visible through the foliage, is the beach with wide emerald waves curling in and foaming pleasantly over the sparkling sand, just as though it had been waiting for them to arrive, and there also are the twenty-five Germans. Marcello is dumbfounded. Did the Germans get up before daylight? Did they come hiking out here by the light of the moon, singing their German songs all the way?

The Germans are playing some sort of leapfrog game, running back and forth and shouting at each other and tearing up the beach.

Marcello looks at them with disgust. Even their haversacks, all in a row, are disgusting. On top of each haversack is a neat pile of clothing. Up and down go the Germans, around and around, bounding across the beach, kicking sand, hauling and slapping and jumping over each other with their long Germanic hair flying like pennants in the breeze. Their yellowish masculine bodies, covered only by a loincloth, are impossible to look at without revulsion. They ought never to get undressed, Marcello thinks. They look like halibut. They ought to wear wing collars and boiled shirts and go about their Teutonic business of teaching mathematics and philosophy and that sort of thing. They should leave bathing to people who know how. He notices that one of the Germans has seen them and is waving. Come here! the German shouts in English. Then another one shouts the same thing in French, and then in Italian, at which all the Germans begin to laugh.

It's funny, is it? says Marcello bitterly. You're glad I brought the girls, yes—and what about me? I could show you a thing or two! How is it the Germans know everything? he wonders. What is it about Germans that they know everything right away? I don't even know how the girls found out I was in Cala Ratjada, but the Germans know everything. He looks with distaste at their grinning faces. Just then he notices that Polly is running wildly down the hill toward them, as though she was on skis, she's in such a hurry. She enjoys everything, he admits enviously. Right now she enjoys simply running down this hill, it doesn't matter what's at the bottom. He watches her join the group. Immediately the game resumes and Polly goes leaping over the Germans one after another; then she in turn bends down while all twenty-five disgusting male bodies come flying spraddle-legged across her. Marcello turns to Huguette, meaning to point out what a revolting game this is, and discovers that she is fascinated by the sight.

Now what are you thinking? he demands roughly, but Huguette doesn't hear. She's like a goat, he thinks, staring at her. Why is it I never noticed? She does resemble a goat. Look at her muzzle, how tame she is, a trifle mad and obscene, in fact. Look at those boney shins and the protruding knees. Yes, and those odd feet! She's hypnotized, just like a goat, imagining all sort of things.

Huguette is walking absently down the hill, her eyes fixed on the men. Marcello goes after her.

The beach is ruined. There are footprints everywhere. He stands around a few minutes shaking his head each time the Germans invite him to join the game. Huguette already is in the circle, screaming with delight every time a German grabs hold of her. Well, what difference does it make? It's disgusting, but if that's what she wants, it's her affair. Marcello puts down his wicker basket and announces that he is going up on the promontory. Nobody pays any attention.

I'll let them unpack the lunch, he mutters while struggling up the side of the cliff. They'll get tired of their game soon enough, then I'll come down and we'll have lunch at the other end of the beach by ourselves. Nobody could stand those Germans for very long. After that we'll have a swim and when they're in a good mood I'll see what I can find out. This suspense is too much. They caught me by surprise.

From the top of the cliff he peers through the windblown evergreen trees and sees them still running in circles jumping over each other. He hurls a pine cone at them and then goes to the edge of the cliff and sits down where he can't see them, where the wind comes up from the sea and mutes the sound of their laughter until it's as faint as though it came from another world.

How's this going to end? he thinks, stretching himself out on the rocks. What's going to become of me? And what's going to become of them, too? Huguette, for instance, why did she really come here? To get away from Paris for a little while? Last summer she used to complain about her job, she kept saying she wanted some freedom. So now here she is enjoying it. But she'll go back to Paris, that's where she belongs. She'll pick out one of those musty French bureaucrats and marry him within the year. That's what she wants, she really is quite domestic. She can't run around too long by herself.

Marcello shuts his eyes against the burning noonday sun. He listens to the waves foaming against the base of the cliff and feels the gentle breeze from the Mediterranean. Presently he falls asleep.

The sun is near the top of the forest when he wakes up. Touching himself, feeling the heat of his skin, he winces and sits up carefully. There's not a sound from the beach. All right, they've gone, probably. They've run off with the Germans and here I am all by myself with a sunburn that feels like a turtle shell. I should never have come here. And things are going to get worse. What's the sense of it all?

He picks fitfully at the shelf of rock. The day is almost over. Soon enough summer will be ending, and what then? What does it come to? He flips a pebble into the sea, then another one for Polly, and a third one for Huguette. Nothing remains but the moment, the day, the hour.

Years from now, he thinks, I'll be at breakfast with my wife in Rome and over the morning paper I'll catch a glimpse of something, or there'll be a taste, or a sound, and suddenly all of this will reappear.

He gets to his feet and stands at the very edge of the cliff. He gazes down at the boiling water and wonders if he should jump, but there would not be much sense in that. Instead he begins working his way down through the trees and comes out finally at the end of the beach, having slipped once and scratched his knee. The Germans have gone, there's no trace of them except the devastated sand, but of course the tide will flood the beach—already it's rising—and will take care of that. Huguette and Polly are packing the wicker basket with what's left of the food and wine.

We called to you, says Polly, but you wouldn't come down. It's your own fault if you go hungry. Anyway, it won't be long till supper. What were you doing up there? Huguette says you probably fell asleep.

Marcello looks from one to the other; they look at him attentively. They are not angry. They should be, considering that they are women, but for some reason they are not. Marcello is mystified, but decides to say nothing. So far so good. Maybe they've come to some agreement by themselves. Maybe there's Oriental blood in every woman and the idea of a seraglio isn't repugnant to them at all. What will happen tonight? Who knows?

Let's go, he says. He feels very tenderly toward them. He stands by while they finish packing. Neither of them speaks a word, they gather the wax papers and the crusts of bread and they put everything neatly into the basket. That's one of the marvelous things about them, that they are so meticulous and clean.

All right, he says, and obediently they begin walking up the path, Polly carrying the basket and Huguette carrying her cylinder of straw filled with the many female necessities. Marcello walks behind them. There is a little sand on their legs and it pleases him that they are not aware of this. Perhaps just before they come in sight of the Casa Madrona he will order them to halt and he will brush them off. He watches them marching along and realizes that they are content. They didn't find what they expected in Barcelona, but there are more sorts of happiness than one. He thinks they don't really care how the night turns out; whatever he decides to do will be all right with them. They'll sleep alone or they'll sleep together like three on a bicycle; all right, sometimes life goes pedaling in that direction.

Polly scoops up a stone and throws it at the stump, Marcello does the same. Both of them miss, but it doesn't matter. Throwing is what's important.

What a lovely beach, says Huguette.

What handsome Germans, you mean, says Marcello. And so many of them. What did you do while I was gone?

At this both Polly and Huguette burst out laughing. They continue laughing all the way back to the Casa Madrona.

All right, thinks Marcello as he follows them into the hotel, it was foolish of me to ask. Probably they played leapfrog all afternoon, just that and nothing more, that's my opinion, but if I say another word I'll never hear the end of it. They're curious girls.

Aiee! cries Tia, looking out of the kitchen. You're as red as a cabbage!

Italians live in the shade, says Don Juan Hector. Is it painful, that skin? Does it hurt?

Of course it hurts, says Marcello, don't be stupid. He hesitates at the kitchen, sniffing the odor of paella. Overhead the Germans are singing and stamping their boots; they've got the entire second floor.

Hurry up, says Polly, there's just time for a shower before we eat. Or aren't you hungry?

Of course I'm hungry, says Marcello.

Well? asks Huguette. What now? Why are you looking around so strangely? Is anything wrong?

Marcello shakes his head. How could it be explained? I'd planned to escape, he thinks, and believed I was successful, yet life found out where I was and came to me. Therefore I think that no man can escape. It's summer for us still, though it won't be forever. There may be clocks to keep the hours, but it's a moment such as this when life is measured.

I'm coming, he says to nobody in particular. Don't rush me.

1963

THE SHORT HAPPY LIFE
OF HENRIETTA

HENRIETTA HAD a marvelous time in Paris. She came from a very small town in Nebraska and did not understand a word of French, but this did not bother her in the least. No matter what was said to her she would eagerly nod her head and begin laughing.

Henrietta enjoyed everybody, and she explained to whomever she met that when she had seen and done everything there was to do in Paris she was going completely around the world by herself. She could be seen at almost any time of the day or night scurrying through the Latin Quarter or sitting in a café on Montparnasse, laughing, nodding excitedly, sharing her table or her umbrella with all kinds of people—Arabs, streetwalkers, students, tourists—it did not matter.

Somewhere near the Seine, probably in an alley, she met two jolly little men from Algiers. She was seen wandering about the streets with them, all three laughing heartily. These Arabs spoke no English.

Some weeks later, when one of the Algerians was located, the story of their hilarious evening came to be known. The three had gone from café to café, from the Latin Quarter to Pigalle, drinking vermouth—Henrietta buying—and laughing till the tears rolled down their cheeks. None of them had ever had such a good time. Late in the evening one of the Arabs proposed they get a wicker basket, a great big wicker basket, and go out to the Bois de Boulogne and there they should cut off Henrietta's head and stuff her in the basket. Henrietta did not understand a word they said, but thought whatever they were suggesting must be enormously funny, and when pressed for an answer she agreed.

The Arabs slapped each other and screamed.

They asked her again if she would like to be murdered and stuffed into a big wicker basket. Henrietta said yes indeed.

The two Arabs could scarcely believe she meant it, so they described with their fingers what they meant to do to her, whereupon Henrietta was overcome with laughter. So, after a time, they got into a taxicab and they went in search of a wicker basket.

The three of them entered various shops that were still open, and in one of these they found exactly what they were looking for. It was a fine, stout basket. They put it down in the middle of the floor and one of them helped Henrietta climb into it. She sat in the basket with her knees drawn up to her chin and she laughed until her eyes brimmed with tears while the shopkeeper shrugged.

If one wishes to buy a wicker basket—so the shopkeeper later explained to the police—one is entitled to buy a basket.

The Arabs put on the cover and found that it contained Henrietta quite nicely. So Henrietta climbed out of the basket and bought it, and her friends carried it to the taxicab and put it in the trunk. They had the driver take them to the Bois de Boulogne.

If one wishes to go to the Bois de Boulogne with a girl and a wicker basket—so the taxicab driver later explained to the police—there is no law against it.

After the taxi went away they stretched out on the grass, Henrietta and her friends, and they rolled around helpless with mirth, for it was a truly wonderful evening they were having. Then the question was once more put to Henrietta, and once more she was certain their idea must be a fine one, whereupon they picked up their basket and went staggering into the woods and it was there the police found her body in the basket.

1957

MADAME BROULARD

APARTMENTS, IN PARIS sometimes explode, even so they are better than hotel rooms. For a number of weeks after my arrival I lived in a hotel near the Seine. The room was quite long and narrow, tapering like a coffin, was papered with orange fleurs-de-lis, and with its medieval window closed smelled like a rabbit hutch. During those weeks I knew only one person in Paris, an American college friend who had been in the city about three years working for the U.S. government, and when he telephoned one morning to say I might possibly get an apartment—not much, he cautioned, but an apartment—I told him several times that I would take it. A friend of the French family he had lived with when he first arrived had decided to rent her place. On the phone he advised not being too eager or she would increase the price, but I was very eager indeed and told him that if the price went up I would do without a noon meal in order to get the place. Apparently he had never lived in a room lined with orange fleurs-de-lis because he did not sound sympathetic, all he said was to meet him at the Pasteur metro stop about 6:30.

Madame Broulard was also at the metro stop though I did not know it at the time; I noticed only a woman of perhaps forty-five with extremely coarse red hair and a complexion like cork who strolled back and forth swinging a black handbag and stopping often to look at sweets in a bakery window. I assumed she was a prostitute.

Presently Max emerged from the underground station. He was carrying in one hand a green fish net full of lettuce and onions, two empty wine bottles and some American PX toilet paper, and in the other hand a brief case of painted Italian leather. While in Paris he had grown a thin, snarled beard but otherwise was unchanged from the days when he had been intercollegiate pole-vaulting champion. He saw us both at the same time; with a crisscross nod he indicated to each of us who the other was.

"*Enchantée, monsieur,*" said Madame Broulard, smiling at me and holding up, either to shake or kiss, a freckled white hand that felt like a chicken breast.

At the time I spoke textbook French, a language most Parisians profess not to understand, yet her smile remained brave when I carefully pronounced a return greeting. While we walked the several blocks to her apartment she and Max talked steadily and too rapidly for me to understand.

The apartment was a seventh-floor walk-up and consisted of a cordon of rooms which became smaller, darker and more mysterious the farther one proceeded, terminating in a kitchen-bathroom where it was necessary to switch on the light. The front room had six thick red draperies which swept the floor and sometimes stirred as though people were hiding behind them. I suggested to Max that Poe must have lived and created some of his ghouls in these chambers. Madame Broulard understood no English but caught the name of Poe and exclaimed that *La Chute de la Maison Usher* was formidable.

The walls of the second room were massed with what may have been the dingiest collection of pictures in the world—sepia and gray Fragonard-ish prints which appeared to have been placed on the roof every time it rained, as well as a number of those stiff Virgins painted on cracked wood which summer tourists buy at the Clignancourt flea market and take proudly home to Kansas City or to the Bronx. There was also a reclining nude with a skin of rancid butter. Madame clearly was fond of this picture. She asked Max a short question and he said to me, "Does the picture offend you? Tell her it's beautiful."

I said, "*Très belle!*"

"Don't overdo it," said Max.

We went on for a look at the kitchen-bathroom. This contained the tub, over which a boxlike gas heater was suspended, the toilet, stove, bidet, washbasin, a big medicine cabinet (on the way up Max had remarked, "She thinks she has liver trouble. Everybody in France thinks he has liver trouble.") and a coil of pipes on the underside of which hung concentric circles of stalactites. There was also the electric meter, a trash carton, a porcelain coffee grinder with cherubs painted by Madame, a frosted window, and what I took to be a bird cage but which proved to be the thing they put lettuce in after it is washed. They then hold this cage out the window, said Max, and angrily swing it around and around and the water is hurled off, splattering on the ledges of all the windows below. These were the larger objects in the kitchen; shelves and recesses contained rows of pots and condiments and labeled bottles.

I leaned across the bathtub and looked from under the water heater out the window: there was the Eiffel Tower. I had known all along I wanted this apartment, now it was foolish to pretend any longer.

Max told her I would very much like an apartment where one could take a bath while looking at the Eiffel Tower. She thought this a rather peculiar reason but was pleased that I was pleased. She made a pretense of considering but unquestionably she wanted the rent money as much as I wanted to get out of my hotel. The price was 15,000 francs, truly reasonable. Max said that by admiring the nude I had probably saved myself 5,000 francs. Madame, however, gave another reason for the price: she had never rented before and was more interested in finding a sober, respectful tenant than in making lots of money. I said to tell her I would take good care of her property, that I drank little, and would be reading most of the time. The fact that I was a student pleased her and so before long it was agreed that I might move in whenever I wished. An hour later I returned with my suitcases.

I decided to begin my stay in Madame Broulard's apartment with a bath. Remembering instructions given me on the operation of the heater, I first pulled open the drawer and lighted the pilot, then closed the drawer and after making certain that the little flame had not gone out I sat on the edge of the tub and began to open the tap. Finally the water came into being, a few drops leaked from the nozzle, a trickle, and when the handle had been cranked until it wobbled there could be seen a flow about the size of a baby's finger. Yet the gas had not ignited. I continued leisurely twisting the handle; at the time I had not learned that one turns this handle furiously. To turn it slowly is to allow gas seepage. I was gazing at the Eiffel Tower when the gas exploded. It was rather like diving off a springboard and landing flat. The blast moved a cup and saucer several inches along the drainboard. A few seconds later when I had recovered from the shock the gas was roaring and the nozzle spitting steam.

That same afternoon Madame Broulard returned. I thought she must have forgotten something, but her manner was vague. I could not guess what she wanted.

I poured two glasses of wine and offered her a chair. She brought out a paper and pencil. After a while I understood that she wished to make an inventory of the silverware. She was embarrassed but after all she did not know me, she said—though I thought her three-year acquaintance with Max should be sufficient security—and it was therefore quite necessary to mark down the number of pieces. I would then sign the paper. Clearly the silver was valuable; I did not understand all she said about it, which was considerable, but gathered that it had belonged to her family for generations and could never be replaced. So, taking our wineglasses and paper and pencil, we walked into the back room where she opened the polished wood chest and began laying out the pattern. Un. Deux. Trois. Quatre . . . and so on through the teaspoons and the snail forks and then into the butter knives. We were about half through this set when she folded the paper, slipped it into her purse and with a smile said all this was unnecessary. Taking our wine, we returned to the front room and conversation, but she was not at ease and finished her glass quickly and said she was sorry to have deranged me. The silver of her *grandpère,* she was positive, would be secure in my hands. I told her it would be. Was there anything I needed? No, I replied as best I could, the apartment was fine and I was very content to be in such a place. I did not see her again until an evening in late November.

She came by about dusk. I poured two more glasses of wine and we sat down for a chat. She asked if I were enjoying Paris, if I had been to the opera and to the Comédie Française and if I had made the trip to Chartres to see the famous cathedral. We talked for possibly an hour. She found my French improved and gave me a lesson in the correct pronunciation of the letter *r.*

Eventually she mentioned the necessity for visiting the toilet, or cabinet as they delicately put the matter, and having excused herself, she disappeared into the back rooms. The lid of the silver chest creaked as she lifted it.

A moment afterward came the sound of the toilet chain, of the door opening and closing, and Madame reappeared rubbing her hands as though she had just finished washing them. We drank another glass of wine. Was there anything I needed for the apartment? No. Could she do anything at all for me? No, I said, I was well satisfied; the quarters pleased me. I then recalled having broken one of her champagne goblets and asked if I could pay for it, or if not, where I might find a replacement, but she threw aside her hands, exclaiming that the goblet was nothing. In renting, she continued, one must expect a certain breakage and I was not to let the matter worry me.

At the door she said, *"Bon soir, monsieur. Vous êtes trop gentil."* And I also said good evening and that she was very agreeable.

The next time Madame Broulard visited was at my invitation after an accident in the kitchen. The washbasin had been cracked before I moved in; a streak like the photographic negative of a lightning bolt ran down one slope, across the bottom and up the opposite side. If water stood in the bowl long enough a few drops would seep through and form a puddle on the floor. It had been that way, she had remarked when Max and I first looked at the place, for twenty-two years— Monsieur Broulard had dropped a syphon bottle and created this crack. But as it was not serious and she felt plumbers' fees to be outrageous the basin had never been fixed. I had paid no attention to it other than not allowing water to stand, but apparently the crack had weakened the bottom. I was washing a sweater when the basin, too, exploded. Now a porcelain washbasin does not break like a china plate or a drinking glass, it goes off like a light bulb dropped on a concrete floor. All at once a bucket under the basin was full of porcelain shards and I was reaching through a jagged hole. My shirt sleeves were ripped as if they had been sliced with razors and both arms were badly scraped.

As I did not know how to contact Madame Broulard at that hour of the evening and as neither Max nor I had a telephone I took the metro to his place near Montmartre. He was entertaining some artist friends. I told him about the accident and said I would replace the basin but that Madame should probably be notified. He said he would call her in the morning from his office; for the present I should join the party. I knew very little about art but he said the same was true of artists. He introduced me around the living room where everybody was on the floor—a collage of plaid shirts, hairy arms, sandals, girls' legs, and many blue packs of Gauloises cigarettes. Max and I then went into the kitchen where he had been uncorking bottles.

"How are you and Madame getting along?" he asked. "She's unreasonable sometimes, you know. She's been that way since the war."

I said that we'd had a nice talk the time she stopped by. She found me droll and genteel. I mailed a check for the rent on the first of every month and a few days later always got a pleasant acknowledgment written by her employer in eighteenth-century English. I didn't know anything about her life during the war.

"Her husband was killed. He was starting to walk across the Boulevard des Capucines when a German lance corporal shot him in the testicles. I shouldn't think that would be a fatal wound but anyway Monsieur Broulard died, maybe from heartbreak. Madame could never find out why he was shot. Nobody ever knew why. Nobody ever does." Max had been getting red and swollen as he pulled at a cork. He was steadying the bottle between his feet and had one big hand wrapped in a towel. When he finally got the cork out he continued: "Things like that have been going on in Paris for a long time. Paris has always been an occupied city. At present of course it's us, the Americans with their purple nylon shirts and chewing gum and three-hundred-dollar cameras and American Express tours. Why, in places like Concorde and Pig Alley and over on the Champs you can't find a Frenchman on the streets. Before us it was the Germans, and before them somebody else, and so on back to Hannibal or Attila or whoever it was first knew a good thing when he saw it. Always this city has been dominated by some foreign power. Always."

He popped open another bottle and began twisting the cork off the screw. "Now there was some point I intended to make but I can't think what it was." He finished unscrewing the cork, placed it in line with others that stood in a half-circle atop the stove, and smiled faintly as he remarked, "Perhaps it's this: as long as you're in Paris you've got to realize that you're part of the occupation force. You'll be treated as such. Now let's join the others."

As we entered the front room a fat, bearded sculptor wearing rope sandals was describing Spain. I remembered that his name was Julian and that he was having his first one-man show somewhere in the St. Germain district. He accepted a bottle from Max and shouted: *"Bueno! Bueno, hombre!"*

A few minutes later an English boy who wore a loose black turtleneck sweater and who had been eating peaches turned to me and said, drawing out the words, "I'm David. David. They tell me you have an apartment? Isn't Madame Broulard the libertine!" As to why she was a libertine David continued after folding a peach skin and placing it atop a stack rising from the ash tray. "But Max has told you *why* she's renting, I mean he must have told you . . . " David was annoyed that I hadn't heard. His voice grew sharp. "Because her employer has wearied of the little wife! And imported Madame Broulard! Into his own home. Now think of the children, won't you? I do feel that Parisians are at once the most wonderful and despicable people on earth." He began to lick his fingers while he stared at a dirty Siamese cat that had gone to sleep on the couch.

Several more artists came to the party and they all began talking about a new movement called Fragmentism. An hour or so later, realizing that I had not yet completed a paper that would shortly be due at the Sorbonne, I located Max reading a book in the kitchen. My intention had been to tell him good night, instead we got to talking of the war, of how it had affected the people we knew. Max said that when the United States dropped the atom bomb he had almost renounced his American citizenship. Almost, he said, but finally he had not. "I don't know," he said, "even now I am not sure what I ought to have done. Civilized people don't destroy cities. No matter how you rationalize it. Speak of Belsen. Speak of Hiroshima."

We could hear Julian's laughter from the front room, and the confused argument that never would end.

"Well," Max said, "I'm like the others. I, too, am terrified and am scratching at life. Attempting to piece together something significant. Take Madame Broulard: her nephew was in the resistance but on his first assignment he became so frightened that he surrendered, not only himself but two others. The Germans tortured and killed all three. Nothing any more is secure or comprehensible to Madame; she is so much alone, trying to hold on to something, anything, that retains a shred of meaning. In America the group announces a pattern for life; in Europe there are no more groups, there are individuals, each in his own way striking out at everything that has wounded him and each in his own time picking from the ashes whatever bagatelle will reassure him.

In the front room a girl shrieked, "Look at the time!" It was, in fact, just eight minutes before one in the morning. The metro stops at one.

We heard David say, "Everybody can sleep here. Max doesn't mind one bit." And there in the kitchen Max smiled.

But in spite of David's invitation the guests began crowding out the door and as they went stumbling down the steep circular staircase in absolute darkness I followed.

Once on the street we all ran for it and inside the station split up without pausing for goodbyes to go our separate directions. I ran alone through an echoing corridor, the wall frames of which had been rented by a mustard company and filled with replicas of the same poster in alternating colors, first in bile and then in mustard. The metro agent at the portillon saw me running toward him just as the last train rumbled into position. He knew I was not French, probably he knew I was American, and he shut the gate a moment before I reached it.

In my best French I asked: "It's the last train?"

"*Oui*," he said contentedly.

"But then . . . " I protested.

"You're too late, monsieur," he said, gazing beyond me. There was still time for him to open the gate and allow me on the train. I pointed out this fact.

"It's not possible," he said.

There was nothing to be done. He would not let me through although he would have let a Frenchman through. As I started back along the corridor he said politely, "*Bonsoir, monsieur.*"

I turned around to look at him. His face was expressionless.

Several blocks away there was a taxi stand. I got in the first cab and gave my address. We drove for perhaps a half mile along the Seine. Here and there on the barges a light could be seen, and the bridges reflected in the water, and I was thinking of what Max had told me.

At the corner of Pasteur and Lecourbe I got out. The meter read 320 francs. I would tip the driver thirty francs. I counted out four one-hundred notes and asked for fifty change. He dropped a large gold coin in my palm and I had walked off several steps before realizing it was not heavy enough. It was a gilded two-franc. He was drawing away from the curb when I ran into the street, caught the handle and jerked open the door. He stopped the taxi and again I met the bland face of the metro agent.

The argument about the fraudulent coin began but I was angry by this time, more angry than he, and in addition I had no other change in my pockets, so at last he admitted he might possibly have given me the counterfeit. He was apologetic, examining the coin and shaking his head. He would report this thing to the police, this swindling. He gave me a genuine fifty-franc piece, selecting it from a handful, not quite concealed, of gilded two-francs.

Madame Broulard appeared the following morning with such an anxious look that I suspected Max had embellished the story of the accident. I showed her the basin and demonstrated how it happened. But had I not been injured? Well, my arms were a bit swollen and stiff. She must have a look at them. Oh, this was terrible. No, Madame, it's nothing. Nothing. At last we got back to the basin. She was unable to believe it could have happened. Americans astonished her. They were savages. No Frenchman would ever have an accident like that. Never.

Although the bowl had been cracked to begin with she had used it for twenty-two years and I was certain she could have made it last that much longer, therefore it seemed I should pay the cost of replacement; however, she reminded me of the crack and in the end we decided to divide the cost.

She came back the following Monday with news that it would cost altogether 20,000 francs. I knew that 10,000 would be difficult for her, but she only smiled and with her hands inadvertently outlined a butterfly. At such moments she was no longer a coarsely red-haired woman with limbs rather like mushroom stalks but one of the legendary Parisiennes, a proper descendant of Maintenon and Sévigné.

Before she left I told her that the following month would be my last in Paris. My year of study abroad was complete and I would be going home. She was intensely interested in the United States and began asking about my home and my plans and before she left I had brought out snapshots of the house and my sister's baby and the cocker spaniel pups. When I first moved into the apartment I had admired a tiny wood Franciscan who sat brooding among the yellowing paperbound editions of Maupassant and Baudelaire; now she hurried across to it and said I must take it to remember her by. Although I protested she would not listen; she put it into my pocket. I complained that I had nothing to offer in return, and she threw out her hands in despair, a moment later saying I should send her a snapshot of myself before the Statue of Liberty. This would be simple enough because the boat would go past it into New York Harbor.

"It is from us to you, this statue," she told me, and I said I knew and that all Americans knew of the good wishes of France.

At the door she said once again how desolate she was that I must leave, how she hoped my stay had been pleasant. She would try to come by on the morning of my departure but her boss was formidable, *un véritable tigre,* and so it would be doubtful. If not, then I could simply leave the keys with the concierge, and if I failed to write from America she would never forgive me.

It seemed during those final weeks in Paris that I was living in Utrillo's city—from the street of the agile rabbit to the pale nipple of the church of Sacré Coeur, and the olive-green book boxes propped open along the *quai* to the sienna chimney pipes high on the mansard roofs. The sun, large now for summer, patinaed walks and grilles and glinted on metal vases bolted to plaques inscribed, *Ici Est Tombé Pour La France* . . . followed by a name, a date, and nothing more.

The veritable tiger of a boss gave Madame Broulard part of the morning off on the day I was to leave. Shortly before noon she arrived carrying a black satchel like a doctor's instrument bag and she put all the silver in it, excepting a knife and a fork and a teaspoon which I was to use for my lunch.

She said, "I have been wanting to have it cleaned for such a long time." She zipped up this bag, placed it by the door and turned to me with a smile. "At what hour does your train depart?" It was to leave for Le Havre late in the afternoon. "And you will write to me from New York? I'll worry because the sea, they say, is so rough this time of year." We talked a few minutes more and then we shook hands and I promised to leave the key with the concierge downstairs.

"Then, monsieur," she told me, smiling a little sadly, "goodbye. I am so sorry you must go." And taking up her bag she started briskly down the stairs.

Max had recently bought a jeep and was driving me to the station. I heard the tires and next the horn; he was late as always. I had been waiting almost an hour, sitting with three pieces of silverware in my hand, wondering what to do. I had thought of hiding them somewhere in the apartment, perhaps behind one of the sepia etchings where she would never think of hunting, then in a month or so sending her a postcard revealing where they could be found, but I remembered Max saying that in this crucified land human hope and reassurance take unaccustomed forms, therefore I only washed them and carefully dried them and placed them in a row on the exact center of the table—one knife and one fork and one silver spoon.

1959

THE VOYEUR

LOVE OF THE UNUSUAL, the remote, and the exotic belongs exclusively to civilization. It is because of the greater nervous restlessness and sensitivity of civilization—at least that's what psychiatrists tell us—that civilization had given birth to Karl Baum. He could not be imagined in a primitive country, nor in a village, not even a small town. He belonged to the world of numberless windows, mirrors, muffled noises, corridors, whispers, unclean violence, and the singular pleasures of the brain. So it was inevitable that he should be found where he was, that he should sit in his chair behind a table at the Café Medallion with his back to the wall, secure as a spider in its deadly tunnel.

Away from the street, half-hidden by the stove in winter, overlooked during the brilliance of summer, always alone, always silent, he sat and watched everything that moved.

How old he was, nobody knew, or where he came from, or how long he had been sitting at the Medallion. Some thought he had arrived recently, but then someone else would say no—no, Baum was here last winter and the summer before.

He was not unfriendly. If somebody sat down at his table and began talking to him he would answer, but never offered a word about himself; nor did he ever greet anybody or wave his hand. It was as though he had no idea how to form a relationship with another living creature. Either that or he understood perfectly, knowing that in a little while he would be left alone.

Certain afternoons he brought into the café a small black portfolio tied with black ribbons, so it was assumed that he must be an artist, or at least that he liked to draw, yet nobody remembered seeing him in the ateliers near the Medallion, nor did any of the models from the neighborhood recognize him. And he was not asked to show his drawings, or photographs, or whatever it was he carried in the portfolio; Baum was not asked to reveal his soul by displaying the work he did, he was not asked because if he opened the portfolio there would be something unpleasant inside.

He had no friends. He had not one friend. Because of this he drew attention, such solitude was thought unnatural, but he was noticeable for another reason—because he so seldom moved, unless it was to turn his head. In a crowd of talkative people it's easy to see one who remains quiet. He was quickly noticed. Newcomers to the café soon saw him and said: Who is that?

Then somebody would answer: That's Karl Baum. Nobody said: He's Karl Baum.

Seldom did they ask much else about him—if he had a job, where he lived, whether he was married. The answers to these questions were commonly understood. That he should be married was unimaginable. Somewhere in the neighborhood he lived but the address was not important, it would be a hotel room or a musty little apartment choked with the odor of half-eaten food, dark with cobwebs. As for money, he had enough; the tip he gave his waiter was not generous but it was adequate, so apparently he didn't need to work.

When he got up to leave the Medallion nobody knew where he was going, yet nobody was curious enough to follow him. He would be back, everybody knew he would come back. What he did in the meantime was of no interest. If he failed to appear for a day or so there was some talk, but not much. A few people might wonder if perhaps he had died, or if the police had gotten him. Why this thought should occur—Karl Baum in trouble with the police—could not be explained because all he did at the café was to watch what was going on, which is what others were doing as they sat there together drinking Pernod, coffee, or cognac. The difference was that they came to enjoy themselves. They came to meet friends and talk and drink while they observed the boulevard; but he was there only to watch, and in the shadows he looked bloodless. This is why they distrusted him, why they suspected he would one day be in trouble with the police.

He was German, of course, with that name and with his accent. He spoke French stiffly, as though he had memorized what was necessary, and his blue eyes were the eyes of a foreigner. His skin resembled cheese. Hair grew thickly out of his nostrils and out of his ears although he was beginning to get bald. The hair on his head was not like human hair so much as it was like a soft yellowish fiber. It was his own hair yet it seemed artificial, carefully arranged to conceal the baldness, giving him the appearance of a figure in a wax museum. This one sign of vanity, the awareness that he would soon be bald, this together with the dark green vein crookedly climbing his temple marked his humanity. Otherwise, unless he moved, there was no suggestion of life, no expression on his face or in his posture to suggest that he was thinking about anything while he watched.

That was the way he was, he never changed. That was all he presented of himself and nobody expected to learn much more.

Then one day a model discovered that he went to the atelier Dufau on the other side of the city, that he went there twice a week and made small ink drawings. But she said he did not draw very often; while she was on the stand he looked at her and only occasionally did indifferent little sketches with an air of boredom or annoyance, as though by doing this he proved his right to stare at her. Each time he began to draw, she said, she felt a sense of disgust. It was disagreeable to see him pretending. It demonstrated that he knew the meaning of shame, and because he was ashamed of himself she could not overcome a feeling of disgust, as though in some way she were part of it. This pretense showed that he was aware of people around him and that he cared what they thought of him; it made an individual of him, an actual man instead of that remote figure in the back of the café, and she did not like this individual—just as you do not like many creatures close at hand, worms, centipedes, lice, grubs, and so forth, which don't bother you from a distance. She avoided meeting his eye, and turned her back on him whenever possible. She did not know if he recognized her from the Medallion. She said he gave no sign of ever having seen her and she was thankful of this, but at the same time she felt it would be more natural if they spoke to each other. As long as he was a human being and not a spider they ought to communicate with each other. They should get acquainted, she thought, even if they had nothing to say. However, she refused to approach him. If he would walk up to her while she was resting between poses, if he would walk across the room and say hello, she explained, that would be enough. Then she would invite him to join the group at the café. Then all of them would talk to him. They could criticize his drawings, have Pernod with him, and finally believe that he existed.

But he never spoke to the model, and as she went again and again to the atelier she discovered something about him that seemed to her very strange. She realized that now and then he got up and left the room. He would be gone for a few minutes, then he came back and sat down behind the drawing board. Of course it was possible that he went outside for a smoke, or to visit the men's room, or it was possible that he got nervous in a crowd with so many people pressing around and sometimes needed a few minutes by himself; but she thought none of these reasons explained why he slipped out of the room. She thought that from somewhere outside he was watching her.

At the Medallion everybody was amused when she said this.

Karl Baum leaves the studio in order to climb up on the roof and peek in through the skylight—that's very good! No, this is how it is: Karl Baum goes outside so he can have the satisfaction of opening the door and coming inside again to stare at you! Once isn't enough, he wants to do it four times every session!

The truth is, they said to her, the truth is just what you've told us yourself. He goes out for a smoke. No doubt he's also got a weak bladder. Those are explanations enough. And maybe it's true he gets nervous with people all around.

You're wrong! she said, because she could not escape the feeling that while he was away his eyes were fastened on her. She felt the lifeless gaze. She knew that he went outside in order to see her from a distance so that she would be reduced to a small, meaningless figure. Inside the studio she was a living woman, too intimate for Karl Baum. Being this close to her he was destroyed, only at a distance could he enjoy her. From outside the atelier he could not sense the heat of her body or notice that she was breathing. She must look to him, wherever he was, as naked and helpless as some kind of larva.

Then one day she came to the Medallion saying that what she had suspected was the truth. Convinced that he was watching, she had begun to investigate. When the studio was empty she had examined the walls for peepholes, but the walls were solid. She had climbed up a ladder to look closely at the skylight, although it was impossible to get on the roof. And besides, as somebody pointed out, you could hear his footsteps. But she had known he was somewhere, and after looking at the walls and the skylight she examined the doors. There were two doors, one of which opened into a closet filled with the janitor's equipment. The other door opened into the hall. This was the door he used, the door used by everybody. She expected to find a crack of light, but it was tightly joined and the keyhole was filled with putty. But she discovered that this door had once been used somewhere else. It had window panes which were now thickly painted over. By carefully searching the glass she found a hole scratched through the paint. The hole was not much bigger than the head of a pin, but by putting your eye next to it you could make out a few blurred shapes inside the studio. This of course was where he stood, but to be sure there was no mistake she wet her finger, picked up some dust from the floor and rubbed it over the hole. The next afternoon Karl Baum got up and went outside. He was gone for about five minutes, then he came back as usual and continued drawing. When the session was over, on her way out, she looked. The dirt had been wiped away.

Now listen, she said, after she finished telling the story to her friends at the Medallion, he has been doing this not just to me, because I am meaningless. I'm nothing to him. Nothing. He has done this to every model, to all of us.

They turned around to look at him; he was sitting motionless with his hands folded on the table.

You understand, she said, what I'm telling you. He has done this to each one of us.

1965

AU LAPIN GROS

BEING UNSPEAKABLY TIRED of—no, no, dissatisfied with myself— yes, that's it. Being unspeakably dissatisfied with myself, I happened upon the simplest possible solution. And what was that? Nothing could be more obvious. I would re-create myself.

Why had I failed to think of this sooner? I don't know. I can't imagine. It's mysterious. In any case, I resolved that no longer would I tell the truth about myself provided I could think of a plausible lie. Well, how does one prepare to substitute fiction for truth? After much thought I grew a little beard which I trimmed to a point like a Russian anarchist and I began to wear tinted glasses. I bought a shabby overcoat that I wore all the time. I obtained a job as menial factotum to a druggist and I rented a musty room in the shadow of St. Sulpice.

What attracted me to this terrible room? A pot of starving geraniums on the window ledge and one disconsolate ray of sunshine that hesitantly approached the moth-eaten rug each afternoon between four and five o'clock. It seemed to me that the person I had decided to become would live in just such a room. The bed, I concluded, would be suitable for a dying leper. As to the armoire, leaning for support against a mildewed wall, it appeared to have been constructed during the reign of

Charlemagne. There was, I admit, a handsome oval washbasin embellished with painted roses and a decorative brass faucet. This excellent basin, owing to an ancient fracture, was capable of holding water up to a certain level but no higher. If the handle could be persuaded to turn, which on certain days proved inexplicably difficult, there came an agonized shriek followed by guttural music from below, followed at last by a spitting noise, then a blast of water that a thirsty horse would view with suspicion. Of the indomitable cockroaches who for countless generations had patrolled the baseboards, I say nothing. In short, a clochard accustomed to life under the Pont Neuf would turn up his nose at such quarters. Consequently, having rented this room, I asked myself what I had done, a question to which there was no reasonable answer. Nevertheless, I reflected, even if I could get my money back, which I could not, the next place I rented might be worse. Life is, after all, the study of contradictions.

Because I have no instinct for cooking I took all my meals at a restaurant from the Dark Ages that smelled of cabbage and mice and also of disinfectant. Among its distinguished patrons this establishment boasted five or six gentlemen with hairy arms who seemed to be playing chess with their knives and forks and whom I had observed at work on a sewer, various picturesque ladies who did not appear until after sunset, and a tribe of students less notable for brains than for bawling voices and the lack of civility one would expect in a railroad station. What a detestable place. Three times a day I went there, shuddering as I entered and clutching my stomach in pain as I departed because the meals filled me with gas. Then, after strolling along the quai belching and fouling the air like a policeman's horse at every intersection, I proceeded to the Lapin Gros in search of adventure. There I would select a table with a nice view of whatever might happen and I would sip coffee while pretending to read *Le Figaro*. That is how I became acquainted with Meretricia Istanapoulos, whom I shall never forget.

She strode into the café one rainy night like a murderess, water dripping from her long black trenchcoat. She walked toward me with gigantic strides and sat down at the next table. Already I felt myself enslaved. I observed that her sandals were huge, which did not surprise me because she was tall as a flagpole. Around the pages of *Le Figaro* I smiled in the most ingratiating manner, but she did not notice. She was muttering to herself in Greek, a language of which I understand scarcely more than five words.

All at once she turned her passionate gaze upon me. Monsieur, she demanded with a voice like a cello, if you please, a match?

I was astounded. Certainly, I replied, and like the most obsequious servant I scuttled to the counter. When I returned with a packet of matches she seemed to have forgotten me. In one hand she held a cigarillo black as the devil's own, which I hastened to light. Four bony fingers of the other hand, bristling with imitation gems, tapped the marble surface of the table as though despatching a message.

Permit me to introduce myself, I ventured. My name is Arturo Sanchez de La Coruña. But having said this I trembled. I am not adept at lying. When I was a child my parents could tell immediately if I was lying; they would look at my feet, which I found myself unable to control. My tiny feet would begin to creep in circles as though ashamed of my behavior. Now I felt them growing restless and was thankful that if she glanced down she would not know what had aroused them.

For some reason she ignored my overture. Possibly she had not heard me. Whatever the explanation, I determined to press forward. And as she continued muttering to herself I took advantage of the situation to study those black Greek eyebrows, the nose, the lips, the chin. I imagined her profile on a vase. I saw her wearing a peaked gold helmet and carrying a long spear as she advanced upon her enemies, who fled in terror. This woman, said I to myself, is a goddess, the daughter of Athena. I risked another peek at her sandals. Again she failed to notice. How was I to proceed? Audacity is not part of my temperament, nevertheless it seemed imperative to act.

Mademoiselle, I began, and made an effort to fortify the voice that was dying in my throat. Mademoiselle, I repeated, forgive me but you appear somehow vexed. On the chance that I might be of service I throw myself at your feet.

Ah! cried this extraordinary creature. It's nothing, monsieur. I have just now come from a meeting of the Opposition. Tell me your name.

I braced myself for the lie. Arturo Sanchez de La Coruña, I repeated. But to my amazement I felt almost no discomfort.

You do not sound like a Spaniard, she said, puffing on her cigarillo. In fact, you do not look like a Spaniard.

I am—as perhaps you deduce from my surname—a *gallego,* I continued boldly. I was brought to France while a mere infant, which is why you discern no accent. My parents, God rest them, were obliged to flee the war.

Your father, then, he was a Loyalist?

I hesitated. I had not expected her to know anything about that struggle which concluded long before she was born. Indeed, I myself knew next to nothing about it. Caution seemed advisable. I screwed up my eyes as though deliberating. Through a cloud of purplish smoke I could see her staring at me like a basilisk. I had no idea what to say. I wanted to hide behind the newspaper. My heart thumped against my ribs. I'm no good at fakery, I said to myself, I have no panache. Then, to my alarm, this Amazon hitched her chair a few inches closer and it became obvious that she was unaccustomed to bathing, but whether the somewhat agricultural fragrance was intoxicating or repugnant, or both, I was at a loss to decide.

Have you not failed to introduce yourself? I inquired with mock reproach. And from the confidence of my voice one might assume that somebody else was speaking.

She sucked in her breath. Ah! Meretricia Istanapoulos.

Meretricia! whispered I to myself. It was a name one could not forget. Meretricia! Meretricia! I felt an urge to embrace her. I wanted to stroke and squeeze those colossal feet. After so many solitary evenings at the Lapin Gros perhaps I was on the verge of a conquest.

Your profession, monsieur?

Please, I said, not "monsieur." Arturo.

Arturo, she repeated thoughtfully. Arturo.

What did she mean by that? Twice she had pronounced the name. I felt encouraged.

Your profession?

Correspondent, said I. After all, if she knew what I did for a living the affair would end in a moment.

She glanced at *Le Figaro* and the significance of this did not escape me. I reflected that it would be unwise to claim a position on *Le Figaro*. If, by chance, she was acquainted with somebody at the paper and inquired about me—well, I would be finished. Nor could I say, for example, *Paris Soir.* On the other hand, having represented myself as a journalist, something further was expected. I had no idea what to do. I decided to take refuge in evasion.

Figaro? I remarked as though the subject merited no discussion. Oh, it can be entertaining enough, but hardly sufficient to engage one with serious concerns. It lacks—what should one say?—a certain depth? And I made a disparaging gesture.

Then you do not, monsieur, write for this—as you express it—"entertaining" journal?

I smiled politely, indicating that I had no wish to condemn *Le Figaro.* As to the publication which employs me, I said, let it remain anonymous. No doubt you agree, mademoiselle, that under certain circumstances one may wish to avoid scrutiny by a repressive and stupid government.

But of course, she murmured, leaning toward me as though we were conspirators.

At this moment, I confess, I found myself hypnotized. Always I had championed the cause of free will, but if just then Meretricia had commanded me to annihilate myself I would have rushed to do so. At the same time it occurred to me that she was less than intelligent. Her admirably bright eye—like that of a seagull—was vacant.

I would love a Campari, she said, so naturally there's no waiter. How are they able to vanish? She looked around the café, squinting. I realized that she was nearsighted.

Allow me, I said and was about to rise when five red talons sank into my arm.

Don't move! she hissed. We are being watched. Behind you is a fat man with the Legion of Honor who has been ignoring us while drinking chocolate.

Could you be mistaken? I asked.

Monsieur, I am not mistaken.

You say he ignores us?

Ah, you fail to understand! The fact that he pays no attention is absolute proof. Furthermore, they work in pairs, although just now I don't see the accomplice.

Meretricia, I said as calmly as possible. Meretricia, luxuriant flower of Ionia, be kind enough to listen. Were it not for a single consideration I would beseech you to clasp my arm throughout eternity.

Monsieur, what is that consideration?

Your fingernails are draining my lifeblood.

Presumably she understood. In any case, she withdrew her claws while I gave thanks to a God whose supervision of the universe appears at times incomprehensible. I then had the impression, although I do not know why, that she was about to serenade the café with an exuberant Greek folk song. This, I suspected, might not be well received by Madame Ponge behind the cash register so I asked if she would care for a sweet—an ice cream, a pastry of some sort.

Ah, oui! The millefeuille! she sang with that melodious voice. Ah, I adore the millefeuille!

Scarcely a minute had elapsed since she was dying for Campari. Well, I thought, women are capable of jumping like mountain sheep from here to there. How they do it is impossible to learn.

A millefeuille, said I. Of course.

By the time I returned after ordering a pastry the fat man with the Legion of Honor had vanished. I asked where he had gone.

That one! she exclaimed. Who knows, monsieur? And then her resolute face grew pensive. I have been thinking about you. Yes, she went on while stroking my sleeve with her talons, it is true.

Meretricia, zephyr of the Aegean, said I with my heart in my throat, will you call me "Arturo"? Say that you will.

If you wish it. Naturally, monsieur.

You were thinking about me? I asked before she could forget.

I have come to a decision, she said. I believe you are one of us. I'm prepared to risk everything.

This disturbed me. If she chose to be a revolutionary, which I suspected might be the case, well and good, but it was no concern of mine. I am not one to mount the barricades. Let others give heroic speeches and get shot, that's how I view the matter. Frankly, what attracted me more than all the political manifestoes in Europe were those two indescribably long feet underneath her table. It was with the greatest difficulty that I prevented myself from staring at them.

Monsieur, she said, would it be correct to assume that you have been outraged by the unjust trial and false imprisonment of Jacques Chatelet?

Who, I wondered, is Jacques Chatelet? I had never heard this name. I was on the point of asking, but the manner in which Meretricia pronounced it—as though he were a saint—warned me against such a question.

For reasons I cannot disclose, I said, I have been prevented from following the progress of this shameful affair.

Just then, by good luck, the millefeuille arrived. Meretricia did not hesitate. I observed with fascination the tiny silver fork traveling rapidly between the plate and her voluptuous mouth—back and forth, back and forth—as though it had developed a life of its own. Her eyes half-closed with pleasure. What provocative noises she made while munching! How I envied those crisp little flakes of pastry! I intend to begin writing epic poetry, I said to myself, which I shall dedicate to this imposing and excitable foreigner.

Suddenly the fork came to a stop in midair while Meretricia gazed frantically at the plate. I could not imagine what was wrong. Her bosom heaved. You must pardon me, monsieur, she said. You must pardon me. You must—I am about to sneeze.

Neither of us moved. Well, I said after a moment, how goes it?

She lifted the fork. Next, a cataclysm.

Listen to that! she exclaimed. And having rubbed her nose like a child she turned once more to the task of devouring pastry.

You are prepared to risk everything . . . ?

Ah! You made me forget. What a little goose I am! Then with the majestic dignity of enormous women she leaned toward me. I reflected that every patron of the Lapin Gros, to say nothing of Madame Ponge, must be watching.

The trial, she whispered. A disgrace! The government will do anything to discredit the Opposition.

Why did she choose to whisper? Possibly she was an actress. I would be honored to make the acquaintance of Jacques Chatelet, I remarked while staring at a flake of millefeuille that clung like a moth to that monumental bosom.

If you wish to wait nine years and three months, she said.

Having considered her statement I began to view these sans-culottes differently. My passionate conspirator evidently belonged to an organization devoted to more than the deliverance of furious speeches. What Monsieur Chatelet had done, or to whom, I had not the faintest idea, but I believe he had not merely disobeyed a traffic signal. I recalled that on some festive day of the previous year a bomb had exploded in front of the stock exchange. All right, I said to myself, I've been hoping for adventure, let's see what happens next. But it then occurred to me that my companion may have been correct about the fat man drinking chocolate. Well, to be identified as the associate of a bona fide anarchist wasn't what I had in mind. One shouldn't antagonize the authorities, that's how I look at it. Life under any circumstances is problematic, so it's best to remain invisible. Nothing would give me greater satisfaction than to be informed that the government had absolutely no record of my existence. In short, I felt torn between my desire for this Mt. Everest of a woman and a quite sensible desire for anonymity.

How do you know, said I, that you are not discussing this business with an agent of the national security? How do you know I am not an accomplice of the fat man with the Legion of Honor? It was you yourself who assured me that he was not alone.

You are not an agent of the national security, she said. If that were the case you would behave more cleverly. For one thing, you wouldn't exercise yourself by peeking at me while you think I am unaware.

But that is unavoidable, I said.

For what reason is that unavoidable?

Because I am bewitched.

Ah, monsieur, she said, you are very wicked.

But how could I fail to admire you? I replied while stroking my beard. Where you are concerned, I admit to being without shame. I think of you as a mermaid swimming through the maelstrom that Paris has become.

No, my complexion is too dark, she said. I am unattractive, as you see. And she touched her hair.

Allow me one liberty, I said.

What is that liberty, monsieur?

Permit me to devour you. Permit me to feast upon you like a millefeuille.

I will consider it, she said. In the meantime, I permit you to accompany me to the metro.

What about the rain? I asked because I felt that my position was not yet established. Look, there's a waterfall outside and you didn't bring an umbrella.

That's true, she said. But you have one.

I hadn't expected such a logical remark. Perhaps, I suggested, I may accompany you beyond the metro?

As to that, it will depend. We shall see.

All right, let's be off, I said, putting on my beret. And with the umbrella under my arm I stood up. The situation was progressing. I had extracted no promise, nevertheless a certain something in her attitude gave me hope. Besides, the rain might prove useful. I would remind her that upon emerging from the metro she would again appreciate the value of an umbrella. And whose umbrella was it?

Meretricia stood up.

I had known, of course, from the moment she strode into the café that she was a giant, and when it became obvious that she had her eye on the adjoining table I had said to myself, very good, she's marching this way, I look forward to the challenge. Now, as the saying goes, it was a different story.

Sit down, she said, and she pulled me down. We are being watched.

This, in fact, was so. A theatrical audience could not have been more attentive than the patrons of the Lapin Gros. Madame Ponge herself had turned a crocodile gaze in our direction.

Pretend you do not know me, Meretricia commanded. I have located the accomplice.

Does he wear the Legion of Honor? I asked.

He's Algerian, she whispered while pretending to search for something in the pockets of her trenchcoat. I know the type. Be careful. Don't look at me.

Obediently I stared at a poster for the Comédie Française. Why do you think he is the accomplice? I asked.

There's no mistake, she whispered. This is dangerous, monsieur. You have been observed with me.

Our lives are entwined, I said while inspecting the handle of my umbrella. Authors a century from now will write of us as another Héloïse and Abélard.

He's getting up, Meretricia said between her teeth. He's approaching. Pay no attention.

I am prepared to sacrifice myself a thousand times, I replied in a menacing voice. I will bite his hand.

He has turned around, she murmured. I believe he is going to the lavatory for a conference with the other one. Let's get out of here.

This I thought was a splendid idea. Because of a shy disposition I feel uncomfortable on stage. Also, I did not care to have a strange Algerian walk up behind me, especially after I had been talking with this remarkable woman about whom I knew nothing. I recalled my first impression of her—a murderess—and it occurred to me that I was planning to accompany this formidable creature to an unknown destination. Always, throughout my life, I have taken discreet pride in my judgment, but now I began to wonder if it had evaporated. Still, I reflected, had I not come to the Lapin Gros in hopes of some such adventure? Very well, Arturo, said I bravely to myself, proceed. The truth, however, was a little different. After considering various possibilities my natural cowardice reasserted itself and I wished that I had been less anxious to escort her as far as the metro, or perhaps beyond.

Meretricia, you shall teach me Greek, I announced when we emerged on the rue St. André des Arts. I will become your favorite pupil. Every lesson will be a joy. And having spread the umbrella I held it high in the air.

Ah, but you are droll, she replied. Wait! There's another! And she squinted toward somebody getting out of a cab.

It's a conspiracy, I said. We are surrounded.

We must go back. There's no time to lose.

What do you mean? I asked. What are you talking about? Are you suggesting that we go back into the café?

We'll go out the other side. Hurry! she exclaimed, giving me such a push that I staggered.

Inside the Lapin I dared not look toward Madame Ponge who, I felt certain, must be eyeing us with displeasure. All the same, since Meretricia was leading the way I had no choice but to follow. I could see nothing except her broad shoulders.

Well, what do you think? I asked when we once again stood outside, having entertained everybody by marching like comedians in one door and out the other.

Soon enough they'll catch on to our trick, she said. It would be wise to take the Odéon metro. Then like a goddess she contemplated me with an expression that was possibly amorous and said, Monsieur, no matter what happens I won't betray you.

I could not imagine what she meant.

I understand why you must keep quiet, she said. You are an assassin.

These words astonished me so much that I was unable to speak. My thoughts, which until that instant had pirouetted with the grace of ballet dancers, now bumped clumsily against each other. Having no idea what to do, I tugged my beard and glanced shrewdly all around. I was then still more astonished when Meretricia bent down and kissed my forehead. Naturally I attempted to fling myself upon her but she muttered something in Greek and brushed me aside. I am not a large man.

With stupendous strides she set off toward Odéon while I trotted alongside throbbing with desire. Her monstrous feet splashing through puddles reminded me of salmon. I could hardly control myself. Villains! Pigs! I cried, doubling up my fist to show how much I believed in the cause. Leeches! Termites! We will crush them! I imagined us marching side by side against enemies of the Opposition.

She did not respond. As we approached the rue Danton she murmured in a sorrowful voice: Nine years. They will stop at nothing, monsieur, nothing.

I wondered why he had been imprisoned although I was reluctant to ask because I had hinted that I knew about the government's infamous behavior. As a matter of fact, I had no idea which government was responsible.

Brunetti! she exclaimed in a tone of scorn. Who could believe that Jacques Chatelet would be represented by Eugenio Brunetti? I tell you it's unbelievable!

Brunetti, I thought. Chatelet. Istanapoulos. This sounds like the Internationale. What next? A Bulgarian? A Portuguese? I began to regret that I had neglected to follow the trial in the newspaper. I could recall absolutely nothing about it. Not a word. Also, I was afraid to ask what we were opposing. Sooner or later it will come out, I said to myself. What's important at the moment is to demonstrate solidarity.

The world is a bottomless cesspool, I heard Meretricia saying in the words of, I am positive, Jacques Chatelet. Regard the deputies, she went on. Serpents! Regard the advocates. Behold how they mortgage their souls for a sou! Can anyone deny this?

I replied that I was too overcome with disgust to speak.

Ah! There you have it! The police walk around hoping for an excuse to crack the heads of workers. Innocent people find themselves detained. It makes one sick!

The masses are content to sleep, I said. To wake up the common people would require an earthquake.

Or a volcano, said Meretricia. Beyond doubt you've put your finger on it. Then she gazed over my head with a feminine expression. In the café, surely, you didn't find me attractive?

Meretricia, I said, I am overwhelmed by the need to abduct you. To run away with you. To hold you captive. I am engorged! Yes, exactly, that's the word. If instead of being a journalist I were a poet you would comprehend my passion.

I don't think I believe you, she said. I'm not at my best. I didn't sleep comfortably last night. You should see me when things are going well.

Tell me about yourself, I said. From the first day, from the first instant of your existence. How do you come to be in Paris? Why have we not met before? Tell me everything. Withhold nothing. Exclude only the men you have loved because they no longer have meaning.

Ah! she gasped with that suggestive intake of breath which drew me to the brink of madness. You wish to know about my life? I summarize my life in three words. Resistance. Purity. Rebellion.

The second word appalled me. As a matter of fact, I cared for none of it. I had a feeling she was altogether under the thumb of that imprisoned Svengali. This disposition to subordinate themselves is something about women I have never understood. In any case, Meretricia's politics interested me less than her exceptional stride—like that of an American basketball player. The flapping of those immense sandals on wet pavement reduced my brain to pudding. I found myself out of breath while attempting to keep up with her.

Don't allow yourself to become excited, she said. It's not the most important thing in the world. What's important, monsieur, is to lift the yoke of capitalism from the necks of our brothers and sisters everywhere. That is our mission.

She kept talking while I shook my fist and nodded enthusiastically, although I confess that political rhetoric makes me yawn. Justice! she exclaimed with great bitterness. Tell me, monsieur, what chance has the worker? None! And she went on about government abdicating its responsibility abetted by lackeys of God in lace collars who would drink a poor man's blood if it would please the rich, and so on and so forth. Well, I said to myself, that's all true enough and I wish things were different, but they aren't, and so far as I can see they won't be much better tomorrow. In my opinion it wasn't going to make the least difference whether Monsieur Chatelet spent the rest of his days in the Bastille or whether he was appointed Minister of Finance.

Why did they do away with him? she asked. Because they feared him, that's why. Because he, alone, understands the truth. Don't authorities always fear the truth?

Exactly! I cried. You've got it just right! And I wondered what sort of impression I made by shouting. With my little beard and tinted glasses, wearing a beret worth less than a centime and a discouraged overcoat, it seemed to me that I might easily be mistaken for a disenfranchised radical, possibly a bolshevik. I noticed Meretricia squinting along the boulevard. We were very close to the Odéon metro.

What's your opinion? I asked while trying to slip an arm around her waist. Are we out of danger?

It looks all right, she admitted, but of course that's what they want us to believe. In any event, you'll allow me to borrow the umbrella, will you not? It's a long walk to my apartment from Gare du Nord.

Now wait a minute, I said. In the first place, I don't live right around the corner and this is a torrent. What about me?

A few drops won't hurt you, she said with a playful expression and before I knew what was happening she had seized the umbrella.

Now don't be hasty, I said without letting go. Look at it this way. We've been observed together. The fat man was watching us and also the Algerian. You yourself said it was dangerous. I'd better come along to protect you.

I assure you I'll be fine, she said while twisting the umbrella away from me. I'll meet you next Wednesday at the Lapin. Don't worry, monsieur, I know how to take care of myself.

Well, it was an awkward situation. What was I to do? I'm not good at taking the initiative. Wednesday? I called while she descended the steps. You'll be there?

She waved and said something in Greek before disappearing.

I should have been forceful, I thought. I should have asserted myself. But everything happened so fast. She was too quick for me.

I returned to my room shivering and wet as a cod, already counting the days until I would see her again. I remembered that when she entered the café she had seemed distraught. Why? She had just come from a meeting of the Opposition, therefore something disagreeable must have occurred. What? I tried to imagine the meeting. Fifteen or twenty malcontents packed into a squalid closet reeking of wine and department store cheese. There would be a Scandinavian because there are Scandinavians everywhere—perhaps a sallow boy with a bad complexion who carried a guitar and cleaned the wax out of his ears with a little finger. I had seen such a boy at the café. An American Negro with a booming voice and huge white teeth and hands that could strangle a horse. I imagined him playing the bongo drum. Several of my countrymen would be there, stingy and quarrelsome and dissatisfied as always. Another Greek. Russians, naturally. Germans. Yes, anything political attracts Germans. They would attempt to dominate the meeting. And what would be the purpose of this stupid affair? Would they pass a resolution to hurl a bomb at the Palais Nationale? Or, since I did not know which government was to be opposed, they might resolve to attack the embassy of Greece. Or that of the Netherlands. What difference did it make? I wondered if the Opposition had an official song.

However, I spent most of every day thinking about Meretricia. I planned to be at the café well ahead of time. I imagined her pushing through the door with my umbrella, squinting in the direction of our tables, marching toward me like a basketball player. I would put aside the newspaper, rise, press my lips to one of those baguettes on her fingers. No doubt she would ask for another millefeuille. And this time our conversation would make more sense because I had prepared a list of interesting topics to discuss.

Wednesday. A day I thought would never arrive. When it did, I grew convinced that it would never end, but at last the supper hour approached.

After a hasty meal of putrid lamb flavored with venomous herbs accompanied by a poultice of exhausted spinach and wine that would corrode a shovel, followed by a dish of scabrous chocolate—doubtful that I could survive many more such meals without submerging my stomach in lactates and sulphates and mineral water—I all but trotted along the rue St. André des Arts.

Finding our tables unoccupied, I seated myself with an air of nonchalance and pretended to read *Le Figaro* while sipping coffee, although in fact I comprehended nothing. Each time the door opened I held my breath.

Not until past midnight did I give up hope and no sooner had I returned to my room than I felt convinced she had been delayed and even now must be hurrying to meet me. Next I told myself that I had failed to pay attention—that she had said we should meet not this Wednesday but the week following.

Night after night I waited at the Lapin Gros.

It was only much later that I learned she had run off with a Turk. A wrestler. I knew I would never see her again.

1992

THE CORSET

I THINK THAT you are, she had said, enunciating each word, unutterably disgusting. I think, to tell the honest truth, that never in my entire life have I heard such an inexpressibly vulgar suggestion. Just in case you care for my opinion, there it is. To think that any man would even propose such an idea, especially to his wife, which, just on the chance that you've forgotten, I happen to be, is, to put it in the simplest possible terms, unutterably disgusting.

Mosher shrugs. Okay, never mind. It was a thought, Alice.

What you did while you were in the Army, and the type of women who prey upon lonesome soldiers in foreign countries, or for that matter, how foreign women in other countries behave with their husbands, are things I'd just as soon not care to hear about. I don't know if I'm making myself clear. It simply does not concern me, first of all, and then too, I don't see why you keep harping on these things, as though I were merely some sort of concubine. I guess that's the word. To be perfectly frank, because certainly I've always wanted you to be frank with me whenever anything was bothering you about our relationship, and I'm sure you've always wanted me to express my feelings just as frankly, I appreciate the fact that you thought enough of me to mention it, but it's just so revolting, I mean, I honestly do not know quite what to say.

I thought it might be fun, says Mosher. Overseas the women would—

Fun! Did you say *fun?* When we've always had such a marvelous relationship? I can't understand you any more. You've changed. We used to agree that we had the most beautiful relationship in the world, at least you said so every time I asked, but now I don't know whether to believe you or not. I should think you'd want to keep it the way it was. When two people sincerely respect each other they surely oughtn't to jeopardize their affiliation, do you think? A moment ago I could scarcely believe my ears. I never dreamed that you could be so—so—

Vulgar?

Exactly! Not by any stretch of the imagination.

Then you think it's an unreasonable request? asks Mosher after a pause. Listen, Alice—

What you did in Europe is one thing, and I try not to dwell on it, which is more than most wives would do, but now you're home and we ought to go on the way we did before.

Alice, it's a damned strange thing, says Mosher, that my own wife should know less about me than a whore on the rue de la Paix.

For a moment she gazes at him. Then all at once she remarks: Tell me what you want. I love you, you must know that. I'll do anything on earth for you. Tell me specifically what would please you and I'll agree to do it, on the condition that it means preserving our relationship.

I don't want it that way! Mosher shouts, and bangs his fists together. Can't you understand? Oh my god, don't look so miserable, he adds. You look like I was getting ready to flog you.

That wouldn't surprise me. Nothing you do any more could possibly surprise me. I don't know what's come over you. Honestly, I don't. You're a perfect stranger.

Mosher, enraged and baffled, lights a cigarette.

Smoking isn't good for you.

I know it isn't, I know, he says, puffing away.

You never listen to me.

Alice, he replies with a gloomy expression, I don't miss a word, not a word. Oh hell, I love you as you are. Don't change. You're probably right, we'll go on like we used to. I don't want you to change. Forget I said anything.

But you *do!* You do want me to change, and I've got to be everything to you, otherwise our—

Don't! Mosher groans, falling back on the bed. Don't keep calling the two of us a relationship, as though we were a paragraph in some social worker's report.

For better or worse, she says as though she had not heard him, I've made up my mind to behave exactly like one of those European women. I'm quite serious. I mean that.

Mosher, rising on one elbow, gazes at his wife curiously.

I do mean it. I'm going to be every bit as depraved and evil as they are, you just watch!

What the hell's got into you? he demands. You're out of your mind. You're as American as Susan B. Anthony. Then he continues: But if you want to, fine. Go ahead.

What do I do first?

I don't know. Don't you?

No, this was your idea. Give me a suggestion.

Well, says Mosher uneasily, I'm a spectator, so to speak. I don't really know. He realizes that she has started to unbutton her blouse. What do you think you're doing? he asks. I mean, good God, it's three o'clock in the afternoon and the Haffenbecks are coming over.

I don't care, she says. I simply don't care about a thing anymore.

But wait a minute, Alice. We invited them for drinks and a barbecue, remember?

I don't care! I don't care about the Haffenbecks. And she takes off her blouse, asking: Shall I take off everything?

Oh, yes, yes, everything, everything, says Mosher absently, gazing at her shoulders. With his chin propped in his hands he watches her get undressed.

I really should have paid a visit to the beauty parlor this morning, she says. My hair is a fright.

The beauty parlor! he shouts. What the hell has a beauty parlor got to do with this? Life's too short for beauty parlors!

However, she's doing her best, he thinks, all for me, because she does love me and wants to please me, isn't that odd? She's not a bit excited, she's just ashamed and embarrassed, so I am too. He feels deeply touched that his wife is willing to debase herself for him, but at the same time he is annoyed. Her attitude fills him with a sense of vast and unspeakable dismay. In Europe, now, romping in a bedroom, there would be no stilted questions, no apologies or explanations, no pussyfooting about, no textbook psychology, nothing but a wild and fruitful and altogether satisfying game. Alice, though, after the first embrace, customarily looks to see if her clothing is torn or her hair has been mussed.

Why, he asks with a lump like a chestnut in his throat, do you wear that corset?

It isn't a corset, it's a foundation.

Mosher waves impatiently. Alice, I hate these Puritan bones. Those Boston snoods. You haven't the slightest idea how sick and tired I've become of Aunt Martha's prune-whip morals. Whenever I touch you while you're wearing that thing it's like I've got hold of a bag of cement. Didn't I ever tell you how much I hate that corset? Didn't you ever realize? I mean to say, I think of you as flesh and blood, but that freaking thing makes you look like a python that swallowed a pig. Why do you wear it? You have such a marvelous shape all by yourself. It would look wonderful to see you out in public without that damned corset.

I should think a man wouldn't want his wife to be seen on the street bulging at every seam.

Well, I would, says Mosher with great bitterness. I'd love it. Anyway, right now I want you to take that bloody thing off.

She does, with no change of expression; her eyes remain fixed on him rather like the eyes of a frightened tigress, bright and watchful and unblinking.

Do you love me because of this? she asks.

Because of what?

My figure.

Yes, he says earnestly, I certainly do. A moment later, to his amazement, a tear comes wandering down her cheek.

I hoped it was me you loved, she says, weeping a little more but holding her head high.

I should have been a monk, he thinks. I'd have a nice quiet cell with bread and porridge and books to read—it would all be so simple. On the other hand I wouldn't make a very successful monk. I know what I'd spend every day praying for.

You can leave those beads on, Alice, he says, I like the effect.

He gazes at her body with immense interest; it is as pale as a melon. In the undergloom of her belly, he thinks, a little bird has landed—a fierce little falcon with tawny wings. He lifts his eyes once more to her face and sees a lock of hair almost, but not quite touching the lobe of her ear. She is as divine and inimitable and perfect as a snow crystal or an April leaf unfolding.

You mentioned some girl over there who was a dancer, who used to dance for the soldiers.

Oh yes, yes, and she was magnificent, Mosher answers. Her name was Zizi. She used to go leaping around like the nymphs on those Greek vases, and when she wriggled across the floor you'd swear she was made out of rubber. I never saw anything like it.

Well, look at me, says Alice. And to Mosher's astonishment she lifts both hands high above her head and turns a perfectly splendid cartwheel.

What do you think of *that*? she demands, on her feet once again, tossing her hair over her shoulders.

I didn't know you could turn a cartwheel, says Mosher. He sits up briskly, spilling cigarette ashes on the bed.

You haven't seen anything yet, she calls from the other side of the room, and bending backward until her palms are flat on the floor she gives a nimble kick and is upside down.

I didn't know you could stand on your hands, says Mosher, looking at her in stupefaction. Even with your clothes on you never did that.

Does it please you?

I should say it does! Mosher replies.

Men are so peculiar. Why should you want me to do these things?

I don't know, Alice. Somehow it makes me love you all the more.

I simply cannot understand you, she remarks, and begins walking around the bedroom on her hands. Could your old Zizi do this?

I don't know, he mutters. I can't remember. You've got me confused. I don't think I ever say anything in my life like this.

Not even in Paris?

Not even in Heidelberg. You look strange upside down, Alice. What else can you do?

Just then the doorbell rings.

Oh my word, she exclaims, that must be the Haffenbecks!

No doubt, says Mosher. Either it's the Haffenbecks or the police.

What on earth are we going to do?

I don't know, he replies, unable to stop staring at her. Who cares? Do you?

I suppose not, she answers, still upside down.

The corset is lying on the edge of the bed. Mosher picks it up, flings it out the window and, reclining comfortably, takes a puff at his cigarette.

Now, he commands, turn a somersault.

1961

THE FLAT-FOOTED TIGER

WHEN PEOPLE discovered that Willie ran a freight elevator they always looked at his feet and then began to make jokes, but Willie didn't mind because jokes were a fine thing. There was only one thing he treasured above good jokes and that was Gloria. Gloria had long brown hair and eyes as big as the knobs on the elevator. Her skin was as nice as milk. She wore lilac perfume and she was kind and as gentle as a Christmas carol.

When in the line of Willie's duties there were boxes to be checked or a number to be remembered he counted on his fingers, a mannerism which irritated Big Chuck no end, but which had moved Gillis to observe quite soundly that although Willie might be no tiger he always solved his problem.

Willie had no illusions about becoming president of Comer's, but there was pleasure in contemplating the fact that if he stopped his elevator between floors and refused to deliver, Comer's would soon be out of string, cardboard, pins, envelopes, and any number of important things. On slow days he often filched a scrap of brown wrapping paper from the storeroom and made lists of all the things Comer's would run out of if he stopped the elevator between floors. Undeniably no department store could do without men in his position.

Added to this was the fact that Big Chuck and Gillis and Wop were his friends. Big Chuck worked in the basement, where he moved barrels. He liked to tear decks of cards and thick magazines in half. Gillis worked up front selling shoes. Having had a year of college, Gillis smoked a pipe with an amber stem and was very smart. He wore bay rum on his hair. Wop worked on the second floor and he had a finger missing from his left hand and he could tell jokes for an hour. Wop's last name was Glorioso, a fact which interested Willie immensely and which had caused him to sound out Gloria on several occasions as to whether she had any brothers she didn't know about.

Willie was indeed pleased to have such a distinguished group of friends. And in January Gloria had promised to marry him. Whenever he thought about all this Willie's ears would turn red with happiness. Not often did one have so much to be thankful for. Truly he was the most fortunate man at Comer's.

So it was that he hummed *Cowboy Jack* as he parked on the second floor waiting for Wop to lock up. It was just after six o'clock. As he hummed and waited he amused himself by counting the rivet heads in the opposite wall of the elevator. Strong rivets they were. Strong. Hard and black. Good rivets.

When Wop pulled his coat off the nail and got into the elevator Willie dropped to the main floor for Gillis. Big Chuck had already closed the basement and was waiting for them outside.

"It's getting cold," said Big Chuck as they came out.

Gillis considered and then said, "Yes. It is inclement." He filled his pipe.

"Well, let's go eat," said Wop and he walked off toward the Dine-A-Mite.

They sat in a rear booth and Willie managed to sit next to Big Chuck. Carefully he slid his hand along the tablecloth to where he could compare the size of their knuckles. It would be fine to be as strong as that—to have long black hairs on one's wrists and fingers strong enough to bend bottle caps. Gillis sat across from them and he thought, too, that it would be fine to be as smart as Gillis. Or as handsome as Wop. Oh, it was fine to be in such company, and so he grinned.

"What you grinning about?"

He grinned wider.

"Our undersized friend is musing about waitresses," said Gillis.

Willie shook his head.

"Then what?"

The grin almost split Willie's ears. "N-nothing."

"Willie's dumb," said Big Chuck. "Ain't you dumb?"

Willie picked at the tablecloth. He was not dumb. "No."

Gillis said slowly, "People can be dumb in different ways. Now possibly he's only dumb on the outside. Maybe he's got a lot of stuff we don't know about. Possibly he collects stamps."

"You collect stamps?" demanded Big Chuck.

Willie shook his head.

"See!"

"B-but I used to—I collected postcards and buttons and ha-hammers too and n-needles."

They all turned to stare at him.

Willie's ears got red. They didn't understand about the needles. "Needles," he said. "For designs."

"Oh," said Gillis, and thought for a minute. "Why don't you collect things like Wop does?"

"What?" asked Willie. They all laughed.

They looked away from him then and he sniffed toward the fry cook's window. The Mite smelled good. And there were cowboy songs on the juke box and blue lights in tubes on the ceiling. Waitresses, too, and although he was engaged to Gloria still it was all right to look at waitresses. Everybody was allowed to look at waitresses. Men were. After dinner he'd go over to Gloria's. He'd sit around and listen to the radio until late and then Gloria would smooth her long brown hair and her eyes would shine and she would kiss him goodnight, maybe ten or fifteen times. He'd rather kiss Gloria than almost anything. Ten or fifteen times! Willie oozed down in the booth and closed his eyes.

II

AFTER DINNER they went outside. It was cold and black, for the moon had not yet risen. Big Chuck hung an arm over Willie's thin shoulders. "So you're going to get married on us, eh buddy?"

Willie nodded.

"You got a picture of her?"

Willie produced a picture, but he did not show them the blue fountain pen Gloria had given him. That was secret.

Big Chuck stepped under the streetlight. "Wow! Get a load of this tomato." He passed the picture around for inspection. "Look what our old buddy's got himself lined up with."

Willie was pleased. He stood on one foot and industriously scraped the back of his ankle. He felt called upon to say something. He announced: "We're going to get married."

"Ah! When?"

Willie puckered his lips while he thought. "January."

"January, eh? Getting all set for those cold winter nights."

Willie shuffled his feet. He was not certain about such things.

Big Chuck nudged him. "Tell us about her. You can tell your old buddies, can't you?"

Willie meditated. "We're in love," he said.

"Sure. Sure. But tell us about her."

Willie reached for the picture.

"Now hold on a minute." Big Chuck hooked him by the armpits and lifted him away from the picture. "Now this here—what's her name?"

"Gloria."

"Gloria. That's a good name. Now this Gloria looks to me like a real sweet little lady and it seems to me you ought to know how to take real good care of her comes January." A thought came to Big Chuck. "Willie, you ever made love to a girl?"

Willie began to grin.

"Well, how about that! Old buddy's all fixed to get married to this nice cabbage and here he's never even made love to a girl." Big Chuck smacked his palms together. "We got to do something about that."

Willie puckered his brows and thought hard. Then he shook his head.

"Sure we do. Absolutely. We got to get you smartened up."

"No. Give me the picture."

"Now wait a minute. Don't go getting excited. You're always getting excited. You got a problem and we're just going to help you in solving it."

"No. No."

"Sure, sure," said Big Chuck soothingly, "and I know just how to do it."

Willie reached again.

"Hold it, Gillis. Don't let him have it. We're going to take our pal down to the carnival so he can learn some things. Yes, sir." Big Chuck grinned and thumped him across the shoulders. "Yes, sir. Soon as we get you squared away you'll get that picture back."

Gillis leaned over until Willie could smell his bay rum and whispered, "Ever seen a girlie show?"

Willie scraped his ankle.

"Well, I guess we really are doing you a favor then. Everybody ought to see at least one."

It was true he did not know much about girls and this might be good to know. Still— "No I don't think I wa-want to go—I think I'd just rather ma-marry Gloria."

"You just *think* that," said Gillis.

"Absolutely," said Big Chuck. "We're going to the carnival."

"No! All I want to do is marry Gloria."

Big Chuck took his outstretched arm and twisted it behind his back. "We're doing you a favor, old buddy. Go get the car, Wop."

Willie's lips quivered and Big Chuck began to laugh.

III

THEY SAW the ferris wheel first, like a sparkling bottle cap. Then they could hear music coming over the loudspeaker. As they approached the carnival grounds Big Chuck drove on the wrong side of the highway and blew his horn several times. He had taken the regular horn off and installed one that sounded like a train. Everybody turned to look as they coasted into the grounds.

Big Chuck sounded the horn once more, then rapped Willie on the skull with his knuckles and got out of the car. "Here you go, old buddy. Tonight you're going to grow up. Help our buddy out of the car, you guys."

Willie climbed out and stood looking around the carnival. Wop patted him on the shoulder. "Let's get a coffee, huh?"

"Naw," said Big Chuck, "Willie's not hungry, are you?"

"—only for a vixen," said Gillis, chuckling.

Willie reached into Gillis' pocket and Big Chuck slapped his hand and then broke off the end of a cigar. "Now don't be in such a damn hurry. Why are you always in such a hurry?—Gillis'll take good care of Gloria, won't you Gillis?"

"With ardor."

"Don't be such a rube, Willie. Here—eat this." Big Chuck pushed a bag of popcorn into his hands. "Okay now, come on." And he stepped off toward the midway.

The tent flap of the girlie show billowed slightly as they stopped at the barker's stand. Big Chuck leaned down and squinted through the opening.

"Six bits," said the barker, tapping Big Chuck in the ribs with his cane.

"The Dove is a friend of mine," said Big Chuck, still stooping and peering through the flap.

"Everybody's a friend of La Paloma," said the barker. "Six bits."

Gillis said, "Our small friend here drinks nitro-glycerin. Don't make him mad."

"Six bits. Each."

"What a prune," said Big Chuck and paid his admission.

"Who buys for Willie?" asked Wop.

"He buys for himself. Gloria's worth that much to him."

They stopped at a rope in front of the stage and Big Chuck hooked a thumb through Willie's belt strap. Wop and Gillis stood near them. Gillis looked very intelligent. He cupped a match to his amber-stemmed pipe and began to blow smoke rings.

First of all there were three girls who danced and skipped and climbed through hoops while somebody behind a screen played *Tales from the Vienna Woods* on a saxophone. Everybody clapped. There were many questions shouted at the girls. Willie stood quietly in a puddle of mud.

"He's eating this up," whispered Gillis.

Next there was a lady in a leopard skin. She was named "Queen Oog" and she began to dance and wave a spear while the saxophone player pounded on a drum. In back of Willie a voice said "Wow!" and a fat man in blue overalls started to climb up on the stage. Queen Oog jabbed at him with her spear and the point broke, but the fat man fell off the stage and lay in the mud. Then the barker walked on the stage and said if that happened again the show would not go on. Everybody booed. Willie's faintly frostbitten nose twitched, but he did not say anything.

La Paloma was dressed in feathers. She had pink hair and wicked eyes and a mole on her forehead. Big Chuck yelled " 'Ray for The Dove!"

" 'Ray-for-dove," said the fat man and went to sleep.

In spite of being nudged, poked, jostled and thumped, Willie remained silent, slowly munching his popcorn. He did not move until La Paloma began to sing. She had a voice like a tearing window shade. Willie covered his ears. Then La Paloma began to pluck her feathers. She touched her lips to each one and her eyes got very sad as she blew them out toward the audience. Feathers began to fall on Willie. Gloria would not like this. Gloria would not like this at all. Willie stood on one foot and made small clucking noises.

"*Regardez*," whispered Gillis.

" 'Ray Dove!" shouted Big Chuck.

No, Gloria would not like this one bit. Willie pursed his lips and frowned in tremendous thought. Gloria would be at home now; she would be waiting for him. She would have the radio on and she would be curled up in the big red chair, warm and soft. The lamp would be shining on her arms and she would smell nice. Oh, nice.

The muddy water was seeping into his shoes. He was cold and tired and thirsty and lonely and ugly and The Dove was throwing feathers at him. Willie extracted his feet from the mud. He was going.

Then enormous hands gripped his collar and the seat of his trousers and he heard Big Chuck bellowing into his ear. And suddenly his arms began to churn and Willie found that he was flying through the air. He floated upwards through a haze of cigar smoke and popcorn, described an arc, and descended, coming to rest on one heel on the boards of the stage. His other foot swung forward and for a minute Willie thought he was punting a football. His arms were flapping and his hair was in his eyes. It came to him then that he was starting to fall down so he reached out for support. The only thing nearby was La Paloma, but he clutched and hung on.

The feathers flew and Willie and La Paloma hit the boards with a terrible crash.

When the light bulbs stopped whirling he discovered that he was sitting next to La Paloma and that she did not have any more feathers. The stage was covered with buttered popcorn. Willie was not sure what to do. He had never been on a stage with a naked woman before.

IV

HE FELT that perhaps he should apologize. Looking down he found that he had a fistful of feathers. This was an opening: he held out the feathers.

It was at about this time that La Paloma recovered from both the physical and emotional jolt of Willie's attack. She began to scream. She held both hands to her cheeks and pointed her mouth at the top of the tent and howled. The noise appeared to help her recovery: she gained range and volume until the canvas began to vibrate. The noise fascinated Willie. He sat on the stage and peered down her throat. He wished she would stop because the noise hurt his ears, but he did not have the faintest idea how to stop a naked woman from screaming.

"Shhh," said Willie, hopefully.

But La Paloma's shrieks increased, so he looked around for Big Chuck, who would explain to her that it was an accident. Big Chuck was gone. So was Gillis. And Wop. However, the barker was coming through the tent flap. That was fine; now he could explain. He stood up. The barker, he saw, had a shotgun. That was strange. Very strange.

Suddenly he sensed that the barker was going to blame *him* for what had happened. Willie decided to leave and explain later. The tent flap, however, was located directly behind the shotgun, so he looked about for another exit. He could not find one. All of a sudden Willie was scared. He coughed and shuddered and said, "Oh God!"

The barker, he saw, had one leg over the rope and would very soon be on the stage. Willie did not have an extensive knowledge of guns, but this particular one was quite long and black and possessed of two gigantic holes at the end. All in all it was the sort of tool one might use to hunt crocodiles. Willie forgot all about the exit; he commenced to run around the stage in little circles. He wished Gloria were here. And then climbing onto the stage was the shotgun followed by the barker who looked very angry and who was roaring terrible oaths.

Then something spoke to Willie—telling him that if he, the gun, and the barker remained together long enough the gun would go off and he, Willie, would get shot. At the time of this message he was in a running position and aimed at the side of the tent. It required no change of direction for his 131 pounds to hit the canvas like a terrified ostrich, and with a loud screech the canvas gave way to allow him passage to the outside. He struck the ground on all fours and took out from there, with the barker two jumps behind.

The moon had just risen and it was a beautiful evening indeed, but Willie did not stop. He hurdled a fence and a briar patch just as the barker let go with one barrel. Probably the buckshot traveled faster than Willie, but there could be no argument about which went farther. Willie was running low and pointed into the wind, and with each leap his shoes picked up momentum until they were bounding over the furrows in a truly magnificent fashion. The barker did not give up the chase.

Activity at the carnival had come largely to a standstill and it must be said that no attraction there could compete with Willie, the barker, and the shotgun zigzagging over the fields in the moonlight. At the crest of the hill they were silhouetted for a moment against the moon, and then there came a bang from the shotgun and a horrible scream that sounded like Willie and then all three were over the hill and out of sight.

V

WILLIE DID NOT appear for work the next morning. At eleven o'clock Big Chuck was sitting on the loading dock behind Comer's speculating as to how soon the police would recover his body when Willie turned the corner and sauntered up the alley.

"Morning," he said. He was covered with scratches and bruises and his trousers had been torn in several places. However, each of the tears had been neatly mended and over each scratch was a dab of mercurochrome.

"Morning," returned Big Chuck, somewhat stunned.

"Guess I'm late," said Willie.

Big Chuck nodded dumbly. Then shaking himself he got down off the dock and fished into his pocket. "I—I got your picture—"

"Oh. Thanks."

Big Chuck stood with his hand in mid-air. "What?"

"Close your mouth," said Willie.

Big Chuck collected himself. At length he asked: "How did you get away from the barker?"

"Outran him. He tripped in a gopher hole."

Big Chuck digested this information and then straightened up. "Well!" he said jovially. "Well, at least we came pretty close to getting you squared away. Didn't we, old buddy? Eh?"

Willie yawned.

"By the way—by the way, what happened after you ditched the barker?"

"None of your business."

Big Chuck's jaw dropped again. He studied this new casual Willie for some time. At last he said, "Willie. Willie, where did you go after—"

Willie snapped without a stutter: "None of your business!" Then he frowned. Somehow that did not seem the complete reply to such a question about a man's personal life. Slowly, but quite firmly, he reached out a lilac-scented hand toward Big Chuck's face and gave to Big Chuck's nose a terrible tweak.

It was as Gillis had said: Willie might be no tiger, but he always solved his problem.

1948

BÉBERT'S NEPHEW

"Leon, I'm terrified," said Bébert. "I'm frightened out of my wits."

"Once and for all," Leon replied, "kindly relax, will you? If you want my advice, there it is. The little monster doesn't get here for almost an hour. Any number of things could happen between now and then."

"I've always been afraid of that boy," said Bébert. "When he was a year old he could look right through me."

"What have you got to be afraid of? He's your nephew so he undoubtedly idolizes you. He probably sees you as being very sophisticated and worldly."

"Oh, but I'm not!"

"Who said you were? I know you're not. Everybody else knows you're not. You're about as sophisticated as Mrs. O'Leary's cow. What I said was your nephew assumes you are. It makes all the difference. How old is he?"

"Sixteen. No, he's just seventeen because I forgot to send him a birthday present. I didn't forget, truthfully. I was so alarmed by the idea of sending him something inappropriate that finally I couldn't bear to send him anything at all. Then of course I had to write and apologize and pretend it had slipped my mind."

"What did he say?"

"He wasn't fooled. He wrote back and said: That's quite all right, Uncle Bébert. Oh, he wasn't fooled one iota. Leon, what are we going to do?"

Leon, who had been hunched over his beer, straightened up uneasily. "We?"

"You've got to help entertain him. I've been counting on you."

"Well, now," said Leon, "you're a good friend of mine and all, don't misunderstand, Bébert, and under any other circumstances I'd be only too—"

"You're deserting me, I can tell."

"I don't think you should express it quite that way."

"It's the truth."

"Come now," Leon said after a few moments, "you'll be able to entertain him without any help from me. In the first place, he doesn't even know me. He'd think of me as just some elderly friend of his uncle."

"Yes, but you could *talk* to him, I know you could. He needs somebody to *talk* to. He's not interested in what you'd expect a boy of that age to be interested in."

"Such as what?"

"Oh, girls, to cite one example. Frankly, I doubt if he's ever taken a girl to the movies. Things of that nature simply don't exist for him. He's going to become an astrophysicist. But I've already told you that—you see how nervous I am. Furthermore, he's been accepted at the Massachusetts Institute of Technology. You've got to help me, Leon."

"In case you want my opinion, I'd say you've developed an exaggerated sense of respect for this kid. Not knowing any more than what you've told me, I'd guess that he's bright and a bit fruity, but otherwise natural enough. Let's have another beer. That'll make you feel better. You'll see the situation more clearly. It'll put you in shape to meet him at the station."

"I don't dare. I'm going to eat a bag of peppermints before we go to pick him up. I'd be so ashamed if he suspected I'd been drinking."

"Now, look, Bébert," Leon said, "you'd better pick him up by yourself. I mean, I'd love to meet him and so forth, but you see I've sort of been planning to spend the remainder of the afternoon here at the club and then tonight, well, I just thought I might send out for a pizza so that I can more or less stick around and play chess or dominoes. You know how it is, Saturday's the most sociable night of the week."

"I understand," said Bébert, looking away. "I don't hold it against you."

Leon finished his beer and they sat a while in silence. The Po-Po Club was filling up with the late afternoon trade. Leon and Bébert nodded to acquaintances.

"Feel like a round of darts?" Leon asked.

"I just couldn't," said Bébert.

Leon signaled for another beer. "You know, Jason is an odd name for a boy. It's a name you don't hear too often."

"It's Greek," said Bébert unhappily. "It was my sister's idea. It fits him, though."

"I associate it somehow with the Golden Fleece. Jason owned some golden fleece, I believe. Beyond that, however, it more or less escapes me. Was it a gift from the gods or something? Also, the word 'quest' comes to mind."

"I know it by heart. My sister was a classics major in college and then of course when she named the boy Jason we all wondered why, so she then had the most gorgeous opportunity to display her erudition. Privately I suspect that's the reason she named him Jason. However, in answer to your question, he was the famous leader of the Argonauts. He was the son of the lawful king of Iolcus in Thessaly and he was spirited away to Mount Pelion there to be raised by a wise and just centaur because he had to have some protection from the attacks of Pelias, who was his father's half-brother."

"Um'm," Leon said. "I'd pretty well forgotten."

"It's a famous story. Jason resided with the centaur till the age of twenty, whereupon he returned home to confront his uncle, who, however, in order to gain time, craftily assigned the youth what was adjudged an impossible task—bringing home the Golden Fleece."

"Like bringing home the bacon?" said Leon, laughing.

Bébert didn't seem to have heard. "Oh, I suppose," he answered with a vague expression. "Leon, I'm so depressed. I can't for the life of me imagine what I'm going to do. I honestly don't know the first thing about astrophysics."

"Nobody does," Leon said firmly. "You shouldn't let that worry you. Look at the situation this way: there must be countless subjects he doesn't know fact number one about, so what you could do is you could study up on a few of those and then confound him the minute he unbuttons his lip."

"But he arrives in less than an hour."

"All right, then get him a date. That's the simplest and most practical solution. Andrea's kid sister. She's a sweet little girl. Why, if I was five years younger I'd jump on that chick like the quick brown fox. I would anyhow, except they'd probably jail me."

"But he'll be here for two weeks."

"I thought you told me two days."

"If so, I was distraught. He telephoned last Wednesday announcing he'd arrive today and was planning to visit for two weeks. That's virtually all I know."

"He sounds like a pushy little bastard," said Leon. "I'd let him know who's boss, that's what I'd do if I were in your position. A kid like that can spell trouble. Next thing you know, before two weeks are up you'll find yourself serving him breakfast in bed."

"He does run people around. He's been like that since the day he was born. He has this utterly commanding intellect, which becomes perfectly obvious to everybody who meets him, even for an instant, so it's difficult to argue. You always feel that you're in the wrong."

"I'm afraid this may sound rude," Leon remarked, "but I'm telling you, Bébert, if I meet that kid and he tries to shove me around he'll get the shock of his young life, prodigy or no prodigy. And as long as we're on the subject, I'm far from being convinced that he is the intellectual giant you claim. I'm willing to grant without ever having laid eyes on him, just on the basis of your word, that he's a smart kid; however, there are plenty of those around. For instance, what concrete proof have you that he's actually exceptional? I'll venture to say he's a decent everyday boy who discovered he could bully his folks and you by shooting off his mouth. In fact, as I think about it, I'm halfway inclined to demonstrate the point. I might even go to the station with you. I'd sort of like to catch a glimpse of him because I've got a pretty fair hunch he's nothing special. I'm sorry if my attitude offends you, Bébert, but you've got to forgive me for being a bit skeptical. I'm not claiming kids like Jason are a dime a dozen, but I'm willing to bet you've overstated the case."

"You're not offending me, but you're wrong. I thought I'd told you—there was an article about him in *Life* magazine when he was eight years old. Maybe it was in *Look*. I never can remember which magazine it was, they have all those pictures. Anyway, it showed him doing schoolwork and playing around in the backyard, and then there was a picture of my sister cooking supper. They were forced to put him in a private school, he was so intelligent."

"Lots of kids go to a private school. I went to one, myself, for a year, but that doesn't make me a genius."

"It certainly doesn't," said Bébert. "However, Jason's IQ has been tested and places him in the top one per cent of the population."

"IQ tests don't mean a thing. I tested very high, myself. I was in the top four per cent or something like that when I was in school. They don't mean a thing. I don't regard myself as being particularly outstanding. I say this in all humility. For instance, you take chess players. The great chess masters you would suppose would be equally brilliant in other fields, but case histories disprove this."

"Well, all I'm saying is that everybody who's ever met Jason has been impressed, and by the time he was ten he could recite the Greek and Hebrew alphabets backwards or forwards."

"I had to do that, too," Leon said. "It's one of those things I had to learn for my fraternity initiation."

"You weren't ten at the time."

"I imagine I could have memorized them at that age, but there wasn't really much point in doing so. It's one of those useless tricks like swallowing oysters on a string."

"Yes, except that Jason decided to read Homer in the original, that's why he learned the Greek."

"Well, with a name like he has I suppose he'd naturally be interested. What did he learn Hebrew for? Did he decide to read the kabbala?"

"I haven't the foggiest notion," Bébert said miserably. "I never was able to understand him. He likes nothing better than to humiliate me. It's dreadful to be related to certain types of people."

"What prompted him to come visit you? I mean, assuming he likes to lord it over you, even so that wouldn't be a sufficient motive. Is it the lake? Did he just figure he'd get a free bunk at Uncle Bébert's and spend a couple of weeks swimming? Besides, why isn't he in school?"

"It's a very progressive school. The students go on vacation whenever they feel the need. But I really don't know what his motive is, he's never cared to visit me before. He may have had an argument at home."

"Does your sister know about this? I guess she must."

"Oh, yes, he freely announces to all the world what he's going to do next. Neither my sister nor her husband have ever been able to control him, and of course if he decided to leave home for a while they'd much rather he came up here than go batting off somewhere else."

"He may enjoy it so much he'll announce that he's staying. You'd better give it some thought. What would you do then? I mean, there's the lake and plenty of girls."

"I told you, Leon, he's never paid the slightest attention to girls. You're projecting your own desires. You assume that merely because it's your principal occupation in life it must also be everybody else's. Which isn't true at all. Jason, for instance, is the perfect example. He'd rather read. I'm going to get him a temporary library permit, that's the least I can do."

"All right, you know the kid, I don't. The world's full of nuts."

"He isn't a nut, he's just a nice, introverted boy who has the misfortune to have this unusual head."

"He won't fit in here at the lake."

"I don't think so either, but you never can tell. I grant you it would be terribly awkward if he decided to remain. Two weeks is more than enough, even for a nephew."

"I'll bet you he hits his folks for money to buy a sailboat, and if they've got it they'll give it to him and before you know what happened he'll have turned into another young slob. God, there must be a hundred of them around here that don't do anything but sail back and forth and swagger around town looking for somebody to punch in the nose. I've been thinking about moving away, this area's beginning to give me the creeps. I thought I might move to the Caribbean, it sounds nice."

Bébert did not say anything.

Leon belched and thoughtfully scratched his stomach. A few minutes later he said, "I'm a little embarrassed about this but the fact is, I'm not sure I'm altogether positive what an astrophysicist *does*. I mean, technically, what's his job?"

"Oh, he computes things. Wouldn't you say?"

"Well," Leon said, "that sounds logical. Does Jason use a slide rule?"

Bébert frowned. "Possibly. Though I'm under the impression that engineers are the ones who use the slide rule. I remember seeing them at college."

"Me too," said Leon. "They always wore them hooked to their belt like a six-shooter. It struck me even then as an affectation. They could have carried them the way other people carry books, but no, invariably you could spot an engineer—he'd have a slide rule dangling from his hip."

"I didn't have much fun at college," Bébert said. "I believe I worried too much."

"I had a great time," said Leon. "Jesus Christ, what a marvelous time I had! When I think back—oh, when I think back! Those were the days. I mean, really, Bébert, do you know what I mean?"

Bébert had not been listening. "I could ask Jason," he said, "except that I'd feel awfully foolish."

"About whether he uses the slide rule, you mean?"

"No. About what an astrophysicist does."

"Oh. Well, my guess would be that he sits at a plotting board of some description, either at a university or in an observatory. By the way, have you ever been inside that one on Mount Kincaid?"

"No, and it does look forbidding," Bébert said. "I doubt if there are any people in there."

"There must be," said Leon. "I expect they allow visitors. Let's take a drive up someday."

Bébert considered. "All right, that might be fun. Although for some reason the very sight of an observatory is enough to unnerve me, I don't know why. I can't help thinking it must be filled with electrical apparatus and gloomy old men running around in white aprons. Then, too, there's the dome—I suppose that's what alarms me, not having any corners. However, that's a good idea, Leon. Jason might enjoy it. In fact, he should be able to introduce us to whoever works there."

"Don't be ridiculous. He wouldn't know Dr. Hubble from Mickey Mouse."

"Dr. Hubble?" asked Bébert.

"A very famous astronomer. I cut out a portrait of him from a magazine cover a long time ago. There was a big finger behind him pointing straight up at the sky. I think maybe he's dead now."

"Is that so? Well, anyway, my guess would be that astrophysicists do an enormous amount of calculating. They coordinate various problems such as the relationship between astronomy and physics. That sort of business."

"I guess," Leon said. "It wouldn't appeal to me, it's too abstract. But everybody to his own taste. I need something I can get my teeth into."

"Or your hands on to," remarked Bébert, laughing. "Gloria told me about your date the other night."

"Gloria," said Leon. "What a wasted evening. She's always so friendly and congenial that naturally I assumed we'd have a profitable time together. Women are the worst hypocrites of all," he continued after pausing for a drink, "smiling suggestively the way they do and wiggling around even when the very sight of you turns their stomach. I consider the ones that live here at the lake to be the worst I've ever encountered. I really am contemplating a move to the Caribbean. Possibly next autumn," he added reflectively.

"What time is it now?" asked Bébert.

"Twenty after four. Stop fretting, you make me nervous. Look at it this way: the train might be late or something bizarre could happen, like Jason having a heart attack. These scholarly types are never in the best of health."

Bébert sighed and shook his head. "Wild horses couldn't prevent Jason from arriving. In his own way he's virtually an irresistible force."

"Look, I'll tell you what," Leon said and picked up a half dollar from the bar. "Being that you're so concerned, if this comes up heads I'll accompany you to the station." He spun the coin and they both watched as it slowed down, wavered and wallowed to a stop, head down.

"I might as well go along anyhow," Leon said. "What the hell, why not? You understand, though, I'm not wasting my entire night helping you entertain this kid.

I'm coming back here, understand. However, this'll give you a start and frankly all he's going to want in my opinion is to be let alone. Obviously he needed to get away from the home environment and I dare say the last thing he wants is Uncle Bébert rushing back and forth trying to see that he isn't bored. Leave him to his own devices and the problem will solve itself, that's my suggestion, for what it's worth."

"I must admit, you've often been right," said Bébert.

"Ignore the kid. Show him his bunk, point out Walgreen's drugstore and forget about him. Two weeks'll go by like a shot. Kids are nothing but animals, the only thing they need is enough to eat and room to turn around in. They're extremely simple, once you grasp these elementary facts. They're far less complex than we are."

"He won't join that bunch at Walgreen's. He's too advanced."

Leon unwrapped a cigar and lighted it. "Here's this ordinary kid," he said without taking the cigar out of his mouth, "that got his picture in a magazine because he scored high on some IQ test. Well, all of a sudden his parents and his uncle decide if he holds up one hand the grass would stop growing." Leon blew a smoke ring gently toward the neck of his beer bottle, then he continued. "Now, Bébert, you know as well as I do that's silly. Listening to you, I can tell a great deal about this young boy. I might even go so far as to guess what he looks like. Spindly, horn-rimmed glasses and a smart-ass expression. Does he lisp?"

"No," said Bébert. "And you're absolutely wrong."

Leon slapped the bar. "I've seen a million kids like him! Tell me, what have you observed about him that you'd consider typical? In what specific way is he typical, would you say?"

"That's a hard question to answer."

"I'm asking for one instance."

"Oh," Bébert said, "I'd have to think. The telephone is the only thing that comes to mind. But he doesn't in the least resemble your description. He's terribly handsome. In fact, he's the absolute picture of health. He's already as tall as you are and he has broad shoulders and seems to be just brimming with vitality."

"Let's get back to the telephone," Leon said with some annoyance. "Specifically, do you mean he's always on it?"

"Day and night, if you want to know the truth. It drives my sister half out of her mind. He does do that, Leon, I admit. He's always telephoning somebody. He doesn't often call me, but occasionally he does, and at the most inconvenient moments. Of course I say that I'm delighted to hear from him, and I am, but I can't forget that it does cost money. Once I suggested that he call after six in the evening and place it station-to-station because there's nobody in my apartment except me, but for some reason the idea didn't seem to make a dent. Whenever he calls it's person-to-person. He has a friend in Utah or Nevada, I never remember which, and Jason likes nothing better than to telephone him. My sister says they've begun subtracting the phone bill from his allowance, but even that doesn't stop him."

Leon blew another puff of smoke, took a long swallow of beer and wiped his lips on the back of his hand. "Bébert," he said, "what you've got without realizing it is a typical nephew. A shade smarter than the majority, perhaps, otherwise very typical indeed. You'll see that I'm right, and you're not going to have any problem. Show him where Walgreen's is and you'll scarcely know he's alive from then on."

"I sincerely hope you're right," said Bébert.

"I'd even make you this bet: walk past Walgreen's after he's been there half an hour and I'll bet you see him in the general vicinity of the telephone booth. As for myself, I was never like these teen-agers we have today, running around hollering and riding motorbikes and so forth. I was an individualist. I didn't hang around Walgreen's hour after hour."

"Your certainly spend enough time in here."

Leon frowned. "That's different. We don't have a jukebox in here, for one thing. Anyway, it's altogether different. Now as far as Jason is concerned, as I say, I'll go to the station with you but that's the extent of my participation. Incidentally, why does he want to be an astrophysicist?"

Bébert shrugged. "His parents both would like for him to become a surgeon."

"They make a good living, surgeons do. I used to fancy myself as a prominent psychiatrist."

"I seem to recall you once mentioning that you were a pre-medical student."

"Not exactly. I was taking freshman and sophomore courses that would lead to pre-med, but then I had a kind of bad-tempered chemistry professor who flunked me, and the thought of taking his course over again was extremely disagreeable so I didn't."

"You're very different from Jason. He decided years ago that he would be an astrophysicist and ever since then he's shown unswerving determination."

"I'm beginning to hate that kid," said Leon.

"He can talk about Messier 33 or the horse's head nebula for hours on end. You never heard anything like it. It's simply unbelievable."

"I saw a flying saucer once," said Leon.

"You're joking!"

"Not in the least. It was a bright moonlit night and this shimmering object passed almost directly overhead giving off this strange luminous blue flame."

"I don't believe you."

"I seldom mention it because I'm sick of hearing the same identical comments. Everybody attempts to be amusing. All you need to do is mention flying saucers and some stupid jackass will make a reference to 'little men.' You can practically depend on it."

"What do you think it was?" Bébert asked with a serious expression.

"All I'm prepared to state is that I saw this object and that it was not a hallucination. Nor was I drunk at the time. Nor was it an airplane or St. Vitus light."

"St. Vitus light?"

"It's something pilots used to observe on their wing tips during the war. It's a mysterious electrical discharge. It's been verified. Thousands of pilots reported seeing it. I'm not making this up, Bébert."

"I realize you're not. I've heard about it, although somehow it doesn't sound quite correct. In any event, and with all due respect, Leon, I must confess to being a trifle skeptical about your saucer. It certainly is eerie, though. Suppose we ask Jason for his opinion."

"The last thing I need is the opinion of some sixteen-year-old genius," Leon said. "They exist, saucers do. I could even give you a couple of examples. In Hungary a few years ago during a storm there was this mass of ice that dropped to the ground which was three feet wide and three feet long and approximately two feet thick."

"What has that to do with flying saucers?"

"They aren't directly related. It was just the first thing that came to mind. Although there's a possibility that this ice was jettisoned by a saucer. No matter how it came about, I find it extremely curious, don't you?"

"Not terribly," said Bébert.

"What I was getting at is that the universe has these inexplicable phenomena. Certainly you wouldn't deny that, would you?"

Bébert thought about this. Finally he shook his head.

"I just now remembered a more pertinent example," Leon continued. "There was this businessman from Boise, Idaho, by the name of Mr. Arnold who was flying his private plane to Yakima. Well, when he was in the vicinity of Mount Rainier he saw nine silvery discs. That was in 1947. His report, which I've read, stated that these discs were clearly visible against the snow."

"We can ask Jas—"

"No, we won't!" said Leon. "To be honest with you, Bébert, I'm getting fed up with Jason."

"I think you're uneasy about meeting him, that's what I think," said Bébert, smiling.

"You've talked about him too much. If he was an accredited scientist with an established reputation, that would be different. If I was going with you to pick up Dr. Oppenheimer at the train, very well, I'd be nervous. Dr. Oppenheimer is smarter than I am. I'd be the first to admit. He puts on that pork-pie hat of his and he looks at the camera with those eyes and it makes a person feel uncomfortable merely being in front of the newspaper. It's an absolutely different proposition. Absolutely."

Just then the bartender called out Bébert's name and pointed to the telephone alcove.

Bébert, looking very puzzled, slid off his stool and hurried into the alcove.

Leon turned around and gazed out the window at the sailboats on the lake. The wind was decreasing, there were few whitecaps. It would be a balmy evening. He puffed at his cigar and considered whether he should go to a movie after supper or return to the club for dominoes. Andrea might be available, or the new girl from Brooklyn. There were various possibilities.

Bébert was gone for quite a while. When he came back he said in a strange voice: "It was my sister." He remained standing beside the bar. Obviously he had been shocked by the call.

After a few moments Leon said, "I gather something's happened. I'm sorry. I hope it's nothing serious."

Bébert did not move.

"I hope nothing's happened to your nephew," said Leon.

"Well, it has."

"Some kind of an accident?"

"No," Bébert said. "The fact is, he's run away."

"I thought you said he'd informed his parents."

"He told them he was coming here but apparently he boarded a train going some other direction. Not only that, he's run away with one of the telephone operators. He called my sister just a few minutes ago and refused to say where he was, only that he was planning to get married and was sorry if they disapproved of his decision. Leon, I have trouble believing it. He sounds like an altogether different person. Not only did he refuse to divulge his whereabouts but he wouldn't even tell my sister the name of the girl. All he said was that she was a long-distance operator. I scarcely know what to think, I'm so confused. This is just too awful for words, and of course my sister has no idea how to cope with the situation."

"In case you're interested in my opinion," Leon said, "your nephew's really had himself an accident. Or he's going to pretty soon." And with that he began laughing.

"Go right ahead," said Bébert. "If it amuses you. Personally, I see no reason to be vulgar. My sister's simply crushed. She had such high hopes. She's afraid they're headed for Niagara Falls."

"Well," said Leon, who was trying to control himself, "it's probably a very nice girl." But then he began laughing again.

"I suppose he can still be an astrophysicist," Bébert said. "Although it was so foolish of him, really. I must admit I'm practically as upset as my sister."

"Maybe they'll stop by to visit you after the honeymoon," Leon said, and almost knocked over his beer.

"Frankly, I don't find this situation the least bit amusing," said Bébert, "and I wish you'd stop making a fool of yourself."

Leon was doubled across the bar, gasping for breath. "How—how—little prodigy!" he gasped, and rolled helplessly from side to side. "Jason—you—he—get—get him a—get him a library card!"

Bébert did not say anything. He sipped at his beer with a disturbed expression.

After a while Leon recovered and took out a handkerchief to wipe his eyes. "I'm sorry, Bébert," he said, chuckling, "I know how you must feel."

"I have my doubts," Bébert answered. "But never mind. I accept your apology. I can see your point of view. I admit that on the surface at least it does appear a trifle incongruous."

"It does that," Leon said. "It does indeed."

"My sister doesn't want me to allow him in, in case he should arrive. I'm supposed to tell him to go right back home."

"Ungrateful youth!" cried Leon, sitting up straight and pounding on the bar with his fist. "Go! Take your telephone operator and begone! Never darken this door again!"

"I wish you'd stop acting childish," Bébert said. "In many ways, Leon, you're infinitely less mature than Jason."

"All right," Leon said, "I'll do my best."

"I'm sure he won't come here now. I certainly hope not," Bébert added, pinching his lip and frowning.

"I doubt that he will. I know I wouldn't if I was in his shoes. Not if I'd just made off with a long-distance operator. I'd head for the Caribbean and live it up. That's what I'd do!"

"I'm sure you would," said Bébert. "But you and Jason have precious little in common, if you don't mind my saying so."

"I don't mind a bit—not one bit," said Leon as he began to break up in laughter again. "Astr—Astrophys—."

1964

THE PROMOTION

"THE TROUBLE with you, Lester, is," she had said almost as soon as he got in the door; and she did not stop talking while he took off his coat and his shoes, loosened his necktie, fixed himself a double martini, and scanned the headlines of the evening paper. He knew what she was saying so there was no reason to listen. Sylvia didn't expect him to answer, she assumed he was listening and she would be annoyed if he tried to interrupt. It worked out very nicely.

"— and take your feet off the sofa!" she concluded. "How many times must I tell you! Suppose somebody should walk in and find you lounging around like a factory worker."

Lester put his feet on the floor.

"If you must take off your shoes the moment you get in you might at least wear your slippers. Is that asking too much?"

Lester set his drink on the table and walked into the bedroom to get his slippers.

"You don't like them, do you?" she called after him. "You've never liked those slippers. The fact that I spent half of one entire morning shopping for them doesn't mean a thing."

"I like them," he said, coming out of the bedroom. "But why is it that I always have to go and get them? Can't you put them beside my chair?"

"If you think for one instant I have nothing better to do than trot back and forth waiting on you, Lester, you'd better think again. I'm not a servant, after all. And I do wish you wouldn't walk around with a cigarette in your mouth. Honestly, there are occasions when you show remarkably little consideration."

"It's one of my worst faults," said Lester.

"I'm in no mood to endure your sarcasm. I've had a frightful day."

"Me, too. Air conditioning broke down at the office."

"It looked simply impossible outside. I cancelled my appointment with the hairdresser."

"Hundred-and-three at two o'clock. Fourth day in a row it's topped a hundred. That office felt like the inside of a casserole. I thought I was going to have a coronary."

"You spoke to Mr. Gumbiner?"

Lester glanced down into his martini.

"You didn't ask, did you? You promised me, Lester—you gave me your solemn promise."

"It was too hot, Sweetie. It was just too hot. He'd have thrown me out. This was no day to nudge the boss. Maybe tomorrow, if it cools off."

"There are times, Lester, when you make it impossible for me to respect you. I suppose I really shouldn't blame you for being what you are. I suppose it isn't entirely your fault, but really, you're such a weakling."

"You've told me before."

"If it weren't true I wouldn't say it."

"Plenty of people in that organization would be delighted to change jobs with me. Plenty of them!" Lester added, nodding significantly.

"How self-satisfied you look! It would never occur to you to try to improve yourself."

"I earn enough to pay the bills, don't I? You aren't going hungry, are you? I don't see why you have any complaint."

"Are you accusing me of trying to ruin you?"

"I am not."

"Then why did you bring up the subject of bills? I get sick and tired of hearing about bills! If you had your way I'd be wearing last season's clothing one year after the next. Do you expect me to do my shopping in the ten-cent store? And as long as you've brought up the subject, suppose you tell me just exactly what you do expect of me!"

"Come on now," Lester said mildly.

"You make me wish I'd never divorced Roger. Whatever his faults, Roger wasn't stingy. And he wasn't a weakling. Roger had his faults but in many ways he was three times the man you are."

"So you've told me more than once."

"You're not a man at all."

"I'm a chicken."

"You disgust me."

"I'm a capon."

"I won't say what you are."

"Sylvie, all in the world I'm trying to do is hang on to a pretty good job, that's all. I work like a bloody slave but at least I'm working, and jobs aren't so easy to find."

"Roger wasn't afraid to ask for what he wanted."

"I'm a bit sick of hearing about precious Roger."

"Then let me tell you something, Lester. I'm sick of your whining and I'm sick of your dilly-dallying. I don't know why I put up with it. There are times I could scream. And for goodness sake stop toying with that olive, either eat it or leave it alone!"

"It's too bloody hot to argue," Lester said as he began chewing up the olive.

"I'm going to cry."

"You've never cried in your life. You're hard as a rock. Hard as nails. If you were a man you'd march into old Gumbiner's gilded palace and let him know who the boss really is. Tell him there's going to be a promotion and a big raise in salary right now, otherwise he can take his job and shove it."

"Do you have the slightest inkling how utterly I despise your vulgarity, Lester? No, I don't suppose you do. I don't suppose you could. Furthermore, I believe you're proud of it. Actually proud of it! I believe you are."

"That's right," said Lester.

"Stop it! Stop it this instant!"

"Okay," Lester said, "but as you keep pointing out to me, I can't be anything except what I am."

"I was trying to be helpful. I don't enjoy being humiliated, nor do I intend to put up with it, do you understand? Do you understand? Are you listening to me?"

Lester nodded.

"Then open your eyes."

"Sylvie, I'm tired. This heat. I feel like a leg of mutton, I just want a chance to relax."

"Sit up and pay attention to me. I'm not going to speak into a vacuum. I won't be ignored. You're not the only person who had a wretched day. Do you think for one single instant that it gives me pleasure to sit here hour after hour waiting for your arrival? Frankly, Lester, I'd far far rather be a number of other places. And for the last time—stop scattering ashes on the carpet! Roger, do you hear me?"

"My name isn't Roger."

"It was a slip of the tongue, Lester. I'm sorry. But you do infuriate me. Now, where was I?"

"On the subject of my faults."

"I will not listen to any more of your sarcasm. I will not. If I criticize you it isn't because I enjoy it."

"No?"

"One more such word will be one too many."

"Sylvia, it's too bloody hot for this. Four days in a row, one right after the other."

"According to the weatherman on television we'll have more of the same to-morrow. I wish you'd stop saying 'bloody'."

"Tomorrow morning I'll grab old man Gumbiner by the throat and strangle him. Beat his bald head on his big walnut desk, smear his brains all over the walls. Would that satisfy you?"

"I've been trying to point out that if Roger had been working at the same job for as many years—"

"Please!" Lester said with a look of anguish. "Please please. Not after a day like this."

"Are you the only one who feels the heat? How do you think I feel? Do you suppose I've enjoyed myself?"

"I imagine so. You haven't accomplished a bloody thing. You lie around half the day watching the idiot box and spend the other half giving orders to the maid. Who are you to be complaining?"

"Thank you."

"Sweetheart, I'm sorry," Lester said. He reached over and took her hand. "I didn't mean to say it, really I didn't. Forgive me."

"I forgive you, Lester."

"Sylvia, truly I am sorry. Believe me."

"I'm a parasite. Is that what you're saying?"

"I called you no such thing."

"Now I'm a liar as well. How very nice. At last I've discovered what you honestly think of me."

"I didn't say you were a parasite. I didn't call you a liar."

"Don't repeat it. I'm not deaf. Now if you have finished cataloguing my faults for the moment, let me tell you a thing or two."

Lester sighed and leaned his head against her shoulder.

"Well," she said, "if you imagine I take any pleasure in these arguments you couldn't be more mistaken."

"Then let's have no more."

"Promise me one thing."

"What's that?"

"Ask Mr. Gumbiner. I want you to promise me faithfully that you'll ask."

"Done. I swear."

"Are you making fun of me again?"

"Absolutely not. I'll ask the old crook. I'll walk in there, sit right down, lean back and put my feet on his desk."

"Tomorrow."

"Well, it depends," said Lester, letting go of her hand.

"That's what I thought. That's exactly what I thought. I wish I'd been a man."

"You'd have been something, you would."

"I wouldn't be the sort of man you are. I'd make a success of myself."

"Thank you, thank you, Sweetheart."

"Lester, at certain moments I wish I'd never laid eyes on you."

"As they say, the feeling is you-know-what."

"Damn you, Lester. God damn you!"

"Well, who started this?"

"You're the most despicable man I've ever met."

"And you've met plenty."

"Every word you speak reminds me of something I prefer not to think about."

"But you do think about it, don't you? Don't you?"

"Thanks to you."

"The pleasure is mine. Every ounce. Every gram!"

"You've never cared for me. You've never cared. You treat me as though I was a creature you'd picked off the street."

"That's a lie and you know it!"

"It's how you make me feel."

"Sylvia, I love you."

"I want to believe that," she replied after a moment. "I do want so very much to believe it."

"It's a fact," said Lester, reaching for his drink.

"Then why don't you prove it?"

"I do my best."

"When was the last time you told me you loved me?"

Lester glanced at her in astonishment. "What are you talking about? I just now told you. Just this minute."

"No, I mean really, Lester. You weren't sincere just now."

"Certainly I was sincere, why else would I say it? Don't be stupid."

"Lester? Lester, tell me something. Do you have somebody else?"

"Somebody else?"

"Are you cheating on me?"

"My God," said Lester, "what kind of a joke is this?"

"I wouldn't put it past you."

"My God," said Lester, "you're kidding!"

"Don't lie to me."

"After a full day in the office? What do you think I am, some sort of nineteen-year-old international galloping stud? Look at me! All I want when I get away from that office is a chance to sit down and have a few drinks. My feet hurt. My back hurts. Everything hurts. My God, Sylvia, you're out of your mind!"

"I can remember when you used to say you could hardly wait to get away from the office so we could be together."

"Yes, well," said Lester uneasily, "you've got quite a memory."

"You never say things like that anymore. You don't care for me."

"Yes I do," Lester said, "yes I do."

"Other men find me attractive."

"I'm sure they do. You're a very attractive woman, Sylvia."

"Only yesterday a man followed me in the street. I was ready to call a policeman. I didn't want to tell you because I was afraid it might upset you."

"Why didn't you call the cop?"

"Just exactly what is that supposed to mean?"

"Nothing."

"Lester, I want to know where we are. I don't like this situation. When are we going to get married?"

"I've told you before, as soon as I'm free. Nine in the morning as soon as I'm a free man."

"You keep saying that, but I don't really believe you want to marry me."

"I do, you know I do. You know I've spoken to Louise about a divorce, what else can I do? You know the situation as well as I do. My hands are tied. It's up to her. She's promised to think it over, but until she makes up her mind we're helpless. I don't like this situation either."

"We could be so happy."

"I know, Sweetheart. Already you've made me very happy. Happier than I've ever been in my life."

"Think what it will be like when we're together constantly."

"I often do," said Lester.

"We'll be married as soon as she lets you go?"

"I wish it could be sooner."

"Are you eager to marry me, Lester?"

"I just said so, didn't I? Why do you keep asking?"

"I need to be sure. You do care for me, don't you?"

"I do. You know I do."

"How can a woman be so self-centered?"

"Louise? I don't know, nobody knows. That's how she is. I suppose she was always that way but when I met her I didn't recognize her true nature. I was blind. I must have been blind."

"Did you love her?"

"In a way, perhaps, although we were both kids. I've almost forgotten."

"Only a man would forget."

"That was a long time ago," Lester said. "These last few years with her have been hell on earth. Absolutely hell on earth."

"Will you forget how you feel toward me?"

"Of course not, Sylvie. You're everything Louise isn't. I've wished a thousand times that we'd met before I happened to run into Louise."

"That's how I feel, too, Lester. I mean, concerning me and Roger."

"It's not much fun when you get married and then afterwards you meet the right person."

"I wonder if it happens to very many people."

"Probably. Probably it does."

"How tragic."

Lester nodded and finished his drink.

"Darling, I'm sorry if we argued. It must not be easy for you—living with that woman."

"Every night when I get home she starts right in. Nag nag nag. If it isn't one thing it's another. Lester, you drink too much. Lester, you said you were going to have the car washed. Lester-this and Lester-that! You wouldn't believe it, Sylvie. Nobody could believe it."

"I can imagine."

"The way she pecks at me! Peckety-peck-peck! I wish I didn't have to go home."

"I wish you could stay."

"Ah, that would be marvelous!" Lester said. He bent over to reach for his shoes but winced and straightened up cautiously. "It's nothing," he said. "Just my spine."

"You work too hard."

"Well, it wouldn't be any easier if I was promoted."

"You're going to ask, though. You told me you would."

"All right," Lester sighed, rubbing his back. "I'll ask."

"Tomorrow?"

"Tomorrow."

"I don't want you to think I'm nagging. It's simply that as soon as Louise lets you go and we're married we ought to move to a nicer place. We'll need new things. These drapes won't do," she began, gazing around the room while Lester fumbled for his shoes.

1966

SAINT AUGUSTINE'S
PIGEON

TOO LATE *loved I Thee, O Thou Beauty of ancient days, yet ever new! too late I loved Thee! And behold, Thou wert within, and I abroad, and there I searched for Thee! deformed I, plunging amid those fair forms which Thou hadst made . . .*

Muhlbach closes the book sharply. How long must this continue? he asks of himself. Everywhere and always this theme recurs, spirit opposing flesh. I'd thought I would escape, but as Augustine would say, Alas! Yes, indeed, alas. Here am I dressed up for the twentieth century, affluent, reasonably affluent, stuffed with trivial comforts, with a home in a borough, two children, and my wife is dead. The pain of deprivation subsides neither more nor less quickly, I suspect, for me than it did for him; and the body's flesh does not care for sentiment more now than in past millenniums, conscious only that it has been deprived. What is more selfish than the body's appetite?

He taps the book with his index finger, a bit didactically, and puts it on the shelf. Rising from the depths of his green leather reading chair, he walks to the window; there he stands for a long time with a meditative and dissatisfied expression. From across the river Manhattan confronts him.

It's possible, he says aloud, that I ought to acquire a mistress. I've said to myself that I should live moderately, which I have done, but too long. My spirit is suffocating. I've all but forgotten the taste of pleasure. It's as though I'd eaten plain bread for a year. What is ordinarily sweet and natural to other men seems as exotic to me as frangipani or a glimpse of Zanzibar. My senses are withering. My finger tips have memorized only the touch of paper. I need to court an Indian dancer with bells strung to her ankles, I need to go out shooting tigers, smoke hashish, explore the Himalayas. God knows what I need.

He turns from the window and looks critically at the room where he spends so much time. It is a comfortable room, this study he has established, a sanctuary, a rectory filled with books, a few photographs, records, a humidor, the substantial chair—yes, and it has become odious.

Muhlbach suddenly clasps his hands as though he were about to drop to his knees before an idol and offer up some passionate supplication. There are times a man must liberate his soul, otherwise he's in for trouble.

If I do not, he says, but persist in guiding my life, the reins of it beneath my thumb—well, who knows? It is not moderate or reasonable to live as immoderately as a demented anchorite plucking thistles for a shirt, suffering voluptuous hallucinations. A woman could save me from myself. And surely it should not be difficult to find one, not if I proceed logically.

Just then Mrs. Grunthe, that paragon, that archetype of sense and logic, brusquely raps at the study door.

Eight o'clock. Supper's on the table.

Whereupon she departs, muttering. But Mrs. Grunthe always mutters, whether the day has been good or bad. The plink of mandolins sounds no different to her than the crash of lightning; in fact it would be alarming, thinks Muhlbach, if her disposition improved.

Eight o'clock, he says softly. I'm sure it is. Exactly eight. This, too, is my own doing. How many times has Mrs. Grunthe laid out supper at eight? The hour does suit me, the emanations of the day are gone, it all seems natural. The children are ravenous by six and I'm never home by then, so we eat separately. It's as though I have no family any more. Yes, I'm exiled from delight, he thinks, opening the study door.

And what do we have for supper? Chicken à la king with peas. Hardly a banquet. Mrs. Grunthe for some reason likes to prepare chicken à la king. We have it too often, I wonder if I should let her know. The problem is, she's not good at taking hints. What was last night's supper? He pauses, napkin half unfolded, and tries to remember what he was given to eat twenty-four hours ago, but cannot.

I believe I'll have a little wine, Mrs. Grunthe.

This isn't Sunday, she answers, Sunday being the day he is in the habit of opening a small bottle; nevertheless she plods off to fetch it.

This isn't Sunday, he remarks when she's out of hearing. Has my life sunk to such a pattern? I ask for a bottle of wine on Saturday night and my housekeeper comments. She may even tell her friends about this strange occurrence. Next thing you know, Bertha, he'll take to drinking on Monday and Tuesday and Wednesday and every other blessed day of the week. You can go a long way to hell with little steps.

And furthermore, Muhlbach announces silently when she re-enters with the wine, I intend to go to hell, Mrs. Grunthe—very quickly, if I may say so. I'm planning to catch myself a little something, Mrs. Grunthe. What d'you think of that, eh?

Will you be wanting anything else?

Muhlbach is startled. The wine, of course, that's what she means. Will I be making any other odd demands, that's all. She wasn't reading my mind. And he is tempted to ask: Why? Are you going out? For a moment the thought has come to him that Mrs. Grunthe is about to take a lover. She's going to slip away from the kitchen and run barefoot through the night, one hundred and eighty pounds of nymph, to the eager arms of Salvador, the mechanic. Salvador has been seen drinking coffee in the kitchen when he should have been flat on his back on a dolly beneath an automobile at Sunbeam Motors; God knows what intrigue has been prepared.

No, no, nothing else, Mrs. Grunthe. How are the children?

Both quiet. Donna's gone to sleep. Otto is in his room building a model airplane.

That's fine. Oh, by the way, Mrs. Grunthe, I'll be going to the city for a little while this evening.

No response.

Muhlbach feels a trifle let-down; after all, when one is setting out to discover a mistress, and gives a hint, it's justifiable to expect some curiosity. He pushes his fork at the creamed chicken and eats without appetite. It is not the stomach that's hungry.

When he has finished eating he doesn't linger with a cigarette but immediately goes upstairs to Donna's room. She is thoroughly asleep, too beautiful to be real. No doubt she is dreaming of princes and castles and white horses with flowing manes.

Otto in his room is just as quiet; he is gluing an insignia on the airplane and cannot be distracted by much conversation.

I'll be going out for a while, Otto.

Okay, says Otto.

I won't be late. If you want anything, Mrs. Grunthe will be here.

Okay, I know it, says Otto.

Incidentally, have you finished your homework?

At this Otto looks bemused, as though he has never heard of any such thing.

Speak up. Is it done?

Practically, says Otto, and quickly adds that he can do it tomorrow. But the rule is that he does his weekend homework on Saturday because he tends to disappear on Sunday.

I think, says Muhlbach, you'd better do it now. A short, fierce, querulous discussion follows, which ends with Otto sighing heavily.

Okay, but it's nothing except some stupid decimals and junk that any moron could do with one hand tied behind him.

In that case, my friend, if you are such a mathematical prodigy, why did your last report card show a C minus in arithmetic?

But to this there is no answer. Muhlbach does not insist. The horse has been flogged enough. Otto is on his feet with a gloomy expression rummaging about for a textbook.

So the house is in order, the inhabitants making their usual rounds, and Muhlbach considers himself free to do what he pleases. He heads for the shower, thoughtfully, fingering his bald spot. I'm going out to attract a woman, he thinks, and not by the use of my wallet; that may not be easy, I do look a bit professorial, but still it's true that women aren't so fussy about appearances as we are. And I'm not ugly, it's just that I look uncommunicative, as though I had a briefcase full of government secrets. I wish I didn't always look so stiff, but what can I do? Maybe I should try to smile more often, my teeth aren't bad. Well—step up, ladies! One insurance expert in average health, slightly bald, slightly soft at the hip, more perceptive than most, but also more constrained than most, seeks passionate and exotic companion between ages of eighteen and—now really, let's not be absurd! Begin again. Between ages of twenty, no, twenty-three, for instance, and, ah, thirty-five. Thirty. Twenty-six. Must be, ah, sophisticated and, umm, discreet. Abandoned. Lascivious. Dissolute. The more dissolute the better. Everything that I am not but would like so much to be. A young lady experienced in each conceivable depravity, totally intemperate, unbuttoned, debauched, gluttonous, uncorked, crapulous, self-indulgent, drunken and preferably insatiable. Never mind if it is an adolescent dream, never mind. There may be no such woman this side of Singapore, but I won't settle for less. Not for a little while. What about Eula?

Thank you, I believe not, he says to himself in the mirror, cautiously parting his hair and frowning. Eula Cunningham is comfortable as a pillow is comfortable, which at times is quite enough, but sometimes is not. Eula is yesterday's bouquet. Eula is a loaf of bread, unleavened and thirty-eight years old, if I'm any judge. Thirty-two, she claims. Maybe. She gives me the feeling of thirty-eight. I don't say she's stale or hard, no, no, it's just that she's like any domestic beast, or a geranium on the window sill, and let the metaphors fly where they choose.

Straightening up, he draws a long breath and studies his chest. It is not impressive. He exhales. No, it is not impressive at all.

He turns the shower handle, tests the water with one hand, shivers and wraps a towel about his pale shoulders. There he stands meditatively naked, curling his toes into the fluffy blue rug while he waits, a sight to inspire terror in nobody, the image of no feminine dream. He thinks again of Eula. Madame Everyday, that's what she is. Eula has the instincts of Mrs. Grunthe and fifty million others. Proper sisters, all of them. Eula won't be pinning an orchid in her hair or shimmying across the room, not now, not ever, because she never has, because it would attract attention, would be rather flamboyant, cause eyebrows to lift. She won't fly away to Las Vegas to play roulette, she won't practice the Lotus position. She is, in fact, just like me, reason enough to catch a cat of another color.

Muhlbach flings away his towel and thrusts himself beneath the shower as though he were plunging into a waterfall.

Mrs. Grunthe is downstairs waiting, arms folded, when he descends. Miss Cunningham has telephoned. What about? Mrs. Grunthe didn't ask, obviously doesn't care. I'm expected to call, he thinks, Eula's hoping I'll return that call, but I won't. I have other plans. Tonight I hope for the taste of Hell.

Good night, Mrs. Grunthe. If Miss Cunningham calls again, you can say that I'll get in touch with her soon.

Ten minutes later, underground and attached to a metal loop, it seems that he is already halfway to Hell. Rocking through the tunnel, he reflects once again that the professional aestheticians have been wrong, utility does not equal beauty. Some opposite dictum may lie closer to the truth. What is most useless or inefficient, say, is most appealing. What is more wasteful and extravagant, for example, than that epitome of sexual allure known as the chorus girl? But again, how is sex identified with beauty? It's a knotty problem.

Emerging from the subway, he sees just ahead, or thinks he does, a familiar profile. It's difficult to be positive, the crowd is gathering, shoving through the turnstile, and she is gone. He hurries a few steps further, stands on tiptoe, looks and looks, then turns around, searching every ramp, but she's disappeared. He goes to the phone booth.

Yes, she's listed in the book. In fact, she is listed twice. Blanche Baron on East Seventy-third, Blanche Baron on MacDougal Street. Which Blanche is real? Which is the red-haired Blanche with the poise of a lacquered mannequin whose husband killed himself? Chances are that she would not be living on MacDougal, not with her taste for elegance. He studies the number on Seventy-third. Here is the opportunity. Of course, the opportunity is not new; it is just that he's never thought of calling her, she has seemed so Continental and gelid, distant and expensive and bathed in rumor, a mistress of shadows. She is a figure in a French novel and he could not visualize himself with her. She must think of him—if ever she does think of him—as an office grub who has yet to recognize the exceptional perfumes of life. Persuading a woman that she has been mistaken can be a tedious process. Muhlbach hesitates.

If it was indeed Blanche getting off the subway, then *ipso facto* she can't be at home and therefore to call her now would be a waste of time. On the other hand, she probably doesn't ride the subway, ever. She might be home. Still, it's Saturday night, very unlikely that she's there, she's more apt to be at somebody's penthouse.

He cannot make up his mind. But then suddenly he puts a dime in the slot and dials. The telephone rings just twice. A male voice answers.

I think there must be some mistake, says Muhlbach. What number do I have?

The voice reads off the number he has dialed.

I'm calling Blanche Baron. Is she at home?

The voice asks who is calling Blanche.

It occurs to Muhlbach that this would be a good point at which to hang up. Something is wrong. If a man answers, hang up, that's the classic advice. But it has never happened to him—he has never called a woman without knowing the circumstances—and he finds that the idea of simply hanging up the receiver is both rude and cowardly. It smacks of being in some woman's home and dashing out the back door while the husband comes in the front. It's a bit farcical. He wants no part of it. Blanche is single, so far as he knows, a widow with whom he is acquainted and whom he has every right to call. He cannot bring himself to hang up, although he is certain that has the correct number and also that Blanche's situation has changed. The male voice has such a proprietary sound.

He introduces himself to the unknown, explaining that he is acquainted with Blanche. Then he listens, expecting a congenial response, and hears nothing but hoarse breathing.

Is this by any chance her husband? he inquires, for it's possible that she has remarried.

The owner of the voice evidently is too confused or annoyed to speak. The receiver at the other end of the line is clumsily dropped in its cradle; Muhlbach, at once a little surprised but yet not too surprised by this treatment, is left holding a dead instrument. He feels insulted by such tactlessness and for a few moments does not hang up. However, there's nothing else to do. Nor would there be much point in calling again. Does Blanche have a new husband or a lover? He suspects it is the latter, and this is oddly gratifying. All right, she has found someone, so will he.

Out of the phone booth, he pauses to settle his hat and straighten his tie before the mirror of a chewing gum machine, then briskly walks up the steps toward the surface world. Blanche might not have been an appropriate mistress in any case. Probably she wouldn't. It's just as well. He feels a bit relieved. Talking to her could have been quite awkward; no doubt she would have thought he was calling in regard to her policy. And for a woman she's tall, close to being a flagpole. She's graceful and sensuous, true, her movements are feline—she knows what men are all about. Isn't it a pity that this experience couldn't be housed in the satin corpulence of Eula Cunningham—that amiable Venus of Willendorf, steatopygous as an Upper Paleolithic figure. Now there would be a woman, thinks Muhlbach, there would be something!

Exactly what sort of a mistress should a man have? The possibilities are infinite. A ballet mouse, agile and quiet and seldom noticed? Or a more heroic piece of goods? One of the great madams, say, regal and unforgettable, with a cold eye and a bank account and scattered parcels of real estate, supporting her amplitude behind black corsets like a formidable gift from faraway provinces. Or an actress dressed up in hats and veils. A society girl?—somebody you could introduce to senators. Well, he thinks, who or what's waiting for me? My shoes are polished and there's money in my pocket. Not a great amount, but enough for tonight. I'm ready for adventure. Now, let's see, where shall I find it?

He stops walking and looks around, for it occurs to him that he doesn't have a plan in mind and has allowed himself to be carried half a block by the crowd. Well, the logical place to begin hunting for an available woman is in the middle of town, is it not? Yes, all right. What happens next?

I'm going in this direction because of the people alongside me, he reflects, but this is foolish. Suppose I work my way into the contrary stream, where will that lead me? What should I do? I ought to do something, I ought to make a positive gesture. Take the ferry to Staten Island? That doesn't seem appropriate; if I should meet a strange woman on the ferry she'd be apt to have a book tucked under her arm. She'd wear spectacles and her hair would be a tidy bun. No, no, I've come to Carthage for the sizzling and frying of unholy love. I won't go to Staten Island.

He studies a billboard advertising a musical comedy on which there is a chorus girl fifteen feet tall. The corner of the billboard is streaked with birdlime. This does not add to her appeal, but it can be overlooked. What sort of mistress would she make? Avaricious she is, there's that look in her wickedly tilted eye. But also there's little doubt that she is passionate, probably given to illegal practices. This, he thinks, is the sort of woman I'm after, the question being merely how she's obtained. Must I buy ticket after ticket to the same seat and sit through this absurd entertainment for God knows how many weeks until she can't help but notice me? Is she worth all that? Six dollars for each performance. It would cost a hundred dollars before she so much as recognized my face.

If not a chorus girl, what? A cigarette girl, possibly. That would not be so glamorous, but after all I won't be taking her to Sun Valley or the Riviera where she would need to be introduced. And philosophers tell us that one's like another, attraction is where we find it. What about a model? A Tintoretto creature living in a cold-water flat, whose friends are intellectual and consumptive? That might be stimulating, a substitute for the youth in Paris that I never had. It's not too late. I'm just past forty, and artists and their kind are notoriously indifferent to age, among other things. Yes, that might do. Well now, I could pay a visit to Washington Square and see what's going on. I don't want a receptionist or a secretary or a teacher or a female executive or Eula Cunningham. What I require is something in spangled tights—a cocktail waitress, for example, who works at some extraordinary place with a shadowy reputation, where they ring a bell and girls come sliding down a fireman's pole. That sort of thing. Something on that order. Yes, or a flamenco dancer from Valencia.

Where does one meet these women? They exist, one sees them on the stage, sees their pictures in magazines or in the Sunday supplement as a result of some affair under the most bizarre circumstances, hears of them having leapt naked into the Tivoli fountain. But otherwise, where are they concealed? Why are they not more available? Are there not enough of them to go around? Do they live secluded in Hollywood harems and in Fifth Avenue apartments with gold plumbing? Occasionally one does see them on the street near the entrance to Saks, say, or in the lobby of an elegant hotel. But they are unapproachable. They are guarded by watchful eyes, by the very mystique of their existence. They are not for the man who works conscientiously in his office at Metro Mutual, now and then removing his glasses to pinch the bridge of his nose and wonder where life has gone. They are not for him, they are not seen with men who carry briefcases and who ride the subway hopefully reading the *Wall Street Journal* for news that a moderate investment is prospering.

I have forty-five shares of General Motors, says Muhlbach to himself, and I have sixty—thanks to the split—of Allied Potash, plus several bits of this-and-that. It's a tidy egg, for years I've watched it hatching, but there's a certain type of woman who'd gobble it up. I must remind myself to be careful. Yes, I'll be cautious.

It seems to him that already he has compromised his security, and quite possibly Mrs. Grunthe suspects him of squandering funds that must be kept safe for Otto and Donna. But Mrs. Grunthe, he reflects, has assumed more significance than she deserves. A housekeeper she is, that's all, yet she functions like a guardian of virtue, implacable, honest, devout in her brutal Anglo-Nordic way, and a terror to every spot of grease, every germ that seeks to invade the house. Mrs. Grunthe is priceless, of course, but her rectitude is stifling. No doubt the germs expire as much from guilt as from the incessant and terrible roar of Mrs. Grunthe's vacuum cleaner.

It occurs to Muhlbach that he needs a drink. At home he customarily has a daiquiri before supper, and because he did not have one this evening he thinks he will have it now. There is a nice place that he remembers on Lexington so he turns in that direction, and presently is seated at the bar with the daiquiri between his fingers. The place is busier than he remembered, he has not been here for almost a year, and it has been remodeled. He observes the comings and goings through a gilded mirror and sips his drink. Then, because nobody is looking at him, he has a look at himself. It is luxury for a man to gaze at himself in public; women are allowed the privilege, men are ridiculed. Well, he decides, women are also ridiculed, but with affection. There's a difference.

He glances from side to side. Nobody's noticed, so he continues to study the image in the mirror: it appears to be that of a man who is either ill or exhausted. The lips are compressed. The eyebrows lean toward each other. And at this moment, Muhlbach thinks, I could not possibly smile. My head feels molded, each feature set. I do believe I'm made of papier-mâché.

Just then two Hollywood people walk directly behind him and are ushered to a table. The woman's face and body are recognizable, although he cannot recall her name and does not think he has ever seen one of her movies. She is wearing a white leather trench coat open halfway to the navel and may not be wearing anything else. Of course it's impossible not to stare at her and inevitably their eyes meet. She looks at him boldly, for so long that he feels the blood rising to his face and is relieved when she looks away. Was there some meaning to this look? Can it be that she is tired of the pudgy director or producer, or whatever he is, and has issued a discreet invitation? Could it happen?

Muhlbach again stares into the mirror; the actress obviously is bored, she is yawning. Her lips are tinted not red but white, and have been outlined with a pencil; there is something inordinately sensual about this, the hollow of her mouth is suggestive.

She is offered a cigarette. She leans forward, the leather coat bulges, parts at the breast, two broad soft globes of flesh come pouring into view and rise slowly rather like poached eggs against each other. Down that phenomenal bosom the crease deepens and lengthens until, thinks Muhlbach, one could mail a letter in the slot.

Desperately he watches her preposterous body. She is not amusing, however ludicrous. Grotesque she may be, but amusing she is not; only fools, hermaphrodites and jealous women pretend to find her so.

Quickly he steps down from the bar stool and avoids glancing at her while he makes his way to the street. She will having nothing to do with him; if she stared at him with such insolence and challenge it was merely what she had taught herself to do; she would return any man's gaze.

But what he has seen cannot be forgotten and he strides along angrily, sober and baffled. It seems to him unjust, unjust that he must spend his life and energy among women such as Eula, ordinary women—unimaginative, average, modest women. It is not right. He feels obscurely cheated; it seems to him that if he were given the chance he could prove himself with the half-mad actress in a way that he has never proved himself before. He clenches his fists, halted by a red light at the corner.

Indemnities, cordial handshakes, briefcases, promises, raincoats, percentages, statistics, a drink before supper—too many years of it, too many years, he thinks bitterly, and discovers that he is walking along Fifth Avenue. There's a bus approaching; he realizes that he has been intending to get on this bus and go to the Village. All right, why not? He has not been to the Village in years.

He rides down the avenue with a fixed, irritable expression. He sees nothing. He does not know who is sitting next to him. He thinks again of the actress, of her flesh and the white leather coat. He has been on the periphery of another kind of existence, one infinitely more exciting, one that he is not privileged to share. He has not enough money to buy himself into it, does not have any creative talents that might win a place for him, nor friends who already belong. He is excluded, he can come no closer to this actress than imagination will take him; it is no good saying to himself that she is stupid and vain, that within a decade she will be meaningless. It is dry comfort every night to turn a book's thin pages.

He is surprised that the bus has stopped. The driver is looking at him strangely. Everybody else has gotten off.

Muhlbach steps down and brushes against a young girl in black leotards and a turtleneck sweater who is dismounting from a motor scooter.

Alors, she cries, *prenez garde, s'il vous plâit!* But the accent is American.

I'm sorry, says Muhlbach, I should have watched where I was going.

Just then an odd-looking youth appears, dressed in a cape and a plumed hat, takes the motor scooter and wheels it away; apparently it belongs to him and she had borrowed it for a ride around the square.

Sale cochon! exclaims the girl, snapping her fingers at Muhlbach.

He looks down at her with annoyance. The insult is nothing, the fatuous expression of youth, but he is irked by her pretense. She's not French, he doubts that she has been farther from home than the Cloisters. She is not more than seventeen, undeveloped, with delicate rebellious features. On her flat breast hangs a chunk of turquoise at the end of a leather thong. Very well, she has chosen to play at being what she is not, so will he.

Et vous-même, ma petite? Est-ce-que vous êtes si propre? he answers crisply, gratified that he has not forgotten everything learned in school. He sees at once that she is startled; her assumption had been that he would not understand. Now she gazes at him respectfully and he guesses that she has exhausted her knowledge of French. Her Village sophistication is badly torn, she may be even younger than she looks.

Are you a Frenchman? she asks, a bit derisively; but it's plain that she wants to know. She wants to believe that he is. She wants to believe that he has just arrived from Paris.

I'm twice as French as you, says Muhlbach.

Dad, you're too much! she replies, suddenly at ease. I mean, like, you're making the scene!

Muhlbach flinches slightly at being called Dad. It's true there's considerable difference in their ages. Well, it is true that chronologically he might be her father, but still she shouldn't call him that.

As a matter of fact, yes, says Muhlbach, since you put it in those terms, I am making the scene.

Well, dig, dig, Daddy. I mean, go!

This doesn't make sense. Is she suggesting that he leave, or what? Maybe she's wishing him a pleasant evening.

Comment t'appelles-tu? he inquires.

Je m'appelle Rouge, she grins. Too much, Pop! You're the most!

Rouge? That can't be your name.

She shrugs, very French. That's the bit. You want to paint the top, I'm Rouge.

Is this an invitation? What does she mean?

Rouge settles the question. You got some wherewithal? I mean, that is, you want to stand this chick to a little spread, let's make it. I mean, *por exemplo,* they chop the grooviest cheesecake at the Queen's Bishop, dig?

Fine, says Muhlbach. She means to take him somewhere. He will be expected to buy her a piece of cheesecake. All right, fine, why not? He feels exhilarated. He is being picked up. A tough little Bohemian in Greenwich Village has picked him up. For the first time since leaving the house he smiles. Let's go, Rouge, lead the way. Take me to the Queen's Bishop, whatever and wherever it is. I'll buy you a wedge of cheesecake, Rouge, I'll buy you the whole pie if you want it.

Across the square they go. Muhlbach glances at each passerby to discover whether or not he is making a fool of himself, meanwhile half listening to Rouge, who's more talkative than he suspected. He cannot understand everything she says; she speaks an ephemeral dialect. If he could recall the patois of his own youth, which at the moment he cannot, would she comprehend? He thinks that when they are settled in the Queen's Bishop he will try to remember a few expressions and will try them on her.

The Queen's Bishop, what sort of place could that be? And then, as they walk by the last benches in the park he notices the chess tables. Of course! Coffee, cheesecake, sandwiches, interminable discussions about God, Communism, Art, Free Love, and a chessboard for the asking. That's the sort of place it will be.

Rouge, talking enthusiastically, as though they had known each other for at least a week, leads him down one street and up another and finally down a flight of worn stone steps to a basement with a brightly painted door.

In they go, and the emporium is quieter than he'd anticipated. There are no loud discussions, no arguments. It's like a library with everyone bent over chessboards instead of books. There's an Italian coffee urn on the counter, a case of pastries, a door leading into what appears to be a little kitchen, travel posters on the wall, and the proprietor—a dwarf wearing an apron and a checkered vest—carefully sweeping the floor with a broom taller than himself.

Bonsoir, Rouge, says the dwarf, grinning.

Bonsoir, Pierre, says Rouge.

Good evening, says Muhlbach, and takes off his hat.

Monsieur, the dwarf replies courteously, but goes on sweeping the floor.

So, the Queen's Bishop is very much as I guessed, he thinks, pleased with himself; and though he is not hungry he joins Rouge in a slice of cheesecake—which is, as she claimed, delicious. He tells her so.

The most, Pop.

Muhlbach looks about the Queen's Bishop and wishes that he had not worn his business suit. With an old pair of slacks and a sweater he wouldn't feel so out of place; he might even have passed for an artist. But it's too late now, and if Rouge does find his suit rather bourgeois she has not yet commented on it. Anyway, this is the Village where unnatural couples are common enough.

How about a game? he asks.

She hesitates, glances narrowly across the table at him, and Muhlbach's heart beats heavily. What has he said? Does "a game" have special significance?

Man, says Rouge, nobody's going to believe this! You mean you really cross the board? What I mean is, like, I tell myself this cat's flaky, dig? I mean, you pulling me around?

I'm not a bad player, Muhlbach answers. How about it?

Oh, ah! says Rouge, making a face, you are just the rookiest. You're greater than pot!

Yes, she's very young indeed; but it seems that she is willing to play chess, at least she has not said anything altogether negative, so he signals for the dwarf, who brings over a board and a cigar box filled with chessmen.

The game's not free, however. Thirty cents per hour, per player. Muhlbach pays, amused. One hour with Rouge for sixty cents, change that one might leave for the bartender uptown. Has he ever found a better bargain?

He takes a pawn in either hand, shuffles them, holds out his fists side by side, and Rouge taps one.

White.

She arranges the white pieces while Muhlbach, having glanced about the Queen's Bishop and found no one watching, begins to set up the black.

Rouge opens King Knight to Rook 3.

Highly unorthodox. What has she in mind? He bends his attention to the board, fingers in a steeple.

Hey wow! she whispers. Great claws!

He discovers that she is staring with admiration at his hands. They are strong, neat, graceful hands; he is proud of them and has himself often looked at them and thought that he should have become a surgeon. These sensitive hands of his seem wasted when they have nothing more to do than shuffle papers, zip and unzip a briefcase, button a stiff white collar. Yes, it's a waste. They're the hands of an artist, of a musician, of a philosopher.

You do tricks? she asks, and he realizes that, incredibly, she is wondering if he is a magician. A magician! If only I were, Rouge, if only I were.

I sell insurance, fire insurance mostly, he says, and waits.

Too much, she answers.

Muhlbach opens his defense with pawn to King 4.

That figures, she remarks, nodding.

Does she know me so well? he wonders. Am I that conservative? He's tempted to recover the pawn and start again, but too late. She moves quickly, Queen Knight to Rook 3, and Muhlbach stares at the board. What's the significance of this curious ploy? An expert counterattack would make short work of such a beginning; its weakness will soon be quite evident. But he hopes that she will somehow strengthen her position. He is indifferent to winning or losing, so long as the game lasts—it's playing with her that counts; and while he pretends to concentrate on the board he imagines a crumbling apartment on Bleeker Street where roaches climb up and down the rusty pipes and the odor of gas seeps from a blackened stove, and the blankets on a sagging iron bed are worn through and frayed. Late Sunday morning, he thinks, we'd have orange juice, coffee, and croissants, if that would please her. Read the *Times*, listen to Mozart. If I seem elderly and repugnant, Rouge, I'll give you a present.

She has moved again; he answers.

The game proceeds, pieces deploy, are taken and dropped in the cigar box. But Muhlbach does not play with much enthusiasm. He is depressed by lecherous fantasies of Rouge; and that she resembles his niece is mortifying. Furtively he stares at her. She doesn't notice. She squints and glares at the board, savagely gnawing her lips.

He has felt, meanwhile, crawling over and around his feet, a small living object that demands attention. Rouge's foot? Could that be? With infinite tact beneath the table, concealed from the rude eyes of other chess players, has she sought him out? Her little foot, slipped loose from its sandal, creeps across his shoe, rubs affectionately against his ankle. He feels a gentle tug at his trousers, deft and knowledgeable, not the blind, clumsy tug of a human foot—there's a beast down below. He bends down to look. There is a hamster nibbling at his cuff.

Does this belong to you? he asks.

Rouge doesn't answer. One of her pawns is threatened.

Go away, whispers Muhlbach, go away, go away, you silly animal! and he nudges the hamster, which pays no attention. He discovers that it has eaten a series of little holes in his cuff.

Queen, says Rouge thoughtfully. *En garde,* Pops.

Muhlbach surveys the board. The attack is obvious, has been so for the past six moves. Check, he replies, a bit reluctantly because he doesn't want the game to end; but she has obliged him to close the trap. He leans down again and pulls the hamster off his foot, worried that he may receive a nasty bite, but the hamster patiently returns to its task. Muhlbach hisses at it, thinking that perhaps it is frightened of cats. But the hamster with beady eyes fixed on his trousers cannot be alarmed.

With a sigh Muhlbach returns his attention to the game. The cuff already is ruined, another few holes won't make much difference. He tries to ignore the gentle weight on his foot and the soft, persistent tugs. If only I had a piece of lettuce, he thinks; and says aloud to Rouge as he moves a pawn, Check. And, I'm afraid, Mate.

She doesn't give up. She has one move left, that's true. It's inconsequential, a bit embarrassing. She should have the grace not to insist on making it, but she does, she retreats grimly. He realizes for the first time that this game has meant something to her; it must have been important that she defeat him. Well, it's too late. He can't possibly lose, there's just no way to lose, none at all. He searches the board. Perhaps he could pretend that he was working on a more intricate and aesthetically satisfying Mate and thus justify the forfeit of a piece.

He looks up, aware of two spectators. They have come out of nowhere and now stand one on either side of the table, ragged and solemn, the natural companions of Rouge. One is the boy who owns the motor scooter, still wearing his cape and plumed hat, and smoking a stogie. The other, who appears to be about Muhlbach's age or a little older, is a bearded Negro with a beret and a snaggly grin. Why are they here?

Muhlbach cautiously picks up the enemy bishop, replacing it with his own. There's no need to speak. Rouge looks at him for just an instant, she is cold with rage. He attempts to smile; he feels guilty.

Cha-boom! murmurs the Negro.

The boy in the plumed hat removes his stogie and puffs a row of tiny smoke rings.

Thank you for the game, Rouge, says Muhlbach.

Oh, rookie, Dad, rookie. Cool the crap.

Cha-cha-cha! exclaims the Negro. Ba-zoom-ba!

Rouge, still peeved, introduces the visitors. They are named Quinet and Meatbowl. It seems they would like to sit down; in fact, without being asked, they do, and Muhlbach finds three pairs of eyes trained on him. Something is now expected of him. What can it be? He looks from one to the other. Quinet clears his throat and inspects that magnificent cigar. The Negro, who is humming and tapping his fingers on the table, does not once remove his gaze from Muhlbach. Nor does Rouge. They're waiting. But for what?

Muhlbach begins to feel uncomfortable. After a few moments he takes off his glasses, wipes them with his handkerchief, holds them up to the light, carefully hooks them on again. It is almost as though he were being initiated.

Perhaps—could it be? Has he been accepted? The defeat of Rouge might be significant. Yes, now that he thinks it over, no one in the Queen's Bishop paid the slightest attention until the end of the game was near, until it was plain that Rouge couldn't win. It was only then, he recalls, that a few heads began turning their direction. Everyone in this place must be acquainted, they come here every night and have learned to communicate with each other as mysteriously as bees or ants; they've known what was going on. Rouge isn't a good chess player yet she must hold some position of authority here and I've made a spot for myself by defeating her! For a moment he imagines himself coming to the Queen's Bishop night after night, growing bolder, being less concerned with appearances, imagines himself in a beret and a suède jacket, with a mustache and goatee, saluting Quinet and Meatbowl and Pierre with casual familiarity.

Muhlbach realizes that he is smiling, first at Rouge, then at her two rococo companions, for no reason except that they have welcomed him to the sanctuary of the Queen's Bishop. It is flattering, really. Do these people care about his business, his habits, his background, whether or not he has money? No. No, they are interested in him for himself alone.

He sees that Meatbowl is grinning; Quinet grins, too, if not as pleasantly. Just then Pierre arrives, his head on a level with the table. Pierre is carrying a dented aluminum tray on which there are four large bowls of minestrone and some crackers. Obviously this is the rite, the moment when he becomes a catechumen. Now they are to break bread. Muhlbach feels powerfully moved; he feels within himself something that he has virtually forgotten—a flow of love toward his fellow man. And that he should have rediscovered this community at such a humble crossroads! His eyes are moist with tears; he is tempted to reach over the table to take Meatbowl and Quinet by the hand. It is all so unexpected.

He blinks, looks down at the steaming minestrone. He is not hungry, and as a matter of fact the minestrone does have a doughy appearance, but he will eat it and love it because this soup is symbolic.

When he lifts his head he finds the dwarf standing at his side, gazing at him attentively with one hand outstretched, palm up, ready to be crossed with silver.

The silence is profound. Every chess game has stopped.

At this instant many things become clear to Muhlbach, just as chemicals in a beaker of liquid turn instantaneously to one great glittering shard of crystal. Life is as it is, not as man wishes it to be. He has entered this house, which is not his own, which he had no prerogative to enter, and has been promptly recognized. I've been false, he thinks, and they have known it from the first. They knew me before I knew myself.

Now he is docked for this audacity, for having intruded. Now he must pay.

The dwarf is waiting.

No one speaks. Muhlbach wonders how he could have been so stripped of sensitivity. He, alone, is out of place. Even that old man in the corner who has not said a word to anyone, but has sat motionless with a tattered overcoat buttoned up to his chin and speckled arthritic hands folded over a cane—that old man belongs to the Queen's Bishop. The gangling boy in denim work clothes and flowered cowboy boots who is sipping coffee at the bar, with a guitar case at his feet—he is part of it. The fat girl in a muumuu who is absently reading a newspaper and scratching herself—she is welcome here. Even the two lesbians with crisp silvered hair and masculine suits, withdrawn, hostile, frightened—yes, they are made to feel at home here, they are given refuge from the terror and confusion of the outer world. Why am I different? he wonders. Why am I not welcome? Why is it that I represent the enemy? What do these disparate people communally own that I do not share? Is it poverty? No. That must be subsidiary, it's not the principal. These people are like odd patches on a quilt, how curious they won't accept another. Well, what do I stand for? A nation's hypocrisy? The tribes of Philistia? Can they despise me as an individual because I am dressed like a bureaucrat? Am I the corporation executive gorged on stolen figs who never serves a sentence? Is it not hurtful to be accused by outcasts?

So his thoughts chase each other over and under with the alacrity of tigers in a circus.

And she has signaled these two—Quinet and Meatbowl, he thinks angrily. That leaves the sourest taste. The question now is whether to accept the imposition and pay for everybody's minestrone, or not. To do so is to avoid embarrassment, but at the same time to acknowledge a personal ignominy. Either way, I lose. If I object and complain that I've been taken for granted, if I point out that no one consulted me, say to the dwarf what he knows perfectly well—that he and they are in league to pluck me cleaner than a squab, just as they've plucked other innocents, no doubt—if I do raise my voice, what's gained? What's to be saved? Well, two dollars, but what else? Self-respect? Is this a thing that strangers are qualified to evaluate?

He looks at the dwarf's untrembling hand, the right hand of iniquity. In the Tenth Book of Augustine it is written that our fellow citizens must be also our fellow pilgrims—those who have walked before equally with those that are on the road beside us, and with those that shall come after us. We are meant to serve them, if we elect to live in the sight of God; to them we are meant to demonstrate not what we have been, but what we are and continue to be. But neither are we to judge ourselves.

Muhlbach reaches for his wallet.

Oh, Daddy, says Rouge, this gruel's the greatest. Quinet nods approvingly. The Judas kiss. Ba-boom-boom! says the feeble-minded Negro.

All of them are sure. They never doubt.

And when they have finished spooning up the soup, when the last noodle has disappeared, the final bean devoured, without one further word they get to their feet and go. He is left to reign over the table, over four bowls—three of them as empty as the day they were lifted from the potter's wheel—four bowls and the mock ivory pieces of a lengthy intellectual triumph. The flesh—the flesh he coveted—is gone. Everything considered, it's been not unlike a vision in the desert.

Tell me, what's your name? he hears himself inquire again. Not Rouge, what's your Christian name?

That's it, she seems to say. Like what else is there, you know? A chick's got a short time and then it's night, you dig? So, like, express it uptown, Pop, because you and me, we beat a different skin.

But are not the senses of our bodies mutual, he wonders, recalling Saint Augustine, or is the sense of my flesh mine, and the sense of your flesh yours? If we are not the same, how could I perceive all that I do, even though we have our separate organs?

Muhlbach disconsolately picks at the flaking table. His strength is gone. If he were at home he would fall into bed exhausted. How long he sits at the table he does not know. When he walks out of the Queen's Bishop no one looks up.

A warm wind is blowing through the trees. An ice cream vendor waits at the corner. An artist who paints bucolic scenes on colored velvet stands hopefully beside his merchandise in the light of a theater marquee and the reflections from a thousand automobiles.

Muhlbach sits down on a bench in Washington Square. Through the arch he sees the flow of traffic. He hears, as though from a considerable distance, the noise of the city. He feels slightly chilled, as though he had been without food all day. It is a weakness of privation, abstinence that chills to the bone. The sickness is deep. It will pass, of course, and it's not fatal. Yet the cure is absurdly simple. The body of a woman, that is all. That is all.

I'm both parts of a man, he reflects, body and soul. I think that the interior of me is the better, but it is also the weaker. How does any man resolve the conflict that continually rages between the exigencies of his body and the burning pod of the soul? I am famished for love and I despise myself, although it is much too easy to call myself dust and ashes. I know that there are things about myself that I do not know. Certainly now we see through a glass darkly, not yet face to face.

After a while he gets to his feet and walks to the curb where he waits for a taxi. He feels as though he has been mildly poisoned, or has had a quart of blood withdrawn; he sees his wife again, as though in a mirror, her taut body stretched across his own, her mouth yawning with excitement; but he cannot summon her warmth, and the weight of her thighs is no heavier than dust.

A taxi veers aside and stops. Muhlbach climbs into the back seat and orders the driver to take him to some night club—any one that's close by—so long as there are women in the show.

The taxi swerves and lurches through the Village, the driver cursing, and turns north.

Very soon he finds that he is being delivered to the Club Sahara. Apprehensively he considers the fluorescent sign, the doorman costumed as a sheik, and wishes that he were not alone. The club looks ridiculous but also a trifle dangerous. He has not been in any such place as this for several years.

Effendi, says the doorman, bowing and making a vaguely religious gesture with one hand. Don't miss the harem dancers. Exotic entertainment once seen only by caliphs in the privacy of the seraglio!

Muhlbach gives him a quarter and marches up the staircase to be met by another sheik. There's an admission charge, after which the curtains are drawn aside and he steps into darkness. The show has begun. On stage sit four musicians, each wearing a tasseled red fez.

This way, *effendi,* says a voice. Muhlbach discovers that he is standing next to a figure in a white burnoose.

He is led to a table in a corner. The stage is partly hidden by a post. He shifts his chair, is nudged by some invisible party whose view he has blocked, and so resigns himself to what he has. The table interests him; he has never been seated at a table so small. It is round and is about the size of a pancake griddle. A slave girl arrives by flashlight to take his order.

Meanwhile to the wicked clink of finger cymbals, Nila, direct from Beirut, Lebanon, has undulated into the spotlight. Muhlbach polishes his glasses, settles them on his nose, and after crossing his arms he prepares to watch the dance; just then the slave girl reappears with his drink. One dollar and fifty cents. He is a bit shocked. Considering the admission fee, this is too much. However, there's nothing to do but pay. She goes away to get change for the bill he has given her and returns almost immediately.

I'm afraid you've made a mistake, says Muhlbach when he has counted the change she holds out on a platter. It was a ten I gave you, not a five.

The slave answers that it was a five.

It was a ten, he knows, because he is meticulous about such things. He does not make mistakes of this sort, he never has. He remembers having looked at the denomination of the bill when he handed it to her. For a moment he wonders if he should simply give up and go home. The night to this point has been nothing if not a disaster. At best it has been a disappointment and at worst he has suffered humiliation enough to last the year. He looks helplessly at the ruins of his ten-dollar bill.

Will there be anything else, sire?

Not at the moment, thank you. For the time being this is quite enough.

Very good, sire. The slave girl switches off her flashlight and steals away.

On the stage Nila is swaying like a viper to the music of oud and darabukka. Flutes are wailing, cymbals clink. Her costume, which may or may not be authentic, consists of loose transparent pantaloons tied at the ankle, a gilded halter with loops of coins that dangle to her navel, and a Cleopatra bracelet squeezing the tawny meat of her upper arm. She dances as sinuously as though she were remembering the pasha who came to visit last night, and Muhlbach finds that he enters into the soul of her dance: America becomes distasteful—an insensate, vulgar, flatulent, bloodless subway nation of merchants, thugs, Protestants, and barbers. He considers giving up his position at Metro Mutual and moving to Lebanon.

Nila melts to the floor, heavy strings of brass coins flowing. Her pale orotund belly possesses a life of its own. The jewel in her navel winks at him. Truly it is a wondrous belly—throbbing, heaving, pulsing, quivering. It trembles, it palpitates, it almost weeps, and then mysteriously vanishes but soon returns larger than ever, rolling languorously from side to side. Muhlbach is quite fascinated; he leans forward.

However, the slave girl is at his table. Would he like another drink?

No, he replies, but changes his mind. Yes, do bring me another. Mindful that money disappears in the Club Sahara as if it were dropped on a shifting sand dune, he searches his pockets to collect the exact amount, nothing extra. Not a surplus peso, not a drachma, no gulden, no dinar, no yen, no reis—in brief, not a pfennig.

When she comes back he is prepared for an ugly scene; but having collected for the drink, the slave girl slips away into the night without saying a word, so there would seem to be an arid truce between them.

Will she serve me again? he wonders. I suppose I'll be ignored from now on, or possibly bounced. We'll find out soon enough.

A new harem dancer is on the stage. Lisa from Port Said, direct from a triumphal tour of the capitals of the Middle East, the personal favorite of Sheik Ali Bey. She is slender and charming, with a sensitive face. Muhlbach feels himself half in love with her. She's as delicate as a fawn. Her eyes are edged with kohl. A jeweled pendant glitters on her forehead. He is positive that she is looking toward him while she dances; it seems to him that she is entreating him to go with her. They will go together, hand in hand, back to the days of King Solomon; they will live in a whitewashed hut, or a tent, and mind a herd of goats. Anything becomes possible when Lisa dances. Anything. The ringing of her tiny cymbals destroys him, he does not know if he can stand this passion. She is calling him to Paradise.

Lisa, ladies and gentlemen! Lisa! A nice round of applause for the little lady.

Lisa bows, smiles like the carnival courtesan she is. As she walks into the wings she peels off the diadem.

And still, thinks Muhlbach, she's what I need. Maybe she was born in the Bronx and has no more danced in triumph through the capitals of the Middle East than I have been shot out of a cannon or gone parachute jumping, but I need her. If there's a God, a God with compassion, He knows. I cannot help it if I lust after the favorite of Sheik Ali Bey—who's probably better known as Mick, Abe, or Louie, who at this moment is lounging at her dressing table paring his nails with a switchblade knife. Yes, each inordinate affection becomes its own torment.

The question no longer is one of aesthetics or of sensibilities. The question is: how do you acquire a belly dancer for a mistress? Do you send a note concealed in a dozen roses? How should it be addressed? Do you ask the slave girl for the dancer's true name? Then what do you write? Dear Lisa Goldberg, et cetera, et cetera, signed Your Faithful Admirer. This must be ancient fiction; furthermore it would necessitate coming back again to occupy the same table, becoming a spectacle yourself, the butt of obscene jokes. Suppose that is the procedure. Consider the implications.

I can't do it, he thinks. I cannot do it. Suppose she replied, and told me to wait for her outside the stage door, in the alley, among the trash cans and mewing cats. The truth is, I simply don't understand how these things are accomplished. I just don't know how. I'm pricked and urged along by this degrading appetite and I drag after me a great load of doubt. I know that what I'm following is not happiness, or even satisfaction, but a state in which I am free of my mortal goad. This is the simulacrum of content. I think that I would settle for it. At least, thank God, I am not altogether ignorant of my ignorance.

Another dancer's on the stage—Riva, she is called, the toast of three continents, direct from Istanbul for an exclusive engagement at the Club Sahara. She, too, has a tender belly possessed of demons which she sets about to exorcize, but the slave girl has come around again and Muhlbach is distracted; not knowing whether to say yes or no, he orders a third drink. Or is this the fourth? What difference does it make? He does not feel well. He inspects the rim of the glass and wonders if he has swallowed a little something that he did not pay for. Riva fails to interest him—excepting the magic belly, which he observes with remote concupiscence. Otherwise he is not moved, she lacks the grace of Lisa, she is not half so Byzantine, has not the deep conviction or felicity. Riva does not promise much.

Just then like an evil flower blooms the thought that perhaps he could attack some unknown woman. Incredible! Muhlbach adjusts his glasses, as though he might be able to see the origin of this insane conceit. He tries to remember if some previous thought has brought up such a criminal idea from the depths of himself, or if he has overheard or seen anything that nourished it. Nothing. Nothing. The woman swaying on the stage has summoned it, but why? Already the idea has become unreal, impossible. Of course I never would, he reflects, but at the same time how interesting that I should think of it! Yes, very interesting indeed. So in spite of my intelligence I'm not much different. There, spattered across the front pages of the tabloids, but for the grace of some inherent power go I—good God! Good God, are we so near the precipice, each one of us?

He squints against the smoke, realizing for the first time just how crowded, uncomfortable, and perfidious the Sahara is. And to say that it is expensive is to put it courteously. He looks at the leader of the four musicians, at the great beaked avaricious nose and snapping black eyes, the trimmed mustache, the tassel on his fez.

Abdul Somebody. Abdul, nodding and smiling rather like a crocodile, leads the authentic Arabian band while Riva slithers around the stage to a flute obbligato of sorts. She is barefoot, with fingernails like the talons of the phoenix and the profile of a hawk. She is fierce and she is mean, there's little doubt; also, she looks dirty, as though she had spent her life in the back rooms of the club. He thinks again of Lisa: no matter if she's a fraud, her lithe body was altogether genuine, and because he will never enjoy that body—and he knows he will not—he wishes he had never seen it.

The lights go on, the musicians put away their exotic instruments. The next show will begin presently, but Muhlbach decides he will not be there. He joins the crowd struggling through the curtained exit and while he is being jostled and elbowed and struck in the back, and perhaps fondled, he asks himself what he has gained by coming here. Nothing, of course, except a clearer knowledge that his temptation has not ended.

Once outside the club he asks himself what to do next. He is standing on the corner with his hands clasped tightly behind his back when someone speaks to him—a naval officer, a stoop-shouldered lieutenant commander with a Southern accent, and Muhlbach recognizes the adult face of the boy who used to be his closest friend, who had been his college roommate twenty years ago.

Puig, for that is his name, promptly insists that they have a drink together.

He'll ask what I'm doing, thinks Muhlbach, if I'm married, if I have a family, and so forth. I know every question he's going to ask.

What is it that's disappointing about Puig? Is it that he's changed so little? He does look older, yes, and his face is still disfigured by those hairy brown warts. He looks somehow depraved, the cold agate eyes blurred by a hundred barrels of sour mash bourbon, the ribbed stomach of youth collapsed and grossly distended. Puig's khaki uniform is wrinkled, the little black shoulder boards are perched askew. His cap is set too far back on his head and he is perspiring. And he's so delighted, Muhlbach reflects, that we've run into each other after all these years.

The longer he looks at Puig, the more it does appear that Puig has changed; but still, the first thing he'd noticed was not any outward modification but that, apart from having physically aged, he might still be mingling with college boys. There's been no inner growth, merely this deterioration of the surface. Muhlbach remembers that Puig had been very fond of music, particularly of Victor Herbert and Sigmund Romberg; now he guesses that although twenty years have elapsed Puig's not yet graduated. He loved the jingles and the macabre stories of Poe; probably he still does. Puig reached his highest point of sensitivity with Rodin. That's real carving, he used to say.

Any old port in a storm, Puig is saying.

Muhlbach follows him across the street into a dank saloon, and there they sit on high leather stools. Puig insists on paying for the drinks, then he swivels back and forth and talks and appraises every woman that walks by. He's married and has four boys. He's executive officer of the U.S.S. *Huxtable* which dropped anchor only last night. After the war ended he stayed in the Navy, it seemed the simplest thing to do; now the pay is good, there are benefits, and when he's not at sea he gets in quite a few rounds of golf. Life's all right in the peacetime Navy, not really bad, claims Puig.

Well, probably it's neither more nor less satisfying than the insurance business; and certainly to be based in Casablanca one year and on the other side of the world the next is far more stimulating than year after year in the dust-free, odorless, subdued and regulated neutrality of Metro Mutual.

Just then with a lecherous little squeak Puig slides off his stool and whispers that he will be back in a moment.

Muhlbach nods and remains at the bar, contemplating his drink. He is envious of Puig, who has no scruples, who has never been concerned with dignity. Puig is at home in the gutter because he does not recognize it as such; if asked, he might very well admit to being in the gutter, but of course to identify a place or a condition of the soul doesn't mean that it's been recognized.

Minutes go by. Muhlbach has finished his drink. What's become of Puig? Foul play? Is he stretched out unconscious in a back room? Not likely. His uniform implies that the total weight of the United States Navy would fall on any malefactor unwise enough to despoil its wearer. Whether this is true or not, Puig never was the type to be victimized. Wherever he is, and whatever he's doing, he's all right. It's almost certain that during these past twenty years nothing unfortunate has happened to him, nor will anything damage him more than temporarily until the day of his death; even that he may turn to some account—triple indemnity taken out the day before, something similar.

It is this blithe ease and fortune of Puig that annoys Muhlbach, that causes him to turn restlessly on the leather stool; because Puig is so average, so direct and ponderous, and because tonight his snuffling chase is similar to Muhlbach's own, equally discreditable. This is not comforting.

Both of us suffer the muddy cravings of the flesh, he thinks, the bubblings and foggy exhalations that demean the spirit. Only he is not aware of how he has fallen; he sees nothing despicable or ridiculous in his acts. The truth is that I must be considered inferior to him because whatever it is possible to corrupt is inferior to what cannot be corrupted. Whatever cannot be damaged or lessened is undoubtedly preferable to what can be, just as whatever suffers no evident change is better than what is subject to change.

Restless in his weariness, Muhlbach can do nothing but wait.

Puig returns, but not alone. He brings Gertie, with the inevitable shiny black handbag. She is as drunk as the grape can make her.

You're all alike! shrills Gertie. No good sons-of-bitches, every blessed one of you. Always after the same thing, by Christ! Only one thing ever on your mind! I should've listened to my first husband. He's got the number of guys like you! Who needs you? Answer me that! Triumphant in her rhetoric, she leans soggily against Puig, who has trouble holding her upright.

Stand by, Gert, we're casting off. See you, buddy, murmurs Puig, somewhat apologetically. Together they go leaning out the door.

What about me? thinks Muhlbach, once more abandoned. I was hoping he would invite me to go with them. I'd share her, God help me. I would have, if I had been invited. Then he looks around—for the first time seeing the bar in which he has been seated—and realizes with amazement that he's been descending: it resembles the entrance to a sewer.

He does not know how he got here, but what alarms him is not that he has reached this low step but where the next might take him, since he has not descended deliberately; some inner force has been diligently at work, a despotism too deeply buried and silted over to be uncovered. Realizing this, he believes he should be able to control it, but is not sure.

Immediately he gets off the stool and walks out.

The city air is not clean, and it seems to have become much warmer during the past hour; it is almost uncomfortable, as though summer would begin again. A polluted river breeze hangs in the soot-blown street. His suit feels thick, the collar tight.

There's a taxi parked at the curb. The driver, like a messenger from above or below, is looking directly at him.

Times Square, says Muhlbach without enthusiasm and climbs into the back seat. I've got to get off these dark avenues, he thinks. I've been too long at the periphery. Other people are finding happiness, they evidently know where it is; strange that I don't. And stranger still, I've the feeling that I too could have found it, if I'd been able to recognize the form it takes. Doubtless the saint was right in telling us that those things are not only many but diverse which men witness and select to enjoy by the rays of our sun, even as that light itself is one, in which the sight of each one beholding sees and holds what pleases; so, too, there may be many things that are good, and also differing aims of life, out of which each chooses as he will. Now, in matters of the flesh, it's said that whatever you perceive through the flesh you perceive only in part, and remain ignorant of the whole, of which these are parts; yet still these parts do delight you.

Times Square, says the cabbie, taking off his yellow hat to scratch his skull.

So soon? Muhlbach is surprised. He sits forward, blinks in the artificial light, and reaches for his wallet. However, his pocket is empty. Never, in fact, has a pocket felt so absolutely empty. The wallet has been stolen. He is positive of the moment when it was stolen—as he was jostled by the crowd leaving the Club Sahara. He remembers that in the bar with Puig he started to reach for it but Puig caught his wrist; the last time, therefore, that he touched it was in the Sahara. But this is merely the deduction of the conscious mind, which is a useful tool but a blunt one; the wallet was lifted by somebody in the crowd, and now that he has been informed by the emptiness of his pocket that it is gone he realizes that the perpetually vigilant self within himself has been trying to notify him ever since it happened.

To placate his incredulous brain he methodically feels through all of his pockets, then, with the cabbie's assistance, searches the back seat. The wallet's not found, of course.

The cabbie is prepared for a struggle, since nothing's half so important as being paid. You want to go back?

No, says Muhlbach, take me to the Tyler Plaza. I'll cash a check.

You know somebody there?

I do. The manager's a friend of mine.

You better hope so, pal.

There's more insolence than sympathy in this remark. Why did I attempt to justify myself? Muhlbach asks while the taxi works its way through the crowd. What business is it of the driver who I know at the hotel, or if I know anybody at all? That's not his concern. He'll be paid. I'm stripped of my money and all at once I'm as insecure as a schoolboy. As for going back to the club, I'd rather lose a dozen wallets. I'll telephone and ask, I can do that. But I couldn't walk up those steps again. This has been a wretched night. Good God, I've been robbed. Robbed!

The cab driver follows him into the Tyler Plaza.

May I please speak to Mr. Sproule, says Muhlbach to the clerk.

Mr. Sproule, according to the clerk, is not there; he's at home sick in bed with the flu. Could Mr. Ascagua be of any assistance?

I need to cash a check, says Muhlbach. Sproule is a close friend of mine. I'm sure it will be all right.

Just let me speak to Mr. Ascagua, suggests the clerk, who is unctuous enough to run a mortuary. He then disappears for ten minutes. Finally it develops that, most unfortunately, Mr. Ascagua has stepped out for a little while.

What time do you have? asks Muhlbach.

Almost two in the morning.

Call up Sproule and I'll talk to him.

The desk clerk is afraid he couldn't do that.

Then you give me the number because I cannot remember it, and I'll damn well call him.

Reluctantly, peevishly, and with a look of insane discomfort, the clerk agrees. So the call is made.

David, says Muhlbach, I'm sorry about this. It's a long story and I feel like an imbecile. Somebody took my wallet and here I am. I need help. He listens, nods to the cabbie, and hands over the telephone to the clerk.

Yes, sir, of course, begins the clerk, I'll be glad to. Yes, sir! Right away, sir!

Muhlbach has no difficulty visualizing Sproule propped up in bed, eyes bulging, mustache and jowls aquiver with indignation.

No trouble at all, sir. Certainly, sir. Not a bit, sir! I certainly will do my best. And a different breed of clerk comes off the telephone.

By the way, says Muhlbach, are there any rooms left? Because I think I'll stay overnight, provided you can locate something away from the street.

The clerk is positive that he will be able to find a very nice room, meanwhile the cashier will be delighted to take care of Mr. Muhlbach's check.

In a few minutes the cabbie is paid and tipped and goes on about his nocturnal business; and Muhlbach with a modest roll of bills lodged carefully in his trousers pocket feels somewhat better. He calls home to tell Mrs. Grunthe that he has decided to spend the night in town.

Mrs. Grunthe is not asleep as he had supposed she might be; she is wide awake. He is oddly touched by this, but also slightly irritated. She has been sitting in her favorite chair, watching television and knitting and every once in a while no doubt lifting her eyes to the clock on the mantel.

How are the children? he inquires. They're asleep, naturally. Everything is under control; as usual, nothing is ever much out of control while Mrs. Grunthe is present.

I'm tired, he explains. I don't feel like riding the train back at this hour. I've decided to stay overnight, that's all.

Mrs. Grunthe does not take to this idea; she suspects something. Muhlbach remembers that she now and then preaches against the wickedness of gambling;

probably she thinks he has become involved with a bunch of card-playing Italians. She always has been suspicious of Italians. Puerto Ricans, Greeks, Negroes, Chinese, they're very much the same, they are not devils, however foreign; but Mrs. Grunthe knows that sinfulness dwells in the Italian breast.

So be it. Good night, Mrs. Grunthe. Dream of Salvador.

Now there is only one call to make, and it will be futile. He calls the Club Sahara, explains that he was there earlier and that his wallet is missing. Just by chance has it been found? No answer. He hears the clink of glasses, laughter, remote voices, and once more the music of oud and darabukka inscrutably beckoning him across the wire. Time goes by while he holds the receiver and blinks his eyes to keep awake. Finally, without explanation, somebody at the other end of the line hangs up.

This insult is one too many. He had planned to go to bed but now, after this, there is only one possible resolution to the night—he will get drunk. He has not been filled to the brim since his wedding day and that was fourteen years ago. Now seems like a good time. No doubt the time was long past. Probably a man's anguish and his troubles are best washed away once in a while, since they are bound to return. In any case, where's the nearest cocktail lounge and how fast can it be achieved? He calculates that half a dozen ought to finish him, after which he'll get a good night's sleep. It may be joyless, that's not the point. I'm half out of my senses, he thinks, with grief and shame and mummified passion. I'm a coward and a celibate. I don't have guts enough to approach a kootch dancer, I don't have either the brains or the sex to interest a Bohemian girl. I'm a fake, a pompous ass, a stuffy bourgeois pedant and a—well, what's the use? I could go on and on. And a blessed son-of-a-bitch not the least of these. Oh, but I am miserable! How miserable I am.

This causes him to feel a little improved. He heads grimly for the cocktail lounge. To his surprise it's nearly deserted. There are a few lonesome men at the bar, who look around as he comes in, a waitress, and two bartenders. The thought of joining his fellows on a stool is disagreeable; he selects a table in the darkest corner.

The waitress begins walking toward him. She does not wear a dress but red mesh stockings to the hip, a black Merry Widow, and a marvelous blond wig.

Muhlbach knows that he is staring at her like a provincial, but he does not care. Frustration, disgust, anger, disappointment, the badly stained and spattered image of himself, mauled dignity—whatever the night and this impossible city have proffered is wrapped up and tied in one vulgar bundle which he might throw away if he can bring a light to the eye of this steamy wench. Pride and confidence may then be restored, may grow and flourish. He knows in the midst of his dejection that such a thought, such hope, is madness, that he will fail again. Yet he is a man, no matter what else; lecherous and unrepentant in the depths of exhaustion; desirous of much more than can be reckoned; muddied by concupiscence; made wild with shadowy loves; halted by the short links of his mortality and deafened by conceit; seldom at peace; adulterous and bitter; stuck and bled by thorns on every side; rank with imagined sin; exiled forever and yet ever returning, such he is. Brambles of lust spring up on all sides while he plots the course. He learns that Carmen is her name.

As she walks away her fat thighs torment him and he is heavily swollen by lascivious plans. With a dull, furious gaze he follows the gathered pink chiffon decorating her extravagant rump like a rabbit's flag and wonders if he will explode from passion before she comes back. Jesus, oh Lord! I've been taken prisoner by this disease of my flesh, he says to himself, and of its deadly sweetness, and I drag my chain about with me, and I dread the idea of its being loosed.

Carmen doesn't wear a ring, he notes when she returns. He introduces himself, but she replies with a shrug.

He mentions that she could be the sister of someone he used to know years ago in Washington. She doesn't say a word.

Well then, says Muhlbach, tell me, what time is it?

She doesn't know.

I'll be wanting another drink as soon as you can get it, he says, leaning back against the cushions, and is grateful that she goes away without so much as a glance at him. He swallows most of the drink and looks around. The lounge is not uncomfortable, in a rather calculated way, as though it had been designed to solace defeated men. Muhlbach shuts his eyes. It's true that Carmen does remind him of somebody in Washington; he tries to remember, but cannot. He remembers that he had been attracted to whoever it was, but then, just as now, nothing came of it. The reason was the same, as it is invariably the same. It never will be different.

I'm trapped like a bird in a loft, he thinks.

Carmen is returning and it occurs to him that she, too, is a bird—a glorious bird of the jungle with plumage as indescribable as a tropic dawn. When she bends over to serve him he seizes her wrist. She utters a little cry and draws back; there is a momentary struggle before he lets go, more shocked than she.

Porfirio! she calls.

That one word brings out of some gloomy recess in the lounge a dapper, swift, and unmistakably dangerous Latin with a diamond stickpin on a white silk necktie.

He stares at Muhlbach through tinted glasses and inquires if he may be of service, although this is not why he has come to visit. He conveys a very different message.

Muhlbach, shaken doubly by his own conduct and by the implied threat of violence, has difficulty answering. Exposed to Porfirio's pitiless gaze, he takes out his handkerchief and weakly pats his face. He is glad that Carmen has gone. If anyone must witness his shame, it should be another man.

I'm afraid I feel a little sick, he says.

You had enough for tonight, says Porfirio, not unkindly.

Muhlbach nods, perspiring.

You make it to the door by yourself?

In a few minutes I will. Let me sit here until I recover.

Take your time, says Porfirio, and sidles away.

Oh my God, asks Muhlbach during his moments of grace, what has become of me?

Before getting up he reminds himself that he is seriously drunk, at least that is what the evidence suggests, and if he has not acted nobly anywhere else tonight, he will manage somehow to leave this place unassisted. I'll do that, he says, if I drop dead one step beyond the arch.

Cautiously he gets up. He walks with unspeakable dignity past the piano and the bar and so into the lobby to the desk where he asks for his key, while the meditations of Saint Augustine sing loosely through his head. There is no place that I can rest, he thinks; backward or forward, there is no place. I have dared to grow wild and touch a multiplicity of things in order to please myself, but each consumed itself in front of me because I exceeded the limits set for my nature. But is there not attraction in the face and body of a woman that is very great and equal to the face and body of gold? For the flesh has like every other sense its own intelligence.

Holding the key in both hands so that he will not drop it, he heads for the elevator. He does not know what time it has become, except that it must be quite late; and he is amazed by the determination of his body, which does not care whether it is three or five or twelve but would as soon walk out again into the street.

In the elevator he is relatively certain that he is going to vomit; he concentrates on other matters in the hope of deceiving his stomach, and once inside the room he does not feel quite so sick. In fact, after a very few minutes, there seems to be no reason he should not refresh himself with a shower and go out. Really, a man's luck changes. Yes, of course, things should improve.

But this is the voice of the Devil—that wheedling tone is familiar. Muhlbach refuses to listen. He sits down on the edge of the bed to examine the cuff of his trousers. The hamster has eaten more of it than he thought. Tomorrow he must buy a new pair of pants. But tomorrow is Sunday. All is wretchedness and cross-purpose.

The softness of the bed soon affects his body. He lies down but immediately gets up and walks back and forth wrestling with the devilish proposal. He mutters, squeezes his hands, turns around, explains to himself that it is all a fabulous absurdity. Some time later, fully dressed, not able to sleep naked if there is no other body for companionship, he stretches himself on the floor. Hours pass. He sleeps nervously, aware that he is alone; it is as though the troubled evening continues.

By morning the night phantoms have not been vanquished; at breakfast he scarcely tastes his food but sits gazing through the window of the coffee shop at the sensual movements of women on the street. Even their shadows on the pavement suggest and hint at Babylon. The morning is brilliant, and morning is reflected everywhere, but he cannot enjoy its splendor. This is Sunday, he reflects, a time for Christian worship, but I am obsessed. This is the seventh day, yet I am unable to rest.

Then, whether it is a hallucination or not, he believes that he sees Rouge across the street, accompanied by Meatbowl and Quinet. If he is not mistaken, and he wonders, they are standing outside a bookstore. Quinet and Meatbowl are gesticulating—stock characters in an old folk comedy—while Rouge, like Columbine, perhaps invisible to mortal eyes, stands just apart as though waiting for Harlequin. Now imploringly she looks toward him; she has discovered him at his table. He cannot remain where he is. He quickly pays for his breakfast and hurries out.

Yes, they are there. They do exist, all three of them, outlandish spirits. And has Rouge truly seen him? Is she beckoning? Is there something that she wants? A book, a meal, a game of chess, a diamond to exchange for a night of love? No matter, he will give it to her. How different from the pains of youth. Here is no thought of pressed flowers, moonlit walks along the beach. Here is the meaning of the body's work, its need; the rest is wasted time.

Impatiently he waits for the light to change, worried that Meatbowl and Quinet will wander off and she will follow and be lost forever.

But Columbine is there, looks up with great grave eyes at his vigorous approach. Bright indeed is this morning, fortunate are those who have found each other. Is not the very air filled with clapping wings?

So the deus ex machina, a pigeon, one gray pigeon otherwise quite nondescript and indistinguishable from the millions, unaware or indifferent to the magnitude of its act and to the finality with which it will score a human life, possibly two lives, briskly cocks its head, winks once, and without a ruffled feather sends down from Heaven the fateful message.

Muhlbach, in mid-stride, hears the liquescent thunder against his hat. He takes it for a distant earthquake because the sky is blue. But no! Informed by Rouge's insane shriek of laughter, by the looks of horror, sympathy, and stupefied amusement from passers-by, as well as by his own desperate inner certainty, Muhlbach takes off his hat. One glance certifies the pigeon's mighty blow. After this, what can befall a man?

With the hat held upside down in one hand as though he were collecting coins he stalks up Broadway. Perhaps, he thinks, this is for the best. I've hoped for what was never meant to happen. I have spent one whole night attempting to distort the truth which was born in me; now I have learned. Whatever I touch henceforth— whether it is the body of the earth or the air itself—I must be sure that it is within my province and does not belong to any other. But still, knowing this was not meant to be, does not, nor ever shall diminish the yearning. I know this, as I know that seven and three are forever ten.

1962

NOAH'S ARK

IN THE BOOK of Genesis it was written that a man ought not to be alone—he should have a helpmeet. Tessie often thought about this while vacuuming the carpet or washing dishes and the idea troubled her. She tried to imagine what it would be like to marry one of the boys she had known while growing up on the farm. Some had been nice enough, yet they always pressed her to go for a walk with nobody else around; they wanted to kiss her on the mouth and fondle her body, which would be indecent. So she had been polite to them when they invited her to dance or go to the movies, and once in a while she had permitted her hand to be held, but nothing more, because according to First Corinthians it was not good for a man to touch a woman. And she recalled the passage from Deuteronomy which said that when a man has taken a wife, if she finds no favor in his eyes then he can write a bill of divorcement and send her out of the house. This was painful to think about. However, since she had moved to the city and gone to work for Dr. and Mrs. Stocking it seemed to her that she had been excused from marriage. Surely the Lord understood what was in her heart and would not be angry if she went through life alone. Still, this meant that some young man would have no helpmeet. The whole thing was a puzzle. She wondered if the Lord might be watching with a displeased expression.

Whenever Tessie thought about Dr. Stocking she wagged her head. Dr. Stocking was a skinny little psychiatrist with a shrill voice and the face of a chipmunk. In the hall closet he kept a gorilla costume and every so often he would put on this costume and take a walk around the block, which set the neighborhood dogs to barking.

Mrs. Stocking was just as peculiar. She taught Religious Studies at the college but she paid no heed to the Holy Bible, nor did she go to church. Usually she sat on the porch smoking French cigarettes and reading. Books—some written in foreign languages—were scattered upstairs and downstairs, all over the house. Tessie was annoyed by this because books ought to be arranged neatly on shelves, but Mrs. Stocking had told her to let them alone.

Days never seemed long enough. If it wasn't Tweetwee the canary needing attention, or the guppies' aquarium, or Scraps the fox terrier who needed a bath, there was the laundry, or shirts to be ironed, or the grocery list, or a delivery boy ringing the bell, or the gas meter reader, or the postman with a package. Then, likely as not, Gigi would arrive in a terrible rush, even though she didn't have much to do. If she wasn't begging money from her parents she wanted something tucked away in the attic or the basement—phonograph records, clothes, pictures from her school days. A sweet child and playful as a kitten, Tessie said to herself, but she married so young. Well, who am I to judge?

Now and then as she went about her chores Tessie would pause in the breakfast room where half a dozen colored glass bottles decorated the windowsill. There she would stand admiring the colors and chatting with Tweetwee, who sang to the sunshine from his green wire cage or fluffed his feathers or crept from side to side on his wooden perch and cocked his head with such impudence that she could not help laughing.

Oh, goodness! What a naughty fellow! Dirtying your paper! Don't you know I got more than enough to do without changing your paper again? Such a rascal! You want more seeds? I expect you do. If it ain't one thing, it's another. Mrs. Stocking will be after me for not finishing the carpet and what am I supposed to tell her? Answer me that, will you? And what about the guppies? The poor little things take sick if I don't look out for them. That moss just keeps growing. Now what are you up to? First you hop off your perch and then you hop right back up on it. Goodness, you are a trial! And where is that Mr. Scraps? Chasing all over the neighborhood, I imagine, barking at delivery boys and getting his feet muddy. I declare he is the feistiest dog a person ever saw. Now I've got to get on with my work. I ain't dusted upstairs and then it'll be time to fix lunch.

In the evening after she had cleared the dinner table and washed and dried the dishes and put them away, Tessie climbed the dark narrow staircase to her room in the attic. There she turned on the electric fan or the heater, according to the season, pulled off her shoes and settled in the rocking chair beside her bed. From here she could look at the trees in the backyard through a little round window resembling the porthole of an ocean liner. Sometimes she gazed at television or listened to gospel programs on the radio before going to sleep.

Every Sunday night she listened to Reverend H. L. Hunnicutt whose program emanated from Chattanooga, and one night Reverend Hunnicutt spoke on the Book of Revelation. Tessie listened drowsily to his powerful voice while rocking in her chair. Gog and Magog were at this moment preparing to wage battle against the kingdom of the Lord. Led by Satan, loosed out his prison after one thousand years, these enemies of God whose number was as the sand of the sea were girding their loins for combat. And was not the dreadful hour imminent? Was it not fast approaching? O yea! Was not heaven itself alight with shooting stars? Were not the silhouettes of four horsemen visible at dawn? Had not the very moon suffered eclipse? Were there not devastating floods? Volcanic eruptions? Hurricanes? Tidal waves? O yea! O yea! cried Reverend Hunnicutt. And the sea shall give up the dead which were in it. And death and hell shall deliver up the dead which were in them. And on that fateful day shall every man be judged according to his works.

Monday morning while doing the breakfast dishes Tessie thought about what Reverend Hunnicutt had said. Later as she was dusting furniture she thought about it again. And just before noon while she stood at the kitchen sink peeling apples she looked out the window and saw Mrs. Stocking in the garden with a trowel and shears and the sprinkling can. Tessie frowned because Mrs. Stocking wore dirty old slacks, one of her husband's cast-off shirts, and a ragged straw hat.

Far be it from me, said Tessie. After drying her hands she straightened her apron, walked out the back door and marched across the lawn to ask if Mrs. Stocking knew when Gog and Magog would threaten the world.

You appear disturbed, Mrs. Stocking said. Or could it be my imagination? Is something wrong?

There shall be earthquakes in divers places and famines and troubles, Tessie replied in a stubborn voice. Heaven and earth shall pass away, but the word of the Lord shall not pass away.

Mrs. Stocking was on her knees beside the rose trellis. She took a deep breath and said: Oh, dear.

The number of God's enemies is as the sand of the sea.

Mrs. Stocking smiled politely. Yes, I'm sure that must be so. Tessie, what would you think of a hearing aid? Dr. Stocking and I have discussed the matter and both of us believe it might help. Naturally we would take care of the bill.

After a few moments Tessie returned to the house. In the kitchen she picked up an apple and the paring knife but discovered that she could not see very well because her eyes had filled with tears. She put the apple and knife on the drainboard, climbed to the attic and sat in her rocking chair. Through the round window she could look down on Mrs. Stocking trimming the rosebush.

Wasn't no cause, she whispered. She sniffled and blew her nose. Then she began to sob because Mrs. Stocking had been rude.

Underneath the bed was an old suitcase that served as home for packets of Christmas cards and letters from long ago neatly tied with colored ribbons, a leatherette album containing snapshots of the farm, a plaster bluebird she had won by tossing rings at the county fair, a baby's shoe coated with bronze, a tiny pair of mittens, the eighth grade report card when she got a B for spelling, and her mother's cameo brooch. There, too, slumped cheerfully in the suitcase—his brown button eyes shining with mischief—was a rag doll named Sailor Boy. His puffy hands were soiled and his cloth face stained because she had so often held hands with him and had kissed him goodnight so many times. Here and there Sailor Boy had split at the seams, but she had sewn him together again.

With the doll clasped to her breast she rocked gently beside the bed while talking about the end of the world. What do you think, little fellow? How much longer you expect we might be around? Lord alone knows. We just best hope. Well, now, if you ain't a rascal—sailing everyplace under the sun! A person couldn't never guess what you been up to. You been good? And don't you fib! Them as speaks the truth got nothing to fear. Only sinners stand to be punished.

Then she remembered what Mrs. Stocking had said. Wasn't no cause to talk like that, she told the doll.

Gigi arrived one afternoon while she was making fudge cake.

Fudge cake! Gigi cried, and tap-danced across the floor. Is Mother home?

This is Wednesday, said Tessie. What's wrong with your mind?

Right! She teaches until three. I always forget. Gigi stooped to pet Scraps, who dozed beneath the kitchen table with his muzzle on his paws and his ears twitching.

That dog, Tessie said. He all but took a bite out of the postman yesterday morning. He does and his name won't be Mr. Scraps no more, it'll be mud, let me tell you. I give him a bath not three days ago but would you just look. Goodness, what a trial.

Gigi laughed. When I was here last week I saw you talking to Raymond. Why don't you go out with him?

Raymond?

Sure. You might have a jazzy time. After that, who knows? Maybe a passionate flaming insane romance.

Oh, my! Tessie said and tried to keep from smiling.

Don't you think about getting married?

Can't say as I do.

Weren't you ever in love?

Years back, said Tessie. There was a fellow named Sylvester Voss. But he drank. Then he'd chase around half the county shouting and breaking things. Scared the life out of folks. I wouldn't choose to marry that sort of fellow.

But you must get lonely. I mean, night after night.

I'm fine, Tessie said while peering into the oven. Just fine, thank you.

That's weird. When I was a kid you used to tell me how much you wanted children.

That's so. There was a time.

Gigi grew thoughtful. You must have wanted to smack my bottom more than once. I always asked for something different. If Mother and Dad were going to have pancakes for breakfast I'd ask for a waffle just to be different.

Children love to fuss, Tessie said. You had your share of tantrums.

You know what used to make me feel sad? We'd be eating dinner together at the table and you'd be in the kitchen all by yourself. I used to leave the table and come out here to talk to you. Mother didn't like it.

I recall.

I was afraid you felt neglected. It didn't seem fair.

Now Gigi, don't you make me cry.

I wanted to invite you to sit at the table with us, but I couldn't.

Now stop, Tessie said. You run along.

I thought you were really special. You never criticized me or tried to improve me the way Mother did. Her big mission in life was to make me perfect. What a laugh!

She wanted to bring you up right. You ought to be grateful she cared.

Gigi made a face. Teaching meant more to her than I did. She was always reading and taking notes. She never had time for me.

What's got into you? Tessie asked.

That's how I felt, Gigi said. I can't help it. You were the one who taught me how to sew and bake. All those girl things I learned from you. I remember watching you fix those goodies at Thanksgiving and Christmas. I used to watch you basting the turkey and wondered if I'd ever learn how to cook. And once when I got sick you held me on your lap and told me stories about what it was like on the farm when you were a kid my age. Mother just put her hand on my forehead to see if I had a temperature and then went back to her desk.

Now you know she loves you more than anything in the world.

Sure, I know it, Gigi said. Once for my birthday you made a red flannel night-gown with angels on the collar. I was thrilled.

You looked cute as a bug.

And one morning you invited me up to your room and told me to guess what was in the tree, so I looked out the window and I could see right into the robin's nest. There were those little pale blue eggs. They were simply darling. Do you remember?

I do. You wasn't but maybe nine.

I was eight. I'll never forget. And Saturday nights we'd watch the Lawrence Welk show. Wow, did you have a crush on him!

Goodness, Tessie said. Why bring that up?

One time I asked if you'd marry Lawrence Welk and you clapped your hands and said, "The minute he asks!"

That's so, I did. He had a real nice smile.

Listen, Gigi said after tasting the fudge cake, why don't you give Raymond the eye? He'd invite you out.

You scamp! I couldn't never do a thing like that. I wouldn't know how.

Get Myra to show you.

Myra?

I've seen how she ogles the delivery boys and telephone linemen and Jehovah's Witnesses and anything else in pants, especially when the Fitzgeralds aren't home. She's a hot number.

Shame on you, Tessie said. Shame on you for such talk.

But what Gigi had said was true. Myra did flirt. And this was strange because Myra had a mustache like a twelve-year-old boy and her left arm was two or three inches shorter than her right arm. Well, Tessie thought, the Lord does move in mysterious ways.

Now you best run along about your business, she said. I've got more than enough to do.

Gigi laughed and hugged her. You're so shy! Get Myra to fix you up on a double date. You spend all day doing housework and then hibernate in the attic like a nun. You don't ever go out.

I'm not missing a thing, Tessie said. In case you forget, young lady, I attend Bible class twice a month.

Bible class, said Gigi. Bible class. Okay, it's your life.

Gigi was right, Tessie thought. Still, there was no sense going out just to be going out. And there was no reason to make eyes at Raymond or any other man. It would seem forward. Raymond was decent enough. When he came around to do yard work he was always polite, but spending the evening with him would be different. He might get ideas.

A few days later Tessie was in the dining room polishing silver when Mrs. Stocking returned from the college with a satchel full of books.

Oh, good for you! she exclaimed. Silver does tarnish, doesn't it?

Tessie nodded.

A while ago, Mrs. Stocking went on in a careful voice, I sensed that something important was on your mind. I felt that perhaps you wanted to have a talk. I could have been mistaken, but are you in difficulty?

I hear fine, Tessie said.

Of course you do, Mrs. Stocking went on in the same voice and placed her satchel on a chair. I've simply been wondering if—well, you've mentioned that you contribute to a radio ministry.

Reverend Hunnicutt, Tessie said and began to polish the soup tureen.

What you do with your money is your own affair, but Dr. Stocking and I have discussed this. Frankly, we're concerned. We haven't the slightest idea how much you contribute, or how often. Your donations may be appropriate. Nevertheless, some of these radio evangelists can be remarkably persuasive.

The kingdom of God is nigh, Tessie said and continued polishing.

After a few moments Mrs. Stocking said, Well, I've no wish to intrude. She glanced at her wristwatch. We're going to a cocktail party at the Woodruffs and I should get ready. My hair is a fright. If there's anything you wish to discuss, please don't hesitate. You know you're almost a member of the family.

Tessie decided to ask about Gog and Magog, but when she looked up Mrs. Stocking had disappeared.

Sunday night after clearing the table and washing the dishes she climbed to the attic, shut the door, and arranged herself comfortably in the rocking chair to wait for Reverend Hunnicutt's broadcast. On the dresser between a tinted photograph of her parents and a pink glass angel with lace wings stood a little globe filled with water. Inside the globe was a miniature Swiss chalet surrounded by tiny evergreens.

Hearing aid, Tessie said with contempt. She picked up the globe and gave it a fierce shake. The evergreens and the chalet vanished in a blizzard.

After the opening hymn of his broadcast Reverend Hunnicutt pointed out that the cost of keeping his ministry on the air had been rising steadily and he urged those who believed in Jesus to express their love. This meant a pledge. He described those listeners who were contributing ten percent of their income as soldiers in a growing army of the Lord which daily girded itself to battle Satan. Beyond doubt Jesus heard the prayers of these generous listeners. But would not the Lord listen yet more closely to those who found in their hearts the charity and wisdom and love to contribute twenty percent? For what is charity? Reverend Hunnicutt inquired. What is charity if not the Holy Spirit?

Twenty percent, Tessie murmured. Gracious, wouldn't that be a sum?

Yea! O yea! sang Reverend Hunnicutt. Blessed are the charitable! Blessed are the generous!

Whenever Tessie mailed an offering, no matter how small, she received a gilt-edge postcard assuring her that the Lord would not forget. Twice she had enclosed a note asking when to expect the Second Coming, but Reverend Hunnicutt had not answered. She reminded herself that he must get thousands of letters.

Now, as she listened, she felt that he had mysteriously entered the room and was stroking her hand, comforting her. With Sailor Boy on her lap she rocked dreamily and whispered to the doll: Where are you sailing, precious thing? Where will you sail this evening, precious child?

Dear friends in radioland, Reverend Hunnicutt continued, do you know the story of Noah's Ark? Of course you do. You have heard it told and retold. But let us take a moment to reflect upon the significance of this instructive story. Ask yourselves, each and every one of you, what it means. What does it mean? Dear friends, the meaning is clear. Almighty God saw that this earth was corrupt and filled with violence and therefore He vowed to destroy everything that He had created, both man and beast, yea, and the creeping things and the fowl of the air. God saith I will bring a flood of waters upon the earth to destroy all flesh, and everything that is in the earth shall die. But with thee will I establish my covenant, and thy wife, and thy sons and thy sons' wives. So saith the Lord God. And the Lord commanded of Noah to make an Ark of gopherwood to the length of three hundred cubits, of breadth fifty cubits, of height thirty cubits. And when Noah was six hundred years old this flood lay upon the earth but the Ark was lifted above the earth—it went upon the face of the waters. And the waters prevailed. The waters prevailed, dear friends, for one hundred and fifty days. And when the windows of Heaven were stopped and the waters assuaged, the Ark came to rest upon the mountain which is called Ararat. Yea! It came to rest.

Reverend Hunnicutt paused. Whenever he did this Tessie felt surprised and thrilled; her eyes widened with pleasure. She felt that she had known him all her life and it seemed that he was speaking to her alone. His reassuring voice was that of someone who kissed her forehead while she was falling asleep many years ago. Her eyes closed. Precious, she sighed, dear child. Drowsily she waited for him to continue.

Praise the Lord, he said. Dear friends, all of you in radioland, how I wish we might clasp hands on this glorious occasion because there is good news tonight. O yea, let us praise the Lord because the news is great. Alleluia! The Ark of Noah unseen by any mortal eye since God threw open the windows of Heaven—that Ark which came to rest upon the mountain of Ararat when the waters were assuaged—the Ark of Noah has been found! Alleluia! Praise the Lord!

Next morning after breakfast Tessie stayed in the kitchen until Dr. Stocking left for the office. Then she returned to the breakfast room with a dish towel in her hands and told Mrs. Stocking what Reverend Hunnicutt had said.

At first Mrs. Stocking did not answer. She was working a crossword puzzle in the newspaper. After a while she took off her reading glasses and looked at Tweetwee, who chirped merrily in his cage.

Not again, she said.

The Ark lies buried deep in snow high upon the slopes of Mount Ararat, Tessie said.

Mrs. Stocking took a sip of coffee and gestured at a chair. Do sit down. Is this what you've been wanting to discuss?

Tessie obeyed reluctantly because it did not seem proper. She spread the dish towel across her knees and waited.

I hardly know how to approach this, Mrs. Stocking said almost to herself. Tessie, dear, we don't take the Bible literally. For instance, the wife of Lot didn't turn into a pillar of salt—not really. Nor did the Pharisees actually swallow camels. You understand the impossibility of such a thing. Nor did the Red Sea roll apart for the Israelites. As a matter of fact, we believe this passage might refer to the Gulf of Suez rather than to the Red Sea. Be that as it may, no power on earth can negate the laws of physics. In other words, Biblical anecdotes should be regarded as a source of profound philosophy and quite marvelous poetry.

The Lord rained fire and brimstone upon Sodom and Gomorrah, Tessie said. He overthrew them cities in which Lot dwelt. His wife become a pillar of salt. Genesis nineteen.

Mrs. Stocking tapped her pencil on the newspaper. Finally she said, Both of us—and Gigi, of course—all of us are so fond of you. And we do respect your faith. However—oh, really, I find this quite distressing.

The waters prevailed one hundred fifty days.

You can be so obstinate, Mrs. Stocking said. You are positively medieval. I'm sorry. Please excuse me. Mount Ararat rises seventeen thousand feet above sea level. Seventeen thousand feet! Oh, never mind.

They seen the Ark, Tessie said.

Who has seen the Ark?

This man from Dothan, Alabama. Reverend Hunnicutt he read a letter this man wrote over the radio. It was during the war. He was in the Army over there some-place and he made friends of this family and one day they took him up the moun-tain to show him where it was at. He seen it. He seen pictures about the Flood in this cave they went into high upon the slopes of Mount Ararat.

Pictures, you say. Murals?

I beg pardon?

Tell me about these pictures. Who painted them?

Tessie considered. I expect it was likely Noah or the sons of Noah. His sons was Shem, Ham, and Japheth.

Yes, Mrs. Stocking said. Can you describe the Ark?

It was of a piece until the beginning of the war, according to this man from Dothan. There was these cages inside. He seen little cages for the birds and big cages for lions and tigers and elephants. Also, there was a good many hammers and ancient tools from the days of Noah. No mortal eye has beheld them tools since the days of Noah. Also, there was ice because it was high up on the mountain. And there was pitch. He seen all this pitch.

The seams had been caulked?

I didn't catch what you said.

The cracks between the boards were filled with pitch?

Tessie nodded. Rooms shalt thou make in the Ark, and shalt pitch it within and without with pitch. I expect it's up there. This man from Dothan he seen it.

I do not question the man's sincerity, Mrs. Stocking said. Now, has Reverend Hunnicutt suggested that in exchange for—oh, the entire business is utterly exas-perating! I hesitate to ask, but is this evangelist selling splinters from the Ark?

Tessie's mouth tightened.

Mrs. Stocking twirled the pencil between her fingers. Tessie, are you familiar with St. Bernard of Clairvaux? I assume you are not. St. Bernard informs us that no creature can be intelligent save by the aid of reason. In other words, it is prudent to reflect critically—I might even say skeptically—upon what we are told.

Tessie considered the dish towel on her knees and discovered a loose thread. She snatched it out.

For example, Tessie, are we not informed that Noah took into the Ark clean beasts by sevens? Yet we have been told also how they entered two by two. Perhaps a firm editorial hand was needed while the Bible was being assembled! Mrs. Stocking laughed crisply. Or take Jesus—was he crucified at the third hour, as related by Mark? Or about the sixth hour, as related by John? And what about Saul's daughter Michal, who had no child until the day of her death, according to Samuel. Yet she bore five sons, this also according to Samuel. And we have been assured in Paul's first epistle to the Corinthians that when the trumpet sounds the dead shall be raised incorruptible. Yet we read in Isaiah how the dead shall not live when they are deceased—they shall not rise. Well, then? Which are we to believe?

Three times six is the sign of the Beast.

Mrs. Stocking pretended not to hear. What about the Deluge? Similar legends abound in the folklore of such diverse people as American Indians, Fiji Islanders, and Australian aborigines. Or, should you choose, ignore this diffusion but reflect on the chronology. The tradition of a catastrophic flood antedates Christianity by quite a while. In 1872 the British philologist George Smith deciphered the inscription on some baked clay tablets from the ruins of Nineveh. These tablets relate the adventures of a hero named Gilgamesh who, seeking eternal life, spoke to one of his ancestors, Utnapishtim—the only survivor of a gigantic flood. The tablets tell us that a ship at last came to rest on the mountains of Nizir. And what do you suppose happened next? A dove was sent forth, but could find no resting place, so it returned. Then a swallow was sent forth, but it too returned. Then a crow was released, but did not return. In other words, despite variations in detail, what we have is a version of the Deluge from the library of King Assurbanipal who reigned seven centuries before Christ. What do you make of that?

It wasn't no crow, Tessie said. It was a dove. Noah sent forth a dove. And the dove came in to him in the evening; and, lo, in her mouth was an olive leaf pluckt off: so Noah knew that the waters were abated from off the earth.

You have a remarkable memory, Mrs. Stocking said.

I can recite the presidents of the United States, said Tessie.

All of them?

Every single one, Tessie said. And she began, but Mrs. Stocking interrupted.

All right, all right. I believe you. Now where were we? Let me think. What I was attempting to point out is the antiquity of the flood legend. It is much older than the Assyrian tablets. Scholars have traced the Gilgamesh epic back five thousand years. So what does this mean? Quite possibly the persistence of such a tale expresses our search for understanding in the face of catastrophic disasters.

It wasn't no crow, Tessie repeated. It was a dove. Genesis eight.

Mrs. Stocking gazed at the crossword puzzle. Then she picked up the newspaper, but immediately put it down with a look of annoyance. Let's start over, she said. The Bible tells us the water was fifteen cubits deep, which is about twenty-six feet. Now, Tessie, in 1929 the famous archaeologist Sir Leonard Woolley probed a layer of silt in Mesopotamia that had been carried down from the upper Euphrates valley and beneath this residue he found traces of reed huts dating from the Erech dynasty. According to Woolley's calculations, this flood must have been at least twenty-five feet deep. The implication is unmistakable. Our famous Christian legend originated in a prehistoric Mesopotamian flood. Wouldn't you agree?

The time draweth nigh, Tessie said. The beast come up out of the sea having seven heads and ten horns and upon his horns ten crowns and upon his heads the name of blasphemy.

Revelation? Mrs. Stocking asked.

Thirteen, said Tessie.

I don't doubt you for an instant. Be that as it may, the legend occurs also in Greek mythology. Deucalion, the son of Prometheus and Clymene, ruled over a kingdom in Thessaly and when Zeus resolved to inundate the earth Deucalion constructed a ship for himself and his wife Pyrrha. Now, when the vessel came to rest on Mt. Parnassus, Deucalion was instructed by the oracle at Themis to cast the bones of his mother behind him. But how should this be interpreted? Deucalion concluded that his mother was the earth. Therefore he and his wife cast stones behind them. The stones hurled by Deucalion became men, while those cast by Pyrrha became women. I think that's an exquisite parable. Don't you?

Tessie winked at Tweetwee, who cleaned his feathers and trilled happily in the warm sunshine.

Mrs. Stocking spoke rather sharply. According to the Koran, the wife of Noah is Waila. This woman attempted to convince people that her husband was out of his mind. Do you find this amusing?

Tessie gazed at her like a tombstone.

After a long silence Mrs. Stocking said: Dr. and Mrs. Joggerst will be here for supper next Friday.

Dr. and Mrs. Joggerst?

Dr. and Mrs. Joggerst. Surely you remember them? They raved about your coconut meringue pie. Do you suppose you could make coconut meringue pie for us next Friday?

Coconut meringue?

Coconut meringue. They'd be delighted. I—it's simply that—oh, I've got to run, she continued after a glance at her watch. I've a class at ten.

After Mrs. Stocking drove off to the college Tweetwee cocked his head in such a funny way that Tessie could not help laughing. She wagged a finger at him. What are you up to, you rambunctious thing? Two of your ancestors was in the Ark, did you know that? Yes, sir! In the seventh month on the seventeenth day the Ark come to rest upon the mountain of Ararat. My goodness, how you scatter them seeds! You are a caution! Well, I can't waste half the day chattering with you. But Mrs. Stocking she don't have no right to poke fun.

That afternoon Myra whistled, which meant the Fitzgeralds were not home. Tessie was at the sink washing lettuce. She dried her hands and went out the back door so they could talk across the hedge. And no sooner did she begin telling Myra what Mrs. Stocking had said than she started to cry.

Myra frowned. Lordy Lordy, you do gush worse than my grandma. What was it she called you?

Medieval. She got no cause to say such a thing.

Medieval. Why, that's a compliment, Myra said while tapping ashes from her cigarette. Medieval means you can work miracles.

I don't care, Tessie said. It ain't nice.

Stop blubbering, Myra said. Holy Maloney!

Well, it ain't, Tessie said, and pulled a handkerchief from the pocket of her uniform and wiped her nose. What kind of miracles?

Why ask me? Myra said. I don't know. Probably any kind.

To work miracles a body needs faith.

That's true, Myra said. But you got faith enough for ten ordinary people.

I believe in the Lord.

I do, too, Myra said. Only not as much as you. I never saw anybody with more faith. I expect you could work a miracle.

That would be a calling, Tessie said.

Myra released a perfect smoke ring. Likely if you set your mind to the matter you could do it. I expect if you prayed hard enough you could be touched with the power. I wouldn't be surprised but what the Lord might bless you.

Tessie caught her lip in embarrassment and looked away.

Well, I don't see why not. Give it some thought. Only for Pete's sake stop blubbering. Seems like somebody always hurts your feelings. You do beat all. You want some gum?

Gum? No, thank you.

I believe I will, Myra said, if you don't mind. She stripped the paper from a stick, bent it double, and began chewing. Guess what! I got a chain letter.

You got what?

Chain letter. Now if you ain't the limit! Everybody knows what a chain letter is. It's where somebody sends you a letter with the names of these five other members included. So you send this first member a dollar and pretty soon other people they send you a dollar. Then after a while this list gets around all over the country—maybe all over the world—and all these members they send you a dollar. That's how it works. You get millions of dollars. Of course some people they break the chain so you don't normally receive that much.

Millions of dollars?

So they say. Emmaline who works for the Knapps in that white brick house with the Airedale—I helped out there at a party and she told me her aunt got twenty-six dollars in three weeks!

Twenty-six dollars?

Yeah, Myra said. I'd buy me a new pair of shoes. These is killing my bunions. Anyhow, what was we talking about?

Chain letters.

Myra chewed thoughtfully. No, before that. Oh! It was miracles. Well, a month or so back you was telling me you seen devils fly out of people's mouths. Now is that a fact?

People use bad words, devils fly right out.

Real ones? Horns and wings and a tail and so on?

Real as can be.

Now that's amazing, Myra said. That truly is amazing. I never could figure out what devils looked like except them pictures you see. Bats. That'd be my guess. You ought to squash a couple. That'd show you got the power. If you could do that you could work miracles all right.

It's something to think about, Tessie said.

Myra coughed and began to adjust the straps of her brassiere. Now would you just look at them pretty white clouds! Couldn't hardly be a nicer afternoon. What you got in mind for vacation?

Vacation? I hadn't give it much thought. Vacation don't come round till next summer.

I'm going to Colorado Springs, Myra said. I'm going up Pike's Peak. I always did want to go up Pike's Peak.

Colorado Springs. That must be a distance.

Colorado Springs here I come! Myra said. You never know, I could meet somebody on top of Pike's Peak.

You just might find yourself in a nasty fix.

I sure hope so, Myra said. I'm rusting away like some old tin can. Hey, let's us go to Danceland.

Danceland?

Saturday a week ago I was there and met this fellow Purvis. We did some stuff, if you know what I mean, but I didn't appreciate his attitude. He kept grabbing things and telling me let's get married and how much he loves me, but I heard that before.

You best watch out.

I don't get buffaloed, Myra said. I look out for number one. Hey, let's you and me go. I love to dance. I just hope that Purvis don't show up.

Oh, Tessie said, them fancy twirls and steps these days, I wouldn't scarcely know which way to turn.

I could teach you. Nothing to it. Also, it helps to lose a few pounds of flesh. I notice you have a tendency to put on weight. Besides, I'm dying to try out this new mascara I got called Queen of Sheba.

A place such as that don't sound decent.

You're so proper! You and Mrs. Fitzgerald. Hey, we could go bowling. Bowling alleys is full of men.

Tessie glanced at Myra's shriveled arm.

Foo! said Myra. That don't stop me. You don't need but one. Let's us go some night.

Most likely it would cost a peck.

Myra rolled her eyes. I declare I never did see the equal. One extra penny in your purse and you send it to that preacher.

Reverend Hunnicutt he serves the Lord.

Excuse me if I step on a few toes, only it wouldn't surprise me none if he lives in some big marble mansion and rides around in the back of a limousine with a chauffeur. They do, some of them. I'm not saying he's like that, if you follow me. Only some of them, they do.

Reverend Hunnicutt he spreads the Word.

Now that's a good cause, Myra said, except you don't spend nothing on yourself.

Oh, well, Tessie said. Ain't much I need.

Myra aimed a plume of smoke at a butterfly. Seems to me you'd ought to do more for number one.

Judgment is nigh. The armies of the devil is assembling this very minute at a place they call in the Hebrew language Armageddon.

Now how do you know? I believe as much as the next person, but there's stuff nobody can't be sure about such as Adam and Eve, and that's a fact. I mean, just taking the first example that come to mind, how do you know what he looks like?

Does who look like?

Myra coughed and pointed upward. What color of beard has he got? Likely gray or white, at least that's my opinion.

This annoyed Tessie. God had a beard, but talking about it did not seem right. She frowned and replied in a determined voice: His only begotten son come down to earth on our account.

I ain't about to deny that, Myra said.

The Lord is our savior even unto the end of the world.

Suppose he's watching us this very minute, how does he know what's going on over there in China? Or what them Eskimos is up to? Myra was triumphant.

That ain't none of our business. You got no cause to ask.

It don't hurt to wonder, Myra said. That's my opinion. Anyway I sure hope he's merciful because there's things I ain't too proud of. A while back there was this fellow Stanley. Him and me got acquainted at the Silver Saddle and he had this tie clip like a horse head and this diamond in one ear. I didn't treat him too nice, if you know what I mean. He was a Polack and religious as all holy Maloney—talking to God whenever he run into trouble. Anyhow that's what he told me and I felt like asking what language was it. I mean, how is God going to talk Polack?

That is just plain blasphemy, Tessie said with a severe expression.

Well, a party does wonder, Myra said. I expect I shouldn't ought to mention this, but has he got that thing? You know, the Bible says how men was made in his image, and men they got that thing. What do you figure he does with that thing all by hisself?

Shame! Tessie cried. Watch your tongue, Myra! The trumpet is fixing to sound.

Myra wagged her head. Well, if you ain't the voice of doom, I swear! You and Mr. Fitzgerald. Listening to you a person would think if it ain't Judgment Day or Satan's army it's earthquakes or floods about to drown us in our tracks or the sky falling down like some old circus tent or killer bees flying up from South America to sting us all to death or whirlwinds or I don't know what. I never in my life met anybody so full of doom as you—except Mr. Fitzgerald. With him it's the Democrats. He got more money than you could poke a stick at, only he turns red as a beet and yells how the Democrats is trying to put him in the poorhouse. He all but has hisself a stroke at the word.

He's Republican, ain't he?

I hope to tell you that man is Republican. He got so many guns in the game room I'm scared to go near. Nothing he cares more about than shooting—aiming them guns every which way. He's still mad about that Vietnam war, you know, how some of the boys run off to Canada. He says they'd ought to be shot because they was traitors to America. He's fixing to set up a flagpole over there by the barbecue pit.

Dr. Stocking he says Mr. Fitzgerald ought to be put away.

Is that how psychiatrists talk?

I heard him. Clear as a bell.

I'm surprised, Myra said. I truly am surprised. You just never know.

The way he goes on about Republicans, if he was my little boy I'd clean his mouth with soap.

The two of them don't hardly speak, I notice. What kind of car is that he drives?

Now it ain't Buick, Tessie said. I believe it come from Italy.

Myra nodded. I supposed as much. I said to myself the minute I saw that automobile there's a Democrat. I bet him and Mrs. Stocking don't even watch television. Mr. Fitzgerald swears the both of them is Communists.

Communists, Tessie said. That would be a thought.

I never did see one—not to my knowledge. Anyhow, Dr. Stocking best take care when he dresses hisself in that gorilla suit or Mr. Fitzgerald will shoot him. I like to suffered a heart attack first time I seen it. Maybe he's the one ought to be locked up. What kind of normal person puts on a gorilla suit? Answer me that! Myra tapped the ash from her cigarette. I wouldn't mind borrowing it, though. I sure could scare the lights out of that Purvis. Hey, you want to see the moose Mr. Fitzgerald shot? Ugliest thing that ever was. He got the head stuffed or whatever they do and stuck up over the fireplace.

I don't care for such things, Tessie said. Thank you anyway. My little brother Gaius he was a hunter, always bringing home squirrel and rabbit.

I never did taste squirrel. Rabbit braised in wine is real tasty, though. Gaius, there's a nice name.

He's a sailor.

So you told me. You told me one day he packed up and left the farm without hardly a word. Is that right?

Goodby and off he went. Gaius, he was the quiet one.

A sailor. Fancy that.

He's been just about everyplace on earth, I expect. China and I don't know where all. He sent me this picture postcard of some heathen temple. Did I show you?

Twice, Myra said impatiently. I wished I had a brother, but there wasn't nobody in the family except me. Sailing around, that's what I'd do if I was a man. I wouldn't stop for nothing. Anyhow, I ain't, so that's that.

The Lord knows best.

I suppose, Myra said with a gloomy expression, but it don't seem right men get all the fun. I bet anything Dr. Stocking can go a hundred miles an hour at least in that automobile. Boomer, sometimes he lets me drive his Ford pickup.

Who's Boomer?

I guess you never met. I'll introduce you when we get better acquainted. Myra stopped chewing and stood on one foot. I might slip off these shoes if you don't mind. Them bunions is murder.

Feel free, said Tessie. I do the same.

Thank you, Myra said and stepped out of her shoes. Excuse me for getting personal, but is Tessie your real name? I was always afraid to ask because it ain't none of my business, only now seemed a good time. I don't mean to pry.

It's Therese.

Therese. That's real pretty. I wish I had a pretty name.

Myra's pretty.

It's common—like I wasn't nothing.

Well, you're not common. You're very special. I think you're a very special person.

Thank you. I could call you Therese.

Oh, now, Tessie said, that ain't necessary.

I don't feel like my name ought to be what it is. I do feel special, though. Thank you. Nobody before ever told me I was.

What do you feel your name ought to be?

Jacqueline.

That's pretty, too.

I ought to of been named Jacqueline. I can see pulling up to Danceland in one of them automobiles with a convertible roof and the men, they'd be crawling over theirselves like I was the queen bee. Myra shuddered. "Oh! Oh!" they'd say. "Here comes Jacqueline!" You know what I'd do? I'd honk the horn and drive off. Leave them standing there bug-eyed, every last one. That's what I'd do.

Tessie thought about this with her lips pursed.

Hey, how much you suppose that automobile cost?

That automobile? I don't have no idea, Tessie said. Quite a sum, though.

I expect, Myra said while smoothing her eyebrows. Dr. Stocking he must do right well listening to all them lunatics.

Tessie frowned. The Lord Jesus can heal. Folks as bring their troubles to the Lord got no cause to spend a dime.

I sure wish the Lord would fix this arm, Myra said. I used to pray when I was little, asking Jesus to make me like everybody else, only nothing happened so I quit. I mean, there's got to be certain things beyond the Lord's power.

Jesus is Lord, Tessie replied in a confident voice. Ain't nothing beyond His power.

Well, foo! Ask the Lord to make me no different.

That'd take a miracle.

You got the faith. Give it a try.

Tessie looked doubtful. Somehow that don't seem right.

Myra lifted her withered arm. See if you can do it. What have I got to lose? And at that instant a ray of sunshine broke through the clouds.

Jesus! Tessie screamed. Jesus God!

What's going on? Myra asked.

Tessie clasped her hands. Sweet Jesus! Come round to this side, Myra. The Lord is here.

Myra slipped on her shoes, opened the gate and walked through the hedge.

He is here, Tessie whispered. Do you feel His presence?

I don't know, Myra said. I guess so.

Praise Him!

Praise the Lord, Myra said. Are you sure?

Tessie whimpered and trembled. Lord! I got the rapture! She pointed at Myra's arm.

What's happening? Myra asked.

Lift up thine eyes!

Myra squinted at the clouds.

Kneel down! Tessie shouted.

Boy oh boy, Myra said, this is nuts.

Tessie gripped her arm with both hands and started to pull.

Ouch! Myra said. That hurts!

Thy will be done! Tessie cried.

Let go, said Myra.

Don't it feel longer?

For the love of Pete, Myra said. The spirit sure enough got you. Let go.

How does it feel?

About as usual, Myra said. Anyhow, that's enough. Let go.

Tessie was breathing passionately. Can't you feel it? Don't it feel longer?

Sweet gooseberries, Myra said. Do you know what you're talking about?

Alleluia, Tessie murmured with her eyes closed. Oh my! Oh dear me! Thank you, Jesus. Dear Lord, thank you. Through the open window of the breakfast room she could hear Tweetwee chirping.

I believe! Tweetwee sang. I believe! I believe!

All at once Tessie understood that she was able to speak a marvelous foreign language. A torrent of strange words poured unexpectedly from her tongue and when she gazed upward she saw God on His throne looking down with approval.

1993

MRS. PROCTOR BEMIS

MRS. PROCTOR BEMIS—lineal descendant of a Revolutionary War general, wife of a Kansas City merchant prince, mother of two boys and a girl who would inherit the Bemis fortune as well as the farm implements company founded by grandfather Suddarth—Mrs. Bemis, in spite of her social eminence, distinguished lineage, prominent husband, attractive children, and stately home, was exasperated; and what further exasperated her was the knowledge that her husband did not share this feeling. He, on the contrary, looked as complacent as an overfed dachshund.

Mrs. Bemis, angrily watching her husband while he lounged in his favorite chair beside the fireplace reading the Kansas City *Star,* thought about General Benjamin Suddarth—friend and neighbor of George Washington—whose gold-framed portrait by Rembrandt Peale hung in the dining room like a religious icon. It seemed to her that if General Suddarth were alive he would do something about the violence and liberalism that threatened to destroy society. General Suddarth would insist upon capital punishment for dangerous criminals instead of patting them on the wrist. General Suddarth would sweep the streets clean of beggars, thieves, drug addicts, vandals, prostitutes, alcoholics, and pornographers. He would restore pride and dignity to the United States. He would abolish the food stamp program. He would crush welfare cheats as though they were insects. And the graffiti was awful. General Suddarth would do something about that.

Mrs. Bemis, vexed by the lack of expression on her husband's face, demanded to know how he was able to sit there reading the paper.

Mr. Bemis did not find this question unreasonable. They had been married a good many years and he was seldom disconcerted by anything she said even when he could make no sense of it. He peered over the top of his spectacles as he waited for her to continue.

In the grocery, Mrs. Bemis said while trying to restrain the anger she felt, I saw a young couple buying everything they could put their hands on. They paid for most of it with food stamps.

Mr. Bemis waited attentively because he expected more, but that was all she said. He nodded, cleared his throat, and returned to the newspaper.

Mrs. Bemis thought about going to the dining room to speak with General Suddarth. Large areas of the Midwest were flooded because there had been weeks of rain. Television showed vast tracts of midwestern farmland inundated. The Mississippi, Missouri, Ohio, and any number of tributaries were overflowing, thousands of people had been driven from their homes; yet this young couple, without a care in the world, had bought imported cheese and wine. They had been laughing while they rolled the grocery cart up one aisle and down another. Mrs. Bemis had followed them and had seen them pick up whatever appealed to them; she had followed them to the checkout counter and had seen the young man give food stamps to the cashier. He appeared to be in perfect health, perfectly able to work for a living. So was the girl. Why were they entitled to food stamps?

This outrage reminded Mrs. Bemis of the President. She had been willing to give the man a chance, despite the fact that his private life was a disgrace and everybody knew what would happen if he was elected. Now, of course, taxes were being raised. And how would this money be used? To support loafers and chiselers.

Chrysler plunged two-and-a-half, said Mr. Bemis. I don't like the way things are shaping up. That damn Fed chief. I'd better give Eliot a call.

Is he a Democrat? Mrs. Bemis asked.

Is who a Democrat?

Whoever you were talking about.

The chairman of the Federal Reserve? I have no idea. Why?

I was just wondering, Mrs. Bemis said. She closed her eyes and lightly massaged her temples while she thought about two young Negroes she had seen drifting around the Plaza. Apparently they belonged to a gang because they wore baggy trousers and nylon jackets with some kind of insignia and baseball caps turned backward. They had no business on the Plaza. The police should have questioned them, but the police did nothing. Once upon a time the Plaza had been charming. People were well dressed and polite. Now it was unsafe. Shoppers had been accosted by alcoholic beggars and shabby eccentrics—which was the reason Mrs. Bemis carried a whistle in her purse. If someone had suggested a few years ago that she carry a whistle she would have been puzzled, but times had changed. Now there were mysterious symbols and ominous messages spray-painted on park benches and trash cans and mailboxes. Kansas City had been quite different while she was growing up. Of course there had been a certain amount of vandalism and crime—burglaries, an occasional murder in the North End—but nothing serious in the Country Club district.

The situation on the Plaza has become just intolerable, she said. Almost anything could happen.

Her husband did not respond.

Mrs. Bemis frowned as she thought about the colored boys. They had a legal right to be on the Plaza, yet there was no good reason for them to be there. They did not intend to buy anything. She had followed them and knew they did not intend to buy; they were loitering, gawking at displays in the shop windows. They might have been planning a burglary. They might have been armed. They were not the first Negroes she had observed in the Country Club district but these two were by far the least presentable. Obviously they did not care how they looked. Years ago they would have been rounded up and warned not to come back, otherwise they would be arrested as vagrants. Their attitude said all too clearly that they would go where they pleased, and their presence in an area where they did not belong was menacing. Mrs. Bemis had carried the whistle in her hand while she followed them.

Mr. Bemis abruptly lowered the newspaper. Marguerite, he said, what could happen on the Plaza?

There have been so many incidents. Just the other day Helen Gamble saw a man loitering near the entrance to Swanson's.

Why don't you carry a gun? That tin whistle wouldn't scare a chickadee.

This annoyed Mrs. Bemis. In case of emergency she would be able to alert bystanders to what was happening, but she did not want to carry a gun. A man should protect his family so it was appropriate for a man to carry a gun, but it would be inappropriate for a woman. Besides, he was joking. Nancy Reagan reportedly carried a pistol and for some reason he was amused by this.

She decided to think about how nice Kansas City had been when she was a child. How very secure she had felt. How pleasant and comfortable everything used to be. She thought about her parents. She thought about her brown and white dog Hopscotch. She remembered one Sunday in April when all of them got into the car, including Hopscotch, and they drove to Swope Park for a picnic. She had made a collar of dandelions for Hopscotch and a butterfly landed on the potato salad. Now everything was different. So much was unfamiliar. Movies used to be entertaining, but now they emphasized violence or sex. Popular music was romantic and couples danced together, but now the young musicians seemed to lunge and shout while people danced alone. Artists painted women with lopsided faces. What did it mean?

I feel sick about Robin moving in with that boy, she said.

Ah, said Mr. Bemis from behind the paper and it sounded as though he had yawned.

What they are doing is indecent. If they live together they should get married. He is taking advantage of Robin.

Umm, said Mr. Bemis.

Why is she supporting him? Why doesn't the boy get a job?

Alex wants to paint and Robin tells me she doesn't mind working.

I realize that times change, Mrs. Bemis said, but I cannot begin to tell you how much I disapprove of this arrangement. It is immoral.

They're happy, said Mr. Bemis. Let them alone.

Mrs. Bemis plucked anxiously at her necklace. It isn't right, she said. If they are in love they ought to get married and Alex should look for work. What will happen if she becomes pregnant?

Mr. Bemis sighed.

I don't care for his paintings, Mrs. Bemis said. I don't pretend to be an art critic, but I think they are hideous. Who on earth would buy them?

Why ask me? said Mr. Bemis.

He hasn't sold a single one. Do you think he's a Communist?

Ten years ago, Communism. Today, enlightenment. Alex and Robin probably eat carrots and meditate.

We never behaved like that when we were young.

You didn't know me when I rode a motorcycle, said Mr. Bemis.

Well, I do not approve, Mrs. Bemis said. I thought Robin would marry Tyler Pence. They went around together for such a long time. I felt sure they would become engaged.

Mr. Bemis rustled the paper. Marguerite, listen to this. Members of the school board in Tavares, Florida, wherever the hell that is, after reciting the pledge of allegiance to the flag, voted to teach Lake County students that American values are superior to all others. New policy shall include and instill appreciation of patriotism, free enterprise, freedom of religion, et cetera. One board member says teaching supremacy will make the boys enthusiastic about going to war.

Don't you think America is worth defending? Mrs. Bemis asked. I certainly do. And anybody who burns our flag ought to be prosecuted.

That's what Hitler thought.

I do not care what Hitler thought. This isn't Germany.

Madame Chairman of the Tavares board objects to deep-breathing exercises which could induce in the student an altered state of mind. Also, they figured out a way to save money—dropped sex-education program for retarded kids.

There is no reason for sex to be discussed in school, Mrs. Bemis said. It encourages children to experiment. Nothing but trouble can result. She twisted her wedding ring and frowned, wondering if the colored boys were retarded. That would explain why their shoelaces were untied and why they shuffled aimlessly around the Plaza. It was a shame the Negro district didn't have better schools. The boys might be able to make something of themselves if they received a good education, so it wasn't altogether their fault. America was not perfect by any means. Colored people were discriminated against, which wasn't right; they should have the same opportunities as everyone else. But it did seem that at times they went out of their way to cause trouble. The boys had been encroaching and they knew it.

She remembered a big Negro who passed her on the sidewalk while she was going to the post office. He brushed by so closely that she could smell him. He had almost touched her. She had been afraid that he might follow her. Inside the post office she spent more time than necessary, and before going outside she took the whistle from her purse. Of course he might have meant no harm, but he did come unusually close—as though he intended to frighten her.

Why is it, she asked herself, that so many colored people were changing their names? And why did some pretend to be Muslims? They were Christian, probably Baptist, so why should they adopt outlandish Arabic names and pretend to be what they were not? Supposedly it had to do with resentment over the way their ancestors were treated, which was understandable. But what did they expect to accomplish by changing their names? Apparently they were determined to make an issue of the past.

Then—just as vividly as if they were on a movie screen—Mrs. Bemis saw the welfare cheats. She watched the young man select a bottle of wine and saw him roll his eyes at the girl, who laughed. It was quite obvious what they intended to do. And who would pay for their enjoyment? At a time when taxes should be cut, what did this Administration want? Middle-class citizens who did not ask for government help were expected to support idle young men, unwed mothers, the United Nations, socialized medicine, career criminals, foreign aid programs, missions to Mars, and whatever else appealed to the left wing. Mrs. Bemis angrily drew in her breath and closed her eyes. What earthly reason could there be for supporting the United Nations? Foreign governments had no business telling America what to do. General Suddarth would put a stop to such nonsense. However, ultra liberals controlled the media and Congress and now they had gotten into the White House. Nobody should be surprised that taxes were going up or that good manners had become a thing of the past. Conservative values were ridiculed or ignored. Abortion had been legalized, although it was a crime and a sin. Pornography was displayed on magazine racks. Homosexuals boasted of their unnatural acts and lobbied for special privileges. Homosexuals. The word itself was disgusting. Why would a normal person decide to become homosexual? Mrs. Bemis shook her head. Nothing made sense. America was no longer one nation under God. School prayer had been prohibited and children were taught evolution because the textbooks were written by secular humanists.

I'll be damned, Mr. Bemis said. Get this. Two kids in upstate New York killed a swan. Broke the bird's legs and stabbed it forty times. Forty times! Cut off the head. Swan's legs snapped just like twigs, according to the younger kid. Umm, they left the bird's head on the steps of a police station.

Mrs. Bemis grimaced. Why would anybody want to kill a swan?

Mayor of the town says people demand maximum punishment for the kids. Death threats and so forth.

How old are they?

Fifteen. Seventeen. Father of one kid says he can't understand the big brouhaha. "All this over a duck," he says.

But why did they do it?

Drinking. Jumped a fence, caught the swan, broke its legs, stabbed it. Younger kid told police he blacked out, claims he doesn't remember much.

Proctor, in Heaven's name, what is happening? Has the world gone mad?

Umm, said Mr. Bemis.

Well, Mrs. Bemis remarked after a long silence, I agree with the townspeople. Those young hoodlums ought to be paddled within an inch of their lives and locked up until they learn to behave. Alcohol is no excuse.

It occurred to her that instead of being punished the boys probably would be released on probation. No doubt a psychiatrist would testify that because they had been drinking they should not be held responsible. That happened so frequently. No matter what crime had been committed there would be a psychiatrist to explain why the offender was innocent. What he had done wasn't his fault because he had been unable to control his emotions. In fact, so they argued, the criminal himself was a victim because he suffered from depression or multiple personality disorders, or drug withdrawal symptoms, parental abuse, alcoholism—one thing or another. It was infuriating. Criminals ought to be imprisoned and they should not be released. Most crimes were committed by a small percentage of the population so it would make sense to keep those men in jail, but they always seemed to get out. Again and again and again they were pardoned or released on parole, which only encouraged them to continue robbing and murdering. No sooner was one locked up than some psychiatrist or clever attorney or liberal judge would find a reason to let him out. This was absurd. If the prisons were crowded, which might well be true, why not build more? Tax money was wasted on all sorts of ridiculous social programs. Why should the federal or state government subsidize artists, for example, when ordinary citizens were afraid to walk the streets? Why not use that money to build prisons? The federal government ought to maintain the armed services and the interstate highway system; everything else could be left up to individual states and local communities.

Teamsters, Mr. Bemis muttered. Picketing the Fairfield assembly plant.

I do not approve of picketing, Mrs. Bemis said. They should settle their differences some other way. Those strikes usually end in violence.

She had expressed her feelings about pickets and strikes quite a few times in the past, but it was worth repeating. Unions were legal and the law must be obeyed, even though union members themselves frequently violated the law. Of course nobody should be forced to join a union. If a laborer decided to join, that was his privilege, but those who did not wish to become members should not be denied an opportunity to work—which happened quite often. Union members blocked the entrances to factories, jeered and threw stones, overturned cars, and attacked people who wanted to work. This was not right. Everybody knew this was not right, but the union leaders did not care about anything except getting their way. And most of them were corrupt.

I wish General Suddarth were alive, she said.

Umm, Mr. Bemis replied. Ha! Star Wars budget reduced. Reagan's Maginot Line in the sky could be kaput.

Proctor, that makes me simply furious! Liberals waste our tax dollars coddling criminals and Heaven knows what else when the money ought to be spent on national defense. We could be attacked at any moment.

By whom?

This exasperated Mrs. Bemis; she waved the question aside. We ought to be prepared. Russia cannot be trusted. Stalin was worse than Hitler. We've got to remain on guard. Is there anything in the paper about tax reduction?

Not likely, Mr. Bemis muttered. Well, well, another JFK book.

That's one I can do without, Mrs. Bemis said. Why must they glamorize him? He should have been imprisoned.

Why not the whole bunch?

The Kennedys?

All those humbugs we put in the White House.

I thought you meant the Kennedys.

JFK and Bobby worried folks, no doubt about it. More than once I've heard somebody say Oswald deserved a medal.

I don't approve of assassination, Mrs. Bemis said, but I most certainly do not approve of immoral conduct. That is one thing I find inexcusable.

Mr. Bemis gave her a peculiar look and she turned away. John Kennedy had been promiscuous and she could remember what she felt—along with shock—at the news of his death. She remembered feeling that he had gotten what he deserved. His behavior was disgusting. And he had been Catholic just like all the Kennedys. They might not be Jews or atheists, but neither were they true Christians.

I admired President Nixon, she said.

Tricky Dick, said Mr. Bemis. Nine lives.

The liberal press was always after him. It made me so mad. He was one of the first to point out the threat of Communism. He and Senator McCarthy. I suppose that's why the liberals were out to get him. They hated him because they knew he wasn't afraid to stand up for America. He should never have been forced to resign. I wish he could have remained in office forever. I always believed he was telling the truth about Watergate. And of course he did put an end to the Vietnam war.

She tried to remember when the war had ended. The draft evaders would be middle-aged by now. A few of them probably were still living in Canada and it would be just as well if they never came home. They had given aid and comfort to the enemy. They were traitors. The United States did everything imaginable to help South Vietnam and if the country had remained united behind President Nixon the war effort would have been successful. But Communist sympathizers had organized riots and protest marches and the liberal media supported them. How many American soldiers died because North Vietnam thought those protesters represented America? And somebody in the Pentagon had stolen classified documents. Mrs. Bemis tried to think of his name, but could not. Whoever he was, he had made the situation worse.

She thought about the long-haired filthy students taunting President Nixon, the subversive peace symbols, the caricatures and horrid photos—the naked Vietnamese girl seared by napalm, the televised execution of a handcuffed prisoner, the embarrassing helicopter escape. And at these memories she felt almost as irritated as she had felt during the war.

What we did was right! she said bitterly. We have nothing to be ashamed of. We were only trying to help.

Ancient history, Mr. Bemis remarked. Vietnam sounds like the Peloponnesian War except when some farmer trips over an old mine or an unexploded bomb.

He was referring to a television special. The pictures of mutilated children and peasants had been horrifying. Mrs. Bemis gazed out the window. I suppose all they can do is watch where they're going, she said. But don't you agree that our intentions were good?

I do, I do, he agreed, although his tone indicated that he would prefer to read the paper.

Mrs. Bemis, with hands folded in her lap, reflected on the amount of time she had spent watching newscasts and listening to various analysts explain why North Vietnam would lose the war. It would be impossible, they had explained, for a small impoverished country like North Vietnam to defeat the most powerful nation on earth. She thought about the pictures of huge bombers dropping what appeared to be tiny sticks on Hanoi. Emaciated little captives—none of whom seemed to be more than five feet tall—were guarded by brawny American soldiers.

Mrs. Bemis suddenly realized that her husband was talking about a Presbyterian conference in Minneapolis. Two thousand women had convened to discuss and celebrate feminine religious beliefs.

Ritual affirming the sensuality of women, he said. Shared milk and honey. Laughed at patriarchal traditions. Methodists there, too. Well, well. "Our maker Sophia, we are women in your image. With the hot blood of our wombs we give form to new life. With nectar between our thighs we invite a lover." So on and so forth. Warm body fluids remind the world of its pleasures and sensations. Revolutionary way of perceiving God.

Everybody has gone insane, said Mrs. Bemis.

Sophia a personification of God found in the Book of Proverbs. "I was set up, at the first, before the beginning of the earth"—whatever that's supposed to mean. Conference organizers insist the meeting was a thoroughly Christian effort to dramatize a feminine Biblical metaphor. Ha! One speaker invited lesbian, bisexual, and transsexual women to join her on stage. Denounced as blasphemous by evangelical wing of the church. Ha! I'll bet!

Mrs. Bemis, with lips pursed, wondered about the women in Minneapolis. That they should publicly celebrate their immorality seemed not just vulgar but a deliberate attempt to offend and shock respectable people. They were nearly as perverted as men. She remembered a poetry festival on television where an old man with a white beard chanted about his love for adolescent boys. Now, of course, those homosexuals were diseased and ought to be quarantined. Why were they permitted to infect other people? Negroes and Communists and homosexuals and every other minority under the sun insisted upon their so-called rights, but what about the rights of decent men and women?

It isn't fair, she said.

Her husband did not reply and she discovered that he had left the room. Perhaps he had gone to call Eliot about the stock market. She closed her eyes and imagined Kansas City as it had been many years ago. She thought of a green bicycle she got for Christmas, and Hugh Puckett who gave her an orchid, and her best friend Chessie. She remembered pedaling around Mission Hills with Chessie, who had a blue bicycle. One afternoon they stopped beside a pond to watch some boys who were fishing. After a while they tossed pebbles at the boys and rode away as fast as they could. She thought about the neighbors and the colored maid, and Francisco who came around once a month during summer to cut the grass. She remembered vacations at Lake Quivira when the children were small, and the time Robin sprained her ankle. The time Peter was arrested for speeding. Mark's beautiful wedding. None of it seemed so terribly long ago. In those days Kansas City was quiet and safe. People were courteous. Nobody used drugs. Maybe some of the colored people did, and perhaps a few Italians in the North End, but drugs had been unknown in the residential area. There were no lesbians, bisexuals, or women masquerading as men. There weren't any male homosexuals. There had been two or three effeminate boys in high school and one of them was chased into a vacant lot by some football players and given a bloody nose, otherwise the sissies were ignored. Most of the boys had been nice. Several of them drank and drove too fast, but none of them carried knives or guns. There wasn't much vandalism, except at Halloween. There weren't any beggars in the Country Club district. There weren't any armed guards in the banks, or television cameras or security guards in the shops.

Mr. Bemis grunted. Mrs. Bemis opened her eyes and noticed that he had returned with a drink.

Immigrants, he said. Boatload of Chinese got ashore near San Francisco. Scattered like rats.

I do not understand how that can happen, Mrs. Bemis said. How many were there?

Who knows? Dozens. Hundreds.

Can't anything be done?

Pai gow fat chance, Mr. Bemis said. They probably had fake identification cards before they jumped ship. Relatives in Chinatown. How do you catch them?

Immigration laws ought to be enforced, Mrs. Bemis answered in a determined voice because it seemed to her that the Coast Guard had not done its job. Possibly the Coast Guard didn't have enough ships, but somehow these illegal aliens ought to be stopped, otherwise more and more would arrive and the economy would suffer. Mexicans waded across the Rio Grande, boatloads of Negroes sailed up from the Caribbean, and hordes of Orientals—Chinese especially—managed to elude the Coast Guard. It was not right. They knew they could earn more money in the United States so what they did was understandable but they ought to be stopped. Immigration laws meant nothing to them, all they cared about was getting in. Quotas were necessary because there must be limits, and the law should be obeyed.

Couple of juveniles found a corpse near the railroad tracks, Mr. Bemis said. Can you guess what they did? Reported a body to the cops? Wrong. They toyed with it—poked it with sticks—invited their pals to have a look.

Mrs. Bemis sighed. Proctor, what is going on? What is wrong with those children?

Where are they leading us? Mr. Bemis asked.

The educational system is to blame, Mrs. Bemis said. Discipline has become a thing of the past. And as she considered this it seemed undeniable. The lack of discipline in schools was appalling so the children did as they pleased and neglected their studies. They learned almost nothing. Permissive educational policies were devastating. High school graduates scarcely knew how to spell. Few of them could put together a coherent sentence. Some of them would be unable to find the

United States on a map of the world. Some could not do elementary arithmetic. They had no manners, no ambition, no education. European schools might be just as good as American schools, possibly better. Yet these rude, self-indulgent, hostile American children would be awarded diplomas because the liberals did not believe anybody should fail.

Mister Softee murdered.

What? said Mrs. Bemis.

Philadelphia. Ice cream truck driver robbed and murdered. Customers laughed while he bled to death.

You are making this up, Mrs. Bemis said.

First came familiar music of the truck, then an argument. Gunfire while the music tinkled on. Word spread that Mister Softee was shot. Iranian immigrant with three kids, first week on the job. Undisclosed amount of cash stolen. Group of teenagers improvised songs about the dying driver. Sounds like a ghetto neighborhood.

We need more police, Mrs. Bemis said. We need more and more and more police, that's all there is to it. This sort of thing seems to happen day and night.

Send for the Marines, Mr. Bemis said. Swamp the country with gung-ho leathernecks.

That might not be a bad idea, Mrs. Bemis said, although I'm sure the ACLU would object. Why do they wear beards?

Mr. Bemis lowered the paper. Beards?

Every single one of them. I realize that during the nineteenth century it was normal for a man to have a beard, but we do not live in the nineteenth century. I assume they are attempting to make some kind of political statement, but they look silly.

Who are we talking about?

You know perfectly well who I mean. Those ACLU lawyers. All of them wear beards and they always stand up for the troublemakers.

And this reminded Mrs. Bemis of how she despised socialists. She remembered Harry Bridges who had come to the United States from Australia and was forever organizing strikes on the west coast, just as Eugene Debs and other socialists had tried to overthrow capitalism early in the century. They were not satisfied unless they caused trouble and most of them secretly belonged to the Communist party. They should have been deported or imprisoned. Instead of being grateful to America they attempted to destroy it. They had no respect for private property, they did not want anybody to succeed. They wanted to take everything away from those who were willing to work and give it to those who did nothing. And there had been Roosevelt to back them up. And then more Democrats—which resulted in more government interference with the lives of ordinary citizens. Now the middle class was being taxed out of existence. Why should those who had worked hard throughout their lives be expected to subsidize abortions for lazy unmarried colored women? The minute those women got out of the hospital they became pregnant again because they knew the government would provide. And some of them already had five or six children but no husband. Why should decent citizens pay for the rehabilitation of drug addicts who had nobody to blame except themselves? Why should respectable people be obliged to support idlers and cheats who had no self-respect? But of course that was what liberal socialists wanted and if they got their way the nation would go bankrupt. Liberals were anxious to spend every cent. Tax and spend. That was how they reasoned. But why not use tax money sensibly? Marijuana and other drugs were grown in South America and smuggled into the United States, so why not cancel offensive programs such as the National Endowment for the Arts and use that money to curtail drug production? It should not be difficult to locate the fields and it should not be difficult for the Air Force to bomb them. That ought to teach the drug dealers a lesson.

Proctor, Mrs. Bemis said, when the United States invaded Panama didn't it have something to do with drugs?

Mr. Bemis cleared his throat. As I recall, the problem would be solved if we could apprehend Noriega.

But it seems to have gotten worse.

That's right. Our troops accomplished their mission and now you can buy heroin from your friendly neighborhood dealer.

Well, Mrs. Bemis said after thinking about this, I'm sure President Bush knew what he was doing.

Mr. Bemis nodded and murmured to prove that he was listening. Pre-dawn vertical insertion, he said a few moments later.

What?

Panama reminded me of Grenada. According to the Pentagon, Reagan's attack on Grenada was a pre-dawn vertical insertion.

Mrs. Bemis realized that she had practically forgotten about Grenada. She frowned, trying to remember. There had been some American medical students on the island who asked to be rescued—or was that right? And it had been necessary to bomb a mental hospital. Or was the hospital bombed by mistake? In any case, it happened quite a while ago and no longer mattered; President Reagan had taken care of the situation. She tossed her hands in despair. At times, Proctor, I believe you go out of your way to provoke me!

Umm, he said. Nasty situation in Walla Walla. State decided to hang somebody but the fellow wouldn't cooperate. Struggled. Had to spray him with pepper and strap him to a board. Strapped to a board—ye Gods! Sprayed with pepper? Death penalty supporters outside the gate whooping and cheering. Prison authority complained, said an air of decorum should prevail. Two hundred and forty-first execution since capital punishment resumed in 1976.

I have no idea what the man did, Mrs. Bemis remarked, but I'm glad he wasn't paroled. He got just what he deserved.

Another one in North Carolina. Gas chamber. Cyanide. Fellow dressed in diapers and socks. Socks? Damned if I understand the socks. Sounds like a fraternity initiation. Face covered by leather mask. Screams continued five minutes.

I don't believe that, Mrs. Bemis said. The man does not feel a thing. After one breath he simply goes to sleep.

Supreme Court earlier rejected argument that gas chamber is cruel and unusual. Harry Blackmun dissented.

Both men should have received lethal injections, Mrs. Bemis said. Lethal injections are painless and merciful.

Mr. Bemis silently turned a page.

Capital punishment was a deterrent. Common sense proved this beyond a doubt and there was no reason the sentence should not be carried out at once. Why did murderers have a right to appeal? A person convicted of a terrible crime had absolutely no rights. Sooner or later there would be more justices like Blackmun. Then, of course, one vicious criminal after another would be pardoned or paroled in order to attack somebody else.

Proctor, she said, what do you suppose will become of the middle class?

Ah, Marguerite, he said, that's a provocative question.

Do you know the answer?

Mr. Bemis reached for his drink. No, he said. No, I don't.

You are so blasé. You can be utterly maddening.

Mr. Bemis swirled the ice in his glass.

Proctor, she continued in a firm voice, the time has come for us to sell our stocks. Every single one.

Mr. Bemis was astonished. What? Why? For God's sake, Marguerite, are you losing your mind?

I think we would be safer owning gold.

If the market crashes it'll recover.

But I just don't know what might happen. I dreamt of General Suddarth.

Ah, said Mr. Bemis. And how is the old boy?

You think I'm overwrought. You think there must be something the matter with me. Do you find nothing wrong with gangs of hoodlums roaming the streets and pornographic films and drive-by shootings and child molesters and drugs and soaring taxes and a President whose personal life is a national disgrace? Do you think I am hysterical?

Not in the least, Mr. Bemis said. We're going to hell in a handbasket. As he said this he glanced across his spectacles and felt surprised because the face of the woman he had known intimately for so many years conveyed something unexpected. It seemed to him that he was looking at a confused, terrified child. The dangers of the world—dangers both real and imaginary—had overwhelmed her. She had withdrawn. In the wrinkled face of this woman with whom he had lived for such a long time were the eyes of a child wakened by a threatening sound in the night. He felt touched and dismayed by her anxiety.

Mrs. Bemis covered her face with both hands. I'm so upset, she whispered through her fingers. I'm afraid to have lunch on the Plaza.

Yes, well, he said uneasily.

I want Hopscotch.

What? he asked. You want what?

1994

CANTINFLAS
AND THE COP

V IRDEN STUDIED the red dots on his handkerchief as if they were specimens under a microscope. Twice he had been hit in the mouth and this was the result. The dots puzzled him because he had expected more blood. Gently he touched his lower lip with a fingertip but could not feel anything unusual; the lip was not swollen. His briefcase had fallen into the gutter so he picked it up and continued walking.

When he entered the lobby of the Meridian Plaza it seemed to him that people were aware of what had happened and were amused or contemptuous. He brushed his sleeve and walked rapidly through the lobby toward the grill with an air of haughty indifference. Ascher and Guthrie were at a corner table. As he approached he could hear Ascher talking about KLM options while Guthrie frowned at the menu.

Sorry to be late, Virden said, I was delayed at the office. He dropped the briefcase on an empty chair and seated himself.

Why don't they ever change this thing? Guthrie asked. The chef has no more imagination than my wife.

Virden took a deep breath and opened the menu.

Last week you were touting Bendix, Ascher continued. You catch the report in yesterday's *Journal?*

Guthrie ran a palm over his nearly bald head and looked thoughtful. Earnings are pretty good. Equity rising. It might be close to a bottom.

Risky, risky. Too much debt and all that preferred. I like KLM.

Fuel goes out of sight if the Saudis cut production.

No chance. Those sheiks trust each other like spiders in a bottle. So what's your latest table-pounding buy?

Zamboanga platinum futures, Guthrie said. How the hell do I know? The last company I recommended struck an iceberg. He sighed and loosened his belt. I never thought I'd be eight months pregnant. I used to have a stomach like a washboard. I could do fifty push-ups. He beckoned to the waiter. How's the shrimp remoulade?

An excellent choice, sir. Excellent.

Make that two, Virden said while brushing his sleeve. And a glass of chardonnay.

Turkey club sandwich and mineral water, Ascher said. Inflation at this level, what in God's name is the Fed up to? That's what I want to know.

Hocus pocus. Crystal ball experts, Guthrie said. Our research department predicts a gradual strengthening.

Where have I heard that before? Last fall it was up-trend, up-trend. Everybody was singing up-trend. Then what? We drop almost five hundred points. I wanted to hide under my desk. I thought about switching to real estate. Ascher reached for a bread stick and smeared it with butter. I didn't eat enough breakfast. I'm starving. Bob Faldo told me to short the domestic oils. Did I listen? Coulda, shoulda, didn't. Hey, one of my clients is hot for a drug issue called Celtron. What have you heard?

They landed a high-profile CEO but their first product is pre-clinical. It's at least three years from market. Tell your client to buy bingo tickets.

I wasn't delayed at the office, Virden said. I got in a fight.

Guthrie and Ascher stopped talking.

Actually, I didn't get in a fight. If you want to know the truth, I was hit in the face, that's all. It's quite simple.

Guthrie and Ascher stared at him.

This isn't a joke, Virden said. I'm in no mood to joke. He thought about showing them the handkerchief but changed his mind. He took off his glasses and began to polish them with a napkin. The whole thing came as a shock, he said carefully. I wasn't prepared, as you might imagine. He glanced from one to the other before hooking on his glasses.

Ascher pointed the bread stick at him. You got hit in the face?

Virden tilted back in his chair. He noticed that he could see himself in a mirror across the room and he felt surprised by his appearance—as though nothing had happened. He straightened his tie. I had left the office and crossed the street, he said while watching himself. I was on my way here—more or less preoccupied—when a filthy bum grabbed my arm. It didn't amount to anything. I don't know why I mentioned it. What do you think of those GM warrants?

Why did he hit you?

Why? I'm not sure. Presumably because I wouldn't give him any money. It wasn't as though he simply asked for spare change, it was more like a hold-up. I thought he might have a knife.

Mamma mia! Guthrie said.

Virden tried to smile. I decided the best thing to do was ignore him and hope he would go away, but he walked along beside me calling me every name in the book. He smelled like a cesspool. I couldn't believe it. Then he grabbed my sleeve so I pulled loose and that's when he hit me. As a matter of fact, he hit me twice. It didn't amount to much.

He must have been high on something, Ascher said. These days it could be grandma's cologne. Here we go, bub, don't take this personally. Blap! So after he hit you, what?

Virden coughed into his fist before answering. Well, as you might imagine, I was astonished.

So what did you do?

I asked him to let me alone.

What? You did what? Ascher was incredulous. Asked him to let you alone? Tell me, sir, when did you leave Turnip Junction?

He caught me off guard, Virden said angrily and thought again about showing the handkerchief.

So where did he hit you?

Virden pointed to his lip.

Guthrie's pumpkin features assumed a theatrical squint: No damage, you handsome dog.

It's a bit sensitive, Virden said, but I'm not asking for condolences. I just have trouble believing somebody assaulted me. I mean, I was near the entrance to Mayberry's and there were people all around but everybody ignored what was going on. I felt like the invisible man. The bum was so small that at first I assumed he was a child.

Black?

Brown. He had a wispy mustache—just a few hairs at the corners of his mouth. He reminded me of Cantinflas.

Who's Cantinflas? said Ascher.

Sort of a Mexican Charlie Chaplin, Guthrie said. You're too young to remember. The Mexicans thought he was hilarious.

There was nothing hilarious about this punk, Virden said. I asked him several times to let me alone but for some reason that infuriated him. It was like being attacked by a wasp. I thought if I could get here he wouldn't follow me inside. I knew the doorman would stop him because he was quite obviously a bum—a stinking rotten filthy bum—so I started walking faster and—this sounds ridiculous—he trotted along beside me like a hyena. If I had a gun I might have shot him. The whole thing was unbelievable. Some of his teeth were missing. I could see that he hated me. I don't know what I would have done if I had a gun. I can't begin to tell you how persistent he was. Suppose I'd picked him up and smashed his head on the concrete—he was about half my size. I could have split his skull. I could have smeared his brains on the pavement. Then what? Cops. Ambulance. I'd be arrested. If he died I'd be charged with manslaughter. Well, it didn't amount to much. I'm sorry I mentioned it.

You're babbling, Guthrie said.

I wish you'd been there, Virden said furiously. I wonder how you'd have reacted. What would you do if you were walking along the street when some punk grabbed you by the arm? Laugh about it? Or would you give him whatever he wanted. Would you give him some money to get rid of him? Suppose you tell me what you would have done. I truly would like to know.

Keep your voice down, Guthrie said. People are turning around.

Let them listen, Virden said. I wonder how they'd react. I was walking along minding my own business when he grabbed my arm and then he hit me.

Guthrie took a sip of water.

Yes, go ahead, Virden thought, watching Guthrie's eyes. Ignore me. Pretend nothing happened. All right, he said and clasped his hands on the table. I get the message. I won't embarrass you. I'll stop talking. I apologize.

Ascher groaned. Man, you sound like the family pooch just died. Lighten up. We understand how you feel. Pass me the butter. *Passez moi le beurre.*

You understand, do you? Virden said and handed him the butter. How could you conceivably understand? If you understand, why not give me an example. Have you had a similar experience? Ascher's face all at once seemed offensive; Virden gazed with hatred at the soft predatory eyes and the bearded muzzle.

What kind of lunch is this? Guthrie asked. We get together for an hour, talk about the world series, brag about the kids, maybe exchange a few ideas on the market. These lunches are supposed to be pleasant.

I'm sorry, Virden said and looked down at his plate.

Ascher was annoyed. You want an example? I'll give you an example. A couple months ago after work I stopped at Chelsea West for a drink and some guy thumps me on the back. I'll buy the first round, he says. My God, I'm wiped out, really bad day at the office, so in a polite way I try to explain I'm not in the mood for talking and he says who are you? Lifts the eyebrows. You're some big shot? You're too good to drink with me? Listen, pal, I say, I'm in worse shape than Humpty Dumpty. Then he calls me a jerk plus other things. Okay, where's the bartender? Out of sight. On vacation. So I think to myself I don't need this and I leave. I let a prick intimidate me. And you know, sometimes I wake up at night wanting to murder the bastard. Two months ago, I got a heart full of murder. I should take karate lessons.

Will you gentlemen cease and desist? Guthrie said. Who's going to pitch for the Phillies?

Why should I give a damn about the Phillies? Virden asked. I can't forget that panhandler's voice or that terrible odor. He was coughing and his nose was slimy and next thing I knew he hit me in the face. I couldn't believe it! I just—Virden looked down and saw that he had been twisting the napkin into a rope, strangling the bum. It was an unpleasant incident, he said calmly, but I should be thankful it wasn't worse. I feel quite fortunate.

Let me give you another example, Ascher said. He inspected the olives, selected one, popped it into his mouth and began chewing. When I was ten, maybe eleven years old, I got into a beef with this kid named di Lucca—I forget why. All I know is I wanted to punch his lights out. I mean, terminate! Joey di Lucca. I see him like he was in this room. Curly hair, black and white jacket with a skull and crossbones. I wanted to kill di Lucca so bad I could taste it. You know what I mean?

Ah, the persistence of memory, Guthrie said and wrinkled his brow like an actor. This conversation reminds me of a Russian story. A couple of hussars are riding across the steppe. "Comrade," says Yuri, "what troubles you?" Boris groans. "Fourteen years ago this very afternoon, comrade, I received a slap on the cheek. And my enemy still lives."

A stinking bum grabbed me and hit me, Virden said. I'm not hurt, but I feel unclean, as though he did something on my sleeve. What am I supposed to tell Laura when I get home tonight? Both of you are married. What do you say when you walk in the door? You tell your wife you got hit in the face? How does that sound? And what do you tell your kids? I'd like to know.

Wait till the kids are in bed, Ascher said.

My advice is keep your mouth shut, Guthrie said, otherwise you upset your wife. How old are the kids?

Sean is twelve. Melody is nine. She wants to be a horse trainer. She's always buying dimestore horses. Plastic horses. Glass horses. Horses. Horses. She's absolutely out of her mind.

What does Sean want to do?

What? Virden said. Oh, I was thinking about that bum. Well, one day it's professional hockey and the next day nuclear physics. Sean doesn't want to follow in Dad's footsteps.

Neither does my boy. Steve graduates next spring with a political science degree and talks about becoming Governor.

I'll vote for him, Ascher said. I'd vote for Nancy Drew. Anything to get rid of that zebra in the executive mansion.

Hear! Hear! Virden exclaimed and watched himself in the mirror lifting a wine glass.

You're not eating much, Guthrie said, although that's understandable. This remoulade must be two weeks old. I believe they served better food in the Army. How's Laura?

Virden shrugged.

Martha bought a croquet set and wants to challenge somebody. We might arrange a barbecue one of these weekends.

Great idea, Virden said. Why don't you invite Cantinflas?

Guthrie leaned back in his chair and sighed.

I didn't mean that, Virden said. I apologize. Maybe I need a vacation. I wish I was in Hawaii. I'd like to be anywhere else. He realized that he had been twisting the napkin again.

All right, what the hell, Guthrie said. Let's enjoy lunch.

Hawaii, why not? Ascher said. Ukelele music, hibiscus, sunset on the beach, plenty nice wahine you bet!

Virden took a sip of wine. He poked at the food on his plate and decided he could not eat anything else. The smell of the panhandler would not go away. He could feel the hand grasping his sleeve. He remembered how his briefcase lay in the gutter. He tried to remember being hit. None of it made sense.

Either of you know Pete Catherwood? Ascher said. Pete's a big stud, used to play fullback in college. Anyway, Pete and his wife are headed for the theater when he decides to cut through an alley because of traffic. So halfway through this truck pulls out from a loading dock. Pete opens the window and asks the guy to back up enough for him to get by and this truckdriver hops out of the cab and runs over and grabs Pete by the lapel and shows him a fist. Pete doesn't know what to do. There's his wife sitting in the car and this guy has grabbed him. So does he get out of the car and start punching this truckdriver? What if the guy has a wrench in his pocket? Maybe Pete's lying in the alley with his skull split and his wife screaming. What do you do?

I give up, Guthrie said.

Pete thinks to himself why get killed over something like this? But at the same time he's worried about what his wife thinks. Maybe she wonders what kind of man she married. A truckdriver threatens him and he sits there like a wimp. What kind of man is this? Ascher plucked a bread crumb off the table and rolled it between his fingers. There's Pete saying to himself twenty years ago I was a football player afraid of nothing and now I don't know if I ought to take on this redneck. Is my wife going to respect me if I don't fight? So here's old Pete in the alley trying to make up his mind. What does he do?

The suspense is too much, Guthrie said. Kindly pass the ground pepper. I should have ordered a bowl of soup.

What does old Pete do? He backs out. Backs out of the alley and he's so humiliated he can't get over it. Blames himself for acting like a pansy. Now you take the ladies, Ascher went on and held up a spoon for emphasis. They complain about how unfair it is being a woman, but they never have to deal with this. They don't have to meet the gorilla. A woman finds herself trapped, what does she do? Screams bloody murder, cries, runs away—all of which is excusable. But anybody at this gathering yelps or whimpers, he becomes non grata. Right?

Norm Leach! Guthrie exclaimed, holding out a hand. Last time I saw you was at the symposium. Pull up a chair.

Leach nodded to Ascher and Guthrie. I can't stay. What do you chaps make of this GBI spin-off?

Not much book value, Ascher said. Take the money and run. I like your suit. Nice cut.

I've a crackerjack Chinese tailor, Leach said. He tipped his large British head to one side and stroked the bristling ginger mustache. Business has been rather good, you know. I recommended Chrysler last August, so I've quite a few satisfied clients.

I seriously thought of recommending that stock, Ascher said. Coulda, shoulda. I ought to get into another line of work—maybe sword swallowing. Hey, I was just talking about Pete Catherwood. Pete got shoved around by a truckdriver, got himself bent out of shape. Similar fate overtook this gentleman a while ago.

Virden cleared his throat before speaking. An aggressive panhandler hit me. It didn't amount to anything. I'm okay. It was nothing.

Really? Leach contemplated him from a distance.

Popped him in the kisser, Guthrie said. Twice, according to what he tells us. Pow! Pow! Frankly, I suspect the bum hit him with a marshmallow.

Virden slapped the table and pretended to laugh. I was on my way over here for lunch with these comedians. It was like a stick-up. I wasn't sure what to do. If I'd had a .38 I might not be here. I might be explaining things at the precinct station and that bum might be on his way to the morgue.

Guthrie belched. Ah! One dreams of revenge. It's a condition of life.

Well, I keep analyzing the situation, Virden said. I might have given him some change if he'd asked in a decent manner, but he threatened me. Then he hit me. However, it's of no consequence.

Little guys, Ascher said. Little guys are without doubt the worst. Napoleons. They hate the world. I'm standing in line at the ballpark when this midget turns around and glares at me like it's my fault he's short. I ask myself what next? I look over his head. He gets so mad he starts to hiss. I mean, talk about unreal!

Napoleons—oh, hah! Very good, Leach said. I'm just back from Calcutta, had to go there because we're opening a branch. Incredible spot. Blokes die of hunger before your eyes. Musgrave booked me at the Royal Eastern. Dandy hotel, I must say, first class, but quite a scrum outside. Dozens of spindly little wretches wearing loincloths converged like vultures whenever I stepped out—clawing at me, shouting five rupees or whatever. Ricksha men, you know. The poor fellows wanted to lug me about and grew absolutely infuriated when I wouldn't oblige. Little buggers tormented me until I caught myself pushing one aside. Dreadful. I confess I've never felt so ashamed. India will do that.

The bum who hit me looked like Cantinflas, Virden said.

Cantinflas! Extraordinary! I've not heard that name in a while. Londoners were a bit puzzled by him.

I was afraid he might pull a knife, Virden said. These days you never know.

Let's not play it again, Guthrie said. He rattled your cage, shook you up. The only thing wounded is your self-esteem.

At first I didn't realize I'd been hit.

Guthrie rolled his eyes.

You weren't there, Virden said, attempting to speak without emotion. You have no idea what it was like. But then he remembered that Guthrie had served in Korea. I've been wanting to ask. When you were in the Army, how did you feel?

Out of place.

Somebody told me you were in combat. Is that true?

I believe so.

Now this interests me, Virden said and folded his arms. It must have been an overwhelming experience.

I didn't care for it, Guthrie said.

No, of course not. Forgive me if I sound inquisitive, but did you—that is to say, I'm not quite certain what I'm trying to find out.

Neither am I, Guthrie said.

I suppose I'm wondering how you reacted. You must have been angry and confused. Were you frightened?

Oh, Guthrie said after a meditative silence, on the first patrol we walked into a mortar barrage and I wet my pants, otherwise I didn't feel alarmed. I thought I was somebody else, that's all.

Did you get over it?

Yes and no, Guthrie said. You can't pee in your pants forever.

Concentrate on the market, Ascher said. That's my advice. Concentrate on making millions. Don't lift your eyes from the tape all afternoon. I'll have some more butter.

Concentrate on making millions, Virden thought. I don't know who I am anymore. What am I going to tell my wife?

Several times during the afternoon he got up from his desk and went to the men's room to examine his lip. There was no swelling. He considered the handkerchief and thought about washing away the blood, but there was no other evidence that he had been attacked. When he studied his face in the mirror he could not see anything unusual. He appeared perfectly calm, unmarked, unchanged.

On the way home he remembered what Guthrie had said: The only thing wounded is your self-esteem. That was true. He told himself that he would be out of the city in a few minutes. Nineteenth Avenue to Marsh Road, then the expressway. Another half hour and he would be home. I could use a stiff martini, he thought. I'll find out what the kids have been doing and catch up on the news. I've got to stop thinking about a worthless derelict. He isn't important. But what made the punk attack me instead of somebody else?

After merging with the expressway he tuned the radio to background music and kept time by patting the wheel; and he decided that he had been imperceptive. What did Cantinflas see? he asked himself. A successful executive in a tailored suit, somebody who never had to paw through garbage or ask the Salvation Army for lunch. Did he notice my shoes?—these expensive Italian shoes? Did he notice how my hair is styled? What about my hands? Virden lifted one hand and rubbed his thumb across the palm; it felt as agreeably soft as his wife's hand, the fingers tapering, immaculate, the nails manicured. Whoever owned this hand did not drive a truck or clean sewers. All right, he thought, so be it—I look like the enemy. The idea was ridiculous. What would Cantinflas think if he could see me now?—en route to the suburbs in a sporty Japanese hatchback. Dirty rotten capitalist scoundrel! Yet every morning I go to work, put on the harness, obediently pull my load. I don't loiter on a park bench hating the world. I'm entitled to a few comforts, a few luxuries. I don't cheat, I don't lie or steal. Does it matter? Why should it? Well, I chose the career I wanted, so did he. I ought to ignore what happened, I don't need a rat gnawing my entrails. Ascher was right, concentrate on the market. Think about making millions. Think about Laura and the kids. Pretty soon, God willing, we can shop for a larger house—maybe in Brookside near the country club, maybe on Circle Drive.

But once more he could hear the voice at his side and felt a hand on his sleeve. Abruptly he slapped the wheel. The bum staggered backward, sprawled on the sidewalk like a broken puppet. Virden quickly opened a knife and slashed the bum's throat, blood gushed over the pavement. He cut off the head, picked it up by the long greasy hair.

Why am I doing this? he asked aloud.

In the rearview mirror he noticed a red dot that developed into a penetrating red light. The speedometer registered less than seventy, which was a bit fast but not enough to draw attention. He watched without interest until the light drew up behind him. Over a microphone the cop ordered him to take the next exit.

He slowed for the unfamiliar curve and realized that he was near a suburban mall. It was embarrassing to be stopped and now there would be an audience.

The siren began winding down. The cop turned on a high-intensity white light.

Come to a stop. Remain in the vehicle. Do not attempt to leave the scene.

It occurred to Virden that he might be delayed. The cop might decide to go on stage and pretend that a minor infraction of the speed limit was a serious crime. He glanced at his watch. Laura probably was in the kitchen starting to prepare dinner.

Several minutes passed before he was ordered out of the car and told to place his hands on the hood.

I wasn't much over the limit, he said while shielding his eyes from the light.

Comply with instructions, sir.

He shrugged and obeyed. After a while he heard footsteps. When the steps came very close he was about to ask why he had been stopped when he felt the muzzle of a gun against the back of his neck. The cop swiftly fondled him around the torso and between the legs.

I resent this, Virden said. What's going on?

This vehicle is reported stolen.

There's been a mistake, Virden said. The car is not stolen.

Have you been drinking, sir?

No. I had one glass of chardonnay at lunch, but I am not drunk.

May I see your license?

Of course, but I insist on knowing why you stopped me.

Sir, you will comply with instructions.

Virden fumbled through the cards in his wallet and noticed that his hands were trembling. Then for the first time he saw the cop—a bantam rooster. The cop's boots were waxed. He wore amber sunglasses. He had pimples. He could have been a high school sophomore with pimples and a Hitler mustache.

Here, Virden said, holding up a card.

That is a credit card. You have been instructed to produce a valid driver's license.

I can't see what I'm doing, Virden explained and held up another card. Is this it?

After a long silence the cop said: That is an insurance card.

I am attempting to locate the license, Virden said politely, but that spotlight is giving me a headache. Would you please turn off the light?

The cop did not answer.

Okay, I found it, Virden said. Here. And I have the registration someplace, if you want that. This car isn't stolen.

The cop inspected the license, but instead of returning it he tapped it against the barrel of his gun. How fast do you think you were going?

Maybe two or three miles over the limit.

Although the cop did not move, he appeared to be strutting. To overtake this vehicle, sir, it was necessary to accelerate to a speed of ninety-six miles an hour.

Virden lifted his eyebrows. I doubt if I could have been going seventy. I might have been going no faster than sixty-five.

The cop stiffened with authority. Sir, you were clocked at eighty-eight miles an hour.

Virden squinted at his name tag: Sweetness. The cop's name was Sweetness!

Stand on your left foot, sir. Extend both arms.

I had one glass of chardonnay, Virden said while balancing himself. It certainly wasn't enough to make me drunk.

Count backward from twelve.

Virden began to count in a loud voice edged with sarcasm, enunciating each number. When he finished he said: I could have recited the Greek alphabet backward.

Officer Sweetness took one quick step forward with his toes pointed like a ballet dancer and slipped his gun into the black leather holster. He was posing. He imagined himself as a frontier sheriff—dangerous, impassive, brave, dedicated to the law.

Return to your vehicle. Remain seated in the vehicle until further notice. Both hands shall be kept visible at all times.

Virden eased into the car. The back of his head was pounding and he felt nauseated. He could see the cop writing out a ticket.

Officer Sweetness glanced up, alert, pretending to sense trouble. The sunglasses glinted. After a menacing stare, he spoke:

You have been issued a citation because you have exceeded the posted speed limit. You have been clocked at eighty-eight miles per hour. I will cite you for going eighty-three.

Thank you very much, officer, Virden said. I'll try to be more careful. Can I leave?

Sweetness approached cautiously, waxed boots crunching gravel. One hand dangled suggestively near his gun.

Violation of the posted speed limit may result in loss of license and—or—incarceration. Then with great dignity, aware of himself on stage, Sweetness offered the ticket.

You son of a bitch, Virden thought, I'd like to blow your head off.

After easing into expressway traffic he watched the rearview mirror. The patrol car followed at a distance for several miles.

By the time he got home it was nearly dark. Laura would be in the kitchen wondering why he was late. Melody and Sean would be motionless in front of the TV.

Suddenly he realized that he had been talking aloud and it occurred to him that he had behaved like an actor in some grotesque spectacle. He decided he would say nothing to Laura and the children about what had happened.

As he pulled into the driveway he saw the cat—the dainty white neighborhood puss that very often seemed to be waiting for him. The cat would approach, not quite close enough to be petted. Virden parked the car, got out and walked toward the cat.

How about it? he said. Come here, you little sucker.

The cat trotted forward with surprising speed, obviously happy to see him, and stopped just out of reach.

I won't hurt you, he said. Come here, you little bastard.

The cat lashed its tail.

For the last time, Virden said.

The cat stared at him, its tail moving delicately.

Virden looked around. Near the backyard fence a semicircle of stones marked the boundary of Laura's flower garden. He chose a smooth round stone that fitted heavily into his palm.

What do you think? he asked. Have you made up your mind? No?

The instant he lifted his hand the cat raced up and over the fence. The stone thumped against wood.

For a while Virden stood with his head bowed, considering the day. He understood that he had tried to break the back or smash the skull of a friendly little cat because he had been insulted and humiliated, so what he had done could be explained. Nevertheless, it was disturbing. I'm weak, he thought. I'm not a man, I'm weak. He touched his lip, and it seemed to him that he was not quite as tall as he had been when he kissed Laura goodbye in the morning.

1993

VALENTINE'S DAY

McCRAE LOOKED at the delicate tissue paper collages Julie had pinned to a slab of cork above the sink. She was a twenty-year-old art student who thought the world was beautiful. Now listen, he said, you shouldn't be living in this place.

I've only been here three weeks, she said. I like it. Well, there are things about it I like. Well, actually, Uncle Mac, I might not stay if I hadn't signed a lease. Do you want some coffee?

Sure, McCrae said. He looked around the room while she went to the stove. A folding screen that she had bought for eight dollars at a discount warehouse partly concealed her bed. The screen was sunset orange and she was trying to decide if silver tissue glued to the panels would create an Oriental effect. Above her bed the ceiling sloped and a crack in the plaster angled down like a lightning bolt.

What about that ceiling? he asked. Does it leak?

She squinted at the lightning bolt. I'm not sure, Uncle Mac. We haven't had any rain since I moved in. I guess I should have asked, but Mrs. Karpov didn't seem very anxious to let me have the room so I just told her everything was neat.

McCrae looked at the warped and scarred thrift shop coffee table. One leg was fractured, bound with adhesive tape. On the table, enthroned among art magazines, sat a plaster Buddha holding a metal cup. In the cup lay a green pellet of incense discharging a filament of nauseating smoke.

That's called "Mandalay," she said. I just love incense. Maybe I can get a job teaching art in some foreign country like Mandalay. I told you Mrs. Karpov was almost murdered in here, didn't I?

In this room?

Yes. Go look at the bloodstains by the door if you don't believe me. That's probably the reason she didn't want to rent it. I mean, you know, the memories—ghoulish and all.

McCrae thought about this while Julie settled herself on the frayed couch. Her thick auburn hair gleamed in the lamplight. Her Pre-Raphaelite face might have been painted by Rossetti or Alma-Tadema. Pumpkin the cat jumped on the couch and nestled in her lap. He watched her stroking the cat.

When you called me you were scared. What happened?

Nothing, she murmured. Oh, Pumpkin Pumpkin! We do love each other so much, don't we!

Come on, McCrae said. What happened? Last week you told me there was an ex-convict in the next room. Did he scare you?

No. He doesn't live there any longer. He had a gun so the police arrested him. I couldn't believe he was a criminal. Maybe it was the Scandinavian—the old man who lives up there, she said, gesturing toward the ceiling. Every time I pass him on the stairs I can feel him watching me. You think I'm paranoid, don't you?

What I think, McCrae said, is that if you go on living in this tenement full of losers and victims and ex-cons and God knows what else, you could become a statistic. You are a gorgeous young woman and you know that. You couldn't possibly be unaware of it.

I guess I am, she said while frowning at the cat.

Ever since you were born you've drawn a crowd. You wouldn't remember, but people stared at you while you were sucking your thumb.

It isn't my fault, she said angrily.

McCrae rolled his eyes. It isn't anybody's fault. That isn't the point. The point is, you've got to learn to be careful. You don't pay enough attention to what you do or where you are. I'll tell you something. A lot of men in this neighborhood have found out by now that you live in this Victorian firetrap and some of them have found out that you live alone. And some of them are turning over ideas. I could tell you what those ideas are, but I'd rather not. Are you listening?

I'm listening. I just want to be left alone, that's all.

McCrae heard the resentment. I know how you feel, he said.

Do you?

No, he said after thinking about it. Of course I don't.

Take a look in the wastebasket.

The floor groaned under his feet as he walked toward the wastebasket and for a moment everything seemed unreal. When he looked into it he saw half a dozen muddy polaroids.

Don't laugh, Julie said from far away. I mean, they're utterly gross. Somebody pushed them under the door last night. I didn't know what to do except—well, I didn't know what to do. So when I got back from school this afternoon and saw them again I practically threw up.

McCrae went to the door, opened it, and squinted down the gloomy hall. One lightbulb dangled from an exposed wire. A strip of rotting linoleum led to the toilet and he could smell disinfectant. The silence was menacing. From the shadows a woman emerged slowly, as though hypnotized, with no expression on her waxy face. Long orange hair flowed across her shoulders. A sullen baby rode on her hip. She advanced like a ghost and passed within a yard of him, leaving an odor of decay. McCrae shut the door.

Julie, he said, what was that? The girl with orange hair and a baby.

Oh, isn't she weird! I don't know who she is. She never speaks. I tried to make friends but she ignored me.

You have no more brains than Little Red Ridinghood, McCrae said. They could film a horror movie in this place. Tell me about the Scandinavian.

Julie shrugged. Mrs. Karpov gives him his room in exchange for maintenance but he never does anything. The toilet is filthy—I just hate going down there. All he does is walk back and forth half the night and curse and drink beer, I guess, because he throws bottles at the wall.

How old is he?

Ancient. Seventy at least. He reminds me of Boris Karloff in those old movies. I hold my breath when I pass him on the stairs.

Why did you do this?

Do what?

You know very well what I mean.

Because it was inexpensive.

Inexpensive, McCrae said. Inexpensive. Who owns this flophouse?

Mrs. Karpov.

I thought she was the manager.

She is, but she inherited the building when her husband died. Or else they owned it together. I don't know. I told you about him trying to have her killed, didn't I?

I couldn't make sense of it, McCrae said.

Well, there was a knock at the door and when she went to find out who it was somebody hit her over the head with a hammer. The man kept hitting her until he thought she was dead, but she recovered. I told you to go look at the bloodstains.

I noticed them, McCrae said. What I don't understand is what you are trying to prove.

I'm not trying to prove anything, Uncle Mac. This room is really cheap and I want to be independent, that's all.

What happened to Mrs. Karpov's husband?

He was sent to prison for thirty years because he hired the man who tried to kill her. That's what she told me. Then a few years ago her husband died of a heart attack, so now she owns the building. She looks kind of crazy, one of her eyes is upside down or something, I guess because she was hit over the head so many times. Did you notice the liquor store across the street?

What about it?

There was a burglary and the clerk was shot to death.

How nice, McCrae said. What I did notice on the way up was a hooker. And judging by your neighborhood there must be quite a few.

Melissa?

I didn't ask her name. Fur coat. Red leather skirt. Stiletto heels. Fishnet stockings.

You certainly got an eyeful. What makes you thinks she's one? She told me she represents a company that sells specialty items.

Specialty items, McCrae said and began to stroke the cat which was trying to wind itself around his leg.

Melissa is darling. You'd like her. She's so funny. She's a riot.

I'm sure, McCrae said. Have your parents seen this dump?

I told them to wait until I could get it fixed up. Actually, I don't want them to see it. Daddy would just about have a stroke and Mother would pretend it's charming because she always pretends. She drives me out of my mind. I'm sorry, Uncle Mac, she's your sister and all that, but you know what I mean. Oh, Mr. Pumpkin! Whatever would I do without you?

She doesn't look twenty, McCrae thought. She looks sixteen. She loves that cat and she believes Art is what truly matters and life ought to be as uncomplicated as it was when she was a kid. He remembered her dangling from the limb of a tree when she was nine or ten, all feet and elbows. Then, magically, the promise had been fulfilled. But she doesn't understand, he thought. She knows men look at her and she knows some of them follow her, but she doesn't think beyond that.

Pumpkin moved in a couple of days ago, she said. He meowed at the door so I gave him a saucer of milk and he stayed. He likes it here. I'm going to paint Mr. Pumpkin's portrait.

McCrae got up and wandered to the window. Across the street was a burned-out apartment. I could smell that on the way up, he said. You're lucky it didn't spread. These tenements are a collection of matchboxes.

It was scary, Uncle Mac. I heard a siren while I was asleep and usually they go away, but this one got louder and louder. Then it stopped and when I opened my eyes I just felt petrified. Right across the street was this fire engine with smoke and flames pouring out of that apartment. Mrs. Karpov said it was arson.

McCrae looked down. Far below he could see Melissa standing on the corner with her fur coat unbuttoned.

Julie, do you have a fire escape?

I guess so, she said. Actually, I never thought about it.

McCrae walked to the other window. What a splendid view, he said. I can see the liquor store. Now pay attention. From here to the sidewalk might be fifty feet and there is no fire escape. Not even a ladder. If a fire shoots up that stairway you will be cooked like a Christmas turkey. No fire escape is a violation of the safety code. I don't know how the regulations define it, but this is a violation. I'm surprised the city hasn't condemned this trap.

Pumpkin darling, she said. Here, precious.

McCrae turned around to look at her.

I heard you, she said. I guess there ought to be a fire escape, but Mrs. Karpov is really tight. She probably doesn't want to spend the money. I put a sixty-watt bulb in that light at the end of the hall so it wouldn't be so dark and she made the Scandinavian change it.

I'm beginning to sympathize with that woman's husband, McCrae said. Now listen to me. Get out of this joint. Get out tomorrow.

I can't, she said.

Why can't you?

Because I signed a lease for six months.

I will give you a check to pay off Mrs. Karpov so you can get out, McCrae said.

You can pay me back sometime in the distant future or you don't need to pay me back at all. I don't care.

I want to be independent. It matters a lot.

I understand that, McCrae said. And I understand why this room appeals to you—torn windowshades and a ceiling that probably leaks and that sick woman with orange hair and a drunken Scandinavian upstairs and a hooker on the street— very artistic. Very Bohemian. But what I am trying to explain is important.

I don't want to borrow money, she said, even if you are my uncle.

McCrae waved impatiently. One can of benzene in the corridor and this ginger-bread palace would explode. Besides, you have mice. A lot of mice. They stink.

I know, she said. I caught one. Actually, two. And the strange thing is, the second one died of a broken heart. I guess they were husband and wife.

Husband and wife, McCrae said. Go on.

Well, a few nights ago I heard—you know, Snap!—so I got out of bed to see if I caught one, and there he was, so I went back to sleep. But in the morning when I looked at the trap there was this other one. They were lying face to face, Uncle Mac, with their noses practically touching. Like this, she explained with her index fingers almost touching. And they were just—you know—together. I felt awful. I cried and cried.

Let's get back to the pictures, McCrae said. Do you have any idea who shoved them under the door?

I saw a naked man in the hall.

When?

Sunday.

What did he look like?

I don't know.

What do you mean you don't know?

Actually, I didn't see anything except a behind.

McCrae threw up his hands. Tell me again about the ex-convict. When I talked to you last week you said he tapped on your door late at night.

Yes.

And with your usual sophistication you opened the door. What happened next?

He asked me to change the lightbulb in his room because he couldn't reach it. He was just tiny. At first I thought he was a little boy, but then I saw this weird bristly mustache.

So you went to his room?

Yes.

You went to this midget's room late at night because he asked you to change a lightbulb.

Yes. I had to stand on a chair.

You changed the bulb. Then what?

He thanked me and said to let him know if he could return the favor. He was as polite as could be. You'd have liked him.

I'll take your word for it, McCrae said. Now tell me, have you met any normal people since you've been here? In other words, what do people do in this loony bin except run around naked and change lightbulbs and stuff dirty pictures under your door?

Did I tell you about the Puerto Ricans?

No, you have not yet told me about the Puerto Ricans, McCrae said. Do tell me about the Puerto Ricans.

They lived in the room next to the toilet and they were screaming at Mrs. Karpov. I could hear them all the way up here.

Why were the Puerto Ricans screaming at Mrs. Karpov?

She blew out the candle in their room.

McCrae thought about this. A votive candle?

I guess so.

Mrs. Karpov was afraid it might set the building on fire?

Maybe, Julie said. I turned on the radio so I couldn't hear. They were absolutely furious. They were calling her all kinds of names in Spanish. Then they threw everything into cardboard boxes and moved out. It was just bizarre. Here, Pumpkin.

Does Mrs. Karpov know you have a cat?

She adores Pumpkin. I was afraid she wouldn't let me keep him. Seriously, Uncle Mac, the room will look really neat after I get it fixed up. I thought it would be fun to make curtains, and I'm going to change that horrible shelf paper. You won't recognize the place.

Yes, I will, McCrae said. The cockroaches are big enough to have names. If they get any bigger they'll eat the mice.

Mrs. Karpov promised to call the exterminator. After the roaches are gone I'll invite you for spaghetti.

All right, fine. We can stick a candle in a wine bottle and eat spaghetti and sing a duet from *La Bohème*.

Seriously, Uncle Mac. Can I make spaghetti for you some evening?

Let's wait until you have a decent apartment.

Oh, please! she said. Not again. This isn't as bad as you think and I love the neighborhood. There are delivery trucks and people sitting on the steps outside and—oh, Uncle Mac, I've spent practically my entire life in the suburbs so this is exciting. Just the other day somebody handed me a gift certificate for a tango lesson. Isn't that neat?

Since when have you wanted to tango?

It's free, she said. I might as well.

Sure, go ahead. Explore the big city, McCrae said. It had not occurred to her that after the free lesson she would be guided to a private cubicle for a chat with the instructor who would say that because she was unusually talented she qualified for a reduced price on the three-month course. And if she did not accept this magnanimous offer a disagreeable scene might follow. She had not thought that far ahead.

Oh! she exclaimed. I almost forgot. Do you remember what last Tuesday was?

Valentine's Day.

Yes. And do you know what? Right outside the door I found dozens and dozens of tiny paper hearts! One of the boys at school probably found out where I live and sneaked into the building. I've been trying to guess who it was. Dwight Huddle, maybe. I have a feeling he calls me sometimes at night.

What do you mean?

When I say hello, nobody answers.

I want you out of here, McCrae said. Don't give me an argument.

Don't you give me orders, she said with a frown.

Somebody has focused on you. Some geek is watching you and dreaming about you and meanwhile you pet your cat and trust anything that moves and if you open that door once too often I will be reading about you in the newspaper.

Don't yell.

I'm sorry, McCrae said, but you are being obstinate and foolish. No, I'm not sorry. You are obstinate and foolish. What do I have to do to get your attention?

Thank you so much. I appreciate your concern. I'll look for another apartment.

When?

As soon as possible.

What does that mean?

When the lease expires.

That's not soon enough.

I know what's on your mind, Julie said. You think if you tell my parents about this neighborhood they'll make me leave, but I won't. I won't even talk to them because we have these incredible arguments. They don't care anything about art. All my father talks about is politics and making money. And you know how Mother is. She wants me to play tennis at the club and marry a boring young businessman. But I won't do it, Uncle Mac. This is my life, not somebody else's life.

McCrae got up and wandered around the room while she continued talking. On a shelf lay her psaltery. He stopped to look at this quaint instrument which he had not seen for years. The metal strings appeared to be taut and he wondered if the room occasionally reverberated with a plaintive twang. His sister and brother-in-law had given the psaltery to Julie one Christmas and he remembered thinking that it was a strange gift, but it was what she wanted. She had learned to pick out a few melodies and would accompany herself by singing in a shrill voice not unlike the falsetto of a choir boy.

He considered the sagging bed and the cheap refrigerator and the faucet dripping into the sink. Near the stove was a mousetrap, but she felt so guilty about having killed a mouse—two mice—that there was no bait in the trap.

Magazine reproductions of famous paintings had been stuck to the grimy plaster walls with masking tape. She had constructed a bookcase out of bricks and boards. Half a dozen awkward mobiles dangled from hooks in the ceiling. Everywhere was the odor of mice and incense and from outside came the distant waterfall of city traffic.

Pumpkin and I will be okay, she murmured, gliding toward him with both arms outstretched.

She's terrified, he thought, but she's too stubborn to admit it.

Give us a hug, she said. Julie needs a big hug.

McCrae hesitated. I don't feel right about leaving you here, he said. Why not come home with me? There's plenty of room. I'll drive you to school in the morning.

She sniffled and shook her head.

Julie, he said, you're acting ridiculous. You're scared silly. You'll lie awake half the night listening for noises in the hall and wondering what that geek will do next.

No, I'll be fine, she said while rubbing her nose like a child. Mr. Pumpkin and I will be just fine.

All right. All right, McCrae said uneasily. But if anybody tries to break in, what you do first is call the police. Then call me. I can get here in twenty minutes. It would take your parents an hour. Do you understand?

She nodded. Got it, Uncle Mac.

Shall I dump those pictures?

Please.

Are you sure you won't stay at my house tonight? No roaches. No mice. A pleasant room. I'll cook breakfast for you.

No. Thanks just the same.

If you were still a kid I'd blister your bottom, McCrae said. He walked over to the wastebasket and realized that he would have to pick up the photos. He stooped quickly, gathered the pictures without looking at them and stuffed them into a pocket. Julie was watching, her eyes large and vulnerable.

As he went down the staircase he heard somebody coming up and knew it would be the Scandinavian. The old man climbed each step with difficulty, clutching the rail. He wore a stained pea jacket and he reeked of beer.

Good evening, McCrae said.

The old man gloomily regarded him from the depths of a knitted wool cap, but did not speak. McCrae went down a few more steps and paused. The old man muttered as he shuffled by Julie's room.

The instant McCrae stepped outside he knew that Melissa was conscious of him. She patrolled the sidewalk like a spider, her expensive coat frankly unbuttoned despite a few snowflakes tumbling out of the darkness. Have a polaroid, he said to himself. You can have them all. How do I get rid of them? I wonder if she recognizes me. She might or might not have seen me go into the building. And then he realized that he would have to walk past her to get to his car, either that or walk the opposite direction and go completely around the block, which would be absurd. Good evening, Melissa, he thought. I'm Julie's uncle. How's business?

She murmured as he went by.

Not tonight, McCrae said, although he had not intended to say anything.

Who you savin' it for? she asked.

McCrae kept walking. I shouldn't have said a word, he thought. She might be a decoy. Suppose a cop jumps out of a doorway and books me for soliciting a prostitute. Suppose they search me, what do they find in my pocket? I'll burn that stuff as soon as I get home.

He thought again of how vulnerable Julie was and it seemed to him that he had been too lenient. I should have dragged her out, he told himself, slung her across my shoulder like a sack of wheat. But the fault was hers. He had tried to explain that she did not belong in a tenement but she refused to listen—she went right on playing with the cat. Maybe I should have talked to Mrs. Karpov, he thought. Then he began to wonder if Julie had been lying. Melissa was real enough, so were the photos. What about the rest of it? He tried to remember if she made up fantastic stories when she was a child. Nothing significant came to mind. She had been normal. She had loved puppies and roller coasters and soap bubbles and chocolate sauce. Now she loved tissue paper collages and mobiles twirling in the breeze and possibly some art student named Dwight Huddle.

At home he dropped the pictures in the fireplace and struck a match, wondering if he should burn them or take them to the police. He imagined himself walking into a precinct station with a fistful of pornographic pictures. It might not be a pleasant experience. Where did you get these, Mr. McCrae? How long have they been in your possession? You obtained these from your niece? Where does your niece live, Mr. McCrae? Where do you live?

He lit the fire and stepped back to watch. One polaroid lay on the hearth. He nudged it away from the fire with his shoe and picked it up. Already the paper had curled and was changing color but it showed a stiff penis gripped by what appeared to be an artificial hand.

He was nearly to the door when the telephone rang.

Uncle Mac? she said. I didn't wake you up or anything, did I?

No no, he said, I was just coming to get you. Are you all right?

Of course. Why shouldn't I be?

Julie, listen, McCrae said. I'm taking you out of that place tonight. Don't argue. I'll be there in a few minutes.

You always try to boss me around, she answered in a peevish voice. I'm perfectly able to take care of myself. I'm not half as unsophisticated as you think. I just called to let you know about something terrible that happened. I told you how the siren stopped outside when there was a fire? Well, this time it was a police car and when I looked down I saw that girl lying on the sidewalk with her hair spread out like the girl in the shampoo ad. That girl with long orange hair—the one with the baby. I guess she jumped.

Don't go out of your room, McCrae said. Keep the door locked. Don't open the door for anybody until I get there.

I'm perfectly safe, Julie said. There's no reason to worry. Mrs. Karpov was baking cookies and promised to bring me some.

Cookies? What are you talking about?

She asked if I wanted some. She was baking when she heard the siren.

McCrae glanced at his watch. It was almost midnight. Never mind the damn cookies. Is the girl all right?

I don't think so, Julie said. They put her in the ambulance and drove off but they didn't turn on the siren. Something else happened. A couple of minutes ago I heard a knock at the door so I thought it was Mrs. Karpov but then I heard somebody run away and you'll never guess what I found on the linoleum. I almost got hysterical. It was this rubber hand. Dwight Huddle probably got it at one of those shops where they sell Dracula masks and plastic spiders and stuff. It's too gruesome for words. I put it on the coffee table. Oh! Somebody's at the door. That must be Mrs. Karpov.

Julie? McCrae said. Julie! Julie! he shouted.

Then he could do nothing but wait. He told himself that Mrs. Karpov had brought some cookies. Or was Julie going mad? He thought about the paper hearts, the murdered clerk, the screaming Puerto Ricans, bloodstains on the floor, a naked man running down the hall, the mute creature with orange hair. Some of it was true, but how much did Julie imagine? How much had he himself imagined? Was she losing control? Or was he himself sliding helplessly toward madness? He remembered a dream in which he had crawled through a window and drifted like a ghost toward her bed. What lay beyond?

He could hear nothing except the crackling fire which grew louder while he waited.

1993

THE SCRIPTWRITER

KOERNER LEANED against the glass wall of the booth and stared at the moonlight on Malibu beach while he listened to the telephone ringing. Somebody picked up the receiver and a woman's voice said, "Yes?"

"Dana?"

"Who is this?"

"I'm calling Morris Reisling," he said because the woman did not sound like Dana. "Do I have the right number?"

"Who are you?"

"My name is William Koerner."

"It's you," she said. "Where are you?"

"On the highway near the ocean. Not far from the house."

He expected her to turn away from the telephone saying, "Morrie, Bill Koerner's here!" or "Morrie, guess who's calling!" And then Morris would be on the telephone asking if he remembered how to get there, saying the extra bedroom was waiting and there was a pot of chili on the stove.

"I suppose you remember how to get here," she said.

"I'll find it."

"Are you staying in Malibu, or just passing through?"

"I'm on the way to Mexico," Koerner said. It was not what he should be saying and not what Dana should have asked, though more than a year had gone by without a word from them. He wondered if they had been divorced.

"I look forward to seeing you," Dana said as though he was nothing but an acquaintance.

"How's Morrie?"

"Morris died."

Koerner blinked. Then he said: "What?"

"I told you," she answered in a flat voice. "He's dead."

"Morrie?"

"Yes, Morrie. How does that grab you?"

After a few moments Koerner said, "I didn't know."

"I realize you didn't. I'll look forward to seeing you. Goodby." Then she had hung up.

Koerner walked across the highway to his car and started driving slowly toward the house where he had spent so many nights. The house with those two people in it had meant as much as almost anything he knew, but now he did not want to see it again. Morris was dead and she had remarked "How does that grab you?"

Several minutes later he coasted to a stop in front of another telephone booth and sat for a while without moving, but then continued on the highway and presently turned into a canyon. The night was warm and a deer sprang over the road, bursting through the headlights like an image on a movie screen. Going up the hill the lights followed a furry shape lumbering along, probably a small brown bear, which soon disappeared among the trees. Koerner put his head out the window to smell the pines. All of this he could remember and he had wanted to experience it again, but now none of it was pleasant.

Morris is dead, Morris is dead, he thought. Yet it might be a joke. They both were there when I called and Morris decided to give me a scare. Or he's working on a script and needs to know how people react to shocking news. He could do that because he uses people. He's experimented on me before, but it never hurt like this.

Dana was alone, wearing the ragged sweatshirt, dungarees and sandals. She shook hands calmly and asked what he wanted to drink. After that she sat down on the hassock where she always used to sit and listen while they talked; and she asked how he was, and Koerner wondered how soon he could leave.

"You were suspicious on the telephone," he said.

"I've become afraid of the telephone. There were so many bad calls after it happened. Anonymous obscene calls at night. I began to hate people. I can't pick up the receiver anymore without being frightened. But that doesn't concern you. I suppose you want to hear about Morris. He died a year ago September. It was in quite a few papers. Not as many as I expected, but quite a few."

Koerner remembered that Morris was overweight and at times his breathing sounded like a locomotive.

"Did he have a heart attack?"

"No."

"An accident?"

"Not an accident."

Koerner wondered if she expected him to guess again.

"Morris was murdered."

He realized that instead of being shocked he was annoyed. She had deliberately tried to shock him. Morris, who had been his friend and her husband, was dead and she had played a scene. He tried to excuse her because she had been an actress.

"Nor do I mean it figuratively," Dana said, looking at him with one eyebrow lifted.

Then he understood that she was playing not a scene but a role, and had been playing it ever since Morris died. Her questions on the telephone, the remoteness and the artifice, shaking hands instead of throwing her arms around him, forcing him to ask about what had happened.

"Morris was shot."

Koerner knew she would go on with it. He had done his part, now it was her turn. How many times had she behaved like this? Since Morris died how many friends had driven up the canyon road to the light burning above the door like a backstage entrance? Dana there to greet them with both hands outstretched, the palms turned down, perhaps, if the visitors were movie people, or if she happened to feel that way. Now she was sitting on the leather hassock as indifferently as a cat.

Suddenly she glanced up and said, "I know who did it."

Koerner hoped the exasperation he felt did not show on his face. She had resorted to acting because she had been hurt, and knowing this he knew he would not get angry, but still he wished she would stop.

"Actually there's no mystery. The man was tried for what he did and acquitted. He's walking around free today. He's a film cutter named Huggins. Poor little man. Morris was shot to death by a little film cutter. What do you think of that?"

Koerner said, "This isn't what I asked for. Please, Dana."

"It happened in a cheap motel on the beach. Morris was in bed with the film cutter's wife. It seems that Huggins suspected his wife was having an affair so he hired a private detective. The detective found them together one afternoon when Morris had told me he was going to the studio. The detective did something that is not ethical. He told Huggins exactly where they were, with the result that the man left the studio and took a taxi to the motel. He was not supposed to be in possession of a gun because he was an ex-convict, nevertheless he had one. He proceeded to kick open the door of the cottage and begin shooting. He shot Morris only once, but he shot his wife seven times. Both of them were naked. She was very fat. Isn't it amusing?"

"Not to me," Koerner said.

"I realize that."

"Dana," Koerner said, and waited until she would look at him. "Dana, for God's sake."

"You wanted to hear about it. I'm simply telling you. The man's wife died immediately. Morris lingered for nearly three weeks and for most of those three weeks I was at the hospital. He died in agony. His stomach was bloated like a sausage. I knew he was going to die. I knew before the doctors knew. I knew it even when they told me he was going to recover. Morris didn't believe them either, although he would nod his head when they told him. Do you know what he said to me one morning? He said 'It was a roll in the hay.' That's all the affair meant to him. Don't you find it amusing? People we know aren't murdered, are they? Gangsters are murdered and South American generals are murdered and occasionally a Brooklyn grocer is murdered by a boy who was trying to rob the cash register, but people you and I know aren't murdered, are they? Are they, Bill?"

Without any expression or any tears she was crying.

Koerner looked at the row of framed certificates on the brick wall above the fireplace and said, "Did he get another one?"

"Two since you were here. The one at the end is from a Brussels festival. He was killed before the awards were announced. Everything seems like such a waste."

Then she talked about it some more, and played a record of songs from a new musical comedy which was very popular, and before midnight Koerner was driving out of the canyon. He had hoped when he telephoned to find them both at home and if that had been so they would have insisted that he stay with them. He had hoped this is how it would be. Next, after learning that Morris was dead, he expected Dana would invite him to stay overnight in the guest room; but she had not offered and after a little while he would have refused. He thought then that he would stay at some place near the beach and perhaps go for a swim during the middle of the night as he and Morris used to do. But when he turned out of the canyon onto the Malibu road he did not slow down. From that house something was seeping like a poison and he felt it staining everything for miles in all directions. Whatever he looked at became disagreeable—the trees, the beach, the moonlight on the water—and the ocean wind had a foul odor.

Morris died without speaking, she had said, but he knew what was happening because he put on his glasses. Those horn-rimmed glasses, Koerner thought, mounted like a machine gun on that enormous nose. How could he meet Death without being able to see its visage? And he had died because of a lapse of taste, as well as poor judgment; died in a hospital, a setting he had used more than once in his scenarios, with a white plastic tube curling from his intestines into a pail beneath the bed, wagging his head slowly from side to side because he believed none of it.

She was sitting beside the bed when Death finally got around to his room. She had been reading a magazine when she knew Death was in, and quit reading and turned the magazine over on her lap and looked at her husband. Everything had been done for him that could be done, so with no particular surprise, and not much sorrow, she observed the meeting. She had loved him but her esteem for him disappeared when he was shot. He had been caught so stupidly. She had respected his intelligence, it had been the foundation of her love for him. They had lived together eighteen years and she had admired him even when she felt critical of things he did or said, but then one afternoon he was caught in bed with an overweight tramp in a roadside motel. He was caught like a foolish sailor. The stupidity of it disturbed her; three weeks she spent reading magazines and watching him suffer, and she began to feel insulted. She had selected as her husband a man who turned out to be a fool. She could not forgive him this. She might have forgiven his poor taste, because that was a thing men were often guilty of, but she could not forget or forgive his stupidity. She would have taken him back if he had believed he was in love with the woman, because men are easily confused; often they think they are in love when a woman knows it is only the body that absorbs them. If Morris had believed he was in love there would have been some dignity to the affair, at least there would have been that if nothing more. But he knew he was not. Or she might have overlooked it if the woman had been beautiful, but she was not. She was fat and ordinary, while he was a superior man. So she had quit reading that afternoon and dispassionately watched while Death strangled him, sorry that he was in such pain but otherwise not caring.

I never dreamed he would plot against me, she had said. I knew he plotted against other people, but not against me. Not in my wildest dreams. Not against me. As long as we were married I never once considered another man.

Then she attempted to explain something, which Koerner understood easily enough, although she was not sure she had made it clear. It was how she had observed herself, Dana, observing her husband's death. Did that make sense? Morris used to observe himself, many times she had noticed him doing it, and from him she had gotten the habit. He used it professionally. He would step out of himself and stand distinctly to one side observing Morris. In fact he made notes of his own behavior, she said, and later in one of the scenarios she would read what he had discovered about himself. Was this clear?

Yes, Koerner said, because he too had seen it.

As he was dying, Dana said, I did what he had taught me. I stood far away. I could see him suffering from where I was, and I was curious to learn what would happen next. As though my husband was the subject of a script. How could I be like that? Do you know?

She did not expect an answer. Koerner was looking at her and noticed how neatly her brown hair was parted and how carefully she had plaited it and closed the long braid hanging down her back with a rubber band.

Really, she said, it's a shame he never knew. He had such a sense of humor. He would have loved that touch of irony, and probably would have found a way to use it. He was so clever. But he was occupied with himself during those last few minutes. He didn't pay any attention to me. And there were other touches which were terribly reminiscent of his scenarios. He always employed at least one scene of violence—shots, screams, a door slammed, the sound of running feet. Imagine him doing the motel. The woman shrieking and collapsing on the bed while her husband was firing shot after shot into that enormous body. She was quite dead when the police arrived. She must have been as bloody as a Spanish crucifix. Morris would have enjoyed writing it, if he had lived. People used to say he was a genius. He wasn't, as we both know, but he was awfully smart. Isn't it amusing that he was shot to death by a nobody?

That doesn't amuse me either, Koerner had said.

Then he stood up and she walked with him to the door where they said goodby. She seemed to know he would not come back again. She was not blaming him for this. She had discovered within herself certain thoughts and feelings that she had never known existed, and no doubt the same was true of everyone.

The light still burned above the door when Koerner turned the car around and started through the canyon.

Halfway to Mexico he took one hand off the wheel, pointed a finger at the moon and said while wiggling his thumb: "Pok pok pok pok!" the way Morris used to do when reading one of his scripts aloud, as though by such a gesture he might get rid of the disgust and the oppression, but the moon would not fall into the sea.

1966

FILBERT'S WIFE

IN CLAIBOURNE SQUARE, before the mailbox, there stood a man with his head bowed. The park was abandoned but for this one man. He stood looking at the space between his feet, the fingers of one hand touching the lapel of his dark brown suit.

All around him on the streets of Lee's Ferry warm raindrops descended like melted glass marbles, falling on housetops, gables and dormers, dripping over doves bent into gray bullets for the night, clearing wrought-iron balconies and railings, tracing their hesitant paths to the mint-covered ground and the street. Lights in the windows burned orange, as if they would hasten the coming of Thanksgiving.

Though the raindrops touched him this man did not lift his head. When the clock on Bienville Tower thoughtfully counted ten he did not hear it.

His name was Filbert, and he was vice-president of a small progressive company which made paper boxes. These boxes were well known throughout Georgia and Alabama. Filbert was vice-president because he followed the advice he frequently gave his friend, Aaron Sifting: "Aary, when you tackle a job do it all the way. Don't change horses in midstream."

Filbert's wife had died that afternoon. She had been sitting on the sofa with a book turned upside down in her lap and her head hanging forward when he came home from work. He had sailed his Panama toward her. It landed on the carpet by her feet with a wispy sound, almost like a baby's sigh, and then rolled quickly into a corner.

"Hey, Duchess, aren't you going to love the old man any more?"

She did not move.

"All right. Don't talk to me." And he had walked into the kitchen to smell what there would be for dinner. Things had been laid out. Since Filbert liked to cook, he first watered the peas and asparagus and set them on the stove. He tied on his wife's ruffled apron in order to do a better job, smiling as he thought about her. He kept very quiet in the kitchen, handling the knives and spoons with care. While the chops were frying he opened the bag of candy pumpkins he had bought and hid them all through the cupboards, in dishes and bowls, in her apron pockets—every place where she would find them for days to come. He did this because she liked surprises.

It had grown dark by the time the chops and vegetables were finished. He set them on the table and they smelled fine. He looked into the living room but she had not moved.

Filbert grinned and tiptoed back to the kitchen. He climbed on a stool to reach a bottle of wine. Then it seemed everything had been made ready. He put an apple in his mouth, hung a pair of cherries over each ear and with a candle in each hand went in to wake her.

THE DOCTOR'S NAME was Hooper. He stopped at the edge of the living room and looked at the candles and fruit scattered on the floor. He was a bald man with cardboard lips who did not understand jokes and who spent each weekend blasting ducks with an enormous shotgun before they could get off the water. He wore a crisp pinstripe suit and striped shirt.

He picked up a brace of cherries and twirled it in his fingers. Then he stared at Filbert, but did not say anything. He nudged a candlestick with his toe, not taking his eyes off Filbert.

"She was thirty-eight." The doctor had not asked for this information, but it was somehow important. It meant a great deal, her being thirty-eight, even though Filbert did not know exactly why. Filbert wanted to explain to the doctor that once she had been fourteen years old. Then he had first seen her running through the rain in flat heels. How the puddles splashed. The exercise she was getting, how it excited him. Her legs did not quiver as she ran because she was still almost a boy. He wanted to explain how she was holding the dress up in order to run, how the dress seemed to wave at him. Her name was Suanne.

Next she had been seventeen, and at the birthday party had wanted to cry because she was so old but he had made her laugh. That was the first time he had said her name out loud. Then she had been eighteen, twenty-one, and the leanness on her had become smooth. Somehow she had become like those passages in the Bible.

The doctor was going out the door, pulling a hard derby hat down on his head with both hands and looking up at the sky to see if it would be a good weekend for killing ducks.

Filbert had gone out to the kitchen then to squeeze some oranges, because he suddenly thought it would be a splendid idea. But the juice made a pool on the drainboard because he did not remember to put a glass under the machine. Then he cut a slice of pork and chewed for awhile, but it tasted like newspaper, and when he swallowed, the pork would not go away from his mouth.

All he could think about was what she used to do after they were married. She would watch him until he couldn't think about the paper-box accounts. That was the way it began—she just looked at him. And then when he threw down the pencil she would come across the room with her arms stretched out like a sleepwalker and get into his lap. She would take hold of his ears and push his head back and say, "Close your eyes and hold up your mouth." Then she would give him a kiss that rolled down him like a stone. It would jar so that he could not move for several seconds. That was the way it had happened.

THE RIVER STEAMER'S WHISTLE hung in the black locust limbs that made a net over Claibourne Square. Filbert dropped the hand that had been touching his lapel. He noticed that he was standing in front of a mailbox. There was a sticker on it that read, "Think." The mayor had started a People's Improvement Campaign. There were stickers on other mailboxes.

Something felt cold in his palm. He found that he was carrying a stone, and it was cold because it was wet. He put it slowly in his suit pocket. He remembered having walked upstairs and down again, down to the basement and up again, remembered that he had left the house to take a little walk.

Gray Spanish moss hung from the trees. She loved the moss and said it would be her shawl in Heaven. He reached for some and realized it was yards above his head. His toe bumped on something. Looking down, he saw it was the snout of an iron alligator which stuck through the grill fence and was grinning up at him.

Beyond the square he stopped in front of a house whose door was of cypress, studded with bolts as big as hammer heads. Beside the door were mosaic windows—through them he could see green bead curtains. In the courtyard a brass arm reached up through clipped camellia stems, and in its palm rested a pink glass ball, candied by the rain. Mint covered all the ground. How she would go walking each Sunday afternoon to see these things. The dignity of her. Now, somehow, she was gone. On the sofa she had not made any noise. If only they had known she was going to die.

Filbert's arms were numb from leaning on a thing cold and hollow. He did not want to look at it. He walked quickly down the street but knew it had been a stone urn. He did not walk fast for very long. Soon he had stopped on a curb and was standing with his head bowed.

Each morning he had to leave her, but once in the office he would take a moment to dream, lean his jaw on one hand and stare at the papers on his desk. No one bothered him. From a distance, as if they were at opposite ends of a tunnel, he would hear the singing of her voice from the choir loft of the Riverside First Congregational Church and see her round face on the collar which looked like a platter. Or he would see her as she had been one Saturday morning—a tan wicker basket by her ankles and clothespins like Halloween teeth in her mouth, soft arms reaching above her head, while an October wind stuck sheets together and snapped drops of water from their corners.

Sometimes, as he dreamed there in the office, he would not move until his elbow slipped and he almost cracked his jaw on the desk. Then he would rub his eyes and gravely pinch the bridge of his nose, not smiling at such memories but considering them, not ashamed of who had seen.

LOOKING UP, Filbert found himself standing in front of a shoe store. On a pedestal were slippers like hers, and behind them, brown pumps just like those she had bought for their trip to Atlanta.

He clenched his fist, but then, because it was like throwing rocks at the wind, he let go. There was nothing to be done; every sound and every scent, like hounddogs, shagged her memory. There was not anything at all to do. He shuffled into a doorway, where he turned his face to the wall and began to wait.

While standing there, the rain fell less heavily. After a time, mist glittered by the street light. Near the river a blind street singer had begun to play on a guitar and sing. A wind carried his words lightly over the house tops:

"—buzzin' of the bees

"In the cigarette trees,

"Near the Soda Wahhh-ter fountain—"

The wind curled but in a moment straightened itself.

"—in the Big Rock Can-n-ndy Mountain!"

Listening to the words, Filbert understood that he and his wife had spent many pleasant years together, understood that it had been lovely, every minute of it, and that he was very lucky indeed.

Standing in the shadows with his face to a wall, vice-president Filbert comprehended death as clearly as if he had punched it out on his adding machine. The figures were, after all, rather simple.

By the river, where cypress trailers dragged the dark water, the blind man was again pulling the strings of his guitar. His nasal voice came wildly through the papaw trunks.

"I'm going away

"Where Life is eternahhhl—"

The song stopped. It was as though the singer could not remember what came next. He repeated the words but stopped again.

Raindrops were thumping beside the doorway like little drums. Abruptly, Filbert trotted out of the shadows, and as he passed a street light, hooked himself to its post with one arm. Those fine things he had so clearly understood went zigzagging off into the darkness.

He remembered the moment he bent over her, putting one hand on her shawl, the odd knowledge that she was not alive, remembered straightening up, seeing in the mirror his lips stretched and the smooth apple punctured by his teeth, how the apple rolled down his chin. How it fell on his toe. How the grackles laughed outside the window.

Filbert leaned against the post of the street light. "But it's only two days until Thanksgiving," he said in a bewildered voice.

Across the street a baker was locking the door of his shop; a very tall skinny man named John Roland, who smelled of brown sugar and hot piecrusts. Turning around the baker saw a man in a soggy suit who was making noises like a clogged drain and who must be drunk because he was holding onto a street light.

The baker's eyes became like cracks in a loaf of bread. All forms of begging and drinking disgusted him. He shook both fists; the overcoat jigged around his thin legs. He waited to see what would happen.

The sloppy man coasted down the street light, taking with him a "Keep Smiling" sticker.

This enraged the baker who was a member of the People's Improvement Committee. He ran across the street, his long feet splashing puddles. "You, get up now!" he shouted. "Get up!"

Filbert's jowls hung loose as dough. He was on his knees because he had decided to pray. "Our Father—" he said, but he could not get the next sentence beyond his tongue. He took hold of the baker's shoe.

John Roland jerked his foot away. He quivered with hate. "You're all alike!" he shouted at the big cinnamon eyes. Then his throat began to constrict with rage and, recalling that he must speak at the flour festival in two days he turned around and walked furiously into the darkness.

But Filbert had not even heard the baker: *She* was coming across the room to get into his lap.

All over the streets of Lee's Ferry rain was falling. It fell on gables and dormers, azaleas, trellises, by silent doves and dripped from Spanish moss onto the back of a gaunt man in a brown suit who lay on the curb covering his face with his hands. It fell noncommittally, with a soft and constant sound like leaves on a ruined temple.

1949

THE MOST BEAUTIFUL

RAMON SAT on his bed and blew hard at the soggy valentine lace to dry the paste underneath it. He opened his mouth and sucked in air until his eyes started to roll back into his head and the blood ran out of his cheeks and then he blew until he thought his lungs had turned inside out. He pressed his round brown fingers into the white lace. The lace was wrinkled and crooked, but it covered up the furry edges of the cardboard and Ramon was pleased. He said, "Oh boy!" Soon he would not have to look at the hole where the plaster had dropped off the wall. Soon the wall would be beautiful as a garden, and if the pipes leaked a little gas and the rats gnawed behind the plaster when he wanted to sleep it would be all right. If Mr. Silver threatened to fire him again and called him Greaseball it would be all right. He held up the square green cardboard. In the middle of the cardboard was a heart-shaped opening that had taken a long time to cut and in the opening was Jeannie. "That's the ticket!" said Ramon.

He pushed the picture of Jeannie down further so that the page number by her shoes was hidden, and then he blew on the valentine lace again. When the lace was dry and stiff he cut some pieces of adhesive tape and stuck the lace and the card-board and Jeannie to the wall above his head. Then he lay down on the bed and looked up at her. She was so beautiful. She was big and round as a woman should be, and her legs above the black stockings were very white and looked as soft as a marshmallow. It was too bad the magazine only said "Jeannie" because there were many girls with that name in the world.

The magazine had answered his letter: "We are obliged to inform you that it is against our policy to give out any information concerning the models who appear in *Beauty Forever.*"

So there it was. He could not write to Jeannie and tell her how much he loved her. He could not even send her a little present. But some day he would see her and he would bow very low like a rich gentleman and he would say to her, "You are Jeannie. I know you. You are the most beautiful in the world, it is true." And then with tears of joy in her gentle eyes she would sigh, "Ramon," and he would take her arm and they would walk through gardens to the Mission of Dolores while the iron bells played "La Golondrina" and they would be married and live forever.

Without taking his eyes from the picture Ramon reached both hands back over his head and groped around on the table. He felt a glass jar: olives. He pushed it away. He felt the cellophane wrapping of the figs, but he moved his hands on. Then he found the paper bag: cookies. He took some cookies out of the bag and lifted them onto the bed, where he licked the sugar off the crust and slowly ate all the cookies while he looked up at his girl. He lay on the bed for a long time with cookie crumbs on his chin and his neck and his collar.

After a while he rolled over to look at the newspaper page, which was stuck on the opposite wall and had the Gettysburg Address printed in curly letters. He was looking at the printed letters when he heard the man coughing in the next room. All week, ever since Ramon had moved into the hotel, he had heard the man walk around and around groaning and coughing. Every night. The coughing was as thick and low as the old seals on the Seal Rocks and sometimes the man would choke and spit like he had swallowed hair.

Ramon turned to Jeannie. "He is pretty sick, I bet. Maybe we should take him some figs, eh?" But Jeannie did not answer and so he said, "You don't like the sick man. O.K., he does not get the figs."

He got up off the bed and walked with little pigeon-toed steps to the window, his shoelaces flickering along the boards. At the window he pressed his forehead against the cold glass. Fog was coming around the bottom of Telegraph Hill. A gray battleship was going by the point and would soon be out of the Golden Gate, going a long way, maybe to China. On the battleship, dressed in buttons and guns and gold, would be the officers. By the window Ramon stood a little straighter. In

China the officers would buy everything. He would take Jeannie to China some day. He would buy her everything: tiaras of diamonds because diamonds were the most expensive things in the world, a hundred of them as big as watermelons; they would eat rice with chopsticks, and he would see why the Chinamen did not fall off the bottom of the world. He turned slowly from the window to the table and got some olives out of the jar. Whatever she wanted he would buy for her and she would love him very much because all the Chinamen would bow when they walked by and say, "Hey, everybody look, here is come the very distinguished Mr. Ramon Barbara and Jeannie."

There was a squeaking in the room. Ramon threw the olive pits into the wash basin and began to walk around the room, looking. He looked under the bed, in the closet, in the corners. His eyes got narrow; he remembered the detective in the moving picture whose eyes got as thin as needles. He walked to the wall and listened. There it was. The man was keeping mice. So. Ramon looked over his shoulder into the mirror to see if his eyes were thin. Then he listened some more. Yes, squeaking. The man was playing with his mice. But no, because the mice could not make a song. It was a violin. Ramon looked into the mirror again: his eyes were very thin. He would be a movie star.

"Eh!" he said. "A violin." He folded his hands behind his back and began to pace up and down the room. "Is pretty beautiful." He paused at the mirror and tried to look at his profile. He stuck out his chin and then pulled it down into his collar. He began to stroke his chin, and he said, deep in his throat, "You will force to play this violin all the night or I, famous detective, will send you off to electric chair." He said, very deep in his throat, "Electric chair, electric chair."

The violin played slowly and gently. Ramon climbed up on the bed and bowed to the picture. "You will like little dance? Sweat Heart?" Jeannie smiled. "Oh, ho!" said Ramon, "You are little dancer, eh?" He slipped her from the cardboard and holding her carefully by the edges he danced from the door past the bed to the window and back again, stepping sometimes on his own toes. He began to sing with the music but the music stopped. He banged his palms on the wall. "Play the violin! Play the violin! Why are you stop play? Who are you? We are having little dance." And then he added, "Or I will hit you in the nose."

Suddenly glass crashed against the other side of the wall. Dust drifted from Ramon's wall and the rats behind the plaster stopped moving. He said to Jeannie, "Pretty soon I will go in there and cut off the man's ears." But gas was leaking from the pipe again and it was late at night, and he was tired, and Mr. Silver had thrown a fish head at him. He lay down and closed his eyes. Jeannie would love the violin:

it would make her sad. She would cry very soft as a woman should. She would lie on the bed and her hair would look like red wine. She would smell like flowers, like spring flowers on the hills above Nogales, and he would light a candle for her and open the window so she would not smell the gas from the pipes. He would bang on the wall until the man played "La Golondrina," and then he would put his arms around her and whisper into her hair, "You are the most beautiful."

Ramon ground his fists into his eyes and said slowly, "We will go take little walk." He put on his big fur-and-leather jacket that he had bought in the army-navy surplus store, and carrying the picture under his arm he went out the door and down the stairs. In front of the desk he passed the little old man who had one arm and the silky beard. The little old man was whistling "Cowboy Jack," and when he saw Ramon he bowed and his beard wiggled, but he did not stop whistling. Ramon said to him, "Was just lonely cowboy—" and the little old man stopped whistling and sang, "—with a heart so brave and true," and Ramon sang, "—love the beautiful maiden—" and the little old man sang, "—with eyes of Heaven's own blue," and he bowed again and went on whistling. Ramon walked into the street.

With Jeannie under his arm he walked toward the piers. Oakland was shining across the bay and a chain of gray battleships and destroyers was sliding northward in front of the yellow lights. They moved slow as a column of turtles, one behind the other with their guns sticking out. North they curved under the Golden Gate and floated without a sound into the fog.

Ramon and Jeannie walked north along the Embarcadero and looked at the fishing boats rocking and nudging the pilings. "All the strings will break and fly against the man's nose," he muttered. When they passed an old woman she was putting each foot down carefully.

At the Colombia-West Indies wharf, Ramon sat on a coil of rope in the shadow of the *Sanford Thomas*. Jeannie lay against his chest.

Pete the lame watchman called, "Who's that there?" and he answered, "Ramon," and Pete said, "Who's that you're talking to?"

"Oh, is just my girl."

"Lover Man." Pete's footsteps went away.

Ramon whispered, "If I am little late getting home from work you don't worry because the big fish are coming here pretty soon. And I have got a lot of important things to do."

Jeannie smiled.

The searchlight in the bay swept around and around the cloud bottoms and the bay water gobbled and sucked on the rocks under the pier.

IN THE NEXT few days the boats began to come back to the wharfs later every night, heavy and shining with fish. Ramon worked hard with his knife. It would be dark when he ate dinner and walked along the Embarcadero into the dark scuffed street that coiled behind the army-navy store and up the steps to his long thin room. He would fall on the bed in his fur-and-leather jacket with his eyes closed and his hands dangling over the sides of the bed, and he would lie there not moving until the foghorns in the bay woke him, or a drunk man stumbled along the hall, or the Italian boys began to shoot holes in the trash barrels. Behind him on the table was a salmon can with its lid bent back. The can was half-filled with water. There was a rose in it that leaned over the table edge toward the picture on the wall. Oil and scraps of rust made a film on the water and made a scum that clung to the stem of the rose, and because the room was hot the rose petals rolled themselves into little fists and fell on the floor.

One night when the Italian boys were playing in the alley, Ramon woke up and found that he was crying. It was hot in the room and his shirt under the jacket was sticky. He got up, opened the window, and stuck his head out to breathe some fresh air.

When the room had cooled off, he closed the window and sat down at his table and took his Bible out of the drawer. He took a little paper sack from the pages of the Bible. He emptied it on the table. Dimes and quarters rolled out and when he shook the sack three one-dollar bills fell out. He counted the money several times, stacking the dimes on one side and the dollars and the quarters on the other. He thought for a while and counted on his fingers, and finally he said, "Eleven bucks," and he put the money back into the Bible and into the table drawer. He stood in front of Jeannie and said, "You are having good time this evening?" Jeannie smiled at him and Ramon's tan nose spread almost all the way across his face. He said, "You don't know what is going to happen to you pretty soon, I bet," but Jeannie did not answer. Ramon crossed himself and lay down on the bed and lay still for a long time. Some day he would find Jeannie and they would be married in the Mission of Dolores. Then he slapped himself on the stomach and grinned. "Pfoo! Jeannie will not marry you in the Mission." He rolled over to look at himself in the mirror. "What do you think you are? Eh? Robert Taylor. You are ugly I see in this mirror."

He got up and put some figs in his mouth and walked back and forth from the door to the window. Soon the violin began to play. Ramon chewed his figs slowly. The man began to play louder, so he hummed along with the music. The music stopped. Ramon pounded on the wall as hard as he could. Dust flew from the cracks in the plaster, and the light bulb swung in circles on its cord, throwing shadows in and out of the corners. Ramon beat on the wall until his hands felt puffy. "What is the matter with you?" he shouted. "You are crazy, I bet! Maybe you think is the violin that is keep me awake. No! Why are you stop the playing?"

But the man did not answer and, after a while, when the dust was settling and the light bulb had stopped swinging, Ramon took off his shirt and dropped his trousers on the floor and stepped out of his lumpy shoes. Then he picked up the shoes and threw them one at a time at the wall to make sure the man understood.

Beneath the picture, in his underwear and socks, he knelt on his fat knees, and his toes in back of him turned together like a big arrowhead. "Father of mine," he said, "this is I, Ramon, talking for you. I will thank you and the gold angels for beautiful Jeannie. Is because I love her. In her eyes are kindness of the Madonna or Holy Mary and Jesus." Ramon paused and looked at the picture, and then bowed his head and went on. "I am very ugly, Father. Is when I say some day we will be marry in the Mission of Dolores, you know is joked, because I am very ugly like a lobster and got thin brains. Jeannie is so beautiful. We will never be marry. I love her more than anything in the world, but I think it is pretty good she does not know I am living because I am so ugly. She will say, 'Ugh! Ramon Barbara who lives in the room which look like the coffin loves me. Ugh!' And she will be sad and cry. Father, I cannot stand her to cry unhappy. Is better she does not ever see me. Never. Father, Father, protect Jeannie from everything."

Ramon thought for a minute and then said, "Goodnight," and crossed himself and got up. He sat on the bed rubbing his knees, and he listened to the stairs squeak, and then somebody went by the door jingling keys. The room was cold. Ramon took off his socks and turned out the light and went to sleep.

THE NEXT NIGHT when he came home from work he carried a new rose for the salmon can and a little brown package. He laid the package carefully on the table and did not touch it until he had taken a nap. The ferryboats in the bay were hooting and the fog bells were ringing when he woke up. His room was hot again so he opened the window and looked out. Fog was coming from everywhere. It came creeping over the hills, covering the box houses, floating in front of the orange and pale blue street lights, turning them into colored cotton balls that showed the direction the mist was falling. Ramon sucked in the wet air and left the window open. He pushed the transom rod beside the door and at first it would not move, but he hit it with his fist and said "Ugh!" and the transom rod screeched and the little window opened. Ramon said, "You will learn better pretty soon. Don't fool with me, guy."

He rolled a long cigarette and held a match under the end of it. "Real cigarettes," he said, blowing soot, and then he untied the string around the brown package. There was a cardboard box with "$11.00" marked in pencil on the bottom. In the box was a bundle of tissue paper. He took it out and held it in both hands. The man in the next room coughed and choked like a chain had been tied around his neck and then water began to bubble in his basin. Ramon smoked and waited for him to stop. Rats were chewing behind the plaster again; he could hear their bodies scrape on the laths when they moved. He heard a girl's footsteps come running down the street and into the alley by the trash barrels, where they stopped. In a minute big footsteps came running down the street and passed the alley and went on down toward the bay.

In the next room the man was quiet so Ramon began to open the tissue. Suddenly he stopped. He found a shirt in the closet and tucked the sleeves between the wall and the cardboard so that the shirt covered Jeannie's eyes. Then he opened the tissue paper and took out a gold crucifix. He held it up to the light. It dangled and swung on a chain that was thinner than the string around the box. The crucifix caught the light from the bulb and sparkled through the dark smoke in Ramon's room. He did not touch it, but held it by the chain and the gold cross dangled and swung, glittering in the light like a piece of yellow ice.

After he had put the cross carefully back into the tissue and wrapped it up, he found a pencil in the closet and with great care he printed on the brown paper: "This is little present for Jeannie. Magazine *Beauty Forever.*" He put a stamp on it and went downstairs and to the street corner where he pushed it through the slot in a mailbox.

When he got back to his room he took the shirt from the front of the picture. Jeannie was smiling at him. Ramon clapped his hands. "Oh, ho!" he said, "Wait until tomorrow."

Down the hall two men were laughing and pounding their fists on a door, and their laughter came up the corridor like bouncing ping-pong balls.

Ramon lay on the bed and folded his hands on his round stomach. "I will tell you little story," he said. "Sweet Heart. Once upon the time in Mexico—in Guadalajara, I think—lives the wisest man in the world. His name is—eh, I have forgot his name. Anyway, he is fine man with lots of friends and everybody is ask him questions because he is smart. Only trouble is with girls because they don't like him because he is the ugliest man in the world too. And he is lots of times sad and lonely. Then one day he see the most beautiful girl in the world." Ramon paused. "Eh, but this girl, all the rich guys and the good-looking guys have got her sewed up. So this man does not know what to do because he is very much in love with her. And then one day, when the flowers are bloom and everybody is feel jimdandy, he meet this girl in the park, or in the garden—someplace. He is not afraid being ugly and he goes up to this beautiful girl and he says, 'Hello. I am in love with you. We will go get married.' And this girl says, 'No! I do not want to marry you because you are ugly. Who are you? Who do you think you are?—ask me to marry you. Go away. Or I will scratch you.' But the man does not go away. He is too smart. You know what he says to her? Eh? He says to this girl, 'A long time before you are born, the Father is talking with me and says what kind of a girl I want, and I tell him, "The most beautiful girl in the world," and the Father says, "O.K., only you have got to be the ugliest man in the whole world." And so I am ugly, but the Father is feeling a little bit sorry for me too so he is give me the deepest heart in the world so I can love you forever. More than all the other guys put together.' That is what the wise man say to this beautiful girl. And she says, 'O.K., come on, we will go get married.' It was in Guadalajara. Was a long time ago." Ramon looked at Jeannie. "Yes. Was a long time ago." And after a while he grinned and said, "You like the story, Sweet Heart?"

Jeannie did not answer and Ramon slapped himself on the stomach and chuckled. "Eh! You are patient girl, listen to dumb stories."

Then he heard the man moving in the next room and soon the violin started. Ramon lay on his bed watching Jeannie's face while the music played. He said, "I like the music of the violin. Is pretty good player next door." He began to hum softly and wave his thumbs to the melody. "I will like to hear the 'La Golondrina.'" He turned his face toward the man's wall and said loudly, "The 'La Golondrina' is very nice." The music stopped. Ramon waited a little while and listened, but it did not begin again so he went to the wall and said, "The 'La Golondrina.'" He paused. "Play it!" He pounded on the wall to make sure the man understood, and then he lay down on the bed and folded his hands on his stomach and put his feet on the iron footrail. "Play music!" he shouted. But the violin did not start. The man next door was very stupid. Ramon sighed. He stood up and tucked in his shirt. He combed his hair, with a little oil. He put on his tie with the pink horsehead and he walked out the door and directly to the room of the violin player. He knocked one-two-three, standing very straight. When the door opened he had to look up. The man was tall and thin with light blue eyes and elastic suspenders. Ramon held out his hand. "I am Ramon Barbara, your neighbor who is just move in a little time ago. What is your name, neighbor?"

The tall man was silent. His light blue eyes looked Ramon all over.

Ramon asked again, "What is your name, neighbor?"

The man said slowly in a hoarse voice: "Reynolds."

"Hey! Joe Reynolds?"

The man did not say anything.

"What? Bill?" Ramon was delighted. "What is your name, neighbor? What's cooking?"

The tall man held his throat. He said at last: "Edward."

"Eddie Reynolds! Wonderful!" The man was wearing bedroom slippers and he had a book in his hand. Ramon said, "I was reading the paper in English the other day." He waited. "Eh, the paper said that it was going to be cold." But Reynolds did not say anything. "I have gone to school. I like the Gettysburg Address." Reynolds was holding his throat and could not talk so Ramon wandered into the room. It was bigger than his and had wall paper. Sheets of paint did not hang down from the ceiling. Eddie had toothpaste and a box of soap. Ramon said politely, "I hear the violin play every night. Is beautiful. I don't know why do you stop all the time. You don't feel O.K.? Why is the violin not play?" On the table he saw a picture of the man holding a baby on his knee and a woman standing behind the chair with her hands on the man's shoulders. "Hey! You are very handsome. Who is this?" Ramon reached for the picture and the man slapped his hand.

"Oh, ho!" Ramon said, "You are very tough, Eddie. You are prize fighter, eh?" He began to snort and thumb his nose.

The man said: "Get out." He began to gag and he held a yellow handkerchief against his mouth.

Ramon stopped boxing and patted his shoulder. "Eddie, play the violin for me, Eddie. Pretty soon you will feel on top of the world."

The man said through the handkerchief: "Get out."

Ramon crossed his arms on his chest. "Not until I hear the music." He remembered to stand a little straighter so his tie with the pink horsehead was not hidden by his chin. "How about it, neighbor? Sure!"

The man went toward the door. His back was turned so Ramon scooped the violin bow off the table and quickly pushed it up his sleeve. With his arm straight against his side he walked to the door. "O.K., neighbor. I am going. Sleep tight."

Inside his own room Ramon laid the bow on the table and clapped his hands over his mouth to keep from giggling. He sat on the edge of the bed to wait. When footsteps stopped at his door he opened it and bowed very low. "Come in, neighbor! Come in! Ramon Barbara makes you extra welcome." He grinned hugely at the joke. "Come on in, Eddie! See my room. I have got something to show you."

He grabbed Reynolds' sleeve and tugged him into the room. It was the first time company had visited him. They would sit down and have a little talk and smoke some real cigarettes, talk about the weather and what the newspapers said, talk about China. They would call each other Son-of-a-Gun. He would say, "Old Son-of-a-Gun Eddie, come down to the wharf and watch me butcher all the fish." And Eddie would say, "O.K., tomorrow, old Son-of-a-Gun," and they would shove each other in the stomach and be the best friends in the world. Ramon looked about for something to offer his guest. There were the olives on the table. He grabbed the jar and held it out. Eddie slapped his face and Ramon stumbled backward and tripped on his shoelaces and sat down with a thump that made dust spurt from the boards. The olives had spilled out of the jar and were rolling around in little circles and the jar rolled under the bed and stopped against the wall. The light bulb was swinging. The man's head almost touched the ceiling. Ramon started to get up, but the man stepped over him and lifted the bow, so he sat down again.

Reynolds looked all around the room. Then he looked down on Ramon and said weakly: "God, but you smell." Then he walked out the door.

Ramon scrambled to his feet, climbed on the bed and tore the picture from the wall and ran desperately out into the hallway. "Eddie!" He held up Jeannie.

Reynolds turned around. He closed his eyes. He did not say anything.

"Is my girl."

Reynolds said in a voice as thin as wire: "That's disgusting."

Ramon began to grin, but the grin felt like it was made of clay. He was not sure what to do. He said, "Is like your girl, Eddie."

Reynolds whispered through his teeth: "Get out."

Ramon stood on one foot like a stork. He had done something wrong.

Reynolds said: "You filthy slimy beast."

"Eh—"

Reynolds shouted "Get away from me!" He spit on the picture and then he grabbed his throat and stumbled into his room and banged the door. Water began to run in his basin.

Ramon stood in the hall. He wiped off the picture with his thumb, but Jeannie's legs began to wrinkle and get puffy. He looked at his thumb and soon his knees trembled and got as soft as chili and he went back to his room and sat on the bed. Jeannie lay on the bed beside him. He stared at the floor and twisted his ankles first one way and then the other. The olives rolled in circles when he kicked them. Finally he went to the mirror. He pushed his lips apart and saw that his teeth were brown with little bits of fish stuck in them. He looked at his underwear in the basin and the scum circles on the porcelain. He looked at the towel on the bed and then he got down on the floor and looked under the bed and there was a sock, and a piece of sandwich, and the olive jar with paste all over it, and some licorice straws.

The man in the next room was crying and groaning and twisting the handles of the water faucets.

Ramon went downstairs holding the picture underneath his jacket. Sitting in the lobby and whistling was the little old man. When he saw Ramon his silky beard quivered. He sang, "—your sweetheart waits for you, Jack—" but Ramon walked pigeon-toed across the lobby and out the door.

At the wharf Ramon sat on the coil of rope. Pete the lame watchman called, "Who's that there?" and he answered. From far away Pete said, "Lovin' again. Lord. Lord." His feet went step-thump step-thump as he walked along the wharf knocking the pilings with his stick.

Ramon stumbled down the ladder to the platform below the pier, but in the darkness he tripped over his shoelaces and fell down and a nail ripped the picture. The platform rocked with the weight of his fall and his knees were bruised. He reached over the edge of the platform until he could feel the water and then he put the picture in the bay. It began to curl and uncurl. Jeannie's face went under. The foghorns hooted as she rolled back up. Her eyes glistened and she looked at him. Then she rolled slowly into a tube and sank.

Ramon lay on his stomach underneath the wharf with his arms dangling in the cold greasy water. The water wet his fur jacket and licked his elbows and the bay searchlight went over him again and again as it swept the cloud bottoms, but he did not move until Pete hit the moss-covered ladder with his stick and said, "Wake up, Lover Man. She's gone."

1948

THE SUICIDE

S INCE NOON a cold rain had been falling, and the ducks floated as silently and stiffly as decoys among the reeds at the edge of the lake. The sailboats were moored; the village shops were closing for the night.

Leon, having ordered supper, was warming his hands over a candle. He felt chilled and exhausted. He had been playing cards most of the day at the Po-Po Club. As soon as I've eaten, he said to himself, I'll go straight home, take a warm bath and get a long night's sleep. He rubbed his hands and shut his eyes, shivering as a gust of rain swept across the colored glass windows. The more he thought of going home to bed, the more agreeable it seemed. When he opened his eyes, there stood Bébert, dripping wet.

"I've been looking everywhere for you!" Bébert exclaimed. "They told me at the club that you'd been there and left, saying you were going to eat, but nobody knew where."

Leon gazed at him in surprise. "Is anything wrong? You look anxious about something."

"Well, yes, I'd say so," Bébert remarked, sitting down at the table. He pulled out a handkerchief and wiped the rain from his face and then mopped his hands. "Yes, indeed, I'd say there's something wrong," he continued. "And if you want to know the truth, there's plenty of reason for me to look anxious. There's plenty of reason for you to look anxious too, as far as that goes. The fact is, just a few minutes ago I received a call from Maggie, who says that Andrea is extremely distraught and is threatening to kill herself."

"Is that right!" said Leon, looking at him with interest. "I had no idea Andrea was feeling depressed."

"Nor did I," said Bébert. "You can imagine how the news astonished me."

"I'm not altogether surprised," Leon said. "I admit that you startled me, but of course we both know that Andrea isn't the most stable person on earth. In fact, the more I think about it, the more it seems to me I've halfway suspected she'd do something like this sooner or later."

"Really?" Bébert asked. "Well, there are various ways of looking at it. But suicide's a nasty business in any case." All at once he sneezed. "Excuse me! You wouldn't believe how cold it is outside. I'm stiff as a board. It's nice enough in here, though."

"Did you walk all the way from the club?"

"Yes. As a matter of fact, I ran part of the way. I'm supposed to get you to go and see Andrea. Apparently it's a matter of life and death."

"But what am I supposed to do?" Leon asked. "Incidentally, who told you to come and get me?"

"Maggie said that you were a close friend of Andrea, and naturally you should be notified. She assumed you'd know what to do. I don't remember her exact words. The whole affair is confusing. I haven't had much experience at this sort of thing."

"But I really don't have the vaguest idea what to do," Leon said, pinching his lip and frowning. "Why didn't Maggie take care of the situation?"

Bébert shrugged. "She was terribly upset. She asked for you; it's as simple as that. Everybody knows you and Andrea are good friends."

Leon smiled. "Not in the way you seem to be suggesting. We're friends, true enough. We've gone out together occasionally. She's very attractive and I'd be the first to admit I've had ideas, but that's as far as things went, believe me."

"I'll take your word for it. Of course, people do assume that you and she are closer than you pretend. But that's neither here nor there."

"It's the truth. I'm not just saying so."

"All right, I'm only repeating what I've heard."

"I can't understand why Maggie sent for me," said Leon after a pause.

"Possibly Andrea asked her to locate you."

"That doesn't make sense. It isn't like Andrea. And if you want my opinion, I'd say she's despondent because of Schumann getting married."

"Schumann?" cried Bébert. "You mean to say that Andrea has been seeing Schumann!"

"That's what I hear."

"I don't believe a word of it. Not one word."

"Well, I don't know," said Leon. "Stranger things have happened. I once knew a girl who seemed like a perfectly ordinary sort of girl, but later I heard that she had fallen in love with an acrobat. You just can't tell."

"That reminds me—did you know there's to be a carnival in town next week?"

"Yes, I noticed the poster at the club."

"Are you planning to go?"

"If there's nothing better to do. Frankly, I don't care much for spectacles of that sort." Leon stretched out his hands again to the candle. "You know, I really don't understand why Maggie was asking for me. It's as though I had something to do with all this, but I assure you I haven't. This morning I was working on the boat and this afternoon I was at the club. I haven't seen Andrea for at least a week, come to think of it. And as soon as I finish dinner I'm going home. I don't want to catch cold. It's a bad night."

"I'm only doing as I was asked," said Bébert.

"H'm'm. Well, to be honest about it, I feel more or less inadequate. Ever since I was a child I've had a feeling of being somehow not too effective when it comes to emergencies, I don't know why. Of course, nobody's perfect; we all have our weaknesses."

"I'm the same," Bébert replies. "I have the best of intentions, but I never know quite how to proceed. A fire, let's say, well! That's enough to throw me in a panic. I gallop back and forth explaining to everybody that there's a fire, but of course that's hardly the way to put it out. Now in this particular case—Andrea, I mean—I came dashing up the street with a message, but beyond that I didn't have an idea in my head! So you see I know exactly what you mean. But I don't really think of you as ineffectual. You've always struck me as being very calm and collected. That's a good thing. I envy you, in fact."

"Well," said Leon, "in any event, it's disturbing to know about Andrea. On the other hand, I find myself wondering if she's really as depressed as Maggie says."

"Oh, there's no doubt of it! Not a doubt in the world. Maggie told me that Andrea was completely hysterical. Threatening to slash her wrists! Just the thought of something like that is enough to terrify me."

"Did it come on suddenly?"

"I'm so upset I can hardly think. Did *what* come on suddenly?"

"Has Andrea been in this state for some time, or did she collapse without warning?"

"I don't know. If Maggie told me I've forgotten. If a thing's important you can trust me to forget it."

"She's planning to slash her wrists, you say. That's unusual."

"How so?"

"Andrea's fastidious. She seems to me the type that would take poison."

"Really? How awful! You could be right. But then I don't know her too well."

"Women rarely shoot themselves, either. Did you know that? They jump off buildings or take too many sleeping pills, but they don't care much for guns or knives. I don't know why it is, except that there's something basically different about them. And they often go in for gas. They shut the windows and then put on a transparent negligee and arrange themselves on the sofa. You read about it in the papers every day."

"I can't bear to think about such things," said Bébert. "It gives me cold chills."

"Getting back to Andrea, didn't Maggie give you any clues as to just why she happens to be in this condition?"

Bébert was silent for a while. "No," he said at last, frowning. "All I know is that she was weeping and creating a scene, so Maggie telephoned the club, and it was just my luck to be there. I shouldn't say that, but it's true. There I was playing chess with some fellow from New York, when they came around asking if anybody knew where you were. Well, I made the mistake of being curious, so they assumed I must know. That's how I got involved. I shouldn't have said a word. At any rate, before I knew what was happening I found myself on the telephone talking to Maggie, and as she seemed so desperate and kept asking for you I thought to myself, the simplest way to get out of this mess is to try and find you. That's the story in a nutshell. So here I am, wet as a dog! And I had a good game going for me, if I do say so. I'd pinned his rook; he didn't have any idea what to do—you should have seen him twisting his hands together and studying the board." Bébert laughed.

"Who did you say you were playing?"

"You don't know him. He's visiting that tennis player with the red mustache. They came into the club just after you left, evidently. Then I happened to come in, and this New Yorker for some reason challenged me to a game; I don't know why. You'd think he'd rather play with his friend, but he took one look at me and said,

'What about you? You look like a chess player.' I had to admit that I was, although not a very good one, and I told him so. Well, he gave me a superior little smile and I must admit that annoyed me. I wasn't pretending to be modest. The fact is, I scarcely ever win a game. Practically everybody beats me."

"Is that so? I had the impression you played very well. I wouldn't take you for an aggressive player, but I should think you'd win your share."

"No, I almost always lose. But tonight I got off to a good start, and that makes all the difference. I offered a bishop pawn, and to my surprise he took it, which is exactly what I was hoping he'd do. Then I moved out with the queen and threw him in check right away. He was completely startled—you should have seen his face! It knocked him off his game, I suppose. One isn't expected to open with the queen attack, you know; the textbooks advise against it. But it worked. Whatever he had in mind, he didn't have a chance to get started. There he was with his back to the wall. And things moved along from there quite nicely. It's the beginning that's important."

"Ah! Excuse me, here's my soup," Leon said, and placing both hands on the table, he leaned forward to smell the soup.

Bébert watched attentively. Leon stirred the soup, lifted a spoonful and blew on it.

"Looks very hot," said Bébert.

Leon nodded and then tasted it. "But it's good."

"There's nothing better than hot soup on a bad night," said Bébert.

"Not many things, at any rate."

"Aren't you coming to see what you can do about Andrea? I thought you were planning to cancel your order."

"I've been thinking about it," said Leon. "But of course if she's firmly made up her mind to kill herself, why, chances are that she'll do it. Look at the case this way. Suppose we go to see her and tell her things aren't really half as bad as she thinks, and so on and so forth. Now, if she's determined to kill herself she won't believe a word we say, will she? Women are like that."

"I wasn't planning to go," said Bébert immediately.

Leon took another spoonful of soup.

"I'm just running an errand, so to speak," Bébert continued. "That's the extent of it. You could think of me as a messenger."

"I thought you wanted the two of us to go and see her."

"Oh, no!" exclaimed Bébert. "You misunderstand!"

Leon was annoyed. "But why did they send for me? That's what I can't understand. You'd think I was her lover."

"I believe you," Bébert said, who had placed both elbows on the table and now sat with his chin cupped in his hands watching Leon eat the soup. "Don't you think we ought to go see her?" he asked after a little while. "It sounds like a crucial situation. Not that it's any of my business, of course. They asked if I could find you, and I thought perhaps I could. I remembered that you liked this place."

"Yes, the food's good here," Leon said. He began grinding pepper into his bowl.

"I shouldn't think you could taste anything, not with all that. I take very little seasoning. I read somewhere or other that pepper weakens the senses and leads to any number of complications, some of them quite serious. There was one fellow who sprinkled paprika on everything until finally he developed pleurisy, and the doctors say it was the paprika that caused it. That doesn't sound reasonable, but you never know. As for myself, I'm not afraid of pleurisy, but I do get cramps if I eat certain things. Well!" he exclaimed, straightening up. "There was a flash of lightning if ever I saw one! What a storm! And it's odd for this time of year. Usually the weather isn't too bad, nothing like this anyhow."

Leon wiped his lips with the napkin. "Hand me the bread, will you?"

Bébert silently gave him the basket.

"You're worried about Andrea, aren't you?" Leon asked, as he twisted off a piece of bread.

"I certainly am. You should be too. I don't know how you can sit there placidly eating your dinner as though nothing in the world was wrong when she could be slashing her wrists at this very instant, for all we know."

"But you've forgotten one thing."

"What's that?"

"Maggie is there. Maggie wouldn't let her do anything foolish, so as I see it there isn't much to worry about."

"How can you be so sure? There was simply this telephone call, you understand, and Maggie was excited—I could tell!"

"That's bad, I admit. It isn't like Maggie to be excited."

"Furthermore, I can't positively state that Maggie was with Andrea. It's conceivable, you know, she simply received word that Andrea was planning to do something drastic. I should have asked; that's my fault. I didn't think of it. You see what I mean when I say I'm not good at emergencies? I just came flying down here to try to locate you. I'm so impulsive. It seems as though I'm always rushing off in one direction or another, and then people such as yourself who have a naturally phlegmatic nature are able to calmly butter their bread and ask about specific items, and then I'm forced to confess that I don't know. It's embarrassing. Whenever something like this happens, I promptly say to myself that I've got to take action when, of course, the intelligent thing is not to go running around helter-skelter."

"I don't regard myself as phlegmatic."

"You're always perfectly in control of yourself."

"Well," said Leon, "that's different. Anyway, you know how it is. We each have a varying tempo, different ways of doing things, so to speak. It's true that you're more or less impulsive—at least that's been my observation—but there's nothing wrong with that. In fact, I wish I could be more like you. I'm perhaps inclined to be a trifle sluggish. Right now, for instance, you could be right and I might be absolutely wrong. Here I am, as you point out, buttering a piece of bread when at this very moment Andrea might be lying in a pool of blood. Suppose, for example, this really turns out to be the case and we find out that a tragedy occurred while I was here eating supper. How would I feel? You can imagine. I'd feel a sense of guilt for the rest of my life."

Bébert nodded enthusiastically. "And you wouldn't be alone! Even though I really haven't anything to do with all this, I'd feel a sense of guilt right along with you. I know exactly what you're trying to express. When these things occur, it's simply no use telling yourself after it's all over that you weren't to blame. You know in your heart that you should have done something about it. You should have been able to avert the tragedy. People are pretty much alike in that respect, at least this is my own opinion. Their hearts are in the right place, but somehow they don't behave the way they know they ought. It's queer. I've often thought about it. You're right. You're absolutely right."

"Shh!" Leon whispered, holding up a finger.

"What's the matter?"

"Can't you hear the ducks?"

"Ducks?"

"It sounds as though they're taking off. I thought they'd stay where they were, considering it's such a bad night."

"Well, I don't suppose they mind the weather," said Bébert.

"Ah! This looks worth waiting for," Leon remarked as the waitress placed a large salad in front of him.

"What do you have there?" Bébert asked, looking at it closely. "Is that a Roquefort dressing?"

"Yes. My favorite. I never get tired of it."

"Salads are good for you. When I was a child my mother told me they were, and naturally, just like a child, that was enough to put me off salad for years. I refused to eat one for no reason except that they were supposed to be good for me. But now I must admit I love them."

Leon was grinding pepper on the salad. Bébert watched with a look of disapproval.

"What do you think ought to be done?" Leon asked.

"As far as Andrea is concerned?"

Leon paused and looked at him curiously. "Well, what else did you think I was talking about?"

"You needn't be snappish."

"I apologize," Leon said. "You've got me on edge."

"As I've previously explained with utter clarity, this entire affair has nothing to do with me personally. Strictly speaking, my job is finished. I've notified you, that's all I set out to do. From here on it's up to you for better or worse. But frankly, I don't see how you can go right on eating at a time like this."

"Don't be ridiculous," Leon said with his eyes fixed on the salad.

"Well! If that's how you're going to act," said Bébert, "I'll just be leaving. I can't honestly say I enjoy being spoken to in that tone of voice. Furthermore, I certainly don't feel that I was being ridiculous."

"Let's not argue. Perhaps you misunderstood what I meant. Now look here—the important point is whether or not Andrea actually plans to end it all. What do you think? Is she, or not?"

"I'd say there's not much question about it."

"By the way, you know she's divorced, don't you?"

"One hears rumors. I don't believe everything. Repeating rumors can be malicious."

"I know for a fact that she is a divorcée. I don't know what the husband was like, but if he was anything like Andrea, they must have made a pair. You were at the beach that time she started kicking sand at everybody, weren't you? No reason for it, she just decided she disliked everybody. She flies off the handle every once in a while."

"I wasn't at the beach, though I did hear about that episode. I remember being surprised, because I'd always thought of Andrea as not being the type to raise a fuss. She seems so mature."

"She's not as old as she looks. She's twenty-three."

"No! Are you sure?"

"Positive." Leon took a sip of wine and inspected the bottle. "Here, this is very good. Have a glass."

"No, no. Thank you. I never can guess how wine will affect me. At times it disagrees with my stomach. I believe I'll just have a cigarette, though, if the smoke won't disturb you while you're eating."

"Go ahead; one gets used to it nowadays. You'd think we were all living inside a furnace. I'm as guilty as the rest. Puff-puff-puff, morning, noon and night. The first of the year I'm going to quit."

"I've tried to quit several times," Bébert said as he struck a match. "I simply don't have the will power. But you say Andrea is only twenty-three? That's amazing!"

"She's been around. Probably that's why people tend to associate her with me. Since I have a poor reputation they probably assume the two of us have something going."

"What makes you say you have a poor reputation?"

"It's true, isn't it? Be honest."

Bébert looked thoughtful. "No worse than anyone else who spends a lot of time at the club. I'm there half my life, you know, so I'm hardly in a position to be criticizing. On the other hand, it's probably true that certain persons who don't go there very often think that some of us are wasting a lot of time, if that's what you mean. Otherwise, though, I don't feel that you have a bad reputation. We're all in the same boat. Practically every night the club's full of the same old faces."

"What else is there to do? That's what I answer when anybody asks why I'm always around."

"And it's true!" Bébert exclaimed. "You can only go to the movies every so often, and what else is there? The club's a nice place to spend your time. It isn't too expensive and there aren't many fights."

"Even so, the first of the year I'm going to stop spending so much time there," said Leon. "It repels me. Here, try a bite of this salad."

"All right," said Bébert, laughing. "How often do you eat at this place, by the way?"

"Oh, twice a week, more or less. It depends on the chef's special. I almost always have the special, although you have to get here early; otherwise it's gone. I've been here as early as six o'clock some nights and the special was gone."

"I've never tried it. I don't come here often, maybe once a month. I do enjoy the lobster tail. I suppose you've tried that, haven't you?"

"Yes, it's delicious. But it costs too much."

"It certainly does! What's on the special tonight?"

"Baked sugar-cured ham with bread crumbs and cranberry sauce."

"What an odd combination!"

"You get to trust the chef. He improvises, and sometimes it's a little strange. For instance, last week he cooked a chicken risotto that had an unusual taste. I've been wondering what he put in it. But ordinarily the special is a good bet. The baked ham is fair, although he does better with the pocket of veal."

"I don't know why they don't serve dinners at the club," said Bébert reflectively.

"I've wondered. It must be the cost of outfitting a kitchen."

"You know how much plumbers and electricians are making these days, I suppose?"

Leon held up both hands. "Don't say a word! They earn six times what I do."

"You wouldn't believe it. Just last week an electrician's helper came into the bank to deposit his weekly check, and I was absolutely dumfounded. I thought he'd stolen it."

Leon shook his head and continued eating the salad. Rain swept across the windows. Bébert sat watching a drop of wax roll down the candle; every little while he shivered as though remembering the cold outside. Presently the waitress brought Leon's baked ham, and with it the cranberry sauce, some parsley and Mexican beans and a dish of corn pudding. A little cloud of steam rose above the plate.

"I don't have much appetite," Leon said. "I don't know why."

"It looks delicious," Bébert said. "In fact, if you don't mind my saying so, I could almost eat it myself."

Leon picked up his knife and fork and said, as he prepared to attack the dish, "I was thinking about Andrea. There wasn't a thing on my mind, but then you came in here and told me about her being so despondent, and since then I haven't felt particularly hungry." He cut a slice of ham, which he put into his mouth and began to chew with an expression of pleasure.

Bébert looked at him and then at the ham on the plate.

"Why don't you have some of that corn pudding?" Leon asked. "I'm not really very hungry."

"I'm not either, in fact," said Bébert. "It's just that suddenly the ham looked very good, as you say. How is it?"

"Excellent!" said Leon. "Excellent." He began to cut himself another piece, but then lowered the knife and said, "Look here, I've got an idea. While I'm having dinner you could run up to see Andrea. You could find out how she is and come back and let me know. How does that sound? I should have thought of it before."

"I don't think that's a good idea," said Bébert.

"No? Why not?"

"Well, first of all, you've got to consider her feelings. You're the one she's expecting. How does it look when you're expecting a certain person and all of a sudden there's somebody else at the door? That can be quite a shock, particularly so when you're in a bad state. It might even be fatal. You yourself told me just a little while ago that she's unstable. There'd be no way of guessing what she might do. There's a knock at the door, she thinks it's you and she flings open the door, and there I am! What happens next? It could be extremely awkward; you can see that."

"You're forgetting she's desperate," said Leon, who was cutting another piece of ham. "There's nothing worse than feeling desperate. I ought to know; I've had that feeling myself once or twice. It's terrible. You don't know which way to turn."

"Those are the truest words ever spoken," said Bébert.

Leon helped himself to the corn pudding. "Just let us suppose," he went on after a little while, "that Andrea is by herself. You say you forgot to ask Maggie whether she was with Andrea or not. All right, suppose there's nobody with her; what about that? Wouldn't you be glad to see anybody, no matter who it was, even though it didn't happen to be exactly the person you were expecting?"

"You're right," Bébert admitted, nodding. "I hadn't thought of it like that. I agree with you one hundred percent. But still, the main thing is that she's expecting you. That's the important point."

Leon stopped chewing and gazed at Bébert curiously. "But you said it was Maggie who asked where I was. Did Andrea herself ask for me? There's all the difference in the world."

"You're right again; I should have asked specific questions. I never think about those things until it's too late. It's just the way I am. I forgot, that's all. The first thing I thought was that here was an emergency and something had to be done immediately."

"Well, it's nothing to be embarrassed about," Leon said and resumed eating.

Bébert frowned. "As a matter of fact, I remember one time six or eight years ago I was witness to an accident, and virtually the same thing occurred. It must have been at least six years ago, because I was going around at that time with a blond girl by the name of Claudine, but I don't think you knew her. She was a very good swimmer." He paused and then shrugged. "There. You see? Already I've forgotten what I was going to tell you."

"An accident. Something about an accident."

"Oh! Yes. A taxicab ran over this fellow who was selling newspapers. Papers flew all over the street. I never saw anything like it. It was a windy day too. The confusion was unbelievable. Everybody honking and traffic tied up for blocks. You can imagine the scene. At any rate, I just happened to be standing on the corner waiting to go across when the taxi hit this fellow. I've never seen anything so horrible. He turned a somersault in mid-air and came down sitting. Well, he just sat there in front of the taxi and leaned back slowly on his elbows with the oddest expression on his face. I was petrified. I simply stood there and gawked at him like an imbecile. The only consolation was that everybody did the same. It was just as though nobody wanted to get mixed up in it. Of course everybody felt sorry for him, but at the same time they didn't quite want to get involved, seeing it was none of their business. They were pretty thankful they weren't the one who'd got hit. In fact, I remember thinking at the time that this was the reason I didn't make a move to help him. I was afraid I'd get some blood on my hands, in case he was bleeding. Then, too, you could be called into court and involved in lawsuits and so on. One thing leads to another, particularly in cases like this. There's just no telling."

"What happened?" Leon asked without looking up from his plate.

"Oh, the spell was finally broken, so to speak. Everybody gathered around and started offering advice, but naturally one person said to wrap him in a blanket and somebody else said not to move him and somebody else thought he needed a drink. I must say, I certainly could have used a drink right at that moment. At any event, an ambulance finally arrived with the siren on and the lights flashing, and there was a great deal of commotion before they managed to get the poor fellow loaded on a stretcher and carried away. I never did find out what became of him. Some woman fainted, and at first the ambulance stewards supposed she was the victim. Oh, it was a pretty mess!"

"I can imagine," said Leon.

"Frankly, I'm terrified of accidents. Except for that one time, I've never gotten involved; I always seem to be somewhere else when anything happens. It's almost mysterious. It isn't that I go out of my way to avoid incidents; it's just that I'm almost always getting there after it's over, or else I leave not five minutes before something occurs. It's amazing, when I think of it."

"That's so. There are certain people who do seem to miss everything, just as other people are always breaking a leg or having their house burn down, or getting robbed. Nobody knows why it is, but it does make you wonder."

Bébert nodded.

"Now, take Andrea, for instance," Leon continued, filling up his wineglass. "Wouldn't you say she's a perfect instance of what we're discussing?"

"I don't know," said Bébert promptly. "I'm not well acquainted with her, as I've already pointed out. We've run into each other a number of times, yes, and we're on friendly terms, but aside from that I can't truthfully say I know much about her. This thing tonight was a great shock."

"Yes, it was for me too," said Leon thoughtfully.

"There I was playing chess at the club, when all of a sudden I find myself mixed up in a business that's completely foreign to me and have to come flying down the street getting soaked to the bone trying to find out where you are. It was no picnic. I don't care for things of this sort. I don't have the temperament for it. But as to what you were saying, you could be right. Divorced, and then that scene at the beach, and now this! It makes you wonder what will happen next."

"She's not realistic, that's her trouble."

"Well, who is? Take my uncle on my mother's side, for example. An absolute mystic! I remember him quite well, although he died when I was little. He used to interpret dreams and read tea leaves, and he could read your history on the palm of your hand so that you'd swear he'd been following you around. It was absolutely incredible! Even my father was impressed, and there were very few things on this earth that could impress my father. Why, when the *Hindenburg* crashed at that airport in New York—or New Jersey, I think it was—anyway, my father when he heard the news didn't so much as bat an eye. 'That's quite a tragedy,' he said. Those were his exact words. 'That's quite a tragedy.' Everybody else was simply horrified and went around telling people, but not my father. That's the way he was about everything."

"I remember the *Hindenburg* disaster," Leon said.

"People discussed it for weeks! The thing caught fire and exploded. There were photos in all the newspapers and magazines. They were using helium instead of hydrogen."

"No, it was hydrogen instead of helium."

"Are you sure? Well, it doesn't matter. I just recall that the whole thing caught fire and blew up. People trying to escape, twisting red-hot metal bars with their bare hands! It's remarkable what people can do when they have to. I remember reading somewhere about a man who picked up a three-thousand-pound safe and threw it out a window because the building caught fire and there were some valuable papers in the safe. The funny thing is, if he'd simply stopped a minute to think, he'd have realized the papers would be all right where they were because the safe was fireproof. But he got excited and just picked up this enormous object and flung it out the window as though it was a cigar box. Later on, of course, he couldn't begin to budge it."

"That's the adrenaline in the bloodstream. When you get excited about any-thing, the body secretes adrenaline. It's some sort of a survival response. It goes back to the time of the cave man. It gives you additional strength for emergencies."

"Yes, that's what I've heard. It's a good thing, I guess."

"Here, why don't you have some of this wine? Really, I should have ordered a small bottle. Ordinarily I do, but tonight I felt extravagant for some reason. Maybe it was the bad weather. The weather affects me that way. I'm subject to moods."

Bébert shook his head, but then after a moment he said, "All right, I will. Usu-ally I don't drink wine on account of my stomach, but I'll make an exception." He plucked a glass from the next table and neatly wiped the rim with a napkin. Leon filled the glass and Bébert held it to the light.

"I never can tell a thing by doing that," said Leon.

"Neither can I," said Bébert, "but I do it just to be on the safe side. You never know. It could be full of sediment."

"There's a great deal to be learned about wines," Leon said. "I keep telling my-self that I ought to take time and brush up on a few things. It gives you a better sta-tus with women. They appreciate a man who knows all about wines and fabrics."

"You're right, particularly about fabrics. I've noticed that a woman will be im-pressed if a man can glance at a dress or a suit and make some intelligent remark about it. That's because they don't expect men to know about such things."

"Women have a great many misconceptions. I could give you a list as long as my arm; it wouldn't any trouble. You can't be too careful about dealing with them, because you can't predict what will happen. They do things without a reason. Then, if you make the mistake of asking why they've done this or that, they attack you. It's just the way they are."

"Like birds in flight," said Bébert.

"Exactly," said Leon, although he did not see the resemblance. "You've nailed it down. That's how they are. Andrea's the perfect example. But she might be feeling somewhat better by this time. What do you think?"

"I should think so," Bébert agreed, "after all this time."

"That's right. She's had a chance to think it over and realize how foolishly she was behaving. I'd even go so far as to make a guess that she's laughing over it by now. They're very changeable, you know."

"They're just like chameleons. They get over these things. Take my sister. Why, you wouldn't believe it, but when we were children it seemed to me that five times a day, at least, my sister was screaming about something or other, but then the next thing I knew she was playing with her dolls as though nothing had happened. They have extraordinary powers of recuperation. They're much stronger than men, as a matter of fact."

Leon smiled. "You don't know how right you are."

"What do you mean?"

"Never mind. At times they're feeble enough."

"Feeble, did you say? That's not a word I'd use in connection with them. Of course, your experiences may have been different."

"I imagine we all have the same experience."

At this Bébert burst out laughing. "Well, you were talking about having a reputation, and in that respect I must admit that you certainly do. Everybody knows your favorite dish isn't printed on the menu, if you don't mind my saying so."

"Oh, I'm no worse than the rest. We're all alike. It's just that I'm not as discreet."

"It pays to be cautious, I've found. It's easy to get yourself in a jam." Bébert snapped his fingers. "It can happen just like that! One minute you're all right and the next minute you hardly know what hit you. You've got about as much chance as a pig in a butcher shop."

"It's not all that bad," said Leon thoughtfully, "not if you keep on your toes. Anyway, you can't do without them, so you've got to run a few risks. That's how I feel about it. You can criticize me if you like; I'm only being truthful. It's no fun being left out in the cold."

"There's something to what you say," Bébert remarked. "I should be more like you. You always know what you're up to. I can't help admiring you for that."

Leon, who had eaten everything in sight, swallowed the rest of the wine and patted his lips with the napkin.

"It's foolish to get excited about things," Bébert continued. "I should have learned by now that if you let well enough alone, why, sooner or later the matter will straighten itself out, chances are. But women in particular don't realize this. If you simply let nature take its course, though, there's no reason to get upset. What do you think?"

Leon belched. "I don't know," he admitted. "It seems as though every time I eat too much I have trouble concentrating. My head feels strange."

"It could be your pancreas. They say that if you develop a bad pancreas you have any number of symptoms."

"Maybe," Leon said doubtfully. "I think, though, that I just ate too much."

"Well, you ate quickly too. I noticed that. It's bad for you. I have a cousin who eats as if the world was coming to an end, and there's always something wrong with him. Backaches, hangnail, pinkeye, warts—if it isn't one thing it's another!

He's always running off to the doctor. I've told him what the trouble is, but he doesn't listen. 'Mind your own business,' he says. So I don't even speak to him any more. It's not my affair if he wants to kill himself by gobbling. Furthermore, it shows. He's terribly overweight. He used to be thin as a rail. That's what happens when you're too proud to accept advice."

"How many people can you name who do take advice? They all think they know what they're doing."

"Right!" said Bébert. "I've observed the same thing, and it never ceases to amaze me."

"You take this case we've been discussing. What about that?"

"Andrea?"

"Yes."

"I'm afraid I don't follow you."

"Simply this: What sort of advice could you give her?"

Bébert sank back in his chair. "That's quite a question. You asked a hard one that time."

"Let's assume she's right here at the table and it's as plain as the nose on your face what she's up to. She's on the point of doing something drastic. Now then, how are you going to approach this hypothetical problem?"

"To tell the truth," Bébert replied after some moments of thought, "I wouldn't know how to begin."

"So you'd leave it all up to her, is that right? You'd simply let nature take its course?"

"I see what you're getting at. What would you do? How would you handle it?"

"Oh," Leon said, "I'm not trying to give the impression that there's an easy way out. If one thing didn't work, you'd have to try something else. In a sense, you'd find yourself caught between two fires. You might do the wrong thing very easily. It would be touchy, to say the least."

"Judging from what little I've seen of her," Bébert remarked, "I'd say she's very strong-willed, and in a situation such as you were describing she might even grow dangerous. She's capable of anything. In fact, although I don't know whether you agree with this or not, it might not be a bad idea to leave her utterly alone, because she might not want to be disturbed. The more I think of it, in fact, the more I think that's the proper course to follow. People frequently wish to be left alone, especially if they don't happen to be feeling up to par. My cousin used to complain about his intestines, but then he'd get furious when I tried to help. It makes you wonder. You want to help people, but the first thing they do is turn right around and virtually bite your head off for trying to be of some assistance. It's happened to me more than once. On the whole, if a person isn't quite up to snuff, the best thing for them is to be left alone. No telephone calls or visitors. I sometimes lie down with a damp cloth over my forehead and rest for several hours without thinking about anything in the world. It restores your confidence."

"Well, anyhow," said Leon absently, "I don't think we ought to go up there. Besides, she's probably had enough excitement for one day."

"I agree one hundred percent! After all, we wouldn't want to be held responsible for complicating matters."

"That's rather a droll thought," Leon said, and began picking his teeth with a match.

"I see nothing droll about it," said Bébert crisply. "My father once told me about some man who met an old friend unexpectedly while he was out swimming, and suffered a heart attack then and there. He drowned right in the water! It goes to show, you can't tell how people are going to react."

Leon had been examining the check while Bébert was talking. He opened his wallet and said, "As soon as I pay this, I think perhaps we ought to go back to the club and find out if there's any news. I can't get over a feeling that this whole business ought to be looked into."

"I agree with that wholeheartedly," said Bébert. "We'll gather some firsthand reports and see what's up. Incidentally, I notice it's stopped raining."

"I noticed," said Leon, unwrapping a cigar. "Well, then. So the matter's settled."

"Yes," Bébert said, "and to put it mildly, I feel relieved. I couldn't begin to tell you how much. Let's rush back to the club and find out what's what."

"That strikes me as a good idea," said Leon.

1963

ACEDIA

I WAS SEATED on a flat rock overlooking the yacht harbor when it occurred to me that my thoughts were unnatural. I did not want to go anyplace or do anything, and it seemed to me that tomorrow would be the same—and the day after that, and the day after. Tomorrow and tomorrow and tomorrow would be identical.

Just then somebody called my name. It was Billie Serapis in a red leather miniskirt and pointed white elf boots, her small oval face sagging beneath eight ounces of cosmetics. She looked more than ever like yesterday's movie starlet.

Crawford, why are you sitting there? she asked. Aren't you coming to the party?

I knew nothing about a party.

It's Oliver's forty-ninth birthday, she said.

Well, I thought, who cares? I didn't dislike Oliver, but on the other hand I could get along without him. When he was sober he could be amusing, especially when he talked about his adventures in the merchant marine, but all too often his eyes were glazed and he mumbled. Oliver is forty-nine, I thought, so what difference does it make? I patted the rock and invited Billie to sit down.

I can't, she said, holding up both pale hands to protect her face from the sun. I'm late. Magda will be furious.

Of course Billie would be late. If one used to be in show business and might at any instant receive a telephone call from an agent or a producer one must always give the impression of being late. One could not be observed sitting on a rock doing nothing.

Have you seen Albert Defanbaugh? she asked.

I hadn't seen Albert Defanbaugh for months. Maybe he had moved to Costa Rica. Maybe he was in jail. I didn't care.

Everybody's frantic, Billie said. Albert and Joyce have separated.

She made it sound as though the sky was falling. Albert and Joyce, I said to myself. Albert and Joyce. The names sounded odd. I asked myself what they looked like but couldn't remember. Billie herself—if she had not been standing in front of me I couldn't have described her features. Evidently she meant nothing to me, which seemed strange because I liked Billie. She lived alone in a gloomy two-room apartment behind the hardware store and collected old purses. Occasionally she invited people to her place for spaghetti and I had been there a few times and noticed twenty or thirty purses dangling from hooks on the wall—red velvet bags with drawstrings, miniature tapestries called reticules, purses of woven gold or tarnished chain mail. They were the ugliest things I had ever seen. They reminded me of thrift shops and the mouldering nineteenth-century gowns you see in museums. I kept away from the wall where they hung because I was sure they smelled bad and while I ate spaghetti I would look at them with disgust. I had an idea that Billie collected old purses because once upon a time her life had been exciting. No more. There wouldn't be any telephone call from an agent or a producer and Billie would hide the wrinkles with more and more cosmetics. She was, in her feminine way, like the bearded man who stood alongside Bridgeway with a challenging expression and stared at people driving into town. He was waiting for an important person to stop in amazement and exclaim My God, what presence! I must have him for my next film! Being in California, of course, everybody relates to the film industry.

We're afraid Albert might have—oh, you know, Billie said. Because he's despondent.

Drowned himself? Is that what she was afraid to say? Albert Defanbaugh, disappointed in love, flung himself into the Sausalito yacht harbor at midnight with a despairing shriek. Excellent, I thought. Good riddance.

I insist that you come to Oliver's party, she said, pulling a theatrical face. Magda has ordered an extra-special birthday cake.

I don't want to, I said. I'm tired. I'm just going to sit here.

Pish! Billie said. Pish tosh!

I explained that I felt exhausted. I could barely keep my eyes open.

As you like, she said. Ta ta, *cheri*!

She hurried away like a little vampire shrinking from daylight, waving her hands angrily at the sun. She very seldom left her apartment until after dark. Then she would emerge and wander along Bridgeway, pausing at all of the restaurants and bars to chat with friends. She didn't have a job so everybody assumed she lived on a small inheritance. In my opinion her life was meaningless, although from a certain point of view one might argue that absolutely everything is meaningless.

I'm bored, I said aloud. Yet it seemed more serious than boredom. The Slough of Despond—I believe that's what Bunyan called it. This was what I had fallen into. Christian sank deeper and deeper because of the burden on his back and there arose in his soul many doubts and fears and apprehensions—which is about as far as I got. What a dreary book. I wondered how I could have stumbled into Christian's swamp. Somewhere along the way I must have taken a wrong turn. I reviewed my life. College. Army. A few romances. Tedious jobs. Unsuccessful marriage. No children. Divorce. A bit of travel. How ordinary. I could not see where I had made an important mistake, my life was commonplace. Well, then, what about the future? I could not imagine any because I had nothing to anticipate. My past was a heap of slag, my future a bottomless pit. If I remembered Bunyan correctly, from the Slough of Despond one entered the Valley of Humiliation.

As far as I could see across the harbor everything appeared natural but at the same time unreal. Sailboats were dipping with the breeze. Fishing boats rocked in the swells. A freighter on the opposite side of the bay ploughed heavily toward Oakland. San Francisco gleamed like Byzantium. Sausalito bristled with cheerful tourists. People went about the business of life wherever I looked and I addressed them as though I were John Bunyan. Oh yes, enjoy yourselves! Oh yes, by all means! But do not forget that the path of indulgence is strewn with traps to catch the unwary.

I contemplated the gulls flapping and screaming over some half-submerged treasure in the bay and it occurred to me that they might be quarreling over Albert Defanbaugh's corpse. Yes, indeed, I thought, old Bunyan knew what he was talking about.

At that moment a familiar voice cried: Behold yon Crawford!

Roscoe and Pax were approaching. Roscoe, costumed as Father Time in a bathrobe with a rope around his middle, carried an hourglass and a scythe. Pax, daisies in her hair, wore an extremely short nightgown and sandals and was clutching a book to her breast. I had no idea what or whom she was trying to represent—maybe Sappho. They both could have been mistaken for escaped lunatics. Here it was Sunday afternoon and the town full of people from Iowa.

Didn't Magda get hold of you? said Pax. She told me she called and called.

I haven't been answering the phone, I said. I haven't felt like talking.

Oh, you! Pax exclaimed. Everybody's going to Oliver's party.

Arise! Roscoe cackled, reaping the air with his scythe. Arise, thou sluggard!

I told them I didn't have a costume.

Now, Crawford, you don't need one, Pax said. Come on, get up. It's going to be a marvelous party with champagne punch and dancing girls. It's on Bambi's houseboat. All your friends will be there.

I couldn't imagine going to a party. Something's wrong with me, I said. I believe I have Acedia.

Pax took a little step backward. You have what?

It was a medieval illness, I said. I've forgotten exactly what it means. Sloth. Weariness. Torpor. It's much worse than boredom. I can't seem to get over it.

My goodness, Pax said. She tried to sound sympathetic but I knew she was wondering if it might be contagious. Roscoe looked at me suspiciously.

All right, I said and got up. Why is Magda giving a party for Oliver on his forty-ninth birthday? Why didn't she wait until he was fifty?

Roscoe lifted the hourglass. Ho ho! She was afraid he'd be too old to enjoy it.

That's right, said Pax. She's mad at him because she wanted to go to Tahiti and Oliver said maybe next year they could go and she said she didn't want to go to Tahiti with a fifty-year-old man. She hired an organ grinder with a monkey.

I couldn't understand what they were talking about. My head felt like a gourd. I didn't want to go to the party but I didn't know what else to do. I'd been sitting on the rock for at least an hour and I could hardly walk. My legs were half paralyzed and my tailbone ached.

Pax took me by the arm. She had not quite made up her mind about Acedia and if I did anything odd she was ready to scream. You'll have a fabulous time, she said. There was a man at the bakery who spent four years in Tibet and met the Abominable Snowman so we invited him.

Nepal, said Roscoe.

I thought it was Tibet, said Pax.

Nepal, Roscoe said. He didn't tell us he met the Abominable Snowman. Anyway, that isn't what they call it. Yeti is what they call it.

Oh, whatever, Pax said. I thought he was nice. He looks awfully quaint, but he's nice.

I'm going to sit on a bench in the park, I said. Both of them were getting on my nerves. Roscoe kept reaping the air and Pax never stopped talking. Everybody within a hundred yards was waiting for a good breeze to flip her nightgown.

No, you're coming to the party, she said. Roscoe held up the hourglass and bellowed Ho ho! and if he did that once more I was going to hit him. I asked myself why they were leading me along the boardwalk to Bambi's houseboat when all I wanted was a comfortable bench where I could think about how miserable I felt. I couldn't remember who they had met at the bakery—not that it mattered.

I forget his name, said Pax. Stonewall or something. He told us the Abominable Snowman actually kidnapped a girl and carried her off to his cave. Isn't that thrilling?

Some villagers tracked him down and killed him, Roscoe said. This guy bought the hide and both feet.

How repulsive, said Pax.

I told them I was going home to take a nap.

Oh, there he is! Pax cried, waving at a lanky individual who was shambling along the boardwalk with a grocery bag in one hand. He wore bottle glasses and his head swayed back and forth as he walked.

Stonewall! Yoo hoo! she cried.

The man's triangular little head drifted from side to side like a viper as he peered through his glasses.

This is our friend Crawford, Pax said when we caught up with him. Crawford, meet Stonewall.

I said hello.

My name's Jackson, he said.

I knew it was something like that, said Pax. Oh, listen! You can hear the organ grinder!

Be careful with that apparatus, Jackson said. He was leaning away from the scythe.

I've got a headache, I said. I'm going home. I really am.

You are not, said Pax. Magda and Bambi have made just oodles of champagne punch. We're going to get you drunk, that's what we're going to do. You'll forget all about your silly disease.

What's wrong with him? Jackson asked, peering at me uneasily through the bottles.

Acedia, I said.

Jackson looked relieved. I've had that, he said. It can be serious. How long have you had it?

I'm not sure, I said. It crept up on me.

Yes, that's what you've got, he said. I recognize the symptoms. I had a terrible attack in Kathmandu.

I didn't realize people still got it, I said. I thought it disappeared during the Middle Ages.

Not at all, said Jackson, not at all. As a matter of fact, I knew a woman in Goa who nearly died of it. You should take precautions. Do you know anything about the Hindu concept of Chakras? For example, are you aware that your alternative energy flow might be obstructed? Do you feel tired?

I'm exhausted, I said.

He asked about my vision, whether things occasionally got sort of blurred. I had to admit they did. Then he said the imbalance of organic force might not be evident at a structural level but it could be apparent in the electromagnetic field. His head swayed back and forth and I could not get over the idea that he was a rattlesnake. He began talking about meridian points of the body and deficient kidneys and I had the feeling that he would recommend acupuncture or something, so I asked what took him to Nepal. He said he'd been an industrial chemist for twelve years—get up, drive to the lab, put in his hours, drive home—and finally decided the hell with it, he wanted to see the world. Well, that made sense. I envied him. I wanted to see more of the world myself, but it takes money. He looked surprised when I pointed this out and said it wasn't difficult, what you have to do is take advantage of stock market fluctuations. All right, I thought, tell me how. But we were near the houseboat.

You'll have such fun, Pax assured me. Oh, there's Magda. Magda, we're here! Guess who we found sitting on a rock!

Magda swept down the gangplank with her vast muumuu billowing. It was an awful sight. She reminded me of the Winged Victory of Samothrace.

And this is Stonewall, said Pax. We found him at the bakery.

How do you do, Stonewall, Magda said and graciously extended one hand as she had been taught to do at finishing school, I'm so pleased you were able to join us. She glanced at the grocery bag. But really, you needn't have brought a thing. We're afloat in wine.

My name's Jackson, he said. I didn't bring any wine. Jackson had not been to finishing school.

After just the faintest pause Magda said, Do come in, won't you? Or "come aboard" as they say. We're trying to keep Oliver away from the punch.

Oliver had not been kept away from the punch. His eyelids drooped, his hair looked like an abandoned bird nest, and his mouth hung open. He was seated on a crude plywood throne that I guessed had been hammered together by Sonny Bippus. There was a pasteboard crown on his head and a moth-eaten purple cloak draped around his shoulders. A broken scepter lay on the rug.

You might introduce Jackson, Magda suggested to Pax. I'm sure you must be acquainted with everyone. Bambi needs help in the kitchen—the "galley" I believe it's called. Make yourselves at home.

Jackson was looking around. Thirty or forty birthday guests had arrived and more were marching up the gangplank two by two like animals entering the Ark. Jackson looked at the organ grinder who had a great black Sicilian mustache and sparkling black eyes and he looked at the monkey attached to the organ by a chain. The monkey wore a green pillbox hat and was picking its nose while staring at Bambi's Persian cat. Bambi had decided to impersonate a ballerina but the costume did not fit very well, or maybe it was not the costume's fault. Bambi's shoulder blades stuck out like chicken wings and the lavender tutu hung lopsided. Jackson contemplated Norwood Hovarth who weighed about three hundred pounds and fancied himself a jockey. Norwood and knock-kneed Sarah in a belly dancer costume were dipping into the punch bowl. Jackson looked at several other guests.

These are your friends? he asked.

I thought about it for a while but couldn't make up my mind, so I shrugged.

Who's the pipe? he asked.

I knew he must be talking about Marvin Wetbush who never went anywhere without a long ivory meerschaum that resembled an upside-down question mark. Nobody ever had seen Marvin without the pipe. I thought he probably took it to bed. Marvin was all right, except that conversation was difficult because he would always fold his lips around the pipe stem and suck on it before responding to anything you said. Whenever I talked to him I tried to avoid watching his lips. He was on the opposite side of the punch bowl listening to Bambi's ex-husband who sold used Cadillacs in San Rafael. Marvin had been a high school teacher in Ohio or one of those places before moving to California. Now he painted enormous abstract pictures that none of the local galleries cared to handle. I believe some of them may have been too big to get through the door.

He's an artist, I said.

Jackson was not happy. I feel that I don't belong here, he said. Who's the dwarf?

I never saw him before, I said. He looks mean.

That's how they are, Jackson said. It's because of the distribution of chromosomes. The meanest dwarf I ever saw was a cook in Australia. Everybody hated him.

I thought about going someplace else for a drink, but the party wasn't quite as bad as I'd expected. In fact, there were several attractive women and men with interesting faces. The organ grinder was drawing a crowd. He cranked with one hand and caressed his mustache with the other and turned those big white Sicilian teeth in all directions, but I noticed he kept an eye on Billie Serapis. The monkey stared at everybody and jumped around. When it stared at me I stared back with what I hoped was an ugly expression. I had a feeling it would bite and I was in no mood for trouble with a monkey.

I've been studying you, Jackson said. You don't appear to be in good health. What sort of work do you do? Office work?

I told him I was unemployed, at the moment unemployed. And not that this is any of my business, I said, but what have you got in the bag?

He offered me the bag and said take a look, but I didn't care for that idea. I suggested maybe he could put whatever it was on the piano, so he turned the bag upside down and a long black hairy foot dropped out. I knew it, I said to myself. I knew it would be something like that.

For a minute or so the foot just lay there on the piano and I had the impression we were actors in a surrealist movie. Then the dwarf saw it. He waddled over and rested his chin on the piano. What you got there, buddy? he asked, grinning at Jackson.

Jackson didn't like being called buddy and said his name was Jackson.

Eric, the dwarf said. They shook hands. What you got there, buddy?

Figure it out, said Jackson.

You joker, Eric said. I know a gorilla's foot when I see one.

Jackson looked at the foot with a thoughtful expression and I could tell he didn't want to talk to Eric. I felt pretty sure the foot didn't belong to a gorilla because it was too narrow. The toes were strange, not exactly like a man's toes, but almost.

Magda walked out of the kitchen with a silver tray full of munchkin sandwiches cut into circles and oblongs and diamonds and triangles. I guess she and Bambi used cookie cutters. She smiled at us as she went by and then she saw the foot. She dropped the tray on the piano and said, Dear God in Heaven, I'm going to faint. Help yourself, everybody. Oh, sweet Jesus.

Eric grinned at her. He snatched a sandwich and peeped inside but didn't like what he saw and tossed it back on the tray. He was so rude that I started thinking about his chromosomes, but also I was wondering how Jackson got the foot through customs because you can't come back from Nepal with a package and walk right through. He must have bribed somebody.

Magda was hanging on to the piano lid with both hands and gazing at the foot. What on earth! she said in her finishing school voice. Just then a man in a turtle-neck sweater who looked like a movie star came over and Magda presented him.

Jackson, she said, may I introduce Dr. Ledoux? Dr. Ledoux is an orthopedic surgeon.

Hello there, Dr. Ledoux said and displayed a condescending smile. I under-stand you're a primate biologist.

No, Jackson said. I used to be a chemist.

Dr. Ledoux studied the foot, but kept both hands clasped behind his back. It was obvious that he did not intend to pick it up. Do you have X rays? he asked. Jackson said no. Dr. Ledoux cleared his throat and said, What's the story on this? Jackson explained about the Yeti kidnapping a girl. She was alive when the villagers found his cave, but she was in a coma and died three weeks later raving mad.

What a joke, Eric said scornfully. I've heard that one before. When she woke up she began screaming "Why doesn't he call? Why doesn't he write?" That's an old one.

Jackson tried to ignore him.

Hey, pal, Eric said with a disagreeable grin, I want to show this to somebody, okay? What a great gag.

Keep your paws to yourself, said Jackson.

Dr. Ledoux was still considering the foot. Remarkable, he said. He cleared his throat again, nodded politely, and walked away.

What did you do with the hide? I asked. Roscoe told me you bought the whole thing.

I hung it in a closet in New Delhi and somebody stole it, Jackson said. I don't care, though, because it was full of bugs.

Bambi's cat leaped on the piano and Magda clapped her hands. Oh, such a naughty kitty! Shoo shoo, Noodles!

Eric had been inspecting the sandwiches and eating the ones he liked. That damn organ grinder, he said with his mouth full. I hate "Come Back to Sorrento."

Several other people gathered around the piano. They were drinking punch and laughing and discussing the foot and one woman kept referring to Jackson as Pro-fessor Stonewall, so the professor had a lot of questions to answer.

Two business suits joined the group. One of them asked if it was real. I pointed to Professor Stonewall. The other suit was trying to think of a funny remark, I could see it working on his face. Finally he grunted and pretended to be scratching his armpits. I decided I'd had enough so I refilled my cup at the punchbowl and stepped outside. A couple of women were standing by the rail. One of them turned to me and asked how anybody could live on a houseboat. Well, she had a point because the bay smelled worse than a privy when the tide was out, but I didn't want to talk to her so I wandered toward the stern and there was the monkey chained to a deck chair. It didn't like me and bared its teeth. You bite me, I said, you little peckerwood I'll throw you sixty yards in the bay. Then I noticed Billie Serapis and the organ grinder curled up in a lifeboat. I thought they wanted to be alone so I went back inside. Jackson's foot was still drawing a crowd, but for the moment he wasn't answering questions.

I didn't expect this, he said. This is grotesque.

It seemed to me a fairly typical houseboat party, although I could understand how he felt. A little girl with a tambourine was prancing around Norwood and Sarah who were dancing—which was a terrible thing to watch because neither of them could dance and there was no music, unless you counted the tambourine or a different kind of music in the lifeboat. A bunch of executives were clustered in a corner probably talking about Atlantic Richfield preferred stock and Bambi was shouting at Roscoe because she was afraid he would decapitate somebody. People were coming up to congratulate Oliver on being forty-nine years old, but he was so drunk that he only smirked. It was just a matter of time before he fell off his throne. I could smell perfume and fried chicken and marijuana and whatever had been exposed when the tide ran out. There was a lot of noise in the kitchen. I saw Magda waving a broom and all at once I understood what Jackson meant. We had gotten on board a ship full of nuts. The Germans have a word for that, but I couldn't remember what it was so I asked him.

Narrenschiff, he said, looming over me like a gargoyle. How do you feel? Are you plagued by unusual thoughts?

There were none I cared to mention. By the way, I said, is Acedia contagious?

He hesitated, but then said there had been an epidemic not long ago in Uttar Pradesh. Fortunately the victims recovered. Chaucer mentions the affliction, he said. Agayns this roten-herted sinne of Accidie and Slouthe sholde men exercise hem-self. I would say that in your case the subcutaneous particles might be negatively charged. Let me see your tongue.

Well, I couldn't think of a reason not to, so I stuck out my tongue. He stared at it and evidently disapproved of what he saw. Hold up your left hand like this, he said and demonstrated. I felt a little silly, but nobody seemed to be watching.

Close your eyes, he said. So I did, and he stroked my palm a few times. How does that feel? he asked. Not bad, I said, it sort of tickles. That's because of the intrinsic texturization of subcutaneous movement, he explained. Have you considered a lengthy sea voyage? I couldn't afford a lengthy sea voyage so I asked if I could open my eyes and he said yes. This probably doesn't interest you, I said, but I've been sleeping ten or twelve hours a day or sometimes more.

Jackson nodded and said he had felt like that in Kathmandu. His Acedia got so bad that he spent most of his time under the bed. Then he met Dr. Hari Das Gupta who advised chewing twelve almonds every morning to cleanse the intestines. I thought that might be worth a try. Actually, I was feeling a little better. Jackson went on about color meditation or something and how Dr. Das Gupta's name in Brooklyn was Mort Zelinsky until he became enlightened, but I didn't follow much of it because Magda was clapping for attention.

People eventually quieted down and Magda announced that this was Oliver's forty-ninth birthday, which everybody knew. She said no speeches would be allowed. Then she blew a whistle. In marched Willis Schnittke and Bubba Pierpont and two other guys. They were dressed like Roman slaves and were lurching around trying to carry a cake about three feet high and three feet wide. It appeared to be made out of orange crate slats and from the way they were staggering and the cake was rocking back and forth I thought I knew what was inside. Finally they managed to put it down in front of the guest of honor who was so drunk that Bambi was standing behind the throne with her hands on his shoulders to keep him upright. Then the little girl with the tambourine pranced around and suddenly did the splits. Magda blew her whistle, the lid popped off the cake and up jumped a naked blonde shrieking Happy Birthday. I'd been afraid that would happen. Everybody cheered and clapped. Oliver's birthday present was lumpish and awkward and for some reason she reminded me of a turnip. She had trouble climbing out of the cake. I never saw a clumsier woman, but she made it and then decided to sit on his lap but accidentally knocked off his crown. It was dreadful. He didn't seem to know what was happening.

Jackson asked if I had experienced palpitations or dizzy spells. I wished he would quit trying to diagnose me because I could feel a trickle of energy returning.

The Holy Roman Emperor Rudolph suffered from Acedia, he said. Were you aware of that?

No, I said, and of course he knew all about Rudolph.

It used to be one of the seven capital sins, he said. You might not have been aware of that either.

I was getting a little sick of Jackson so I challenged him to name the other six, which was foolish. He knew them. Avarice. Lust. Hubris. Gluttony. Wrath. Envy. Well, I was surprised that Lust could be a capital sin. I'd been afflicted by it now and again, at times extremely afflicted, although it hadn't bothered me since contracting Acedia. Gluttony, not very often. The others were occasional problems. Wrath, yes, but everything considered I didn't know why Wrath should be sinful. Or maybe that proved I was guilty of Hubris.

Jackson kept talking. Acedia was described not only in the Septuagint Bible but in the works of various pagan authors and so on. Evagrius Ponticus wrote about Acedia in the year 383. John Cassian reported it—whoever he was. St. Thomas called it a capital sin because it activated or created other sins. Well, I'd heard more than enough. I had a feeling Jackson could name the Seven Wonders of the Ancient World, he had that sort of mind. When he was a kid everybody must have hated him. Probably he could multiply 329 by 486 without a pencil. There's a kid like that in every class.

I don't know why I asked—maybe it's a symptom of Acedia—but I did and he reeled them off like a schoolteacher. It seemed to me that his triangular skull behind those bottle glasses looked even more weird while he was reciting Colossus of Rhodes, Mausoleum at Halicarnassus, Temple of Artemis, and all the rest.

Tell me about the Colossus, I said. I didn't care about the Mausoleum, or the lighthouse at Alexandria or the Hanging Gardens or the others, but Colossus of Rhodes had a majestic sound. So the professor rambled on about Chares of Lindos who designed it, and Strabo and Pliny the Elder and an earthquake during the third century B.C. and a thousand camel loads of bronze et cetera while I emptied another cup of punch and wondered why I was on Bambi's houseboat listening to this eccentric who had come back from Nepal with a Yeti's foot. I could hardly make out what he was saying because an old man wearing a World War aviator's costume with a leather helmet and goggles and a long yellow scarf had started to play the piano, but it didn't matter. I understood by now that Jackson was a bit cracked, although he wasn't the only one. Somebody in a cowboy suit was trying to stand on his head while Marvin was doing his Zorba imitation—holding a chair in his teeth and flapping his arms. Marvin imitated Zorba at every party. Meanwhile the slaves were waiting for the blonde to get back inside the cake so they could put on the lid and carry her away. It was a squalid performance. I don't know why artists like to pretend that naked women are graceful.

Dr. Ledoux came by just then. He had been marching around the room with his arms folded and a contemptuous expression. Well, I thought, instead of acting superior why don't you just leave?

Jackson had begun talking about endorphin release and Ayurvedic needle therapy and for all I knew he had a syringe in his grocery bag. We were near the punch bowl so I nodded to give the impression that I was listening and dipped up a fresh cup. A very attractive woman on the other side of the piano was talking to an idiot dressed like Pancho Villa and I thought I might butt in on their conversation if I could get away from the professor.

Suddenly there was a lot of yelling outside. Somebody said call the cops and Magda blew her whistle. Oliver woke up, gazed around with a stupefied smile and toppled off his throne but nobody paid much attention. The monkey had gotten loose and Eric was chasing it. I noticed Bambi stretched out on the couch with her eyes shut. She was pressing her temples with her fingertips and there was barbecue sauce all over her tutu. She looked like a wounded grasshopper.

The monkey scared her cat, said one of the business suits. It ran down the gangplank mewing, that's all I know.

Jackson turned to me and said, My God, this is like something from the eighteenth century.

Magda hurried out of the bathroom with an armful of towels so I asked what happened. She said Billie Serapis and the organ grinder had fallen into the bay. I guess that should have surprised me, but it didn't.

Thank goodness the tide is out or they might have drowned, Magda said. Both of them are covered with mud. Billie looks like the bride of Frankenstein and she's hysterical. She says it's the organ grinder's fault.

They could catch diphtheria, said another business suit. The bay is alive with diphtheria.

I'm going home, Jackson said.

All right, I thought, go on home. Nobody promised you a meeting of great minds. It seemed to me that the party was getting livelier and being around Jackson wasn't much fun. His head drooped and he stared at the rug like a whipped dog. I asked if he felt all right because he'd been eating a lot of barbecued turkey.

I was hoping for intellectual stimulation, he said. These people are frivolous.

Of course there was a certain amount of truth in that, but I didn't want to discuss it. Pancho Villa's lady had been watching me over Pancho's shoulder and made it clear that before long she would be available.

How about another cup of punch? I asked.

Jackson sighed and wrung his hands. I don't know what's wrong, he said, my head feels peculiar.

Standing up for a long time can be exhausting, I said. Why don't you lie down on the couch?

He didn't answer. I felt sorry for him and also a little worried. He looked sallow. I believe he was naturally sallow, but in addition to that he was slumping. I thought maybe he needed a breath of fresh air so I suggested a stroll around the deck, but he wagged his head and said he didn't have enough energy. It occurred to me that a dozen almonds might help, or maybe a cup of tea. There was a bowl of mixed nuts on the piano and Bambi might have some tea in the kitchen.

I haven't felt this tired since Kathmandu, he said. It's a struggle to keep my eyes open.

I asked if there was anything I could do, but he wanted to be left alone. He seemed to have wilted. I could barely hear what he was saying. He looked awful. Pancho Villa's lady was staring at me and the message was pretty clear. Besides, I felt a lot better. Life didn't seem as bleak as it did when I was sitting on the rock.

See you around, Professor, I said and patted him on the back.

He mumbled something about taking a nap.

1991

THE CARIBBEAN PROVEDOR

A T FOUR O'CLOCK the sun was burning like a green lemon above the coconut palms. The ship's rail was too hot to touch. Koerner stood in the shadow of a lifeboat with a cigarette between his teeth and looked around. In the water alongside the stern some garbage was floating. On shore a few Negroes in straw hats sat on boxes in the shade of the customs house. Nobody else was in sight. There was no breeze, and not a sound except the hissing ball of the sun. Aboard ship nothing moved and there was a smell of hot canvas.

Koerner felt suddenly that his skull was as empty as a gourd. He looked at the deck to be sure that if he fainted he would not hit his head on a piece of iron. Then the feeling passed, but he thought it would be a good idea to go inside. A cold drink would be a very good idea. For almost eight hours he had been playing chess with the surgeon from Ohio. Neither of them had eaten since breakfast. They had played without stopping and were planning to continue until dinner time as usual, but the surgeon's wife got angry. After five days at sea the score stood 23 to 17 in the surgeon's favor, but he was going as far as Vigo and if his wife did not cause too much trouble there would be time enough to overtake him.

Koerner squinted at the shore to see if there was anything he might have missed but the town looked worse during the day than it had the previous night, and there had been nothing worth seeing even then. It was a port of call and they would leave in a few hours. The loading had been completed.

He dropped his cigarette into the water, stepped back inside the ship and descended to the lounge where he took a stool at the bar next to a fat man who was wearing a short-sleeved shirt. The fat man was stroking a little bottle of champagne as tenderly as though it were a cat and talking to the bartender in Portuguese. He stopped talking but continued playing with the bottle, wiping away the moisture with his fingers.

"Um Magos," Koerner said to the bartender.

The champagne was good and very cheap and it was cold and he thought he would be drinking a number of these little bottles while crossing the Atlantic.

"Are you on this boat?" the fat man asked in Portuguese.

Koerner nodded. The man was probably a merchant seaman, both of his thick hairy red arms were heavily tattooed. On his left wrist was a bright new watch which looked as though he had just that afternoon put it on.

"Are you a passenger?"

The heat, no lunch, and so much chess had been exhausting and Koerner did not want to get into a conversation. Besides, the man was anxious to talk and therefore probably did not have much to say. He began to roll the bottle between his palms and tried to remember when the ship was scheduled to arrive in Vigo.

"It's nice to be rich," the fat man said in a voice that was almost threatening. "I'm poor. I work for a living. I can't afford to go on a voyage."

Reluctantly Koerner looked at the man directly for the first time. He was about fifty years old, with a flattened nose and protruding lips and skin that burned but would never tan. Underneath the fat he was solid. He could have been a wrestler. Koerner noticed that the top of one of his ears was missing, sliced off quite cleanly.

"What do you do on this ship?" the fat man said.

"Not a thing."

"You don't do nothing at all. Is that what you tell me?"

"I play chess."

"Ah! You play chess, do you?"

"Every day. I've been playing this entire day since breakfast and I'm very tired."

"Every day. So you been on board a few days. You didn't come on board this ship last night?"

Koerner shook his head.

"I can't waste time playing around. I got a lot of work to do."

"All right," Koerner said.

"When you are not playing games what do you do?"

"I travel."

"That's all you do. You don't do nothing else?"

Koerner took a drink of champagne and then said, "Nothing else."

"You don't work on this ship?"

"No," Koerner said.

On a shelf behind the bar there were trinkets for sale. Portuguese galleons with billowing sails of filigreed gold, carved wood boxes inlaid with ivory squares, black lace Spanish fans, postage stamps from different countries in cellophane packages, flags, and miniature cork life preservers with the name of the ship. Some of the postage stamps were quite beautiful, especially the Japanese which looked like tiny woodcuts. There was snow on Mount Fuji, and waterfalls, and animals. He thought he might buy a package of them.

"I have business here. I'm the provedor," the man said. "I finished loading eight tons of food and drink on this ship. It's all done. I was working while you were asleep in your very pleasant cabin."

Koerner continued to look at the stamps.

"Now everything is on board so I'm having a drink. I'll buy you a drink, too."

"Thank you," Koerner said, "but I've already got one."

"I have been supplying this ship, all the ships of this line, and a lot of other ships for sixteen years. You don't know what it means to work hard like that. I have never done anything wrong. I have made friends all those years. Tomorrow I give the company my bill, then in a few days they pay me everything. Just sign the papers. I asked to buy you a drink. If you don't want to drink with me it's your business. I don't give a damn."

"Dois Magos," Koerner said to the bartender and took out his wallet, but the fat man pushed it aside.

"I can do this much," he said. "You don't get yourself in trouble drinking with me. You got nothing to worry about. Anyway, nothing worries you."

Koerner didn't answer.

"What's your name?" the fat man asked.

Koerner told him.

"That's what you call yourself. All right, if that's what you tell me it is. You say you're a passenger on this ship."

"I am."

"If you're a passenger on this ship where are you going?"

"Lisboa."

"Then you come back again?"

"Maybe."

"Traveling. That's what you said."

Koerner nodded.

"You work in Martinique?"

"I don't work in Martinique."

"You don't work for the French?"

"No."

"You look French, whatever your name is. Are you a tourist?"

The word was a little degrading but Koerner decided to accept it. "All right, call me a tourist."

"Where do you live? You live in Lisboa?"

"No."

"You don't live on this island. I'm sure about that."

"You're right, I don't live on this island."

"In Curaçao?"

"No."

"I seen you once in Curaçao. A long time ago. Maybe three years ago."

"I was there once," Koerner said while he tried to remember when he had been in Curaçao. Then he remembered it had been about three years ago.

"In a café holding a newspaper, pretending to read. But you was watching somebody. I don't forget."

Koerner had not thought of it for three years but now he remembered sitting in a café with a newspaper, although he could not remember that he had been watching anybody.

"It was some English newspaper."

"Sure," Koerner said in English.

"Sure. Me too. Hell, yes," the fat man said in English but then continued in Portuguese. "I speak eight or nine languages. I don't know how many, maybe more than that. Spanish. German. French. Just about anything. In my work I got to. You didn't see me in Curaçao?"

"No."

"I can see you like a photograph. In Curaçao I could show you what table you was sitting at. I could tell who you was watching."

"You notice a lot."

The fat man stopped talking. Koerner drank some more champagne, then without turning his head he glanced at the wristwatch.

The man said immediately, "You want it?"

"No."

"You want this watch I'll give it to you. It don't mean nothing to me." He was starting to unbuckle the strap.

"I don't want your watch," Koerner said. "I've got no use for it."

"Listen, whoever you call yourself, you know what my little girl said to me this morning? She said 'Papa, I know you have to go to work today because loading the ship means plenty of money for you, I know that.' Do you know what I said to her? I said 'No, Sweetheart, the ship means you can go to school and it means nice things for you. It don't mean the money is for me.' That's what I told my little girl this morning. But you don't know what I'm talking about because you don't have no little girl. You don't have no idea at all what it means to bring a present to a little girl. A little ten-dollar watch from Switzerland. You don't know how much that means to a child. Something she can show her friends and tell them her Papa got this for her and it comes from Switzerland. A little ten-dollar watch. A ten-dollar watch! But you don't care about these things. They don't mean nothing to you."

Well now, Koerner thought, I believe he's going to smuggle that watch past customs.

"You want it? You want this watch I'll take it off and give it to you if that's all you want," the provedor said. He was breathing heavily.

"Keep it. I don't need it."

"A man like me works from the day he's born but he don't get very rich. What do you want?"

What is he saying? Koerner wondered.

"I don't forget you, not for one minute. A long time ago in Curaçao I told myself 'There he is. That's him.' I feel sorry for you, William Koerner, if that's what you tell me your name is. I feel sorry for anybody like you that goes around like you do, doing what you do. Not having any wife to come home to, not having a little girl throw her arms around your neck when you get off work. Eating by yourself every night. It don't make no difference to you, I know that, but I feel sorry for you. I'd rather be in my place."

Koerner waited to hear what the man would say next.

The provedor shrugged his shoulders. "A cheap watch. What difference does it make? Who cares? It don't hurt nobody. You want another Magos?" he asked in a voice that tried to be friendly.

Koerner shook his head.

"A man like me. What am I? All my life I work hard, but I don't amount to nothing. Maybe you're important. Probably that's what you think you are. You're proud of yourself, but I don't envy you. I don't want to trade places with you."

He realizes I know about that watch, Koerner thought, and he's afraid I'm going to tell the customs officer. But why should I? It's no business of mine. He can smuggle half the watches in Switzerland for all I care. I don't work for customs. He knows that.

Or does he?

And then everything the man had said gradually began making sense.

He believes I'm an inspector. This man thinks I work for the shipping company or for some government. He doesn't believe a word I've told him.

"Maybe you like what you do," the provedor was saying. "Maybe you don't. You do it just for the money? If that's what you do it for nobody's going to care if you live or die. A man like you could get killed and nobody cares. What good does money do? Sure, plenty of things. A lot of things. I know. I know that. But what kind of a life have you got?"

Suppose I were an inspector, Koerner said to himself, and suppose I had just now caught him with this watch. At the moment he's not guilty of anything because he hasn't taken it ashore. So why is he worried? I don't understand. Suppose that in a few minutes he does try to take it through without paying duty and he's caught, what would happen? Nothing. They wouldn't let him keep the watch, that's all. I can't understand why he's worried. Of course if he'd made a habit of this, if he'd been smuggling things ashore for sixteen years that might be a different kind of horse.

So that's it! Not just a wristwatch this afternoon, my fat friend, you've got a business going on the side. Coming aboard and going ashore day after day, one ship after another, for all these years. No wonder you're worried. I would be, too. And you don't know who I am, do you? If I were in your britches I'd be scared to death.

It mounts up, doesn't it? Sixteen years multiplied by how many ships? How many people do you deal with? And what do you bring ashore? What were you and the bartender talking about when I walked into the lounge, and why did you stop talking? Will there be a few cases of cognac hoisted ashore late tonight? That ten-dollar watch is nothing. That's a peanut, isn't it, my friend? You've finished work and you feel so good you decided to wear it ashore right past the customs officer, right past his nose because you feel so good. Ordinarily you'd slip it into your pocket and nobody would search you because you're the provedor. Everybody knows you. After all, you've been here sixteen years.

Yes, indeed, it does mount up, doesn't it? But something else mounts up too, my friend, my ambitious businessman. Every day you've got to worry, like every other ambitious businessman. And you wait, and you wait, because you've juggled the accounts, and each day the waiting is a little harder. But you've got to keep on because you're not quite strong enough to let it go. Just one more time. One more time. Then suddenly I'm here.

Koerner put his elbows on the bar and smiled.

"William Koerner," the provedor said, "if that's what you call yourself, I feel sorry in my heart for anybody like you. Nothing makes any difference to you. I got to pity you."

"Ah," Koerner said, and shrugged.

"Sure," the fat man said, "you can be like that. How many people you hurt don't mean a thing in the world. You don't care for nobody. You got no family. No little girl waiting at home asking her Mama when you're coming in."

He loves his daughter, Koerner thought. She's the only person or thing on earth this man loves.

"Why don't you get married?" the provedor asked. He was trying to pull his face into an expression of intimacy but he could not get rid of the fear. "When a man gets married he knows what's worthwhile. He don't run around hurting people."

Whenever I please, Koerner told himself, following the idea slowly, as though it was a speared fish pulling him through the water, I can destroy this man. I can ruin his life. I can destroy his business, his reputation, and probably his marriage. Whenever I want to, from now on. I can do it because he thinks I can. He himself gave me the power, which means he can't possibly doubt it. I'm powerful because he thinks so. And whatever I want to do with him, I can do. If I order him to go ashore and wait for me, he will. If I stand up and beckon to him he'll follow me like a toy on a string.

"Give me a cigarette," he said.

The provedor picked up the package and offered it; Koerner took one and waited and the provedor lighted it for him.

So this is how it feels, Koerner thought, this is the way it feels. I'd never have guessed. I can actually destroy a man and I can hardly keep from laughing. I can put an end to a man's life and I feel a kind of elation. I feel as though I'd like to do something nice for this man. I don't know why, but I rather like him.

"What do you call yourself?" Koerner demanded, and smiled.

The provedor gave him a curious look, almost of surprise, or of some deep and sudden confusion.

"Oh, come on now," said Koerner, trying to control his excitement.

The provedor continued to look at him with a speculative expression, but finally said, "I am Hans Julio García."

It had been a stupid question Koerner realized too late.

"Ah," he said, turning his face aside, "for some reason that sounds familiar. Did we meet in Curaçao?"

The provedor didn't answer.

Koerner looked into the mirror behind the bar. He could see the fat man's ear. The top of it appeared to have been taken off with a razor swipe, and he remembered his first impression of the provedor, of how solid he was under the creases of fat. It occurred to him that Hans Julio García probably was a very dangerous man, and that he had been threatening this man.

I wonder what might happen, he asked himself, when this man decides I'm not who he thinks I am. I don't know. What happens probably will depend on how he feels about me. If he thinks I never suspected the truth he won't have any feelings about me and he'll forget me. No, not that. He won't forget this afternoon, or me, for a long time. I'll be the tourist he talked to in the bar.

But if he thinks I did suspect the truth? If, let's say, he thinks I've guessed. What then?

I don't know that either. I don't want to think about it. I don't know how I got into this but I don't like it. I feel like I've put my hand inside a jar full of spiders. I didn't realize what I was doing. This could get ugly. I don't know how it got started. It was that watch. I noticed the watch because it was new and it didn't belong on his wrist, his wrist is too big for it. Then I looked at it again because I was hungry and wanted to know how soon I could eat but he didn't know that. I should have asked the time instead of trying to see the dial, but I didn't want to talk to him. How was I to know this would happen?

But if I go on pretending to be an inspector how could he find out I'm not? He's afraid of me, he's quit asking questions. He's pretending more than I am. Sorry for me, he says. I pity you, he says. He doesn't pity me, he hates me. He's terrified of me, his hand was shaking when he tried to light my cigarette. He thinks I know everything about him. By God, why couldn't I turn him in? Why not? I didn't ask for this, it's his fault. I came here to get a drink, that's all, and now he's involved me with his guilt.

Damn this man's soul, Koerner thought, and felt himself becoming angry. I could see this man in Hell! Why should I care what happens to him? He means nothing to me. Nothing! All right, by God, let him suffer! He deserves it—the lousy thief!

But could I do it? Say I have the power, can I use it? If I ruin him who else is ruined? His daughter, for one. His wife. I don't have any idea who else. What difference does it make to me? For all I know they're both as rotten as he is. Yes. The little girl, too. And how do I know she exists? Because he talked sentimentally about "my little girl" and what she'd said to him this morning. How do I know it's true? How many lies have I heard since he started talking?

Koerner had been leaning on his elbows, rocking the stool slowly backward. He glanced at García. The fat man was gazing at him very seriously.

He's waiting. I've got to make up my mind. Suppose on the other hand I let him off. But how? He's never admitted anything. Just the same he's guilty and he knows I know it. He's waiting to see what I do. Suppose I've decided to let him go. What do I say? "I feel sorry for you, Hans Julio. I pity you. I don't want to hurt your daughter. I'm not going to do to you what I thought I would." Oh yes. He'd believe that on the day he'd believe my name is William Koerner. He'll believe me only when I act the way he expects me to act, whether it's false or not. And if I've come here to get him I'd never let him go, not unless I was corrupt.

Suppose I hinted about a bribe. And say he agreed to pay me. What's to stop me from being twice as corrupt? Turn him in as soon as I get the money. Or come back later. Bleed him again and again.

I must be out of mind, Koerner thought and shook his head. I'm trying to figure out whether I can untangle this mess by accepting a bribe. I must be going mad. This is a dangerous man beside me who assumes I'm somebody that I'm not. If he ever finds out how much I've guessed he might kill me. Right now he's wondering. He knows I've learned something and he realizes that I'm playing with it. He's about to lose control. He thinks he's already lost, he has no more to lose. This man is brutal, he could put a knife into me. He's almost ready. I can feel it. I've got to do something, there's not much time. I can't take a bribe. As stupid as I've been so far, that would be worse. The ship leaves tonight. He has people on board who will know about me.

What's left? If I try to turn him in, exactly what do I do? Go ashore with him following me like a sick bulldog and present him to the customs officer? "Look here, officer, just have a look at what I found!" Oh yes. Sure. Oh hell yes. We're at the bottom of the world and I've cornered a man who thinks I'm Death. He's waited for me. He's been waiting all these years. Once he saw me in Curaçao and he believed I was Death. Oh yes, we understand each other. There's no need to speak. But at this moment what's he thinking? I don't know. All I know is that he believes in me and therefore he must hate me. It was he who gave me this authority, yet he hates me because I have it.

Koerner went over the situation carefully with himself.

I have an authority that I don't want and I'm not able to give it away. I'd throw it in the water if I could, there's nothing I want less. What do I do?

Say I can't accept a bribe, and say I don't dare to let him go. I've made one false move already; one more and he'll sense the truth. I'm no actor. Why hasn't he found me out already? Because he wants so much to believe, that must be it. And because I made no effort to persuade him, which makes it hard to doubt.

All right, say that's the case, yes, and I couldn't possibly turn him in. Supposing I did act well enough to lead him off the ship, where's the proof? There's none. Only what I've guessed. He'd get rid of that watch in a minute. And maybe the customs officer is his partner, I don't know. It doesn't matter. I can't finish him. I should never have started this. But I didn't; he was the one. He built this into what it is. The fault's not mine; he can't blame me. When I learned what was going on I helped a little, but not much, and I didn't think it would come to anything like this. I didn't realize. He can't blame me. But he will. He will.

Why argue with myself? There's not time, and that's all I've got. He's got the rest. No, there's one more thing, the knowledge that I have. If I could use that. If I understood how to use that.

I'm trying to be logical, but I can't think. My head's full of mice scrambling in every direction. How much longer will he believe? I can't even guess. My strength exists in his imagination and when he no longer believes in its existence it no longer exists. Then how much longer do I have it? He must have told himself I wouldn't be here unless I was confident. He imagines I have every exit blocked. He imagines he can't escape unless I allow him to, which is the reason for the servility and fright and the lies dripping and sliding from his lips, yes, and the threats I heard. Only through me can he escape. And I have this power over him precisely as long as he believes.

Koerner had been gazing almost stupefied at the Japanese stamps, at the waterfalls and the tiny white cone of Fujiyama. He blinked and looked at himself in the mirror and was relieved to see that he appeared unconcerned. He picked up the bottle, poured out the rest of the champagne and drank it quickly. The champagne was warm and he knew he was beginning to get drunk.

Either I make use of what I know or I don't, he said to himself, and I think I'd rather not. I'd rather back out of this without getting my skull crushed or a knife in the ribs. I'm not a hero with celluloid teeth. When we get to Lisbon I could talk to somebody who might be interested. I don't know who, but somebody ought to be interested. I could do that much, although I doubt if anybody will listen. But I can't break this up by myself.

Then if I'm not going to use what I know, and if I don't dare let him know what I know, I've got to get out of this by seeming ignorant. How easy is that? I don't know, I've never tried. But if I can give no hint of understanding what both of us have sensed, he'll never ask directly. I'll be the simple tourist that I am. I travel and I play chess and I see no evil and time itself takes care of me. This man can't believe forever. He's got to know. He's got to ask. Already he's suspicious. Soon he's going to ask more questions. If ever in my life I've been careful, I'll be twice as careful now. All right, William Koerner, clever enough to move into the mind of another man, are you clever enough to be a fool?

"You're just traveling," the fat man said. "That's what you told me."

Koerner nodded.

"You said you were on vacation."

Koerner shook his head.

"That's right," García said, "you didn't tell me that. I forgot. If you're not on vacation what kind of work do you do?"

"I work at a desk."

"In Lisboa?"

"New York."

"I don't know what kind of work you do," the provedor said finally. "I never got a chance to have a job like you, so I could go traveling around playing games. I work hard."

Koerner listened carefully.

"You got friends on this island?"

Koerner knew instantly that he must not hesitate about answering, or show the slightest caution.

"No," he said, "in fact I couldn't give you the name of anybody within a thousand miles of this place."

"No? Who do you play games with?"

Koerner laughed. "Right you are! I do know somebody's name."

Hans Julio García smiled.

"You told me your name, too, a while ago," he said, "but I forgot."

Koerner told him again.

"Sure. I got a bad memory."

Then suddenly García said, "You're not Poigt."

Koerner appeared puzzled. The provedor began to laugh. He pounded Koerner on the back.

"Listen, William Koerner, I want to buy you another drink. I'm going ashore pretty soon but I'll buy you another drink."

"It's almost time to eat. I didn't have any lunch."

"That's right. You're a chess player," said Hans Julio García laughing.

Koerner grinned.

"Well, you go eat dinner," said the fat man, and he was laughing to himself. "Goodby, whatever your name is."

"Goodby," Koerner said.

He walked out of the lounge and went up on deck instead of into the dining salon. The deck still smelled of hot canvas but the late afternoon air seemed not so deadly. Beyond the breakwater the Caribbean lay dark blue-green and slightly broken like a stained-glass window.

So somebody exists, he thought, whose name is Poigt, or who calls himself Poigt, who causes the fat provedor to wake up in the middle of the night. It's for him that Hans Julio García waits. And one afternoon Poigt will step into the lounge as quietly as I did. Yes, the day will come. Or maybe it won't. It might never. What a shame, I'd like to know. Not that it concerns me very much, but still I would like to know.

He wandered to the other side of the deck. The sun looked larger and was wedged between two palm trees like an orange or a pomegranate. A few gulls were soaring above the ships in the harbor. On the quay some people were getting out of a taxi. He put his elbows on the rail and waited. Presently he saw the fat man go ashore. The watch was not on his wrist.

It must be in his pocket, Koerner decided. Isn't that curious. He's not so sure of himself anymore. I took the edge off his confidence. In fact I believe what I may have done was make things more difficult for Poigt. My fat smuggler is going to be much more cautious from now on. I hadn't expected that.

The provedor waved to somebody in the customs office, then walked through the gate and into a warehouse.

1966

THE WALLS
OF ÁVILA

Thou shalt make castels in Spayne,
And dreme of joye, al but in vayne.
— ROMAUNT OF THE ROSE

ÁVILA LIES only a few kilometers west and a little north of Madrid, and is surrounded by a grim stone wall that was old when Isabella was born. Life in this town has not changed very much from the days when the earth was flat; somehow it is as though news of the passing centuries has never arrived in Ávila. Up the cobbled street saunters a donkey with a wicker basket slung on each flank, and on the donkey's bony rump sits a boy nodding drowsily in the early morning sun. The boy's dark face looks medieval. He is delivering bread. At night the stars are metallic, with a bluish tint, and the Spaniards stroll gravely back and forth beside the high stone wall. There are not so many gypsies, or *gitanos,* in this town as there are in, say, Valencia or Seville. Ávila is northerly and was not impressed by these passionate Asiatic people, at least not the way Córdoba was, or Granada.

These were things we learned about Ávila when J.D. returned. He came home after living abroad for almost ten years. He was thinner and taller than any of us remembered, and his crew-cut hair had turned completely gray although he was just thirty-eight. It made him look very distinguished, even a little dramatic. His skin was now as brown as coffee, and there were wind wrinkles about his restless cerulean blue eyes, as though the light of strange beaches and exotic plazas had stamped him like a visa to prove he had been there. He smiled a good deal, perhaps because he did not feel at ease with his old friends any more. Ten years did not seem long to us, not really long, and we were disconcerted by the great change in him. Only his voice was familiar. At the bus station where three of us had gone to meet him only Dave Zobrowski recognized him.

Apparently this town of Ávila meant a great deal to J.D., although he could not get across to us its significance. He said that one night he was surprised to hear music and laughter coming from outside the walls, so he hurried through the nearest gate, which was set between two gigantic watch towers, and followed the wall around until he came to a carnival. There were concessions where you could fire corks at cardboard boxes, each containing a chocolate bar, or dip for celluloid fishes with numbered bellies, and naturally there was a carousel, the same as in America. It rotated quite slowly, he said, with mirrors flashing from its peak while enameled stallions gracefully rose and descended on their gilded poles. But nothing was so well attended as a curious swing in which two people stood, facing each other, grasping a handle, and propelled themselves so high that at the summit they were nearly upside down. The shadow of this swing raced up the wall and down again. "Like this!" J.D. exclaimed, gesturing, and he stared at each of us in turn to see if we understood. He said it was like the shadow of some grotesque instrument from the days of the Inquisition, and he insisted that if you gazed up into the darkness long enough you could make out, among the serrated ramparts of the ancient wall, the forms of helmeted men leaning on pikes and gazing somberly down while their black beards moved in the night wind.

He had tales of the Casbah in Tangiers and he had souvenirs from the ruins of Carthage. On his key chain was a fragment of polished stone, drilled through the center, that he had picked up from the hillside just beyond Tunis. And he spoke familiarly of the beauty of Istanbul, and of Giotto's tower, and the Seine, and the golden doors of Ghiberti. He explained how the Portuguese are fuller through the cheeks than are the Spaniards, their eyes more indolent and mischievous, and how their songs—*fados,* he called them—were not more than lazy cousins of the fierce flamenco one heard throughout Andalusia.

When Zobrowski asked in what year the walls of Ávila were built, J.D. thought for quite a while, his lean face sober while he gently rocked a tumbler of iced rum, but at last he said the fortifications were probably begun seven or eight hundred years ago. They had been repaired occasionally and were still impregnable to primitive force. It was queer, he added, to come upon such a place, indestructible when assaulted on its own terms, yet obsolete.

He had postal cards of things that had interested him. He had not carried a camera because he thought it bad manners. We did not completely understand what he meant by this but we had no time to discuss it because he was running on, wanting to know if we were familiar with Giambologna, saying, as he displayed a card, "In a grotto of the Boboli Gardens not far from the Uffizi—" He stopped abruptly. It had occurred to him that we might be embarrassed. No one said anything. None of us had ever heard of the Boboli Gardens, or of the sculptor Giambologna, or of the Venus that J.D. had wanted to describe.

"Here's the Sistine Chapel, of course," he said, taking another card from his envelope. "That's the Libyan sybil."

"Yes," said Zobrowski. "I remember this. There was a print of it in one of our high school textbooks. Good God, how time does pass."

"Those damn textbooks," J.D. answered. "They ruin everything. They've ruined Shakespeare and the Acropolis and half the things on earth that are really worth seeing. Just like the Lord's Prayer—I can't hear it. I don't know what it says. Why wasn't I left to discover it for myself? Or the Venus de Milo. I sat in front of it for an hour but I couldn't see it."

He brought out a postal card of a church tower. At the apex was a snail-like structure covered with what appeared to be huge tile baseballs.

"That's the *Sagrada Familia*," he explained. "It's not far from the bull ring in Barcelona."

The *Sagrada Familia* was unfinished; in fact it consisted of nothing but a façade with four tremendous towers rising far above the apartment buildings surrounding it. He said it was a landmark of Barcelona, that if you should get lost in the city you had only to get to a clearing and look around for this weird church. On the front of it was a cement Christmas tree, painted green and hung with cement ornaments, while the tiled spires were purple and yellow. And down each spire ran vertical lettering that could be read a kilometer away. Zobrowski asked what was written on the towers.

"There's one word on each tower," said J.D. "The only one I recall is 'Ecstasy.' "

Dave Zobrowski listened with a patient, critical air, as though wondering how a man could spend ten years in such idle traveling. Russ Lyman, who had once been J.D.'s closest friend, listened in silence with his head bowed. When we were children together it had been Russ who intended to go around the world some day, but he had not, for a number of reasons. He seemed to hold a monopoly on bad luck. The girl he loved married somebody else, then his business failed, and so on and on through the years. Now he worked as a drugstore clerk and invested his pitiful savings in gold mines or wildcat oil wells. He had been thirty-two when the girl he loved told him goodby, tapping the ash from her cigarette onto his wrist to emphasize that she meant it; he promptly got drunk, because he could not imagine anything else to do, and a few days later he began going around with a stout, amiable girl named Eunice who had grown up on a nearby farm. One October day when the two of them were walking through an abandoned orchard they paused to rest in the shade of an old stone wall in which some ivy and small flowers were growing. Eunice was full of the delicate awkwardness of certain large girls, and while Russell was looking at her a leaf came fluttering down to rest on her shoulder. He became aware of the sound of honeybees flickering through the noonday sun, and of the uncommonly sweet odor of apples moldering among the clover, and he was seized with such passion that he immediately took the willing girl. She became pregnant, so they got married, although he did not want to, and before much longer he stopped talking about going around the world.

J.D., handing Russell a card of a little street in some North African town, remarked that on this particular street he had bought a tasseled red fez. And Russell nodded a bit sadly.

"Now, this is Lisbon," J.D. said. "Right over here on the far side of this rectangular plaza is where I lived. I used to walk down to the river that you see at the edge of the card, and on the way back I'd wander through some little shops where you can buy miniature galleons of filigreed gold."

"I suppose you bought one," said Zobrowski.

"I couldn't resist," said J.D. with a smile. "Here's a view of Barcelona at night, and right here by this statue of Columbus I liked to sit and watch the tide come sweeping in. An exact copy of the *Santa María* is tied up at the dock near the statue. And whenever the wind blew down from the hills I could hear the butter-pat clap of the gypsies dancing on the Ramblas." He looked at us anxiously to see if we were interested. It was clear that he loved Spain. He wanted us to love it, too.

"One time in Galicia," he said, "at some little town where the train stopped I bought a drink of water from a wrinkled old woman who was holding up an earthen jug and calling, '*Agua! Agua fría!*'" He drew a picture of the jug—it was called a *porrón*—and he demonstrated how it was to be held above your head while you drank. Your lips were never supposed to touch the spout. The Spaniards could drink without swallowing, simply letting the stream of water pour down their throats, and after much dribbling and choking J.D. had learned the trick. But what he most wanted to describe was the old woman who sold him the water. She could have been sixty or ninety. She was toothless, barefoot, and with a rank odor, but somehow, in some way he could not get across to us, they had meant a great deal to each other. He tried to depict a quality of arrogance or ferocity about her, which, in the days when she was young, must have caused old men to murmur and young men to fall silent whenever she passed by. He could not forget an instant when he reached out the train window to give her back the clay jug and met her deep, unwavering eyes.

"The train was leaving," he said, leaning forward. "It was leaving forever. And I heard her scream at me. I didn't know what she said, but there was a Spaniard in the same compartment who told me that this old Galician woman had screamed at me, 'Get off the train! Stay in my land!' " He paused, apparently remembering, and slowly shook his head.

It was in Spain, too, in a cheap waterfront night club called *El Hidalgo* — and he answered Russell's question by saying that Don Quixote, for example, was an *hidalgo* — it was here that he fell in love for the only time in his life. The cabaret was in an alley of the Gothic quarter where tourists seldom ventured. J.D. often spent his evenings there, buying lottery tickets and brown paper cigarettes and drinking a yellowish wine called *manzanilla*. One night the flamenco dancers were in a furious mood — he said he could feel the tension gathering the way electricity will sometimes gather on a midwestern afternoon until it splits the air. An enormously fat gypsy woman was dancing by herself, dancing the symbols of fertility that have survived a thousand generations. She was dressed in what he likened to a bedspread covered with orange polka dots. Raising and lowering her vast arms she snapped her fingers and angrily danced alone; then all at once a savage little man in high-heeled boots sprang out of the crowd and began leaping around her. The staccato of his boots made the floor tremble and caused the *manzanilla* to sway inside the bottles.

"Everybody was howling and clapping," said J.D., and he clapped once as the gypsies clap, not with the entire hand but with three fingers flat against the palm. It sounded like a pistol shot. "Somebody was looking at me," he went on. "I could feel someone's eyes on me. I looked into the shadows and saw her. She was about nineteen, very tall and imperial, with her hair in braids. She began walking toward me, and she was singing. She sang to me that her name was Paquita—"

"She was improvising a song," said Zobrowski.

J.D. nodded. "It had the sound of a lament. Those old tragedies you hear in Spain, they're paralyzing."

"Just what do you mean?" Zobrowski asked.

"I don't know," said J.D. "It's as if a dagger was still plunged to the hilt in her breast."

Zobrowski smiled. "Go on. No doubt this young woman was beautiful."

"Yes. And she never stopped looking at me. I don't remember, but she must have walked across the room because I realized I was standing up and she was standing directly in front of me, touching my lips with one finger."

"I have had similar dreams," said Zobrowski.

Russell was listening avidly. "I didn't think Spanish women could ever get away from their chaperons."

"*Dueña,* I believe, is the word," Zobrowski said.

"There was no *dueña* for that girl," answered J.D. He was silent for a little while and then concluded his story. "Later that night I saw her walking the streets."

"Well, that explains everything," Zobrowski smiled. "You simply mistook her professional interest in you for some sort of transcendental love."

J.D. looked at Dave Zobrowski for a long time, and finally said, "I didn't think I could make you understand." To Russell he said, "I find myself repeating her name. In the night I see her everywhere. In Paris, or in Rome, or even in this town, I see a girl turning away and my heart jumps the way it did that night in Barcelona."

"You should have married her," said Russell.

"I think he has done enough foolish things as it is," Zobrowski replied, and that seemed to end the matter. At least J.D. never referred to Paquita again. He spoke of the Andalusian gypsies, saying that they are a mixture of Arab and Indian, while the Catalonians are almost pure Sudra Indian. He gave this information as though it were important; he seemed to value knowledge for itself alone. But, looking into our faces, he saw that we could not greatly care about Spanish gypsies one way or another.

He had a pale gray cardboard folder with a drawing of St. George on the cover. Inside was a map of the geographical limits of the Catalan language, and this inscription: "With the best wishes for all the friends of the Catalan-speaking countries once free in the past they will be free and whole again thanks to the will and strength of the Catalan people."

This was a folder of the resistance movement; it had been given to him, at the risk of imprisonment and perhaps at the risk of life itself, by a charwoman of Valencia. Zobrowski inquired if these were the people who opposed Franco. J.D. said that was correct. In Algiers he had met a waiter who had fought against Franco and barely escaped the country; this waiter had been in Algiers since 1938 and had no hope of seeing his family again, though he believed, as the charwoman believed, that one day Spain would be free.

After inspecting the pathetic little folder Zobrowski suggested, "I can easily appreciate your concern for these people. However you might also spend some time considering your own situation. Frankly, time is getting on, while you elect to dawdle about the waterfronts of the world."

J.D. shrugged.

"I've been meaning to ask," said Zobrowski. "Did you ever receive the letter I addressed to you in Vienna?"

"I don't remember it," said J.D.

"It concerned an executive position with the Pratt Hanover Company. They manufacture farm implements. I spoke to Donald Pratt about you and he was very much interested."

"No, I never got the letter," said J.D., and he grinned. "I was traveling quite a bit and I guess a lot of letters never caught up with me."

"Would you have come back if you had received the offer from Pratt?"

"No, I guess not," said J.D.

"We've known each other a long time, haven't we?"

J.D. nodded. "Since we were kids, Dave."

"Exactly. I would like to know how you manage to live."

"Oh, I work here and there. I had a job at the American embassy in Switzerland for a while, and to be honest about it, I've done some black marketing. I've learned how to get along, how to pull the levers that operate the world."

Then he began to describe Lucerne. It seemed far distant, in every dimension, from the days when we were children and used to bicycle down the river road to the hickory woods and hunt for squirrels. Each of us had a .22 rifle, except J.D., who went hunting with a lemonwood bow. He had made it himself, and he had braided and waxed the string, and sewn a quiver, and planed his arrows. He did not hit many squirrels with his equipment, and we would often taunt him about losing the arrows among the high weeds and underbrush, but he never seemed to mind; he would go home to his father's tool chest in the basement and calmly set about planing another batch of sticks. We would watch him clip turkey feathers into crisp rhomboids and carefully glue them into place, bracing each feather with matchsticks until the glue hardened. We would sit on the wash tub, or on his father's workbench, and smoke pieces of grapevine while we studied the new arrows.

When he fitted on the bronze tip and banded each arrow with hunter's green and white Russell would watch with an almost hypnotized expression. But Dave Zobrowski, even in those days, was puzzled and a trifle impatient with J.D.

Remembering such things as J.D.'s bow and arrow we could see that it was he, and not Russell, who was destined to go away. We thought he had left a good deal of value here in the midwest of America. Our town is not exotic, but it is comprehensible and it is clean. This is partly due to Dave Zobrowski, who has always been vehement about cleanliness. That he grew up to become a physician and a member of the sanitary commission surprised no one. He likes to tell of disgusting conditions he has seen in other cities. While he was in Chicago at a medical convention he investigated a hotel charging the same price as the Pioneer House here in town, and he reported, all too graphically, how the ceiling was stained from leakage, how there was pencil writing on the walls, together with the husks of smashed roaches, and how he found a red hair embedded in the soap. Even the towel was rancid. Looking out the smoky window he saw wine bottles and decaying fruit in the gutter.

Visitors to this town often wonder how it is possible to exist without ballet, opera, and so forth, but it usually turns out that they themselves attend only once or twice each season, if at all. Then, too, if you are not accustomed to a certain entertainment you do not miss it. Russell, for example, grew up in a home devoid of music but cheerful and harmonious all the same. To his parents music was pointless, unless at Christmas time, when the phonograph would be wound up, the needle replaced, and the carols dusted off; consequently Mozart means nothing to him.

A Brooklyn police captain named Lehmbruck drove out here to spend his vacation but went back east after a week, saying it was too quiet to sleep. However he seemed to be interested in the sunset, remarking that he had never seen the sun go down anywhere except behind some buildings. And he had never eaten old ham—he studied the white specks very dubiously, and with some embarrassment asked if the ham was spoiled. The Chamber of Commerce later received a wistful little note from Captain Lehmbruck, hinting that he might have another try at the prairie next summer.

Christmas here is still made instead of bought, even if we think no more of Christ than anyone else. And during the summer months the sidewalks are overhung with white or lavender spirea, and we can watch the rain approaching, darkening the farmland. Life here is reasonable and tradition not discounted, as evidenced by the new public library which is a modified Parthenon of Tennessee marble. There was a long and bitter argument about the inscription for its façade. One group wanted the so-called living letter, while the majority sought reassurance in the Doric past. At last we chiseled it with "Pvblic," "Covnty," "Strvctvre," and so forth.

J.D. knew about all these things, but he must have wanted more, and as he talked to us about his travels we could read in his restless blue eyes that he was not through searching. We thought he would come home when his father died, at least for a little while. Of course he was six thousand miles away, but most men would have returned from any distance. We did not know what he thought of us, the friends who had been closest to him, and this was altogether strange because our opinions about him were no secret—the fact that Russell envied him and that Zobrowski thought his life was going to rot.

Russell, to be sure, envied everybody. For a time after the marriage we believed Russell would collect himself, whatever it was needed collecting, because he went around looking very pleased with himself, although Eunice seemed a bit confused. He began to go shooting in the hickory woods again, firing his old .22 more to ex-ult in its noise than to kill a squirrel. Yet something within him had been destroyed. Whether it could have been an insufferable jealousy of J.D.—who was then in Finland—or love that was lost, or the hard core of another sickness unknown to anyone on earth, no one could say, but it was to be only a few years after J.D.'s visit that we would find Russell lying in the garage with his head almost torn off and a black .45 service automatic in his hand.

"Here is where Dante first met Beatrice," said J.D., adding with a smile that sev-eral locations in Florence claimed this distinction, even as half the apartments in Toledo insist El Greco painted there. And he had a picture of Cala Ratjada where he had lived with a Danish girl named Vivian. We had forgotten, if indeed we had ever realized it, that in other countries people are not required to be so furtive about their affairs. We learned that Cala Ratjada was a fishing village on the eastern end of Majorca. Majorca we had heard of because the vacation magazines were publicizing it.

"I understand there's a splendid cathedral in the capital," Zobrowski said. "Palma, isn't it?"

J.D. agreed rather vaguely. It was plain he did not care much for cathedrals, un-less there was something queer about them as there was about the *Sagrada Familia*. He preferred to tell about the windmills on Majorca, and about his bus ride across the island with a crate of chickens on the seat behind him. We had not known there was a bus across the island; the travel magazines always advised tour-ists to hire a car with an English-speaking driver. So we listened, because there is a subtle yet basic difference between one who travels and one who does not.

He had lived with this Danish girl all of one summer in a boarding house—a *pensión* he called it—and every afternoon they walked through some scrubby little trees to a white sandy beach and went swimming nude. They took along a leather bag full of heavy amber wine and drank this and did some fancy diving off the rocks. He said the Mediterranean there at Cala Ratjada was more translucent even than the harbor of Monte Carlo. When their wine was finished and the sand had become cool and the shadows of the trees were touching the water they walked back to the village. For a while they stopped on the embarcadero to watch the Balearic fishermen spreading their nets to dry. Then J.D. and the Danish girl returned to the *pensión* for dinner. They ate such things as fried octopus, or baby squid, or a huge seafood casserole called a *paella*.

"Where is she now?" Russell asked.

"Vivian?" said J.D. "Oh, I don't know. She sent me a card from Frederikshavn a year or so ago. She'd been wanting to go to India, so maybe that's where she is now."

"Didn't she expect you to marry her?"

J.D. looked at Russell and then laughed out loud; it was the first time he had laughed all evening.

"Neither of us wanted to get married," he said. "We had a good summer. Why should we ruin it?"

This was a kind of reasoning we were aware of, via novels more impressive for poundage than content; otherwise it bore no relation to us. What bound them together was as elementary as a hyphen, and we suspected they could meet each other years later without embarrassment. They had loved without aim or sense, as young poets do. We could imagine this, to be sure, but we could not imagine it actually happening. There were women in our town, matrons now, with whom we had been intimate to some degree a decade or so ago, but now when we met them, or were entertained in their homes, we were restrained by the memory of the delicate past. Each of us must carry, as it were, a balloon inked with names and dates.

So far as we knew, J.D. looked up only one of the women he used to know here in town. He called on Helen Louise Sawyer who used to win the local beauty contests. When we were young most of us were afraid of her, because there is something annihilating about too much beauty; only J.D. was not intimidated. Perhaps he could see then what we learned to see years later—that she was lonely, and that she did not want to be coveted for the perfection of her skin or for the truly magnificent explosion of her bosom. When Helen Louise and J.D. began going around together we were astonished and insulted because Russell, in those days, was much more handsome than J.D., and Dave Zobrowski was twice as smart. All the same she looked at no else. Then he began leaving town on longer and longer expeditions. He would return wearing a southern California sport shirt, or with a stuffed grouper he had caught off Key West. Helen Louise eventually went into the real-estate business.

He telephoned her at the office and they went to dinner at the Wigwam, which is now the swank place to eat. It is decorated with buffalo skins and tomahawks and there are displays of flint arrowheads that have been picked up by farmers in neighboring counties. The only incongruities are the pink jade ashtrays that, by midnight, seem to have been planted with white, magenta-tipped stalks to remind the diners that a frontier has vanished. And well it has. The scouts are buried, the warriors mummified. Nothing but trophies remain: a coup stick hung by the Wigwam's flagstone hearth, a pipe smoked by Satanta, a cavalry saber and a set of moldering blue gloves crossed on the mantel, a tan robe laced to the western wall, a dry Pawnee scalp behind the bar. The wind still sweeps east from the lofty Colorado plains, but carries with it now only the clank of machinery in the wheat fields. The Mandans have gone, like the minor chords of an Iowa death song, with Dull Knife and Little Wolf whose three hundred wretched squaws and starving men set out to fight their way a thousand miles to the fecund Powder River that had been their home.

There is a gratification to the feel of history behind the places one has known, and the Wigwam's historical display is extensive. In addition, the food is good. There is hot biscuit with clover honey, and the old ham so mistrusted by Captain Lehmbruck of Brooklyn. There is Missouri fried chicken, spare ribs, venison with mushrooms, catfish, beef you can cut with a fork, wild rice and duck buried under pineapple sauce, as well as various European dishes. That evening J.D. asked for a certain Madeira wine and apparently was a little taken aback to find that the Wigwam had it. Travelers, real travelers, come to think of their homes as provincial and are often surprised.

Helen Louise had metamorphosed, as even we could see, and we knew J.D. was in for a shock. Through the years she had acquired that faintly resentful expression that comes from being stared at, and she seemed to be trying to compensate for her beauty. Although there was nothing wrong with her eyes she wore glasses; she had cropped her beautiful golden hair in a Lesbian style; and somehow she did not even walk the way she used to. The pleasing undulations had mysteriously given way to a militant stride. Her concern in life was over such items as acreage and location. At the business she was quite good; every real-estate man in town hated her, no doubt thinking she should have become a housewife instead of the demon that she was. But apparently she had lost her desire to marry, or sublimated it. At the lunch hour she could be seen in an expensive suit, speaking in low tones to another businesswoman, and her conversation when overheard would be, " . . . referred the order to me . . . Mrs. Pabst's opinion . . . second mortgage . . . bought six apartments . . . "

We guessed that J.D.'s evening with Helen Louise might be an indication that he had grown tired of wandering around the earth, and that he wanted to come home for good. Helen Louise, if no longer as voluptuous as she had been at twenty or twenty-five, was still provocative, and if she married was it not possible she might come to look very much as she had looked ten years before? But J.D. had very little to say about his evening with her; and after he was gone Helen Louise never mentioned him.

"Did you know that in Cádiz," he said—because it was to him a fact worth noting, like the fact that in Lisbon he had lived on a certain plaza—"Did you know that in Cádiz you can buy a woman for three *pesetas?*" Whether or not he might have been referring to Helen Louise we did not know, nor did anyone ask.

"Once I talked with Manolete," he said, as though it was the first line of a poem.

"I've heard that name," Zobrowski answered. "He's a toreador, is he not?"

"I think 'toreador' was invented by Bizet," J.D. replied. "Manolete was a matador. But he's dead. It was in Linares that he was *cogido*. On the twenty-seventh of August in nineteen-forty-seven. At five in the afternoon, as the saying goes." And he continued, telling us that the real name of this bullfighter had been Manuel Rodriguez, and that after he was gored in Linares the ambulance which was taking him to a hospital started off in the wrong direction, and there was a feeling of bitterness in Spain when the news was broadcast that he was dead of his wounds.

"What you are trying to express," Zobrowski suggested, "is that this fellow was a national hero."

"Yes," said J.D.

"Like Babe Ruth."

"No," said J.D. instantly and with a vexed expression. He gestured helplessly and then shrugged. He went on to say that he happened to be in Heidelberg when death came to Manolete in the town of Linares. He looked around at us as if this circumstance were very strange. As he spoke he gestured excitedly and often skipped from one topic to another because there was so little time and he had so much to tell us. In a way he created a landscape of chiaroscuro, illuminating first one of his adventures and now another, but leaving his canvas mostly in shadow.

"One morning in Basel," he said, "it began to snow while I was having breakfast. Snow was falling on the Rhine." He was sitting by a window in a tea shop over-looking the river. He described the sunless, blue-gray atmosphere with large white flakes of snow piling up on the window ledge, and the dark swath of the river. Several waitresses in immaculate uniforms served his breakfast from a heavy silver tray. There was coffee in a silver pitcher, warm breads wrapped in thick linen napkins, and several kinds of jam and preserves; all the while the snow kept mounting on the ledge just outside the window, and the waitresses murmured in German. He returned to Basel on the same morning of the following year—all the way from Palermo—just to have his breakfast there.

Most of his ten years abroad had been spent on the borders of the Mediterra-nean, and he agreed with Zobrowski's comment that the countries in that area must be the dirtiest in Europe. He told about a servant girl in one of his *pensiones* who always seemed to be on her knees scrubbing the floor, but who never bathed herself. She had such a pervasive odor that he could tell whenever she had recently been in a room.

He said that Pompeii was his biggest disappointment. He had expected to find the city practically buried under a cliff of lava. But there was no lava. Pompeii was like any city abandoned and overgrown with weeds. He had visited the Roman ru-ins of North Africa, but the names he mentioned did not mean anything to us. Car-thage did, but if we had ever read about the others in school we had long since stored their names and dates back in the dusty bins alongside algebra and Beowulf. Capri was the only celebrated spot he visited that surpassed all pictures of it, and he liked Sorrento too, saying that he had returned to the mainland about sundown when the cliffs of Sorrento become red and porous like the cliffs of the Grand Can-yon. And in a town called Amalfi he had been poisoned—he thought it was the eggs.

All this was delivered by a person we had known since childhood, yet it might as well have come from a foreign lecturer. J.D. was not trying to flaunt his adventures; he described them because we were friends and he could not conceive of the fact that the ruins of Pompeii would mean less to us than gossip on the women's page. He wanted to tell us about the ballet in Cannes, where the audience was so quiet that he had heard the squeak of the dancers' slippers. But none of us had ever been to a ballet, or especially wanted to go. There was to us something faintly absurd about men and women in tights. When Zobrowski suggested as much, J.D. looked at him curiously and seemed to be struggling to remember what it was like to live in our town.

A number of things he said did not agree with our concept. According to him the Swedish girls are not in the least as they appear on calendars, which invariably depict them driving some cows down a pea-green mountainside. J.D. said the Swedes were long and gaunt with cadaverous features and gloomy dispositions, and their suicide rate was among the highest on earth.

Snails, he said, though no one had inquired, have very little taste. You eat them with a tiny two-pronged fork and some tongs that resemble a surgeon's forceps. The garlic-butter sauce is excellent, good enough to drink, but snail meat tasted to him rubbery like squid.

About the taxi drivers of Paris: they were incredibly avaricious. If you were not careful they would give you a gilded two-franc piece instead of a genuine fifty-franc piece for change, and if you caught them at it they became furious. But he did say that the French were the most urbane people to be found.

He had traveled as far east as Teheran and as far north as Trondheim. He had been to Lithuania and to Poland, and to Egypt and to the edge of the Sahara, and from the animation of his voice we could tell he was not through yet. While he was telling us about his plans as we sat comfortably in the cocktail lounge of the Pioneer House, a bellboy came in and respectfully said to Dave, "Dr. Zobrowski, the hospital is calling."

Without a word Zobrowski stood up and followed the boy. A few minutes later he returned wearing his overcoat and carrying his gray Homburg. "I'm sorry, but it's an emergency," he said to us all, and then to J.D., "Since you are not to be in town much longer I suppose this is goodby."

J.D. uncrossed his long legs and casually stood up.

"No doubt you lead an entertaining life," Zobrowski observed, not bothering to conceal his disapproval. "But a man cannot wander the face of the earth forever."

"That's what everybody tells me," J.D. answered with a grin. "It doesn't bother me much any more."

Zobrowski pulled on his yellow pigskin gloves and with a severe expression he began to settle the fingers as carefully as though he had put on surgical gloves. "In my opinion," he said suddenly, and lifted his eyes, "you are a damn fool."

They stared at each other not with hostility, nor exactly with surprise, but as though they had never quite seen each other until that instant. Yet these were the two men who, about thirty years previously, had chipped in equal shares to buy a dog, a squat little beast with peculiar teeth that made it look like a beaver.

"From birth we carry the final straw," said Zobrowski at last.

J.D. only smiled.

Zobrowski's normally hard features contracted until he looked cruel, and he inclined his head, saying by this gesture, "As you wish." He had always known how to use silence with devastating force, yet J.D. was undismayed and did nothing but shrug like a Frenchman.

Zobrowski turned to Russell. "I had lunch with my broker the other day. He has some information on that Hudson's Bay mining stock of yours that makes me feel we should have a talk. Stop by my office tomorrow morning at eight-thirty. I have had my receptionist cancel an appointment because of this matter."

Russell's mouth slowly began to drop open as he gazed at Zobrowski. He never made reasonable investments and several times had been saved from worse ones only because he confided his financial plans, along with everything else, to anybody who would listen. Then, too, the making of money necessitates a callousness he had never possessed.

"That stock's all right," he said weakly. "I'm positive it's all right. Really it is, Dave. You should have bought some."

"Yes," Zobrowski said, looking down on him with disgust. And turning to J.D. he said, "Let us hear from you. Goodby." Then he went striding across the lounge.

"Oh, God!" mumbled Russell, taking another drink. He was ready to weep from humiliation and from anxiety over the investment. In the past few years he had become quite bald and flabby, and had taken to wearing suspenders because a belt disturbed his intestines. He rubbed his jowls and looked around with a vague, desperate air.

"Whatever happened to little Willie Grant?" J.D. asked, though Grant had never meant a thing to him.

"He's—he's in Denver," Russell said, gasping for breath.

"What about Martha Mathews?"

This was the girl who rejected Russell, but J.D. was abroad when it happened and may never have heard. He looked astonished when Russell groaned. Economically speaking, she was a great deal better off than if she had married Russell. She had accepted a housing contractor with more ambition than conscience, and now spent most of her time playing cards on the terrace of the country club.

J.D. had been in love, moderately, in the abstract, with a long-legged sloe-eyed girl named Minnette whose voice should have been poured into a glass and drunk. Her mother owned a bakery. We usually saw Minnette's mother when we came trotting home from school at the noon hour; she would be standing at the door with arms rolled in her apron while she talked to the delivery man, or, in winter time, we would often see her as she bent over, pendulous, tranquil, somehow everlasting, to place chocolate éclairs in the bakery window while sleet bounced indignantly off the steaming glass. At such moments she looked the way we always wanted our own harried mothers to look. If the truth were known it might be that we found her more stimulating than her daughter, although this may have been because we were famished when we passed the bakery. In any event he inquired about Minnette, so we told him her eyes still had that look, and that she was married to the mortician, an extremely tall man named Knopf who liked to underline trenchant phrases in the little books on Success that you buy for a quarter.

Answering these somehow anachronistic questions stirred us the way an old snapshot will do when you come upon it while hunting for something else. Later on Russell was to say that when J.D. mentioned the yellow brick building where the four of us began our schooling he remembered for the first time in possibly a decade how we used to sit around a midget table and wield those short, blunt, red-handled scissors. We had a paste pot and sheets of colored paper, and when our labors were done the kindergarten windows displayed pumpkins, Christmas trees, owls, eggs, rabbits, or whatever was appropriate to the season. J.D. could always draw better than anyone else. When visiting night for parents came around it would be his work they admired. David Zobrowski, of course, was the scholar; we were proud to be Dave's best friends. Russell managed to remain undistinguished in any way until time for the singing class. Here no one could match him. Not that anyone wanted to. He sang worse than anyone who ever attended our school. It was as if his voice operated by a pulley, and its tenor was remotely canine. The class consisted of bluebirds and robins, with the exception of Russ who was placed at a separate desk and given no designation at all. Usually he gazed out the window at the interminable fields, but when it came to him that he, too, could sing, and his jaw began to work and his throat to contract, he would be warned into silence by the waving baton.

Going to and from the business district ordinarily meant passing this musty little building, which had long since been converted into headquarters for the Boy Scout troop, and which now related to us no more than the Wizard of Oz, but until J.D. spoke of it we had not realized that the swings and the slide were gone, and crabgrass was growing between the bricks of the front walk.

When we were in high school J.D. occasionally returned to wander the corridors of the elementary school. The rest of us had been glad enough to move on and we considered his visits a bit queer, but otherwise never paused to think about them.

These were the streets where we had lived, these the houses, during a period of time when today could not influence tomorrow, and we possessed the confidence to argue about things we did not understand. Though, of course, we still did that. On winter nights we dropped away to sleep while watching the snow come drifting by the street light, and in summer we could see the moths outside the screens fluttering desperately, as though to tell us something. Our childhood came and went before we were ready to grasp it. Things were different now. The winged seeds that gyrate down from the trees now mean nothing else but that we must sweep them from the automobile hood because stains on the finish lower the trade-in value. Now, in short, it was impractical to live as we used to live with the abandon of a mule rolling in the dust.

In those days our incipient manhood had seemed a unique power, and our single worry that some girl might become pregnant. We danced with our eyes closed and our noses thrust into the gardenias all the girls wore in their hair, meanwhile estimating our chances. And, upon discovering literature, thanks to the solemn pedantry of a sophomore English teacher, we affected bow ties and cigarette holders and were able to quote contemporary poets with a faintly cynical tone.

On a postcard of a Rotterdam chocolate factory, sent to Russell but addressed to us all, J.D. scribbled, "I see nothing but the noon dust a-blowing and the green grass a-growing." If not contemporary it was at least familiar, and caused Zobrowski to remark, with a certain unconscious measure, "As fond as I am of him I sometimes lose patience. In a furrow he has found a feather of Pegasus and what should have been a blessing has become a curse."

Now J.D. was inquiring after one or two we had forgotten, or who had moved away, leaving no more trace than a cloud, and about a piano teacher who had died one sultry August afternoon on the streetcar. Yet his interest was superficial. He was being polite. He could not really care or he would not have gone away for ten years. He wondered whatever became of the bearded old man who used to stand on a street corner with a stack of Bibles and a placard promising a free copy of the New Testament to any Jew who would renounce the faith. We did not know what happened to the old man; somehow he had just vanished. Quite a few things were vanishing.

J.D. cared very little for the men who had once been our fraternity brothers, which was odd because in our hearts we still believed that those days and those brothers had been so extraordinary that people were still talking about them. Yet we could recall that he took no pride in being associated with them. The militant friendship of fraternity life made him surly. He refused to shake hands as often as he was expected to. We had been warned that, as pledges, we would be thrown into the river some night. This was part of learning to become a finer man. When the brothers came for us about three o'clock one morning, snatching away our blankets and singing the good fellowship song, we put up the traditional fight—all of us except J.D. He refused to struggle. He slumped in the arms of his captors as limp as an empty sack. This puzzled and annoyed the brothers, who held him aloft by his ankles and who bounced his head on the floor. He would not even open his eyes. They jabbed him stiffly in the ribs, they twisted his arms behind his back, they kicked him in the seat, they called him names, and finally, very angry, they dragged him to the river and flung him in. But even when he went sailing over the bullrushes he was silent as a corpse. Strangely, he did not hit the water with a loud splash. Years later he told us that he twisted at the last moment and dove through the river scum, instead of landing flat on his back as Russell did. They vanished together, as roommates should, but Russell was again audible in a few seconds—thrashing back to shore, where the brothers helped him out and gave him a towel and a bathrobe and a drink of brandy.

J.D., however, did not reappear. Even before Russell had reached the shore we were beginning to worry about J.D. There was no moon that night and the river had an evil look. We stood in a row at the edge of the water. We heard the bullfrogs, and the dark bubbling and plopping of whatever calls the river home, but nothing more. And all at once the structure of the fraternity collapsed. The last vestige of unity disappeared. We were guilty individuals. Some people began lighting matches and peering into the river, while others called his name. But there was no answer, except in the form of rotten, half-submerged driftwood floating by, revolving in the sluggish current, and, beyond the confused whispering, the brief, crying shadows of night birds dipping in wild alarm over the slimy rushes.

When we saw him again we asked what happened, but several years passed before he told anyone. Then he said—and only then was his revenge complete—"Oh, I just swam under water as far as I could. After that I let the river carry me out of sight." He swam ashore a mile or two downstream, and by a back road he returned to the fraternity house. Nobody was there; everybody was at the river searching for his body. The fraternity was almost ruined because of J.D.

Now he had climbed the Matterhorn, and we were not surprised. He knew what it was like in Venice, or in Copenhagen, and as we reflected on his past we came to understand that his future was inevitable. We knew he would leave us again, perhaps forever.

Russell, tamping out a cheap cigar, said boldly, "Eunice and I have been thinking about a trip to the Bahamas next year, or year after." He considered the nicotine on his fingertips, and after a pause, because his boast was empty, and because he knew that we knew how empty it was, he added, "Though it depends." He began picking helplessly at his fingertips. He would never go anywhere.

"You'll like the Bahamas," J.D. said.

"We consider other places," Russell said unexpectedly, and there were tears in his eyes.

J.D. was watching him with a blank, pitiless gaze.

"I think I'll go to Byzantium," Russell said.

"That doesn't exist any more."

Russell took a deep breath to hush the panic that was on him, and at last he said, "Well, gentlemen, I guess I'd better get some shut-eye if I'm going to talk business with Dave in the morning."

"It's late," J.D. agreed.

Then we asked when he would be coming home for good, although it was a foolish question, and J.D. laughed at it. Later, in talking about him, we would recall his reason for not wanting to live here. He had explained that the difference between our town and these other places he had been was that when you go walking down a boulevard in some strange land and you see a tree burgeoning, you understand that this is beautiful, and there comes with the knowledge a moment of indescribable poignance in the realization that as this tree must die, so will you die. But when, in the home you have always known, you find a tree in bud you think only that spring has come again. Here he stopped. It did not make much sense to us, but for him it had meaning of some kind.

So we asked when he would be coming back for another visit. He said he didn't know. We asked what was next. He replied that as soon as he could scrape together a few more dollars he thought he might like to see the Orient.

"They say that in Malaya . . . " he began, with glowing eyes. But we did not listen closely. He was not speaking to us anyway, only to himself, to the matrix which had spawned him and to the private god who guided him. His voice reached us faintly, as if from beyond the walls of Ávila.

1955

THE COLOR
OF THE WORLD

I F YOU'D ASK Mrs. Passen about Shannon McCambridge, she'd likely fold her veiny hands together and say, "The Lord will destroy him." If you'd asked her about the Widow Gorman, she might turn away without even answering. Mrs. Passen is sort of the link between God and Cow Lake.

Cow Lake was built in 1827 in the middle of the prairie. Now it's in the middle of the Kansas wheat fields, but outside of that nothing much has changed. Only two things break up the squares of wheat. One is the creek bed that cuts behind the gravedigger's shack, and sometimes has water in it during March. The other is a bunch of black pins that stick up off to the south. Those are oil derricks, but the oil men quit a long time ago. The derricks are rusting. Life comes pretty hard in southern Kansas. Maybe once a month some of the folks go over to Wichita.

Dust covers almost everything. If a car goes by, dust winds up from the concrete and settles on the silent dogs that lie against the curbs. If one of the dogs walks somewhere its trail is marked for several minutes by a row of dust mushrooms.

There's no saliva on the lips of the women who go to Mrs. Passen's every Wednesday to gain strength from the Gospel, and there's no sweat on the Widow Gorman when she comes into town, except under her arms. There's no whisky on the counter in back of Dummy's pool hall, but the folks who like to drink make Dummy keep the counter there. They like to look at it. The farmers never talk about it, but when they're in town they go over to Dummy's to look at it. They feel of its slick brown top and suck at their teeth for a while.

A little bit after the sun comes up the side doors of the houses open and old women come out. They have celluloid fans that advertise a hardware store. They sit on the porches until sundown, waving the fans. Most of them sit in swings that have chains screwed into the roofs. When they get up at noon or when they pull at their cotton stockings the chains squeak.

All day the sun is blue-white. It crumbles the thin dirt roads into a powder that sticks to everything. On the highway the tar strips turn to jelly, and blue flies cover the little animals killed by touring cars.

Nobody ever looks for clouds.

The Widow Gorman lives out beyond the edge of town. When it begins to cool off around five o'clock she'll sometimes drive in for things like a packet of raspberry coloring or a movie magazine. The young men who sit on the steps of the houses late in the afternoon don't say anything when she goes by. After she's gone they begin to pick at little clots of mud, or they sit on their fingers, or look at the cement. They never look at each other. The old men don't say anything. The women who sit on the porches don't say anything. The chains never squeak when the Widow goes by.

Finally the sun goes down and the people begin to take off their clothes.

MRS. PASSEN is five feet eleven inches tall and her ankles are almost as big around as her neck. She owns the boarding house. The shades are always pulled. Folks who've lived longest in town say they don't know what would happen to religion if Mrs. Passen should ever go to her Reward, but it doesn't seem like she ever will.

She sings at all the men's funerals. She sings at weddings, too, but sometimes she'll drive clear to Parallel if there's a big funeral for a man scheduled. It's close to fifty miles to Parallel, but Mrs. Passen takes time to go over and sing hymns. She never takes any money for her singing, although it's sort of understood that whenever she sings at a man's funeral his widow gives her a photograph of him. She keeps them in a black tin box in the cellar. But she says they give her a deeper Meaning, so now and again she brings them up and spreads them across the dining-room table.

Mr. Passen disappeared just three weeks after their daughter was born. He disappeared in Oklahoma City, where he used to drive to sell more insurance. Some officers came up on the train from Oklahoma and told Mrs. Passen they'd found a body, only they weren't satisfied it was the body of Mr. Passen. They stayed several days, asking if he'd ever looked at the ladies more than was right and wanting to know if he'd gotten mail from out of town. But finally they looked at each other and went back to Oklahoma.

After they'd gone Mrs. Passen told how she'd had a Visitation. The Savior had come and said because her little girl had been born with a crooked foot she should be named Faith, and the Savior had begged Mrs. Passen to pray for the child.

ALL THROUGH her early grades in school Faith was at the top of her class, and even as far as fifth grade she was pretty well along, but then she began to get shy. So when company came to the boarding house Mrs. Passen liked her to skip rope for them instead of reciting "Hiawatha" or "The Children's Hour" as most of the other little girls did. She said that was the best thing for her shyness. The guests always clapped, even though Faith sometimes got tangled up in the piece of clothesline she used for rope.

When her tenth birthday came around she asked her mother for a box of paints and a brush, but Mrs. Passen said the Lord had painted the world. She said now that she was ten it was time to learn about the Lord, and she said Faith should be proud because the Savior had given her one of his crucified legs.

When she was twelve Faith's hair began to grow silky, and took on more the color of wheat just before it was cut, and her breasts swelled so the older boys watched her, and her lips turned more red and she began to laugh and sing a little sometimes, and she learned to carve kittens out of soap. But life doesn't come easy in southern Kansas. Mrs. Passen had to cook the kittens into lumps so the soap could be used.

That summer Faith met the Widow Gorman. She was standing outside R. L. Boehm's bakery when the Widow came out with a sack of cakes, and they looked at each other and both of them smiled, and the Widow said if she'd carry the cakes to the car she could have one. When Faith began to walk the Widow clapped her hand to her mouth. She didn't look at Faith's foot, but she took the cakes and said she had some shopping to do, and she hurried into the lobby of the movie house. Faith started to follow her. Then she quit. She put her arms around the post of a streetlight on the curb and hugged the iron.

The Widow came back out. She asked Faith who she was, and after Faith had told her the Widow didn't say anything for almost a minute. Then she said, "Good

God!" She took Faith into the ice-cream parlor where she bought her a root-beer soda and gave her a dollar, and kissed her on the forehead.

Faith bought a box of paints in Keeven's dime store. She took the box to the elm trees in back of Leroy Bates' house. Bates' is on a little rise and there under the elms she could see almost to Wichita. She looked out across the fields until dinner time, and she hid the paint box in a stump before she went home.

That night Mrs. Passen asked for the dollar, and when she didn't have it Mrs. Passen took her out next to the garbage cans and together they knelt, asking forgiveness of the Lord. While they were kneeling Mrs. Passen said the Widow Gorman would be struck by the hand of the Almighty because her soul was more diseased than garbage.

Faith began to spend all her afternoons in back of Bates' under the elm trees. She'd sit there painting big golden pictures of the wheat fields and orange and purple sunsets.

It almost never rains in Cow Lake during the summer, so she rolled up her paintings and wrapped them around the handle of the black umbrella in the closet. She left the boarding house early every morning so she could be out in the fields when the sun rose. She told her mother it was like church on Christmas Eve. Mrs. Passen thought for a while, but didn't say anything.

WHEN SHE WAS almost fourteen, one of the boys asked Mrs. Passen if he could take Faith to his high school party in the gym at Wichita. But Mrs. Passen said no because when Faith finished high school she was going to study at the Eternal Heart, and it wouldn't be right. She told Faith she was sorry, and she invited the boy to stay a while, but he blinked a few times through his heavy glasses and then said he had to go home. Faith told him goodby at the front door; she thanked him for asking. Then she took the Bible she had gotten for her birthday and went out to the twin elm trees, but she didn't read the passages her mother had told her to memorize; she only sat there until way after sundown, her eyes round and empty like she was blind.

Oron Duchein brought her a box of peanut brittle on her fifteenth birthday, but Mrs. Passen gave it to the gravedigger after Oron went home because it had gone sour in the heat. She patted Faith on the head and told her she was sending clear to Kansas City for an eight-dollar shoe for her foot.

It was three days after that when Mrs. Passen sprang open the umbrella to see if it needed mending, and the pictures of the sunsets unrolled and dropped to the floor. She called Faith home from school. Then she looked at the pictures for a long time while Faith sat cross-legged at her feet. Faith's eyes were soft and big while she waited, and her lips quivered. She sat on the floor waiting to throw her arms around her mother's neck and cry and kiss her, and cry some more—to cry in her mother's arms until the pain was all gone, but Mrs. Passen got out her shears and cut each of the pictures into eight oblong pieces that would fit into the black box with the photographs of men. She said again that the Lord had painted the world.

MRS. PASSEN had more than her share of troubles. Everybody in Cow Lake had troubles. Some of them had sickness every year during the rainy season, others would lose their crops, and some would always be living on a mortgage. But everybody said Mrs. Passen had the most troubles, especially after Faith drowned.

It was at night. Shannon McCambridge found her next morning on his way home from the Widow Gorman's. Faith had drowned in the wading pool. Her hair was still tawny and wonderfully soft, like the wheat, and Shannon McCambridge said it floated under the surface of the pool like the wheat fields sometimes rippled and seemed to float under the wind. Her bad foot was all doubled up, he said, but the specially built shoe from Kansas City was safe on the bank.

Mrs. Passen had a portrait of Faith painted from an old photograph and she hung it in the parlor, and over the portrait she hung a framed piece of crepe that had her favorite passage woven into it: "O Lord, how excellent is thy name in all the earth!"

The Widow Gorman sent a note asking if she could buy a little rose garden for the church, but Mrs. Passen burned the note and flushed the ashes down the toilet. She got into her black dress again, the same dress she had put on when her husband went to his Reward. She ordered a purple candle from a funeral house in Denver, and she hung it under the portrait so some light would always shine on Faith.

Everybody in town came to comfort Mrs. Passen and they all told her she was the most courageous woman they had ever known. Generally when they told her Mrs. Passen would fold her veiny hands together and murmur, "The good Lord giveth and the good Lord taketh away."

1946

DEATH

AND THE WIFE

OF JOHN HENRY

J OHN H ENRY was wakened in the middle of the night by the sound of
someone bitterly weeping. He turned on his side and saw it was his wife,
whom he loved more than anything else in the world.

John Henry took his wife in his arms, and he said, "My love, what is this?"

"I have had a dream," said she.

"Pray, tell me it," said he.

"I dare not tell thee what it was," the wife of John Henry replied. "But promise
me one thing and never will I ask another: tomorrow stay at home with me."

"That I cannot do," John Henry said, reproving her.

And he held her motionless in his arms till the sun rose, for she could not sleep,
nor keep from weeping.

Then, while John Henry was eating his breakfast, there came a knock at the
door, and she went to open it, and she found an old man in a black cloak and a
steeple-crowned hat, and breeches and buckle shoes, and a hoary beard descended
on his breast. The old man carried a musket in the crook of his arm, and he spoke
to her courteously, but he spoke in accents long disused.

"This morning I go hunting with thy husband," the old man said. "Now, mistress, I bid thee tell the good man I am here, and am ready to go."

"He goes alone," she said. "He has told me so, himself. Now go away. Go far away and do not return, for I know thy image, and will not let thee in."

"Just over the hill," the old man said, "shall he find me."

And he made a threatening gesture as she closed the door.

"Who was that?" John Henry inquired. "Who was that at the door so early?—was it the ghost of Old Noll?" inquired he, laughing. "For the blood is drawn away from thy sweet face. Methinks a kiss may restore the color there." So saying, John Henry grasped his wife about the waist and sought to plant a kiss on her cheek.

"'Twas a stranger," she said. "Asking directions. Do not go hunting today, my love."

"Pray," said he, surprised and perplexed, "Why not?"

"Stay with me," she replied. "I beg. This day, of all days in the year." Then, seeing he meant to go, she cried: "Oh, listen! I will tell thee my dream!" And so she told it to him.

This is the dream she dreamt. The dream of the wife of John Henry.

It is afternoon in the spring of the year 1689. In King street there is a crowd. The people of each parish stand close around their minister, and a rumor is spreading: "The Pope of Rome has given orders for a new Saint Bartholomew!" Suddenly a double rank of English soldiers appears, all in red, with shouldered matchlocks, and matches burning, and the drummers are drumming them down the street. Behind the red-coated soldiers ride Sir Edmund Andros and his favorite councillors. At his right comes Edward Randolph, and to the left is Bullivant, and Dudley, with downcast eyes—Dudley the American—comes riding in the rear. Down the long street they come riding, to the rolling tap of the drums, the tap and clack, and the puttering roll, and the horses neighing, shaking their English bridles and tossing their foam while the birds wheel wildly overhead. Now comes the Episcopal clergyman of King's Chapel, and he is riding among the magistrates in his priestly vestments, holding a crucifix to his bosom. Behind him come more soldiers, all in the red coats of the Governor's Guard. Now there is seen an old man in a black cloak and a steeple-crowned hat, with breeches and buckle shoes, and a beard descending on his breast, and he gesticulates as he walks. He seems to be threatening all those who walk and ride before him. The procession passes. At the end of King street looms a prison. The doors swing wide and they all march in, and the doors fall to, locked forever. They are gone, they are gone, the Governor and his councillors, the magistrates in their wigs and robes. James has abdicated and William is King of England.

That was the dream she had. The dream she told to him. And John Henry laughed and said, "Not time, nor use, have I for riddles." And he made ready to leave her.

"There was an old man at the door," she cried, "and I know who he was, for the gun on his arm was thine. Now I pray thee, as my love endures, do not go away. For if this be, thou never will return!"

"And I have failed to return before, my love?" asked he.

"Never," said she, holding him tightly.

"Amen!" cried John Henry.

"Yet do not go!"

"Even as I have promised before, so shall I return from this day's work," John Henry said, and he smiled down on his young wife. "Sweet Mistress, the savages take their ease, and for my part I do believe the Devil himself lies sleeping behind the church. God rest the bones of Increase Mather! On this day, therefore, I cannot fail to keep covenant with mine own resolve."

Having said this, he put on his broad-brimmed Puritan hat and he took down his musket from the pegs in the chimney corner, and he went to the door. He looked out and he looked all around, and presently he came back to his young wife. With his musket in the crook of his arm he considered her most tenderly, and he played with the pink ribbon of her cap.

"Thou hast dreamed again, my love," John Henry said. "There are no footprints at our door. Unbroken lies the snow from here to the top of the hill. Which Sabbath dost thee keep? For, methinks, last night late, thy sweet body was anointed with juice of smallage, and cinquefoil, and wolf's bane."

"I am mine own self, and no other," she replied.

"Amen!" John Henry shouted, and the rafters rang with the joy of his voice. "My faith," said he in a more humble tone, while his face glowed red, "my hat is all but dislodged from my head." Whereupon he straightened it, and he said, "I must go. For if I listened, sweet wife, to such words as come from thy tongue, midday would find me here yet. And if I stayed today, wouldst thou not have another dream tomorrow? And yet another on the day after? So would we be together all the time."

"And thee would mind so much?" she asked, holding him fast.

"Ah, that I dare not say," John Henry answered. "But yon table, I swear, would long lie empty."

So saying, he laughed again, and took up his horn of powder, and he went away to the hill where the snow lay deep, where no man had gone before him.

Then the wife of John Henry flung herself down and she lay bitterly weeping, weeping not for this day, but for tomorrow, and tomorrow.

1957

I'LL TAKE YOU
TO TENNESSEE

L OGOS JACKSON'S GRIN kept on growing until it almost slid off his face. "Sure," he said, "sure we can have a picnic." He unwrapped his big bony hands from the pump handle and grabbed Roy and Dutch-rubbed him, and all the kids piled onto Logos, laughing and shouting. And all the while Logos kept grunting and grabbing an arm or a leg and threatening to have them all thrown in jail for picking on him.

"Picnics—" said Logos, "—ugly kids!" He stood up, shaking them off. "Go on. Go away."

"Come on, Logos! You said you would—you said you would!"

Logos wagged his head, but then the grin crept back. "Eleven o'clock," he said. "Now get. I got work to do."

Roy was the first to get back to the shed where Logos lived with his three Tennessee hound dogs. Roy got there just before ten-thirty. He hugged the two-by-four that propped up the porch and yelled for Logos to come out, but Logos didn't answer. The other kids got there pretty soon and they all yelled and banged on the door so much that finally the door opened a crack and Logos's big hand shot out and grabbed Boulton Polk by the britches. Everybody yelled and jumped off the porch while Boulton screamed as he was dragged inside. Everything was quiet. But then Luanne giggled, so they all ran up on the porch again and began to beat on the old plank door.

Logos poked his head out and the crooked scar around his neck stretched. He blinked like one of the possums he was always telling them about. "What you all want?" he asked. He saw Maxine Crowe standing in back of the gang. Maxine was almost sixteen. She wore sandals and a dress with a Mexican belt.

"Picnic! Picnic! Come on, Logos, you said you would!"

"Picnic?" said Logos. He sneaked out a long stringy arm and grabbed Betty Su by the ear, and Boulton wiggled out through the door. "What picnic?"

But they all yelled again and poured in to rescue Betty Su, and Bert Rice announced he was going to pry off the hinges of the door with his sheath knife, so finally Logos turned her ear loose. "Come on," he said. "Perch ain't going to bite all day." He lifted to the rust-covered shovel from behind the door and ambled out of his shed to the dumping ground.

"Naw," he complained, "dismals come back. Can't go. All wore out." He stuck the shovel in the ground and reached down to lace his white canvas sneakers.

"Worms!" shouted Roy. He grabbed onto Logos's belt and tried to swing from it. "Worms, worms, worms, worms—"

"Yeah, get us some bait, Logos!"

"Yeah!" And Georgia Lee Small hopped around, hitting Logos in the ribs and back. "Yeah, yeah, yeah—"

So Logos grinned again, showing his good teeth, and without saying anything else he began to spade up the dump for worms.

Logos had been born in Tennessee, way up near Three-Forks-of-the-Wolf, he used to say, way high in the Tennessee mountains. He'd been raised there. He'd worked a little place, but it was so rocky that the crops wouldn't grow much, so one day Logos had just called his hound dogs together and they'd walked south and west until the rocks and the hills and the lightning storms had drifted back out of sight. They'd walked to the edge of a plain where there were farms, cut through with creeks and hollows, and a river and a town. There the sun was a long way off. Logos had stopped. That had been eight years ago. He was forty-three now; two of his hounds were buried behind the shed.

Usually in the afternoons, when the sun had cooled and the tree locusts were scratching, the kids would straggle over to Logos's place for a story about Tennessee. They'd squat and sprawl in the dust in front of his porch, sharpening their pocket knives on their pants, or frogging each other on the arm while Logos leaned back against the two-by-four and settled himself. When he'd begin to talk, the boys would stop pretending there weren't any girls in the gang and they'd all fall quiet, listening. He'd lean against the timber on his rickety porch and squint out into the red sun, like he was remembering a million years ago, and he'd tell stories in his Tennessee voice that somehow hadn't ever learned that folks don't care much about the handyman in a dusty little southern town.

He'd tell about the gimpy nigger who'd worked the place in back of his, and the Pentecostal baptisms in the river with the preachers spelling each other sometimes, yelling and ducking the sinners. He'd talk about sitting on a hilltop at night, listening to the dogs chase a fox over the ridges. Sometimes he'd talk about how lightning broke in the hills, or how everybody tried to raise a good mule. A good mule would bring three or even four hundred dollars, Logos said.

Evered Evans liked to hear about the tobacco barns, so almost every evening Logos would have to tell him about the hickory fire leaking smoke through the cracks in the roof. Boulton Polk wanted to hear about the smokehouse and how side meat was hung. Ella wanted to hear how potatoes were heeled in and dug up when winter came.

"Tell us about the trees," would say Luanne. "How do the trees feel when you touch them?"

So Logos would have to tell her all over again about the white oaks and the gray cedars, or the dogwoods with their rough checkery bark. And to the gang it seemed as though Logos Jackson was at least a million years old. They'd tell him he was a million, but he would just laugh. "I'll take you all to Tennessee someday," he'd say.

The rusty shovel glinted once or twice in the sun as Logos spaded up the dump. The sweat began to smell and his blue shirt with the sleeves cut off got limp. He'd turn up a spadeful of the dump and Roy and Boulton Polk would each jump for it, pulling out the worms and dropping them into the can.

"We got sixteen," whispered Betty Su.

"I can't put worms on the hook," said Luanne.

"Logos, why do we have to take girls on the picnic anyway?" asked Sidney Thomas.

"Got to like girls," said Logos without looking up.

Maxine smiled. "Why?"

He wiped the sweat from his mouth and chuckled. "Account of you came from my rib, honey. We're all God's children."

"We only got sixteen worms still," said Roy. "Get some more."

Maxine played with her hair. "Don't you like me, Logos?"

"Sure, I like you. Like all you kids—all you ugly kids."

"I don't mean that. I've grown up. I'm a woman."

Logos turned to his shovel. Maxine watched the muscles of his shoulders bunch and slide under the wet shirt.

Boulton Polk looked up from the worms. "Phooey!" he said.

"How many we got?"

"How many we got, Betty Su?"

"Twenty-three," answered Roy.

"That's enough."

Georgia Lee wiped her hands on her jeans. She grabbed for the can. "Let me carry them."

"You'll spill them," decided Sidney. "I'll carry them. Girls always spill things." He pushed a worm back.

"I get to carry them part way," said Boulton.

Logos stuck his shovel in the dirt and grinned.

Georgia Lee wiped her hands again and looked at the can and then at Sidney. Logos headed the gang toward the path that zigged through the dirty brown weeds.

"Are we going to catch perch today, Logos?"

"I brought a sandwich, Logos."

"What part of the creek are we going to, Logos?"

"THAT'S NO WAY to string a worm." Logos took Luanne's hook in a hand that was almost as hard as the barb. He threaded the worm and dropped the line into the sunny pool. Luanne studied the cork. She crouched on the bank with tense wrists.

"Now you let him get a hold before you jerk him out of there."

Luanne nodded quickly, never raising her eyes from the cork.

Roy plowed through the briar patch. "I got one, Logos! I got one! I got one!"

Logos inspected the catch. "Throw him back. Too small to eat."

Roy unhooked the tiny perch and laid it carefully in the shallows. "Whillickers!" he said.

"Logos, will you put on my worm?" Maxine seated herself on a log where she could watch as Logos adjusted her tackle. "I hate worms. They're so slimy."

Logos grinned down at her. His hands moved quickly, the fingers throwing shadows. Maxine watched. Her wide mouth smiled, thanking him.

"Lay off that fire, Mr. Polk. Cooking fire's small." Logos reached into the can for another worm. "You catch us a mess of fish. I'll fix that fire." He handed a line to Boulton and pulled a stick from the fire.

Maxine's hand closed over Logos's on the stick. "I'll fix it. I don't care about fishing." Then she said to Boulton, "Go on. You heard what Logos said." She stooped and poked at the blaze, moving her knees away from the heat.

Luanne jumped back, whirling her bamboo stick. "Logos!" she shrieked, and ran to bend over the sunfish flopping on the bank.

"That's not so big," observed Sidney. "I've caught bigger ones than that."

Ella poked interestedly.

Maxine spoke. "Kill it."

They all turned around and looked at her.

"Hit it on the head." She rocked forward. "Or do you want to eat it alive?" She tossed a branch toward the group.

Sidney picked up the branch and looked down at the little fish, squirming in the dust and dry beard grass. He shifted the branch to this other hand and doubled up his fist.

"Well," said Maxine, "go ahead. Smack it."

Sidney spit on the ground and mashed his toe in the spit. "I will," he said. "I will, okay."

She stood up, placing her palms deliberately on her angular hips.

Sidney mashed the spit again. He dropped to his knees and took hold of the fishing line. The fish wriggled. Sidney put down his branch. "He threw water in my eyes. I can't see."

"Kill it!"

"Well—*you* kill him."

Maxine picked up the branch and stunned the fish. She ripped the hook from its mouth, and turned to find Logos staring at her.

Evered Evans came around the bend with a turtle. Bert showed up with a perch and another one that Logos said was diseased. Georgia Lee didn't catch anything, but Logos told her that if it hadn't been for her sandwich they couldn't have cooked the fish with bread crumbs. The fish were just right.

AFTER DINNER Roy asked for a story.

Logos poked at the fire and grinned and said he didn't know any more stories, but Roy grabbed his wrist and curled up his knees and said he wasn't ever going to let go until Logos told a story. So Logos said all right because he sure didn't want such a dumb ugly little roughneck swinging on his arm all the rest of his life. He sat down on a patch of turkeyfoot and told the gang to get settled because they were making too much rumpus. They spraddled out flat around him, mostly on their stomachs with their chins in their hands, except Maxine. She walked across from where Logos was facing and sat on a log and drew up her legs to get more comfortable.

Logos started off by saying he was so old that when he was born his mother couldn't think of anything to name him, because way back then nobody had names. All the gang laughed except Maxine. She smiled and leaned on her hands. She asked Logos how old he was. Logos looked up, but he couldn't see her face behind the fire. He rubbed his long thin nose. Then he grabbed a chip of wood and tossed it at her and the kids laughed again, only Maxine took the chip and dropped it down the front of her blouse. Logos looked into the fire for a minute and broke a stick, but finally he went on talking. He told all about a fox hunt, the best fox hunt they'd ever had in the Tennessee hills, and how when they skinned the fox he was eleven feet long.

Maxine leaned back on her hands again. When the kids had stopped yelling and booing she said she wished she could find a man that big. She ran her tongue over her upper lip and sucked in her breath until the blouse stretched tight. Logos went on talking, only sometimes his stories wandered. Roy asked him what was the matter.

Bert and Evered whittled. "How big is the jockey yard?" asked Evered.

"Tell me about Mule Day in Columbia," whispered Betty Su. She sat with her ankles crossed under her in the dust. Her solemn gray eyes seemed even bigger behind the thick glasses. "Do the ladies really ride the mules in the parade? Do they ride the real mules?"

Logos pushed a finger down inside one of his sneakers and popped out a twig. Then he told how the pretty girls jumped on the jackasses and rode in the big parade when Columbia had Mule Day back east in Tennessee.

"Tell me about the revivals in the strawpens and the cunjur doctors."

So Logos told Ella about the revival meetings back in the hill country, about the niggers getting baptized; and why you should always plant a garden in the full of the moon.

"How do I catch a husband, Logos?" asked Maxine.

Logos grinned and spit through his teeth. "First day of May hold a mirror over a well."

Maxine smiled, tangling her hair with one finger. "I'm grown up. I don't want to wait on my honeymoon that long."

Logos tried to grin again. "Sleep with a beef bone under your pillow—" He threw another stick of wood at the fire.

"Aw, whillickers! Cut out that mush. What's a cunjur doctor, Logos?"

Then Logos told about the cunjur doctors selling "hands" and "tobies" to the niggers to ward off spells and to catch witches.

"What about the cunjur doctor with the three birthmarks on his arm?"

"Father and Son and Holy Ghost," Logos answered, but he didn't seem very interested in telling stories any more.

"I got a wart," announced Georgia Lee.

"Black calf lick it three times on three days."

"What do they do in the revivals, Logos?"

"Oh, jump, roll around, wrestle with the Devil," he answered, poking at the fire. Luanne cried happily,

> *"I'll tell you who the Lord loves best—*
> *It's the shouting Methodist!"*

And Roy countered,

> *"Baptist, Baptist, Baptist—*
> *Baptist till I die.*
> *I'll go along with the Baptists*
> *And find myself on high!*

Isn't that right, Logos?"

"Do you go to church, Logos?" asked Maxine.

"They don't have his church here," said Evered.

"I belong to all churches that knows the Word of God," he answered.

Maxine slipped off her sandals and squeezed dust between her toes.

"Maxine's got a dimple in her knee! What does that mean?"

Logos chuckled and his good white teeth showed again. "Means there's the Devil in her," he said. But nobody laughed.

The sun was going down. Maxine ran her tongue over her lips and rubbed the outside of her thin thighs. She looked at Logos across the firelight. She turned around to look at the sun, and the fire reflected the color in her hair.

"Maxine's got pretty hair," said Roy, "for a girl."

Evered snorted and looked sideways at Bert.

Maxine stood in back of the log. She stretched her arms until her blouse pulled tight again. "I've lost my fishing tackle. Don't you reckon I better find it before it gets dark?"

Logos didn't say anything.

"I can't recollect exactly where it is. Maybe—you better come along. I might get lost."

"You can find it."

"All right," said Maxine. She eased her palms down over the bones of her hips. She opened her mouth to say something, but then just licked her teeth. "All right," she said at last. She left her sandals on the log and turned and wandered off into the darkening hollow.

"She didn't lose no old fishing tackle. She didn't even go fishing. She said worms are slimy." Sidney appealed to Logos for confirmation.

"Maxine Crowe," said Roy. "Ugh! Maxine Scarecrow."

"She sure has got pretty hair," said Bert. He glanced over at Evered.

Sidney pulled up his socks. "I don't like her."

"Neither do I," said Ella.

"She is a lamb lost in the wilderness," murmured Logos into the fire.

Night drifted in over the farmlands and the smoke faded from black to gray-blue. Beyond Jess Phillips's land the weak yellow lights of the town popped through the darkness, one by one. A breeze sneaked across the creek and wiggled the smoke, but there weren't many leaves to rustle. Down the field an owl screamed and a dog barked. A train whistled over somewhere near the sun. A mouse ticked a dry branch, and the sky changed from red to purple and finally died.

"Sing us a song, Logos."

So Logos hummed for a while, and sang words, but they weren't connected.

When he had finished the gang didn't talk. Bert remembered to pick up the stick he had been whittling on, but he didn't cut any more. He laid it down softly.

The night was quiet; the fire didn't crackle very loud.

"Reckon I better go find her," said Logos at last. "She's been gone a long time." He roughed Roy's head and stepped over Ella and wandered off toward the dark hollow.

"Maxine!" they heard him call, and heard it drift with the wind. "Maxine, honey!"

A star began to shine over in the east just above the briar, but there weren't any other lights. A branch snapped down in the hollow and another dog barked way off over the black fields, and then they couldn't hear any more.

"Whillickers!" said Roy sleepily. "He's been gone a long time."

"Yeah."

"Think we ought to go after him?"

"No," said Evered. "We'd just all get scattered out. We better wait."

Ella and Betty Su and Luanne sat close together. "Put some sticks on," said Betty Su.

"You're afraid of the dark," said Sidney disgustedly.

"So are you."

"I am not!"

"Are so!"

"The moon's coming up—"

"Shh!"

"What's the matter?" hissed Ella.

"Shh!" Bert peered into the night. "No, I guess it's nothing."

"What did you hear?"

"Nothing. I thought I heard them."

"Put some more sticks on."

Roy pulled out his knife and thumbed the edge. "I bet this is the sharpest old knife in the world." He jabbed at the ground, popping up little chunks of dirt.

"I had a knife sharper than that once."

"You did not."

"Did so!"

"Shh—"

"Are they coming?"

"Can you hear them, Bert?"

"I don't know. There's something." Bert stood up. "Push that big branch on." He walked to the edge of the circle of light and squinted toward the hollow. "Logos! Hey, Logos! Is that you?"

Evered stood up. "Hey, Logos!"

Luanne bit her lip. "I don't think he's ever going to come back." She coughed and ground her fists in her eyes. The owl screamed again and she took Betty Su's hand. "He's not ever going to come back."

"Oh, cut it out." Boulton stood on the log, smacking his fist into the palm of his other hand.

Luanne began to sniffle. "No, he's not. Something's happened."

Roy sat staring into the coals with his knife balanced on one knee.

"Poke it up."

"Oh, who's cold?"

"I'm not, but poke it up anyway. I can't see."

Roy pushed a branch farther in with the blade of his knife. He rubbed his forehead.

Bert ran out into the night. "Logos! Yea, Logos!"

Luanne and Georgia Lee jumped up and stared into the dark. "Logos?" called Georgia Lee.

Maxine walked into the light of the fire. She was crying. Logos followed her in. He carried his blue shirt in one hand.

"Hey, Logos," exclaimed Evered, "we thought you'd got lost yourself!"

"I have lost myself, boy."

"Gee, Logos, what's the matter? You look funny."

"Put on your sweater, boy. You all pack up."

Luanne began to cry.

They collected their pocket knives and their shoes and their rubber gun pistols in silence. Logos stood by the fire with his eyes closed, the red light of the flames deepening the scar around his neck.

"I guess that's everything," said Bert.

Logos scattered the sticks of the fire and walked heavily on the embers until there was just moonlight.

"You didn't even go fishing!" blurted Roy. He turned around and kicked at Maxine's sandals.

Maxine put her fingers in her mouth.

They all went home. Logos opened a can and ate. Then he filled his pockets and called his hound dogs and started walking.

1947

THE ANATOMY
LESSON

NORTH FAYER HALL stood on the final and lowest hill of the university, a little askew from the other buildings as if it were ashamed of its shabbiness and had turned partly away. Its windowsills were pocked by cigarette burns and the doors of its green tin lockers had been pried open for so many years that few of them would lock any more; the creaking floors were streaked and spattered with drops of paint, dust lay upon the skylights, and because the ventilating system could not carry off so many fumes it seemed forever drenched in turpentine. Mercifully the little building was hidden each afternoon by the shadows of its huge, ivy-jacketed companions.

Just inside the front door was the office and studio of Professor A. B. Gidney, head of the art department, who taught ceramics, bookbinding, fashion design, and lettering. Professor Gidney's door was always open, even when he was teaching class somewhere else in the building, and in his studio were teacups and cookies and a hot plate which the students were free to use whenever they pleased. There was also a record player and a soft maple cabinet containing albums of operettas and waltzes; every afternoon punctually at five the music started.

Behind his office were the student ateliers, each with twenty or thirty short-legged chairs placed in a semicircle around the model's platform, and at the extreme rear of the building next to the fire escape, and reached by a dim corridor which multiplied every footstep, stood the studio of the other instructor.

This final studio was shaped like an upended coffin. In the rafters which surrounded its skylight spiders were forever weaving, and because the window had not been opened in years the air was as stale as that of an attic, always cold in December and always close in July. The window as a matter of fact could not even be seen because of the magazines and newspapers heaped atop a huge, iron-bound trunk with a gibbous lid. In one corner of the room a board rack held rows of somber oil paintings, each nearly the same: marshes in the center of which one hooded figure was standing with head bowed. The first few strokes of another such painting rested on an easel in the center of the room, and around this easel a space had been cleared, but the material that was banked against the walls and rose all the way to the ceiling threatened to engulf it at any moment. There were gilt picture frames, some as large as a door; there were crocks and pails half filled with coagulated liquids, cartons, milk bottles, splintered crates covered with layers of dust and tobacco crumbs, rolls of linen canvas with rectangles ripped out, jugs of varnish and turpentine lined up on an army cot with a broken leg, brushes, rags, tubes, apple cores, wrappers of chocolate bars, Brazil nuts, toothpicks, and pictures everywhere—glued on the walls or on boxes or, it seemed, on whatever was closest: pictures of madonnas, airplanes, zebras, rapiers, gargoyles, schooners, adobe pueblos, and a host of others. There seemed to be no plan or preference; a solarized print of a turkey feather had been stuck to the trunk so that it half obliterated a sepia print of the Bosporus. The glue pot itself could be traced by its smell to a cobwebbed corner where, because it had cracked and was leaking, it sat on a piece of wrapping paper. On this paper was an inscription, printed at one time in red Conté but now almost invisible. Beneath the glue and ashes the letters read:

> *I am here,*
> *I have traversed the Tomb,*
> *I behold thee,*
> *Thou who art strong!*

Here and there on the floor lay bits of what looked like chalk but which were the remains of a little plaster cast of Michelangelo's *Bound Slave*. The fragments suggested that the statuette had not fallen but had been thrown to the floor. Also scattered about were phonograph records; most of them looked as if someone had bitten them. Several rested on the collar of a shaggy overcoat which in turn was draped over a stepladder. The phonograph itself lay on its side, the crank jutting up like the skeleton of a bird's wing and the splintered megaphone protruding from beneath one corner of a mattress like some great ear. In the middle of the night when the university campus was totally deserted there would occasionally come from the rear of North Fayer Hall the muffled sound of plainsong or Gregorian chant, to which was sometimes added for a few bars a resonant bass voice in absolute harmony, that of the instructor whose name was printed in gold on the studio door, a door that was always locked: ANDREV ANDRAUKOV, DRAWING & PAINTING.

Nothing interested Andraukov except paint. Each thing he saw or heard or touched, whether it writhed like a sensuous woman or lay cold as an empty jug, did not live for him until he, by his own hand, had given it life. Wherever he happened to be, in a class or outside, he paced back and forth like a tiger, and when with hands laced into a knot at the tail of his sack-like tweed coat and his huge, bony head bowed as if in prayer he stalked the corridors of North Fayer Hall, or the streets of Davenport below the university, he created a silence. Always he walked with his head bowed, and so far had his slanting eyes retreated into their sockets that few people had met his gaze. His teeth were as yellow and brown as his leathery skin and it seemed as if flesh were too much of a luxury for his bones to endure.

It was his habit to start each drawing class in the still-life room, a damp, chill studio with shelf upon shelf of plaster and bronze casts. He always took his students there the first morning; they stood about uncertainly, their young faces rosy from the September air, clean pencils and papers and new drawing boards clutched in their arms.

"Here," he would say, unrolling a long, cold finger. "Rome. Egypt. Greece. Renaissance. You will copy."

The students looked at him, a haggard old man whose head by daylight could be no more than a skull in a leather bag, and one by one they settled themselves before a statue. Around and around behind them went Andrev Andraukov, taking from awkward fingers the pencils or sticks of charcoal, drawing with incredible delicacy tiny explanatory sketches in a corner of the paper. When he leaned down to inspect the drawings of the girls they stiffened and held their breath fearing he might somehow contaminate them. To them he might have been the Genghis Khan. Slowly and with a kind of infinite patience he wandered from one to another, shaking his head, trying to explain, never taking from his mouth the stub of a brown cigarette which protruded from his drooping and streaked mustache like an unfortunate tooth. The moment he heard the chimes which ended each class he halted his explanation even though in the middle of a sentence, and without a single word or another look he went out. The sound of his footsteps echoing in the corridor ended with what seemed like the closing of a hundred distant doors.

When he saw that his students were losing interest in the plasters and so could gain nothing more, he took them into the life atelier. On the walls of this room were tacked reproductions of masterful paintings. Helter-skelter stood drawing boards and student paintings, and on a platform rested an electric heater and a stool. Here, in this studio, he commenced his instruction of the living human body: on the blackboard he drew diagrams and explained for several days, as best he could through the net of language, how it was that men and women functioned. Then he got his students a model. Each morning one would arrive carrying a little satchel in which there was a robe or a cloak to wear during the rest periods and sometimes an apple or cigarettes or even a book.

Generally the models did as others had done for three thousand years before them, so there faced the class each morning a noble though somewhat shopworn pose. With earnest faces the students copied, bending down close to their paper the better to draw each eyelash and mole, their fingers clutching the charcoal as if they were engraving poetry on the head of a pin, and one after another they discovered that if charcoal was rubbed it would shine. In two days every drawing gleamed like the top of a candy box. All the while their instructor, a cigarette fixed in his smelly mustache, paced the back of the room or walked up and down the corridor.

Although the students did not know it, he was waiting. Year after year as students flowed by him this old man watched and waited; he waited for the one who might be able to understand what it meant to be an artist, one student, born with the instinct of compassion, who could learn, who would renounce temporal life for the sake of billions yet unborn, just one who cared less for himself than for others. But there were good foods to eat, dear friends to chat with, and pretty girls to be seduced, so many fascinating things to be done and discussed, thus Andrev Andraukov could only watch and wait.

It was as if a little play never ended, wherein, to his eternal question, *Is it not important?*, the young people answered, *Yes! Yes! There must be one who cares!* And he asked, *Will it be you, then?* But they replied, *Ah, no! Not me! Someone else. You see, I have so awfully many things to do. . . .*

ONE NOVEMBER MORNING the members of Andraukov's class found lettered on the blackboard in his square hand, TODAY: ANATOMY. As a result they did not open their lockers but sat in a semicircle facing the model stand and waited.

Andraukov hurried in several minutes late; beside him walked a strange model who went behind the Japanese screen in the corner and began to undress.

Indicating a six-foot plaster man, stripped of skin and flesh, Andraukov asked two of the students to lift it onto the model stand. Next he pointed to the wooden cabinet where a skeleton dangled by a bolt through its skull, and said, "Mr. Bones." Two more students carried the rattling skeleton onto the stand. There was a half-smoked cigarette clamped in the jaws. Andraukov patiently removed it, as he had removed hundreds of others.

"Now," he said, "Miss Novak, please."

His model walked out from behind the screen and stepped onto the platform where she stood between the skeleton and the cutaway. She was a huge peasant girl with tubular limbs and coarse red hair that hung down her back like a rug. Between her great breasts was the tattoo of a ship. Her Slavic eyes were expressionless.

Andraukov took up a position behind the semicircle of students. From one of his coat pockets—which was more of a pouch—he brought up a crooked brown cigarette. After he had held two matches under it the cigarette began to sputter, flame, and finally emit blasts of terra-cotta smoke. Now Andraukov was ready to begin the lecture; he walked a few steps in each direction and then blew from his nostrils such a cloud that he nearly hid himself.

"Well," he began, "here is a girl. Young woman. Who does not agree?" He walked out of the smoke, looked around, and then walked back into it. "Good. We progress. On street I look at woman first the head, then down, so we will do here. Who can tell what is the shape of human head? Mr. Sprinkle will tell us."

Sprinkle stood up and fingered his lower lip while he thought. Finally he answered that the human head was shaped like a ball.

"So? Miss Vitale will tell us."

Alice Vitale said it looked like an egg.

"Miss Novak, please to turn around. We will see back of head."

The model gathered her hair and lifted it until the class could see her neck and the base of the skull.

"Mr. Bondon, now, please."

Michael Bondon had begun to grow sideburns, and because his father was very rich he was not afraid to cross his legs and shrug.

Andraukov watched him for several seconds and then without expression continued, "Ball. Egg. Who is correct?" He explained that from the front the human head does resemble an egg and from the rear a ball or a melon, but, he cautioned, the artist must not look at what he sees so much as what he cannot see, and holding up one hand he demonstrated that the students, seeing his palm with their eyes, must also see his knuckles with their minds. He said that the artist must see around corners and through walls, even as he must see behind smiles, behind looks of pain.

"For to what use you shall employ knowledge?" he asked, walking to the window and gazing out at the slopes covered with wet snow. "For what you shall be artist? To draw such as all the world can see? Pussycat? Nice bouquet of lily? Little boy in sailor suit? Then bring to this class a camera. No! Not to this class. Go elsewhere." He looked out the window again at the soggy clouds which were settling on the university buildings, and then with his cigarette pinched between thumb and forefinger as if it were alive and about to jump, he walked slowly across the room where he stopped with his back to the students. "You people, you wish to be artist. Why? That a stranger on the street will call you by name? You would be famous? You would have money? Or is it you have looked at your schedule and said, 'Ah, this is hard! I need now something easy. Yes, I will take drawing.'"

He turned around, looked at the faces of the men, his gaze resting on each for a number of seconds. "You have thought, 'I will take drawing because in studio will be pretty girl without dress!' So? This is reason? Or perhaps in this room—in this room perhaps now there sits young man who in this world discovers injustice. He would be conscience of the world. Mr. Dillon will now stand up. Mr. Dillon, you would draw picture which is to say, 'Behold! Injustice!'? You would do that?"

"No, sir," Dillon murmured.

"You will not be conscience of the world?"

"No, sir."

"If not you," Andraukov asked, gazing at the boy, "then who?" He carefully licked the underside of his mustache and pushed the cigarette deeper into his mouth. His knuckles were yellow and hard as stone. From the town of Davenport the sound of automobile horns came faintly up to the university hills; but for these noises and the creak of the instructor's shoes the life studio was quiet.

Andraukov walked to the stand where he flattened his thumb against the neck of the cutaway. "Sterno-mastoid. Favorite muscle. Favorite muscle of art student." He asked his model to look at the skeleton and as she turned her head the sterno-mastoid stretched like a rope between ear and collarbone.

"*Beatrice d'Este,* how many know this painting, painting by Leonardo da Vinci? Three? Three hands? Disgrace! Now I tell you: In *Beatrice* is no sterno-mastoid. And why? Leonardo da Vinci is painting young woman, is not painting tackle of football team." He looked down on the faces turned attentively toward him and did not think they understood, but he did not know how to phrase it any more clearly. He decided to tell a joke. With a piece of green chalk he sketched on the blackboard a grotesque profile. He peered at it and shouted, "Young man after my daughter. Look like this! No, no—" He had confused the grammar. "Would have daughter, such young man like this." The class did not know what he was doing.

Andraukov felt he should explain his joke. He pulled on his mustache for a while and tried again but there was still only a confused tittering. He decided to continue with the lecture. Having become a trifle warm he unbuttoned his vest and hooked both thumbs in the pockets.

"Well, below head is neck. Below neck is breast. You are afraid of this word. Why? This is God's word. Why everybody—all the young girls say 'bust'? Bust is for firecracker. Not for woman. No! Everybody—class entire together—now say correct word."

He listened to the class uneasily repeat the word and he nodded with satisfaction. "So! Not to be 'bust' again. I do not like that word. For drawing; art student draw like balloon. This is wrong. Not balloon, but is bag to rest on rib cage. Is part of the body like ear is part of head, like peanut butter of sandwich, not to be alone. Who does not understand? Who has question?" No hands were raised.

Andraukov asked his model to face him with her heels together, legs straight, and hands at her sides. He stared. He was pleased with the way she stood.

"Class. Class, consider Miss Novak, fine model, head high. Is good to be proud of body. Yes. This is true!" He struck himself with a stony fist. "No scent on earth is so putrid as shame. Good students, do not fear to be proud." He paused to meditate. "Well, on rib who can tell status of breast? Nobody? There is nobody to speak? There is fear?" He looked around. "Ah! Brave student. Mr. Zahn will speak. Mr. Zahn stands to tell instructor of breast. Good. Speak." With head bowed he prepared to listen, but almost immediately held up one hand. "No, no! I would know direction. I would know angle. Yes, angle. On breast does nipple look ahead like nose on face?"

Logan Zahn was a thin, heavily bearded young man who sat in corners whenever possible. He was older than the other students and wore glasses so thick that his eyes seemed to bulge. There were rumors that he was writing a book about something.

"No," he answered in a surprisingly high voice.

"The nipple, it will look down, perhaps?"

"No."

"Then where?"

"Up."

"And?"

"Out."

"Good!"

Zahn and the model looked at each other, both expressionless.

"You will tell instructor amount of angle. The left breast now, to where it is looking?"

"At the print of Cézanne's apples on the wall."

"And the right?"

Logan Zahn was not afraid. He pointed out the window. "At the Episcopal church."

Andraukov looked at the model and then toward the church. "That is correct." He tugged from his vest a heavy watch and studied it, pursing his lips. Why, he asked, tucking away the watch, why was it that men wished to touch women? To allow time for his question to penetrate he folded his arms across his chest and began wandering about the studio. He picked a bit of chalk off the floor, he opened a window an inch, he stroked a dusty bronze on a shelf, he went back to close the window, and when at last he felt that every student should have been able to consider his question and speak of it properly he invited answers. Nobody volunteered.

"I will tell you," he said. "No, I will not tell you. Mr. Van Antwerp will stand."

Van Antwerp, who was the university's wrestling champion, scratched his scalp and grinned. Andraukov's face did not move.

Van Antwerp grinned some more. "They're fat," he said.

"Man is not fat? Yes, but different. Well, on woman where it is most thick?"

Van Antwerp began to stand on his other foot. He blushed and sniggered. The class was silent. For a few moments Andraukov stood with eyes closed and head cocked to one side as if listening to something beyond the range of other ears, but abruptly he strode across the room to Van Antwerp's green tin locker and wrenched it open.

"These material, it belong to you? Take it now. You will not return! Who else now—who else—" But not being able to phrase what he wished to say he stood facing a shelf while Van Antwerp collected his things and left, slamming the door. Andraukov looked over his shoulder at the students. He turned all the way around and the color began to come back into his face.

"We speak of shape. Shape, yes. Is caused by many things. There is fat, placed by God, to protect child of womb. There is pelvic structure—so broad!" His bony hands gripped an imaginary pelvis. "There is short leg, spinal curve so deep. There is, too, the stance of woman. All these things, these things are not of man. You will not draw man and on him put balloons, lipstick, hair, and so to say, 'Here is woman!' No!"

He continued that woman was like the turtle, born to lie in the sun and sometimes to be turned over. Woman, he told them, was passive. She was not to smoke tobacco, to swear, to talk to man, to dance with man, to love like a drunken sailor; she was to brush her hair and wait. As he thought about the matter Andrev Andraukov stalked back and forth cutting the layers of smoke left by his cigarette.

"Trouser! Crop hair! Drink beer! For ten thousand years woman is correct: gentle, quiet, fat. Now?" He paused to stare at the floor, then lifting his head, said. "Well, today is good model. Consider limbs: not little to break in pieces but big and round like statue of Egyptian goddess, like statue in concrete like *Girl Holding Fruit* of Clodion. This piece, how many know? This Clodion?" He looked over the class and seeing only two hands pinched the bridge of his nose in a sudden, curious gesture and closed his eyes. He instructed them all to go to the library that afternoon and find a picture of the statue. Around the studio he wandered like a starved and shabby friar, the cuffs of his fraying trousers dusting the paint-stained boards and the poor coat dangling from the knobs of his shoulders. The laces of his shoes had been broken and knotted many times, the heels worn round. He stopped in a corner beside a cast of *St. George* by Donatello and passed his fingertips across the face as if he were making love to it. He licked the drooping corner hairs of his mustache. He swung his Mongol head toward the class.

"You do not know Clodion! You do not know Signorelli, Perugino, Hokusai, Holbein! You do not even know Da Vinci, not even Cranach or Dürer! How, then, how I can teach you? Osmosis? You will look inside my head? Each day you sit before the model to draw. I watch. There is ugly model, I see on your face nothing. Not pity, not revolt, not wonder. Nothing. There is beautiful model, like today. I see nothing. Not greed, not sadness, not even fever. Students, have you love? Have you hate? Or these things are words to you? As the artist feels so does he draw. I look at you, I do not need to look at the drawing."

There was no sound but the footsteps of the old instructor. Dust motes whirled about him as he walked through a bar of winter sunlight.

"Good students, why have you come to me? You do not know what is crucifixion, the requiem, transfiguration. You do not even know the simple ecstasy. These things I cannot teach. No. I teach the hand. No man can teach the heart." Holding up his own hand for them all to see he went on, "This is not the home of the artist. Raphael does not live here." Tapping himself on the chest he said, "The home of Raphael is here."

The little sunlight faded so that all the sky was mushroom gray, somehow auguring death and the winter. A wind rose, rattling the windows. The studio's one radiator began to knock and send up jets of steam. Andraukov snapped on the lights. He walked toward the motionless Slavic woman, his eyes going up and down her body as he approached.

"Who can find for instructor, sartorius?"

A girl went to the plaster cast and spiraled one finger down its thigh.

"Now on the model."

She touched the crest of the hip and inside the knee.

"What Miss Grodsky does not say is, ilium to tibia. But is all right because she tries. She will learn."

He asked if anybody knew why the muscle was named sartorius, but nobody knew; he told them it came from the word *sartor,* which meant tailor, and that this muscle must be used in order to sit cross-legged as years ago the tailors used to sit. He asked for the patella and his student laid one finger on the model's kneecap but did not know what the word meant. It meant a little pan, he said, as he drew its outline on the model's skin with a stick of charcoal. He asked next for the scapula; she hesitated and then touched the collarbone. He shook his head, saying, "Not clavicle, not the key." She guessed at the ankle and he shook his head again, placing her finger behind the model's shoulder. There with charcoal he outlined the scapula, saying as he finished it, "So! And Miss Grodsky can sit down. Mr. Zahn will find for instructor, pectoralis major."

Logan Zahn got up again and pointed.

Andraukov said, "Miss Novak does not bite." He watched as Zahn placed a fingertip outside and then inside her breast. "Correct. Easy question." With charcoal he drew the pectoralis on her skin. "Now for instructor, gluteus medius." He watched Zahn touch the side of her hip.

"Gastrocnemius."

He patted the calf of her leg.

"Masseter."

He touched her jaw.

Andraukov looked at him intently. "You are medical student?"

"No."

"Find for me—find pectoralis minor."

With his hands Zahn indicated that it lay deeper in the body.

"So. Where you have learn what you know?"

"Library," Zahn answered in his squeaky voice.

"I have told you to study anatomy in library?"

"No."

"But you have gone?"

"Yes."

Andraukov's nostrils dilated and he blew a cloud of smoke dark enough to have come from a ship; he stood in the middle of it, nearly hidden. When he emerged he began to speak of the differences between men and women; placing both hands on the model's forehead he stretched the skin above her drugged eyes until the class saw how smooth the skull appeared, and for comparison he pointed to the ridge of bone like that of an ape's on the bleached skeleton. He pointed to the angle of the model's jawbone and next to the more acute angle on the skeleton. Below the pit of her neck he drew an outline of the sternum and compared it to the skeleton's longer, straighter bone. He said that the woman's neck seemed longer because the clavicle was shorter, thus narrowing the shoulders, that the elbow looked higher because the female humerus was short, that the reason one could not judge the height of seated women was because they possessed great variations in the length of the leg, that female buttocks were of greater diameter than male because of protective fat and because the sacrum assumes a greater angle. He turned the skeleton about on its gallows and placed his model in the same position. He drew the sacrum on her skin, and the vertebrae rising above it. She arched her back so that he could lay his hand on the sloping shelf. Why, he asked, why was it thus? And he answered himself, saying that the spine of man was straighter. Then for what reason did the spine of woman curve? For what reason did the pelvis tilt? Who would explain to him?

But again he answered himself. "Cushion!" A cushion for the foetus. From a cupboard he brought a length of straight wire and stabbed it at the floor; the wire twanged and vibrated from the shock, but after he had bent it into an S the wire bounced. He flung it into a corner and walked back and forth rubbing his hands as he lectured. The belly protrudes because there resides the viscera of the human body. Fashion magazines do not know about viscera, they print pictures of young girls who cannot eat because they have no stomach, who cannot walk because they have no maximus, who seem to stand on broken ankles. Although paper was flat the students must draw as if it were round; they must draw not in two dimensions but in three. A good artist could draw in three dimensions, a master could draw in four.

He stopped to consider the attentive looks on their faces and asked who understood, but did not wait for an answer. He spoke of how Rembrandt painted a young woman looking out an open window and said to them that she did not live three hundred years ago, no, she was more than one young woman, she was all, from the first who had lived on earth to the one yet unborn who would be the final. He told them that some afternoon they would glance up by chance and see her; then they would know the meaning of Time—what it could destroy, what it could not. But for today, he said, his voice subsiding, three dimensions would be enough. From his baggy vest he extracted a silver thimble. He held it between two fingers.

"For belly, three dimensions. It is not, like paper, flat. So navel is not black dot. It is deep. It is the eye of God. You are going to see." Bending down he pushed the thimble steadily into the model's navel.

Every little noise in the studio ceased. There was no movement. It seemed an evil spell had been thrown by the thimble which retreated and advanced toward the students in brief, glittering arcs.

Andraukov licked his yellow mustache. "Good students, you will forget again?"

The class was still paralyzed. Waves of shock swept back and forth across the room; with the elongated senses of the mystic Andraukov caught them.

"Good students," he said simply. "Listen. Now I speak. You have come to me not to play. You have come to learn. I will teach. You will learn. Good students, each time in history that people have shame, each time in history that people hide from what they are, then in that age there is no meaning to life. There is imitation. Nothing more. There is nothing from which the little generation can learn. There is no weapon for the son to take from the hands of his father to conquer the forces of darkness and so to bring greatness to the people of earth."

Andrev Andraukov put the thimble back in his vest pocket. The thin soles of his pointed, paint-spattered shoes flapped on the boards as he walked to the cast of *St. George* and stood for a time gazing absently beyond it.

Suddenly he asked, "Will you like to hear a story?" and immediately began telling it.

Eleven years ago he had taught another drawing class much like their own where the students drew stiff, smudgy pictures of Greek warriors and made spaghetti of Michelangelo's muscles. But they, too, had worked hard, it had been a good class, and so one day he brought them into the life studio and gave them a woman. He left them alone that first morning and when he returned at noon they lined their drawing boards up against the wall and waited for his criticism.

In regard to the first drawing he observed that the head looked as big as a watermelon and he explained that the human head was nearly the same length as the foot; immediately the class members discovered they had drawn the feet too small. The hand, he told them, demonstrating, would more than cover the face; the class laughed at the tiny hands on all the drawings. How could they have made such mistakes! Well, they would learn.

At the second piece of work he stood facing them with hands at his sides and in a few moments the class discovered what he was doing: they had not drawn the arms long enough. He explained the various uses of the human arm, suggesting that if they would learn to speak truly of function then their drawings would be correct. He looked at their faces and saw the struggle to comprehend. It was a good class.

The next drawing was a tiny thing but when he bent down to peer at it he discovered the streaks which were meant to be veins in the back of the model's hand. He held out his own hand with its great veins of red and green twine.

"These are important?" he asked them, and as he lifted his hands high in the air the class watched the veins recede.

So one by one he criticized those first works. When he came to the final drawing he found the figure had been covered by a bathing suit. He thought it was a joke. He turned to the class with a puzzled smile, but seeing their faces he knew it was not a joke.

"Who has drawn this?" he asked. No hand was raised. He returned to the first drawing and asked its owner to leave the studio; he stopped at the second drawing and asked its owner to leave. One by one the students walked out and finally he was left with two drawings but only one student.

"Miss Hugasian," he said, "you draw this morning two pictures?"

She pointed to the first.

"Well, then, this final drawing?"

Her eyes were brilliant with fright but he was patient and at last she said it had been done by Patricia Bettencourt.

"Miss Bettencourt? She is here today?" Then he left the studio and walked up and down the corridor opening each door until finally in the still-life room, seated between the casts of *Night* and *Day* with a handkerchief held over her face he saw Patricia Bettencourt. Looking down on her he wondered.

She did not move.

"You are ill?" he asked, bringing a bench close to her and sitting down. "For me today you make very nice drawing, but the bathing suit—"

Andraukov paused in telling the story of Patricia Bettencourt, but he did not stop pacing so the eyes of the students swung steadily back and forth. Once again the only sounds in the atelier were the creak of his shoes and the knocking radiator. From time to time the electric heater on the model's platform hummed faintly. Rain trickled down the window panes and, finding cracks in the ancient putty, seeped and dripped to the floor where puddles were spreading. Before continuing with the story he walked to the door and opened it.

"Miss Bettencourt speaks. 'I did not know model was to be—' This sentence she cannot finish because she weeps. I finish for her. I ask, 'Nude?' She does not answer. Shadow like shroud drops on cast of Michelangelo."

Andraukov tasted his mustache and nodded to himself. He walked to the window where he stood with his back to the class; they could see only the thin hair on his skull and his yellow fingers tied into a knot at the tail of his coat.

"Good pupils, the artist is not 'nice.' No, that cannot be. He shall hear at times the voice of God, at times the shriek of each dwarf in the heart and in the soul, and shall obey those voices. But the voice of his fellow man? No. That cannot be. I think he who would create prepares his cross. Yes! It is so. But at his feet no Magdalen. Who, then, shall accuse: 'You are evil!'? 'You are sublime!'? There is no one to speak these words. Miss Bettencourt is in this room? Go now. I do not wish to see your face."

The door to the corridor stood open. Andraukov remained at the window with his back to the students.

"Then I will teach you. I teach of the human body and of the human soul. Now you are young, as once even I was. Even as yours were my nostrils large. Now you shall learn what is the scent of life, and with fingers to touch, with ears to listen. Each fruit you shall taste, of honey and grape, and one day persimmon. I, too, have kissed the hot mouth of life, have shattered the night with cries, have won through such magic millions of years. You will listen now! God is just. He gives you birth. He gives you death. He bids you to look, to learn, and so to live."

The chimes of the university chapel had begun to toll. Wrapping his fingers once again into a knot at the tail of his coat Andrev Andraukov walked out the door. The anatomy lesson was over.

1948

COCOA PARTY

DURING the eleven years that Andrev Andraukov and Dr. Karl Locke worked together they evolved a curious manner of conversation, curious first of all because it was invariably opened and closed by the professor, and second because of its disconnected character. Their dialogue might be likened to an underground river which rushes unexpectedly into the sunlight and as suddenly disappears.

The day before the beginning of one Christmas vacation, for example, Dr. Locke bought a tin of cocoa and two boxes of petits fours and rented a phonograph with some records. Then he typed on one of his file cards and thumbtacked to the bulletin board an invitation for all students with marks of C or better to attend a party in the office when they finished class. Not many students accepted the invitation. He sat in his swivel chair behind the desk, his lips counting the young people as they entered, and there was absolutely no expression on his face.

The party such as it was had not been long in progress when everyone in the office heard Andraukov approaching: the squeak of his shoes and the rhythm of his walk were unmistakable. One step came after another as surely as a night comes after a day. Dr. Locke's mouth twitched; he re-crossed his slender legs, arranging the trousers so as not to destroy the crease or result in a bulge at the knee, then with one hand he shaded his eyes against the brilliant winter sunlight reflected through the windows.

On the phonograph *The Blue Danube* had just begun; to its melody a supple crafty-looking boy named Francis Rheba murmured, "Vich zhoe vill it be doday? Vich zhoe vill it be doday?" This was an allusion to the fact that Andraukov owned three shoes, two lefts and a right, the second right having been lost somewhere in the banks of material that jammed his studio. Both pairs had been identical, indeed everything he bought was as nearly as possible like the thing it was replacing. The shoes were ankle-high, black, even longer than necessary for his extremely large feet, and they were of the cheapest quality. The soles all but vanished every four or five months, at which time he would gravely and unquestioningly buy another pair. He did not seem to realize that shoes could be half-soled, at least he never entered a repair shop; it was as if when a thing gave way it was gone forever and nothing could bring it back. His two left shoes could be distinguished now because the toe of one was spattered with sienna paint while the other was scratched and stained with some kind of glue he had once been inventing. Both, though severely worn, could not compare with the state of the remaining right shoe which had a heel as round as a thumb and so many knots amongst the hooks that it could not afford a bow.

In the corridor the footsteps came to a stop. These sudden halts of the old man were a source of infinite amusement to every class of art students and through the years there had grown up a tradition that they were always to be timed. Seniors could speak of the famous day when he had stopped in the midst of a monologue on the importance of mixing paints properly and had stood before them without moving for almost eleven minutes—stood there still, withered, leaning like a cornstalk in some abandoned field. But on this occasion the pause was brief; the steps resumed and a moment later Mr. Andraukov passed the doorway. Few of the students took time to glance at his shoes, they were absorbed by the haggard face.

"Eev you do nod vadz, nod vadz, nod vadz," Francis Rheba murmured, and then gave off attempting to match the melody, "how you vill learn do draw? Zo?" His imitation of the accent was perfect except that he could not lower it to the proper rumbling bass. "Vaz de pendted zhoe."

"But doesn't Mr. Andraukov know we're in here?" inquired one of the freshmen.

"They talk about still waters," another student whispered, "but if you ask me the old boy's more asleep than deep."

Someone said out loud that Andraukov had lemon juice for blood. This brought an instant of silence to see if punishment would follow but there was no movement behind the desk, the wan and weary face almost concealed by a pale hand seemed to be taking no notice of them.

"Mr. Andraukov reminds me of an undertaker with jaundice." The voice was insolent; the "Mr." a safeguard in case Dr. Locke should stop daydreaming. Another Strauss plopped onto the turntable. The cups clinked softly. The eyes of the students were bright with the promise of Christmas.

"I say that man belongs in a tintype."

"Who wears a stickpin in this age?"

"Mr. Andrev Andraukov of Fischer College."

"Who wears a hardboiled collar?"

"Mr. Andrev Andraukov."

"I say he's got feelings from A to C."

There was one student, sitting by himself in a corner, who did not join the game. He was an ugly and rather stooped boy with a face as pinched and stormy as a captured bat and his name was Logan Zahn. His hair was stiff and black but his eyebrows were shot through with bristles of deep red. He sometimes drew savage little caricatures of his classmates when they were not looking, and in addition there were rumors that he was writing a book about something; in consequence he was looked upon with hostility. He had twice been challenged to a fist fight, though nobody could remember for what reason.

Dr. Locke spoke. He had a nasal tenor voice and faultless diction. "One of you may invite Mr. Andraukov to join us." As several students moved toward the door he swung about in his swivel chair and lowered two elegant index fingers like white pistol barrels at Logan Zahn. Having watched Zahn leave the room he placed his elbows carefully on the armrests of his chair and tapped his fingertips together. "Would you care for some more cocoa, Mr. Triggs?"

"No, thank you," the big fellow answered. His mouth worked before he could emit the words. "This is my second cu-cup already."

"Yes. Of course. A third cup might destroy the accuracy of your pitching arm. Alas for the alma mater. Why do you flush, Mr. Triggs? Miss Jefferson, cocoa?"

She swallowed what remained in her cup and held it out for more. As he poured he asked after the health of her brother who had fallen off a motorcycle, and she said he was much better.

"Fine. Please extend my hopes for the rapid knitting of his leg. Now, Mr. Pocock, you? Yes, indeed, eh? And how is the British cocoa?"

"Afraid I'm prejudiced, sir," replied Arnold Pocock bravely, though softening his answer by a brilliant smile through his beard.

"I," Dr. Locke said, "have been in London. And in Liverpool, for which I did not greatly care." He paid no attention to Pocock's acknowledgment but swiveled in the direction of the door, cocoa pot still in hand, lifted his voice a decibel and suggested, "Come in, Mr. Andraukov?"

The instructor, who had been standing in the corridor, lowered his head so as not to hit the arch and then walked into the office.

"As you see we are having a slight celebration in honor of the imminent holidays."

The students were quiet, staring up at Andraukov.

Locke pointed to the cookies and to the phonograph. "We would be delighted to have you join us." He motioned one of the boys to fetch a chair; Andraukov felt for its seat and then sat down and folded his hands in his lap. A saliva-soaked cigarette wrapped in brown paper jutted through the long dirty hairs of his mustache; its fire had gone out but nearly an inch of ash striated and thick like cigar ash clung to its tip. His eyes, sunken so far in their sockets that they were scarcely visible, were fixed on something below the floorboards.

Pocock who was standing beside the phonograph suddenly looked at it and asked if that was not Katherine Tegtmeyer on the violin; Locke glanced up surprised and pleased and said that indeed it was.

"We almost consider her one of ours, you know. Poor girl. She used to be right good."

The professor set his cup very deliberately back into the saucer. He made a steeple of his fingers and peered over the top, saying, "And still is, young man. Not, 'right good' but the best. The very best there is."

Pocock thought this a matter of opinion but after a look at the peculiar rigidity forming on Locke's face he did not elaborate. Both of them listened to the music for a little while, then the professor said more genially, "So you like Katherine's playing, do you? Then I shall see to it that you meet her."

"I beg your pardon?"

"Surely you have seen the posters announcing her Andromeda concert, Mr. Pocock. Yes. Of course. We discussed them as works of art just a few days ago. Well, sir, she and I were schoolmates long years ago. Alas, how many years."

"You and Tegtmeyer?"

"We attended conservatory together."

"Not meaning any disrespect but—music conservatory? You?"

"Does that strike you as so utterly strange, young man?" The professor snapped a cookie between his fingers and ate half of it before continuing, "For three long years I was under the impression that Destiny was motioning me toward a piano stool. How ludicrous it all seems to me now." He ate the rest of the cookie and smiled on all the students, most of whom smiled back.

The conversation which had lapsed while he was speaking now started up again and the new topic was Katherine Tegtmeyer. Who is she? . . . plays what? . . . the Continent how many years? . . . terribly homely . . . a lesbian . . . a nymph? . . . for the King . . . a *real* Stradivarius? . . .

Dr. Locke, pushing an ash tray across the desk toward Andraukov, asked if he was familiar with the music on the phonograph.

The instructor said he was not.

"Well, it's a delicate thing composed by Boccherini about 1795, if memory serves me well. It is one of Katherine's particular favorites."

Andraukov did not say anything.

After a few moments Locke picked up a half-carved block of soapstone which had been lying on his desk, and opening his pocket knife he resumed work on it. Two of the students came across to have a look and he held it up for inspection. "A water spout for my cathedral. A gargoyle, from the Old French word *gargouille,* meaning 'throat.' Do you like it?" They both found it very sophisticated. He listened to their compliments with a somewhat cynical expression and then continued: "The Gothic purity is most pleasing to me, most pleasing. It is, I feel, the true crown of the Romanesque. Its chief element, in case you youngsters are unfamiliar with the conception, is the ogival vaulting which came to be used in association with the famous, and deservedly so, pointed arches of the twelfth century." As he spoke he had lowered his eyes; now he raised them.

All of the students were again staring at Andraukov.

"Let us consider the renovation of the Ely cathedral," he said, his voice pitched somewhat higher. "The great central tower, built by the first Norman abbot whose dates of office, if I remember, were 1082 to 1094, collapsed in the year 1321."

Several students looked politely in his direction.

He pursed his lips, for a few seconds held them in that position, then he blew away the tiny soapstone chips and dust. He knocked the gargoyle against his palm, settled himself more comfortably in the swivel chair. He looked at Andraukov's cup which was untouched and in the middle of which an island of brown skin was constantly contracting and relaxing. Neither had the man eaten any of the cookies which were arranged on the saucer.

"Can you tell me, by any chance, Mr. Andraukov, who ate what with a runcible spoon?" He had spoken so rapidly that even the students to whom English was native did not understand what he had said.

Several seconds of silence followed his question. Then Andraukov said something.

"I am sorry but you must speak up. I am unable to hear you."

There was another pause, then: "Please?"

"Surely you, in common with all foreigners, wish to learn our language as well as possible, therefore you may not take exception if I remind you that we say, 'I beg your pardon?' rather than 'Please?' In regard to my question, I asked if you could tell me who ate what with a runcible spoon. 'They dined on mince and slices of quince which they ate with a runcible spoon, and hand in hand on the edge of the sand they danced by the light of the moon.'" Dr. Locke puffed at the carving again.

Andraukov licked the underside of his streaked and drooping mustache.

"Yes," Locke continued. "'They sailed away for a year and a day to the land where the bong-tree grows, and there in a wood a Piggy-wig stood with a ring at the end of his nose, his nose, with a ring at the end of his nose.' Tell me, sir, what do you think of that?"

"Well, it is very nice."

"Do speak up, sir."

The old man repeated what he had said.

"Then you like that?"

He nodded gravely.

"Fine. Now can you tell me who it was?"

The faces of the students held something close to awe at the professor's temerity.

"'Twas the owl and the pussycat," Locke said. "Yes, the owl and the pussycat."

Andraukov was gazing down at something far out of sight. His face seemed chiseled from ancient marble.

The sun had by now changed its position, shining directly on the professor's large white head which was bald except for what looked almost like a crow's wing resting on each ear. His skin was so pale and transparent that the temple veins could be seen from clear across the room. He opened one of the desk drawers, took out a leatherette case from which he drew a pair of clip-on glasses, tinted dark green, and soberly attached them to his bifocals. "The tower collapsed in 1321, carrying with it portions of the adjoining bays of the nave, transept and choir. Instead of rebuilding the tower Alan of Walsingham conceived the idea of obtaining a much larger area in the center of the cathedral by taking as the base of his design a central octagonal space, the width of which . . . "

Andraukov was still seated the same way, like a child. Suddenly the ash of his cigarette bent, broke, scattered in gray flakes all down his vest.

Dr. Locke opened another desk drawer and brought out a file no larger than a toothpick with which he began to sharpen the gargoyle's teeth. "Some of the students have been inquiring as to the possibility of your opening a class in finger painting."

At this several surprised faces turned towards him.

"Would you be interested?" he asked as he picked and scraped inside the little green mouth. "It might be arranged. I should not have mentioned it, of course, but for the fact that a serious attitude now prevails in regard to this medium. The psychologists, so I am given to understand, are finding it relevant to patterns of behavior."

The odor of Andraukov had filled the room.

"I understand you have a phonograph in your studio upstairs. I understand, too, that you play certain records on your machine late at night when you think no one is around. What sort of music do you prefer, pray tell?"

After a while Andraukov answered. "It is the music of Yemen, I prefer. The plainsong. And Gregory. These are the music. Such is the music."

"I see. You play an instrument, I believe?"

Andraukov did not say anything.

"Despite the declarative construction, that was a question. What sort of an instrument do you play, sir?"

"It is the psaltery."

"Interesting. And what does one do to a psaltery?"

He did not understand.

"I say, does one blow through the instrument?"

"No."

"Continue."

"There are the strings to pluck."

"Yes. Yes, of course. And how does one pluck strings?" On Locke's wide, bulging forehead the veins were throbbing.

Andraukov held up one finger and plucked the air.

"Splendid. And what about a plectrum?"

He did not understand.

"You might employ one in lieu of your finger."

Andraukov, in his grave bass tones, answered. "I do not favor the plectrum."

Dr. Locke's eyes could not be seen behind the dark glasses, "Your vest is dappled with ashes."

"Please?"

Another record fell onto the turntable.

The party had become still more subdued; occasionally a student would approach the cookie platter with an apologetic expression but it was already evident that a substantial mound of the little delicacies would be left over. The students had formed a circle around Andraukov. Dr. Locke reached across his desk and snapped off the phonograph in the midst of a contralto aria: the woman howled and died away with a groan.

"Do you play the dulcimer?"

Andraukov said: "I do not favor the dulcimer."

Through the tinted glasses a movement could be seen, as if perhaps the professor had closed his eyes. His voice, however, retained its cool stability. "Don't you believe in a well-rounded musical education?"

"No."

Locke placed his gargoyle on the desk. "Nevertheless it is possible that we have some records here you will enjoy." He hunted through the stack and replaced several numbers.

First there was a fox trot which was a popular favorite of the moment and which had been requested by the students several times during the afternoon. Next there were some rhumbas, tangos, and two more waltzes. Though the instructor's face did not change in the slightest it was clear that he did not like them. Dr. Locke added one more record. When this had ended he said, "Are you familiar with that piece, sir?"

"No."

Dr. Locke tapped one fist gently against his mouth while he cleared his throat, then he rocked back in the chair and as he spoke he swiveled from one side to the other in slow creaking arcs: "There is a certain poetic unity about you, Mr. Andraukov. What a pity it cannot communicate itself to others. As it is, you are only a type. Still, after a time we do become types, I suppose, sad parodies of all we have striven to be. With what desperate speed do we rush into our lives and later, bewildered, behold them recede rather like some wave, I suspect, which, not finding a rock whereon to gloriously shatter itself, only puckers its lip on the sand."

The older man did not say anything.

The professor picked up his warm cup, cradled it between his symmetrical hands. "That was the Boccherini again."

Apparently he had nothing further to say; little by little the students resumed their conversation while both the professor and his assistant sat in silence, the latter oblivious to everything, the former, despite the passivity of his features, seeming bitterly unhappy. Some time later he asked what Andraukov thought of Fischer's new president, adding, in case he had forgotten, that President Klein had died of a cerebral hemorrhage while on a fishing trip in the mountains and that a new man had been appointed, a man by the name of E. Brian Smallwood. "Prior to his appointment here this fellow was personnel psychologist at one of the largest meat-packing concerns in the country. He is being referred to, so I understand, as our 'pork sausage' president. Do you have any opinion on that?"

Andraukov had not.

Locke suggested that he would have before much longer because the faculty members had been invited to a barbecue at the president's home, something of a precedent to say the least, he added, smiling toward the students. Those who had heard the pun acknowledged it with a smile. He judged none of the faculty members would refuse the invitation if for no other reason than to affirm or negate the extraordinary rumor that an enormous vulture had recently been delivered to President Smallwood.

"It's true," Arnold Pocock said.

"Ah? So it does exist? I had thought it might be just a wild tale."

According to Pocock the huge bird sat in a little, drooping tree on the west side of the house and never made a move.

"It must be stuffed," the professor said, turning his head toward the instructor again, and with this remark the subject of President Smallwood's pet came to a close, at least officially.

The sun had dipped below the bluff and was slowly drawing its heatless rays across the ceiling when the professor spoke to his assistant again, saying, "I understand you are fond of herring." Several days previously Andraukov had bought two herring in a grocery in Andromeda, but while walking up a path to the school the parcel had fallen from his overcoat pocket and later Francis Rheba had carried the fish into the building and pinned them by their tails to the bulletin board.

"Herring," Andraukov said, "is good."

Locke's face appeared to be alternately draining and gorging with blood. He crossed his legs in the opposite direction. He shook up the trousers about his knees. "And where will you be spending your holidays, Mr. Andraukov? Not here, I should think. There is, as you know, a relapse of eighteen days, thanks to a fortunate coincidence of weekends. For myself, I leave bright and early tomorrow morning. Nevertheless, each of us to his or her particular taste, eh?"

In the office no one spoke.

The professor had for some time been toying with his pocket knife. With a deft movement of one finger he snapped it shut and replaced it in the desk drawer. As the sun had completely disappeared he removed his clip-ons, slid them into their case, and placed this beside the knife. He closed the drawer and quietly stood up. With arms folded on his chest he walked past the loaded bookshelves that lined one entire wall and stopped at the far window where he stood for a time gazing out. The great Kaw valley lay tranquil in the winter twilight. Smoke was rising from the farmhouse chimneys. In one of the fields some men were chopping logs; the far faint sound of their axes came across the river on the curving wind. In a barnyard several children were struggling with a saddle and a bucking colt.

Dr. Locke swung about. His frosty eyes moved rapidly over the faces of his students as if seeking someone or something to criticize, but finding nothing he walked back to the desk where he finished his cocoa and replaced the cup with a click loud enough to command attention, a gesture quite unnecessary. There he stood, fingertips resting lightly on the glass top, his barren smile including everyone. He did not need to speak, all understood that he was wishing them a pleasant holiday and that the party was over.

1950

NEIL DORTU

BÉBERT HAD BEEN dreaming. The telephone was ringing. He could not separate the two, but the ringing went on. At last he opened his eyes and saw midmorning sunshine through the Venetian blinds. He rolled over to peer at the clock on his dresser. It was almost ten. The telephone kept ringing. Obviously the caller knew he was at home. He sat up, pinched his cheeks several times to waken himself, cleared his throat and reached for the telephone.

It was Leon, who asked if he had seen the newspaper.

Bébert replied that he had not seen the paper, he was in bed and planned to remain there until noon no matter what awful news there was.

Leon asked if he remembered Neil Dortu.

Bébert said he did not, he had never heard of anybody by that name, furthermore he did not care in the slightest who Neil Dortu was or what he had done to get his name in the paper.

"You know I'm never up at this hour Sunday morning," he went on. "It's terribly inconsiderate of you to call. Incidentally, I hear singing. Where are you?"

"At my place."

"Isn't that *Un bel dí vedremo?*"

"It might be," Leon said.

"Well, you should take that set into the shop for an overhaul. I think you need a new condenser, and it sounds as though the speaker is gone. I've never heard anything so shrill."

"That isn't the radio. It's Andrea."

Bébert listened again. Then he said, "I'm sorry, Leon, but in all honesty I can't change my opinion."

"She likes to sing while she cooks breakfast."

"How curious."

"She's eccentric in the morning. One morning she insisted on baking an upside-down cake. Another time she thought we ought to go for a swim in the lake. There was snow on the ground. My God, I had a terrible time talking her out of it. Listen, Bébert, I'm sorry to have disturbed you, but something serious has happened and I'm all shaken up. I guess you can tell from my voice."

"You don't sound any different. What's happened?"

"Did you see the morning paper?"

"I've already told you I haven't. Please come to the point. Because to be perfectly frank, I'm rather put out with you. I was up till all hours last night playing dominoes at the Po-Po Club with Keith and two girls from the other side of the lake, and I'm just exhausted. Now, what is it you want to tell me?"

"Okay, okay, I'm sorry," Leon muttered. "I'm so shook I don't know what I'm doing. It's about Neil Dortu. You probably remember him. He used to hang around the club sometimes and he played pool a lot at that place on Caledonia Street. He spoke French. I mean, he knew how to speak it. I think his father is French. The old man owns a big ad agency in Detroit."

"You're practically incoherent, Leon. For goodness sake, what's wrong?"

"He shot himself. The story is on the second page of the paper."

Bébert closed his eyes for a moment and said, "This makes me ill. I didn't know him, but I can't help feeling nauseated. Oh, this is sickening. But are they positive it was suicide?—so many people are being murdered these days."

Leon did not answer.

"Are you there?" Bébert asked. "Leon? Leon? Hello?"

"I had to go to the kitchen for a minute," Leon said. "Andrea wanted me to look at the bacon. I don't like it too crisp. Anyway, I'm sure you met Neil. He was a tall guy with sideburns, and he chewed gum a lot. He had a nervous habit of rubbing his face with the back of his hand. I think you knew him by sight at least.

"Did he wear a blue Norwegian ski sweater?"

"Not that I recall. Usually he wore pinstripe shirts and a suede leather jacket if it was cold. He was a basketball star at St. Anthony Junior College. I heard he was offered a scholarship to Notre Dame."

"I can't be positive," Bébert said. "However, I truthfully am sorry about what happened. I didn't know he was a friend of yours. You never mentioned him."

"He wasn't exactly a friend. I never did much like the guy. I don't mean I disliked him, just that we didn't have much in common."

"Well, I'm afraid this is going to sound callous," Bébert said, "but if you weren't especially friendly why should you be disturbed? No, on second thought I take that back. When a tragedy of this sort occurs even though you may not be well acquainted with the person it can be upsetting. I used to know a boy named Gottschalk who fell off a cliff in Colorado one summer while attending camp and I was very deeply distressed when I heard of it."

"Did it kill him?"

"Instantaneously, I'm sure. As soon as he struck the ground. It gives me chills just thinking about it. But that's neither here nor there. Have you any idea what caused your friend to commit suicide?"

"Hang on a minute," Leon said. "Andrea's calling me."

Bébert put down the receiver, arranged a pillow behind his back and looked around for a cigarette. He noticed sunlight creeping across the tatami mat toward his sandals and it occurred to him that it might be pleasant to go for a stroll along Bridgeway and have a late breakfast at the coffee shop. Then to the pharmacy for shaving lotion and a tube of toothpaste, and perhaps stop at the bicycle shop to price the new models. Then sometime during the afternoon to the laundromat.

So he sat propped up in bed with the telephone in his lap and a cigarette between his thumb and forefinger, smoking and thinking about how to spend the day, until he heard Leon's voice.

"She couldn't get the bread in the toaster because the lever was stuck. That goddamn toaster, it always gets stuck. You asked me a question. What was it?"

"I've forgotten. Oh! I was wondering why your friend did away with himself. Had he been despondent?"

"Despondent? Of course he was despondent! That's a stupid question, Bébert. Anybody who goes so far as to blow his head off is bound to be depressed."

"Please remember, you were the one who called. Not I."

"I apologize," Leon said. "Anyway, yes, he was extremely depressed, and had been for several months."

"Was he in poor health?"

"No, he had a personal problem."

"Of course this is none of my business, but I can't help wondering what would drive a person to such lengths."

"It isn't a very attractive story," Leon said. "I ought to keep it to myself."

"I wouldn't expect you to reveal anything you feel should remain confidential," Bébert said, sitting up in bed. "Although knowing me as well as you do you can be sure I wouldn't breathe a word to anyone else."

"Yeah. I trust you. But the whole affair is—well, the word that comes to mind is 'sordid'."

"As bad as that?"

"I never heard anything more sordid in my life. I better not tell you."

"Do as you like," Bébert said crisply. "Far be it from me to pry, I'm not the type. Although I do think it helps to share one's feelings with a sympathetic listener. And now that I've had a chance to think about it, his name does begin to sound famil- iar. I believe I did know him slightly. I'm almost positive we met. You must have introduced us at the Po-Po Club."

"I doubt it."

"He was a basketball player, you say? A tall fellow in a pinstripe shirt and suede jacket?"

"Yeh. He always seemed to be leaning against a wall with his hands in his pockets."

"I remember him now. Nearly every time I saw him he was chewing gum. Neil Dortu. Of course."

After a pause Leon said, "I guess it might be okay to tell you. But keep this to yourself."

Bébert settled himself more comfortably on the bed and remarked in a solici- tous tone, "Tell only what you feel should be told. Now, suppose you begin at the beginning. You say he shot himself?"

"In the park at the south end of the lake. Near the children's playground."

"I doubt if I'll be able to go near that park again."

"They found his body about dawn, according to the paper. Some kids who were camping overnight heard the shot."

"I'm surprised it got into the paper so quickly."

"Me too."

"Is there a photograph?"

"No. Probably in later editions."

"Did he have a family?"

"His father is still living in Detroit, I guess. It seems to me he said his parents were divorced. And he had an older brother who was in either the merchant marine or the Coast Guard."

"He wasn't married? I assumed he was."

"No. In fact that's why he shot himself. He was in love with this French girl in France. He was over there in the Army for eighteen months and had this affair with this girl and thought they were going to get married after he got out of service, but she locked herself in her apartment one afternoon and turned on the gas and stuck her head in the oven, and Neil never got over the shock."

"Sordid is the word, Leon. You were right."

"What made it worse is that she was pregnant."

"With his child?"

"According to him, it was. My theory is that what drove him to shoot himself was realizing she preferred to kill herself rather than have his baby. There's no way to hurt a man worse."

"I hardly know what to say. This is terrible. I can't remember when I've heard anything as sickening."

"Yeah," said Leon. "It's grim."

"You and Neil must have been rather good friends, if he confided in you."

"No. As I say, I never cared much for the guy. There was something crazy about him. You could see it in his eyes. Probably you noticed. The skin around his eyes gave the impression of being twisted, so he had this mad expression. It made me uneasy to look at him."

"Hmmn," said Bébert.

"He used to come over to talk to me at odd hours."

"I never knew that."

"What was the point of mentioning it? Until now he was just somebody who dropped by and needed to talk. Everybody's got problems and occasionally feels this need to talk. The weird thing was he carried a gun. Anyway he said he did, although I never saw it. Maybe he carried it in his car, because you can't pack a .45 in your pocket without being noticed."

"Why didn't you report him to the police?"

"Half the people in the United States carry guns."

"Yes, but I still think you should have done something."

"He wasn't mad at anybody. He was just sick."

"He must have been so lonely. I know the feeling."

"Well, I've thought about it," Leon said, "and what's really pathetic is that as far as I can tell he considered me his closest friend. I mean, I didn't even like the guy, if you follow me."

Bébert sighed and shook his head.

"He'd talk for half an hour but suddenly without the least warning he'd get up, tell me goodby and walk out. It sure was unsettling. And I never knew when to expect him. He never called to ask if he could come over to talk with me. Suddenly there would be this insistent tapping at the door. I always knew who it was. He didn't ring, or knock a couple of times and wait. He just stood there tapping and tapping like a bird until I let him in."

"He must have been insane."

"I think distraught would be more accurate. There was this overwhelming sense of grief about him. He was dying inside."

"Let me say something, Leon. Please listen. This has been a dreadful experience for you, but for your sake at least I'm glad you and Neil weren't close friends. Otherwise it would be so much worse. Needless to say, I feel awful about what happened to him and how he must have suffered, but at the same time it's relatively abstract. To be quite honest with you, I don't believe I ever met him. I pretended a bit because curiosity got the better of me. However, that's not the point. What I'm trying to say is that I believe you'll get over this before long. Seeing it in the paper the first thing in the morning must have been a blow, but I suspect that after a few days this entire tragedy will take on its proper perspective. In the final analysis you're not responsible for his death."

Leon was silent for a while. Then he said, "I haven't told you everything. The truth is, I am responsible."

"Forgive my skepticism," said Bébert. "How?"

"He came over to see me last night."

"Oh?"

"He was desperate. I realize that now."

"Did he give any indication that he might do away with himself? Very often the potential suicide tries to let people know what he's up to. Do you recall anything significant? Did you observe his socks? Somebody once told me about a man who destroyed himself and not long before doing so he began to wear socks that didn't match. He entire personality was disintegrating. What you or I would consider important had absolutely no relevance. That's why I asked if you happened to notice his socks."

"I didn't talk to him. I didn't even see him."

"I'm afraid I don't understand."

"I pretended to be asleep."

"You surprise me, Leon. That isn't like you. Quite frankly, it seems to me you could have spoken to him for a few moments, even though you weren't in the mood."

"I had my reasons."

"I hope so. Really, I find it difficult to sympathize with your attitude. You knew how he was suffering."

"It was after midnight."

"Leon, you ought to have invited him in, if only for a short while."

"Andrea was here."

"That's hardly an excuse."

"Bébert, listen. I couldn't. I tell you I couldn't."

"Why not?"

Leon took a deep breath and said, "How explicit do I have to be? You're not listening. Of all the times for anybody to knock at the door. My God, we thought he was never going to go away."

"Oh," said Bébert. "Oh. This gets worse and worse."

"What could I do? Under the circumstances what could I do?"

"Leon, I wish you hadn't told me. Never in my life have I heard anything as sordid. I'll never forgive you."

"So after he left here when I wouldn't open the door he went to the park and killed himself?"

"Stop it, Leon! You're trying to implicate me in your guilt."

"Right between the eyes, Bébert. Did you ever fire a .45? I have. It feels like a monkey wrench in your hand. Neil aimed that monkey wrench at his head and let himself have it—*Boom!* I expect you could put your fist through the hole on the other side of his skull."

"You're making me sick."

"Did I ever tell you why the Army developed the .45? Because they discovered a .38 slug wasn't heavy enough to stop the natives in the Philippines. That's why they invented the .45. You probably never saw anybody get hit by one of those things. Well, I did. A big Marine corporal. Blew him right off his feet. Like somebody had tied a rope around his body and suddenly jerked it."

"Leon, you're drunk."

"Drinking."

"I just now realized."

"Gin and orange juice. Half-and-half."

"Leon, I want to ask you something. Are you positive it was Neil Dortu who knocked at your door last night? Couldn't it have been a motorist looking for an address?"

"Neil Dortu with a loaded gun was tapping at my door last night. No motorist. Certain things you know. Certain things there's no mistake about. Neil Dortu right on the edge of the cliff about to fall off came around wanting old Leon to save his life. And what did old Leon do? Did he go galloping to the rescue? He didn't even boost his ass out of bed. He lay there hanging on to little Andrea like she was the last blonde on earth, and neither of them whispered one loving word until Neil Dortu gave up and went away. The last chapter of this refined and inspiring story you will find on the second page of your daily blat. Pictures in later editions."

"Leon, you're too harsh on yourself."

"Bébert, it's my opinion the world is not soft. The world is as hard as a .45 caliber bullet. No harder. No softer. That's how I feel this Sunday morning as I glance out the window and see sailboats and fishermen and seagulls. What a marvelous Sunday morning."

"How much does Andrea know of this?"

"Everything except the pregnant mademoiselle in the oven."

"If I were at your place this moment," said Bébert, "I would break a flower pot across your head. I swear I would. Now tell me, does Andrea consider you responsible?"

"She claims it wouldn't have accomplished anything to talk to him. It would merely have postponed the inevitable. Women can be so god-awful bloodless."

"She's sensible, and I agree one hundred percent."

"I know. You're probably right. Sooner or later—*Boom!*"

"Then why blame yourself?"

"This may not make sense, Bébert, but do you know what makes me feel guilty? What makes me feel guilty is that I don't feel the least bit of guilt. I feel guilty as hell about that."

"Let me ask you. Suppose you were confronted again with this identical situation, what would you do? How would you respond?"

"No different."

"That's hard to believe."

"It's true. I'm a rotten son of a bitch."

"You're not, of course. Life can be so puzzling," Bébert went on reflectively. "Perhaps when all's said and done what it boils down to is how much we genuinely care for other people."

"Do you think I'm rotten? Tell me straight, Bébert. Last night the guy came to me for help and I halfway suspected he was at the end of his rope, but I rejected him just the same. It doesn't matter if sooner or later he may have done it anyhow. What matters is that I didn't care enough to climb off of Andrea for five minutes. And you know what, Bébert? I don't give a damn. What kind of ogre am I?"

"I don't believe you're unique," Bébert said after thinking about it.

"Do you know somebody else who would do what I did?"

"That's difficult to answer. But I don't consider you monstrous. What occurred was dreadful, there's no denying the fact. But you shouldn't brood. In a sense, it's water over the dam."

"No use crying over spilt blood?"

"You needn't be ugly. I'm trying to help. And I must say I think you've been drinking a good deal more gin than orange juice."

"I'm sloshed. Mother, am I sloshed. Listen. Andrea has breakfast ready but let's play dominoes this afternoon. It'll do me good. I'll meet you at the club about one. How's that?"

"Aren't you spending the day with Andrea?"

"She's going to visit her sister."

Bébert glanced at the clock. "All right. I really should answer a few letters and do some laundry, but if I get up now I can manage. Suppose we say half-past. Now if you want my advice, eat something solid and tell yourself that last night was just one of those things."

"Right," Leon said. "Never ask to know for whom the bell tolls. It tolls for thee."

"So many people misquote that poem. The line should be: Never *send* to know for whom the bell tolls."

"Are you sure?"

"I remember distinctly. And I was an English major in college."

"Okay. Anyhow, the wording isn't important."

"I agree," said Bébert. "It's the thought that counts."

1969

PUIG'S WIFE

MUHLBACH LISTENS uneasily to the droll French wit of Huguette Puig. He tries again to interrupt but she's too quick, she's waiting for him to say only one thing and until he says it she will not stop talking. He looks at the clock on his desk. Eight minutes. Eight minutes with scarcely a pause. In the outer office the Hanover agent is waiting, so is somebody else.

But of course, Huguette is saying, you must understand that you would become involved with une vrai femme du monde. . . .

All right! All right! Muhlbach finds himself laughing. He knows he will agree to whatever she wishes; she knows it too and immediately stops.

It's nearly five o'clock now, he says, I expect I could be there by six-thirty.

Marvelous! I shall put on my black peignoir. . . .

So, having given in, having agreed to a closer look at the apple, Muhlbach hangs up the telephone and rocks back in his chair with a thoughtful expression. Is she joking, or is she not? What if she does indeed open the door dressed in a black peignoir? Then what? How far do you carry a joke? And what time does Puig arrive? Muhlbach tries to remember. He remembers asking, but she was vague. Something about eight o'clock, but she was very vague. Muhlbach frowns and taps his fingertips together.

She's joking, of course. But of course! As she would say. Just the same, he thinks, I suggested twice that we meet in the cocktail lounge and twice she kept on as though she didn't hear what I said. I don't like it. I should have said I'd meet them later. I don't like this situation.

The green light on his desk winks importantly; he stares at it for a moment, wondering again how such a simple device could cost so much, and also why he bought it. Then he leans forward and touches the key.

Yes, Gloria, what is it?

The Hanover agent has left because he had another appointment; Mrs. Fichte called a few minutes ago and wants you to call her as soon as possible; a Mr. Arnauldi would like to see you about a new filing system.

There's more. Muhlbach listens without much interest. Finally Gloria runs out of news. Hanover will be back tomorrow or the next day, never fear. About Mrs. Fichte, I'll get in touch with her. I'll see Mr. Arnauldi in a couple of minutes—I want to call home first.

Is it okay if I take off a little bit early?

I suppose, Muhlbach answers, but don't overdo it. Now get my house, will you?

At home Donna answers the telephone and suddenly Muhlbach wishes that Mr. Arnauldi would go away and that the Hanover agent and Mrs. Fichte would elope to Persia with Mr. Fichte in mad pursuit, and Huguette Puig, yes, and Gloria and whoever it was from Chase Manhattan and the briefcase salesman and everybody else on earth would somehow disappear. A world has been shattered by the sound of Donna's voice. But before he has time to answer he hears a light scuffling and an argument and next, inevitably, the asthmatic Scandinavian accents of Mrs. Grunthe lugubriously informing him that this is Mr. Muhlbach's residence.

Mrs. Grunthe, I won't be home for supper tonight.

Ooh?

Muhlbach is just able to keep from echoing this noise. Sooner or later, he thinks, I'm going to do it. Then she's going to feel insulted and quit.

Not coming to supper, you say?

That's right. An old friend of mine is going to be in the city. I've decided to have supper with him and his wife. His name is Commander Puig. I won't be late. I expect I should be home by ten or eleven. If you want to reach me before then, they're staying at the Murray. Commander Puig. That's spelled p-u-i-g. At the Murray Hotel on Sixth Avenue.

He waits, knowing that she has been setting down this information carefully, every bit of it, even the fact that Puig is an old friend.

Now, let me talk to Donna.

Mrs. Grunthe replies that Donna has gone outside to play.

Don't bother her, I just—oh, never mind. What's Otto doing?

Otto is somewhere in the neighborhood playing basketball.

When he comes in remind him of his homework. His grades could certainly stand improvement. Muhlbach pauses, but can think of nothing more. Goodnight, Mrs. Grunthe. You needn't wait up, although as I say I don't expect to be late.

Now there is Arnauldi to deal with, next there is somebody else and somebody else, then mysteriously the office is quiet. The telephone no longer rings. The white plastic hood has been drawn over Gloria's typewriter. As to the demon secretary herself, at this moment where is she? Muhlbach tries to remember where Gloria goes for the evening parade. The Golden Lion? Slattery's? Not that it matters, doors open everywhere very much the same. In she will swagger and promptly be appraised by the men at the bar as though she were a piece of livestock. That's how she wants it, so all's right with the world. Like Donna, she's gone outside to play.

He stops a minute near the window, gazes down on the evening rush, listens to the remote honk of taxicabs, whistles, small voices shouting. Another day ended. Nothing much accomplished. A reasonable amount of money was earned, enough to get by and a few dollars more. It's necessary, nothing to be ashamed of, no reason to feel dissatisfied. After all, no intelligent man can spend his life on a Polynesian beach gathering driftwood. And unless you were born with an IQ of 200, say, or a voice that would make people forget Caruso, or—well, unless you're somehow exceptional what's left but to put in the days of your life like this?

Muhlbach answers the question by sharply tapping the window with his index finger, then turns and goes out the door and rings for the elevator. It, too, is empty. Silence. Emptiness. He looks at his watch and is surprised. Already past six-thirty. He realizes that he's been wasting time, but why? Of course the puzzle's not very intricate. Huguette. How much safer it would be to take the subway home, telephone her and apologize. That's what I'd like to do, he thinks, but I can't. I'm going to see her. I'm cursed with this Protestant conscience that forces me to do what I say I will do, and I hate it. What I want right now is to go home to my children and Mrs. Grunthe's casserole. That's just about all I want. Not that I like casserole so much, at least not every single Thursday. Why on earth doesn't she try something different? But in a way the certainty of it is reassuring. In fact I suppose the certainty of casserole on Thursday is worth the monotony of eating it. What reassuring habits I have. I'm afraid of them and yet I can't give them up. I dislike the strain of defending myself against the unexpected. I suppose I must be getting tired as I grow older. Tonight I don't want to exert myself, I just want to go home. Instead of doing that I'm on my way to see Huguette. I don't look forward to sitting in that hotel room with her, defending myself against whatever she has in mind. I really don't want to sit there for an hour trying to balance a loaded drink until Puig arrives. If he's late I'll be forced to have a second drink, and somehow I think he's going to be late.

Muhlbach looks at a woman getting on the bus. She resembles Huguette—that sharp French profile suggesting both the bulky provincial shopkeeper's wife and the arrogant Madame of the seventeenth-century chateau. The history of a nation, he reflects, is in that face, even to the untidy hair. Other than the profile, what is it about her that reminds me of Huguette? Her coat? The way she stands? The packages? I can't be sure. How long since I've seen Huguette? Two years? No, longer than that. I don't understand why she called. Did I make such an impression? That's a flattering thought, but not likely. Puig must have told her to get in touch with me. But why was she determined to see me alone? Why did she insist that I come to the hotel so early? If he told her to invite me for supper—well, I can't make it out. There's no sense to it. I just don't understand what she wants. I can't believe the obvious, that would be too absurd. Whatever it is, I should have refused, told her flatly I couldn't get there until eight.

He stoops to look out of the bus, finds himself nearly face to face with one of the stone lions in front of the library and straightens up. He looks again at his watch. Another ten minutes, then a long block to walk. Thirty minutes late, at least. Forty if the lights are red. Meanwhile she's drifting around that hotel room in a black peignoir. If she's not decently dressed, he says almost aloud, I won't go into the room. I'll tell her to put on some clothes and meet me downstairs. I should have made it clear on the phone. I'm not an explorer and after so many years I've realized the fact, thank God. Why didn't I make it clear? I should have been firm, but she kept talking. I didn't have a chance to explain. Now I've gotten into this ridiculous situation. Well, I won't go in, no matter what she's wearing.

Huguette, in a short pink bathrobe and slippers, opens the door as soon as he knocks.

You're late, she scolds, pulling him firmly into the room, but then so am I you see! I went shopping, little idiot that I am. . . .

Muhlbach notices that she scanned the corridor while greeting him, a cold survey more revealing than the bathrobe. He feels a nearly forgotten astonishment at the lies women tell. And the most unbelievable part of their role is that they expect to be believed. Of course they don't, not completely, but at the same time of course they do. He almost laughs.

And how have you been? Huguette is saying. So good to see you! Sit down, I won't bite you, at least not yet. Sit down. You haven't changed. But as for me—oh la! pauvre Huguette. . . .

Seated opposite him on the couch she continues talking while she pretends that something is wrong with her slipper. She leans forward and he is gradually presented with a deep, snowy bosom. The act is outrageous, but instead of smiling he finds himself gazing solemnly at the delicate weighted flesh. For a moment it is not Huguette that he sees but the marvel of a woman entering the beautiful middle age of womanhood.

She goes right on talking, perhaps unconscious of what she has done, but just then a white and rather boney knee pops out as though to see what's going on. She covers it and sits erect.

La! she exclaims, patting the knee. Le cinéma, alors.

This invitation to discuss her knee is a bit too direct; Muhlbach clears his throat and takes a sip of the drink she has poured. It tastes like a drug. She must be desperate, he thinks. Why did I come here?—I knew it was a mistake. Now I've got to juggle this woman for an hour. By the time Puig gets off duty and gets to the hotel my tongue's going to be thick as a paintbrush. Why did I let her talk me into this?

But almost as quickly as the question comes the answer. Yes, he thinks, I know why I'm in this room. All these years of hating Puig for what he did to me and now I've got the chance to pay him back. There's no other reason. She didn't persuade me, I wanted to come. I might as well be honest about it. Both of us have been pretending but she's more honest than I am—she's not deceiving herself. She wants another man and decided I might be available. I knew that. I knew it right away, I knew it after the first minute on the telephone, and I was willing to accept but pretended that I wasn't. So that's why I'm here, to use his wife. The timeless insult. These years of waiting for revenge, not quite admitting how much I've hated him. I'd have gone along another twenty years without making a move against him because I didn't really know how I hated him until she called. Now I can use his wife. I can take her in a moment, or put it off a while, just as I please. She's mine. She's told me half a dozen times already that she's mine. Puig's wife! Puig's wife, Muhlbach repeats to himself, tasting it like an oyster in his mouth.

He glances directly into her eyes; she looks back without the least embarrassment.

Do I want her now? he asks himself. Do I want this woman now? Now while the offering is fresh? Or should I wait? Let the sea fruit ripen. When would it be sweetest? Now or later?

But the pleasure of the thought becomes a little sickening; he shifts around on the couch as if the cushions were uncomfortable. Then an ugly thought obtrudes and he glances at her again. How much does she know? Did Puig ever tell her what happened? Probably not. No, probably not, because to him it was never a matter of much importance. He won and I lost, so for him it ended. Ended successfully and therefore insignificantly, so I doubt if he told her about it. In fact, he's probably forgotten. He forgets easily. I was always the one who remembered. Sometimes it seems I don't forget anything that happens to me, Muhlbach thinks bitterly. Not anything. Twenty years and what he did is almost as humiliating now as it was then. Why can't I forget?—throw it away somehow. My God, I've bottled it up and I've smelled it ever since. Twenty-three years it must have been, because that was our second year at college. He laughed about it afterwards and he kept waiting for me to laugh, I can still see his face. He thought the whole thing was a joke. Maybe so. Maybe he was right and sensible and I was wrong. Anyway, he's forgotten. He'd forgotten about it long before he got married and all this time I've never once referred to it. There'd be no point in telling her even if he did remember, so this can't be a plot against me. Besides, the winner doesn't plot against the loser. I read too much into everything. She didn't lure me here so Puig could jump out of the closet and catch us flagrante delicto. What's wrong with her is no great mystery, her husband's been at sea for several months and she's made up her mind to punish him for leaving her, it's that simple. She wants to injure him at the moment of his return. No, a moment before he returns, meaning she won't let him know that he's been punished. And as long as they live together she won't tell him what took place. She loves him, she doesn't want to hurt him; at least she doesn't want to destroy him.

How intricate women are, thinks Muhlbach while he listens to Huguette talking, and yet how naive. This one, for instance. What did she expect her husband to do? Was Puig supposed to call up the Chief of Staff and say he'd rather stay home than go on duty with the fleet? She didn't think about it, not as a man would, she merely had a Feeling. My husband is leaving me alone, so when he comes back I'm going to get even. I'll teach him not to treat me like that! How obvious, yes, but at the same time how extremely curious. So I'm here—I'm here not because she was attracted to me. I'm here to provide a service. And afterwards, of course, the three of us will go out to dinner. I can even guess just how she'll look—delightful! As talkative as usual, brightly witty, the charming continental wife. There would sit Puig full of ignorance at her right hand while I sat full of guilt at her left. And she'd insist I be there. Absolutely. Very curious, Muhlbach reflects as he takes another drink.

Huguette is chatting as though nothing of any consequence was on her mind. She is Mrs. Puig who got home late from shopping; she is entertaining her husband's friend for a few minutes before excusing herself to get ready for dinner.

Muhlbach pokes the ice in his glass and avoids looking at her. He wonders if she will give up, if she will in fact ask to be excused so that she may put on some clothes. It would be awkward if Puig came in just now and found them sitting this close together, with her suggested nudity. He remembers an unpleasant scene not so different from this—visiting a relative, taking off his coat and rolling up his sleeves because the evening was warm, talking with the wife while they waited, at last the door opening and then that sudden suspicion like an evil jewel glittering in the night. Remembering this makes him uneasy; he stands up and wanders around the narrow room while Huguette goes on talking.

Presently the telephone rings but she doesn't answer. Again it rings, and again. Huguette is almost reclining on the couch, her lips pursed, her expression vague and troubled, and Muhlbach begins to wonder if she is insane. It occurs to him that he knows practically nothing about her. Huguette Fanchon. A war bride out of some obscure Breton village, she's been married to Puig for a long time, nearly a full generation. But that's all I know, he thinks. I don't know anything else about her.

With an impatient gesture Huguette reaches for the telephone.

Allo? Yes?

Muhlbach stares at her face, at the profile so totally French, as though etched by the needle strokes of some icy French master. Ingres. David. She will always be French, not American. She is still a Breton woman, oddly transported and far from home.

He realizes that she is speaking in French, completely absorbed by the telephone. She listens, her expression changes, becoming no softer yet unmistakably relieved. She's talking to a man, but not to her husband, who's no linguist.

Muhlbach turns away, slightly embarrassed at having stared, embarrassed that he must listen to the conversation. He sees himself reflected in the window—standing alone near the center of the room, a tall and consciously dignified businessman with a drink held safely in both hands; and it occurs to him that he himself could be the insane party, as mad as any creature beyond the Looking-Glass.

Plus tard! Pas maintenant! Comme j'ai déjà . . .

Quite obviously she is not talking to her husband. But then who is it? and what's the conversation about? Hearing only what she says is rather like trying to read through the slots of a stencil. Is it somebody in the hotel? Muhlbach can hear the man's voice, rising as if he was getting angry. Huguette offers a peculiar hissing noise, sighing between her teeth.

Restlessly Muhlbach walks toward the far end of the room and stands gazing across the city. A short distance away in space his reflection stands gazing into the room with an irritated expression. Then the severe features of the phantom are broken by a smile. He studies himself sardonically. What are you waiting for out there? Are you waiting for a woman to stop talking on the telephone or are you waiting for the end of your life? Which is it? You've been standing around for a long time, why don't you do something? When was the last time you simply did something instead of trying to make up your mind about it? Quite a while. Quite a long while.

I'm too sensible and always have been, Muhlbach decides. I'm too cautious. I can't behave like a simpleton even when I'm drunk, I only double into myself. It doesn't seem fair. Here I stand in a hotel room with a woman who for all I know may be a whore, but I'm too sensible to make a move. I've been talking decorously with a half-naked strumpet. Why? Why is that?

What are you doing? asks Huguette. Are you planning to jump out in order to escape from me? She walks toward him without pulling the robe across her breast. I'll get you something fresh to drink, she says, draws the glass slowly from his hand and walks away.

Not a word about that call, he thinks as he watches her putting ice into the glass. Not that she owes me any sort of explanation but an American wife would probably say something, even if it was a lie. But not a word from this one. How long has she been in the hotel? I wonder. I wonder. I assumed she got here this afternoon, but I wonder if she might have been here several days. If men are calling while you pretend to wait for your husband is he ever coming? Dear Huguette, is my friend Puig really on his way? Or am I one more on your list? Then other questions begin taking shape, questions that previously had seemed not worth asking.

Why didn't I hear from Puig himself? He's been at sea for quite a while, yes, but the fleet must have stopped at any number of ports—he could easily have sent a postcard letting me know he'd be here. When she telephoned why didn't she mention that Puig suggested we get together? But she didn't mention it. She's hardly mentioned her husband. Is he coming? Is he? And if he isn't how soon will she tell me the truth! Yes, that also could explain the phone call. Somebody else wanted in this room, but two men at once is one too many. Isn't that so, Huguette? Or is it? Maybe three at once would suit you!

The implications multiply. Is she—is she a whore? Does she come to New York every so often in order to work here? Maybe that's what it's all about. Muhlbach feels his vitals begin to contract. When she hands him the second drink he accepts it reluctantly, as though the glass was contaminated, and continues to look out the window. It seems to him that her hand is the hand of a whore. The shape of her ankle, the whiteness of her skin. Whatever she says. Each gesture. The open suitcase. Cigarette stubs in the ashtray—how many men have been in this room? The closet door is not quite shut, he can see one of her dresses and maybe that too is not without meaning, meant to excite him. Many significant facts that had seemed as unrelated as the stars now appear to form a constellation. The room key lying on the desk, why is it there instead of in her purse? Why did she look up and down the corridor so efficiently? And he begins to remember the items in the newspaper—women caught in raids, jailed, the men sneaking away guiltily. He begins to feel obscurely frightened. He knows that his feelings do not show on his face, or in his movements, not as they would have shown twenty years ago; nor is he as frightened as if he was a college boy locked in some carpeted suite. But still he feels anxious, tense, and irritated with himself because of it. All in all, how much better it would be to be at home eating Mrs. Grunthe's casserole or playing with the children. Where would they be now? Otto is probably in his room working on another airplane that soon will be hanging by a thread from the ceiling. And Donna? Where is she? Muhlbach feels himself softening. He blinks, looks around, and discovers Huguette gazing at him expectantly. She has asked something. Would you like to sit down?—was that what she asked? He tries to recall her words but can't.

I'm sorry Huguette, I'm afraid I wasn't paying much attention. I was thinking about my children.

Oh! You're excused, she laughs. And do you know that we have four boys? Four!

Muhlbach notices that he is being led to the couch again. Why does she keep pulling at me? he wonders. Doesn't she ever get discouraged? I can't understand why she's so persistent. What does she expect me to do? Do I have to tell her I don't want any part of it? This is ridiculous, and pretty soon I'm going to look like a fool. If I keep on resisting she's going to say what's wrong with him? She'll decide that there really is something wrong with me and then how do I convince her that there isn't? It's what she'll think, I know it. It's what every woman thinks when a man doesn't come bounding toward her at the signal. He's inadequate. He's nothing.

But what am I supposed to do? pull out my wallet and give her some money? Then do I simply get undressed? Is it as simple as that? I should have learned how these things are handled years ago, I should have gone to a cathouse at least once. I wouldn't feel so ignorant. Now I don't know what to do. I've walked into this by myself but I don't know how to behave. She thinks I understood the situation from the very beginning. Probably there were some clues she gave me on the telephone and I accepted them without knowing what I was accepting, now she can't figure out what's wrong. Good God, this is absurd! She must be thinking it was a waste of time to call me—I suppose that's it. Yes, because she's one of them. The Murray Hotel. The Murray. It sounds familiar. There were some professionals in this place, I'm sure of it. Flushed out a few months ago.

Huguette is talking about her boys; Muhlbach takes a long swallow of his drink and gazes at her. To be what she is, that's not amazing, but to sit there on the couch with her bathrobe half-undone and talk about her boys. It's incredible. And Muhlbach has no more doubts, she's a professional. He is deeply surprised, not that such whores exist but that he should find himself in the company of one. Then, too, the fact that she is married makes it all the more unbelievable. Housewives, secretaries—there's no longer a division. The old order has collapsed. Life used to be a reasonably simple business. There were certain things you did and things you didn't, or if you did—well, then, at least you realized what you were doing. It was as plain as the painted line in the middle of the highway, you stayed in one lane or another and if you crossed over you were blind not to know it. But now? An officer's wife! By day a housewife in New Jersey, the wife of Commander Puig. Neighbors see him coming home and they see him when he leaves, wearing the uniform of a United States naval officer. The neighbors know, therefore, that Puig and Puig's wife must be respectable. That's so. It must be so because it must. But is it? What about Puig himself? What does he do when his ship drops anchor at Marseilles?

Muhlbach realizes that he wants to see Puig again. Until this minute it hadn't mattered very much. He had looked forward to Puig's arrival merely because it was expected, with no particular enthusiasm, as if an old movie was returning to the neighborhood, or as if somebody was giving him a book he'd read years ago; but now he does want to see this man who had once been his closest friend. Thinking about the past they shared revives in him the affection he once felt for Puig. Four years of college life, sleeping in the same room practically side by side and waking up together, eating together, shaving one right after the other, borrowing and lending—the proximity seemed convincing, yet was it? Was it really? Puig no doubt will seem as real as ever when he walks in the door, although not what he used to be. When he comes in will he stir up the quietly mouldering leaves? or have they flaked and crumbled? so that he will walk in with nothing but some canvas baggage of the present. Muhlbach wonders. How intimately did we know each other? Perhaps not as well as both of us assumed. Since then how many times have I seen him? Four times. Five times, maybe. The world has gone through another war since we were in college, affecting us in more ways than we could imagine. That, too, was an experience we shared several thousand miles apart, just about as equally as we shared the end of our adolescence. How does he feel about the war? We've seen each other since it happened, but never talked about it. I'll ask him. He must have liked the Navy, otherwise he wouldn't have stayed in. Or is that true? The last time we met—let's see, he talked mostly about playing golf. He got every Wednesday afternoon off and went out to the course. Talked about a set of clubs he'd bought. Except for that—I can't remember but I'm pretty sure he enjoys the Navy. The peacetime Navy, that's what he called it. Yes, he does like it. But how much longer is it going to be a peacetime Navy? I'll ask about that, too. Another war seems to be on the way. Powers forming. We do our part to promote it, testing all possible enemies, trying to make up our minds whether or not to fight, and who. Aim one way, then another, like a bunch of kids with beebee guns, but maybe the indecision is better than any possible decision. Puig might know what's going to happen, he's worked his way high enough that he ought to have some idea. I'll find out what he thinks. It's strange I don't already know what his opinions are. Strange I know so little about him. Suppose somebody asked me about Puig, what should I say? Married to a Frenchwoman and they have four children. Been in the Navy since the war. Likes to play golf. What else?

That's all! Muhlbach thinks with astonishment. I've assumed I know practically everything about him but the truth is I couldn't explain to anybody how he's felt or what he's done during the last twenty years. If anybody had asked me how well I know him I'd have said I know him better than anybody else does, except his wife. Yet this is what it comes to. Married, with four children. A career in the Navy. And that's all I know. What does he look like? Well, he's medium height, sandy reddish hair getting thin, a melon face that used to look like the face of a boxer. And his eyelashes turn white during summer. At least I think they do. It seems to me that every summer he turned red and white instead of brown. After those hours on the sun deck I looked like a Mohawk but he came down like a piece of veal or fish. Covering himself with unguent, wincing, grunting. Yes, I could answer if somebody asked what Puig looks like, but that really tells nothing about him. His wife is what tells about him. Huguette Fanchon. Madame Puig. Madame Huguette Puig.

Muhlbach realizes that he has been tipping the glass and rattling the ice cubes more than he intended. In fact, there's not much left of the second drink. His stomach, however, feels receptive; he decides he might even have a third drink before they step out for dinner, unless Puig shows up very soon. He smiles at Huguette and reaches across in front of her to pick up a cigarette. She lights it for him, holding his hand warmly.

She's beginning to get drunk, Muhlbach thinks. I can tell from the way she's been rambling along talking about nothing of any importance. However, let her talk, I don't care. Reflectively he looks around the room. The situation doesn't seem as ominous as it did half an hour earlier.

Oh la—the time! Huguette exclaims, and claps her hands. You know I should be dressing. If we are going out. . . .

Muhlbach looks at his watch. After eight o'clock! He lifts the watch to his ear with an expression of concern. The watch sounds all right. But seven minutes after eight! That doesn't seem possible. And where's Puig?

Huguette is examining her fingernails. The bathrobe somehow has managed to slip aside and expose one of her shoulders, yet she isn't aware of this. He wonders if he should mention it. But how do you express a thing like that? It would be a good idea to let her know, but what do you say? "Huguette, pull yourself together!" or "Huguette, what's going on here?"

Muhlbach frowns at her shoulder and decides to say nothing. She's old enough to look out for herself. Then, too, there's always the chance that she knows exactly what's going on. They're usually aware of these things, they know how much is exposed. He looks with interest at the curve of her breast—a large amount. Just then the robe slides another inch, still she hasn't noticed. And the way it slipped— Huguette didn't move a muscle but the robe fell down anyway.

Muhlbach clears his throat. The time has passed when he could decently have spoken of the matter; to say anything now would be embarrassing.

What in the world has become of your husband?

Huguette shrugs.

I suppose he'll walk in any minute.

Oh yes, any minute! She appears to be dissatisfied with one of her fingernails. She squints at it, turns the finger around, and sighs.

Muhlbach gets up and walks around the room gazing at the pictures on the walls. How splendid if Puig should open the door and find them seated together like that. It would make a nice tableau. Very nice indeed!

The telephone rings again. This time she answers without hesitation and Muhlbach suddenly understands that there has been an arrangement. Puig has told her that he would call at eight o'clock. That explains why she didn't want to answer the telephone an hour ago—she didn't know who it was. Or maybe she did know but didn't want to talk to him, whoever he was. It also explains why she's been in no hurry to get dressed—she knew Puig wouldn't get here at eight.

Muhlbach listens. Yes, she's talking to her husband.

Only after the call is finished does he realize that he has been listening for some reference to himself, in fact that he had been half-waiting for Huguette to beckon him over and give him the telephone. But she talked to her husband as though she was alone.

He says he will be a little late. . . .

How late? Muhlbach interrupts. What time did he say he would get here?

Huguette looks up in surprise. She explains that there has been an accident aboard the ship. A sailor was injured, that's why Puig will be late, but he will be on his way in a few minutes.

Why do you stare at me? she asks. Have I done something wrong? and she stands up and comes close to him.

Muhlbach feels excited and angry. There's no doubt she is waiting for him to untie the belt of her bathrobe.

What a strange man you are! Talk to me, please. Do say something. I don't like you when you behave like this. She reaches for his hands as though to squeeze them.

He turns away but knows that whatever she is, she's not a whore. Something she has done—something she's said—something he couldn't quite perceive has proved she's not. What was it? What proved her innocence? Innocence! Innocent of being a professional, that's all. She's innocent of very little else. "I don't like you when you behave like this!" Could that be it? Or the moment when she got up from the couch instead of smiling and leaning back. She seemed distressed, worried—he shakes his head, not certain what to believe. If it isn't money she wants, what does she want? because I can't be what she's after. She hasn't seen me for the past two years, so why should she want me? I know how cold I look. Even if she told me that she thought I was attractive I wouldn't believe it. Well, then, is she simply auditioning lovers? Was somebody else here at five o'clock? And after I'm gone who will it be?

He turns toward her and sees that Huguette's face is the face of a woman obsessed—not fixed and professional. Her eyes are luminous. Her eyes remind him of someone else. For a few seconds he stands in front of Huguette, stricken by those eyes, trying to remember, then he thinks of his grandmother as she lay dying. There was that same look a few hours before her death. Nothing else he has ever seen resembles it. The brilliant gaze of an old woman finally emptied of all pretense.

Why do you look at me so?

This is how they ask, but Muhlbach doesn't answer. Plainly she is offering her body, not as a gift, but in exchange for the use of his, a cold bargain. He tries to estimate how much he wants her. The fact is, not very much. When she telephoned the office he first assumed she wanted to buy some insurance, that's how little she means. Not once has he thought of her these past several years except as Puig's wife. Now, tonight, almost inexplicably she shows this naked willingness; instead of a wife she becomes a woman and displays the queer values of women.

If I was twenty I wouldn't hesitate, he thinks. Or would I say to myself that she's too old? She must be at least thirty-five, maybe older. She could be forty. If I was twenty again how would I be looking at her? Not as I do now. I'd think she was a joke. I'd see myself telling about it in the fraternity house. I never had an adventure like this when I was young—it was always somebody else who did the telling—but I know what it would have meant to me. Now? Now is it amusing?

Muhlbach realizes that he is still gazing at her, and that she is trying to interpret his gaze. Why has she arranged this? he wonders. What's happened between her and Puig? and suddenly he's convinced that Puig is impotent. There can't be any other explanation. The endless boasting, chasing after one college girl and then another—nobody doubted that Puig was nailing them to the cross. In the Navy it must have been the same. So many conquests, but all of them too obvious, too apparent. How many were actual and how many did Puig invent? Or were all three hundred of them invented? No, Puig's not that empty. Maybe a few have been so real that Huguette's disgusted.

Well, whatever's the cause, thinks Muhlbach, I'm not going to play my part. I can almost read the script: we're no sooner in bed than the door opens, the husband enters, hangs up his hat and announces cheerily that he's home. Well, Huguette, I'm not very good at farce, so I think I can do without that royal scene. I'm not going to spend ten minutes as your leading man, thank you just the same. Find yourself another actor. Revenge is what you want. I don't know why. I don't know what he's done to you, or what you imagine he's done—I don't know why you're disappointed but look somewhere else, not at me. I'm not the man.

Eh bien. . . .

Somehow she has understood. Muhlbach knows that somehow she has understood his thoughts well enough. It's over. "Eh bien!" As if she has compressed the history of her sex in a phrase.

And because it's over and he has ended it by doing absolutely nothing—exactly as so many other affairs of his life have ended at the beginning, because he has done nothing—he feels his head swelling with anger. What's the matter with me? he demands. Puig's wife is here! Mine for the taking. And I hate him. Christ how I've despised him all these years. So take her! Use her! Use her like the bitch that she is!

But of course the moment has gone, and the anger he feels is toward himself. Once again he has caught up with life too late.

It occurs to him that maybe they should talk the whole thing over. She might like to know how he feels. But she already knows, at least it's probable; she seems to have sensed the situation. The best thing might be to let the curtain drop and simply wait for Puig. Muhlbach shuts his eyes for a few seconds and imagines himself at home in his old green leather chair, the children running around upstairs while Mrs. Grunthe plods back and forth from the kitchen to the dining room as she sets the table. That's where I ought to be, he thinks, that's where I ought to be!

Opening his eyes he discovers Huguette bending down patting a pillow, her great box-like hips solidly in front of him. He looks at her hips in despair. He feels crushed and ruined, and decides angrily that he will go over, throw his arms around her waist and see what happens next.

Just then somebody turns the handle of the door. Puig's voice calls through the gilded panel—he's locked out. Huguette goes to let him in, but before opening the door she pulls her robe together and tightens the belt.

Puig, discovering Muhlbach in the room, is quite obviously dumbfounded. He can't believe what he sees; he remains on the threshold with a Navy overnight bag in his hand and the remnants of a husbandly smile on his peeling face—it's plain that he has been in the sun recently, his nose is bright pink and looks extremely tender. He glares at Muhlbach and breathes hoarsely through his mouth; but Huguette is already at work and within a very few minutes Puig is inside, has taken off his garrison cap and is comfortably seated with a drink in his hand, still confused but gradually accepting the situation—as much of it as she has chosen to tell.

It's been a long time! Puig exclaims. A long time!

Muhlbach agrees.

I didn't expect to see you here, says Puig.

Huguette points out that it was meant to be a surprise.

Jesus! remarks Puig without much sign of humor.

Muhlbach asks where the fleet will be going next. Puig doesn't know, or claims he doesn't; he adds that he has been in the Mediterranean for the past few weeks.

How tired I am of winter! Huguette exclaims. Why didn't you take me? I'm so sick of this cold weather! Snow! But then it snows again. . . .

Puig soon stops listening to her. He loosens his tie and speaks to Muhlbach. When was the last time we met?

You'd just recently been transferred from the *Huxtable*.

Oh yeah, what a scow. And the old man nuts for Navy regs. That was one tour I won't forget. He talks about this for a while and when he has finished Muhlbach asks if he has been playing much golf.

Sure. Every chance.

You should be in the low seventies by now.

Nope. Hooking off the tee, same as usual. I got a weak wrist, that's what kills me. High seventies. Low eighties. He looks thoughtfully at Huguette, who gets up without a word and goes into the bathroom and shuts the door.

How about you? he continues. You still play?

Nope, haven't held a club in my hands for ten years, Muhlbach answers, conscious that he is beginning to sound like Puig.

At school you had a pretty good swing. Pick it up again and see what you can do. You ought to break ninety.

I might. I might start playing again. Being behind a desk most of the day I don't get much exercise. They say it's a good game for us at our age.

Puig laughs unpleasantly. I'm not old. If I had time for a couple of weeks at the gym I'd be as fast as I was in college. Don't make any mistake. I can still handle myself.

Muhlbach looks at him curiously. It's as though Puig is hinting at something, and has switched from golf to boxing.

You weren't bad, Puig goes on in a condescending voice. One time at Lakewood you tied me on the front nine. Both of us shot a forty-three. I had a thirty-six on the back, you had a forty-eight. My shoulder was stiff that morning. It took a while to get warmed up.

Muhlbach remembers, and remembers Puig mentioning his shoulder for at least a month after that day.

I guess I never told you how much it bugged me, you tying me. You never appreciated how competitive I am. I hate to get beat. I couldn't stand losing marbles when I was a kid. I felt like killing the other kid, get him down in the dust and pound hell out of him. Puig laughs and begins unbuttoning his coat. Now how about you? What've you been up to since I saw you last?

Business. I'm never up to anything else.

Whose fault is that?

You say it's a fault. Well, maybe it is. Maybe it is. My days are practically identical. No variety. Lack of excitement. So you could be right—fault's the word.

Muhlbach listens to this lordly pronouncement and decides he has had enough to drink. My own voice, he thinks, but I've lost control of it. Somebody inside me is talking. However, I'm not mimicking Puig any longer, there's that much to be grateful for.

Variety! Puig answers with an ice cube in his mouth, and spits the cube back into the glass.

He's tired, Muhlbach thinks. Or is it nervousness? He hasn't said anything about what happened on the ship. He could just possibly have been responsible for the accident. He's upset, but what about?

I might as well tell you, Puig remarks as though the thought had communicated itself, finding you here doesn't make me too happy.

The remark is almost impossible to believe. Muhlbach tries to believe he has imagined it—Puig didn't actually say that. Yet he did.

I been gone such a long while. Cruising around. Storing it up inside. Then I come back and open the door expecting to find Huguette by herself. Forget it, he adds, scratching his jaw with one finger. Don't pay any attention to me. I'm in a bad mood. You were about to say something. Go ahead. I interrupted. What's on your mind?

I shouldn't be here. Huguette—that is, since you didn't know. You weren't expecting me. I thought you were.

What about Huguette?

The challenge in Puig's voice is unmistakable; with bright watery eyes he watches the wall an inch above Muhlbach's head.

I'm asking again: what about Huguette?

Muhlbach realizes that there have been other scenes like this. Puig suspects her. He suspects every man who comes near her. He has never seemed dangerous so the idea of him in a jealous rage is rather funny, but he is tense and this might not be an appropriate time to laugh. Muhlbach considers how to answer. Puig is waiting. The answer begins to seem important.

Such a violent age! Muhlbach says carefully. How violent we are these days.

Amen! Puig answers, squinting with annoyance.

At that moment Huguette turns on the shower. She has been listening. Puig, however, hasn't noticed; he leans back, rolling his head from side to side as though he was in pain.

Individually, but also as nations, Muhlbach continues, cautiously pulling at the conversation. I've been wanting to ask. Apparently another war is shaping up but for some reason we can't recognize the enemy. Yesterday we thought it was Russia. Today, China. Now what about tomorrow? Name tomorrow's enemy. What would be your guess? India?

Puig doesn't turn his head; he looks across his nose to see if this is a joke.

Four years together—four years! but what makes you tick I'll be diddled if I know. I never could understand you. You used to sit in the library annex with a gooseneck lamp curled over a book. I used to look at you and ask myself what you were really like inside. What makes him go? I asked myself. Is it money? I figured you must want to earn a lot of money after you graduated. Maybe you did. I have the impression you're doing all right.

Let's trade jobs.

Puig laughs and settles more comfortably into the chair. On account of money? We get benefits, sure. Dental work. Cut-rate movies at the base. Except for that it's nothing much. You don't want to trade with me.

Not on account of money. On account of the travel. I'm rotting away behind a desk. At certain times I catch myself trying to guess where you are—envying you because you're somewhere on the other side of the globe. I imagine the fleet anchored off Ceylon. If you've ever gotten there or not I don't know, it doesn't matter. I stop by the fountain in the office for a drink of water but just then I see you in Marrakesh, or walking along the esplanade at Palma. Maybe you're two thousand miles from there, that doesn't matter. I see you in these places.

Hell's bells, says Puig with a cheerful expression, if you want to go why don't you go? Lock up the shop for a while and go! You sit on your butt and complain, just like you always did.

I don't think of it quite that way, but I won't argue. I ought to go. And I would except for my affair—carrying on with that gooseneck lamp.

As soon as the word slips out he knows it was a poor choice; but Puig, tenderly feeling the tip of his sunburnt nose, only looks mildly thoughtful.

What is it about this man, Muhlbach reflects, that bores me half to death? Why don't I care what he believes, or what he's done, or what finally becomes of him? When we were students I was interested in his ideas. I thought he was profound. I thought there were reservoirs in him, but there aren't any. He's commonplace. I suppose he always was. His forehead shows practically no expression, strange I never noticed. It's the forehead of a fascist or of a priest. His mind lacks resonance, I believe; even when he surprises me I realize the surprise is shallow. There's no deliberate evil in him, nor much magnificence. He's like other men. I guess that's why he bores me. He's bored with me, too, because he thinks I'm dull and cold, because I'm restrained, but that doesn't insult me in the least. How could it? I'm not concerned with what he thinks about me. I know there's more of me than there is of him. Remind myself that from a distance we're the same size—yes, but I know better, although I don't know how. Given enough to drink he'd announce that he doesn't amount to much, which is a confession I'd never make. Not now, drunk as I may be, or ever, or anywhere. Not even before Jehovah's throne. Let him abase himself if that pleases him, I respect myself too much. Three gold stripes, considerable prestige, yet his confidence is still that of a sophomore. How is it possible? He doesn't—what is it that he doesn't? A sort of growth must be what I have in mind, the way coral grows. But that doesn't explain him because we're not marine organisms, or plants with rings to count. You can't analogize a man. It must be some lack of human deepening that I can't describe. He hasn't deepened since I saw him last. Two years. He was in a good humor then and now he's annoyed at me for something that isn't my fault, otherwise it's as though these two years had never been. Which means it'll be the same when we meet again. Which means I haven't anything else to learn about him or from him. Which makes me wonder what I ever learned from being around him. Is he a great waste of time? And if he is, can I afford it? My life's half over. Come back as a white bull along the Ganges and I wouldn't mind so much, but I'm not expecting that. So what am I doing here with him? because he's nothing more than he appears to be. I doubt if he's ever gotten absolutely and hopelessly lost inside of himself. Never peeled away the leaves looking for the innermost bulb. He doesn't know it's there, and that's why I don't think about him, only where he is in my imagination. I don't dislike him, not really. I suppose I like him. However, I'm not sure about that either, he's so fatally easy to forget.

How long have you been here? asks Puig, pretending to pick a bit of lint from his sleeve. And it's this—the calculated gesture—that betrays him. The question isn't casual. Puig is troubled; he opened the door and discovered another man.

How long? Muhlbach asks, and pretends to consider. Quite a while. We were beginning to think you'd never get here.

What'd you and my wife talk about?

Not "Huguette" but "my wife." What did you talk about with my wife? What were you and my wife doing before I got here?

To be decently honest, I'll say only that your wife did most of the talking.

Puig laughs.

Why do I sit here acting like a friend? Muhlbach wonders. I manipulate him and consider myself superior. I could have had his wife and that, too, makes me feel I'm better than he is but maybe I'm not as good. He's artless and coarse, and he's destructible, but his passions are honest. Mine are contaminated. Who's better? I don't know. I don't know. Maybe I worry it too much.

In the bathroom the shower is turned off.

Takes them forever, Puig remarks. Hey! Huguette! he calls.

A moment later the door opens a crack, a wisp of steam curls out, and Muhlbach can see her eye.

Somebody wants me?

Snap it up, will you? Puig answers without turning around.

Are you hungry, cheri? I'll hurry. One minute. Okay? And then before disappearing the eye regards Muhlbach. The look is very brief, but unequivocal. The eye of Cleopatra, or of Messalina, gazing across her husband's shoulder.

I should have done it, Muhlbach says to himself. That's what she wanted, so why didn't I? What difference would it make. I should have taken my cheap revenge. Puig would never know.

And then while the steam is clearing he realizes that he can see the interior of the bathroom; not much, because the door is almost shut, but it isn't completely shut.

Getting back to war, says Puig. This "peace" is just an introduction to what's coming up next. We're in the middle of another Hundred Years War, that's how I figure. All right, India. Sure, why the hell not?

Muhlbach can make no sense of what Puig is saying; it's as though the words conceal something more important, but what? Puig is not really talking about war, he's explaining something.

It's not going to blow over, you can lay a bet. Not for a long while. Maybe never. You sit in an office so you forget what most people actually are like under the surface. At each other's throat. That's human nature. You ought to remember that. Puig takes a swallow of his drink, belches and wipes his lips on the back of his fist. People can be bloody unpleasant if they got a good reason.

The meaning becomes clear as soon as he finished; nearly everything Puig says is an allusion to his wife.

You've got to treat people with respect, he adds; but then changes the subject. What kind of food you want? Any preference?

Muhlbach lifts his glass slightly to indicate that he doesn't care.

Pizza's good enough for me, Puig mutters, fumbling around in the pockets of his uniform. Out comes a crumpled package of cigarettes which he holds up with a questioning expression.

Muhlbach shakes his head.

Ten days is all I'm going to be here. I put in for shore duty last October but so far not a word. Ten short days. Then out we go. Ten bloody days.

You must like New York.

What do you mean?

You're here instead of at home.

How did you know about that?

About you buying a house in Trenton? She told me.

Puig settles back thoughtfully and feels the tip of his nose again. I've been at sea such a long while I wanted—oh, you know how it is. Lie in your bunk and think about it and think about it. So I wrote her to meet me here. We'll leave in the morning. I didn't want to lose any time. You know how it is.

I shouldn't have come. I assumed Huguette called me because you suggested it.

That's all right, Puig says awkwardly, and seems to say something else but shrugs and sips at his drink.

Maybe some other. . . .

Sit still, Puig replies irritably. You're here so you're here. If my wife ever gets dressed—I don't know what takes so long. You look like you lost a few pounds, he goes on without much interest.

Muhlbach nods.

You look younger. I usually put on weight aboard ship, he adds suddenly and then calls: Huguette! God damn it!

But, cheri, I am hurrying! she answers from the bathroom. Do be patient. One minute more, I promise.

Did I tell you that last year I was in the Orient? Some difference the way those people look at life. Means nothing to them. So courteous but the next thing you know they're torturing some poor bastard. You remember that time we went to New Orleans?

What's he doing? Muhlbach wonders. It's as though his brain has been short-circuited.

Puig smiles. We bought that old rattletrap car for twenty bucks to drive down. Seems like yesterday. You remember?

Yes. Of course. Muhlbach remembers. Rainy green bluffs along the Mississippi. The soft dialect of the people. Negroes everywhere. Crisp greasy fried shrimp and gray beans with red-eye gravy. Lying on the warm salty beach at Pontchartrain, a Gulf breeze blowing stiffly through the late afternoon. But then he hears Puig mention the street fight. That, too, had been part of the trip. A slow, savage beating more like a ritual than a fight. Muhlbach remembers the grotesque figure in a painted leather vest, with a black nail-studded belt and loose motorcycle boots. The fleshless wolf-like Slavic features, Asiatic eyes peeping out from beneath the dinky cap with a look of amusement while he kicked and beat the victim. A pair of gloves flapped from his back pocket when he swaggered away, the vest dangling from the muscular shoulders. Puig calls it a fight, but it was an assault. And the people standing around asking each other how it started, waiting to see if the thug would come stalking out of the night to attack his victim again—a man sprawled against the curb, resting near the base of the streetlight because he had held on to the streetlight with all his strength while being beaten, but at last slid to the side-walk where he sat gazing up at the spectators until he was kicked in the back of the head and dropped over lifelessly. Muhlbach remembers the deep sexual pleasure in the hoodlum's face, and how slowly the victim was beaten. He remembers think-ing that a man's body is like a heavy rubber ball without much air in it. The body scarcely moved when it was kicked.

Too bad we missed out on the beginning, says Puig, and Muhlbach finds Puig looking at him with mockery or contempt.

Now don't tell me you were going to stop it. Come on, mister, you must think I'm stupid. Nobody was going to—nobody in the whole crowd. That punk was dangerous. You knew it, I knew it, everybody knew it. So don't tell me you were about to step up and shake your finger in his face. You didn't make a move. You stood right next to me quiet as a lamb and watched a man get his brains kicked loose. Let's see—what street was that on? Dauphine, was it? Dumaine? It was close to the convent. We ate someplace near Jackson Square, afterwards we walked around. Bought some pralines for dessert. Listened to a jazz outfit. Then what'd we do?

Puig continues reminiscing but Muhlbach no longer listens. What Puig has said is true, he had stood watching quietly while a man was being kicked in the head. He remembers standing on tiptoe to find out what was going on, wondering if there had been an accident, or if it was a play being performed under the street-light. It had seemed almost like a play, as though at any minute the hoodlum would bow to the applause, then take off his cap and approach for a donation, and the motionless man who lay there bleeding from the mouth and ears would jump to his feet with a grin, wipe away the blood, and the two of them would move along the street to a different corner.

Puig is still talking. You couldn't let the thing alone. After it was done you had to go through it again and again. But while it was actually happening you didn't risk your neck, did you? No, you watched. Then an hour later you decide we ought to go to the cops to report what we witnessed. Sometimes you make me sick at my stomach.

The one act in my life that I'm still ashamed of, thinks Muhlbach with astonishment. How did he guess? After all these years how does he know I've never gotten over that feeling of shame? We did talk about it, yes, and I suppose I was the one who kept bringing it up, but of course we used to talk about all sorts of things. And he himself didn't try to stop the fight.

How many people in the world? Puig inquires. Worry about what happens to one of them and you got to start worrying about the others. I didn't lose any sleep over it. I never pretended I did. I didn't go around for the next two weeks throwing ashes on myself. I'm no hypocrite.

Everything Puig has said is the truth. And yet, thinks Muhlbach, why am I suspicious? He's trying to degrade me, that's clear enough, but I don't know why. He was as afraid as I was, maybe more, because he was the fine physical specimen, not I. He was the one who might have been a match for that thug, but he knew I wasn't. So! Is it possible? Does he feel as guilty as I do? Is he condemning himself?

But why did he bring it up now? What were we talking about—war, for some reason I've forgotten, then all at once he asked about New Orleans. How strange! Muhlbach looks again at Puig. War. Violence. Threats. The shapeless conversation while waiting for Huguette to dress. There it is! Of course! She can hear us talking.

Muhlbach glances toward the bathroom. The door has opened a few more inches and he sees Huguette brushing her hair. As she turns toward the cabinet he sees that she is naked.

What's she doing? asks Puig.

Brushing her hair.

Then there is nothing to do but wait, and Muhlbach waits. One more word may cause Puig to look around.

He knows the bathroom door is open, Muhlbach says to himself, and he knows I've been watching his wife. But that's all he knows. What will I do if he looks around? What could I say—nothing. Good God. And it's her fault, not mine.

Puig mutters. He scratches his jaw, swallows the rest of his drink and seems about to stand up.

He's warned me. This ridiculous talk about fighting in the street—he was telling me how he feels. And he's convinced I've had his wife. He's almost certain. The only thing he needs is some proof. The way he's been peeking at me I should have guessed. If he makes a move to get up I've got to stop him. If he gets up he'll look around. If he sees her like that he'll know we were in bed together. What will I do if he starts to get up?

Then the solution appears, as obvious as a cartoon.

What's so funny? asks Puig.

Your suspicions.

Puig grins uncomfortably.

Now that you've asked, I don't mind telling you. I can practically see them. They're all over you like the measles. What if the bed had been wrinkled when you came in? Let's suppose your wife decided to lie down for a while before I got here but didn't straighten the bed when she got up. You were hardly in the door before you glanced at the bed. Isn't that right?

Puig continues grinning because he has no choice.

You suspected me before you bothered to say hello. And you've kept right on hunting for evidence. You decided I was a cuckoo and all you wanted was proof. Isn't that true? It is, isn't it?

Puig wipes his face, bites his lip, and grins again.

Let's try another example. Let's suppose that while I happened to see Huguette brushing her hair she wasn't fully dressed. Suppose that had been the case, what would you have thought? No doubt you'd have manufactured something from that, too. Am I right?

Puig hesitates, but then accepts the stroke; and now unless he doesn't mind being ridiculous he can't possibly turn around. Muhlbach after studying him decides that the position is fixed. However, there's no particular reason to stop, so he continues.

What might happen, I asked myself, if he started misinterpreting? What might happen if—well, it hasn't been very pleasant to contemplate.

Puig is deeply embarrassed, unable to speak. For the first time he feels defensive.

If I'm going to be hanged for a thief, Muhlbach goes on, I must admit I wish I'd stolen something.

Puig is writhing on the couch.

You practically challenged me to a duel, but I was so puzzled by the way you were acting. . . .

Oh come on, says Puig very miserably. Knock if off, will you?

If you want to drop the subject, all right.

This should be enough, Muhlbach thinks. This should satisfy me. Why do I feel like torturing him some more? But the fact is, I do. I finally got a taste of revenge and I like it. I want more, I guess because of what he did to me.

The scene in all of its glorious and ferocious schoolboy stupidity comes streaming back; wrestling with each other on the dormitory sun deck because half a dozen girls were watching, even though they pretended they weren't. Muhlbach remembers rolling closer and closer to the edge. I gave up, he remembers, to keep us from being killed. If I'd held on we'd have gone over and dropped sixty feet. And he was so pleased with himself. So proud that he'd won. We both knew he'd won. So did the audience. But what was the sense of it? Why did we do it? For what? For the admiration of a few girls who were busily snubbing us both. On account of that one absurd juvenile defeat I've hated him. And of course at the same time I've always liked him. Hated? That's not quite right, because hate is total. I never have hated him. What I feel is the nub of something stiff, like a cork or a corroded plug, that he forced down into me. I think only some kind of revenge could soften it. But I suppose I can go on living with it, I've lived this long in spite of what he did to me. And of course I've always liked him. I couldn't have spent four years in one room with him unless I liked him. With all those sorry masculine traits I like him. He's my friend. He always has been, although sometimes I'd like to split his skull. He always had to prove he was better than I was. He had to prove he was stronger, which he was, and smarter, which he wasn't, and better with the girls which is something only they could answer. Well, that's how he was made, and it's how I was made, and otherwise I guess there's not much to choose between us.

Muhlbach, lifting his glass to finish the drink, because surely Huguette must be ready by now, finds himself looking into the bathroom again. She is standing in full view, leaning toward the mirror to add the last touch of lipstick. Her hair is beautifully brushed and arranged. She has put on her shoes and stockings and a red garter belt, but nothing else. She is watching him from the corner of her eye. She has been standing there waiting.

Muhlbach is too shocked to look away. This is no accidental tableau—if Puig should look. This is not the same as a door that's not quite shut. This is something out of the depths.

For an instant she gazes at him. Then as though he did not exist she turns her back, the worst and oldest insult.

Do you see? she seems to ask. This is what I think of you! And with that she pushes the door shut.

For the rest of her life, Muhlbach reflects, that's what she's going to think of me, because I denied us a round of cheap pleasure—a loveless struggle on a rented bed. Have I humiliated her so much?

A few minutes later Huguette reappears, exquisitely dressed and ready.

I am sorry to take so long but there are certain things a woman must do, she begins brightly. Now if you gentlemen will be good enough to get to your feet. . . .

They stand up, neither saying a word. Muhlbach is too amazed to speak and Puig obviously is bored by the idea of three for dinner.

Huguette takes each of them by an arm.

Alors, she asks, shall we go?

1965

CRASH LANDING

A COLD, SALT WIND blew in from the Gulf of Mexico, carrying a few clouds like puffs of cannon smoke. The wind blew through the pines and swept across the long rows of blue-grey Navy dive bombers, the sturdy Douglas SBDs that had swarmed on the Japanese carriers at Midway, and had sunk the *Shoho* in the Coral Sea. Now the war was almost ended and these planes were old, like the battles of 1942, rusting away in the humid air of Pensacola.

Near the edge of the field, in the shadow of the last bomber, stood a lanky cadet with a badly sunburned nose. His name was Martin Isaacs and he was squinting at a line of Japanese flags stenciled on the fuselage of the plane, wondering where the plane had fought. Perhaps it had flown over Rabaul and Truk, or across the jungles of Guadalcanal. He touched one of the flags. Then he shrugged, spit out his chewing gum, and clambered onto the wing, climbing awkwardly because of the parachute on his back. He buckled the canvas straps around his thighs and straightened up, looking closely at the plane. Long metallic scratches glittered like a spider web through the camouflage paint, and the wing on which he stood was dented as though somebody had been throwing rocks at it. He noticed that a spot of rust was eating away the large white star beside the gunner's ring. He walked up the wing to the forward edge and looked at the corroded cowl flaps. He looked down and saw that the pudgy little tires had been worn smooth—a network of white fabric showed through the black rubber.

Thoughtfully he leaned against the cockpit, and there he paused to make a decision while the wind ruffled his hair and pulled at the white silk muffler around his throat. He studied the clouds and the gently waving boughs of the pine trees and he knew they were beckoning to him. Then he looked at the plane again and he jumped off the wing. He walked all the way around the SBD, stopping to give each wheel a vigorous kick and to poke his thumb through a hole in one of the elevators. He guessed that this was one of the condemned planes that would shortly be broken up for scrap; he would be very foolish to try to fly it.

He ought to go back and get another one. There was plenty of time. He tried to slide the hatch open, but the metal had oxidized, and when this happened—when he found himself locked out—he remembered how often he had wanted something and had been denied. With both fists he pounded on the top of the hatch. Then he lifted one foot and kicked at it with his heavy government brogan until he had broken the rust. He was determined to have this particular plane. At last he was able to force the greenhouse backwards. He squeezed inside and sat for a minute in sulky triumph before closing it over his head.

To his surprise he had no trouble with the engine. It started immediately, coughing and spitting, and soon let out a roar of hoarse authority. He listened carefully, feeling less truculent now that he was in command. He began talking to the engine in a confidential way, as he was in the habit of doing, and he had the familiar sensation that the engine was aware of him. He tested the two magnetos, studying the gauges and listening seriously, and after a while he was satisfied. If trouble developed it was more apt to be in the fatigued metal of the wings and tail, or in the hydraulic system.

The radio began to warm up, filling his earphones with the drone and crackle of electricity. He cranked the handle around, hunting the Pensacola squadron tower. Quite suddenly there was an American voice in the sputtering void, the voice of a Wave in the tower. She was reciting: " . . . Zero. One. One. Zero. . . . " He turned the handle too far and she was gone; hurriedly he cranked backward, passing over her again and entering the void. He scowled because he had begun to feel uneasy. The elusive voice seemed to be taunting him. He noticed with some curiosity that his hands were unsteady, and remembering how he had pounded on the canopy he began to wonder if he was ill. This idea annoyed him. He had forced the airplane open; there was no reason he could not force himself to do whatever he wished. He put his fingertips in his mouth and bit them until the trembling stopped. Then he resumed his search for the squadron tower, and finally, through the crackling and sputtering, he found it. He asked the Wave for permission to take off. She announced the runway number and wind velocity, and she gave him permission to leave.

He released the brakes and went fishtailing out the lane toward the downwind end of the runway. Several other SBDs and a dark blue Corsair were ahead of him. He taxied up to the Corsair, closer than was safe, and followed it enviously. The big fighter swung ponderously back and forth as the pilot tried to see what was ahead, and with every change of direction the stubby SBD rocked in a blast from the Corsair's four-bladed propeller.

At the end of the taxi strip they all parked in an oblique line and waited. The first SBD trundled ahead, swung around with a flourish, and began to shake as the pilot tested the engine one final time before leaving the earth. Soon a green light appeared in the distant tower. The SBD rolled forward, faster and faster, the sunlight glinting on its wings. For a moment or so its wheels dangled in the air, as useless as the claws of a bird in flight, then they folded inward and flattened against its breast.

Already the second SBD was in position. The green light shone again.

Now the Corsair was on the runway. The pilot hunched forward in his cockpit, inside his bubble of glass like an insect in a projectile. The long wings shook gently from the rhythm of the enormous engine, and a few seconds later the Corsair was a black dot climbing high above the tower.

And now it was his turn. The green light was shining, mindless but insistent, like the eye of a Cyclops. He pressed the throttle forward, holding the brakes with his toes until the SBD was quivering. Suddenly he lifted his feet and the SBD leaped forward. He could feel the pavement rolling beneath the wheels. In a few seconds he could see the horizon over the top of the engine and he knew that the tail of the SBD had left the ground. Now he could see where he was going without leaning to one side.

The control stick, which had been nothing more than a length of metal, was coming to life beneath his hand. He could not lose a sense of wonder at this familiar transfiguration. The metal became a turgid, living thing, erect and swollen with power.

A gust of wind tilted the wings—the SBD swerved, bounced, and took off in a low, vicious curve. Immediately he brought up the wheels and waited anxiously until he felt the twin thumps as the wheels folded into the belly.

The wind was increasing; he was well off the ground before he reached the tower. He wanted to have a look at the Wave who was directing traffic, so, instead of holding the engine down and gaining speed, he pulled up steeply and turned his head when he flew past the tower. He saw her there, a dark-featured girl in a wrinkled seersucker uniform, holding a microphone to her lips as if she were about to speak. She was watching him without expression.

When he left the traffic pattern he discovered another SBD cutting inside the arc; he looked again and found it was not one but two planes in tight formation, and they were obviously intent on joining him. He saw that the pilots were his friends, McCampbell and Roska. He shook his head and swiftly banked away. This was to be his last flight at Pensacola. He did not want any company.

He rolled out of the turn and continued on a course where no one could intercept him. He had decided to climb as high above the earth as the SBD would take him. He did not know how high that was. He noticed then, for the first time, a row of crosses scratched along the top of the instrument panel, and wondered what they meant. Had they been drawn by some mechanic idling away the afternoon, or was this a calendar of intense significance to the combat pilot whose name had once been stenciled on the fuselage?

The condemned SBD rose in a flat spiral while Martin looked around with a brooding stare.

The sky had become a deeper blue. From the ground it looked cerulean, and warm; now it was a chill indigo. Except for the steady, reassuring tremble of the engine he might have been asleep in space.

Abruptly he shivered from the cold. He glanced at the altimeter and was astounded to find that it registered fifteen thousand feet; only a second ago it had not yet reached four thousand feet. He slapped himself on the forehead to wake up. Then he strapped the oxygen mask over his face and studied the gauges to make sure he was receiving oxygen. To keep himself awake he began whistling.

Yet, in a little while, despite himself, he was not able to hear anyone whistling. Once more he had begun to gaze, fascinated and witless, into a barren and compelling darkness that varied only when the icy gray cowl of the spiraling bomber floated slowly past the sun. He was so high—the air had become so thin—that the controls were loose. He shoved the rudder pedals to the bottom, first one and then the other, but the SBD barely responded. He unlocked the shoulder harness so that he could twist around in the cockpit and look backward while he kicked the pedals again, and he saw the tail rudder swinging wildly back and forth with a sonorous clang that echoed within the fuselage like church bells in a corridor. He looked at the instrument panel and found that the rate-of-climb indicator was stationary.

THE SBD was revolving, very quietly, on an axis of some kind, like a key in a lock, or like some living thing on a mountaintop. Or was it the sphere below that rotated? The true image was elusive. He was gazing down on the western quadrant, hypnotized by the absence of life. And he dreamed that he could see beyond the swamps where De Soto wandered, beyond the swirling dust of the gigantic western plains, to where the surf came thundering down on the shores of California. Somberly he drifted on. He watched the green volcanic islands of Oahu and Molokai take shape and float beneath him. Presently he saw on the southern horizon the raindrenched valleys of Samoa, and New Guinea, and the lost pyramids of Siam. Now, beyond the mystic Ganges, lay the high plateaus of India, and the water of the Red Sea. And Algiers, and Portugal, from which a thoughtful man in a doublet and velvet hat had looked westward once upon a time, calculating, to the Azores and the jeweled Antilles and to the Florida Keys.

The illusion disintegrated like an opulent dream as he spun toward the earth. The SBD fell more and more rapidly, twisting like a diving hawk, while he sat with his hands folded in his lap. Far below him the earth was enveloped in haze; even so there was a sense of solidity to the earth. He studied the broad arc of the whirling horizon, and felt very near to it, yet not altogether a part of it. It was the home to which he must return after each absence. He looked at it with mild curiosity and with the same benign indifference he used to feel as a child when he considered the world from the gilded saddle of an undulating stallion on a carousel.

Disdainfully he grasped the cold, plump stick and pressed it down until it became rigid and indignant; then he pulled it backward. He rolled to his left, and to his right, and turned over completely in wild abandon. He heard himself groan when the airplane stalled and somersaulted over the top. He dove again, and pulled up so steeply that the blood was sucked out of his head. When there was nothing more to do, and he was beginning to grow tired, he threw the stick from side to side and kicked at the rudder pedals. The SBD shuddered, the engine laboring, the nose dipping like a porpoise going through the waves, until at last it rolled over into a mushy, sickening spin. He pushed the lever that set the wing flaps to opening, and watched with an indolent smile as the trailing edge of the bomber's wing split wider and wider apart with the awesome precision of hydraulic machinery. He could feel the speed decrease. The harness began cutting through the coveralls into his shoulders, and the safety belt, when he tapped it with one finger, felt as hard as a board across his lap. The dive became very slow and very stable, and he was suspended by the harness. He pressed the stick down until it was next to the instrument panel, yet neither the speed nor the angle of the dive showed much increase. He remembered what he had been told about closing the flaps in the midst of a dive. A year or so ago some lieutenant from another field had closed the diving flaps, probably by mistake. No one saw him, but a crew of lumberjacks felt the ground shake and thought a meteor had struck.

NOW THE FLAPS were closing smoothly. The safety belt grew slack. His head was resting comfortably on the hard leather cushion, and he gazed blindly ahead, lost in meditation while the earth came rushing toward him.

The wings of the SBD began hissing in the wind. Martin blinked and yawned, and looked to one side. The painted metal was rippling from the force of the wind. He studied the instrument panel: there were a few extreme readings, but nothing totally unexpected. The compass, however, was gyrating wildly in the amber fluid and he realized that he had forgotten to lock it. He was speculating on whether the dive would affect the compass when all at once he understood that the SBD was going to fall apart. He had not heard anything unusual, or seen anything or felt anything, but he knew that the plane was already destroyed.

He rolled his head on the cushion and stared at the radio mast just outside the greenhouse. At that moment the mast broke off. He scarcely had time to see which direction it went, although he knew it had been left behind, or, since the SBD was in a vertical dive, the mast would now be high overhead, maybe several hundred yards overhead by this time. He thought the mast had struck the fin, although the impact he felt could have been caused by something else snapping off. It was possible that the entire tail section—the rudder, the fin itself and the elevators—had broken off completely. In that case he was now riding to his death. He attempted to twist around and peer over his shoulder, but he did not have the strength. He was stuck like a housefly in syrup. He could barely lift his arms. He felt like sighing, but the pressure against his chest was too strong. He could not make up his mind whether to die or whether to struggle. The day must come when he would die. It might as well be now. This would be a satisfying death, free of thought and pain. He wondered if anyone down below was admiring the dive. It must look very beautiful.

There was nothing to do but sit quietly, and dream a little of everything that might have been. Then he would exist no more, although he might be remembered with a certain awe by everyone who had known him, and by those who had heard the story of the crash. But if he lived and worked for fifty years what could he achieve? Who would especially care what he had said, and who would repeat to strangers the various opinions he held? He would live in obscurity like practically everybody else until, on a day that would be remarked for some other happening, he died.

All the same he decided to struggle. He had been sitting in the cockpit with his eyes tight shut and his arms crossed, ready for death. Now he went to work. He took hold of the control stick. If, when he pulled on it, there was a feeling of resistance, he would know the tail section was intact. And in that case he could recover from the dive. But if the stick flopped around like a broken leg he would know it was attached to nothing but a few cables whipping in the wind.

Martin let go of the stick and folded his arms, afraid to know the truth, while the small gray bomber plummeted toward the earth.

AFTER A WHILE he got restless and reached again for the controls. To his astonishment the stick would not move. He clutched it with both hands and pulled with all his strength; even then the stick did not move. He could not understand what was happening. He let go and rubbed his face. Just then he discovered that a strip of hard black rubber, which protected a seam on the wing where the dihedral commenced, was gone. He knew the strip of rubber had been in place when he left the field. He glanced at the opposite wing and saw the strip on that side starting to peel off. Beneath it the seam was open. The rivets were popping out.

The altimeter now registered eight thousand feet, but the needle lagged; he might be nearer seven thousand. If he was going to do anything at all he must do it within the next few seconds. He looked at the altimeter again and was shocked to see the needle dropping below six thousand. Fascinated by the unnatural speed of the needle he watched it go racing around the dial. When he glanced ahead he saw a country road spiraling toward him. He took a deep breath, despite the pressure on his chest, and tried once again to drag the control stick backward. It had the feeling of life—he knew it was attached to something—but he could no more pull it backward than he could have pulled up a sapling by the roots. Tears crept into his eyes and his chin trembled. He had tried very hard, but no one was helping him. He began to weep, choking on his own sobs. He put both feet up on the instrument panel to get more leverage, and then, with the veins standing out on his neck, he tried again.

His vision grew dim. He could not see his hands, and the dials on the panel slipped out of focus and came floating toward him like black halos.

This could mean only one thing: he had forced the controls backward. The course of the SBD was changing. But he thought he had waited too long and he braced himself for the impact. He expected, for some reason, to ricochet at least once before the final crash, like a stone skipping across the surface of a lake. Through the noise of the wind and the shrill howl of the engine he distinguished what he thought was the baying of a wild dog. He suspected himself of making this terrifying sound. He rolled his head toward the mirror. Why the mirror was turned down into the cockpit he had no idea, but there he saw his face—the mouth hanging open and saliva drooling from the corners. He wore a helpless, earnest look. After that he could not see anything, and he had no knowledge of himself.

When his sight returned the first thing he noticed was that he had the control stick drawn all the way back between his knees, and that he was desperately attempting to force it back still further.

Immediately he thought of the road that had been just in front of the engine; he glanced ahead, expecting to catch a glimpse of the road as it came smashing through. Instead, amazed, he saw nothing but the milky sky. The SBD was soaring upward.

Martin discovered that his feet were still on the instrument panel. Several of the dials were broken. He had crushed them beneath his heels. Pieces of glass were dropping straight back from the panel onto his chest and his face, and he realized that the SBD was now in a vertical climb. In a little while it would stall again, and this time, without altitude, no recovery would be possible. He knew this, but he was reluctant to end such a godlike ascent.

The SBD was standing in the air almost motionless, like a fish on its tail, when he finally brought it over into a normal flying position. The plane was ruined; he could see that. He did not even need to inspect the damage; he could feel it, and hear it. The machine was dead. He had no desire to speak to it, and he could not think of it as anything more than a piece of dangerous junk which should be abandoned as soon as possible.

A few hundred feet above the trees he leveled off and cautiously began to pick the glass out of his muffler. Then, because the plane was flying aslant, he looked around. Part of one aileron was gone and the wing surface ahead of the aileron was torn as though it were made of tinfoil. The other wing showed a crack along the seam where the rivets had burst, and while he was staring at the crack he thought it grew a little wider. From the vibration of the engine he knew that one of the propeller blades had been twisted out of alignment. Even if the wings held together it was obvious that the SBD would soon shake itself apart.

The cockpit was filled with fumes and with smoking, greasy odors, and he was afraid the plane was ready to explode. He could smell gasoline. Something trickled over his lips; he put out his tongue and then began to spit because it was covered with blood. He was bleeding from both nostrils. Otherwise he felt all right and, after wiping his nose on his glove and finding that the blood was still flowing, he forgot about it as he thought over the situation. He could fly back to the station, or at least in that direction, and attempt to land. If permission was refused because of the condition of the airplane—if an attempt at landing would endanger the lives of other people—then he would obey whatever orders the tower gave him. The next step, providing he got out alive, which was doubtful, would be to confess what he had done. And he had knowingly, willfully, flagrantly, violated instructions. He had been told quite explicitly what would happen when the flaps of an SBD were closed during a dive. He had even been shown a movie of the silver-and-blue wreckage in the woods where the lieutenant had fallen, and often since then he had thought of the lumberjacks who paused in their work to hunt for the meteor. But he had done it anyway; he had deliberately closed the flaps in the middle of the dive, and the result was now in his hands. The Navy would expect him to return to the base immediately and accept the consequences.

There was an alternative. He could head for the Gulf of Mexico. When he passed over the beach he could lock the controls and use the parachute. In a few hours—if it held together that long—the SBD would be over deep water and out of gas. There it would crash and sink and the wreckage would not ever be recovered for examination. Meanwhile he would be making his way back to the station, and when they asked what happened he would swear that the engine failed in an area where there was no possibility of effecting a safe landing. That would be a form of truth because the engine would fail over the Gulf. And when they asked where the plane went down he could swear, not only that it had gone down at sea, but that he had sent it there so as not to risk the lives of civilians.

These were the courses before him, diverging sharply. If he chose the first, returning to the base, he must accept the judgment, however unreasonable, of other men; if he chose the second, abandoning and concealing what he had destroyed, he had only to examine himself. The decision was easy.

With a crafty expression he studied the sky, shading his eyes and squinting, searching for the glint of sunlight on metal or glass. But the wind had carried him far beyond the usual practice area and there was not another plane in sight. He was alone. Satisfied, he began a careful climbing turn in the direction of the Gulf of Mexico.

While heading for the beach he rehearsed his story, and it amused him. Never before had he been in a situation where he could lie without literally lying. He began to understand how useful it would be to develop that ability. In the future he intended to profit by it.

So he leaned from side to side as he flew along, because he was afraid to bank the ruined plane, and he looked down and found that the land below him was an unearthly, sulphurous green. He was over a swamp. The hoarse cough of the engine disturbed a great blue heron that came flapping up from the stinking water and swung away to the east, and this big solitary bird that flew so clumsily with its feet dangling down, and its head on its breast, as if in meditation, this heron seemed to be saying that no other living creature had come that way. No one would discover the mendacity which would be his salvation.

HE WAS PLEASED, and smiled as he looked ahead. There lay the deep Gulf. Soon he would be parachuting toward the beach while the SBD thundered out to sea, hour after hour, until at last it came down and left a short scratch on the metallic water.

Martin began to get ready for the jump. He took off the radio earphones and turned up the bill of his scarlet baseball cap. Then he reflected that the cap would blow off when he jumped, so he rolled up the cap and stuffed it into the breast pocket of his coveralls. The oxygen mask was hanging around his neck; it had slipped off his face sometime during the dive. He pulled the mask over his head and hung it on the panel. Everything seemed to be ready. He pushed the radio cords aside so there was no chance of getting tangled up in them. Then all at once he realized he had forgotten the safety belt: he was still strapped to the seat. If he could forget that, what else had he forgotten? There was not much time. He fumbled anxiously at the hasp of the belt and finally managed to throw it open. Next, working furiously, he stuffed the shoulder harness behind the seat. He could not find anything more to do, so he began to practice grabbing the rip-cord handle. He felt restless and impatient; he wanted to jump out and hear the parachute boom open like a cannon. But it was not yet time; he was still flying over the swamp. He thought gleefully of the simple deception he had planned.

The SBD had begun to vibrate heavily. The engine was not going to last much longer; it might destroy itself in another five minutes, but even that would be enough. He was only seconds away from the beach, and if the plane would fly on out to sea for another two minutes it would go down in deep water where nobody would ever locate it.

All at once he felt sick and almost fainted, for he realized that he was not thinking lucidly: he had carefully prepared his escape without once thinking about the canopy over his head. It was closed and locked. He would have butted his head against it when he stood up. He might have knocked himself unconscious. He let go of the controls and grabbed the handle of the canopy with both hands, jerking it backward. It slid open easily, though he could feel the metal edges grinding through the corrosion, and it occurred to him that for the past few minutes he had been doing things more violently than usual.

Then he became aware of the damaged engine and he forgot about everything else. When the hatch was closed he had not been able to hear anything except a subdued roar, and sometimes the wind; now he heard the awful thudding and clanking. He leaned forward tensely, ready to let go and dive over the side. Oil had begun to seep along the cowl and drops were blowing against the windshield. He tried to wipe away the dark green drops, even though he knew that he was wiping the inside of the glass and the oil was on the outside. He tried again to wipe them away. Through the oily glass he saw the beach where the combers rolled in.

So, AT LAST, the time for which he had been waiting was at hand. This was the moment to stand up in the cockpit, cross his arms on his chest, and jump. He was not afraid. There was no reason he could not escape. Nothing bound him. And yet, with a truculent expression, he went riding out to sea.

About half an hour later the SBD commenced a cautious, climbing arc and headed landward, bearing directly for the station.

As he approached the practice area Martin noticed several airplanes converging on him. He did not know why. He could not see the plume of smoke trailing a quarter of a mile behind the SBD. Uneasily he watched the planes angling toward him. He felt accused.

When he got within radio range he picked up the microphone and called the tower for permission to make an emergency landing. He was answered by the same Wave, but a male voice interrupted, advising him to fly over the field so that the damage could be assessed.

Martin answered flatly: "Negative." He looked at the aileron, which was about to fall off, and then he looked to the other side to see if the crack in the wing had gotten any wider.

"Negative!" he heard himself shouting into the microphone. He was ashamed of himself for getting hysterical. Staring at the wing he spoke again, calmly but very urgently: "Request permission to land on first approach."

After a long pause the officer in the tower responded: "Permission granted. Come ahead."

"You got a f-fire truck around there anywhere?" Martin asked. He was becoming excited again and could not hide his fear.

"Crash wagon standing by."

"Well, get out the asbestos!" he cried.

"Take it easy, cadet," said the officer. "Everything's going to be all right."

"That's what you think," said Martin irritably. He was staring at the instrument panel. The cylinder head temperature was far above normal. The tachometer needle was bouncing back and forth across the dial. Most of the gauges were broken. Apparently he had jammed one of his heels through the compass, because the glass was shattered and the fluid was dripping from the bottom of the panel onto his shoes. The entire airplane was shuddering.

"Brother," he muttered into the microphone, "you just don't know the half of it." This was not the proper language to be using on an official call, and from the tower's silence he suspected that the officer talking to him was displeased.

"Navy one-five-six. Navy one-five-six. From which direction are you arriving?"

"Isn't that nice?" said Martin bitterly. "From which direction am I arriving?" He was furious with the stupidity of the officers in charge. It seemed to him they were not doing anything right.

"Say again," the tower called, "We do not read you. Say again. Over."

"Oh, Roger Dodger," he mumbled, and gloomily watched the oil streaming over the windshield. He had no further interest in talking with anyone about the situation; he shrugged and dropped the microphone in his lap. Seeing another SBD drifting toward his left wing tip he glanced at the pilot and was not surprised to see McCampbell. Even before he looked to the right he knew Roska would be there. And there he was, unmistakable with his head tilted back and the lavender baseball cap pulled down over his narrow emerald eyes. He came floating in, judging the distance.

The two of them, McCampbell and Roska, were already flying a tight formation, but they were intent on coming even closer. Martin knew it was dangerous for them. If his plane should suddenly give out, as it was ready to do, he could not help sliding into one of them, perhaps both of them, and they would go down. He glanced at the altimeter; it registered four hundred feet. At that altitude nobody would have a chance. He knew they were aware of the danger. They were closing in to prove their faith in his skill and his courage. But who had given them permission? He motioned them away. Neither paid any attention; they did not even bother to look at his signal. Their eyes were fixed on the diminishing space between his plane and their own. Already they were so close that he could have stepped from one wing tip to another. He wondered if they meant to lift him up and carry him to the field.

The SBD had begun to lose altitude, even though he already had the throttle pressed to the end of the slot. He signaled to his friends that he was going to split the landing flaps. They floated backward a few inches to give him room. Then he saw the water tower rising above the trees and quickly signaled that he was altering course. They had anticipated this. All three SBDs banked slightly to the left, flashing in the sunlight, and roared over the pine trees.

Before long the field was in view. From the tetrahedron and the tower lights Martin knew that he would be going in downwind, but there was nothing he could do about that. He had no time to make the circular Navy approach to the upwind runway; he might not be able to reach the field at all. The tower was calling. He could hear the message although the headset was in his lap. The tower was advising him that one of the wheels had failed to descend. He was ordered to gain altitude, cross over the field at a minimum of one thousand feet and attempt to shake the wheel out of the fuselage. But the news that only one wheel was down came as a shock, because it meant that a crash landing was inevitable. Until then he had assumed that in some way, somehow, in spite of everything, he could manage a safe landing; not necessarily a good one, but one that he would walk away from.

Briefly he considered the fantastic command. He had been flying at full throttle for several minutes and had not been able to maintain altitude, but the Navy had just ordered him to climb safely above the field and start performing acrobatics. He was going down and the Navy was insisting that he go up. With a bellow of rage he snatched the microphone and tried to throw it out of the cockpit, but he had forgotten to disconnect it. He grabbed the cords, jerked them loose, and threw everything out—the microphone, cords, and headset.

Now his friends were leaving. There was nothing more they could do. He watched, a little sadly, as they drifted higher and higher above him. Or so it seemed, although he knew this was an illusion. They were not climbing any higher; it was just that he was sinking into the trees.

Presently he was alone. Sick with apprehension he watched the air speed diminish. The SBD was not far from the stalling point. At any moment it would go. He knew exactly how it would feel: the mushy, passive settling, and a wing dipping, and the bulky little bomber rolling belly-up like a dead fish. Then he would be in the trees, the metal wings grinding and breaking off while the fuselage plunged ahead with the mindless determination of machinery. There would be an explosion when it struck the ground, and he would be somewhere inside the explosion, perhaps alive enough to be aware of it.

He watched the crash trucks leave the parking area and drive in a leisurely way out on the taxi strip. Then someone must have radioed further information about the approaching SBD because both trucks stopped and turned around, stopped again, one of them backed up, and finally both trucks drove across the grass and onto the edge of the landing mat. They looked out of place there, oddly shaped, painted red and white. The drivers were uncertain about where to go. Martin could see the drivers as he came flying through the treetops, and he could not understand why the drivers failed to see him. But it was obvious they didn't; they had stopped again and backed away, off the pavement, and apparently were going to park in the grass and wait for additional orders.

THEN THEY saw him. They lurched forward, throwing mud and clods of turf from the wheels, and swerved onto the mat. The smaller truck almost tipped over, but righted itself and came speeding toward him with a horrible flashing of light. Martin could see the hulking form of a firefighter in an asbestos suit clinging to the side of the big truck. The white asbestos suit with its square hood, and the window in front, made the man look like a robot. And whatever or whoever he was, he was carrying something tucked under one arm.

Martin knew that the time had come. He had not yet reached the clearing, and he had hoped so fervently that he might reach it, because it was so very near, but he could feel the power diminishing. A dark green rain of oil was streaming from the cowl, spattering the glass until he could hardly see through it. Now the wings of the SBD had begun to shudder. He eased the stick backward an inch and firmly held it there. When he felt the plane start to roll he cut the switches and flung his arms up to protect his face.

Like a boat on a choppy sea the SBD broke through the branches, bounced crookedly into the swamp grass and weeds that surrounded the landing mat, and then went slewing across the concrete with a brilliant shower of orange sparks. Even before it had come to rest there was fire growing over the fuselage. Flames danced excitedly around the cockpit where a pine branch was blazing and where the pilot sat without moving. Sluggish green smoke boiled out of the engine. A wing of the dive bomber had broken off—only a stub of it protruded from the fuselage. The wing had turned over several times and was lying upside down on the scorched pavement behind the wreck, showing a large white star and the word NAVY.

The crash trucks sped across the mat and stopped at the windward side of the wreckage where the heat was less intense. The man in the asbestos suit lumbered slowly into the flames, crushing pine cones and the glowing skeletons of branches.

On top of the squadron tower a glassy red beacon revolved. The field was closed.

1954

A CROSS
TO BEAR

"**N**AVY CROSS?"

The lieutenant looked up and flushed. He closed the little box and put it back in his pocket. "Yeah."

I took a good look at the row of campaign bars under his wings, but the blue and white of the Navy Cross was not there.

"Why don't you wear it?" I asked.

He didn't say anything, just fiddled with his drink and stared at the table. The bar was crowded and since I didn't know anybody I sat down and offered him a cigarette.

"Look," I said, "I don't mean to be nosey, but it seems funny you don't wear it. I know a million guys who'd give their eye teeth to own one of those."

"You do, huh?" He smiled a little, but it wasn't funny. It sent kind of a chill down my back. "I'll tell you something."

He told me a yarn then, without emotion, almost in a monotone. He didn't seem to care whether I believed it or not.

Back in the late summer and fall of '44 the Navy had a lot of fighter bases scattered around the Marshall Islands. Besides their regular fighter duties, the planes served as escorts when P-Boats went fishing for water-logged pilots in Jap lagoons.

Occasionally a destroyer or a flock of Japs would try to jump *Old Dumbo*, the Catalina rescue plane, after he'd landed, but usually nothing happened and the fighters would just circle around until the job was completed and then go home. They had another job, too. Unofficially they were used as training squadrons for the boot ensigns fresh from Pearl and the States.

Well, along about the first of September a replacement showed up—a scrawny weak-chinned kid with a timid look and watery blue eyes. You expect a Navy fighter pilot to be a rugged character, so when this sickly boot showed up, the squadron's old hands didn't have much to say. Funny thing about this kid, he never wrote any letters and he never got any. He never got any letters at all. The boys in the squadron made him welcome, of course—except one jaygee by the name of Riley. Riley was a big red-headed loud-mouthed Irishman who had a string of ribbons and wasn't afraid to show them. He'd done a tour on the old *Yorktown* and was slated to hit the States before long. He took a fast dislike to this kid, and when he found out they'd be in the same flight he flipped his lid. "I've flown with a lot of Dilberts in my time," he yapped, "but, by God, they were *men!*"

He kept sounding off like that, and it wasn't hard to see the kid was hurt. He admired that jaygee so much, too. Tried to copy him all the time—the way he yanked his wheels up on take-off, the way he talked over the radio. It was downright pathetic. Some of the boys tried to quiet Riley down, but he wouldn't quit, kept hinting that the kid—his name was Mulhern—was yellow. And so it wasn't long until a story started going around that the kid had jumped out of a burning dive bomber back in the States and left his gunner in the turret. It was like kicking a puppy who followed you around. Maybe it was because the kid admired him so much that Riley talked the way he did.

Things went on like that for quite a while, and then one morning the exec grabbed Riley and the kid and another ensign and said that *Dumbo* was on his way to Ponape lagoon. An F6 pilot had been knocked down there and ASR wanted some fighter cover during the rescue. They took off right away, the exec leading and the kid on his wing. Riley led the other ensign.

They didn't come back for a long time, and when they did there were only three planes. The exec landed and the other ensign followed him in. A third plane powered it in a few minutes later with part of his left aileron shot away. That was Riley. The three of them walked into the shack and dumped their gear and then the exec went up to talk with the skipper.

The ensign didn't have much to say, but as usual Riley began to sound off. "The kid won't be back—pulled out of formation when a flight of Zekes jumped us. I told you that stinking little boot was yellow. I didn't see where he went, but when the Zekes cleared out there was just us three and a Jap DD in the lagoon right near *Dumbo*." Riley paused and scratched his head. "*Dumbo* must have laid an egg in that DD's magazine because she was sure burning. Anyway we circled her for a few minutes and then she blew up and went down. But that little yellow—"

The exec walked in then and ordered some coffee. He didn't say anything, just stared at his cup and listened to Riley shooting off his mouth. Finally he said, "Pipe down, Mr. Riley."

Well, the exec was a lieut.-commander and Riley was a jaygee. The shack was dead quiet for two, maybe three minutes. The exec finished his coffee and turned around.

"It was a nice trap—a Jap DD in a cove and Jap fighters behind a cloudbank, just waiting for somebody to come out to pick up that F6 pilot."

Somebody scratched a match on his shoe and it sounded loud. Nobody said anything. The exec looked at a twisted nail lying on the floor and went on softly, "Ensign Mulhern didn't come back today."

"That boot was yellow! He pulled out and left you sitting there like a clay pigeon!"

"Shut up, Riley!" The exec's voice cracked through the shack. Then he got hold of himself. "That DD you saw burn and sink—it pulled out of a cove when *Dumbo* was sitting on the lagoon taking that F6 pilot aboard. Mulhern pulled out of formation and *crash-dived* it before it could sink *Dumbo*."

The exec dropped his cigarette on the floor and stepped on it.

"I've recommended him for the Navy Cross."

The lieutenant took another drink and traced a little design on his glass. "I guess that's about all there is to it."

"Well," I said, "that's a hell of a story. But what's the pitch? What's that got to do with you not wearing your Navy Cross?"

"Look," he said, and his tone was bitter, "you're wearing a ruptured duck, you were in the service. Do you remember those little forms we all had to fill out that began something like this: In case of death I leave—?"

"Sure."

"Well, this Mulhern kid left everything to me."

"Oh!" I said, and it must have sounded stupid. I looked at him again. The second stripe on his sleeve was shiny gold, the way lieutenants' stripes always look just after they've been promoted from jaygee.

1946

THE MARINE

IN THE OFFICERS' QUARTERS of the naval hospital at Bremerton, Washington, two men lay on adjoining beds. One was a Marine captain who had been wounded in the fighting at Guadalcanal and the other was a Navy pilot with catarrhal fever who had not yet left the United States. The pilot had expected to start for his assignment in the South Pacific on the following day, but now he was delayed by the fever and was asking the marine what it was like on the front lines.

The captain, whose legs had been amputated, did not feel like talking but had answered a number of questions out of courtesy, and now was resting with his eyes shut. He had said to the pilot that many of the men under his command were very young and that many of them were volunteers, and that for the most part they were excellent shots. Some of them, the captain said, were the finest marksmen he had ever seen, although he had put in almost twenty years as a marine and had seen more good shooting than he could begin to remember. Many of these boys had come from small towns or from farm country and had grown up with a rifle in their hand, which was the reason they were so deadly. They had been picking Jap snipers out of trees as though they were squirrels. Often the Japs tied themselves to the trunk of a palm or into the crotch where the coconuts grew, so that if they were hit they would not fall, and when they were hit sometimes it seemed as if there was an explosion among the palm fronds as the man thrashed about. Other times an arm might be seen suddenly dangling alongside the trunk while the man's weapon dropped forty feet to the ground. Or nothing at all would happen, except that no more shots came from the tree. The captain had narrated these things with no particular interest, in a courteous and tired voice.

The pilot understood that he had been too inquisitive and he had decided not to ask any more questions. He lay with his arms folded on his chest and stared out the window at the pine trees on the hill. It had been raining since dawn but occasional great columns of light thousands of feet in height burst diagonally through the clouds and illuminated the pines or some of the battleships anchored in Puget Sound. The pilot was watching this and thinking about Guadalcanal, which he might see very soon. He felt embarrassed because the captain had talked so much and he felt to blame for this. He was embarrassed, too, about the fact that he himself would recover while the captain was permanently maimed, but there was nothing he could say about that without making it worse.

Presently the captain went on in the same tired and polite voice.

Lieutenant, he said without opening his eyes, I can tell you everything you need to know about what the war is like on Guadalcanal, although I don't know about the other islands because I was only on Guadalcanal. Listen. In my company there was a boy from southern Indiana who was the best shot I believe I ever saw. I couldn't say how many Japs he killed, but he thought he knew because he would watch where they fell and keep track of them. My guess is that he accounted for at least twenty. There were times when he would get into arguments over a body we could see lying not very far away from us in the jungle. He was jealous about them. One night I observed him crawl beyond his post, which was the perimeter of our defense, and go some distance into the jungle. The night was not very dark and I observed him crawling from one body to another. I thought he was going through their wallets and pulling the rings off their fingers. The men often did that although they were not supposed to. However I was puzzled by what this boy was doing because he made a strange motion over several of the Jap bodies. He appeared to be doing some sort of difficult work, and when he crawled back into the camp I went over to him and lay down next to him and asked what he had been doing. He told me he had been collecting gold teeth. He carried a tobacco pouch in his pocket, which he showed me. It was half-filled with gold and he told me how much gold was selling for by the ounce in the United States. He said that if he lived long enough and got onto enough islands he expected that he would be a rich man by the time the war ended. It was not uncommon to collect teeth and I had suspected he might be doing that also, but I told him I had been watching and was puzzled by the strange movements he had made over several of the bodies. He explained that he had been cutting off their heads and what I had observed was him cutting the spinal cord and the neck muscles with his knife. I asked why he had done this, if it was just for the sake of cruelty, although the men were dead, and he seemed very much surprised by this and looked at me carefully to see why I wanted to know. "They're mine, sir," he said to me. He thought that the bodies of the men he killed belonged to him. Then he said that he did not sever a head unless the man had died face down. I didn't understand what this meant. I thought perhaps it served some purpose that I knew nothing about, relating possibly to the way animals were butchered, but his explanation was so simple and so sensible that I felt foolish not to have thought of it. He reminded me that the jungle was full of snipers and that he did not want to expose himself more than necessary. In order to get at the mouths of the men who had died face down it would have been necessary to turn them over, and he did not want to risk this. A dead man is heavy and it takes a lot of work to turn him over if you yourself are lying flat, so he had severed these heads which, by themselves, could be turned over easily. You wished to know what the war is like on Guadalcanal, Lieutenant, although as I say, it may be different on other islands.

The captain had not opened his eyes while he was talking, and having said this much he cleared his throat, moved around slightly on his bed and then lay still. The pilot decided that the captain wanted to sleep, so he too lay still on his painted iron bed and listened to the rain and gazed at the fleet anchored in the sound.

There's one other thing, the captain continued. I had not known how old the boy was, except that he was very young. I thought he might be eighteen or nineteen, or twenty at the most. It's hard to tell with some of them. They look older or younger than they are. I've seen a man of twenty-six who looked no more than eighteen. At any rate this boy soon afterward was discharged from the service because he had run away from home in order to enlist and managed to get all the way to Guadalcanal before his mother, who had been trying to locate him, discovered what had happened. He was fourteen when he was sworn in and apparently he celebrated his fifteenth birthday on the island with us, telling his buddies it was his nineteenth. But finally, as I say, it caught up with him and he was sent home. His mother, I was told, was very anxious for her son to finish high school. Perhaps he's there now.

I believe what I'm going to remember longest, the captain added in a mild voice, is the moment he stared at me while we were lying side by side. We were closer than you and I. He was young enough to be my own boy, which is a thought that occurred to me at the time, although it seems irrelevant now. Be that as it may, when I looked into his eyes I couldn't see a spark of humanity. I've often thought about this without deciding what it means or where it could lead us, but you'll be shipping out presently, as soon as your fever subsides, and will experience the war yourself. Maybe you'll come to some conclusion that has escaped me.

The captain said nothing more and when the nurse came around a few minutes later, after looking at him, she held one finger to her lips because he had gone to sleep.

1966

THE YELLOW RAFT

FROM THE DIRECTION of the Solomon Islands came a damaged Navy fighter, high in the air, but gliding steadily down upon the ocean. The broad paddle blades of the propeller revolved uselessly with a dull whirring noise, turned only by the wind. Far below, quite small but growing larger, raced the shadow of the descending fighter. Presently they were very close together, the aircraft and its shadow, but each time they seemed about to merge they broke apart—the long fuselage tilting backward, lifting the engine for one more instant, while the shadow, like some distraught creature, leaped hastily through the white-caps. Finally the engine plunged into a wave. The fuselage stood almost erect—a strange blue buoy stitched with gunfire—but then, tilting forward and bubbling, it disappeared into the greasy ocean. Moments later, as if propelled by a spring, a small yellow raft hurtled to the surface where it tossed back and forth, the walls lapped with oil. Suddenly, as though pursuing it from below, a bloody hand reached out of the water. Then for a while the raft floated over the deep rolling waves and the man held on. At last he drew himself into the raft where he sprawled on the bottom, coughing and weeping, turning his head occasionally to look at the blood on his arm. A few minutes later he sat up, cross-legged, balancing himself against the motion of the sea, and squinted toward the southern horizon because it was in that direction he had been flying and from that direction help would come. After watching the horizon for a long time he pulled off his helmet and appeared to be considering it while he idly twisted the radio cord. Then he lay down and tried to make himself comfortable. But in a little while he was up. He examined his wound, nodded, and with a cheerful expression he began to open a series of pouches attached to the inner walls of his raft: he found dehydrated rations, a few small luxuries, first-aid equipment, and signal flares. When the sun went down he had just finished eating a tablet of candy. He smacked his lips, lit a cigarette, and defiantly blew several smoke rings; but the wind was beginning to rise and before long he quit pretending. He zipped up his green canvas coveralls to the neck, tightened the straps and drawstrings of his life jacket, and braced his feet against the tubular yellow walls. He felt sick at his stomach and his wound was bleeding again. Several hours passed quietly except for the indolent rhythmic slosh of water and the squeak of rubber as the raft bent over the crest of a wave. Stars emerged, surrounding the raft, and spume broke lightly, persistently, against the man huddled with his back to the wind. All at once a rocket whistled up, illuminating the watery scene. No sooner had its light begun to fade than another rocket exploded high above; then a third, and a fourth. But darkness prevailed: overhead wheeled the Southern Cross, Hydra, Libra, and Corvus. Before dawn the pilot was on his hands and knees, whispering and stubbornly wagging his head while he waited to meet the second day. And as he peered at the horizon it seemed to him that he could see a marine reptile the size of a whale, with a long undulating swanlike neck, swimming toward him. He watched the creature sink into the depths and felt it glide swiftly under the raft. Then the world around him seemed to expand and the fiery tentacles of the sun touched his face as he waited, drenched with spray, to challenge the next wave. The raft trembled, dipped, and with a sickening, twisting slide, sank into a trough where the ocean and the ragged scud nearly closed over it. A flashlight rolled to one side, hesitated, and came rolling back while a pool of water gathered first at the pilot's feet, then at his head, sometimes submerging the flashlight. The walls of the raft were slippery, and the pouches from which he had taken the cigarettes and the food and the rockets were now filled with water. The drawstrings of his life jacket slapped wildly back and forth. He had put on his helmet and a pair of thin leather gloves to protect himself from the stinging spray. Steep foaming waves swept abruptly against the raft and the horizon dissolved into lowering clouds. By noon he was drifting through a steady rain with his eyes closed. Each time the raft sank into a trough the nebulous light vanished; then with a splash and a squeak of taut rubber it spun up the next slope, met the onrushing crest, whirled down again into darkness. Early that afternoon a murky chocolate streak separated the sea from the sky. Then the waves imperceptibly slickened, becoming enameled and black with a deep viridian hue like volcanic glass, their solid green phosphorescent surfaces curved and scratched as though scoured by a prehistoric wind; and the pilot waited, motionless, while each massive wave dove under the bounding yellow raft. When the storm ended it was night again. Slowly the constellations reappeared.

At dawn, from the south, came a Catalina flying boat, a plump and graceless creation known as the PBY—phlegmatic in the air, more at home resting its deep snowy breast in the water. It approached, high and slow, and almost flew beyond the raft. But then one tremendous pale blue wing of the PBY inclined toward a yellow dot on the ocean and in a dignified spiral the flying boat descended, keeping the raft precisely within its orbit until, just above the water, it skimmed by the raft. Except for the flashlight rolling back and forth and glittering in the sunshine the yellow raft was empty. The PBY climbed several hundred feet, turned, and crossed over the raft. Then it climbed somewhat higher and began circling. All morning the Catalina circled, holding its breast high like a great blue heron in flight, the gun barrels, propellers, and plexiglass blisters reflecting the tropical sun. For a while at the beginning of the search it flew tightly around the raft, low enough to touch the water almost at once, but later it climbed to an altitude from which the raft looked like a toy on a pond. There was nothing else in sight. The only shadow on the sea was that of the Navy flying boat moving in slow, monotonous circles around and around the deserted raft. At one time the PBY angled upward nearly a mile, its twin engines buzzing like flies in a vacant room, but after about fifteen minutes it came spiraling down, without haste, the inner wing always pointing at the raft. On the tranquil sunny ocean no debris was floating, nothing to mark the place where the fighter sank—only the raft, smeared with oil and flecked with salt foam. Early in the afternoon a blister near the tail of the Catalina slid open and a cluster of beer cans dropped in a leisurely arc toward the sea where they splashed like miniature bombs and began filling with water. Beyond them a few sandwich wrappers came fluttering down. Otherwise nothing disturbed the surface of the ocean; nothing changed all afternoon except that a veil gathered softly across the sky, filtering the light of the sun, darkening the metallic gleam of the Coral Sea. At five o'clock the PBY banked steeply toward the raft. Then it straightened up and for the first time in several hours the insignia on its prow—a belligerent little duck with a bomb and a pair of binoculars—rode vertically over the waves. The prow of the Catalina dipped when it approached the raft and the pitch of the engines began to rise. The flying boat descended with ponderous dignity, like a dowager stooping to retrieve a lost glove. With a hoarse scream it passed just above the raft. A moment later, inside the blue-black hull, a machine gun rattled and the raft started bouncing on the water. When the gunfire stopped the strange dance ended; the yellow raft fell back, torn into fragments of cork and deflated rubber that stained the ocean with an iridescent dye as green as a rainbow. Then the Catalina began to climb. Higher and higher, never again changing course, it flew toward the infinite horizon.

1954

LEON & BÉBERT
ALOFT

"THIS IS madness," Bébert said, "pure unadulterated madness."

Leon was not listening. He had begun to fasten his seat belt when suddenly he leaned forward with an expression of deep interest.

"What are you looking at?" Bébert asked. "Is anything wrong?"

Leon was staring out the window. "Press that button just above you!" he ordered. "Never mind, I'll do it," he added quickly and after pressing the button he turned around to wait for the stewardess.

"I wish you'd tell me what's happening, "Bébert said plaintively.

Leon was beckoning the stewardess to hurry. As soon as she was close enough he seized her by the hand and pulled her down so that she could see out the window. There at the end of its little chain the cap to the gas tank was jiggling and bouncing merrily up and down on the wing.

The stewardess after one look hurried forward to the pilot's compartment. A few moments later the engines stopped.

"Well!" Bébert said after the gas cap had been screwed in place and the engines started up again. "Well, Leon, I must admit I'm glad you're here. There's no telling what might have happened."

"Probably nothing," Leon said. "We wouldn't have lost much gas."

"But it could have been dangerous, don't you think?"

"I prefer having everything in place," Leon remarked. He pushed back the curtain and squinted at the sky. "If we don't run into a lot of holiday traffic we ought to be on schedule. The weather looks okay. A few clouds."

"I still insist this idea is insane. Who ever heard of flying all the way to New York just to attend the opera? Anybody would think we belonged to the jet set."

"We were in a rut," Leon said. "Hanging around the same places, seeing the same crowd. You admitted yourself it would be a change. Anyhow, I've got some of Callas' records but I've never seen her and this seemed like a good chance."

"The last opera I attended was *The Flying Dutchman*!" said Bébert, laughing. "Don't you think that's funny?"

But Leon was once again sitting forward with a serious expression. Bébert gazed at him in alarm. The plane was trundling toward the end of the runway, wallowing slightly in the wind. Leon looked back at the control tower.

"What is it?" Bébert asked. "What now?"

"Some pretty heavy gusts out here. I couldn't feel them when we started. Shielded by the terminal, I guess."

"Is it too windy to fly? Do you think we ought to tell the pilot?"

Leon settled back into his seat. "I very much doubt whether the pilot would take kindly to any more suggestions."

"But if you think there's too much wind . . . "

"There isn't. Besides, I'm not flying it. He knows his business. I was just surprised at how heavy the gusts are."

"I wish we weren't going. I'm sorry I let you talk me into this. I have an awful premonition."

"There's nothing to worry about," Leon said, tightening his safety belt. "Here we go. Hang on."

As the plane began climbing Bébert said, "To tell the truth, I didn't think we were ever going to get off!"

"We took a hell of a long run," Leon said uneasily. "It feels like he's got a load of cement on board. And that number-three engine I don't care for. I think it's missing."

"Missing?"

"One of the cylinders may be dead."

"Is that serious?"

"Oh," Leon answered without much conviction, "I doubt it. Probably everything's all right."

"We're on a jinxed flight," Bébert said. "And please don't tell me to stop worrying because I just worry all the more. It may not bother you, because you know about airplanes, but every time I get off the ground I get terribly concerned."

"We'll be there before you know it!" Leon said with an attempt at heartiness.

"I most certainly hope so."

"Theoretically we should be able to maintain altitude even if that number-three engine does conk out. Unless they've got us overloaded."

"You used to pilot one of these. Isn't that what you told me?"

"No, I was in dive bombers. And that was a long time ago. Flying has changed a great deal since my day."

"I don't ordinarily smoke," Bébert said, "but if you don't mind, I'd like to borrow a cigarette."

At that moment the No Smoking sign flashed on again, then the sign ordering them to fasten their safety belts.

"What in the world is this about?" Bébert asked. "He just turned those lights off. Is anything the matter? I'm beginning to get nervous."

Leon shrugged. "Maybe some turbulence ahead. He'll probably come on the radio to explain."

They waited, gazing at the signs, but the captain's voice was not heard. After several minutes the lights again blinked out.

"I hate riding back here," Leon said. "I like to know what's going on. I wish they'd let me sit up front and look over his shoulder."

"You surprise me. I thought you'd be perfectly relaxed, but here you are practically as jumpy as I am."

"Feeling helpless bugs me. I'd be all right if I could sit near the controls. I get almost this identical sensation riding in the back of a car on the freeway."

"I have practically the opposite attitude," said Bébert. "I prefer to leave my fate in somebody else's hands. I'm not a good driver. You know how erratic I am. Consequently I much prefer being the passenger. Provided, of course, that I have confidence in whoever's driving."

"I trust nobody," Leon said. "Nobody except myself."

"Maybe that's a result of the narrow escapes you had during the war."

Leon smiled.

"Perhaps that does sound funny," Bébert admitted. "But I'm sure that anybody who was a pilot, especially during the war, must have had some narrow squeaks. You can't tell me you didn't."

"There were times, there were times. But they're long gone. I hardly remember anymore. I'm not even certain I could still handle a plane. If I had to I guess I could."

"Is there much chance you'll be recalled for service as a result of the Vietnam thing?"

Leon shook his head. "It's simpler to train some kid than try to untrain and then retrain somebody like me. The whole system is different now. I imagine even the ground troops get a different sort of training. And as far as the air force is concerned, it's totally different. Anyway, if they did call me I wouldn't go."

"I don't understand."

"It's very simple. I'd refuse."

"When our government calls, one doesn't refuse."

"They can try me if they want to."

Bébert looked at him doubtfully. "You must be joking."

"I'm not having any more," Leon said. "I got through it once and I'm not having any more. They can blow all the bugles they want to. I won't be there. I'm not one of Napoleon's boys."

"I admire you for taking such a stand."

"Admire, hell," Leon said irritably. "This is simply how I feel. Certain wars are put together by a few old men."

"I realize you're not apt to be called, but in case they did and you refused, don't you think you could be threatened with prison?"

"It would be more than a threat. However, the food's probably no worse."

"Don't pretend you're not joking."

"Yes and no," said Leon.

"You sound practically treasonous."

"As I told you, I've had it. Right up to the neck, and I'm not having any more. I don't care what anybody thinks, I don't care what anybody does to me. I don't care if I'm called a traitor, because I know I'm not. What we're doing is foul. It's very rotten. No statistics could convince me otherwise, so don't quote me statistics, I know better. I never expected to reach this state of mind, Bébert, but I'm outraged and ashamed and disgusted and shocked and sickened and embarrassed, to say the least. I'm so ashamed when I open the morning paper that I can hardly eat breakfast, it's that nauseating. Besides, every bigot, hoodlum, fascist and professional criminal in the country is in favor of it, which is reason enough to be skeptical."

"Leon," Bébert whispered, "I think the man across the aisle is listening."

"So?"

"He seems interested," Bébert continued in a low voice. "It occurred to me that he might be with the CIA."

"I shouldn't say such things, is that what you mean?"

Bébert looked uncomfortable and scratched the tip of his nose.

"What you actually mean is," Leon continued, "it's all right to flood somebody's land and poison the crops and prostitute ten-year-old children and burn their parents with napalm, and maybe finally let go with another atomic bomb. It's perfectly all right to scatter death and destruction like we were the original Four Horsemen of the Apocalypse—that's all right, only it's not good manners to mention the fact. Is that what you mean?"

"You sound as though it was my fault."

"No," Leon said, "it isn't your fault. I apologize. We just got betrayed, that's all, and I'm so bugged I don't know which end is up."

"I understand," said Bébert. "You haven't offended me. Everybody's upset these days. Incidentally, speaking of the CIA, do you remember my cousin? He visited me last summer. You might have met him, in fact I'm sure you did. Ellsworth Kupperman?"

"Vaguely," said Leon.

"This might interest you. Ellsworth told me that a friend of his in Bridgeport once worked temporarily for the CIA. He was hired to drive a sports car from Bridgeport to Miami Beach. Then he flew back to Bridgeport and was paid a thousand dollars. Isn't that fantastic? But that's only half the story. This car had white leather seats and white sidewall tires and he had to dye his hair platinum blond and carry a tennis racket conspicuously strapped to his suitcase. Furthermore, he never did know what was in the trunk of the car because it was locked when he picked up the car and he had been ordered not to try to open the trunk. There must have been something terribly important inside."

"Allen Dulles," Leon suggested. "Or maybe just some old worn-out spy. Or the suicide kit from one of our U-2s. Let's see, what else?"

"I'm serious," Bébert went on. "Ellsworth told me everything his friend had told him about it. The CIA wasn't joking. They followed him around Bridgeport for almost a week before they finally gave him his orders. This friend told Ellsworth he knew he was being shadowed because there were these two men in a peanut butter truck."

Leon turned his head to look at Bébert but did not say anything.

"Well, I'm sorry," Bébert said, "but it's the truth. There were these two men in a peanut butter delivery truck and they were CIA agents. They had on brown uniforms with the name of the peanut butter on the breast pocket. Ellsworth's friend said no matter where he went he noticed this truck. It was eerie. Then one day he had to walk past this truck and suddenly he was handed a large sealed envelope."

"Bearing the coat-of-arms of the peanut butter king."

"I'm not making this up."

"All right. Did Ellsworth's friend say specifically what the orders were?"

"No. But apparently they instructed him to drive to a certain garage in Miami Beach, so he did. He had a very dull trip, according to Ellsworth."

"No Soviet agent in a black limousine trying to run him off the turnpike?"

"Not as far as I know. He got to this garage and handed over the keys to some attendant and that's all there was to it. Then, of course, he had to rinse the dye out of his hair."

"I've changed my mind," Leon said. "There wasn't anything in the trunk of the car. The message was rolled up in the handle of the tennis racket."

"I think your sense of humor is inappropriate. I admit it does sound strange but the fact is, we have no way of knowing.

"A thousand bucks. A cool thousand bucks!" Leon said thoughtfully. "I wonder how he got that job. Hell, I wouldn't mind driving to Miami Beach."

"Nobody knows how he got the job. He didn't know, himself. But they wouldn't hire you if you were the last person on earth."

"Maybe. Maybe not. Just think, Bébert, our taxes go for things like two grown men riding around in a peanut butter truck. Stop and consider that for a while."

"I suppose they know what they're doing."

"I don't believe it. I used to, but no longer. I don't believe the government has a clear idea of what it's doing."

"That's exactly what you said when Ike was president. Only then you blamed it all on the Republicans."

"This is different. This is really serious. This hasn't got anything to do with being a Republican or a Democrat. This is the most serious thing that ever was."

"I agree. My only claim is that our government does know what it's doing. I do believe that's true."

Just then Leon sat erect and appeared to be listening; Bébert gazed at him.

"The gas cap isn't loose again, is it?"

"Something's the matter with that inboard engine. Hear him fiddling around? Don't you hear? Listen!"

"Engines all sound alike to me," Bébert answered with a look of despair.

Leon gradually began to relax, finally took a deep breath and then reached into his pocket for another cigarette.

"We're not going to get down alive," Bébert said. "I can feel it in my bones."

"That's an interesting figure of speech," Leon said with the cigarette between his teeth. "You may or may not be aware of this, but seamen sometimes develop a sort of feeling in their bones about ships. They can tell whether a ship is living or dead. I remember hearing about a chief petty officer in command of a launch who was supposed to inspect a cruiser that had been torpedoed and abandoned but hadn't sunk. As soon as his foot touched the deck he ordered everybody off and ordered the launch to back away, and about a minute later the cruiser heeled over and went down like a rock. The chief couldn't explain how he knew she was ready to go, but he did know."

"You're worried," said Bébert, "don't pretend you're not."

Leon yawned and stretched. "Sitting back here makes me nervous. The plane's probably all right. Probably what it needs is a good overhaul. It does have sort of a dead feeling, though. I noticed it during the takeoff."

"How much longer do you think we'll be?"

"Not much. Half an hour or so."

"I wish we'd gotten to the airport early enough for a drink."

"I agree," Leon said. "I feel like an old dried-out sponge."

A few minutes later Bébert said, "You know, you've turned into quite the heretic over the past couple of years. Do you realize it?"

Leon nodded. "Only it goes back further than the past couple of years. It started with our U-2 incident. I've forgotten which year that took place but what happened is still absolutely clear in my mind. That was the first time I ever realized our government would lie. It was a big shock."

"I confess I'm hazy about the details," Bébert said, "it seems such a while ago. I do remember there was a great deal of confusion. My opinion's always been that the government merely became confused. It's so gigantic."

"Stop sounding charitable."

"I'm not being in the least charitable, Leon. I hesitate to believe the government would deliberately lie. Consciously, at any rate, unless there was extreme provocation."

"Well, it did, whether you hesitate to believe or not. Some famous French philosopher said: 'One must be truthful in all things, even when they concern one's country.' And our government lied. It knew exactly what had occurred when that spy was shot down twelve hundred miles inside Russia, yet it attempted to lie its way out. With incredible stupidity, I might add. A weather plane accidentally blown off course! Any Mongolian idiot could tell a more convincing lie."

"That's usually the way with governments."

"Maybe. But the thing is, Bébert, until that moment I believed. I was one of the faithful. See no evil, hear no evil, speak no evil. But now I can't believe any longer. I've lost faith."

"Because of that one incident?"

"That was only the beginning. After the U-2 business I began questioning things instead of automatically accepting them and I began to realize we're told whatever part of the truth the government wants us to know. They hide what's left. They simply bury it. Then by the time somebody gathers enough evidence so that the remains have to be exhumed, why, what good does it do? It's a fait accompli! — that's what it is."

"I must admit I've never seen you so impassioned."

"Well," said Leon, "if this isn't the time to be impassioned there never was one. A grim hour's near if you've been led by a Cyclops."

"I predict your pessimism will be temporary. I know I personally have been disenchanted with Washington more than once."

Leon shook his head. "There's something irreversible about acquiring knowledge. I've lost too much faith in the integrity and decency of our government ever to get it back."

"You sound absolutely subversive. You do! If I hadn't known you for so many years I'd swear you were a Communist."

"I guess I'm disappointed, which is why I'm angry. When you've trusted anything or anybody for a long long time but then suddenly learn he's a liar, that's how I feel. It makes me sick at my stomach. You hope for so much from your country and then the enormity of its wrongs—the enormity, Bébert, when you know in your heart! As I say, it makes me sick. I'm so enraged at certain times that I'd like to go to the wharf while a military transport is unloading and direct the coffins to the White House."

Bébert turned his head and whispered: "Please! That man across the aisle is listening."

"Good for him," said Leon sullenly. "I hope he learns something."

"I mean, really," Bébert whispered. "I was teasing before, but, Leon, he is! He's jotting down little notes."

"Maybe he's a poet."

"Poets go by bus."

"Well, suppose he is one of those turtlebrain reactionaries, we're both entitled to an opinion."

"Of course, but you ought to be careful about what you say in public."

"I've signed petitions and written senators and contributed my two cents to every organization I know of opposing this imbecilic war and if the FBI or the CCC is interested in making a dossier on me they've already got it started. I couldn't care less who jots down notes."

"All right, but don't count on much assistance from me if you get called before the House UnAmerican Activities Committee."

"I'll eat 'em alive," said Leon, and blew a smoke ring.

"You might not think it's so funny later on," Bébert said ominously. "They're very serious about their work. They don't think anything is funny."

"So much the worse for them."

"So much the worse for you, perhaps."

Leon shrugged.

"Now tell me honestly, can you honestly suppose that protesting does much good?"

"Of course it doesn't," Leon said, looking at him in mild surprise. "Anybody with the least common sense knows it doesn't. The government isn't aware of my existence—except for income taxes—anymore than a tornado is aware I exist. It'll swirl right over me no matter what I believe or do. I write to senators, for instance, but they never see the letters. Some secretary slits the envelope and if there's no campaign check enclosed she drops it in the wastebasket. However, I've done what I could. And in a way it puts me on record, at least in my own mind. I know what I believe and where I stand. Nobody is ever going to say Leon was too chicken to be counted."

Bébert grew thoughtful. "Perhaps it has an effect."

"It has no effect. None whatsoever."

"You can't be sure."

"Look," Leon said, "there must be fifty thousand artistic masterpieces condemning exactly the sort of foul stupidity we're in the middle of, from Picasso's mural back through Goya and God knows how many more. At least fifty thousand, but a lot of good they've done. The artists and the writers go along hippity-hop century after century blasting the philistines, but who runs the world? You know as well as I do. Don't talk romantic nonsense. Listen, you could mail the White House a petition long enough to wrap six times around the equator, but how much effect would it have on our bloody policy? Tell me, how much?"

"Let's not talk about it. I'd rather not discuss the matter," Bébert said. "Aren't we overdue at the airport? It seems as though this flight has taken months. I'm sure we're overdue. I just pray nothing else happens."

"I doubt if anything will since we've gotten this far. I imagine we'll make it all right."

At that moment the plane rolled into a steep turn and a few seconds later began rolling in the opposite direction. Leon pressed his face against the window while Bébert, with a terrified expression, shut his eyes and gripped the arms of his chair.

"We might as well be locked in a boxcar," Leon said. "I wish I knew what this idiot was doing. I wonder if he got in the wrong lane. I wouldn't be surprised. Nothing surprises me anymore."

"I'd just as soon not know," Bébert said weakly.

Leon continued to glare out the window. "How'd he ever get his license? He flies like a turkey. I could do better with a bag over my head. Honest to God, Bébert, the people that get licenses these days! It's hard to believe."

Bébert didn't speak until the plane was level again. Then he said, "Would you mind telling me what those gyrations meant?"

"Who knows?" Leon replied. "Who knows? Who knows what goes on in this world of ours?"

"Well, you sound so oracular at times that one assumes you think you know everything."

"As I've told you before, I get upset when I'm kept in ignorance. I like to know the why and wherefore. If he'd told us the reason he was turning, all right. It's not-knowing that sends me up the wall."

"I'm sure everybody feels the same, but of course, looking at it from the pilot's point of view, that's not always practical. Every decision can't be explained. That's something we have to put up with in this day and age."

"Not me," Leon said.

"You've certainly changed your opinion about our pilot."

"You assume a man is competent until he proves otherwise. After that, if you go on trusting him, you're a fool. About this particular pilot, I'm beginning to have serious doubts."

A few moments later Leon added, "Well, anyway, here we go, we're starting down. Can you feel the difference?"

Bébert looked at him blankly. "I don't feel a thing except that I'm going to be unspeakably relieved when this is over."

"It won't be long. Maybe ten minutes, maybe less. Frankly, I'll be a little relieved myself. How's the FBI doing?"

Bébert glanced across the aisle and then said, "He seems to be dozing but you never can tell. I do think he resembles J. Edgar Hoover."

Leon looked across the aisle but said nothing and soon resumed staring out the window. The plane had begun descending through a layer of clouds that covered the glass with mist and darkened the cabin. Suddenly beneath the wing the earth was visible. Leon breathed heavily.

"I was watching you," Bébert remarked. "You were biting your lip."

"I do that in clouds," Leon admitted.

"It must be time to fasten our safety belts."

"Almost. Not that a seat belt's going to do you any good."

"Then why does the booklet say to be sure it's fastened?"

"Anything to quiet the troops. Do you still believe whatever you read?"

"You're getting to be more and more cynical and embittered."

"Every day," said Leon, "in every way."

"What a shame."

At that moment the signs flashed on above the door to the pilot's compartment. Leon and Bébert buckled their seat belts. Leon tamped out his cigarette.

"Ladies and Gentlemen, this is your captain speaking," said the captain warmly. "We have a slight malfunction up here. Nothing to worry about, however our landing may be a bit bumpier than usual. All due precautions have been taken. Let me assure you once again, the trouble isn't serious."

"Of course not. Of course not," Leon muttered. "It never is."

"Thank you," said the captain. "Please make sure your safety belts are securely fastened. The stewardess will be there to assist you."

"And we hope you have enjoyed your flight," Leon said as soon as the captain finished speaking.

"What do you suppose is wrong?" Bébert asked. "Do you think it's serious?"

"I don't know, it could be the landing gear," Leon said. "Hydraulic system. Flaps. It could be in a number of areas." He pulled out a handkerchief to wipe the window which had been steamed up by his breath.

"Oh oh!" he continued softly. "Now they've closed the field."

"I don't want to know what that means," Bébert said, slumping in his seat with a dazed expression. "I don't want to know. Don't say a word. Not a word."

"It means," Leon said, peering out the window, "that we've got the entire airport to ourselves. Yes sir, all to ourselves! Isn't that nice?"

"I think I'm going to faint," said Bébert.

"Also," Leon said, "it means just about what I was afraid it meant. Yup! There they are, lined up and waiting for us."

"Who?"

"The meat wagons. The whole apparatus. Fire trucks and everybody. This should be quite a picnic."

"Are we going to crash?" Bébert asked.

Leon spread his hands. "That depends. We're helpless, completely helpless. All we can do is sit here."

"I'm losing my mind, I'm so frightened," Bébert said feebly. "Leon, I'm going out of my mind."

"I don't feel much like dancing either," said Leon.

"Isn't there anything you can do?"

"Give me an example."

"Can't you offer the pilot some advice?"

"Such as how to pull the rip cord after he bails out? Something of that sort?"

"How can you joke at a time like this?"

"Have you got a better idea?"

"Leon," Bébert went on in a choking voice, "this may be our last hour on earth!"

"What do you expect me to do about it?" Leon snarled. "I'm not your scoutmaster. Let go of my wrist, your fingers are clammy."

"I'm sorry," Bébert said, "I didn't realize I was holding on to you. How much longer will it be?"

"About a minute," Leon answered crisply. "Why? Are you in a hurry?"

The plane continued to descend.

"Down, down, down," Leon muttered, glaring out the window. "We're so bloody helpless!" he said furiously, and began pounding his knee. "There's not one bloody thing we can do!"

"Please keep your fingers crossed," Bébert whispered with his eyes shut.

1966

OTTO
AND THE MAGI

IN THE PALLID March sun that leavens her patio Helen Chong reads a ladies' magazine. Muhlbach, having greeted her as a neighbor, nothing more, merely commenting on the weather, keeps his eyes averted from the hedge over which he has seen the chaise lounge, the eloquent Oriental figure in Capri pants and a diminutive blue halter which has caused him to think, inexplicably, of twin bluebirds. From somewhere nearby comes an odor of burning leaves, the scent of spring returning, dark loam newly spaded, life resurgent. The sky has not yet cleared, however; winter retreats but slowly, trailing its ghostly haze. The sun obtrudes, strange fruit in the western quadrant, viable, promising an end to these brief, metallic days. And Muhlbach, his winter-long project almost complete, feels himself mystically stirred, restless, absorbed and yet dissatisfied, anxious for whatever is to be. Is it the attenuate hint of spring? — this early season without his wife? Lately the children have not mentioned her; Muhlbach hopes they are forgetting those last months and, when they do think of their mother, recall only what she once was. For himself, there is no forgetting.

Underground once again, he pauses to contemplate his work: the room is functional, which is its purpose, yet not uncomfortable. He reflects that he might spend summer evenings here; it should be cool and quiet. He reaches up, cautiously touches the ceiling. Good. The paint has dried. What remains to be done?—purchase a shade for the lamp, some additional batteries, gravel to spread across the roof. What else? There are a dozen chores, none vital. The retreat is finished. Muhlbach, having draped a rag over a can of paint, hammers the lid shut, gathers the brushes and turpentine, turns off the light, goes out the door and climbs the narrow steps.

Helen Chong is sitting up, legs crossed, petting an English sheep dog that each afternoon comes wandering through the neighborhood. She glances at Muhlbach and winks, as though there were something to wink about. It is a habit which irritates him; a habit she has copied from her husband. It is, indeed, one of the things about the Chongs that he quite actively dislikes.

"I simply love you to death!" she exclaims, and promptly buries her face in the sheep dog's gray fur. Thus, as she leans forward, the sheer cloth flattens across her thigh and Muhlbach during this moment cannot turn away.

"When are you and Bob to go trout fishing?" she calls while her long fingers, supple and jeweled, fondle the body of the dog. "I've heard about this trip for months!" She laughs. Her laughter is not mellifluous; it is slightly coarse.

Muhlbach replies that he has been looking forward to the fishing trip and hopes it can be arranged before much longer. He adds that the weather should be improving. Saying this, he wonders how she can spend hours on the patio dressed as she is. That voice, the gaudy clothing; she might at one time have been a chorus girl. He considers going over to talk with her. After all, they are neighbors. And if Bob Chong should return—well, what difference would that make? The Chongs have lived next door for a year; both he and they often have told one another they must get acquainted.

Across the dividing hedge he remarks, "I've not seen your boy today." To his own ear this sounds commonplace; she must think him insufferably boring.

Helen Chong glances up in mild surprise. "Isn't he with Otto? I was sure Cecil told me . . . "

"Otto has gone hiking with some older boys. He left quite early."

"Oh?" She is not alarmed, squeezing and stroking the animal.

Muhlbach turns away, repelled by this casual affection. The situation, he thinks, is absurd, although no one else is aware of it. He covets his neighbor's wife; it is as simple as that. Every night he imagines himself with her, acting once again the role of a husband. He wonders how long they have been married; they both must be older than they look, because their son is nearly Otto's age. If a perceptive neighbor discerns no hint of domestic friction, does that mean there is none? Bob Chong appears less than passionate, unless baseball and bow ties and intellectual acrostics may be so considered. He is a graduate of UCLA—summa cum laude, Helen has let it be known. Still he is a poseur, for all his fine credentials. The cigarette holder, offhand gestures, habits unexplained. Curious, thinks Muhlbach, that love of baseball. Friday night does he go bowling? Does he belong to a lodge?—this highly paid chemist from the California wastes, who speaks of skin diving and of surfboarding at Santa Monica, who in expensive and sporty attire, laughing, confident, is rumored to be in line for an important government position. And this wife of his, this empress with lips so pale they are almost white, and Asiatic eyes blacker than Chinese ink, with her immense diamond ring and coiled hair. . . .

She has risen from the chaise lounge, is gathering her things, preparing to go inside. She sees him looking over the hedge. She hesitates, but then: "We're having a few people for cocktails a week from tomorrow. Can you make it?"

Angered with himself for staring, embarrassed that she has noticed it, he replies, "Thank you. I believe I don't feel up to such an evening." But how foolish to reject the invitation! God knows he has been too much alone these past months. Solitude enough, and more. To have accepted would please everyone; friends and neighbors would say that finally he was starting to recover. One must begin again, and cocktails next door would be an easy, inauspicious step. But still, it is easier to say no, to vegetate. Five days are fully taken, caring for themselves and so for him; it has been the evenings and the weekends that needed occupation. Possibly it had been a mistake to employ Mrs. Grunthe as mother surrogate; without her, the children would have used his time. But of course she was necessary, martinet that she is, efficient and scrupulously clean. Otto and Donna do not love her, of this Muhlbach feels certain; however, they are afraid of her, and so order is kept in the home. Yet the concomitant of order has been leisure, and soporifics lose their power. How many books has he read since August? How many magazines? How many times has he listened to the Bach Passions?—the phonograph records have been reduced to strident mimicry; even in appearance they are used and exhausted, as though such comfort as they might proffer is wearing through. And now what? Miss Eula Cunningham?—she of the pink and buoyant shape, adequately dusted, fragrant, reminding him of last week's bouquet. Eula. Is she next? This would please the Forsyths, who plucked her from a sunken garden. Past thirty-two, twice divorced, childless, eager—oh, *anxious!*—to try again. Eula. And she *is* an exciting woman, Muhlbach reminds himself. Men do turn to watch her, this is a fact, indeed more than that—something of a joke. The young men and the old, they turn in their tracks; even small boys are impressed.

"Perhaps you'll change your mind."

Muhlbach, startled, glances across the hedge, wondering if his silence has been too deep, his expression too abstract. He does not want to appear eccentric, unbalanced by the loss of his wife. He manages a neutral smile, thanks her for the invitation. Has she said anything else? If so, he failed to hear. Has another silence marked the distance of his thoughts?

"We're always home. Drop over." She is examining her arms to discover what effect the feeble sunshine might have had.

The Chongs are not always at home. Indeed, fairly seldom. Muhlbach finds himself resentful, though he cannot be sure whether he resents the casual hypocrisy of her statement or the fact that so frequently they go out, leaving their son alone.

Now she has gone, with an indifferent wave of the magazine. Such an informal, bland, Occidental salutation seems to him grossly incongruous; she has gone, leaving a perceptible hint of lilac through the barren hedge of winter. Muhlbach contemplates the tin can of paint he holds, a spattered rag, some brushes that might as well symbolize his present estate, thinking of a life that used to be, a life he knew must end, and did, yet how bitterly! And he remembers, too, a phrase of music, crumbs of madeleine, since these are common properties, the gynandrous quality of a woman's limbs—well, these and more. And how does it conclude? What is it, after all? Children, a quiet neighborhood, a funeral not too ostentatious. Surely, he thinks, there must be more.

A sparrow hops across the frozen flower beds; Muhlbach gloomily oversees this petty search, half impressed by the absence of despair, a ritual less convoluted than his own. Soon enough it will be time to wash and dress himself as expected. The Forsyths, with Eula, are due at seven o'clock. Two drinks, the usual conversation, and away to supper. What is the point of this foolish affair? Eula, no more subtle than the next, pretends to seek nothing except his company. So will he pretend, and she, and the Forsyths, and yet they all four know better. Marriage is her heart's desire. This evening she once again will cultivate the children, more especially Otto, the recalcitrant one, attempting to persuade him of her good intentions. Otto will not be deceived; he suspects. He may not know precisely what he suspects, and he will be civil, but that is all; Eula's voluptuous blandishments bring to his foxy face an expression of studied cordiality, nothing else; he knows that his every word and gesture is supervised by adults. This evening she will exclaim with simulated delight at finding him here, where he lives, as though she expected him to be somewhere else. Otto, in turn, will glance upward, shiftily, from Miss Cunningham to Dr. and Mrs. Forsyth, estimating the situation, perhaps formulating a marvelous idea such as kicking Miss Cunningham in the bottom. But it can't be done, however appealing the thought.

Muhlbach lifts his head. Shadows cover the yard. The sparrow has disappeared. How long ago? The sun provides no warmth, retreating, beyond the tangled housetops, beyond the hooks, ropes, and wires of civilization. Evening comes on. This day is nearly finished. Tomorrow will be Sunday, next comes Monday, Tuesday, the comfortable tedium. Once, he reflects, work seemed vital; now it is the means to fill a day. Suppose he should import Greek amphorae, sell wool, speculate on munitions, design cathedrals, would it be much different?

The voice of Mrs. Grunthe is heard. She is annoyed over something, which is usual. Muhlbach listens. Ah!—the scouts have completed their hike, the aspiring trooper is home. Yes, that is the tone she reserves for Otto. When Donna has contrived to displease Mrs. Grunthe the reprimand is less vehement. Well, Mrs. Grunthe is right, however often one may disagree with her; she is right when it comes to dealing with Otto, whose skin would spoil the edge of a scalpel. The mighty, two-handed sword of a Crusader is the appropriate weapon to convince him of error, and wielded with heroic strokes may even bring a trace of blood. So, Otto has come home. Muhlbach listens to the sounds of discord. Whatever the argument is about, Mrs. Grunthe will win.

Chill as any stone, the sun sinks through cloudy folds, through antennae and chimneys; and Muhlbach after a few minutes enters the kitchen.

"If I'm not mistaken, the prodigal has returned," he says.

"Oh, yes! Look at him, now, would you, sir?" Mrs. Grunthe opens for the prosecution. "Claims he doesn't need a bath! He won't spend the night under this roof without a bath, I can tell you!"

Otto speaks. The defense. He commences to recite a formidable list of reasons for his uncouth appearance. The ice was thin, the ice looked thick; unfortunately the ice was thin. Thus we account for Otto having stepped into the creek—warped shoes, dried over the campfire. They are dry enough now, true, with a crusty look that no polish will soften. One pair of shoes ruined, or at least less serviceable than they were. Yes, yes, the water was cold, no doubt, Otto. Neither Mrs. Grunthe nor I will dispute this statement, thinks Muhlbach. One learns, my son, not to walk on ice until one has tested it with heavy rocks, with the recollection of yesterday's temperature, et cetera. There were no rocks near the stream? Well, we must doubt that. And what has yesterday to do with it? The scoutmaster himself walked on this ice? Indeed? Ah, along the edge of it! Now, what about these gloves? They got wet when you stepped into the creek because you lost your balance, all right. Under the circumstances, all right, but why do the gloves no longer have finger tips? Would you be good enough to explain? Here are the gloves, so called, consisting of cuffs, palms, and the beginning of fingers. Only one question: viz., where are the finger tips? Being wet, yes, we understand, because you were in the creek, yes, please continue. It was very cold, you already have informed us of the fact. As to the gloves, please? You dried them. Commendable. How did you dry them? By the fire, of course. How close to the fire? You don't exactly remember. Not really very close? No? Then why, at the point where the fingers vanish, does the wool exhibit this charred appearance? Charred? Yes, meaning burned. The gloves have been burned. But you don't know how this happened? Suppose you take a moment to reflect.

Silence.

Mrs. Grunthe, arms crossed with Teutonic certitude, awaits the confession.

Well, Otto?

Possibly, that is to say, there might just possibly be a chance that the gloves, while being dried, were hung an inch or two closer to the fire than necessary. Immediate qualifications follow; Muhlbach cuts them short. One pair of shoes, one pair of gloves. What next? The pedometer, lost in the woods at the age of seven months. The pedometer, faithfully logging the distance covered this Saturday, now is resting in one of two places—in the underbrush or in the creek. Otto is of the opinion it is in the creek. Because the ice was thin. Everything is the fault of the ice. It seems the ice should have spoken up. So, the list is increasing. Anything else? A hatchet. A hatchet is missing. Where is the hatchet? The leather sheath is produced. Excellent, the sheath is safe, in good condition. But where is the hatchet?

Silence.

Otto? Speak up.

Otto is not positive that he took the hatchet on this hike; perhaps the hatchet is in the basement? No, the hatchet started off this Saturday morning hooked to Otto's belt. Mrs. Grunthe distinctly remembers. Now where is it? Quite obviously it is keeping company with the pedometer. These artifacts will serve as museum pieces for some future society. Now, is there anything more? Shoes, gloves, pedometer, hatchet. According to Mrs. Grunthe this is merely a beginning. Consider, for instance, the mess kit. The canvas cover is filthy—did it fall into the bean soup? Otto resents this. One David Guckenheim, it seems, having allowed his shoelaces to become untied—David Guckenheim is a big fat slob—all right, never mind, we can do without that. Continue. David Guckenheim, in short, tripped himself, and as he, Guckenheim, happened to be carrying a cup of stew at the time—well, all right, all right. The mess kit cover is not important; it can be boiled and scrubbed. So that's it? No? The compass, too, has been lost. Succumbing to irony, Muhlbach points out the function of a compass, which is to prevent the woodsman from becoming lost, whereas in this case the compass has been lost. Ha ha!

Otto does not grasp the irony.

Never mind, let it go. The list of equipment destroyed, lost, mutilated, or forgotten becomes almost unbelievable. Add to the shoes, gloves, and so forth, the following: waterproof matchbox, good-luck charm—a magnesium horseshoe from a box of cereal—and, among numerous other items, the chipmunk tail. It is this loss which sorely grieves Otto, his most grisly possession. Mrs. Grunthe, not unexpectedly, is relieved to learn it will be seen no more.

The chipmunk tail. Muhlbach thinks of it for the first time since last summer. He thinks of Otto's triumphal return from four weeks at camp in the Alleghenies, full of marvelous accounts of wildlife, carrying a bronze medal—third place in the archery competition—a collection of fishhooks, a broken canoe paddle. What use is a broken canoe paddle? No one knows, even the owner, but still it stands in a corner of Otto's room, a relic not lightly discarded. And the chipmunk tail?—ah, the woodcraft instructor, he who teaches survival in the wilderness, teaches the building of traps—in this case a heavy wooden box, overturned, propped up with a peg, a string attached, bait underneath the box, and the hunter concealed behind a nearby boulder. Enter the rodent. The rest is foreordained. But the tail? Enter the camp physician, a young and ruddy resident from uptown Manhattan. How did he get into the Alleghenies? How did he learn to extract the bone from the tail of a chipmunk? And what then?—it is packed with salt, and thus, up to a certain age, remains pliable. This, therefore, is the trophy whose loss Otto regrets so bitterly.

Otherwise, apart from having lost or destroyed an impressive percentage of your belongings, Otto, how was the excursion? Excursion, yes. That is to say, an outing, a trip, a brief journey, usually for pleasure. In this instance, a hike. What did you eat? Excepting the inevitable chocolate bar. What did you cook for lunch? Well, there was a minute steak, tenderized by the butcher. Times have changed. Muhlbach remembers his own camping trips, and the minute steak, remembers buying them from the grocer, the price was ten cents. He does not know how much they cost these days, that being Mrs. Grunthe's concern.

So you ate a minute steak. What else?

Stew, naturally, and something known as bean-hole beans. No doubt everything was liberally seasoned with ashes and dirt, twigs, insects—or perhaps it was
too early for insects. And did you have a good time, my son?

What a question.

For now, for this Saturday, the hike is over. Details of it we will hear later. The
time has come for a bath and clean clothing. And a word of advice: stay away from
Donna, because it appears she is coming down with a cold, or some such. She has
been in bed since noon, and seems listless. Mrs. Grunthe not being concerned,
Muhlbach is not. Despite certain antipathies, certain reservations about Mrs.
Grunthe, he has utter confidence in her female powers of divination. If Donna
were in the first stages of a serious illness, Mrs. Grunthe would know. Just how she
would know, Muhlbach cannot imagine; it is enough to believe that in this respect
the housekeeper is infallible. He muses on this, recalls having watched Mrs.
Grunthe tuck in the covers of Donna's bed, has observed the clean, capable,
plump, lentiginous hands at work. He compliments himself for having the wisdom to select Mrs. Grunthe from among the applicants.

Off to the bath, Otto, off with you! And pick up your room! Mrs. Grunthe has
enough to do without—yes, yes, all right, all right. Otto heads for the stairs, shirt-
tail dangling, warped shoes creaking. It would not take an Indian to follow his
trail; indeed, the odor would be enough.

And as his son is tramping out of sight Muhlbach remembers when the shelter
plans were delivered, how strangely Otto responded to them—how he seemed to
withdraw. From what? That was months ago, but still there is a sense of cross-
purpose, a dissatisfaction, a lack of rapport persisting between himself and his son.
And he falls to thinking of this, and does not listen to Mrs. Grunthe complain of
one thing after another, of a universe poorly ordered—she is well paid, she will stay.
He thinks of that Saturday morning when the plans arrived, in an outsized manila
envelope, with a handsome seal embossed in the upper left corner, the word RUSH
stamped in red on the front and back, with a Washington postmark. There was a
look of authority to that envelope. Otto had stood by, attentive but inscrutable,
wearing a new sweat shirt, respectful, knowing that envelopes from Washington
may be significant.

Yes, and he had been wearing the ill-starred pedometer, having just received it
for a birthday. The pedometer had been worn each day for about a month, then less
frequently, and now appeared only on special occasions such as the hike. But at first
it was always evident, attached to a sock where it attempted to register every step.
Muhlbach, on the assumption he should display some interest in its calculations,

used to ask. But the answer, customarily, was Otto's favorite; that is, he didn't know, wasn't sure, or had forgotten how far he had gone that day. Then of what use is a pedometer, if you don't know, or already have forgotten? Well, having thought this over, of course, he didn't know. Victory belongs to the ignorant, a variation of Gresham's law. At all events, there he had stood, the solemn Philistine, on the day the plans arrived, dressed in sweat shirt and baseball cap, the pedometer noncommittal and yet somehow malevolent, dangling from a white wool sock on which several burrs were lodged—a surly little machine, bloodless and efficient, ready to click the instant its owner moved a foot.

Eying it from time to time, Muhlbach had been almost overcome by an urge to take advantage of this instrument, to deceive it, to hold it up and swing it back and forth until it died of exhaustion. Indeed, very late one night he did take it up from the bureau where it lay surrounded by marbles and Indian-head pennies, but quickly set it down, for the thing was curiously repellent, seemingly aware of him, and might cry out in a thin metallic voice, crying "Otto! Otto!" in the depths of the night. Then what? How should he explain if Otto should waken and sit up stiff with alarm?

So, if he has not commented on the loss of the pedometer, Muhlbach nonetheless is vaguely relieved that it is gone. It cannot, of course, return of its own volition; it was a ghastly totem, nothing more, inanimate, not a conscious and motile automaton—it only seemed to be.

Thus accoutered, in sweat shirt and pedometer, Otto had watched the opening of the manila envelope, watched the unfolding of the blueprints, examined the drawings in the booklet, looked speculatively at a photograph of a pretty young woman, obviously a professional model, smiling and displaying her personal dosimeter, weight one ounce and a half, compactly and attractively designed as a locket. Like Grandmother's cameo, it hung about her neck to measure both the rate of radiation and the amount absorbed. Otto inquired about the dosimeter, whose function puzzled him, radiation being something he does not comprehend. And he looked long at a picture of someone's basement recreation room, so called, with murals of primitive bison, and a television set recessed, its gray elliptoid screen waiting. Is it this he finds so absorbing?—a television set in the basement? No, nor the mural. And how unconsciously droll, thinks Muhlbach, that the family should be contemplating paleolithic art. Could this be deliberate? No, impossible. Irony presupposes a feeling for humor; there is none here. None. How bizarre, in fact, are these ferruginous animals eternally poised in apocalyptic gloom. Is it the bison which fascinates Otto? No. *Ah!*—it is, of course, the exercycle. Yes, a bicycle without wheels. Of course. And, for the sake of realism, this contrivance has a speedometer attached!

What else have we? What else in this basement? One spade neatly pegged upon the wall, a long-handled pick—what for? A pick looks anachronistic, relevant to the Punic Wars. But still, who knows? The pick appears confident that it will be used. A wrench, too. Well, wrenches are convenient, and screwed down close enough may be employed against a reluctant toothpaste cap. And next to the wrench a battery-operated hot plate. A hand-crank phonograph, records, a book or so. Not many books; television is more direct, opportune, demanding adherence. Who doubts the graven image?

And on the shelf is a rag doll! Muhlbach, prepared to turn the page, scarcely can believe what he sees. Yet there she lies, appealing to every little girl, stuffed legs outstretched and hair of colored yarn. She wears a jumper. Her eyes are buttons. How anachronistic, Muhlbach thinks; he has not seen such a doll in many years. The children of our time amuse themselves with plastic robots which squeal and periodically stain their garments, deliver monologues, walk, throw fits of temper. The marvels of realism. Why was not one of these hideous creatures included, rather than an old rag doll? Why?

Otto has had enough of this page, what comes next? Architectural sketches. Muhlbach is interested, Otto is not. Turn the page. Photographs. Charred steel, smashed concrete, the ruins of a warehouse at Nagasaki Medical College, meaningless to Otto. Roof trusses twisted like dental braces, a streetcar flung off its tracks and lying on its side. What have we next?

A portrait of "Fat Man," sixty inches in diameter, length one hundred and twenty-eight inches, weighing just over ten thousand pounds. He is painted black, stands on some sort of trestle, a box guidance system affixed to his rear. He it was who rode unannounced into the heart of the city, a gift from America, riding bloated with the knowledge of triumph through Persepolis. Otto asks if it is a submarine. No, it is not. We'll talk about it later. That is, in a few years.

And here, cradled, is "Little Boy," the predecessor, the original. Muhlbach stares at this thing which has altered history. It is so recent, yet it has an antique look, primitive, rusty. It appears to have been made by hand. How strange! Conventional bombs of that era had a sleek, well-fed aspect. Why should this appear so crude? It looks as though two boys had built it in a garage with a hammer and pliers and parts from some abandoned generator. It has the look of a device submitted to the government patent office but rejected. So much for that. Turn the page.

Aerial photos, before and after, with concentric rings superimposed. Yes, even the untrained eye can note the difference. Here the bend of the river is the same, otherwise nothing. A city, not unlike Paris, with its rivers and bridges, constitutes Exhibit A. Exhibit B is merely an area. Muhlbach fingers his lip, frowning; this is how the state of Arizona must look from high above.

Otto is impatient. Turn the page.

Grids, screens, additional views of Sodom and Gomorrah. Maps, statistics, drawings—a man dressed in a double-breasted business suit! He appears to be standing in a strong breeze, his hat has just hopped off his head, he is covering his face with both hands in order to protect himself from an explosion. Muhlbach skims the explanatory text, bemused by the double-breasted business suit. How very odd, such attention to fashion, but still a fashion out of date.

Next we have a photograph of a Mr. Wheeler Rosenbaum, a grocer from Sioux City, Iowa. Grocer Rosenbaum is pictured lifting the lid of his shelter garbage can and, at the same time, drinking something from a paper cup. Curious, to say the least. Otto, too, seems puzzled. What is the grocer drinking?

It occurs to Muhlbach that there is about this booklet a feeling of insanity. And the people whose pictures appear, are they inhabitants of an asylum? A grocer, ostensibly, from Sioux City, a portly, self-satisfied grocer stands beside a garbage can. Yes, with one hand he lifts the lid of the receptacle and he soberly drinks from a paper cup. Someone is mad. Surely this pamphlet was composed by the unfortunates of a madhouse.

But let us see what the grocer does next. Surrounded by his five children and his wife, and a neighbor—Miss Holloway, she is called—the grocer is shown seated at an oilcloth-covered table. He is waiting, this is quite evident. Everyone is looking at him. Presently he will do something, or something will happen. Perhaps the others will join him at the table and they will eat scallopini. We cannot be sure.

Grocer Rosenbaum also is pictured out of doors enjoying the sunshine. It would be October in Iowa, to judge from the trees, a few leaves on the ground. The photo has an October feeling. Rosenbaum stands, hands thrust into his pockets, smiling at the camera, beside the emergency exit which, like some prairie rodent, he has most prudently burrowed. For unknown reasons this exit has been camouflaged—a piece of garden statuary adorns it, a concrete cherub holding in its arms a birdbath half filled with water. Would not this hinder the escape? Presumably not. One must suppose the statuary tumbles aside when the grocer and his family and Miss Holloway emerge from beneath the sod.

And we are shown pictures of the Rosenbaum food cache, adequate, more than adequate, which is to be expected.

We have a picture of Doris, the eldest, who is eating what is called a Survival Ration Cracker. It resembles the common graham cracker, we are informed; however, the taste is slightly different. This cracker is composed of 8.4 percent protein, 8.5 percent fat, 79 percent carbohydrates, and 1 percent sodium chloride.

Muhlbach cannot help himself; he knows he must total these percentages. Something is missing. Impossible! 96.9 percent. What has become of the remaining 3.1 percent? Protein, fat, carbohydrate, sodium chloride, yes. What could it be?

Otto asks what the girl is eating. A cracker, Otto. It is a cracker, as you know quite well.

What next? The two Rosenbaum boys, on their knotty pine bunks, pretend to read, eyes carefully averted from the camera in order to give the impression of candid photography, life as it truly is.

Next, our grocer once again, appraising his groceries. Peaches, spinach, peas, jam, soup, cocoa, candy, et cetera. Splendid. Turn the page.

Consumption as well as production, we learn, will be government-controlled. We will not be allowed to purchase food. Therefore the list for stockpiling, calculated to the ounce. How many government employees, loyal and trustworthy, using how many computers, for how many months, have arrived at this conclusion: 448 ounces of sterile whole milk will suffice one child for a period of fourteen days, provided said infant is not more than eighteen months of age? But if he should be nineteen months and sickly? If he has a large appetite? Never mind, let us continue.

A serving of diced carrots in a plastic bag—are you listening, Otto?—subjected to Gamma radiation 2×10^6, has been kept at room temperature for almost three years! One cannot help wondering if the carrots are tasty. We have also a bag containing five—why *five?*—"frankfuters"—yes, that is the way it is spelled—five of these revolting edibles subjected to higher irradiation.

Ah!—here is the famous bottled water, the taste of which, our government informs us, the taste of which may be restored by pouring from one container to another in the same fashion as the Lion's Club magician entertains us. See the water? Otto sees the water.

Mrs. Rosenbaum now enters the activities. She, with one foot on the pedal, has raised the lid of yet another disposal unit. In virtually every picture there has been one or more waste containers. Well, the implications of this are not pleasant. Back to Mrs. Rosenbaum, immortalized with a foot on the pedal. She wears an everyday sort of dress. Her hair, it would seem, has been curled by a Sioux City beautician. Malloy's Beauty Parlor? Gertrude's Beauty Shoppe? One cannot help wondering what things are like in Sioux City. In regard to Mrs. Rosenbaum, we cannot tell too much about her, the photograph being grainy, except that her waist is thicker now than it once was, and her curls appear to be gray. She is fifty, and after five children she is what we expect. Does she doubt that when the moment comes she will once again place her foot on the pedal? Now she only simulates her chores. Can she doubt that everything will function? It is wise to be prepared.

Consider the chemical toilet, privacy afforded by a decorated bamboo screen. Precisely how many rolls of tissue will be consumed by a family of seven, plus one neighbor, during a period of fourteen days? Has this been calculated? What if the government broadcaster, after fourteen days, informs Mr. Rosenbaum that, unfortunately, because of certain unexpected and regrettable conditions, he cannot come upstairs? Well, we are working on these problems, of course. We do the best we can. A start must be made somewhere. A stitch in time, et al.

Thus we leave our good grocer and, having turned the page, receive lessons in first aid. Muhlbach scans the instructions. Eyedrops are sold by druggists under various trade names. True. One does not quarrel with such a statement. A one-ounce bottle, with dropper, is recommended. Very well. For eyes irritated by smoke, dust, or fumes it is advisable to use two drops in each eye. Apply cold compresses every twenty minutes, if possible.

If possible?

A forty-page newspaper folded to dimensions—*what* dimensions?—pieces of orange-crate sidings, or shingles cut to size. Read this again. Oh!—yes, yes, splinting. But a *forty-page* newspaper! Muhlbach attempts to recall the size of his daily, and cannot. He doubts it is forty pages. But suppose it is not only that, but larger. Are the extra pages to be thrust into one of the disposal units? Could a forty-*eight*-page newspaper be folded to these mysterious, unspecified dimensions? However, let us proceed.

In case of shock, dissolve one teaspoonful salt and one-half teaspoonful baking soda in one quart of water. Have patient drink as much as he will. Yes, under the circumstances it is safe to assume there will be a number of rather shocked individuals. But will they enjoy this potion? Will they agree that it is good for them? How much will each victim drink? What if he refuses? Otto, for example, is hostile to unfamiliar liquid; he resists, as a matter of course, whatever is said to be beneficial.

Do not attempt to give anything to the patient by mouth, Muhlbach reads aloud, if the patient is vomiting. Has such advice spewed out of a computer? The booklet does not give us the name of its author. But let us go on. Let us read further. Who can say what fascinating information will be revealed?

Do not use a tourniquet unless you know how to use one.

That is the recommendation.

When bleeding stops, bandage firmly but not tightly.

The mind boggles before such wisdom. Firmly. Tightly. What can be said? So much for first aid.

Here comes Mrs. Rosenbaum again, serious, farsighted, even a bit truculent, on the exercycle. Onward the grocer's faithful spouse! Underground she rides magnificently nowhere. The enemy so high above, will he plot her bearing and speed in order to calculate the destination? Do not worry, Mrs. Rosenbaum. Ride faster. Faster.

Turn the page.

Ace Electronics now has on the market—what is this? Advertising? Collusion? Ace Electronics is marketing a high-quality, yes, it is so described, a high-quality radiation meter, portable, sturdy, battery-powered, selling, mind you, for a mere $59.95. Less than sixty dollars, so long as one does not count the tax. On the eve of Armageddon the precepts of Madison Avenue have not been neglected. The consumer is of the opinion that $59.95 is less than $60. That is true. So it is, indeed. Furthermore, this handy device is pictured. It has a convenient knurled grip and would be a joy to carry through the countryside. The gauge resembles that of a voltmeter; the needle is long, red-tipped, extremely sensitive. When one discovers that one is entering an area of intense radiation one turns around and goes back.

Next we see a photographic enlargement of some chromosomes that have been badly confused by what is happening. One chromosome has sought to trifurcate rather than bifurcate itself, as is the custom.

Finally the checklist. Muhlbach runs through this—Otto long since having become bored—turns the page and discovers an essay on morale. Games, crafts, home movies, and so forth, in consequence of which a deep, quiet satisfaction is promised. There is the government promise in black and white—"a deep, quiet satisfaction."

This is a good time to strike out on new paths which have lured you through the years but which have never been taken or have only been briefly tried because of lack of time.

Ah, now!—don't we know that voice? Consider the limpid, persuasive style! We can almost see you in the fury of creation, scribbling on sheets of foolscap, impatiently crumpling them, one after another. The carpet of that little Washington office is littered. Or could we be mistaken? Do you lean back, comfortably dictating immortal suggestions? Dust and flapping shades, toppled columns, garlands and scepters, prince of scribes, we know you. Could anyone be deceived? Could we mistake the hairy mammoth? Does one confuse the stegosaurus with the ptero-dactyl? Yes, yes, we are listening. Pray continue.

To throw away your own life through lack of preparation for survival is suicide.

Wait, permit us to interrupt. But no! Go on.

To throw away the lives of your family through negligence is murder.

Maxims, apothegms, dicta, precepts, epigrams, cabbages. Memories of Aesop. Shades of the French salon. What next?

If derision is thrown at you for your efforts, just don't talk about them.

Thrown? *Them?* Plural of derision? Oh!—now it becomes clear. Our friend speaks of the efforts. Do not talk about the efforts. Very well.

The care of birds is relatively simple.

Birds?

Actually, it might be wise to put the bird in their cages into the shelter area now but if that area is in a cellar or basement or in another building just make a note of the fact that you must get the bird and post this where you can see it.

Suppose we try that once more. Ready? Begin. Actually, it might be wise to put the bird (singular) in their (its?) cages (singular or plural?) into (yes, in*to*) the shelter area now (no comma) but if that area is in a cellar or basement (where are we?) or in another building just make a note of the fact that you must get the bird and post this where you can see it. When an alert or warning sounds you won't forget.

In quintuplicate. Well, there it is. Government advice. Onward.

Do you like to dance? Get records or take advantage of music which you might get over short-wave stations outside this country or over Conelrad stations broadcasting morale-boosting melodies.

Muhlbach, somewhat stunned, gazes at what he has just read. It cannot be true. Nevertheless, it is. Morale-boosting melodies. The exact phrase. Can this be some ghoulish parody?

If you have family diaries and scrapbooks, heirlooms such as journals and photograph albums and letters, put them in a box and in the shelter.

The box, that is. Put the box in the shelter.

You might find them intriguing as reading material and they might also serve as an inspiration to start you on the road to writing such a journal of current events of your family's experience from day to day.

Oh, how easily we recognize that style! Muhlbach, hypnotized, reads on.

Why not write letters? Of course they won't be mailed as they normally would, but when they are mailed you will have given those who receive them reassurance as to your well-being, your thoughts, your daily problems and your solutions to them.

Unless, of course, the problems turn out to be insoluble. Never mind. Engrossed by this document, this runic dream which might well be preserved on slate tablets, he cannot stop reading.

Otto is restless.

Go outside and play, Otto. Go outside and dance. Take along your heirlooms. Start a journal of current events for purposes of inspiration, by all means, as our favorite author would say.

Thus the booklet accompanying the plans, marked RUSH, from the nation's capital, that bulwark of sanity and prudence, cynosure of all eyes in the midst of these troubled times. Let us repose our confidence in the perspicacity of our nation's leaders.

And the image that has lingered in his mind's eye—a very good phrase, that!—is a sketch of a happy family enjoying their deep, quiet satisfaction after the Event. We behold the earth above, devastation absolute, and the triumvirate below. On the divan Mother takes her ease. Smiling, she holds a letter she has just received. Father, casual in slacks and windbreaker, as though he has completed a round of golf, selects a phonograph record. He, too, is smiling. Susan, let us call her, wearing her school sweater, lounges on the carpet where she works at her arithmetic. We are not astonished that she, too, is smiling. On the wall are four large, beautifully framed prints—early American sailing ships. There are many pillows, triangular, elliptical, the latest thing in pillows. We see also the grocery shelf, the generator, the disposal unit, yes, there it is, right next to the shovel. But where is the pet? Surely such a family would not be without a pet! We must conclude the siren caught the miserable beast away from home. That is to say, Rollo is now a shadow on the pavement.

When the chips are down—ah ha! Here is our author again. We promptly identify that prose. When the chips are down—yes? yes?—you will want to live. The premise. How does one refute such fearsome logic? Impossible.

Insane? This is not insanity, for there is meaning to insanity. And yet, is there not meaning to everything? Muhlbach cannot forget this drawing; and each time he thinks of it he must ask himself if, by spading up his own backyard, by constructing a similar refuge, by implication and association he therefore has committed himself to the company of these placid cretins.

What is the answer?

Unable to reply to his own question, he thinks he might as well ask Otto. Still, he reflects, because I have chosen this road I will go down it some distance further, and we shall see what we shall see.

Again his thoughts turn upon Otto and the indifference, the all but overt hostility, his son displayed toward these plans. Here arrived from Washington a set of blueprints, accompanying it a treatise on living underground with pets, family, and friends, with pictures of explosions, flaming houses, devastated cities—and Otto withdrew! He is fascinated by tree houses, caves, fires, catastrophe of every description, and has demonstrated his affinity for a wilderness wherein one eats out of tin cans. Then why should he view so coldly this exciting prospect?

Why?

He asked very, very few questions about the shelter. This, of itself, is odd. And the questions were unlike his usual queries, which customarily are noted for a certain lack of distinction. Why are trees green?—and so forth. Demotic questions. In short, however capable or ingenious Otto might be, and though he is one's own flesh and blood, it would be excessive to pretend that he is remarkable for his intelligence.

Well, then, how account for the surly bite of his questions regarding the shelter? There was, Muhlbach remembers, a vesicant quality to them; it was as though Otto had been transmogrified and, full of *Weltschmerz,* proposed to doubt everything. Will the roof fall in? This is a question he once asked about the house, but he was then half his present age and it seemed not unreasonable. But that he should ask such a question now! He knows better. He knows, thinks Muhlbach, he knows damn well that the shelter roof will not collapse. He knows what a blueprint is for; he understands. What was the purpose of that question? The boy is growing up. Yes, it will pay to listen more closely. We may ignore the duplicity of the infant, only take care as he grows older.

At any rate Otto now is out of sight, rinsing away the creek water. That hike was rather expensive. One doesn't think of hikes as costing much. Well, so be it. Muhlbach sighs—and is startled by the noise. Perhaps there is time for a nap. But, no, the Forsyths will be coming over, with Eula. What has been planned?—he cannot remember. Oh yes, cocktails here, then out for the evening. They are all four to go out for dinner. He wonders if he might cancel the evening. Women make use of the sick headache and no questions are asked. What does a man do? Ordinarily nothing; he puts up with the situation. And here comes Mrs. Grunthe.

Yes, yes, he replies, I know—they'll be here in a little while.

So, like Otto before him, Muhlbach trudges up the steps, conscious of the housekeeper's eye upon him, as though he too were a small boy.

In the shower, steaming the March wind from his bones, he leans against the warm tile wall and shuts his eyes. It seems so long since Joyce died. It seems so long ago. Times change, we are told, and we with them. How lonely it has been, these past months.

Dressing, he regards himself in the mirror, manages a smile, not that there is much to smile about; the smile is for practice. He will be expected to smile this evening. Everyone wonders to what extent he has recovered from the death of his wife. Well, that is something he himself can wonder over. He walks and talks, goes to the office as expected, eats, sleeps; it is only that life is senseless, as though he had been mildly drugged all this while. Nothing is of much consequence. As to the shelter?—who knows? He has built it not because it was something to do; he could as easily have spent these weekends painting the house with a small brush or picking up autumn leaves one at a time. But because the shelter might possibly succeed, because of the children, on their account, he has built it. And because of his own perversity—yes, that is the true reason. I accept the madness of our time, he thinks. Each age does produce its folly—some scheme, project, or fantasy toward which the blood drains—economic, political, religious. Always. Panniers of mold from the hill of the Crucifixion, flagons of water from Jordan. There is testimony to the madness of an earlier age, but is ours more sapient? Compare us to the men of Urban's time, those that listened, rich with devotion, while he communicated his madness till Europe boiled and the meadows of France were covered with tents. How have we grown? Here am I, dabbling in an art that may soon be lost, the building of shelters against total irruption; one might as well have faith in the power of shrunken heads. But I acquiesce in the name of prudence, which is a sort of wisdom.

So, carefully drawing the noose of a quiet necktie, having been fastidious since he can remember, drawing and placing the knot, Muhlbach somberly contemplates his image.

At last he blinks and draws a breath. His thoughts turn to the present evening, to the curious solicitude of friends. How tentative each suggestion, each invitation. No doubt the Forsyths and Eula discussed this supper before proposing it. Eula, anxious to begin the assault, probably protested nonetheless, out of sham modesty, with Margaret countering, women not wanting other women to go to waste. And Lewis, to whom death is as common as a radish, seeing it approach and seize his patients despite his most valiant efforts—quite probably Lewis ignored this female intricacy. Is it, in fact, too soon? What will the neighbors think? Muhlbach speculatively taps the mirror with a fingernail file as though to elicit some response. The face in the mirror does not speak. Come now, my familiar friend, show a reasonable countenance. This evening we must be genial, we two.

Downstairs again, the night has taken on a winter look.

The Volkswagen is parked next door, Bob Chong is home, the sound of jazz is heard, a tree filled with blackbirds. Every night this charivari, this unspeakable bobbery, emanates from their house in concentric rings, thrusting itself upon the neighborhood, Bob Chong's voice shouting intermittently to some nonexistent personage—*"Bix! Do it, man! Muggsy, go! Go!"* Muhlbach cannot separate them. Who is Bix? Is he also Muggsy? Perhaps they are brothers. Are they figures of speech? Symbols of distress? They cannot be real, only the uproar which is promulgated in their name.

With hands locked behind his back he stares at the lighted window, at the shadows bouncing back and forth across the half-drawn shade, and hopes it will not last much longer. He had thought there might be time for some music of his own choosing, perhaps the Brandenburgs, but nothing—surely not the Stuttgart chamber group—could compete with Muggsy and Bix. Patience, therefore. Goths and Vandals passed away, so must these individuals, whoever or whatever they are.

Guided by his nose, Muhlbach enters the kitchen. Mrs. Grunthe, it is true, resents his presence there. He may be the employer but the kitchen belongs to her; which of course is a proper reason to enter now and again, to impress upon her the fact that it is he, not she, who is the captain of this sloop. Besides, he wishes to know what she is cooking for such a chilly night. He does not inquire; he lifts the lid of the kettle, sniffs, peers, nods, replaces the lid. For all her faults, she most certainly is a cook. He cannot say what is on the fire, but his mouth waters; he is tempted to call the Forsyths and plead a sick headache. How satisfying to spend the night at home with the contents of this kettle, a slice of pie, and coffee, brandy and a cigar; and, once the atmosphere has purified, once the cacophony subsides, to sink into the green leather chair, close his eyes, and keep company with Bach and Vivaldi and whoever else might come to mind. Patience. Patience. There are more ways than one of looking at a blackbird.

The doorbell. Muhlbach goes to welcome his guests. But there stands a young man, a stranger, who thrusts out a hand and begins to talk. I'm sorry. Go away. No. No, whatever it is, no. And as he shuts the door, courteously but firmly, he thinks there should be an ordinance against this sort of peddling. It is not the principle, really, quite so much as the deceit—the insincerity of that outstretched hand. The footsteps beat down the walk and Muhlbach reflects that as he nears forty he has conquered his need to be considered a friendly man. The wasteland roils about us. I refuse, he announces to himself, to shake each hand. And yours, especially, whoever you were. I do not know you, I do not believe you came in friendship but only because you wanted something of me; it is not that I was averse to helping you, or your cause, but you offended me, insulted my intelligence, by your dissimulation.

That smile was unctuous. Am I some address, a potential source of profit? Would you have smiled such a beaming Christian smile and proffered that hand if you had known that I never would buy your product? Therefore I rejected the overture. The door is not so easily opened these days. I am not what I once was.

Minutes later the doorbell rings again; he composes himself, pulls the lingering annoyance from his features, and, to be sure, here are the Forsyths and Miss Eula Cunningham. Ah?—not quite. Margaret Forsyth and Eula Cunningham. Where is Lewis?

"He got a call as we were leaving." Margaret expresses her resignation, her understanding, her years of being the physician's wife; this and more she can express in a single weary sentence. Another minute, she says, and they'd have escaped. Pretend you don't hear it, she advised him, but of course he wouldn't. Some child had found a firecracker left over from last year and had set it off in his ear, of all places. Honestly, it does make you wonder about people.

Mrs. Grunthe is summoned to take the ladies' coats. Muhlbach, already bored by the sound of Margaret's voice, pours her a glass of ginger ale, mixes a drink for Eula, and thinks about the boy—it could not possibly have been a girl—with the wits to set off a firecracker in his ear. It is precisely what might be expected of Otto.

As though materialized by his father's reflections, Otto becomes visible at the top of the stairs. He is en route to the kitchen for supper, but in order to get there he must pass by the living room where he will be subjected to the guests. He knows them well enough, and though he has expressed no opinion about them, except to say that he likes Dr. Forsyth, it is plain that he does not care for the women. Each time he encounters them there is a horny, medieval restraint to his amenities.

How do you do, Miss Cunningham? How do you do, Mrs. Forsyth?

He cannot get away with less than this, and he will volunteer nothing more. He glances sharply about, expecting to see the doctor, but does not ask.

Mrs. Grunthe has your supper ready, says Muhlbach.

"Okay."

However, as long as you are here, make yourself useful. Muhlbach holds up the two cocktails for delivery, ginger ale and ice for Margaret, which, as a drink, is fair enough if taken on its own merits. For Eula—this is what she wanted—bourbon mixed with a commercial preparation whose taste is as noxious to the tongue as its name is to the ear, a magenta-colored syrup symbolic of the aesthetics of America. That is what she ordered, that is what she gets. Each society must endure the crime it deserves. Here you go, Otto, and be good enough not to spill them.

"Okay."

The only living Philistine. My father, thinks Muhlbach, would have rapped me across the skull if I dared answer him that way. Times change. Language deteriorates. The absence of culture becomes a culture.

He sees that Eula deliberately has blocked Otto's line of retreat. She is attempting to—well, seduce him. She is using her female body to overpower him, to win him, and through the son to obtain the father. It is a crass maneuver. And I, he reflects, the ultimate prey, somehow find myself obligated to observe this scene as though indifferent to its significance, to say nothing of its immorality! Can this woman presume I am not aware? If so, if true, the famous intuition of women is a myth.

He watches, silently.

Otto, young Ganymede, you and I know that your desire is merely to reach the sanctuary of the kitchen. I could extricate you, but you are growing up, my son, and soon enough must manage these affairs by yourself. We will observe your performance now. See if you are able to outwit the gross female.

"I'll bet you just hate Saturdays, don't you? No school."

She is being arch. Riposte, Otto. Riposte!

"They're okay."

Outwit her? With such a response? It will be years yet before Otto is capable of outwitting anybody.

"What'd you do all day? I'll bet you played games with your little friends."

"I went on a hike with some guys."

Eula leans plumply nearer and at this instant Muhlbach decides that he will not marry her. He has known, of course, how narrowly she has been calculating, has noted her shrewd, appraising glances at the furnishings of his home; and various oblique questions, ostensibly innocent, have not been lost on him. But until this one moment, seeing her bend that body against a boy, he had not realized how cold she was. There will be no marriage. Miss Eula Cunningham now is wasting her time, exuding spurious warmth, one hand resting with simulated affection on Otto's sleeve. She smiles in what she believes to be a confidential manner; meanwhile she is plotting, unaware that she has no future in this house.

"My! How exciting! Where did you hike to?"

Otto gestures, easing himself away from the clutching hand. "Nowhere. Just sort of out that direction."

"I'll bet you cooked your own lunch, didn't you?"

He nods. "Yes, ma'am."

Muhlbach is startled. Yes, ma'am. That is not Otto speaking. There is some mockery here. Eula as yet has not perceived it, but she will, assuming Otto plays this tune a little longer, which he most certainly will, if he thinks nobody is on to him. Muhlbach clears his throat, and again.

Otto, however, has gone mad with success. He pays no heed to this warning—a malignant gleam has lit his eye, he is set to make a fool of Miss Cunningham. This is slightly incredible. Otto is not that subtle. Muhlbach gazes earnestly at his son, wondering if he has misinterpreted.

"What fun!" exclaims Miss Cunningham. "Then what did you do?"

Otto is insufferably casual. "We went ice skating on the creek."

This leads to something, Muhlbach does not know what, but he is sure that Otto is about to overplay his hand. In a moment Otto will make some curved remark and there will be a deadly silence; both women will perceive the ape, and Otto himself will perceive that somehow he miscalculated. Muhlbach sets down his glass, not too loudly, yet loud enough for communication. This time Otto hears.

He says that he guesses Mrs. Grunthe wants him to come and eat. And as he goes out he directs one brief, inquiring glance at his father, not quite convinced that he has been detected. Muhlbach returns an ominous look, and Otto, to judge by a suddenly altered expression, is convinced; no further verification is required. Exit Otto. In the future perhaps he will tread more softly.

The doorbell again. This would be Lewis. But there, both of them together on the horsehair mat, clasping hands like children, stand Bob and Helen Chong.

"Oops!—Oh!" Helen exclaims, pretending astonishment that he is not alone. "You're entertaining." However, they make no move to leave. The visit, therefore, is not accidental. This would have been her idea, thinks Muhlbach; no doubt she has learned about Eula Cunningham, sensed the machination, and could restrain herself no longer. What is the candidate really like? A neighbor can deduce only so much by peeping from a window corner.

Do come in, have a drink. What a nice surprise. Permit me to introduce you. Margaret Forsyth. Eula Cunningham. Yes, Helen, this is she, this is the one to evaluate. Tell me, what do you think? Is she acceptable?

"We can only stay a moment."

Of course, of course. Now, quickly, manage another look. Shoes, stockings, hands, accessories. What about it? Will she do?

"I was just telling Bob how you seemed so deserted this afternoon, so we thought we'd drop over to say hello."

Very glad you did. For a year, now, we've been promising each other, et cetera. Is she a bit heavy, do you think? A trifle ripe? How about her perfume? Rather challenging, isn't it? And is her suit tailored to your demands, or does it fit too closely across those alarming billows of rubicund flesh? What of her earrings?

"We're headed for the ballet," Bob Chong explains, and goes on to say they will grab a bite at a lunch counter somewhere. Muhlbach understands that this is so; unequivocally it has the ring of truth. It is a clumsily offered, masculine truth, doglike in its honesty; he cannot help smiling, and feels at the same time a surge of affection for this man whose wife is now attempting to conceal her displeasure. She imagines the other women smiling at her, secretly, and quite probably they are. From lunch counter to ballet. Will this anecdote spread throughout the neighborhood? Helen Chong does not look at her husband.

Margaret has asked if Cecil Chong is their son. Yes. Well, it appears that Margaret's boy, Duncan, is a classmate of Cecil Chong. Conversation, such as it is, grows out of this.

Muhlbach, studying Margaret Forsyth, half listens to her talk. In a polka-dot dress that is much too large, limp colorless hair knotted at the base of her neck, she is prim and flat, a married spinster with steel-rimmed glasses and a nasal midwestern voice. It seems to him that she gives off an odor of something stale and sour. He tries to recall if he ever has seen this woman excited, animated for any reason. She does not gesture. At thirty-one she is humorless and old. Is it not remarkable that she has four lively sons? Her eyes are vacant, her body does not exist. She is, he reflects, the most tedious creature he ever has met. Then how is it she happens to be here? Why must he regard this woman as a friend? Why is it necessary to entertain and to pretend affection for someone who bores you? The answer, of course, is that she comes with Lewis. That is the answer, but it hardly seems enough. Why doesn't she stay at home? Why doesn't she recognize what she is?

Muhlbach, having asked himself these questions, begins to wonder if perhaps he has not been drinking too much, or at least too quickly. He adds a squirt of soda to his glass, rattles the diminishing ice, and turns his attention to the Chongs. They seem to him a curious pair, overly American, determined to prove their Occidental sympathies. For instance, how could a man so obviously intelligent and worldly as Bob Chong be obsessed by the sport of baseball? Baseball is the sport of truck drivers and, these past few years, of effete and balding young men who scream with joy—neither of which pertains to Bob Chong, who is not aggressively masculine any more than he is epicene. With his crew-cut hair and argyle socks, his casual slang, and a preference for pastel shirts with French cuffs, with the mien of an Elks Club loyal, he is somewhat bizarre, more than a little contradictory. His attitude is so fraternal. Confidence is implicit in the manner with which he strips cellophane from a pack of cigarettes, taps one into space, and in the ease of long accomplishment flicks the flat gold lighter, cleverly chatting—each insuperably normal remark following another. He was, as one might guess, a pilot during the war.

Muhlbach studies him, not without admiration for the man's intellectual and imaginative achievement. He is, as the saying goes, a brain—the consequence of which, Muhlbach suspects, may have a profound influence on the lives of many people. Infrequently, hardly perceptible even then, Chong seems to reveal a further self, differing from this outer, visible man—chill, withdrawn, imperturbable, insistently at work behind the good-fellow mask. It is a little frightening, somehow. One could not say just why.

Muhlbach suddenly gets out of his chair, draws the emptied glass from Chong's delicate, blue-veined hand and fills it with liquor until it looks like a glass of German beer. He notes with amusement Chong's sharp, questing expression, which instantly vanishes. Yes, another man lives somewhere in back of this chortling neighborhood bon vivant. And this mysterious personage whose face so seldom shows is the one to estimate more carefully; it is he who decides, who directs the gesticulations and inane mouthings which the world assumes are representative. Santa Monica surf rider, indeed! Grab a bite at the lunch counter, indeed. Muhlbach revises his estimate. Even this man's apparent lapses are calculated, decorations on the mask. Toward what end? That by seeming innocuous he may go about his business undisturbed?

And as Chong recounts that dramatic ninth inning, ostensibly for himself and Muhlbach as the only males, for their mutual pleasure—women not being interested in that sort of thing—the narration is, yet, directed toward these women, although he evidently is ignoring them. Thus, deviously, most subtly, the fox doubling across its tracks, he believes himself undetected on the hillside, from which vantage point he will observe the hunter hunting him, not aware of a second hunter at his back. Or is he aware? And by this apparent ignorance perform a further arabesque?

Muhlbach all at once has the sensation of half a dozen eyes peering at him, coldly, through the pupils of Bob Chong, and feels his stomach tighten. This is how the suspect feels, guilty or innocent, helplessly illuminated while the inquisitors remain in darkness. But of course it is his own probing that has alerted Chong, has brought to life the recessed intellect. And at this realization he smiles, and is more at ease; after all, not himself but Robert Chong has been examined. Now it is Chong who must venture forth, must reconnoiter, simply because he has no choice.

Muhlbach tips his glass, nods, clears his throat pedantically and remarks that he has been intending to go to a baseball game. So many people, he says, seem to enjoy it. For one moment he is almost able to believe that baseball defines the full extent of Chong, so convincingly does the man approve this statement. But their eyes have met, long enough. No, there has been no mistake.

So, this initial evening will not be the last. Bob Chong will come back again. Surprised in the course of a pointless neighborhood visit, himself tracked down, he must learn how this happened; he cannot help himself, it is the nature of the scientist. He cannot rest until he knows. Thus, inaudibly, invisible to any but the narrowed eye, a relationship is born. Muhlbach permits himself to laugh aloud, and does not explain; he turns his attention to Helen Chong, deliberately, boldly. Each look and gesture, henceforth, and the response each calls forth, will be slipped beneath the husband's microscope. Helen Chong, he notes, is not drinking. She is here on female business, no doubt of that, lured across the intervening hedge by the presence of Eula.

Margaret licks her lips. She has finished her drink and studiously is examining the empty glass. He takes it from her. Then, just as he begins to fill it up again, he understands that she is alcoholic. He almost drops the glass; at this same instant he feels Chong's eyes like pincers hook the back of his head. The sensation is not pleasant. Nothing will escape Chong's attention from now on. Nothing. No one else has noticed. He takes the glass more firmly in hand, pours the ginger ale, adds a cube of ice, and returns it to her. She accepts with a look of wan gratitude, lusterless, exhausted. She gazes remotely at the bubbles. Is she imagining champagne?

A car draws up outside the house.

Yes, this time it is Lewis. Muhlbach opens the door and waits to greet him, thinking meanwhile of his wife—those pink-rimmed watering eyes, the weary voice. Strange he had not thought of it before, but there can be no doubt. How well kept a secret! And for how many years? Always, when visiting, she asked for ginger ale, always more than one, as if the very act of swallowing was vital. And, waiting for Lewis Forsyth to reach the door, he is fascinated that such a woman could possess depths enough to ruin herself.

Well, Lewis, it's about time, I should say. How are you?

Forsyth stamps his feet on the mat, as though snow still covered the walk. It has been a long winter; habits persist. He removes a glove to shake hands. "I suppose Margaret told you why I'm late. Somebody dared that kid to set one off in his ear. Frankly, I don't hold out too much hope for the human race."

The record isn't encouraging. At any rate, come in. Bob and Helen Chong, Dr. Lewis Forsyth.

The men reach forward, grasp one another by the hand, the ageless mistrust of the male. Having disarmed each other, they withdraw a step. The women smile. There follows a pause.

How's that shelter coming along?

It is almost completed, a few details remain. One could say, really, that it is complete. As a matter of fact, perhaps everyone would like the grand tour? Open house, so to speak. By the way, Lewis, I should appreciate your opinion of the sanitary facilities. Everything is in accord with government specifications, but nowadays one can't even trust the government. Least of all the government! And at this there is a certain amount of laughter. Remind me, Lewis, to tell you some of the things which appear in the booklet of survival instructions. At any rate, I've been thinking I might spend tonight in the shelter. I thought it should be christened! Now, smile.

"Oh?" Forsyth hesitates, glances around.

Muhlbach suddenly is aware of his own loquacity, and that whenever the shelter is mentioned, no matter under what circumstances, everyone grows ill at ease. Why? As though he had mentioned that he intended to sell his business and become a poet, or that he planned to walk from New York to Seattle.

Bob Chong, authority on batting averages and earned runs, the suburban husband, jumps to his feet, ready for the grand tour.

Anyone else? asks Muhlbach, attempting levity. Admission free.

Yes, the others will come along; they scarcely can do otherwise.

Muhlbach beckons, leads the way. Through the kitchen they go; Mrs. Grunthe does not bother to conceal her displeasure.

"Oh, doesn't something smell divine!" This is Eula.

"Good evening, Mrs. Grunthe."

"Good evening, Dr. Forsyth."

And so out the backdoor into the light of early stars. Across the lawn. Careful. There should be a lantern of some sort.

Muhlbach feels in his vest pocket for the key, descends the steps and with a flourish inserts the key in the lock, installed only last week, swings open the door and switches on the light. There is an odor of cement, of paint, the unmistakable knowledge that one is underground.

Without a word the guests walk in like refugees from the plague. Here is a castle hidden in the forest; here they shall occupy themselves with drinking and telling stories until Death has gone from their land. Here they will be safe, and those outside must die.

"What is this?" Chong asks. He, alone, has observed the poem lettered above the door.

> *N'en déplaise à ces fous nommés sages de Grèce,*
> *En ce monde il n'est point de parfaite sagesse;*
> *Tous les hommes sont fous, et malgré tous leurs soins*
> *Ne diffèrent entre eux que du plus ou du moins.*

"It is from Boileau," Muhlbach replies, and waits.

Forsyth now has scanned the lines, but shrugs. "I read very little French," says he, and indicating the shelter, goes on: "Frankly, I dislike such precaution, yet I suppose it is only sensible."

"It is, I guess," says Muhlbach, and Chong, nodding, seems to agree.

Here we stand like Gaspar, Melchior, and Balthazar, thinks Muhlbach. We are stuffed with holy wisdom. Who is there to contradict us?

"A fine sense of irony you have," Chong remarks. "After going to all this trouble you ridicule your work."

"Not the work so much as myself," Muhlbach answers without a smile. Then, in an altered tone of voice, he announces to the women that he has ordered a Navajo rug which should make the room somewhat more cheerful and will soften the noise. He demonstrates by advancing, and his footsteps echo on the unpainted concrete.

Eula exclaims with pleasure; one would think she has always wanted to live in such a place. But then the oppressive nature of this room descends upon her. She cannot sustain her attitude of delight. It is, beyond doubt or concealment of the fact, a dungeon. A colorful rug will not enliven it. Dart boards, lemonade, phonograph records—no, this is a crypt. It speaks of evil, of misery, destruction, violence, life without hope. Eula apprehends this, gradually. Her face is stricken.

Muhlbach observes how she falters, gazes desperately around; then he becomes conscious that everyone is looking at him. Are they wondering why he has brought them here? This terrifying room is of itself meaningless; the evil it represents is of his own construction. They are looking at him. They seem to be waiting for some explanation. "I'm sorry," he begins, embarrassed. He does not know what to say next. "I must have been asleep," he adds. What a thing to say! He cannot imagine why he has said that.

Murmurs, vague condolence. They assume he has not yet recovered from the death of his wife. They think he is distraught; they are being kind.

"What time is the ballet?" Chong asks his wife, pretending not to know.

"We should be leaving, too," Forsyth suggests, and turns to Muhlbach. "Well, my friend! Ready for a hamburger?" This is Forsyth's familiar joke. He is a gourmet, former president of the wine and food society. It has been twenty years since he ate a hamburger.

Muhlbach nods; he does not trust himself to speak. Already he is weary of this evening and longs to be alone, to meditate. But they are going out and he must go with them. All right.

Mysteriously, as though he had been subject to teleportation, he finds himself seated in Forsyth's car, talking with him, answering the women who are comfortably arranged in back. He cannot recall what he has been saying or what anyone else has said; but evidently the habits of a lifetime now preserve him. He listens and responds, that is enough; and sinks again into the dream he has dreamed these passing months.

Death and transfiguration. Meters of time, distance counted. We are like medieval figures dancing and capering across the hill.

He hears himself chatting with one of the women and knows that he is looking at her, yet for an instant it is difficult to think of her name, difficult to recognize the features. He discovers himself patting his lips with a napkin. Supper is ending. Lewis is about to light his usual cigar. At any moment the two women will excuse themselves to visit the lounge. Or have they already gone and returned—Muhlbach looks at them wonderingly.

Soon he is lost again among his thoughts, the body's presence of little consequence. Interesting that Chong should so quickly have noticed the Boileau poem. He, too, must be concerned with the perpetual madness of men, there's no better explanation. Yes, that would be it. Out of his smoking alembics have drifted the weird gases of our time. His robe may be a trifle new, no writing tools in a pouch at his belt, nor the right sleeve pushed back to his shoulder and the hood half lowered around his neck with a long cowl hanging very low. Caged birds, ox hearts, prostrate angels. Red copper, basilisk eyes, human blood, and vinegar. Whose decoctions are more marvelous, or more horrifying? What protection have we? Infatuations and delusions increase, they do not diminish, as the world grows older. It is wisdom to retreat, but madness to face each day. Let us seal ourselves behind seven doors. With the aid of curious devices and varicolored powders of projection we shall make great metals and all manner of substances. Let us form a famous triumvirate, wizard, physician, and digger of graves, typical of our age, deep in correspondence with the capital. Less ignorant than our neighbors, we must diagnose the time in which we live and albify the shadow that now has fallen across the earth.

Muhlbach coughs and gazes about with a feeling of mild astonishment, aware that he is rubbing his hands together as he often does when deeply troubled. He notes that his hands are gloved, that he is wearing an overcoat and a hat. He is standing in the street in front of his house, and dimly he recalls that he has said good night to the Forsyths and to Eula. In fact they are just now leaving—the red lights of the automobile diminish, turn a corner, and he is alone. To judge from the position of the stars it is after midnight. He listens to the sound of the night wind through wires and bushes. The neighborhood is dark, silent. There is one light, far down the deserted street. Perhaps a child is ill. Or someone works late.

He has walked halfway to the corner. Why? Where he was going, he does not know. A few blocks further and the street will conclude in a circular drive; whoever goes that way must come back again. He stops, tucks the muffler more closely around his throat. The silence is profound. The night will be long and hollow. He contemplates the sky. If the stars showed some slight compassion, he could weep. But the stars pay no attention; they offer nothing. They return his gaze.

He finds he has walked around his home and is standing in the backyard staring at the entrance to the shelter. He realizes that he is frowning, and wonders without the least sense of alarm if he is going mad, truly and publicly mad. Would it matter? The insane, we presume, are not unhappy, having made peace with their awful problems. If, he thinks, Forsyth should come waltzing around tomorrow, bright and early, followed by two hulking attendants, and, with his most affable smile, explain that he believes I need a rest, how would I respond? Possibly I would agree. There should be no trouble, Lewis, just call off the dogs. I understand. Nor do I care, especially. Only tell these secondary persons not to touch me, not to put their hands on me, not ever. Never. That is the one thing that could make me violent. Well, but then there are the children. You will see to them, Lewis, will you not? Of course. Now for Mrs. Grunthe. She is a virago of sorts. Who would employ her? Still, she is not helpless; it *is* madness to worry on her account. Concern one's self over Mrs. Grunthe?

Muhlbach startles himself by laughing aloud. He looks around uneasily. Is anyone observing him from a darkened window? Here he stands by himself in the middle of the night braying like an ass. He coughs against his fist, turns abruptly and goes into the house.

From the linen closet he pulls out sheets and a pillow and a blanket. Will one blanket be enough? The shelter might be cold. This March night is almost freezing. Well, there is an electric heater; that will do.

Outside again, he crosses the yard, goes down the steps and into the shelter and switches on the light. The bed has already been made—Mrs. Grunthe must have made it while he was out to supper. Fancy that! Mrs. Grunthe is a gem, an utter gem. He drops the linens across a folding camp chair and turns down the cover of the bed, then hesitates, pinching his lip. Isn't it a little odd that Mrs. Grunthe should have prepared the bed? She is not usually so thoughtful. She ought to have done just what she did, to be sure, considering that she is paid to keep house; and this is, in a manner of speaking, part of the house. Yes, it was her job, no doubt of that, but still it is peripheral. At any rate, it was decent of her.

Muhlbach removes his coat and looks about the room. There are no coat hooks, no hangers. Somehow this becomes amusing. That he could have forgotten such a thing! He laughs again, then drapes his coat across the extra linens, pulls off his necktie and sits down. It occurs to him that he has not brought along his toothbrush. Every night—for how many years?—he has brushed his teeth before going to bed. Every night. Not once has he neglected to do so.

He sits for a long while, his chin resting on his fist, wondering whether or not he should make the trip back to the house to get the toothbrush. He cannot decide. Just how important is it? What is the good of all this toothbrushing? Really, when one comes to think about it, what good has been accomplished? The dentist continues to fill the visible teeth with porcelain and plug the concealed teeth with gold. So what good is all this scrubbing?

Muhlbach pulls off his shoes, which drop to the linoleum with an unfamiliar noise. He reflects that always before tonight he has dropped his shoes on a carpet. This business of dropping his shoes rather than setting them down—this always annoyed Joyce. How could he explain that he needed to do this? There was never any way to explain. It is all a consequence of working at the office and of obeying traffic signals, of being married, domesticated, and so forth and so forth. No, there never could have been an explanation. He recalls that after a year or two she quit objecting. He picks up a shoe and drops it again. Truly, the sound is different. And the air in the shelter—that has a different odor. All in all, this is quite unreal. There is a perception of dampness, of earth just beyond the walls. He holds his breath in order to listen. One almost could hear worms burrowing, and the distant rushing noise of space, the revolution of the planet and the passage of time.

The door has opened! There, with sleep-drugged eyes, wind-blown hair, pajamas giving him the aspect of a badly wrinkled bird of paradise, stands Otto, splay-footed, anxious, the final result of love. What are you doing up at this hour? Where are your bedroom slippers and your robe? You'll catch cold! But most of all, exactly what are you doing here? You are supposed to be asleep.

Otto, it develops, does not want his father to spend the night in the bomb shelter.

Nonsense! There's nothing to be afraid of; there won't be any burglars sneaking into the house simply because I'm out here. And, come to think of it, should one do so, it is a certainty that without warning Mrs. Grunthe would materialize in wrapper and nightcap, more terrifying than a squad of policemen. Go back to bed, Otto. Avaunt!

Blinking, yawning, Otto militantly repeats his request.

Back to bed, at once! It's the middle of the night. Off you go, friend. Muhlbach looks at him sternly, the look that heretofore has been sufficient, the look that puts an end to argument.

But on this occasion Otto ignores the gathering cloud, though its implications are not lost on him. His lip trembles. Muhlbach, quite amazed, calls the boy and takes him in his arms. What is the trouble? He thinks Otto must be lonely for his mother. He waits to discover if this is it. Otto never mentions her, but of course memories may be the source of grief, however mute. Well, Otto, what is it? Tell me. That's what fathers are for, you know. Tell me, did Mrs. Grunthe hurt your feelings? No. Well, then, what?

Otto has only one thing to say, a simple request.

Muhlbach becomes puzzled, then annoyed. Perhaps, Otto, if you can explain *why*, we might come to an understanding. A compromise, even a concession. Tell me.

Otto cannot explain.

What possible difference does it make, Otto, whether I spend the night underground, or in the house?

Otto, with tears streaking down his chin, remains defiant. Furthermore, it is quite obvious that he has no insight into his problem. There is, figuratively, a big black bear in the woods. What this bear is up to, no one can say. But he is there, he is in the woods.

Perhaps Otto would like to sleep in the shelter? — a bed can be fixed up, and the two of them will sleep underground.

That is not satisfactory, either. In fact, if anything, this idea has compounded the difficulty. Only one thing is clear: Otto does not want his father to sleep in the shelter, nor does he want to sleep there himself. That is final. It is unmistakable.

Well, my friend, you're behaving like your little sister, who seldom has a reason for anything. That may be all right for little girls, but it just won't do for a man! Men must give reasons for what they do. They know what they are doing, and why. Or, if not, they should. Do you understand? No. Well, anyhow, that's the way it is. That's all there is to it. So when you decide to come up with a proper reason, then we can discuss this matter. Until that time, mister, nothing doing. Sorry. Now you get back into that house and climb into your bed and don't let me hear one more quack out of you until the sun shines. Is that plain enough? Any questions?

Otto staggers out, more asleep than awake, and bangs shut the door. As the shelter is airtight, the concussion is something of a shock. Muhlbach gasps; he considers going after Otto to put a more definite end to this foolishness. But banging the door that way could have been accidental. Let it pass.

He switches on the blower which will draw fresh air through a pipe that sticks up into the garden. In the summer this pipe will be concealed by flowers; now it stands out of the barren ground like a submarine periscope. And, having finished undressing, he turns off the light and rolls into bed.

As minutes go by it seems to him that he hears Otto singing. How very strange! Otto always has loved to sing, and many were the nights past when Muhlbach and his wife had been wakened by a pagan lament, a dirge full of meaning, no doubt, signifying something. But again, who could tell? What are you singing about? they would ask. I don't know, he would answer. Then kindly don't keep us awake. Remember, you are not a young animal, a wolf or a coyote who is privileged to howl at the moon; you are a human being, civilized, and we wish you would stop this nocturnal serenade and go to sleep. Thus it would stop for the time, perhaps for the night and the night that followed, but eventually Otto again would favor them with his ability. Had he showed some promise they would not have minded, but the operatic stage, it is safe to say, will not ever be graced by the presence of that renowned tenor, Mr. Otto Muhlbach. Not in the lead, not in the chorus. His best notes are indisputably canine.

And now, thinks Muhlbach, he has taken to singing once again. Or is this all a dream? Am I asleep? Can this be a warning? Is there a rustling overhead?—and he believes he is seated at a sumptuous table in an immense dining room and is holding in one hand a heavy linen napkin. There are many diners, and severe waiters dressed in tuxedos; and almost everyone, while eating, is listening to the news over portable radios. Something terrible has happened, that is why they are listening. He is paralyzed with horror; and he feels, too, an imperial sense of rage because this occurred despite every precaution. His hands tremble and he looks at them but cannot decide whether they are shaking from fright or anger. He stands up, thinking he will tell everyone what has happened. No one pays any attention to him. He wonders what is going on. He rushes to the window and looks down. The street just below is filled with police busily directing traffic. Something lands suddenly in the street, very near the middle, like a spear—the heavy point pierces the pavement and the object stands almost upright, but does not explode. The night sky is filled with streaks of light and a furry creature has fastened itself to his throat, attentively sucking his blood. Batlike, with bony wings trailing, rising and falling—he feels them drawing across his chest—the creature is fanning him with its wings as though to console him and persuade him to keep quiet. He struggles, bends backward, but cannot make a sound. He is standing quietly in cold moonlight. Around him are scattered crumbled stones and mortar, statuary, marble pillars half concealed by withered grass. He does not know where he is, but this may be the ruin of Baalbek, or Uxmal. He feels no emotion. He looks at the shattered columns, chipped faces of forgotten heroes. He shivers, perspires, turns from side to side and tries to sit up, but cannot; then finds himself awake—alive on the marble steps of the ruin. They are cold and rough. They are real, made of concrete. Once more he attempts to sit up. His arms do not support him. He believes he is going to vomit, but after a while the nausea passes. He notices that he is outside the door of the shelter, staring up the steps toward the night sky. The night is very cold and this seems wonderful. He thinks that he will sleep awhile.

How much time slips past before his eyes open again? Who can say? The stars are less brilliant, fewer. He turns his head, languorously, toward the dark opening, the rectangular Egyptian entrance, knowing that within are blankets and musty linens. He feels that he has accomplished some immortal act; he has renounced the gods, outwitted them, and survived.

On his knees he crawls up the steps, uncertainly, out of the tomb. Overhead the stars seem to withdraw until only one or two remain; and while he gazes at them they disappear. It is nearly dawn. There must be sunlight on the ocean to the east.

He gets to his feet, awkwardly, not certain that he will be able to stand. Having achieved this, he feels encouraged. He walks halfway to the house. Just then he hears the jingling of Mrs. Grunthe's alarm clock; it stops immediately, throttled by a brawny hand. She sleeps in a tidy room with the shades drawn, with a broom as a weapon posted beside her bed in the event of an amorous prowler. The question as to whether she would flail the intruder or merely sweep him right back out the window has yet to be resolved. Muhlbach, continuing his careful journey toward the house, smiles at the thought of Mrs. Grunthe; however, the smile is tentative. He feels himself to be a patient only now beginning to recover from an almost fatal accident. But given a few hours to get over the shock, and a good hot breakfast, he thinks he should improve.

All at once he stops. He looks at the periscope in the garden. It protrudes to a height of twenty-four inches, just as it is supposed to, a steel intake pipe, and there it stands among the dead leaves of autumn. On the ground beside it, no longer attached, lies the protective screen. Nearby is the little conical cap that makes the pipe resemble a water tower. The cap and the screen have been dismantled. The orifice of the air intake is plugged with a potato.

Muhlbach, even before he has reached the pipe and bent down to inspect it, fully understands, but cannot let himself believe the truth. There is a look of wonder on his face as he examines the potato. How forcefully it has been stuffed into the pipe! How absolutely it has sealed the shelter. One potato. Nothing more was needed. One potato.

He straightens up. He continues to gaze at the potato. There it sits, not quite half visible to the spectator, ensconced like a diadem in the spiky crown of an underworld deity, this fruit of the earth, seed of Pluto. One potato. Muhlbach, staring at it, cannot quite accept the fact. It is a trifle difficult to admit that someone undertook to murder you.

Who could have done such a thing? And why? As to the first, several names present themselves. Helen and Bob Chong. Absurd. Next, the Forsyths. Can one imagine them returning in the dead of night? Hardly. Eula? Mrs. Grunthe? But Muhlbach can proceed no further. He knows who has attempted to destroy him. There is no possibility of mistake. Why seek to blame the innocent? And yet, he thinks, just suppose—still not willing to acquiesce. Dark rivers rise inexplicably from the depths of the soul. It *could* have been Mrs. Grunthe, could it not? No. No, it could not. Her weapon is a broom, together with a vigorous tongue. But it might have been Helen Chong. Yes, yes, it might have been. No, it could not. Women, young and seductive, do not murder for the sake of a concept, an abstraction; they kill out of jealousy, from a nourished grievance, frustration, fantasy, rage. It is not probable that the empress could have become unbalanced over the cause of a somewhat academic, fortyish gentleman who scarcely has spoken to her—has spoken across a hedge, rake in hand, conscious of his paunch, remarking on the weather. A pity, in fact. One might not mind being assaulted by such a woman. Well, her husband, then? Assuming a motive, however implausible, discretion enters. This man is not a simpleton; he knows the consequence of imprudent acts, even when justified. He is far too brilliant to risk his own destruction over a fancied cause. Consider, then, the Forsyths. And Eula—with hopes of marriage, Eula. Later, in disappointment, she might never hesitate. But not now, not before the ceremony. Which leaves only Margaret and Lewis. But why go on? If we discount the unknown, that mysterious Mr. X so beloved of trivial thrillers, there remain but two possibilities, both children—a very little girl, very little indeed, and her elder brother. The little girl has been in bed with fever. She is wan and listless, dependent. She does not halfway comprehend the structure buried in the back-yard.

Muhlbach realizes that he is weeping. Tears are rolling down his cheeks. He has not wept since—since when? And now these tears, as though he were still a child! How odd! He wipes his face on his pajama sleeve. He reprimands himself. Be reasonable. There are no problems that do not have solutions. The question to ask is not who, but why. What could be simpler? Why? Why has this thing been done? Let us choose to regard the individual as an abstract, the Victim, of no significance. From this let us proceed, objectively, as scientists. There is no crime without a motive. Pragmatic, empirical, the contemporary man must inquire.

Having encouraged himself to take a few deep breaths, Muhlbach announces to himself that already he feels somewhat better. The tears are drying up. Once more he resembles a man. He will go into the house. If he should encounter Mrs. Grunthe—well, pretend that nothing is wrong. Truthfully, it may be that nothing is wrong. This problem can be solved; one need only ask logical questions in order to receive answers, which, if not rational, at least are instructive. Soon Otto will be awake. An explanation should be sought immediately.

Yes, of course. Logic. Questions, answers. Surely the boy cannot reject this age of reason.

1959

THE CUBAN
MISSILE CRISIS

RUSSIAN FREIGHTERS were approaching Cuba, but Kennedy had said they would not get there: "All ships of any kind bound for Cuba from whatever nation or port will, if found to contain cargoes of offensive weapons, be turned back." The freighters had been en route for several days. Now they were approaching the point at which they would be stopped.

Koerner thought about the blockade and the Russian ships as he strolled along Broadway. In front of Ristorante Sergio he paused to consider the menu. *Prosciutto e fichi. Zuppa di pesce. Insalata Nizzarda. Fagiano. Costoletto di agnello piccante. Abbacchio al forno. Montebianco.* Everything sounded good, but it occurred to him that he might as well be reading the farmer's almanac. Two weeks earlier Vice President Johnson had stated that if the United States stopped a Russian ship it would be an act of war. Nevertheless, President Kennedy had ordered a blockade.

Just inside Sergio's window a checkered curtain hung from a brass rail. This was intended to give the diners a certain amount of privacy, but the rail was too low. Koerner stood on tiptoe and looked over it. Sergio's was not crowded; there would be no problem getting a table. He told himself that he should go inside and order something but his stomach felt like a cockroach. He had not eaten very much for two days because of Kennedy's decision to stop the Russian ships and the closer the Russians got to Cuba the more difficult it was to swallow. He imagined freighters plunging across the Atlantic and wondered what the men in Washington who had decided to stop them were doing at this moment. In San Francisco it was almost nine o'clock so it would be almost midnight in Washington. No doubt some of the policy makers were asleep. Others might be up late discussing the matter. Kennedy and his wife might be at a party. Maybe they were dancing. On the other hand, he was no fool; he might be going over the latest information with his advisers.

Koerner thought about the presidential election while he gazed at the diners in Sergio's. He had been worried about the election. Nixon was one of the worst—maybe the very worst of all the politicians—so it had been a great relief when Kennedy strode into the White House with that enormous grin and his beautiful wife. As long as he was in the White House it would be possible to hope. Of course he had started out clumsily, stupidly. Following Eisenhower's lead he was crawling into Vietnam, which was about as smart as invading Russia in December. Then there was the Bay of Pigs. You didn't have to be very bright to know the Cubans would object to American interference even if they didn't like Castro. Still, he wasn't Nixon. Even with two strikes against him, he wasn't Nixon. If Tricky Dick got into the White House there would be no hope; the ugliness and corruption could only get worse.

Exactly what were the Russians doing in Cuba? Kennedy said they were building missile sites. His Yankee voice reverberated: "The purpose of these bases can be none other than to provide a nuclear strike capability against the Western hemisphere." When these missile sites became operative they could launch nuclear warheads against Washington, Cape Canaveral, Mexico City, the Panama Canal, or anyplace else within a thousand miles—which meant the entire southeastern United States, Central America, and the Caribbean. McNamara was asked what would happen if a Russian freighter carrying offensive weapons chose to run the blockade and McNamara replied that the United States would use force. In other words, the United States would sink the Russian ship.

Koerner decided that he felt no animosity toward the Russian sailors who were delivering this equipment. They were doing a job—making a living, one might say. It was quite probable that most of them had no idea what was aboard. Trucks or trains delivered containers of various sizes and shapes to the pier; cranes hoisted the containers aboard; the ship transported this cargo across the Atlantic to another pier where it was unloaded. But what about the captain? Without doubt he knew what he was carrying and he understood the implications. Therefore was it possible to hate the captain of a Russian freighter? He, too, was obeying orders and quite possibly he felt that he was doing the right thing. Koerner wondered if the captains of these ships crossing the Atlantic had heard Kennedy's speech. This wasn't likely, but one way or another they probably had gotten the message and must be reflecting on the significance of their cargo.

Why didn't Kennedy go to the UN? There was plenty of time. The first ship wasn't expected to reach Cuba for another couple of days, so there was plenty of time to convoke an emergency session. That's what the UN was all about. It was supposed to handle international problems. Why didn't Kennedy go before the assembly with whatever evidence he had collected and say, look, here is what we've found and we're not going to have Soviet missiles on Cuba ninety miles from our shore and we want the UN to tell the Kremlin to recall those ships. Here's the evidence. Do something and do it quick because if you sit on your hands—if those ships don't turn around—the United States is going to blow them out of the water and nobody on earth knows what will happen next.

But he didn't go to the UN, Koerner thought. At least he hasn't done it yet and apparently he doesn't intend to. All he did was ask the Security Council to approve a measure requiring the Soviets to dismantle those things and get them out of Cuba. He said he'd been studying the evidence for a week. What was he waiting for? Why didn't he go to the UN immediately? Maybe they can't do anything or won't do anything, but at least he should have tried. What he's telling the entire world is that we have no confidence in the United Nations.

Koerner realized that he was glaring over the curtain at an old gentleman sprinkling cheese on a dish of pasta. He turned away from Sergio's with his fists clenched and walked toward Mike's Pool Hall. Mike's had a counter where you could eat and the hamburgers were famous. I've got to eat, he told himself. I had a quart of coffee and one orange for breakfast and coffee instead of lunch. My nerves feel like watch springs. Those people who govern us have lost their minds. They study their maps and charts and push buttons on their electronic toys and at the head of their table sits the Mad Hatter and I can't do a thing about it. I'm helpless. Kennedy may be right, but what if he's wrong? One flash of light—that's all I'll ever know.

He remembered the primitive hole in a neighbor's backyard. Every Saturday the neighbor was out there digging like a dog trying to find a bone. When the hole was deep enough he would pour cement. In another three months, the neighbor had said with cheerful satisfaction, it would be finished. If the alert sounded he and his wife and their daughter would scuttle into the shelter and pull the trapdoor shut. They could live underground for ten days. By that time Russia would be destroyed.

People were scared witless. They dug holes in the ground. They peeked in the broom closet and under the bed. The recited the Domino Theory. They pasted *Better Dead Than Red* stickers on their cars and told each other that Communism had to be stopped. If the Communists weren't stopped in Vietnam, for example, America would have to fight on the beaches of Hawaii or maybe on Sunset Boulevard.

Koerner walked into Mike's and sat at the end of the counter where he could see the pool tables. Half a dozen people strung along the counter were eating, others gossiped while they waited. He ordered a hamburger and a Mexican beer and settled back to watch the games.

After a few minutes he decided that the players were nothing special, no better than himself. He slumped on the counter stool with a bottle in one hand while he listened to the agreeable clicking sounds as the colored ivory balls rolled to and fro. Pool was a silly, comfortable gentleman's amusement like golf, a relic from the Age of Reason.

He was still waiting for the hamburger when one game ended and another began. These new players were good so he watched attentively. It was instructive and interesting to watch people who were good at something. He thought about the odd rituals of sprinters before a race. One might prance and snort and toss his head like a horse. Another would slap his thighs, quiver like a religious fanatic, touch his palms to the cinders, or dance a quickstep toward the finish. Finally all of them knelt at the starting blocks to wait for a pistol shot.

Koerner looked around. Everybody in Mike's was waiting, although nobody admitted it. They drank coffee and beer and ate spaghetti and sandwiches and played pool and nobody spoke of Russian freighters loaded with missiles wallowing toward the blockade. In Cuba by this time it would be midnight. On the Atlantic it would be morning.

Just then the hamburger arrived piled with tomato and lettuce and pickle and bacon and cheese and onion so that it looked as big as a football. Juice seeped through the thick French bread and the aroma would draw cats down from the rooftops, but Koerner knew that eating this majestic sandwich would be impossible. He thought about the first bomb. He remembered what Oppenheimer had said after the thing exploded above Hiroshima: "A few people laughed. A few people cried. Most people were silent." And this complex individual who directed America's greatest scientific accomplishment recalled a line from Hindu scripture:

Now I am become death, the destroyer of worlds.

Now I am become death. I am become death, the destroyer of worlds, and have grown weary from gathering them in.

Kennedy hadn't started this insane waltz, but that wasn't the point. Missiles were on the way, no matter who was responsible, and incomprehensible numbers of people would die if somebody in the Kremlin or in Washington miscalculated.

Why should I hate this man? Koerner wondered. I like him and I think he is our best hope. As long as he's in the White House we can hope for better government. We can hope that the terrible reign of dinosaurs may come to an end. Maybe that's naive. Maybe it won't. Maybe it will never end, but with this clever and amiable president we have a chance. So why do I want to attack him? I understand how a political assassin feels. I hate Kennedy worse than I've ever hated anybody. If a motorcade passed Mike's and I saw him in the back of a limousine—if right now I saw the president of the United States with his wife riding in triumph through the streets of San Francisco and there was a gun in my pocket, what would happen?

He remembered what Admiral Leahy had said after Hiroshima and Nagasaki, that the weapon had been of no material assistance in the war against Japan. The Japanese had lost and were attempting to surrender, but Truman wanted to send a message—not to the defeated Japanese but to the undefeated Russians. What Admiral Leahy said was that by annihilating two cities America adopted an ethical standard common to barbarians of the dark ages. What President Truman said was this is what we will do to Moscow. This is what we will do to Leningrad.

A pool player bent across the table—his long skeletal fingers arched, the cue balanced like an arrow. He was as pale as Dracula and he wore a black motorcycle jacket. It seemed that he was about to shoot, but after a few seconds he straightened up. He appeared to be thinking. Suddenly he whirled and flung his cue with terrific force against the brick wall. Koerner saw the cue explode and saw five or six pieces drift through the air. One piece bounced off the table. Nobody moved. Then the pool player asked in a wondering voice:

Why didn't he go to the UN?

The only noise in Mike's was the sizzle of frying meat. Koerner looked at the fragments of the shattered cue. Before long somebody would pick them up; but now they lay where they had fallen, as though they held some totemic power, and touching them might affect the delicate suspension of life.

1993

THE PALACE
OF THE MOORISH KINGS

OFTEN WE WONDERED why he chose to live as he did, floating here and there like a leaf on a pond. We had talked about this without ever deciding that we understood, although each of us had an opinion. All we could agree upon was that he never would marry. In some way he was cursed, we thought. One of those uncommon men who follow dim trails around the world hunting a fulfillment they couldn't find at home. Early in a man's life this may not be unnatural, but years go by and finally he ought to find a wife and raise children so that by the time his life ends he will have assured the continuation of life. To us that seemed the proper pattern because it was traditional, and we were holding to it as best we could. Only J.D. had not.

From the capitals and provinces of Europe he had wandered to places we had scarcely heard of—Ahmedabad, Penang, the Sulu archipelago. From the Timor coast he had watched the moon rise above the Arafura Sea. He had slept like a beggar beside the red fort in Old Delhi and had seen the Ajanta frescoes. Smoke from funeral pyres along the Ganges at Varanasi had drifted over him, and he'd been doused with brilliant powders during the festival of Bahag Bihn.

Three hundred miles south of Calcutta, he had told us, is a thirteenth-century

Hindu temple known as the Black Pagoda of Konorak which is decorated with thousands of sculptured sandstone figures—lions, bulls, elephants, deities, musicians, dancing girls and frankly explicit lovers. Its vegetable-shaped peak, the *śikhara,* collapsed a long time ago, but the *mandapa* is still there, rising in three stages. It represents the chariot of the sun. This fantastic vehicle is drawn by a team of elaborately carved horses and century after century it rolls toward the Bay of Bengal. Nothing equals it, he said. Nothing. The temple complex at Khajuraho is marvelous, but Konorak—and he gestured as he did whenever he could not articulate his feelings.

What he was after, none of us knew. Seasons turned like the pages of a familiar album while he traveled the byways of the world. He seemed to think his life was uncircumscribed, as though years were not passing, as though he might continue indefinitely doing whatever he pleased. Perhaps he thought he would outlive not only us but our children, and theirs beyond them.

We ourselves had no such illusions. We could see the clean sweep of youth sagging. Not that we had considered ourselves old, or even badly middle-aged, just that there was some evidence in the mirror. And there was other evidence. Zobrowski's son, for example, was in Asia fighting a war that had begun secretly, deceptively, like a disease, had gotten inside of us and was devouring us before we understood its course. We who had fought in the Second World War had gone along confidently supposing that if war broke out again we would be recalled for duty, but now the government ignored us. It was somewhat embarrassing, as if we were at fault. Young Dave Zobrowski did the fighting while all we did was drive to the office. A boy hardly old enough for long pants had been drafted.

The war offered a deep and bitter paradox. We had succeeded. Beyond all possible question we had succeeded: we had defeated the enemy, yet we had failed. Davy, too, attacked the riddle, unaware at his age that an insoluble problem existed, just as it had existed for us and as it existed for our fathers after the war they called The Great War. Maybe young Dave was more conscious of this than we had been, because we were more knowing than our fathers; still, not much had been changed by our evident sophistication. One conflict ended. Another began. Awareness was irrelevant.

So, against this, we were helpless. We could only hope that our bewilderment and dismay were misplaced. The acid we tasted while listening to newscasts and hearing the casualty figures—"body count" the Pentagon secretaries chose to call it—we could only hope that these falsified and shameful statistics would soon be forgotten. During the Second World War we would have thought it degenerate to gloat over corpses. Now this had become official practice. Apparently it was meant to reassure and persuade us that the government's cause was just.

The slow spectacle of ourselves aging, a dubious war, the decay of our presumably stable nation—these matters were much on our minds when J.D. wrote that he had decided to stop traveling. He was planning to come home. Furthermore, he intended to get married.

We were, of course, astonished. At an age when his friends might become grandfathers he had concluded that perhaps he should stop amusing himself like a college boy in the summertime.

Our wives were not surprised. They considered marriage inevitable and they were relieved that J.D. had at last come to his senses. They were merely irritated that he had waited so long. They regarded his solitary wandering as some kind of pretext for taking advantage of women all over the world. If we were in charge, they seemed to say, he'd have been suitably married years ago. The news affected them quite differently than it affected Zobrowski and Al Bunce and the others who used to play football and marbles with J.D. in those tranquil days when it was safe to walk the streets, and the air in the city was almost as sweet as it was on a farm.

Then we didn't think of our city the way we do now. Sometimes in winter or when the earth was soft after a rain we would find deer tracks across a vacant lot, and occasionally we caught a glimpse of what we thought must be a strange dog vanishing into the shrubbery—only to realize that it was a fox. Now we go about our business in a metropolis. The sizable animals have disappeared, nobody knows quite where; but we don't see them, not even their prints. Gray squirrels once in a while, some years a good many, but little else. Robins, jays, bluebirds, cardinals, thrashers—we used to sprinkle bread crumbs on the snowy back porch just to watch a parliament of birds arrive. Today our luncheon guests are the ubiquitous sparrows who can put up with anything.

Smoke fouls the sky and we find ourselves constantly interrupted by the telephone. Billboards, wires, garbage. We have difficulty accepting these everyday truths. How can we admit that the agreeable past, which we thought was permanent and inviolable, has slipped away like a Mississippi steamboat? We like to think that one morning we will see again those uncultivated fields thick with red clover, streams shaded by cottonwood and willow, and butterflies flickering through the sunlight as clearly as illustrations in the heroic books we read when we were eight.

We used to discuss what we would do when we grew up. We made splendid plans. First, of course, we would be rich. Next, we would marry beautiful exciting women with names like Rita, Hedy or Paulette. We would race speedboats and monoplanes, become as famous as Sir Malcolm Campbell and Colonel Roscoe Turner, or perhaps become wild animal trainers like Clyde Beatty, or hunters like Frank Buck, or great athletes like Glenn Cunningham and Don Budge. There were jungles to be explored, mountain peaks that had never been scaled, cities buried in the sand.

One after another these grandiose ideas acquired the patina of dreams. We could perceive as we grew older that we had not been realistic, so it was natural for Bunce to stop talking about an all-gold motorcycle. Art Stevenson would laugh when reminded of his vow to climb Mount Everest. But there were less ambitious adventures which still seemed reasonable. It's not so hard, for instance, to visit the ruins of Babylon; apparently you can go by jet to Baghdad and hire a taxi.

All of us intended to travel—we agreed on that—just as soon as matters could be arranged. As soon as we finished school. As soon as we could afford a long vacation. As soon as the payments were made on the house and the car. As soon as the children were old enough to be left alone. Next year, or the year after, everything would be in order.

Only J.D. had managed to leave. Surabaja. Brunei. Kuala Lumpur. The islands of Micronesia. He had sent us postcards and occasionally a letter describing where he had been or where he thought he might go next, so in a sense we knew what the world was like.

Once he had returned for a visit. Just once. He stayed not quite three days. We felt obscurely insulted, without being able to explain our resentment. He was not obligated to us. We had played together, gone through school together and exchanged the usual juvenile confidences, but no pacts were signed. We couldn't tell him to come home at Christmas, or insist that he stop fooling around and get a job. Nevertheless, we wished he would; bitterness crept into our talk because we knew he meant more to us than we meant to him. We suspected he seldom thought about us. He could guess where we would be at almost any hour; he could have drawn the outline of our lives day after day and year after year. Why should he think about us? Who thinks about a familiar pair of shoes?

Nor could we explain why we so often discussed him. Perhaps we were annoyed by his indifference toward our values. The work we did was as meaningless to him as the fact that our children were growing up. To us nothing was more significant than our jobs and our families, but to J.D. these vital proceedings had less substance than bread crumbs in the snow. When he wrote, usually to Zobrowski, he never asked what we were doing. He considered us to have a past—a childhood involved with his own—but a transitory nebulous present and a predictable future.

During his visit we questioned him as if we might not ever talk to him again. We asked about Africa—if he had seen Mount Kilimanjaro. He said yes, he had been there, but you seldom see much of Kilimanjaro for the clouds.

Millicent asked if he had shot anything. He said no, he was not a hunter. But he had met an Englishman who did some sort of office work in Bristol and every year came down to hunt, and they had sat up all night drinking gin and talking while the clouds opened and closed and opened again to reveal different aspects of Kilimanjaro in the moonlight, and it sounded as though the lions were only a few yards away. This was as close as he had gotten to hunting the big game of Africa he told her with mock seriousness. Unless you counted the flies, which were savage brutes.

Nairobi, he said, was a delightful town, surprisingly clean, and the weather was decent. We had assumed that it was filthy and humid.

The Masai live not far from Nairobi, he said, and you can visit their compounds if you care to. They eat cheese and drink the blood of cattle and have no use for twentieth-century marvels, except for ceramic beads with which they make rather attractive bracelets and necklaces. Their huts are plastered with animal dung, yet you can tell from watching a Masai warrior that once they were the lords of this territory just as you see in Spanish faces the memory of an age when Spaniards ruled Europe. But it's embarrassing to visit the Masai, he said, because they start to dance whenever a tourist shows up.

I should guess they look forward to the tips, Zobrowski remarked.

They get paid, J.D. said, but you don't tip a Masai. And nobody needs to tell you.

Barbara asked how he liked Ethiopia. He said he'd been there but hadn't stayed long because of the cholera and the mud. He mentioned this Ethiopian mud twice. We thought it strange that his principal memory of such an exotic country should be something as prosaic as mud.

Nor did we understand why he chose to cross and recross a world of dung-smeared huts, lepers, starvation and cholera. No doubt he had seen rare and wonderful sights, he must have met a good many unusual people, and he had tasted fruits we weren't apt to taste. Granted the entertainment value, what else is there? His pursuit of ephemeral moments through peeling back streets struck us as aimless. He is Don Quixote, Zobrowski observed later, without a lance, an opponent or an ideal.

Perhaps J.D. knew what he wanted, perhaps not. We wondered if the reason for his travels could be negative—ridiculing the purpose and substance of our lives. In any event, we had assumed that he would continue trudging from continent to continent as deluded as Quixote until death overtook him in a squalid cul de sac. We were wrong.

He was planning to settle down. Evidently he had decided to emulate us. When we recognized this we felt a bit more tolerant. After all, what sweeter compliment is there? Then, too, it should be interesting to learn what the Black Forest was like. Dubrovnik. Kabul. Goa. The South Seas. At our leisure we would be able to pick the richest pockets of his experience.

Leroy Hewitt was curious about Moslem Africa and meant to ask if there were minarets and cool gardens, and if it was indeed true that the great square at Marrakesh is filled with storytellers, dancers, acrobats and sorcerers just as it was hundreds of years ago. Once J.D. had traveled from Marrakesh to the walled city of Taroudent, rimmed by dark gold battlements, and he had gone over the Atlas Mountains to Tiznit and to Goulimine to the lost Islamic world of women wearing long blue veils and of bearded warriors armed with jeweled daggers.

From there we had no idea where he went. Eventually, from Cairo, had come a torn postcard — a cheap colored photo of a Nile steamer. The penciled message told us that he had spent a week aboard this boat and the afternoon was hot and he was drinking lemonade. How far up the Nile he had traveled we didn't know, or whether he had come down from Uganda.

Next he went to some Greek island, from there to Crete, and later, as closely as we could reconstruct his path, to Cyprus. He wrote that the grapes on Cyprus were enormous and sweet and hard, like small apples, and he had bought an emerald which turned out to be fraudulent, and was recuperating from a blood infection which he'd picked up on the Turkish coast. Months passed before we heard any more. He wrote next from Damascus. The following summer he was in Iraq, thinking he might move along to Shiraz, wondering if he could join a camel train across the plateau. He wanted to visit Karachi. What little we knew of these places we had learned from melodramatic movies and the *National Geographic*.

But what brought J.D. unexpectedly into focus was the Indo-China war. We saw him the way you suddenly see crystals in a flask of treated water. Dave Zobrowski was killed.

When we heard that Davy was dead, that his life had been committed to the future of our nation, we perceived for the first time how J.D. had never quite met the obligations of citizenship. During the Second World War he had been deferred because his father was paralyzed by a stroke and his mother had always been in poor health, so he stayed home and worked in the basement of Wolferman's grocery.

Nobody blamed him. Not one of us who went into the service blamed him, nor did any of us want to trade places with him. But that was a long time ago and one tends to forget reasons while remembering facts. The fact that now came to mind most readily concerning J.D. and the war was just that he had been deferred. We resented it. We resented it no more than mildly when we recalled the circumstances; nevertheless we had been drafted and he hadn't. We also knew that we had accomplished very little, if anything, while we were in uniform. We were bored and sometimes terrified, we shot at phantoms and made absurd promises to God. That was about the extent of our contribution toward a better world. It wasn't much, still there was the knowledge that we had walked across the sacrificial block.

After the war we began voting, obeying signs, watering the grass in summer, sowing ashes and rock salt in winter, listening to the six o'clock news and complaining about monthly bills. J.D. had not done this either. As soon as his sister graduated from secretarial school and got a job he packed two suitcases and left. He had a right to his own life; nobody denied that. Nobody expected him to give up everything for his parents' comfort. But he had left with such finality.

Problems sprang up around us like weeds, not just family difficulties but national and international dilemmas that seemed to need our attention, while J.D. loitered on one nutmeg-scented island after another. Did it matter to him, for instance, that America was changing with the malevolent speed of a slap in the face? Did it make any difference to him that American politicians now ride around smiling and waving from bullet-proof limousines? We wondered if he had an opinion about drugs, ghettos, riots, extremists and the rest of it. We suspected that these threatening things which were so immediate to us meant less to him than the flavor of a Toulouse strawberry. And now young Dave was among the thousands who had been killed in an effort to spread democracy—one more fact that meant nothing to J.D. He was out to lunch forever, as Bunce remarked.

While we waited for him to return we argued uncertainly over whether or not it was a man's privilege to live as he pleased. Wasn't J.D. obligated to share with us the responsibility of being human? We knew our responsibilities, which were clear and correct, and hadn't disclaimed them. Maybe our accomplishments were small, but we took pride in them. We might have no effect on these staggering days, no more than we had affected the course of the war, but at least we participated.

We waited through days charged with electric events which simultaneously shocked and inured us, shocking us until we could feel very few shocks, until even such prodigious achievements as flights to the moon appeared commonplace. At the same time our lives continued turning as slowly and methodically as a water-wheel: taxes, business appointments, bills, promotions, now and then a domestic squabble. This was why we so often found ourselves talking about J.D.—the only one whose days dropped from a less tedious calendar. He had gone to sleep beside the Taj Mahal while we occupied ourselves with school bonds, mortgages, elections, auto repairs, stock dividends, cocktail parties, graduations and vacations and backyard barbecues.

Because we had recognized adolescent fantasies for what they are, and had put them away in the attic like childhood toys, we felt he should have done the same. What was he expecting? Did he hope somehow to seize the rim of life and force it to a stop? Implausibly, romantically, he had persisted—on his shoulders a rucksack stuffed with dreams.

He drifted along the Mediterranean littoral like a current, pausing a month or so in Yugoslavia or Greece, frequently spending Easter on the Costa del Sol; and it was after one of these sojourns in Spain that he came back to see us. His plans then concerned the Orient—abandoned temples in a Cambodian rain forest, Singapore, Macao, Burma, Sikkim, Bhutan. He talked enthusiastically, youthfully, as though you could wander about these places as easily as you locate them on a map.

He had met somebody just back from the foothills of the Himalayas who told him that at Gangtok you see colors more luminous than any you could imagine— more brilliant, more hallucinatory than the wings of tropical butterflies. The idea fascinated him. We asked what sense it made, quite apart from the danger and the trouble, to go such a long distance for a moment of surprise. He wasn't sure. He agreed that perhaps it didn't make sense.

He'd heard about prayer flags posted on bamboo sticks, the waterways of Kashmir, painted houseboats, mango trees on the road to Dharamasala. He thought he'd like to see these things. And there was a building carved from a cliff near Aurangabad. And there was a fortified city called Jaisalmer in the Rajasthan desert.

Then he was gone. Like a moth that flattens itself against a window and mysteriously vanishes, he was gone.

A friend of Art Stevenson's, a petroleum engineer who was sent to the Orient on business, told Art that he happened to see J.D. sitting under a tree on the outskirts of Djakarta. He did not appear to be doing anything, the engineer said; and as he, the engineer, was pressed for time he didn't stop to say hello. But there could be no doubt, he told Art, that it was indeed J.D. dressed in faded khaki and sandals, doing absolutely nothing there in the baking noonday heat of Indonesia. He is mad, Zobrowski commented when we heard the story.

This, of course, was an overstatement. Yet by the usual standards his itinerant and shapeless life was, at the very least, eccentric; and the word "madness" does become appropriate if one sits long enough beneath a tree.

However, some lunacy afflicts our own temperate and conservative neighborhood. We meet it on the front page every morning—a catalogue of outrageous crimes and totally preposterous incidents as incomprehensible as they are unremitting. What can be done? We look at each other and shrug and wag our heads as though to say well, suppose we just wait and maybe things will get back to normal. At the same time we know this isn't likely. So it could be argued that Zobrowski's judgment was a trifle narrow.

Anyway, regardless of who was mad, we waited impatiently for J.D. When he arrived we would do what we could to help him get settled, not without a trace of malicious satisfaction. But more important, we looked forward to examining him. We need to know what uncommon kernel had made him different. This, ultimately, was why we had not been able to forget him.

Our wives looked forward to his return for another reason: if he was planning to get married they wanted to have a voice in the matter. They thought it would be foolish to leave the choice of a wife entirely up to him. They were quite in league about this. They had a few suitable divorcées picked out, and there were several younger women who might be acceptable.

We knew J.D. had spent one summer traveling around Ireland with a red-haired movie actress, and we had heard indirectly about an affair with a Greek girl who sang in nightclubs along the Riviera. How many others there had been was a subject for speculation. It seemed to us that he amused himself with women, as though the relationship between a man and a woman need be no more permanent than sea foam. Leroy Hewitt suggested, perhaps to irritate the ladies, that their intricate plans might be a waste of time because J.D. probably would show up with a Turkish belly dancer. But the ladies, like Queen Victoria, were not amused.

We tried to remember which girls interested him when we were in school. All of us agreed that he had been inconstant. It was one girl, then another. And as we thought back to those days it occurred to us that he had always been looking for somebody unusual—some girl with a reputation for brilliance, individuality or beauty. The most beautiful girl in school was Helen Louise Sawyer. J.D. would take her on long drives through the country or to see travel films, instead of to a dance where she herself could be seen. This may have been the reason they broke up. Or it might have been because she was conceited and therefore rather tiresome—a fact which took J.D. some time to admit.

For a while he dated the daughter of a Congregational minister who, according to the story, had been arrested for prostitution. Almost certainly there was no truth in it, but this rumor isolated her and made her a target. J.D. was the only one with enough nerve to date her publicly, and the only one who never boasted about what they had done.

His other girls, too, were somehow distinctive. Gwyneth, who got a dangerous reputation for burning her dates with a lighted cigarette at intimate moments. A cross-eyed girl named Grace who later became a successful fashion designer in New York. Mitzi McGill, whose father patented a vending machine that supposedly earned him a million dollars. The Lundquist twins, Norma and Laura. To nobody's surprise J.D. went out with both of them.

Rarities excited him. The enchanted glade. The sleeping princess. Avalon. We, too, had hoped for and in daydreams anticipated such things, but time taught us better. He was the only one who never gave up. As a result he was a middle-aged man without a trade, without money or security of any sort, learning in the August of life that he shouldn't have despised what might be called average happiness—3 percent down the years, so to speak. It wasn't exhilarating, not even adventurous, but it was sufficient.

Now, at last, J.D. was ready to compromise.

I've expected this, Zobrowski said. He's our age. He's beginning to get tired.

He's lonely, said Millicent. He wants a home.

Are we echoing each other? Zobrowski asked.

On Thanksgiving Day he telephoned from Barcelona. He knew we would all be at Zobrowski's; we gathered there every Thanksgiving, just as it was customary to drop by the Hewitts' for eggnog on Christmas Eve, and to spend New Year's Day at the Stevensons'.

It was midnight in Barcelona when he called. Having gorged ourselves to the point of dyspepsia we were watching football on television, perfectly aware that we were defaulting on a classic autumn afternoon. Somebody in the next block was burning leaves, the air was crisp and through the picture window we could see a maple loaded like a treasure galleon with red gold. But we had prepared for the feast by drinking too much and by accompanying this with too many tidbits before sitting down to the principal business—split-pea soup, a green salad with plenty of Roquefort, dry heavy salty slices of sugar-cured Jackson County ham as well as turkey with sage and chestnut and onion dressing, mushroom and giblet gravy, wild rice, sweet potatoes, creamed asparagus, corn on the cob, hot biscuits with fresh country butter and honey that would hardly flow from the spoon. For dessert there were dense flat triangles of black mince pie topped with rum sauce. Nobody had strength enough to step outside.

As somnolent as glutted snakes we sprawled in Zobrowski's front room smoking cigars, sipping brandy and nibbling peppermints and mixed nuts while the women cleared the table. Embers snapped in the fireplace as group after group of helmeted young Trojans rushed across the miniature gridiron. It was toward such completed days that we had worked. For the moment we'd forgotten J.D.

His call startled us, though we were not surprised that he was in Spain again. He had gone back there repeatedly, as though what he was seeking he'd almost found in Spain. Possibly he knew the coast between Ayamonte and Port-Bou better than we knew the shore of Lake Lotawana. He had been to Gijón and Santander and famous cities like Seville. He'd followed baroque holy processions and wandered through orange groves in Murcia. During his visit he spoke fervently of this compelling, strict, anachronistic land—of the apple wine *manzanilla,* fringed silk shawls, bloody saints, serrated mountains, waterless valleys, burnt stony plateaus, thistles as tall as trees lining the road to Jaén.

We remembered his description of goat bells tinkling among rocky Andalusian hills and we could all but feel the sea breeze rise from Gibraltar. One afternoon he ate lunch in a secluded courtyard beside a fountain—bread, a ball of cheese and some sausage the color of an old boot. He insisted he'd never eaten better.

He imitated the hoarse voices of singing gypsies—a strident unforgotten East beneath their anguished music—and told us about a cataract of lavender blossoms pouring across the ruined palace of the Moorish kings of Málaga. As young as another Byron he had brought back these foreign things.

There's a town called Ronda which is built along a precipice, and he told us that when he looked over the edge he could feel his face growing damp. He was puzzled because the sky was blue. Then he realized that spray was blowing up the cliff from the river. It was so quiet, he said, that all he heard was wind through the barranca and he was gazing down at two soaring hawks.

He thought Granada might be Spain's most attractive city. He had told us it was the last Arab bastion on the peninsula and it fell because of rivalry between the Abencerrages and Zegris families—information anybody could pick up in a library. But for him this was more than a musty fact. He said that if you look through a certain grate beneath the floor of the cathedral you can actually see the crude iron coffins containing the bodies of Ferdinand and Isabella; or if you go up a certain street near the Alhambra you pass a shop where an old man with one eye sits at a bench day after day meticulously fitting together decorative little boxes of inlaid wood.

And he liked to loiter in the Plaza España, particularly while the sun was going down, when swallows scour the twilight for insects.

He had ridden the night train to San Sebastián along with several members of the Guardia Civil in Napoleonic leather hats who put their machine guns on an empty seat and played cards, with the dignity and sobriety peculiar to Spaniards, beneath the faltering light of a single yellow bulb. Outside a station in the mountains where the train paused to build up compression there was a gas lamp burning with vertical assurance, as though a new age had not begun. Wine bottles rolled in unison across the warped floor of the frayed Edwardian coach when the train creaked around a curve late at night, and the soldiers ignored a young Spaniard who began to speak of liberty. Liberty would come to Spain the young man believed—even though Franco's secret police were as common as rats in a sewer.

From everything J.D. said about Spain we thought it must be like one of those small dark green olives, solid as leather, with a lasting taste.

He returned to Barcelona more than to any other city, although it was industrial and enormous. He liked the Gothic barrio, the old quarter. He enjoyed eating outside a restaurant called La Magdalena which was located in an alley just off the Ramblas. Whenever a taxi drove through the alley the diners had to stand up and push their chairs against the wall so it could squeeze past. Whores patrolled the barrio, two by two, carrying glossy handbags. Children who should have been at home asleep went from café to café peddling cigarettes. Lean old men wearing flat-brimmed black hats and women in polka dot dresses snapped their fingers and clapped and danced furiously with glittering eyes on cobblestones that were worn smooth when the Armada sailed toward England.

Flowers, apple wine, moonlight on distant plazas, supper in some ancient alley, Arabs, implications, relics—that was how he had lived while we went to work.

Now he was calling to us from a boarding house in the cheap section of Barcelona. He was alone, presumably, in the middle of the night while we were as surfeited, prosperous and unrepentant as could be. It was painful to compare his situation with ours.

So, Zobrowski said to him on the telephone, you're there again.

J.D. said yes, he was in the same boarding house—*pensión,* he called it—just off Via Layetana. He usually stayed at this place when he was in Barcelona because it had a wonderful view. You could understand Picasso's cubism, he said with a laugh, if you looked across these rooftops.

I'm afraid my schedule won't permit it, Zobrowski remarked.

What a pity, said J.D.

Zobrowski took a fresh grip on the telephone. It would appear, he said, that Spain continues to stimulate your imagination.

Actually no, J.D. answered. That's why I'm coming back.

Then he explained. He wasn't altogether clear, but it had to do with progress. With jet planes and credit cards and the proliferation of luxury hotels and high-rise apartments you could hardly tell whether you were in Barcelona or Chicago. Only the street signs were different. It wasn't just Barcelona, it was everyplace. Even the villages had begun to change. They were putting television sets in bars where you used to hear flamenco. You could buy *Newsweek* almost as soon as it was published. The girls had started wearing blue jeans. There was a Playboy club in Torremolinos.

Years ago he had mentioned a marble statue of a woman in one of the Barcelona plazas and he had said to us, with an excess of romantic enthusiasm, that she would always be there waiting for him.

Zobrowski asked about this statue. J.D. replied that she was growing a bit sooty because of the diesel trucks and cabs and motorbikes.

He said he had recently been up north. The mountain beyond Torrelavega was completely obscured by factory smoke and there was some sort of yellowish chemical or plastic scum emptying into the river with a few half-dead fish floating through it.

The first time he was in Spain he had walked from Santillana del Mar to Altamira to have a look at the prehistoric cave paintings. There wasn't a tourist in sight. He had passed farmers with long-handled scythes, larks were singing, the sky was like turquoise, and he waded through fields of flowers that reached to his knees. Now, he said, he was afraid to go back. He might get run over by a John Deere tractor, or find a motel across the road from the caves.

That bullfighting poster you had, Zobrowski said, the one with Manolete's name on it. Reproductions of that poster are for sale at a number of department stores.

You're flogging me, J.D. said after a pause.

I suppose I am, Zobrowski said.

However, I do get the point, J.D. said. Another decade and the world's going to be as homogenized as a bottle of milk.

Millicent is here, Zobrowski said. She would like a word with you.

J.D.! Millie exclaimed. How marvelous to hear you're coming home! You remember Kate Van Dusen, of course. Ray Van Dusen's sister? — tall and slim with absolutely gorgeous eyes.

J.D. admitted that he did.

She married Barnett Thomas of Thomas Bakery Products, but things just didn't work out and they've separated.

There was no response. Millie seemed about to offer a trans-Atlantic summary of the marriage. Separated was a euphemism, to say the least. Kate and Barnett were in the midst of a reckless fight over property and the custody of their children.

She's asked about you, Millie went on. She heard you might be coming back.

I'm engaged, J.D. said.

We didn't realize that, said Millie without revealing the horror that flooded the assembled women. We simply understood that you were considering marriage. Who is she?

Margaret Hobbs, he said.

Margaret Hobbs? Millie sounded uncertain. Is she British?

You know her, J.D. answered. She's been teaching kindergarten in Philadelphia.

Oh! Oh, my God! Millie said.

We had gone to grammar school with Margaret Hobbs. She was a pale dumpy child with a screeching voice. Otherwise she was totally undistinguished. Her parents had moved to Philadelphia while we were in the sixth grade and none of us had heard of her since. Her name probably hadn't been mentioned for twenty-five years.

We met by accident last summer, J.D. said. Margaret and some other school-teachers were on a tour and we've been corresponding since then. I guess I've always had a special feeling for her and it turns out she's always felt that way about me. She told me she used to wonder what I was doing and if we'd ever meet again. It's as though in a mysterious way we'd been communicating all these years.

How interesting, Millie said.

It really is, isn't it! J.D. said. Anyhow, I'm anxious for all of you to make her acquaintance again. She's amazingly well informed and she remembers everybody.

I think it's just wonderful, Millie said. We're so pleased. I've always wished I could have known Margaret better. Now here's Leroy.

Is that you, young fellow? Leroy asked.

Hello, said J.D. You don't sound much different.

Leroy chuckled and asked if he'd been keeping himself busy. J.D. said he supposed so.

Great talking to you, Leroy said. We'll have a million yarns to swap when you get home. Hang on, here's Aileen.

We look forward to hearing of your adventures, Aileen said. When do you arrive?

J.D. didn't know exactly. He was going to catch a freighter from Lisbon.

Aileen mentioned that last month's *Geographic* had an article on the white peacocks.

After a moment J.D. replied that the connection must be bad because it sounded as if she was talking about peacocks.

Have you been to Estoril? Aileen almost shouted.

Estoril? Yes, he'd been to Estoril. The casino was jammed with tourists. Germans and Americans, mostly. He liked southern Portugal better—the Algarve. Faro, down by the cape.

Faro, Aileen repeated, memorizing the name. Then she asked if he would stop in Philadelphia before coming home.

J.D. was vague. The freighter's first two ports of call were Venezuela and Curaçao. Next it went to Panama. He thought he might hop a bus from Panama, or maybe there would be a boat of some sort heading for British Honduras or Yucatán or maybe New Orleans.

Aileen began to look bewildered. She was sure that he and Margaret would be able to coordinate their plans and it had been a pleasure chatting. She gave the phone to Art Stevenson.

Art said a lot of water had flowed under the bridge and J.D. might not recognize him because he had put on a pound or two. J.D. answered that he himself had been losing some hair. Art proposed that they try to work out a deal.

Neither of them knew what to say next. Art gave the phone to Barbara.

Barbara asked if he and Margaret would be interested in joining the country club. If so, she and Al would be delighted to sponsor them.

Not at first, J.D. said. Maybe later. Let me talk to Dave again.

He was thinking of buying a car in Europe because he had heard he could save money that way, and he wanted Zobrowski's advice. He had never owned a car.

Zobrowski suggested that he wait until he got back. Bunce's brother-in-law was a Chevrolet dealer and should be able to arrange a price not far above wholesale. Zobrowski also pointed out that servicing foreign cars in the United States can be a problem. Then, too, you're better off buying from somebody you know.

J.D. inquired about jobs.

We had never learned how he supported himself abroad. As far as we could determine he lived from day to day. There have always been individuals who manage to do this, who discover how to operate the levers that enable them to survive while really doing nothing. It's a peculiar talent and it exasperates people who live conventionally.

A job could be found for him, that wasn't the issue. What disturbed us was that he had no bona fide skills. Zobrowski was a respected surgeon. Bunce was vice-president of the Community National Bank and a member of the Board of Education. Art Stevenson was director and part owner of an advertising agency. Leroy Hewitt was a successful contractor, and so on. One or another of J.D.'s friends could find him a place, but there would be no way to place him on equal terms. He could speak French, Italian, Spanish, German and Portuguese well enough to make himself understood, besides a few necessary phrases of Arabic and Swedish and Hindi and several others, but language schools want instructors who are fluent. He knew about inexpensive restaurants and hotels throughout Europe, and the best way to get from Izmir to Aleppo. No doubt he knew about changing money in Port Said. Now he would be forced to work as a stock clerk or a Western Union messenger, or perhaps as some sort of trainee competing with another generation. The idea made us uncomfortable.

Margaret would soon find a job. Excluding the fact that Bunce was on the Board of Education, she was evidently an experienced teacher with the proper credentials. She could do private tutoring until there was a full-time position. But J.D. in his coat of many colors couldn't do anything professionally.

I have a suggestion, Zobrowski said to him on the telephone. This will sound insulting, but you've got to face facts. Your capacities, such as they are, don't happen to be widely appreciated.

I'm insulted, J.D. said.

Zobrowski cleared his throat before continuing: Fortunately, our postmaster is related by marriage to one of the cardiologists on the staff of Park Lane Hospital. I have never met this man—the postmaster, that is—but, if you like, I will speak to the cardiologist and explain your situation. I cannot, naturally, guarantee a thing. However, it's my feeling that this fellow might be able to take you on at the post office. It wouldn't be much, mind you.

Well, said J.D. from a great distance, please have a talk with that cardiologist. I'm just about broke.

I'm sorry, Zobrowski said, although not surprised. You enjoyed yourself for a long time while the rest of us went to an office day after day, whether we liked it or not. I won't belabor this point, but I'm sure you recall the fable of the grasshopper and the ant.

J.D. had never cared for lectures, and in the face of this we thought he might hang up. But we all heard him say yes, he remembered the fable.

If I sound harsh, forgive me, Zobrowski said. It's simply that you have lived as the rest of us dreamt of living, which is not easy for us to accept.

J.D. didn't answer.

Now, as we wait to greet him, we feel curiously disappointed. The end of his journey suggests that we were right, therefore he must have been wrong, and it follows that we should feel gratified. The responsibilities we assumed were valid, the problems with which we occupy ourselves are not insignificant and the values we nourish will flower one day—if not tomorrow. His return implies this judgment. So the regret we feel, but try to hide, seems doubly strange. Perhaps without realizing it we trusted him to keep our youth.

1972